"Galloping through the village, he made for the parsonage house which stood a little apart from the other habitations."

ADELINE;

OR,

THE GRAVE OF THE FORSAKEN.

A DOMESTIC ROMANCE.

BY THE AUTHOR OF "THE MILLER'S MAID," "BLANCHE," ETC. ETC.

"They said she of consumption died,
But there was one who knelt
Her weary couch of pain beside,
A sadder influence felt."

LONDON :

PREFACE.

ADELINE; OR, THE GRAVE OF THE FORSAKEN, is one of those "Chapters in Real Life" which, from their truthfulness, seldom fail to speak home to every heart.

Still the author was unprepared for the great amount of patronage the work has received, it having reached, from the first part, a sale of almost unprecedented amount in the history of Periodical Literature.

Mr. Endsleigh, the village curate, is no ideal creation. Such a man lived, possessed of all the rare virtues which made him so beloved and venerated by all.

The author has, from first to last, struggled hard against the necessity of death, at length, robbing his pages of their sunshine, by depriving him and his readers of the gentle, the devoted, the beautiful, Adeline ; but he (the author) felt that by straining at a conclusion, which should preserve to him his heroine, he should be inflicting a vital injury upon his tale by depriving it of its reality.

In announcing a new work which is now in the press, and will be shortly published by Mr. Lloyd, the author can only say, that he is " like his whole tribe," very easily and pleasantly led " by kind words gently spoken," to do his best, and the reception which the public has given to the present work, bespeaks in him an amount of gratified feeling which he trusts will be concerted into amusement and excellence in his forthcoming Romance.

Thanking, therefore, heartily his numerous readers, both of the rougher and gentler sex, he bids them, for the present, adieu.

ADELINE;

OR,

THE GRAVE OF THE FORSAKEN.

FOUNDED ON FACTS.

" Man's love is from his life a thing apart.—
'Tis woman's whole existence."—BYRON.

CHAPTER I.

" THE GRAVE OF THE FORSAKEN."—AN ARRIVAL.—DESPAIR AND SELF-
CONDEMNATION.

It was towards the close of the autumn of the year 1828, that the little village of Bracefield, situated in a romantic and beautiful valley, in South Wales, was thrown into a state of consternation and confusion, by an incident which was unequalled in its simple annals for mystery and horror.

The village was celebrated for its many natural beauties. A little bubbling streamlet took its murmuring course through its main street, and thence— with many picturesque windings,—traversed the churchyard; lending a beauty to the homely graves which reared their flower-decked mounds upon its banks.

There was one grave, however, which, although distant from the rippling

music of the stream, had never failed to be pointed out to the curious traveller as being the last home of one "who had known sorrow," and borne it with
a patient resignation, until her head was laid low in the silent tomb—the
tomb, in her case, of youth, loveliness and virtue.

Upon removing the long grass, which waved in luxuriance around the
simple and low head-stone, these words might be traced :—

A. M.

Aged 19, 1827.

"THE GRAVE OF THE FORSAKEN."

The story of the occupant of that humble grave was but dimly known.
She was one of those who had

"Let concealment, like a worm i' the bud,
Feed on her damask cheek.
She never told her love."

Her life had been one happy dream. But the waking—how awful, how
dreadful had that been. But we must not anticipate. Our task is a painful
one, but we must trace, how, step by step, the guileless happy heart, that lay
silent and calm beneath that grassy mound, was broken.

How soon are the good and virtuous forgotten! One year had scarcely
flown by since the grave—the cold, silent grave, had closed over the fairest
flower that ever bloomed on earth, ere she was all but forgotten. A few only
who had gathered hints of her eventful story, cherished the memory of the
gentle girl who they had seen smile so sweetly, but who now, would never in
this world smile again. This apathy, however, was completely broken in
upon by an incident, which, while it at once awakened the most eager curiosity, brought with it a shuddering terror.

The month was September, and the leaves had plentifully strewed the village churchyard with decay, while the extreme heat of a lovely summer was
sweetly tempered by the delicious coolness of the autumnal evenings ; when,
towards sunset, one evening, a horseman dashed into the village of Bracefield
at a furious pace.

He heeded not the curious gaze of the inhabitants, who rushed to their
doors upon hearing the clatter of his horse's hoofs, but galloping like one
possessed, through the village, he made for the parsonage-house, which stood
a little apart from the other habitations, and had more pretensions to the appearance of a villa than any other residence in Bracefield.

Here the horseman paused, and pulling up his foaming and panting steed,
so suddenly that the animal was thrown completely upon its haunches, he
threw himself recklessly from its back, and lifting the latch of the door,
which in the day-time was not otherwise secured, he rushed at once into the
dwelling ; and for a time was lost to the gaze of the curious and astonished
idlers, who, with gaping mouths, had watched his mad career.

What transpired in the parsonage, no one could guess, but about half an
hour after the impetuous stranger had entered it, there came slowly from its
door two persons ; one was the venerable pastor himself, a man stricken in
years ; his step was trembling and infirm, and upon this occasion there were
the traces of deep feeling upon his venerable and benevolent countenance.
Leaning upon the good pastor's arm, was the young man, who, by his previous career through the village, had excited so much surprise and inquiry.
The energy and fire of his movements seemed all lost, and but for the sus-
taining arm of the aged man of God, it appeared as if he would have fallen to
the earth.

His appearance was eminently interesting ; in age he appeared to be
scarcely twenty ; his hair was of a raven blackness, and clustered in massive
curls around his noble brow ; his eyes were of that deep sparkling hazel tint,
which lends so much fire and animation to the countenance, and his beauti-

fully arched eye-brows might have been envied by many a high-born court beauty.

The outline of his face was purely Grecian; there was the straight nose, the short intellectual lip, and the rounded chin, which, for its feminine beauty, might have belonged to some fine young girl. His hands were delicately white, and his long taper fingers, bespoke high mirth and delicate nurture.

He was above the middle height, and there was a graceful majesty about his form, which at once irresistibly impressed the beholder with a strong prepossession in his favour.

The hue of health, however, sparkled not upon his handsome face; his eyes shone not with the lustre of happiness;—his very lips were pale,—those lips which ere now had rivalled the budding rose;—a deathlike paleness was upon his brow and cheeks, and an universal langour seemed to have taken possession of his frame.

His dress was plain, but by its form and fashion, betokened the wearer to be of high rank. He wore no cravat, and the open shirt-collar betrayed the dazzling whiteness of his Antonius-like neck.

There were the traces of tears upon the face of the aged pastor, as with difficulty he supported his young companion, who evidently needed all the aid that could be afforded to him.

The sun had set, and darkness was beginning to shroud all things in obscurity, although the glorious western sky was still streaked with radiant colours, and there was a beautiful glow over the face of nature from the last rays of the god of day—a glow-like blush upon the cheek of beauty and innocence.

What a contrast did these two persons present as they slowly traversed the little lawn in front of the parsonage-house, and walked from thence into the high road.

The venerable clergyman, with his silvery locks, and plain, old-fashioned attire, supporting the tall, graceful form of that youth, who, in the flower of his existence—the young spring time of his beauty, seemed by some dreadful calamity smitten to the dust.

He clung to the aged man's arm with convulsive energy, and deep sobs burst from his labouring breast.

Now they crossed the high road, and the clergyman opening a small wicket gate, they entered a narrow winding pathway which led to the churchyard.

"Let me intreat you," said the pastor, "oh, let me beg of you to put off this melancholy visit for a time."

"No, no, no;" sobbed his companion; "lead me to her!"

"Let it be till to-morrow;" still urged the clergyman, in a tone of deep compassion and feeling.

"No, no;" still sobbed his young companion;—"now—or—or never!— Where shall I be to-morrow?"

"By the mercy of Heaven," said the old man, "you will be in a better frame of mind. Wait—come back with me now."

"No, no, no;" he still cried. "I have travelled, sir, night and day;—I —I——" Deep sobs choked his utterance.

"My dear young friend," said the clergyman, "for dear you are still to me, notwithstanding——"

"I—I know what you would say," interrupted the other, with sudden energy. "Spare me, spare—I—I know I am a villain!"

"God bless us all," said the aged man; "we are all liable to err, and what are the best of us in the sight of Heaven? I—I have wept—wept bitterly for her—for—she was——"

"Spare me! Spare me!" said the young man.

"Forgive me," said the clergyman; "but my heart is full. Be ruled by me and return to my home, where, in counsel with God, we may learn to bear his afflictions with patient resignation."

"Seven hundred weary miles," cried the young stranger, "I have travelled to come hither. Oh, stay me not now—lead me to her—I implore—I beseech you to lead me to her."

The good pastor made no further opposition; with trembling steps he led his companion along the winding walk.

They soon arrived at another small wicket gate, which opened directly into the humble burial place, and now they stood upon the green sod, beneath which, reposed in peace, the weary, the aged, and the young.

That village churchyard was a fit place for melancholy yet grateful musing. It robbed death of some of its terrors by its quiet chastened beauty. The bending branches of graceful willows hung over the graves, and many of the green mounds were decked with flowers, as tributes of affection for the still forms that slept beneath.

The young man now withdrew his arm from that of his companion, and clasping his hands together, he cast his eyes wildly round the place, crying—

"Where?—where—oh, tell me where?"

"Hush—hush," said the old man; "be calm."

"Take me to her—oh, take me to her," he cried.

"This is no place for the display of the violence of worldly passion," said the aged pastor; "be calm, and I will show where she sleeps."

He took his young companion by the hand, and led him to a retired spot apart from the crowd of graves, and then he paused for a moment, evidently striving to overcome the deep emotion which he felt, and which nearly deprived him of the power of speech.

The young man still looked wildly round him, as if in anxious search for something, and he drew his breath short and thick, as he again said in a voice of unutterable anguish,—

"Where—oh, where is she? Take me to her! take me to her!"

"Be calm," said the clergyman. "Yon house (pointing to the church) is dedicated to God. We are standing now in his presence. This spot is holy. Profane it not with wild passions and fierce despair. Come here with a chastened and meek spirit, or come not at all."

"You—you torture me," replied the other; "if you ever loved her—if you now look upon me with an eye of pity, forgiveness I do not, cannot ask, show me where—where they have laid her."

"Forgiveness?" said the old man, and his voice trembled as he spoke. "May God forgive us all as I forgive thee! Come—I will shew you. This way—this way."

A few steps further brought them to a low grassy mound, which betokened that some one slept the sleep of death beneath it.

The clergyman stood still for a moment, and lifted from his head his hat. The last rays of the departing sunlight fell upon his venerable face, as he said solemnly, and with much feeling,—

"She sleeps here."

A cry burst from the young man. A cry of such intense agony, that the old pastor started and looked around him, for he could hardly believe it came from human lungs.

The stranger threw himself upon the humble grave in a passion of grief that transcended all description.

"Adeline! Adeline!" he cried. "And art thou here? Oh, God—oh, God—oh, God!"

The clergyman waited in silence until he thought the first wild burst of grief was past; and while he so waited, his lips moved in prayer—a whispered prayer for the prostrate form, which, in the deep abandonment of grief, lay at his feet.

Then he stooped, and removing the long waving grass from the small stone which marked the head of the grave, he said—

"Herbert! Herbert!"

"Adeline—Adeline—my Adeline," cried the youth, with bitter sobs.

"See here," said the clergyman; "look on this and you will know all. Look once and then come with me."

The young stranger lifted his head and saw through his tears the initials and words upon the grave-stone.

"'The Grave of the Forsaken,'" he repeated, and a dreadful calmness came over him—a calmness more terrible than the wildest passion and despair.

"Come home with me now," said the clergyman; "you have seen all. Come, Herbert; let me intreat you to come."

"Leave me here for a brief space," said the young man. "I—I would commune alone with my heart by her grave."

His aged companion shook his head doubtingly.

"I cannot—must not leave you, Herbert," he said, mildly.

"My purpose is a holy one," said the stranger; "leave me—oh, leave me for a time. Hark! what hour is that?"

The village clock struck nine.

"'Tis nine," said the pastor; "already the air feels chill and cold. Come, Herbert, come."

"Send for me at eleven," said his companion.

"Well," cried the clergyman, "be it so. God be with you."

The young stranger threw himself again upon the grave with a sob, and the venerable clergyman slowly and with a heavy heart left the spot, and returned to his home.

~~~~~~~~~~~~~~~~~~~~~~~~~~~~

CHAPTER II.

" He went where they had left her
When her last sad pang was o'er;
Ere death had yet bereft her
Of the charms her beauty wore."
HAYNES BAYLEY.

A SURPRISE.—HOPES AND FEARS.—THE MIDNIGHT HOUR.—THE ANCIENT SERVANT AND HIS MASTER.—THE LOST BODY.

MISERABLY and slowly the two hours between nine and eleven passed away to the aged pastor. At length, the three quarters past ten chimed from the church clock, and he rose instantly and left his home to seek the young mourner by "The Grave of the Forsaken."

He took with him an old domestic, who bore a lantern, and with slow steps they passed along the path towards the wicket opening to the little churchyard.

A strange feeling of horror came across the clergyman's mind as he neared the spot where he had left the living to mourn the early dead, and his heart beat, and his limbs shook as he crossed the green space broken by many a rounded mound.

"Faster, Andrew—faster," cried the pastor to his ancient servant, who he had distanced in his intense anxiety.

The old domestic quickened his pace, and the clergyman himself took the light as they came near to the spot, and holding it as high as his arm could reach, he cried—

"Herbert! Herbert! Speak."

No voice replied, and with an exclamation of distress, the aged man rushed forward, and stood by "The Grave of the Forsaken."

"Thank God!" was his first exclamation, as he saw the young man stretched upon the grassy mound.

"Herbert, Herbert! why did you not answer me? Such another moment of intense anxiety would still the beating of my old heart for ever. Come, Herbert, come; the time is past. Come, come."

Still there was no answer.

The clergyman set down the lantern by the head-stone of the grave, and with trembling hands he raised the youth's head, so that the gleam of light fell upon the face.

A cry of horror and despair burst from the old man. *He looked upon the face of a corpse.*

"Dead! dead!" he cried, wringing his aged hands. "He is dead! He, the gifted—the young—the beautiful—he is dead!"

The clergyman covered his face with his hands and wept, while the aged domestic looked on in wondering silence.

After a time he rose, and said solemnly, while the tears trickled down his furrowed cheeks,

"God's will be done; but young hearts now in joy and mirthfulness will bleed for this night's work. There will be weeping and desolation in a noble house, for they have lost their flower—their hope! Herbert Mandeville is dead! dead!"

He then turned to his servant and said—

"Andrew, take thou the lantern, and hasten to the village for assistance. I will watch here the while."

"My dear master," said Andrew, pointing to the body. "Is—is that really him who used to—to—"

"Hush, Andrew, hush!" said the clergyman. "Ask no questions now, but hasten to do as I bid you."

With such speed as his years could make, Andrew hurried from the spot with the lantern, and left his master alone with the dead.

The clergyman stood silent for several minutes, then, with a deep sigh, he said—

"And has it come to this? Good Heaven! The young and the beautiful to be snatched to an early tomb, while the aged and care-worn are left to mourn for them. Here lies the victim and the betrayer alike cold—cold and still. Alas! could I have thought two short years since that I, even I should be weeping by the grave of Adeline the while I watched the body of Herbert Mandeville? Great God! how singular are thy providences!"

The old man let his head sink on his breast, and he wept bitterly as thought after thought of what had been crowded upon his brain.

"I could have died for them," he cried; "yes, I would have died for them. But it was not permitted. They are gone, and I remain to weep. I loved them both as if they were my children. Poor, sad victims of ill-directed passion. May the gates of Heaven open to you both, and that peace and joy which was denied you in your mortal state be yours everlasting in the world that is to come."

Again he was silent, and appeared absorbed in painful thought. Occasionally he muttered their names in a tone of deep grief.

"What tears will flow now," he said. "Charles Leslie, too. Poor Charles Leslie; and she—she, too, must weep—Clara, unhappy, guilty Clara!"

Nearly half an hour had elapsed since Andrew had gone on his message to the village, and still no one came. The striking of the church clock aroused the good pastor's attention to the flight of time, and he started as he exclaimed—

"They are tardy. Where can Andrew be? Ere this, assistance should have been here to convey this lifeless form to a more fitting place."

As he spoke, he walked slowly from the grave towards the wicket-gate, from whence he could obtain a view of the village, and see if, by the gleaming lights, he could calculate upon the speedy arrival of the villagers. He opened the gate and walked into the winding pathway, directing his eyes towards the village.

Lights were streaming from many a little casement, and he could hear the sounds of approaching steps.

"They come—they come," he said. "The body shall be removed to my house. Alas! poor Herbert, that I should have to speak of thee thus."

In his anxiety to hurry the progress of the approaching party, the clergyman advanced some distance down the lane to meet them, and in a few moments he was surrounded by eight or ten of the male inhabitants of the village, some of whom were bearing lanterns.

Andrew had partially explained the errand they were required upon, and there was an expression of fear and consternation upon each countenance as they eagerly surrounded the clergyman.

"Quick, my friends—quick," he said. "Here has been a sad mischance. Follow me to the churchyard."

One or two seemed inclined to ask questions before proceeding further, but the clergyman silenced them by saying—

"Ask nothing now. All will be explained to-morrow. There is one dead in the churchyard, and I wish the body to be conveyed to the parsonage as quickly as possible. Come, my friends, do this for me willingly, and at once. Come—come."

Thus urged, the party followed the clergyman, although it was with fear and trembling, and they huddled so closely together as to impede each other's progress materially.

More than once before they reached the wicket gate the aged pastor had to turn and urge them to be quicker, and each time that he did so he imparted a momentary impulse to their flagging steps, and at length they all stood within the pale of the churchyard.

More slowly than before they now proceeded, winding among the gravestones, until they could not help coming near to "The Grave of the Forsaken."

"Stop," cried the clergyman. "Come, two or three of you, with me. The body lies upon the 'The Grave of the Forsaken.'"

There was a general stare of wonder and alarm as he spoke, and the whole body shrunk back several paces.

"What do you fear?" said the venerable man, in a tone of severity, "Think you the dead can harm you? Shame on you all. You question by this fear the goodness and justice of the Almighty. Come, my friends, aid me to remove the body. I am old and feeble, or I would not ask your assistance in the mournful duty."

"Y—y—yes, sir," stammered one. "I—I will come. I bean't afeard, sir, I—I be coming;" and he reluctantly approached.

Thus encouraged, two more left the main body, and signified their intention of rendering the assistance required.

"I thank you," said the clergyman. "Bring your lantern, Andrew. Follow me, I pray you."

Andrew held his torch high in the air, so as to shed a diffused light around, and in a few moments they stood by "The Grave of the Forsaken."

A cry of surprise from the clergyman attracted the men who had remained some distance off, and curiosity overcoming their fears, they, one and all, rushed forward to the humble grave.

"What can this mean?" cried the clergyman. "What dreadful mystery is this? He is not here."

The grave was vacant. The body of the young stranger was gone!

"Search! search!" cried the old clergyman. "God of Heaven! he was here. Search for him, my friends!"

An active search was immediately made around the spot, but it was quite unsuccessful. Not the slightest traces of the body could be discovered, and after a few minutes' careful scrutiny, the men gathered round their venerable and respected pastor, with fear and wonder depicted upon their countenances, and anxiety at their hearts.

"What be we to do, sir?" said one.

"I—I cannot tell," said the clergyman. "My friends, there was here upon this grave the dead body of one whom I loved in life, even as you know I loved the fair being who sleeps in peace beneath the verdant sod."

"There was indeed, master," faltered old Andrew. "I left you with the body of—of——"

"Herbert Mandeville," said the pastor.

"Yes—yes, it was he, master. I saw him—I saw him."

"That body is no longer here," continued the clergyman. "This is a mystery that time possibly may unravel, or it may please Heaven that it should remain, as it is at present, most inexplicable."

The villagers looked at each other in mute dismay.

"Let us return," said the clergyman. "Our presence here is not required. Come, my friends. All that has happened is by the special providence of God, without doubt."

The villagers were not slow in obeying the hint to leave the churchyard, for if their fears were before awakened, their superstitious feelings were now so completely aroused, that they started in alarm at their own shadows as they flitted over the grave-stones, and they were too much paralyzed by fear even to speak.

Thus in a silent shuddering throng they left the churchyard, and it was with a feeling of inexpressible relief that they passed through the wicket gate, which led from the consecrated ground to the winding lane, conducting them back to the village.

The clergyman paused, and said :—

"I thank you, friends ; good night—good night."

With many "Good nights, sir," and muttered kind wishes, for all loved the old man, who had been for nearly sixty years among them, the villagers retired, and left him leaning in deep thought upon the wicket gate.

Their footsteps died away in the distance, and then the aged pastor spoke to his servant who had remained with him.

"Andrew," he said, "you saw the body?"

"Yes, master ; these eyes saw it as plainly as I now see you."

"It could be no delusion ;" sighed the clergyman. "It seems to me like a troubled dream."

He continued in deep thought for many minutes, and then he said :—

"Andrew, we could not be both deceived. There is some mystery in this that I cannot comprehend. Did you see the face of the body that lay upon 'The Grave of the Forsaken ?'"

"No, master."

"But you—you are sure it was Herbert Mandeville?"

"Quite, sir!—Alas! I knew him well. It was him, indeed!"

"The face bore the hue of death," muttered the clergyman. "The limbs were rigid and cold."

"The night, master," said Andrew, "is wearing on. The wind is chilling."

"True," said the pastor. "Go home, Andrew."

"Without you, sir?"

"Yes, I—wish you to do so. Give me your lantern. I will myself again examine the churchyard."

"I—I—will stay, sir," said Andrew.

"No," replied the clergyman. "Go home, and say I shall return within the hour. I wish to be alone."

The old servant obeyed, and handing the lantern to his master, he, with reluctant steps, left him alone by the wicket gate opening into the churchyard.

CHAPTER III.

"Gold he loved not. He had outlived
The thirst for power, and he lived
But to do good and die in peace."

A RETROSPECTION.—THE CURATE AND HIS FRIEND.—MRS. PLUMPJOY'S INDIGNATION.—BRIGHT PROSPECTS.

Four years and a few months before the startling event we have recorded occurred at the little village of Bracefield, an accession was made to the family of the clergyman by the arrival of a young gentleman at the parson-

No. 2

age, whose distinguished appearance and handsome open countenance won all hearts, and set expectation upon the tip-toe as to who he would like, and who he would not like—who he would visit, and who he would abstain from visiting. The old folks talked about him over their tea. The young maidens whispered together about his face—his eyes—his figure, and his jet black ringlets ; and they looked perpetually in looking-glasses, and sighed and wondered, and sighed again, to think how very impossible it was that he could fall in love with, and marry every one of them.

The young men of the village were eaten up with envy, and they laughed in an excited and hysterical manner whenever the handsome young stranger was mentioned, and found a thousand faults with his figure—his height—his complexion—his dress. In fact, the more they admired and gnawed their nails with envy, the more they found fault, so that, at last, there was quite a tumult in Bracefield ; for some affected great candour, and protested strictly that the young stranger was very passable, indeed ; while the others called him a fop, a dandy, an effeminate individual.

Thus Bracefield became quite divided into two parties, who might not inaptly have been respectively called Mandevilleites and anti-Mandevilleites ; for Mandeville was the name of the young man who unconsciously and unknowingly had become an apple of discord to the village youths and maidens of Bracefield.

In the meantime the object of all this contention, and all this envy, all this admiration, both expressed and unexpressed, was totally unaware of his extremely popular character, and pursued for a time the even tenor of his way, favouring neither the Mandevilleites nor the anti-Mandevilleites with so much as a passing thought.

His position in the parsonage-house is easily explained. The good old clergyman had grown grey, as a curate upon the scanty stipend of seventy pounds a-year, and had been upon the point of uncomplainingly settling himself down in the vale of years, with the conviction that a seventy pounds a-year curate he was, and ever would be, when one day he unexpectedly received an affectionate letter from an old schoolfellow, which, while it altered his prospects, did not in the end improve the happiness of the now aged man.

We transcribe the letter, as it will account for some circumstance in the position of the magnet of attraction, who now sojourned beneath the roof of the Rev. Robert Endsleigh, as the clergyman was named. It ran thus :—

"Portman Square.   May 10th, 1824.

"MY DEAR ENDSLEIGH,—I dare say you have forgotten me long ago, or thought me dead, or ungrateful, for the many happy hours we have spent together when our lives were ' young as a May morning,' and if you do not, or did not think and wonder as I have suggested, you will wonder still more at hearing from me now, after forty years of absence and silence. Forty years, Endsleigh ! What an eternity would such a lapse of time have appeared to us when last we parted at Cambridge. Seriously speaking, I should hardly have thought of ' raking up the ashes of time,' to discover your whereabouts, and that I once knew you well, but for the accidental mention of your name by a gentleman, who I much esteem, by the name of Charles Leslie. Then, my dear Endsleigh, an ancient chord, which had long given forth no melody, was struck in my heart, and it conjured up ' The Light of other Days,' when we used to wander together, hand in hand, by the classic banks of that small stream which washes Trin. Coll. Cam.

" You will excuse me, I am sure, for making some inquiries concerning you, but I am not quite sure you ought to excuse me for not making them twenty years ago.

"I learned that you were 'a curate.' It happens that I am grown well to do, and partly and tolerably rich, and, consequently, in the world's estimation virtuous and great, and estimable, with 'troops of friends,' among whom I am allowed to number a high legal functionary, who, to oblige me, has transferred a snug little rectory, as I am told, of some eight hundred a year to you, at a place called Neesom, God knows where, but I dare say you will be able to find it out somehow, Endsleigh.

"And now, my dear Endsleigh, I have a son—the Benjamin of my old age. He is handsome (more's the pity), accomplished (I can't help it), gay, thoughtless, generous, wild, feeling, extravagant, charitable, heedless, witty. In short, my dear fellow, I don't know what he is not exactly, except thus much, that from my heart I believe he has no vice. He has got among a bad set in London, his age is sixteen (dangerous). Now, my dear Endsleigh, will you take him for a year or two, and—and—teach him a little Latin, and a great deal of discretion.

"Pray let me have an immediate reply.

"The Rev. Robert Endsleigh,   "Your ancient friend,
"Bracefield, Wales.   "CUTHBERT MANDEVILLE."

The curate felt a variety of emotions at the receipt of this letter. He was pleased to hear from his old friend and schoolfellow, whom he had not seen or heard of for so many years; but he was not altogether pleased at the worldly wise style of the letter, so very different in thought and feeling from what he recollected of its writer before twenty summers had passed over his head.

He read the epistle several times over, and particularly that part which alluded to the son of his old friend and playmate—for, strange to say, the offer of the rectory at Neesom, and the eight hundred pounds per annum connected therewith, did not sound charming in the ears of the now aged old man.

He shook his head slightly when he came to that part of the letter, and merely said, mildly—

"There was a time—there was a time, but it has long gone by now. No—no—I will live and die here."

He then passed on to the extraordinary description of the young man who he was asked to take, and the good, simple-minded clergyman was sorely puzzled as he read and re-read it.

"Very singular," he said. "What a strange young man. Take him oh, dear yes, and teach him Latin—with great pleasure. The son of my old friend. Dear me, what a singular character. Heedless, witty, thoughtless charitable, gay. Dear me, how very odd. I must show this to Martha. She is of the world, and can tell me more in half an hour of society and its habits and customs than I can recollect in a year."

So saying, the old man took his spectacles carefully off, and having with due deliberation deposited them in their morocco case, he left his room in quest of his sister, Mrs. Plumpjoy, who lived with him in the character of housekeeper and domestic superintendent, an office which she voluntarily took upon herself upon the decease of her husband, Major Plumpjoy, of the militia, and although the good pastor was very happy in his bachelor establishment before she came, yet she so continually dinned in his ears what a favour she was doing him by residing with him, and "keeping things straight and square," as she expressed it, that at last he began to believe it in the simplicity of his heart, and to look upon Mrs. Martha Plumpjoy as a person to whom he owed great obligations.

Mrs. Martha Plumpjoy is much too important, and in her own opinion, high and mighty a personage to introduce at the end of a chapter, so we shall pay her the compliment of commencing a new one with her most euphonious and gratifying name, a name in which the defunct major greatly rejoiced, and his widow took especial care that its dignity and magnificence should lose nothing while it was in her official keeping. In fact, Mrs. Martha Plumpjoy had had privately printed no less a number than one hundred cards, each one bearing the astounding announcement of " Mrs. Major General Plumpjoy," which cards she used upon extraordinary occasions, and justified herself in adding the " general" to the " major," because the deceased Plumpjoy was in the " general line" for many years, which consists in selling something of everything in a dirty shop.

~~~~~~~~~~~~~~~~~~~~

CHAPTER IV.

THE REJECTED OFFER.—THE CURATE'S HOSPITALITY.—PREPARATIONS FOR AN ARRIVAL.

> " He was so single-minded, and so pure of heart,
> That malice passed him by, or if a shaft was aim'd
> At his pure breast, his virtue like a triple shield, did
> Ward it off."

MRS. MARTHA PLUMPJOY was rather lean than otherwise, in fact an ill-natured person might have gone so far as to call her " scraggy." She was tall, beyond the altitude of women, and there was a wiry action about her neck, and a constant restlessness about her keen grey eyes, that bespoke a vast quantity of fidget and discomfort to all around her.

With the open letter in his hand, the old clergyman approached his sister, and his troubled countenance assured her that something unusual had occurred to disturb his usual calm serenity.

" Martha," he began mildly, " here's a letter."

" Well," screamed Martha, " of course I see there's a letter ;—' next comes a horse to be shaved.'" This was a favourite exclamation of Mrs. Martha Plumpjoy's, and she used it on all occasions, whether appropriate or otherwise ; sometimes, but very rarely, and upon solemn and stupendous circumstances, " and a pig to have his corns cut !"

" It's from young Mandeville !—no—that is—eh dear me, he is young Mandeville no longer—that was forty years ago. An old friend of mine, Martha, has written this letter."

" Who is he, I should like to know ?" screamed Mrs. Plumpjoy.

" Cuthbert Mandeville, Martha."

" And who is he ?"

" An old college acquaintance who I have not heard of for forty years, or more."

" Is he rich ?"

" I believe he is ; but that's no matter."

" No matter, Robert Endsleigh ?—no matter ? ' Next comes a horse to be shaved, and a pig ——"

" Well, Martha, he is rich," interrupted the clergyman.

" To have his corns cut," screamed Mrs. Plumpjoy, finishing her broken sentence.

" Will you read the letter, Martha, and give me your opinion ?"

" Was the post paid ?"

" Why, really, Martha, I—upon my word I don't know."

" I thought as much ; I wonder what you would know if I was'n't here ? You'd be out of house and home in no time, and not know it, that you would. You are the most careless man, really — ' Next comes a horse to be shaved.'"

" Well, well," said Mr. Endsleigh ; " I know all that, however. Well, have you read the letter, Martha? because I ought to send an answer to such an epistle at once."

"We'll see about that," said Mrs. Plumpjoy, seizing the letter, and turning it round and round to examine the post mark."

"Eightpence halfpenny, as I'm a sinner!" she suddenly exclaimed.

"What's the matter?" asked Mr. Endsleigh.

"It wasn't paid!" screamed Mrs. Plumpjoy.

"Very likely not," calmly answered her brother.

"Very likely not? Are you mad? Think of eightpence halfpenny!— Think of it!—'Next comes a ——'"

"Well, well, sister," said the clergyman, who had quite a horror of the horse coming to be shaved, from having the expression dinned into his ears so often. "Just read the letter; if it be not paid, you know we can't help it now."

"Horse to be shaved," said Mrs. Plumpjoy, completing her sentence as usual, whenever the opportunity occurred.

She then generously condescended to read Mr. Mandeville's letter, which, when she had concluded, she folded up with great deliberation, saying :—

"A very proper letter, indeed. Goodness gracious, I'm all of a flutter. 'Next comes a horse to be shaved, and a pig to have his corns cut.' Is it possible? Oh, brother! brother!"

Here Mrs. Plumpjoy fanned herself with the letter.

"Well, Martha," said Mr. Endsleigh, "what is your opinion in this matter? for I think it is one in which your feelings as a resident with me, ought to be particularly consulted."

"What do I think?" cried Mrs. Plumpjoy; "why, what can I think, but that it's the best thing in the world. Write an answer in the clearest affirmitative."

"Affirmative, Martha, you mean?"

"Well, well, it's much the same. It's a most sensible gentlemanly letter as ever I read in my life."

"I am glad your opinion coincides with my own feelings," said Mr. Endsleigh, "for I was really afraid that the description of the young man would not have prepossessed you in his favour."

"Young man?" cried Mrs. Plumpjoy.

"Yes, Martha," said her brother, "the son of my old friend, who he wishes me to take charge of for a year or two."

"Oh, dear me! now I recollect, there is something about a young man of a very troublesome sort of character, at the end of the letter. I skipped most of that."

"You skipped most of that, Martha?"

"Yes, to be sure. I think of the dear eight hundred a year, and the sweet charming rectory; and I'm only surprised you could hesitate a moment, brother, with such a prospectus before you."

"A what—a what?"

"A prospectus."

"A prospect, you mean, I suppose?"

"Well it's all the same. 'Next comes a horse ——'"

"Sister, sister, I fear we misunderstand each other," said Mr. Endsleigh, gravely shaking his head.

"To be shaved," cried Mrs. Plumpjoy.

"I did not come to ask your advice about the Rectory of Meesom," said the poor curate.

"And pray, what may I ask did you come for?" said Mrs. Plumpjoy, in rather an indignant tone of voice

"About this young man, Martha. I was fearful that you would be repugnant to receive such an inmate."

"Oh, dear me!" cried Martha, "I'm sure I don't see how we can well refuse to have him, brother."

"Nor I," said the curate. "He shall come, then."

"Oh, certainly. Really you know it would look so very ungrateful to Mr. Mandeville, after his great kindness. We must take the bitters with the sweet, you know, brother; but I really thought you came to me about that charming offer of a rectory, and the dear eight hundred a year."

"No, Martha, upon that subject my mind is quite made up."

"I should think so."

"I needed no advice upon that matter, for it concerned me and my feelings solely, without reference to any one else."

"Oh, dear, yes, to be sure. Certainly."

"I shall, therefore, decline the offer at once."

Mrs. Plumpjoy was struck dumb by this sudden blow, and she could only gasp for a few moments, and mutter some indistinct allusion to the horse who required shaving, and the pig whose corns were troublesome.

"I repeat," said Mr. Endsleigh, who saw her surprise and indignation, I repeat, that I shall decline the offer, handsome and unexpected as it is. I am an old man now, and worldly advancement has lost its charm to me. I am here, and here I will remain as long as it shall please Heaven to permit me."

"Goodness gracious," screamed Mrs. Plumpjoy, when she did recover the power of speech; "is the man mad?"

"I think I should be," said Mr. Endsleigh, with a smile, "if I were at my time of life to go into a new parish with any expectation of doing good to its inhabitants, when my lease of existence would be most likely run out long before I could acquire local knowledge sufficient to make myself useful at all."

"But the eight hundred pounds?" cried Mrs. Plumpjoy; "you forget the eight hundred pounds?"

"And it is fitting I should do so," answered Mr. Endsleigh.

"But you really can't seriously mean ——"

"To reject the offer, you would say, sister? Yes, I do reject it, of course, with such thanks as such an offer deserves. My mind is made up upon the subject, Martha."

"Well," exclaimed Mrs. Plumpjoy, holding up her hands in surprise, and displaying a pair of well darned black silk mittens. "Well, I never. Goodness gracious Next comes a ——"

Mr. Endsleigh picked up his letter, and hurried from the room, for he knew well what was coming.

"'Horse to be shaved,' screamed his sister, in a loud shrill tone, after him, 'and a pig to have his corns cut.' Was there ever such an obstinate strange man in the whole universal world. Eight hundred a year!—Goodness gracious!"

Mr. Endsleigh had made up his mind thoroughly about the rectory. He was not one of those who had gone into the church as they would go into business, merely with a view to the profits. No; he took a higher view of the duties of a clergyman; and while he considered that the labourer was worthy of his hire, he likewise considered the duties of his sacred office as the first consideration, viewing the stipend he received for them, only as a necessary circumstance to enable him to perform them properly, by lifting him above the practice of any other kind of labour, for procuring himself a subsistence.

By the very next post he transmitted the following letter to Mr. Mandeville, in reply to his which he had received :—

"Bracefield, May, 10th, 1824."

"MY DEAR MANDEVILLE,—Believe me, it was with feelings of satisfaction that I received your kind epistle, and I shall not quarrel with it because it came not twenty years ago, for I have been very happy for those twenty years, and it is very probable that I might not have been so happy under other circumstances.

"I am now an old man, Mandeville. You recollect I am your senior by seven or eight years, and I have lived here for many summers. Permit me, therefore, to remain, where, I flatter myself, I am useful, and in that conviction, find happiness, at least such happiness as may pass under the word content.

"Believe me, I am not regardless of your kind offer. It is a great thing that you have placed within my grasp; but while I feel that it is such, I likewise feel that I am very old. Let me, therefore, live and die here, the humble, but I hope, useful Curate of Bracefield.

"With respect to your son, I say yes, with pleasure. Send him to me, when you please. I will do my best for him; but bear in mind that my home is only comfortable, not luxurious; that we have at Bracefield the necessaries of life, not the elegancies, except you are inclined to believe with me, that what is useful and necessary, is commonly to a reflecting mind the most luxurious and elegant.

"Let your son come, then, and he shall receive such care and attention from me, as I would have bestowed upon a child of my own.

"Believe me, my dear Mandeville,

"Your sincere friend,

"ROBERT ENDSLEIGH."

"To Cuthbert Mandeville, Esq."

This letter was written, and despatched, by the poor curate, to his rich and prosperous friend, with the purest and best intentions. It cost him no pang to resign a rectorship with eight hundred per annum. His whole anxiety was now concerning the young charge that he had undertaken to receive into his house, and he waited with some degree of nervous expectation for an answer to his letter.

That evening was a very uncomfortable one at the parsonage, for Mrs. Plumpjoy was ultimately dignified and remonstrative. She repeatedly summoned the horse to be shaved, and the pig to have his corns cut; and upon the whole, Mr. Endsleigh was much pleased when the hour of retiring to rest arrived, and he could at least calculate upon seven or eight hours of peace from the persecutions of Mrs. Martha Plumpjoy.

CHAPTER V.

" Men of the world, which means men of the meanest
Dispositions, cannot understand self-denial."

GOLDSMITH.

MORE DISCUSSIONS.—THE RESULT.—AN ANSWER FROM LONDON.—THE
ALLOWANCE.—THE CURATE'S SCRUPLES.

THE morning came as morning is sure to come, alike to the happy and the miserable.

Mr. Endsleigh saw, the moment he entered the breakfast-room, that there was a most portentous cloud upon the majestic brow of his sister, or to speak more properly, his majestic sister's brow.

The toast and muffins were handed about for a time in gloomy silence, but Mrs. Plumpjoy after waiting in vain for Mr. Endsleigh to break the silence by an inquiry as to what ailed her, or what was the matter, could endure it no longer, and setting down her empty tea cup with a blow in the saucer, which must have broken one or both, had it not been judiciously managed, she cried with a voice indicative of a highly disturbed and indignant state of mind :—

"Brother !"

"Sister," replied Mr. Endsleigh, calmly.

"Are you," she continued, "as obstinate as ever ?"

"Precisely," answered the clergyman.   "I am not aware of any particular change in me, for the better or worse, lately."

"Do you wish to drive me crazy ?"

"Certainly not."

"Then what do you mean ?"

"As regards what ?" said Mr. Endsleigh, with a face of great innocence.

"Do you see that ?" cried Mrs. Plumpjoy, throwing a card before her brother's face with great emphasis.

"Yes," answered the curate, mildly.

"Well," screamed his sister, "what do you make of that ?"

"A very unfeminine and unchristian name," answered her brother.

"What ?" screamed Mrs. Plumpjoy.

"An unfeminine and unchristian name," repeated Mr. Endsleigh.   "This I see is one of the absurd cards that I conditioned with you, when you came here you were never to presume to use."

"Presume ?" shrieked his sister.

"Yes," he continued mildly ; "it's great presumption I think."

"What, may I ask, do you see presuming in that card ?" asked Mrs. Plumpjoy, shouting with suppressed anger.

"Mrs. Major-General Plumpjoy," replied the curate.

"Well, sir, did I not resign that beautiful title on your account ?"

"Certainly not."

"Certainly not ?"

"I repeat, certainly not.   You had no right to it, putting aside its barbarism and bad taste, and you resigned it rather than be subjected to the bad consequences of keeping it, I apprehend."

"I leave this place to-day," said Mrs. Plumpjoy, rising grandly.

"Very well," said the curate, who was quite well used to such amusements ; "as you please, sister."

"You refuse fortune, Mr. Endsleigh, rank, and aristocrative distinction."

"What distinction ?"

"Aristocrative."

"Aristocratic, I suppose you mean, Martha, and if you allude to the rectory offered me, you are very right."

"You consent to take into the house a young man——"

"The son of my old friend—yes I do most willingly."

"Then next comes a horse to be——

"Well, well, sister, that will do."

"Shaved," persisted Mrs. Plumpjoy ; "and a pig to——""

Mr. Endsleigh made a precipitate retreat, not, however, before he heard the last words, as he escaped from the room of—

"Have his corns cut !"

Mrs. Martha Plumpjoy was all that day occasionally dignified, and rarely condescended to speak to any one, and when she did, it was in the tone of a suffering martyr, who felt keenly, but would not openly complain.

Mr. Endsleigh could not expect an answer to his letter till the following

morning, therefore he controlled his impatience as well as he could until then, and carefully avoided all opportunities of fruitless discussion with his sister, who he saw was quite ripe for a pitched battle upon the subject of the reception, or non-reception of Mr. Mandeville's son, who bore so strange a character.

The second morning arrived, and Mrs. Plumpjoy said, with great gravity and an affection of excessive dignity,

"Mr. Endsleigh, I'm going to-day."

"Very well," he again replied.

"I'm going, *nolus volus*."

"Going where?"

"*Nolus volus*."

"*Nolens volens*, do you mean?"

"It's of no consequence, of course, what I mean in this house," said Mrs. Humpjoy, with a wave of her tolerably muscular arms. "I'm nothing here, no more to nobody."

"Humph!" said the curate.

"I shall go where a relic of a military man," continued the widow, "will be respected, and my card will introduce me into the best of society."

"Humph," again said the curate, eating his dry toast with great unconcern and deliberation.

"This roof," said Mrs. Plumpjoy, casting her eyes to the ceiling, "will cover me no more. I'm going—I tell you, Mr. Endsleigh, I'm going."

"I hear you," answered her brother.

"And you shall hear of me too," cried the widow; "I will go and reign."

"Go and what, Martha?"

"Reign as the star of fashion in my proper spear."

"Your proper sphere, you mean, I suppose?"

"Of course what I mean is neither here nor there," continued Mrs. Plump-

No. 8

joy, gradually working herself up into a fury ; " I'm going—I'm going, I repeat, I'm going !"

" Into a rage," muttered the curate, as he swallowed the last drop of his tea, and meditated an instant retreat.

" I will pay you the compliment," said his sister, with a smile of conscious superiority, " of asking your advice as to my proceedings upon leaving your house, Mr. Endsleigh."

" Oh, thank you," said the curate. " Well, since you ask, I should conscientiously advise you, sister——"

" What ?"

" To go by the waggon, wherever you mean to go."

" The waggon ?" shrieked the widow.

" Yes," continued the curate ; " it's safer—more comfortable I think, and a great deal cheaper I believe."

There is no knowing what Mrs. Plumpjoy would have said or done, had not the door just then opened to admit Jane, the only servant the curate could keep, and upon her immediately all the wrath of Mrs. Plumpjoy turned.

" Hussey !" she exclaimed ; " how dare you ?"

" Mum ?" said Jane ; " what mum ? oh lor, what ?"

" How dare you come into this room with brimstone-coloured ribbons in that trolloping—lazy—idle—good-for-nothing—desolate (dissolute, the lady probably meant)—cap of yours ?"

" Really sister," interrupted Mr. Endsleigh.

" And really, brother," screamed his sister ; " I suppose next will come a horse——"

" Oh, dear," said the curate, rising.

" To be shaved," bawled his sister, standing between him and the door ; and a pig to——"

" That'll do—that'll do, sister, I know ; I know."

" Have his corns cut," triumphantly concluded Mrs. Plumpjoy, and she plumped into a seat, with a shock that shook the little dwelling to its foundations.

" Please, sir," said Jane, addressing her master ; " Andrew told me to bring this letter to you, sir."

" A letter ?" said the curate, eagerly.

" Yes, sir, here it is."

" There, now go, there's a good girl, go—from Mandeville, without doubt ; ah—yes—I know his hand well : I—I once knew it better ; forty years ago, 'tis a long—long time."

Without paying the least attention to his sister, Mr. Endsleigh walked to the window and opening the letter, was immediately absorbed in its contents, which were as follows :—

                                        " Portman Square, May 11, 1824.

" MY DEAR ENDSLEIGH,—So you won't be the Rector of Musam ? I think you are right. You say you are happy ; I would I could say as much ; I would give everything I possess for a little quietness. I took your note to my Lord ——, and the living is already transferred to another person. He was pleased and amused, and offers an augmentation (how to be managed I don't know) of your curacy, to double its present value, and of which you will, of course, receive official notice.

" And now, Endsleigh, to say I thank you for your willingness to take my boy, is to say but little, nevertheless, all I can say is, that from the bottom of my heart I do thank you, for you must be strangely altered, if you are not the very person, of all others, who is most fit to discharge the duty of friend and tutor, to a young man like my son, (by the by his name is Herbert).

"And now, my dear old friend, how came you to imagine for a moment, that I intended, (and it seems to me that you did imagine so by the tone of your note), to impose my son upon you as a burthen—a burthen he may be, but not in a way which your kindness would make him. No, Endsleigh—I consider it a great personal favour for you to take him at all ; and that matter so far settled, of course, you will allow me to make you the same allowance for his expenses, &c., that I should have to give a perfect stranger, without your high qualifications and character.

"I shall, therefore, credit you for four hundred pounds per annum, which shall be paid to you through my bankers, in any way you may choose to point out.

"Herbert then will be with you in a few days, and within a fortnight or three weeks, I will myself contrive to run down, to shake once more by the hand my oldest, and I am convinced, my best and most sincere friend.

"Believe me, my dear Endsleigh,
"Yours faithfully,
"CUTHBERT MANDEVILLE."

"To the Rev. Robert Endsleigh,
"Bracefield."

"This is satisfactory enough," said the curate, "but the sum is enormous. No, no, it would be downright robbery! Four hundred pounds per annum. Oh, dear, a great deal too much."

Mrs. Plumpjoy pricked up her ears, and said,

"What do I hear? Do you talk of—of money?"

"Yes," said the curate. "Mr. Mandeville offers four hundred pounds a-year with his son."

Mrs. Plumpjoy held her handkerchief to her face for a few moments, and then said, mildly,

"Brother."

"Well, sister," said the curate.

"Do you really wish——"

"Wish what?"

"Me to—to—to go?"

"Certainly not."

"Then this once—I—think I'll—stay. Four hundred a-year. Goodness gracious! Next comes a——"

Mr. Endsleigh ran out of the room.

CHAPTER VI.

" I saw young Harry with his beaver on,
Leap on his steed like winged Mercury."
SHAKSPERE,

THE ARRIVAL.—HEARTS TAKEN BY STORM.—THE CURATE'S IDEAS OF HIS DUTY.
—A CONVERSATION.

THE day—the important day on which the young stranger was to arrive, found everything in a bustle at the curate's house, for Mrs. Martha Plumpjoy had, like many ladies, a peculiar talent in keeping everybody out of sorts for a long time, in the very midst of such preparations, when quietness, order, and decorum, were most of all desired.

At length, towards the close of the evening, Herbert Mandeville did arrive, and his appearance at once prepossessed the good curate strongly in his favour, a prepossession which time and adverse acts did not succeed in entirely eradicating.

Mrs. Plumpjoy was very much struck, and bitterly regretted that she had not worn the identical white satin dress which had won the heart of Major Plumpjoy at a county ball.

Jane ran down stairs, and in defiance of everybody, inserted in her cap the identical brimstone-coloured ribbons, assuring herself candidly that young Mr. Mandeville was a perfect love, a dear, and an " Apoller."

There was a winning grace, an enchanting sweetness about young Herbert Mandeville, that it would have required the stoutest philosophy to resist. Nobody thought of resisting it at the parsonage, and within an hour after his arrival, he was installed the chief and prime favourite of every one.

He was welcomed by the curate with paternal kindness, and Mrs. Plumpjoy, as she executed a magnificent sweeping curtsey, belonging to the last century, called up into her countenance as nearly as she could recollect it, the precise simpering expression which she had assumed at the delightful moment, when Major Plumpjoy plumped the exciting question of to marry or not to marry.

Herbert replied with an easy and yet an humble grace to the curate. He bowed faultlessly to Mrs. Plumpjoy, smiled his thanks to old Andrew, the curate's servant, who officiously assisted in carrying his luggage, and Jane was ready, she declared, to take her Bible oath that young Mr. Herbert Mandeville very nearly winked at her, which wink, or projected wink, when translated, could mean nothing else than—how very handsome you are, and how amazingly that brimstone-coloured ribband does become you to be sure.

" I hope your father is well," said the curate to his young charge.

" He is as well, sir," replied Herbert, " as he has been for many years' past : his health has never, to my knowledge, been good."

" Dear me," said the curate, " he used to be very robust."

" I think," said Herbert, " he is very hypocondriacal."

" Indeed !" said the curate.

" Goodness gracious," thought Mrs. Plumpjoy, " what can that mean ? Very—what ? Let me try to recollect—*highpocofryhiscal.* What an extraordinary thing to be ; it's very fashionable, no doubt, though."

" You look older than you are," said the curate.

" I believe it is generally so considered," replied Herbert. " I am nearly seventeen, now."

" Goodness gracious," said Mrs. Plumpjoy.

" Madam !" said Herbert.

" Next came a ——"

" Hem !" said Mr. Endsleigh, " and for once in her life, Mrs. Plumpjoy took the hint, and the horse came not to be shaved, nor the pig to have his pedel excresences amputated."

The good curate was most anxious for some private conversation with his pupil, and after a slight repast, he proposed to Herbert a walk through the environs of the village, to which the young stranger gladly assented, and it was with a mixture of strange feelings that the now old Robert Endsleigh walked forth arm in arm with the son of his old friend who had so often been the companion of his walks.

They walked through the village exchanging only common place remarks upon the various objects which met their gaze ; but when they arrived into the open country, the curate thought—

" Now begin the most important of my duty, which is to ascertain what my pupil knows and what may be the peculiar bent of his mind."

" Herbert," said Mr. Endsleigh, " you are aware of how intimate your father and I were many years ago ?"

" I am, answered Herbert. " He has often expatiated upon that intimacy, and I am quite sure thinks of it always with pleasure."

" The basis of that intamacy, Herbert, was candour and truth telling," said the curate, kindly.

"I understand you, sir," replied Herbert; "without assuming to possess them, I can endeavour to emulate those high virtues."

The curate looked very much pleased.

"Herbert," he said, "we shall get on very well together."

"I do not doubt it, sir," replied Mandeville.

"Now then," said Mr. Endsleigh, "will you permit me to ask you a plain question, Herbert?"

The young man slightly coloured as the curate spoke, but it was only for a moment, and he replied—

"Certainly, sir."

"And you will answer me, candidly?"

"I will."

"Was there any special circumstance then that induced your father so very suddenly to decide upon your removal from London to this quiet and somewhat dull retreat?"

"Yes," replied Herbert. "There was, in my father's estimation, a special reason, although not in mine."

"I thought as much," said the curate, in a tone of slight vexation.

"My father," said Herbert, after a pause, "did not then communicate to you the reason of my rustication?"

"He did not," answered Mr. Endsleigh.

Herbert said nothing, but walked on in silence by the side of the curate, apparently absorbed in his own reflections. In fact, neither of them spoke for many minutes, and they both felt that a little awkwardness had occurred through Mr. Mandeville's want of candour in his written communications to the curate.

"What was the special circumstance, Herbert?" said the curate; "I think fitting I should know, and not be left perhaps to do you an injustice by mere surmises upon the subject."

"I can have no objection, sir," said Herbert, "to tell you candidly all that I know upon the subject of my withdrawal from London."

"I do not ask from idle curiosity," said Mr. Endsleigh; "your father has given me a trust, and I only seek to fulfil it to the best of my ability. For that purpose alone, I seek the information which I am pleased to perceive you betray no hesitation in giving me."

"There is a young lady," said Herbert.

"A what?" cried the curate with a start.

"Only a young lady, sir," replied Herbert Mandeville, with a smile.

"Dear me," said Mr. Endsleigh, "I had not the least idea it was anything of that kind. Well, Herbert, go on."

"Well sir, this young lady's name is Clara Seagrave."

"Clara Seagrave," repeated the curate. "Well, Herbert?"

"She is beautiful as a Houri."

"What?"

"Beautiful, sir; exceedingly beautiful."

The curate gave a groan.

"But do not mistake me, sir," said Herbert, hurriedly; "I am not in love with her."

"Oh, dear, no; certainly not," said Mr. Endsleigh.

"Well, sir," continued Herbert; "she was an only daughter of a very rich man, although not one of high rank; and upon her father's death, which took place within the present twelvemonth's, she became possessed of a large fortune."

"Yes, yes," said the curate; "go on, Herbert."

"She commenced then living in the most costly and extravagant style. She kept a sumptuous establishment, and her wealth won her access to the best of society. She gave—and in fact, I may speak of the present, and may say gives—for she is in full career—the most brilliant entertainments."

"And a single woman, too ?" said the curate.

"Yes," continued Herbert ; "an elderly female relative resides constantly with her, and beyond the love of show and expense, which are her peculiar foibles ; she enjoys, I believe, the most unblemished reputation."

"Humph," said Mr. Endsleigh, which was his mode of entertaining a doubt upon a subject.

"She invited me to her parties," continued Herbert, "and would have me so much in the house that it attracted observation."

"And your father became alarmed ?"

"Precisely so. He thinks her an intriguing woman ; the rest of the world think her an angel."

"Your father is most likely to be right, Herbert," said the curate ; "but what peculiar dangers were you exposed to at this ——"

"Clara Seagrave's ——"

"Aye, Clara Seagrave's house."

"There was high play," said Herbert.

"Gaming, you mean ?"

"Yes, and a general air of dissipation throughout her establishment. In fact, my father thought he saw ample reason for removing me from the sphere of what he calls her dangerous influence upon a young mind uninformed in the world's wisdom."

"I think your father is very right," said the curate. "These glittering, showy, and in most cases, heartless women, are the most mischievous pest of society. They are *ignes fatui* to delude mankind."

"Very true, sir," said Herbert ; "I do not like a constant glitter, and an effort to shine, that while it dazzles becomes painful."

"My dear Herbert, I am rejoiced to hear such sentiments from you," said the curate. "I was afraid your admiration for this woman had gone further than I now evidently see it has."

"I do admire her," said Herbert, "and that is all."

"I am very glad of it, said Mr. Endsleigh. "Is she accomplished, Herbert ?"

"Figure to yourself a faultless form !" cried Herbert.

"I will do no such thing," said the curate.

Herbert smiled as he continued. "She is very beautiful, indeed. A form cast in Nature's loveliest mould."

"Pho! pho! pho !" cried the curate.

"A face of radiant beauty !"

"Hem !" said the curate.

"A complexion—teeth, eyes—all perfect."

"Ha !"

"She sings as if inspired—talks like a philosopher—speaks foreign languages as if they were her own—laughs like a peal of silver bells—dances like a fairy."

"Pho ! pho ! pho !" cried Mr. Endsleigh. "Come home, Herbert. Come home and think no more of the woman. You don't love her."

"I do not, as Heaven is my witness," said Herbert. "I have yet to gaze enraptured on that form—that face which——"

"What ?" cried the curate.

"Which," continued Herbert, his eyes lighting with enthusiasm ; "shall lend a new charm to existence, and——"

"That will do, Herbert," cried Mr. Endsleigh, impatiently. "You forget that I am an old man. Come home, come home."

CHAPTER VII.

" Mrs. Brown.—Have you heard ?
Mrs. Green.—No! have you ?
Mrs. Brown.—You don't say so !
Mrs. Green.—Goodness gracious !"
VILLAGE GOSSIP.

THE VILLAGE IN A COMMOTION.—A MYSTERY.—ROSE VILLA AND ITS
INHABITANTS.—AN IMPORTANT EPOCH IN OUR TALE.

HAVING so far satisfactorily established Herbert Mandeville, who will occupy an important position in our narrative, at the house of the good curate of the parish of Bracefield, we must direct the indulgent reader's attention to other, and if possible, still more important personages in our chequered and eventful story.

The inhabitants of the village of Bracefield, presented but few peculiarities worthy the special observation of our readers, and those peculiarities which might, if recorded, excite a smile of contempt, or a tear of sympathy, were not of an uncommon order ; but on the contrary, incidental to every country village, with few exceptions.

The place, many years since, had been of more repute than it was at the period of the commencement of our tale. By some means or another it had become insignificant by being deserted by several wealthy and influential families, who had resided in the immediate vicinity. All at once a sort of fatality seemed to effect Bracefield. A sudden death from an accident to its heir, caused one family to abandon the place ; another got into serious pecuniary difficulties in consequence of a contested election, and emigrated to Boulogne, according to the rule and customs in such cases, made and provided.

In short, by a series of misfortunes, Bracefield gradually sunk into, not disrepute, for nothing disreputable or disagreeable could be said of the place, but neglect. It became neglected for no apparent cause, and sunk from a rising place into a little straggling village, on the outskirts of which there were a great many pretty little houses to let remarkably cheap.

It is towards these little houses, with their neat latticed windows, and briar little gardens in front, that we would draw the reader's attention at this period.

There were but few of them let, and the tenants of those few presented no peculiar varieties of the human species. There was one, however, which had remained unoccupied for a considerable period of time, on account of the very dilapidated state its garden was in, which prepossessed people against it, although a few days work would have restored it to a state of neatness and beauty.

The agent for letting these cottages resided at a market town, nearly twenty miles from Bracefield, so that the curious villagers, although they always felt a great deal of interest about the cottages, and who came to look at them, and what was offered for them, and what refused, had a great deal of difficulty in arriving at any facts concerning them, and were frequently thrown quite into consternation by the sudden occupancy of one of them, by people they had neither seen nor heard of before, to their great chagrin and annoyance.

This one that we have remarked as having been unoccupied so long, was, one morning, to the intense amazement of the whole village, found to possess inhabitants.

The shutters were unclosed, the windows cleaned, and there appeared altogether an air of comfort about the cottage, which was called Rose Villa, that was quite surprising, and in the short space of time in which it must have been accomplished, quite provoking and very inexplicable and unjustifiable indeed.

Rose Villa is let! There are people in Rose Villa, ran from mouth to mouth, and at one period or other throughout the day, every inhabitant of the village had found occasion, at least once, to pass the door and windows to make observations.

They could see nothing, however, all that day but white muslin curtains, which must have been put up in the course of the night. They were drawn close, which was very provoking, and very wrong into the bargain some thought; for, as they eagerly remarked, if people had nothing to hide, why did they close their muslin curtains?

All this occurred about two months before the arrival of Herbert Mandeville at Bracefield, and the villagers had very nearly got over their ferment about Rose Villa, when he came and stirred the stagnant pool of popular anxiety into a tempest of commotion again.

The whole of the day passed—the important day upon which Rose Villa became inhabited, without affording much satisfaction to the villagers, for the only one of the new household who made her appearance in the village, was an elderly woman, who had much of the air and manner of an old confidential domestic, and who came to make many little necessary purchases.

She was, of course, eagerly questioned, and her replies listened to with breathless attention, as if they had been the oracles of fate.

The old woman, however, was evidently prepared for a cross examination, and had thoroughly made up her mind how much to impart and how much to withhold.

"Who lives in Rosa Villa?" was the first question asked by the butcher's wife.

"I live in it," was the answer.

"Oh, dear, yes, but there's some one else I suppose?"

"Yes, certainly," was the dry reply.

"May I ask who?"

"Yes; my mistress."

"Your mistress? Oh dear me, is she—a—that is, eh?"

"I really don't know what you mean ma'am."

"Oh, I mean is she a single lady or a widow; or—or anything else?"

"A single lady, ma'am; a widow."

"A widow? Bless my heart, a widow."

"Yes," said the servant, "and we will trouble you to send for orders every morning, if you please, ma'am."

"Oh, dear, yes, certainly," replied the butcher's wife. "Mrs.—a—a; what's your missuses name?"

"Mrs. Mordaunt," said the servant, as she left the shop.

This much of information, and no more, was given to all who asked questions, and when those questions were pushed further, they met with a sturdy repulse.

Popular curiosity, therefore, was but scantily gratified, and the day passed off most fidgettily and portentously at Bracefield.

The news of the new arrivals, of course, soon found its way to the parsonage, for Mrs. Plumpjoy was a great lover of small gossip, and doted on anything mysterious.

Jane brought the news to her mistress, exclaiming,

"Oh, mum, mum! what do you think?"

"What do I think?" screamed Mrs. Plumpjoy. "Why, I think you are an ungrateful, idle——"

"But, mum," interrupted Jane, "Rose Villa has let itself, mum."

"What?" cried Mrs Plumpjoy.

"It's true, mum," persisted Jane. "There's people in Rose Villa, as nobody would have, you know, mum, on no account; on account of dirt, you know, mum."

"Dirt?" screamed Mrs. Plumpjoy. "Dirty people?"

"No, mum, the villa I mean," said Jane.

"Next comes a horse to be shaved," cried her mistress. "I thought you said the people were dirty, and nobody would have them."

"Oh no, mum."

"Who are they then? Come, tell me all about it."

"I don't know, mum."

"Not know? what's their name?"

"I don't know, mum."

"Nor who they are?"

"No mum."

"Then comes a pig to have his corns cut! Goodness gracious, I must see Mr. Endsleigh directly."

So saying, Mrs. Plumpjoy rushed wildly into the presence of the curate, exclaiming—

"What do you think? Here's people come into Rose Villa, and nobody knows who they are."

"Well?" said Mr. Endsleigh.

"Well," screamed her sister. "Do you call that well? nobody knows even their names."

"They won't tell their names?"

"I don't know whether they have been asked or not, I'm sure," cried Mrs. Plumpjoy. "But I think it's very dreadful."

"What's dreadful?" said the curate, calmly.

No. 4

" Why, your provoking manner to be sure," screamed his sister, flying from the room in a great passion.

The curate smiled as he heard, in the distance, the usual statement concerning the horse and the pig.

Although Mr. Endsleigh had no vulgar curiosity to satisfy, yet he was not entirely unheedful of the information that Rose Villa was let, for this one reason: It was a custom with him, as curate of the parish, to leave his card at the residence of every new comer to Bracefield, after which he left it to them to make his acquaintance, or not, according as they thought proper, for uninvited, he never afterwards obtruded himself upon their notice, nor would he in that case, but that he considered it as one of his duties as pastor of the village to make the offer of his personal acquaintance to every one of its inhabitants.

Accordingly, towards the close of the evening of the same day on which the new arrival had been discovered, Mr. Endsleigh walked from his own house to Rose Villa.

Before knocking at the door, he was prepossessed in favour of the new inhabitants, for there was evidently 'the pride of name' about them, and it was one of Mr. Endsleigh's maxims, that where people are fond and careful of their homes, they will usually be found to possess domestic virtues, and, on the contrary, people who are careless and disorderly as regard their dwelling-places, will ordinarily possess careless and disorderly feelings in general.

The windows were all scrupulously clean. White muslin blinds, as pure as driven snow, were neatly arranged at them, and there were evident preparations for restoring all the beauties of the little garden which had been so sadly neglected.

" All this looks well," said Mr. Endsleigh, as he knocked at the door.

It was opened immediately by the elderly domestic, who seemed to possess an intuitive tact in knowing a gentleman when she saw him, for her manner was deferential and respectful, as she said—

" Will you please to walk in, sir ?"

" No, I thank you," answered Mr. Endsleigh, " I merely called to leave my card. I am the curate of the parish, and it is my custom so to do when I am informed of any new inhabitants arriving within the limits of my pastoral jurisdiction."

" Thank you, sir," said the servant, as she took the card.

" Good day," said Mr. Endsleigh, in his usual kind and winning manner, as he left the door with a smile.

" Well ?" said Mrs. Plumpjoy, when he returned.

" Well, what ?" said the curate.

" You have been to Rose Villa ?"

" Yes."

" What have you found out ?"

" Why, I think they will undoubtedly do up the garden, and the windows are very clean indeed."

" Pshaw," cried Mrs. Plumpjoy. " Is that all ?"

" Yes, that is all," replied her brother.

" Then next comes a——"

The curate made his escape immediately to his own private room.

CHAPTER VII.

'Twas a loveliness ever in motion that flies
From the lips to the cheek—from the cheek to the eyes."

THE NEW ACQUAINTANCE.—THE NOTE.—THE VISIT AND ITS CONSEQUENCES.—
THE CURATE'S SURPRISE AND ADMIRATION.—THE WILD FLOWER.

THE next morning, after Mr. Endsleigh had left his card at Rose Villa, there came to the parsonage, by the elderly servant, a remarkable neatly folded note, addressed to the Rev. Robert Endsleigh, in which was a card, with the name upon it, 'Mrs. George Mourdant,' and further, the note contained these words :—

"Mrs. Mourdant begs to thank Mr. Endsleigh for his kind call, and to say that she shall always consider it a kindness on Mr. Endsleigh's part to favour Rose Villa with a visit."

"That's all very proper," said the curate, as he handed the note and the card across the table to his sister.

Mrs. Plumpjoy examined critically the card and conned the note, then she shook her head with an air of dissatisfaction, as she said—

"Well, I wonder who could make anything out of that ?"

"I don't see," said her brother, "that it is necessary to make anything further out of it than it distinctly specifies, an acknowledgment of my call, and a very kind general invitation."

"Well, all I have got to say is, that I don't like the new people at Rose Villa," cried Mrs. Plumpjoy, in a huff.

"You don't like them, sister ?"

"No—I don't."

"Why, you never saw them."

"Very well, brother ; I know that. You can't say I'm *prejudicated* against them, I'm sure."

"Prejudiced, you mean, I presume," said the curate, with a smile.

Mrs. Plumpjoy did not deign a reply, but walked with great dignity from the room.

However, after Mrs. Plumpjoy took refuge in offended dignity, or called upon the horse and the pig, from her brother's quiet remarks, which sounded so uncommonly like sarcasms, she always very quickly emerged again, and returned to the subject with renewed vigour.

Thus, on the next morning, she attacked the curate at breakfast, with the remark,

"Well, Robert, so I suppose you will go to-day to Rose Villa ?"

"No," said the curate, quietly.

"Not go ?" cried Mrs. Plumpjoy.

"Certainly not," was the reply.

"And may I presume to ask why not ?"

"Of course you may. I have an opinion that where liberty is given freely, should be very cautiously taken. Now, these new people have made me welcome, as the curate of the parish, doubtless, to call upon them, and I can't be too circumspect in using the privilege ; to abuse it would be shocking the extreme."

"Now, that's one of your oddities, brother," screamed Mrs. Plumpjoy. "You are so uncommonly particular about intruding and all that sort of thing that it's really quite absurd."

"Can any one be too particular about intruding ?" said Mr. Endsleigh.

"Oh, of course, they can," replied his sister. "Especially when I am dying with curiosity to know what sort of woman Mrs. Mourdant can possibly be, as you know to be the fact."

"Oh, indeed," said the curate, with a smile. "If that's the case, I must go, I suppose, in three or four days."

"Three or four days, brother?"

"Yes—to speak as clearly as possible," said Mr. Endsleigh; "I will call on the fourth morning from this, which will be on next Saturday."

"How can you wait so long?" cried his sister.

"Very easily, indeed," replied the curate.

"Goodness gracious, I couldn't. But wonders will never cease—next comes a horse——"

"Yes, I know," said Mr. Endsleigh.

"To be shaved," continued Mrs. Plumpjoy.

"I've heard you say so before," drily remarked the curate.

"And a pig to have his corns cut," continued Mrs. Plumpjoy, determined that he should lose nothing in the shape of annoyance for putting off the visit to the Mourdant's at Rose Villa, to such a unconscionable distance of time as the next Saturday, that day being but Tuesday.

The Saturday at length, in due course of time, arrived, and Mrs. Plumpjoy asked her brother, in a very triumphant tone of voice, if he would then visit Rose Villa, or hold himself for ever a perjured man?

"Yes, Martha," he replied, "I shall go to-day if nothing prevent me," and go he did.

It was in the morning that he thought proper to make his visit, and not knowing well, as a matter of course, the habits of the people he was about to visit, he made it late in the forenoon before he knocked at the door of Rose Villa.

The door was opened, as before, by the elderly domestic, and Mr. Endsleigh replied to the invitation to walk in, by stepping at once into the little parlour.

He proffered his card, which was taken respectfully, and while the servant was about announcing his presence, he had full leisure to examine the remarkable neat and tasteful apartment into which he had been shewn.

There was nothing of a rare or expensive character in the rooms, but the arrangement generally was exquisite. Early flowers bloomed in sweet luxuriance from every part, and the walls were adorned by drawings of extreme beauty and delicacy of execution.

Upon a small table, there lay a guitar, and some pieces of music, and upon another table were various materials for drawing, and an unfinished sketch which lay in an open portfolio, left no doubt upon the curate's mind, that the artist who had so sweetly adorned the walls with the works of his or her penci was a resident in Rose Villa.

Mr. Endsleigh was still admiring the drawings when the parlour-door opened and turning abruptly at the sound, he found himself in the presence of elderly lady, about whom there was that decided air of good breeding, whi at once stamps a person as belonging to, or as having largely associated wi the higher ranks of society.

She wore a widow's cap, and her face was very pale, and altogether the was an appearance of recent mental suffering depicted upon her countenance what might still have boasted of the remains of great beauty.

At the second glance the curate altered his opinion as to her age, and om thinking her past the prime of life, which had been his first impression arising, probably, from her paleness and look of ill health, he began to do't if she had more than reached the middle period of an ordinary existence.

These reflections passed rapidly through Mr. Endsleigh's mind as recovered from the gentlemanly bow with which he greeted the interesting-looking and really handsome widow.

In fact, he was pleased much with the appearance of Mrs. Mourdant, for such he of course, presumed her to be, and inwardly rejoiced at so becoming and apparently respectable an addition to the limited society of Bracefield.

"I have the pleasure," said Mrs. Mourdant, "of receiving Mr. Endsleigh."

"Yes, madam," said the curate, "and I sincerely hope you do not consider my visit an intrusion."

"Certainly not," replied Mrs. Mourdant, as she presented the curate with a chair; "your character and station, sir, precludes such a possibility."

"You are very good, madam," said Mr. Endsleigh, "and such services as may be in my power to render you during your stay at Bracefield, I beg you will always command."

"Of that I feel convinced," said Mrs. Mourdant. "I have heard too much of Mr. Endsleigh to doubt his generosity and kindness."

"May I ask from whom, madam?" said the curate.

"Through Mr. Leslie," was the reply.

"What?" cried the curate; "are you acquainted with my most estimable young friend, Charles Leslie?"

"I am," answered the widow. "My—my husband knew and esteemed him."

Mrs. Mourdant's voice faltered as she spoke, and Mr. Endsleigh had far too high an appreciation of the sacredness of genuine sorrow to interrupt by a single word the silence of a few minutes that ensued.

Mrs. Mourdant at length said—

"Pardon me, sir, but there are subjects that excite pain, unless——"

"Madam," interrupted Mr. Endsleigh, "say no more. I respect your sorrows, as much as I grieve for their origin."

"Mr. Leslie," continued the widow, "promised me that he would write to you a detailed account of who was to be your neighbour."

"I hope you acquit me of any idle curiosity to pry into your affairs, Mrs. Mourdant, but at the same time, I shall receive any communication from my esteemed young friend, Charles Leslie, with pleasure."

The widow bowed, and Mr. Endsleigh then said—

"Is Mr. Leslie now in England, can you tell me, for I have not heard from him for some time, and he spoke of going on the Continent?"

"If he be not in England now," said Mrs. Mourdant, "he will be soon, for he promised to become a frequent visitor to us, here."

"I rejoice to hear it," said the curate. "I know no young man for whom I entertain a greater respect."

Mr. Endsleigh now rose to conclude his visit, and he was upon the point of making his adieu, when the door opened and presented to the wondering eyes of the curate a vision that he was not at all prepared to encounter.

It was a young girl who stood half bending forward upon the threshold of the door, as in doubt whether to enter or not, and it was evident from her manner that she had not been aware of the presence of a visitor in the little flower-decked parlour.

The enthusiasm for female beauty had become much calmed down in the mind of Mr. Endsleigh, but upon this occasion he was taken so completely by surprise, first of all by the appearance of the young girl, and next by her surpassing loveliness, that he stood for several moments perfectly transfixed, and unable to utter a word.

CHAPTER VIII.

" Her form was radiant with pure feelings,
    And her beauty sat upon her like a garment
    Sent from Heaven.''

ADELINE AND THE CURATE.——BEAUTY AND SIMPLICITY.——THE FEARFUL RECOL-
LECTION——A PARENT'S FATE.

MRS. MOURDANT was the first to break the silence, and it was with something of a mother's pride in the beauty of her child, that she said—

"Mr. Endsleigh, this is my daughter Adeline."

Upon this the young girl with a radiant blush walked into the room, and
bowed with ineffable grace to the astonished curate.

The age of Adeline Mourdant was fifteen, but there was a graceful dignity
about her that made her look about one year older than she really was.

She was a creature of exquisite beauty. The graces of the child, the girl,
and the woman were all sweetly combined in her person.

She was not one of those coldly classical beauties who are faultless in form
and feature, and who enforce our admiration because they defy criticisms;
but the beauty of Adeline Mourdant was dear, sweet, loveable domestic
beauty—such a beauty as one could never tire of. It was a beauty of expression and action as much as a beauty of form.

She was fair, and her hair, which hung in waving ringlets nearly to her
slender waist, was of that glowing sunny hue so much esteemed by the an-
cients, and which we may occasionally see represented in some of the finest
heads of " the Virgin" by the old masters.

Her eyes were Heaven's own blue, and they were fringed by lashes, that
when she looked downwards and veiled for a moment the beauty of those twin
orbs of light, hung like silken threads upon her glowing cheek.

She had the sweetest little mouth in the world, and there were the dearest
dimples upon each side of it—dimples worth each a kingdom.

The curate, in fact, was more completely lost in admiration of Adeline
Mourdant than ever he had been in the whole course of his life at anything.
He could not help repeating to himself the exquisite lines attributed to
Herrick :—

" She surely is the youngest daughter of the sun,
    And never can be quenched by envious night.
    The beams she borrows from the glorious sun,
    Upon her velvet cheek the pure light glows.
    Her hair is tinted by a golden beam,
    Plucked from the orient west ;
    There's sunshine in her movements. Her voice
    Is sunshine—and her heart
    Is surely still the shrine of worshipped fires!''

The curate looked at the drawings, and for pure want of something to say,
for he did not like to burst out with, " Madam, how extremely beautiful your
daughter is," he said—

"I presume I may attribute these designs to—to Miss Adeline ?"

" Yes," replied Mrs. Mourdant, with a sigh ; " they are Adeline's drawings.
She devotes her time to music and the pencil."

" They are very beautiful, indeed," said the curate.

Mrs. Mourdant smiled a gratified smile, and cast a look of affection upon
her daughter, as Mr. Endsleigh pretended to be busy looking at the various
sketches of evidently foreign scenery that adorned the walls.

There was one drawing of a wild flower which the curate did not recognise, notwithstanding his knowledge of botany, which was very extensive, and he turned to the widow, saying—

"What flower is this, Madam? It seems a portrait, and yet has some peculiarities of structure."

Mrs. Mourdant glanced at the picture, and her lips quivered as if it called up some painful emotions.

"Dear mamma," said Adeline, throwing her arms round her mother's neck, heedless of the presence of a stranger.

It was the first word the curate had heard come from the lips of the beautiful girl, and so low and sweet was her voice, that it wounded like the exquisite breath of a flute, and the curate longed to say—

"Speak again!"

"I will tell Mr. Endsleigh, mother," said Adeline.

"Do, Adeline," said her mother. "Will you excuse me, sir?" to the curate, who could only bow his acquiescence, and she rose with her eyes swimming with tears and left the room.

"I—I am very sorry," said the curate, looking earnestly in the mild beautiful face of Adeline, "but I——"

"It was a natural question, sir," said Adeline, in her sweet tones, perhaps a shade sadder than before.

"I could not tell that it would distress your mother," added Mr. Endsleigh; "and can only regret what I cannot recall."

"But I will tell you," said Adeline.

"Nay," said the curate, "I will leave you, now, my dear young lady, "but not without a hope of improving our acquaintance."

"But mamma would rather you know about the picture," said Adeline, mildly, "and than she can bear to see you look at it without emotion."

"I will listen with pleasure," said Mr. Endsleigh.

"Have you heard of my father?" said Adeline, in a slightly tremulous voice.

"No," answered the curate.

"He was Captain Mourdant."

"In the army?" asked the curate.

"Yes," replied Adeline. "He—he——"

"Do not distress yourself," said Mr. Endsleigh; "some other time you shall tell me."

"No! no!" said Adeline, endeavouring to recover her composure, and laying her hand with all the innocence of a child upon the good clergyman's arm. "No, no—I will tell you, now."

The curate saw a tear drop from her eye as she spoke, and a sigh arose to his heart, as he thought, "If Heaven had blessed me with such a child!"

"They—they killed my poor father," said Adeline, evidently with a great effort. Then speaking quickly, she added—"Now sir, you know all. It is over now."

"I cannot tell you, you should not weep," said Mr. Endsleigh, kindly; "but I can promise you that Heaven will bless your tears as the offerings of a pure and guiltless heart."

"Thank you, thank you," said Adeline. "I do not weep much now, because I wish to comfort my mother."

"Now then, let me leave you," said the curate, "and be assured of the best wishes—the prayers and sympathies of an old man who has himself known sorrow."

"Nay, sir," said Adeline! "I will now tell you of the picture."

"As you please," said the curate.

"It is then," said Adeline, "a drawing of a peculiar flower that grows in some of the wild passes among the mountains in India."

"I guessed it was not European," said the curate.

"Its history is this," continued Adeline : "My poor father was with his regiment in India, advancing through a mountain defile, when he suddenly came upon one of these wild flowers, and as he had not seen one before he was struck by its beauty and peculiar colour. He stooped to pluck it, when at the instant a shot from some concealed enemy passed over him."

"Then under Providence he owed his life to that little flower !" said the curate.

"He did, sir," answered Adeline ; "he plucked the flower, and brought it home with him about two years since, and I drew it as a memorial of his strange preservation from death."

"It was worth preserving," said the curate ; "such things keep alive holy and good feelings."

"Alas !" said Adeline. "How short a time he was with us. Again he was forced to leave us, and we shall see him no more."

These words were spoken with a mournful tenderness that sunk deep into the compassionate curate's heart, and as if addressing one he had known for many years, he said :—

"My child, be comforted ; we are all in the hand of a just and merciful Providence. And there is a special Providence in the fall of a sparrow, even."

"I know, I know," said Adeline. "Charles Leslie told me so."

"And you may depend upon what Charles Leslie says," replied Mr. Endsleigh : "I have great confidence in his head and heart."

"My father knew him," said Adeline, "and he has been very kind to us."

The curate looked at Adeline as she spoke, but there was no emotion but one of gratitude visible in her countenance.

"She is too young," thought the curate, "for such feelings, or else what a companion for life would she be to the noble and gifted Leslie."

Mr. Endsleigh now took his leave, and left Rose Villa most favourably impressed towards its inhabitants. He was much pleased to hear that they were known to Charles Leslie, who was a young man, held in the very highest estimation by the curate, and who is destined to play an important part in our "Tale of Real Life!"

CHAPTER IX.

"He had that nice sense of honour
Which felt a stain like a wound."—BURKE.

THE CURIOSITY OF MRS. PLUMPJOY.—THE CURATE'S ADMIRATION.—CHARLES LESLIE AND HIS HONOUR.—AN INTRODUCTION.

IT may well be supposed that the curate's return home was looked for by Mrs. Plumpjoy with the most ardent expectation.

"Well?" she exclaimed, as he crossed the threshold of his own house.

"Well," he answered. "Do you not mean to allow me to come in ?"

"There," cried Mrs. Plumpjoy, bouncing into the parlour. "That's always the way with you, brother, when you know one is dying with anxiety."

"If I thought you were really dying of that most common malady," said Mr. Endsleigh, taking off his hat with great deliberation, "I might be inclined to hurry, but as it is——"

"Well, well," said his sister, "who have you seen at Rose villa?

"A very respectable servant," said the curate, "Mrs. Mourdant, Miss Mourdant, and a canary bird, and I'm pretty sure there's a dog too."

"What?" cried Mrs. Plumpjoy, "a Miss Mourdant is there?"

"Yes," answered the curate. "Is that so extraordinary?"

"But nobody even suspected such a thing," exclaimed Mrs. Plumpjoy.

"Is it a suspicious circumstance?" asked Mrs. Endsleigh, drily.

"Now there you go again," cried his sister. "You catch one up in such a minute, as if one spoke high treason."

The curate smiled; for, to tell the truth, he did sometimes amuse himself by tantalizing his sister.

"And what sort of woman is Mrs. Mourdant?" was the next inquiry.

"A very agreeable sort of woman," said the curate. "She is a widow, and seems to feel very acutely the loss of her husband."

"Next comes a horse to be shaved," said Mrs. Plumpjoy. "And pray what sort of minx is the daughter?"

"Minx?" said the curate.

"Well, then, what sort of a person is she? I'm sure most girls are minxes and stuck up things now-a-days."

"I don't pretend to know what a minx is," said the curate; "but Miss Mourdant is a delightful young person."

"Highty tighty!" cried Mrs. Plumpjoy.

"She is, indeed," said the curate. "I never was more agreeably surprised in the whole course of my life."

"And pray how old may she be?" said Mrs. Plumpjoy, who seemed at once to have taken some instinctive dislike to Miss Mourdant.

"Why, really I can hardly say," said the curate; "but she can't be above sixteen, I should think."

"Sixteen!" said Mrs. Plumpjoy. "The odious, presuming chit."

"The what?" cried the curate.

No. 5

" I hate your forward little minxes," said Mrs. Plumpjoy, turning up her nose, as if there was something peculiarly disagreeable under it. " They ought to be kept in nurseries, and put to bed at seven. But, now-a-days, they are always pushing their baby faces before men's eyes."

" Miss Adeline Mourdant," said the curate, firmly, " is the most beautiful and unassuming young lady I ever saw, and I request that you will be particularly kind and civil to her, for, poor thing, young though she is, she has not escaped the lot of all—sorrow."

" Oh, dear, me, of course," cried Mrs. Plumpjoy, in a great rage. " Kind and civil I think you said ? Oh, dear, yes. Perhaps she'll be Mrs. Endsleigh some of these days. Oh, dear me."

" Absurd," said the curate. " Sister, you are very wrong, and very uncharitable, to take these prejudices against people that you never saw ; moreover, you do your own character a great injustice, for I never knew you to behave positively unkindly to any one yet."

The curate rose as he spoke and left the room, not, however, before he heard the usual termination to all his disagreements with his sister, muttered behind his back, of—

" Next comes a horse to be shaved, and a pig to have his corns cut."

From that period, which we have already stated was some time before the arrival of Herbert Mandeville at Bracefield, the intimacy between the curate and the little family at Rose Villa had grown closer and closer. Nay, even Mrs. Plumpjoy would feel a pleasure in talking to Adeline Mourdant, and she was brought at last to confess that, although all other *girls* under thirty-two were minxes and chits, yet Adeline Mourdant was an exception, and was really very much to be commended and admired indeed. Moreover, Mrs. Plumpjoy declared that she took Adeline under her especial protection, for two reasons ; first, that as Adeline's father was a captain, and Mrs. Plumpjoy's husband had been a major, although it was but a militia one, there was a bond of union forthwith growing out of that remarkable coincidence ; and, secondly, as she, Mrs. Plumpjoy, declared Adeline Mourdant was the very image of what she was at her age, with a few trifling and unimportant exceptions.

Mrs. Mourdant was not long in preferring a request to Mr. Endsleigh, which he at once complied with, with great pleasure, which was, that he would at any leisure hour assist in the education of Adeline as regarded some points of classical and literary lore in which she was deficient.

Thus was an intimacy established between the venerable clergyman and the inhabitants of Rose Villa, which was equally agreeable and delightful to all parties.

Adeline came to respect Mr. Endsleigh as she would a father, and with his warm and kind heart it was not surprising that in a little time he felt for her all that affection which he had never had an opportunity of lavishing upon a child of his own.

We must not forget to mention that the curate, shortly after the arrival of the Mourdants at Bracefield, received a letter from the Charles Leslie of whom so frequent mention has already been made, and who it is high time we should properly introduce to the reader.

Charles Leslie was the son of a gentleman, who, from some reverses of fortune, had been compelled to embark in commercial pursuits, which terminated in his bankruptcy and death.

It had so happened that the small sum which the curate of Bracefield had put by for many years out of his small yearly stipend had been, by the advice of some friend, embarked in the hands of Charles's father, and it was hard upon the old man that he should lose all his little savings for many years ;

but he replied not, and continued his career of usefulness without mentioning the circumstance to any one.

His astonishment, however, was very great when, one year after the bankruptcy of Mr. Leslie, he received a letter full of requests from Charles Leslie, of whose very existence he had been before ignorant, stating, that after much trouble he had succeeded in winding up some of his father's debts abroad, and their produce, together with the results of his own industry for twelvemonths, had enabled him to discharge in part some of those debts of his deceased father, which could not be looked upon in a commercial point of view merely.

The letter likewise contained a sum of money very nearly equal in amount to the principal which Mr. Endsleigh had been persuaded to allow to be placed in the hands of Mr. Leslie.

The curate was so pleased with the circumstance, as well as the tone and manner of the letter, that he immediately wrote to Charles Leslie in the warmest terms of commendation, and offered his acquaintance so kindly, that the young man was induced to visit the curate, and cement a friendship which grew up so suddenly and strangely.

Ever after this, it was customary with Charles Leslie to come to Bracefield whenever he could spare a few days from his professional labours ; for he was working hard as an artist, and was rapidly rising into distinction. At the parsonage he was always warmly welcomed, and parted with with regret ; and Charles Leslie was even a favourite with Mrs. Plumpjoy, for he had presented her with several drawings of military subjects, which so strongly reminded her of the halcyon days when "the militia were out," that she forthwith took Charles into high favour.

The letter which the curate received from Charles Leslie shortly after the arrival of the Mourdants, will convey to the reader some idea of the man, as well as imparting information concerning one in whom we would fain hope we have excited some degree of interest—namely, the fair and gentle Adeline.

It was as follows :—

"London, April, 1824.

"My Dear Friend,—By this time you will, doubtless, have become acquainted with some persons who are calculated to win your esteem, and who are beforehand prepared to esteem you. I allude to Mrs. Mourdant and her only daughter, who, at my earnest recommendation, are induced to take up their residence at Bracefield.

"Mrs. Mourdant is the widow of Captain Mourdant, who was a gallant officer, and a good man ;—I knew him well. He was a kind friend to me, and you will be better able to conceive what he must have been by observing how much he is regretted by those he has left behind him, than from any laboured panegyric from my pen.

"Captain Mourdant had nothing but his pay to depend upon, and his wife and child have now nothing but the pension usually allotted in such cases ; which, although just and liberal as far as it goes, is much too little to support them in respectability in London. Mrs. Mourdant's only object in life is, I am convinced, the happiness and health of her child ;—child, however, she is not, for a more perfect character, and a kinder, sweeter being than Adeline Mourdant, I am convinced, does not—cannot exist.

"I will not say, my dear friend, 'be kind and hospitable to the bereaved wife and her dear child,' for that I know you will be without any exhortation ; but I write to assure you of the high character, integrity, and good feeling of the little family whom chance has thrown within your pastoral and friendly circle.

"More, my dear kind friend, I will not say at present, because the same of Adeline is flowing from my pen, and I should write too much, at the same time that I expressed too little.

"Believe me, my dear MR. ENDSLEIGH,
"Your grateful friend,
"CHARLES LESLIE.

P. S.—"I fear some weeks must elapse before I am at Bracefield; but I shall assuredly see you at the very earliest opportunity."

The curate was both pleased and puzzled at the letter, and after a good deal of thought, he came to the conclusion that Charles Leslie very much admired Adeline Mourdant.

CHAPTER X.

"Beware, my lord, of Jealousy,
It is a monster
Which doth mock the meat it feeds on."
SHAKSPERE.

THE ONE FAULT OF HERBERT MANDEVILLE.—RIVALRY, AND ITS INFLUENCE.—MRS. PLUMPJOY'S OPINION OF CHARLES LESLIE.—THE CURATE'S SURMISES.

THUS affairs proceeded at Bracefield, without anything particular happening to disturb the usual routine of events, until the unexpected addition to the curate's little family by the arrival of Herbert Mandeville.

Charles Leslie wrote several times to Mr. Endsleigh, but affairs of importance to his future prospects still kept him in London; and, although in each letter he regretted his inability to come to Bracefield, and promised himself that pleasure very shortly, he came not; and Herbert Mandeville had become quite at home and domesticated at the curate's, before Charles Leslie made his appearance upon his visit to the village.

Before his arrival, however, some events had occurred—or, at least, the dread shadows of some events had shown themselves, which deserve a prominent place in our narrative.

It was on the fourth evening after Herbert Mandeville's residence with the curate, when he and Mrs. Plumpjoy, and Mr. Endsleigh were sitting together in the small parlour at the parsonage, that Mrs. Plumpjoy suddenly burst out with :—

"Well, brother, I've been telling Mr. Mandeville all about the Mourdants."

"Are you sure," said the curate, in his usual quiet manner, "that you know all about the Mourdants?"

"There you are again," said his sister. "Snap me up, do. It wouldn't be you else. You know what I mean, well enough."

"Very well," said the curate.

"I've told him all about who they are, and who the father was, and what an uncommonly nice-looking girl Adeline is."

"She is a very nice girl," said Mr. Endsleigh.

"'Tis very odd to me," continued Mrs. Plumpjoy, "that she has not been here for these few days past."

"I believe," said the curate, "that she is aware we have an addition to our little social circle, and probably feels some reluctance to make her visits so very frequently as heretofore."

"It would grieve me much," said Herbert, "if I were to be the cause of anything of the kind."

"It may, or may not be so," said the curate, "but I will see Adeline to-morrow, poor dear child."

"Child?" said Herbert.

"Yes," answered the curate; "she is but fifteen."

Herbert Mandeville smiled as he said :—

"My dear sir, in London girls of fifteen are planning and plotting for establishments, and are immersed in matrimonial intrigues."

"So I have heard; so I have heard," said Mr. Endsleigh, shaking his head; "and so it will be, so long as mothers bring up their daughters with one sole idea."

"And pray what idea may that be?" said Mrs. Plumpjoy.

"That the only object of his existence is to get married, no matter to who or what, so that they are married."

"That is too true," said Herbert, "and hence the number of unhappy matches. Young women do not marry because they love and admire some particular man, but merely because they have caught a man who is willing to give them his name to save their vanity from the reproach of being called an old maid."

"Well, I'm sure, Mr. Mandeville," cried Mrs. Plumpjoy. "I didn't expect such a speech from you, of all people in the world."

Herbert smiled.

"Now, I do hope," continued Mrs. Plumpjoy, "that you will fall desperately in love with Adeline Mourdant, and be refused."

"Eh?" cried Mr. Endsleigh, looking up.

"If I do," said Herbert, smiling, "if I do fall desperately in love with Adeline Mourdant, and am refused, it will not alter my opinion. I shall still think the same."

"And what will that be?" said Mrs. Plumpjoy.

"Why," said Herbert, laughing, "only that I am too late."

"Too late?"

"Yes ;—that she is pre-engaged."

"Which," said Mr. Endsleigh, gravely, "as far as her youthful feelings can guide her, I should think, is most probably a fact."

"What!" screamed Mrs. Plumpjoy, "Adeline Mourdant going to be married?—Well I'm sure. Next comes a——"

"Sister, sister," interrupted the curate, "you accuse me of snapping you up, and what have you done just now?—converted a mere supposition of a youthful attachment into so serious a subject as a matrimonial engagement."

"Humph!" thought Herbert. "So the beauty is caught up already, is she?"

"I think," continued Mr. Endsleigh, "that Charles Leslie loves Adeline with a warmth of affection exceeding that of a mere friend; and, with his manly virtues, and rare integrity, it's a very odd thing to me if she does not feel for him a decided preference."

"Manly virtues and rare integrity," said Herbert, "do not always succeed in winning hearts."

"I know it," answered the curate. "A glowing tongue and an effeminate exterior, are in many cases stronger weapons; but Adeline Mourdant is no common person. It is not every glittering light that will lead her judgment astray. She is a rare creature."

"You excite my curiosity, sir," said Mandeville.

"And so, brother, you really think," said Mrs. Plumpjoy, "that Charles Leslie is in love with Adeline Mourdant?"

"I hope so," said the curate.

"You hope so, sir?" said Herbert Mandeville.

"Yes," replied the curate, I do hope so. Nothing would give me greater leasure, now that I am at the close of life, than to see those two beings, who stand so high in my esteem, united for ever."

"Dear me," said Mrs. Plumpjoy, "I should like it myself above all things. A wedding is always delightful ; there is such a crying, and such a fainting, and such a fuss altogether. I recollect, when I married the poor dear major, I was in strong hysterics for two days and one night."

Herbert and the curate both laughed, which offended Mrs. Plumpjoy very much, and muttering that " Next would come a horse to be shaved, and a pig to have his corns cut," she gathered up her work-box, and indignantly left the room.

Herbert Mandeville's curiosity was strongly aroused by all that he had heard of Adeline Mourdant, and it may, perhaps, appear strange to the reader, —considering that Herbert had not yet seen Adeline,—to hear that his jealousy was very much inflamed.

The fact is, there was one great blemish in Herbert Mandeville's character, and that consisted in an earnest desire to be first and foremost in everything, and the slightest circumstance would frequently suffice to arouse into violent action his ever wakeful and vigilant jealousy. He was jealous of everybody who excelled him in anything whatever, even if it were something that he really in his heart despised.

Hence his feelings were very much annoyed at the idea that the beautiful and peerless Adeline Mourdant should be already appropriated by somebody else ; not that he was at all sure that he panted for the possession of her hand, but, as usual with him, he unreasonably wanted the refusal of her hand, in the same way that he would have liked the refusal of every pretty woman in the world.

When he retired for the night, the conversation he had had with the curate and Mrs. Plumpjoy recurred again and again to his mind, and he resolved that another day should not pass over his head without his being enabled to come to some personal judgment with respect to the much-lauded charms of the fair Adeline.

The name of Charles Leslie as often as it recurred to his memory, was dismissed with impatience, and sometimes with an execration ; and without having seen him, and having heard everything to his advantage, Herbert Mandeville, after passing half the night in feverish thought, went to sleep at last, with the words " I hate Charles Leslie" upon his lips.

At breakfast the next morning, Herbert took an opportunity of saying to the curate, in as indifferent a manner as he could assume.

" I should like to be introduced to your friend Mr. Leslie."

" He will be here certainly within a week," said Mr. Endsleigh, "and I shall have great pleasure in performing the office. You will like him very much, Herbert. In fact, no one can help liking and admiring Charles Leslie."

" Indeed ?" said Herbert, coldly.

" Yes," continued the curate. " He has so much to much to be vain of, and yet so free from vanity."

" Yes—oh, yes," said Herbert, abstractedly.

" You and him will be good friends, I'm sure," said Mr. Endsleigh.

" No doubt," said Herbert. " I really should like to see him."

" I am glad to hear you say so," answered the curate.

" Is he—" said Herbert, balancing his tea-spoon on the edge of his cup, is he—that is— very handsome ?"

" Handsome ?" repeated the curate.

" Yes," said Herbert. " Is he good looking ?"

" Why, really, Herbert," replied Mr. Endsleigh, " I'm sure I hardly know what answer to make you. His many high qualities, and —"

"Then I can tell you, Mr. Mandeville," chimed in Mrs. Plumpjoy. "Charles Leslie is not handsome at all."

"Indeed!" said Herbert.

"Oh, dear no ; he's rather plain than otherwise."

"Indeed?" again said Herbert.

"He has the best of hearts," said the curate ; "and his face beams with intelligence and good feeling."

"That may be," said Mrs. Plumpjoy ; "but you know, brother, Charles Leslie is not handsome, by any means. He wears his hair perfectly horrid, and has no more idea of dress than an Indian savage."

"I believe Charles has rather a contempt for personal adornment," said the curate, with a smile.

"But he is decidedly plain," persisted Mrs. Plumpjoy. "You know, Mr. Mandeville, all virtuous and high-minded people are plain."

"That's a very sweeping proposition," said the curate.

"But still," continued Mrs. Plumpjoy, "I think Charles would look very well if he paid more attention to dress, and let his hair grow long."

"Upon my word I never noticed his hair," said Mr. Endsleigh. "I believe short hair is considered more comfortable than long ; but it's a very singular thing to me, that anybody notices such things at all."

Herbert, upon the whole, was not ill-pleased at the account he heard of his rival ; for such he was determined to consider Charles Leslie, whether he was or not ; and he repeated to himself a favourite maxim of the witty, but licentious Rochester, as he glanced at himself in the glass :—

> "To one that's caught by a true heart's sigh,
> There's a hundred snared by a laughing eye."

"We shall see," he muttered to himself ; "we shall see if I can't steal a march on the pattern man and the philosopher."

The curate, in pursuance of his determination of the previous evening, departed to call at Rose Villa, for he regretted that the gentle Adeline should think it necessary to exclude herself from his house, where she had ever been so welcome a visitor on any account.

CHAPTER XI.

> "In truth she was the genius of the place,
> And where she moved, moved music,
> Flowers, and perfumes."

THE CURATE'S VISIT.—ROSE VILLA AND ITS ASPECT.—A CONVERSATION—A MOTHER'S FEARS AND DAUGHTER'S LOVE.

THE change exteriorly at Rose Villa, since the arrival of the merchants had been great and striking. The garden in front was now no longer a neglected patch of ground, which might have been imagined to be a refuge for all sorts of destitute weeds, but it presented a charming appearance of neatness and order. The spirit of the fair goddess of flowers herself seemed to have descended upon that little spot of land. There were blossoming plants of all kinds, and so carefully were they all tended, that no garden in or about Bracefield come near in beauty to that belonging to Rose Villa. The windows, too, were prettily and tastefully adorned by creeping plants, and white and red roses, the luxuriant branches of which, when the casements were open, projected in graceful freedom into the rooms, delightfully blending together the beauties of nature and art.

What a change can a pure and beautiful spirit such as Adeline's, effect in a short time upon the sport of earth on which it fixes its earthly home. It seemed as if there was some pervading atmosphere about the good and beautiful, that enlisted even inanimate nature on its side ; for the roses that blossomed under the care of the guileless and gentle Adeline seemed of a richer tint, and a softer perfume appeared to be exhaled by the mignionette which crowded the window sills of Rose Villa.

"I think," said the curate, "we have all been happier and better since Adeline came to Bracefield. The contemplation of innocence and virtue is enough to make all love it."

Thus spoke Mr. Endsleigh, as he laid his hand upon the wicket gate leadng to the Villa of the Mourdants'.

He stepped across the little garden, and was about to knock for admittance, when he heard the sounds of the harp from the open window ; that harp which was ever touched with so much grace and sweetness by Adeline, and which she usually accompanied by the thrilling tones of her beautitul voice in some simple melody.

The curate never asked in vain for a song from his gentle and affectionate pupil, and he might have gone in to the house, and there listened to the sweet strains ; but there was a charm about the mellow glorious voice of Adeline, which tempted him to linger ere he knocked, and hear the ditty to an end.

"Bless her," he said ; "God hath gifted her with rare powers, doubtless for her own happiness, and the happiness of those about her."

There was an ineffable charm about the singing of Adeline Mourdant, because she sang naturally from an appreciation of the beauty and spirit of music. Moreover, she never could, nor would, bring herself to wed trashy sentiments to glorious sounds. She conceived that when words were made into music there should be some similarity of sentiment between the two ; therefore, what she sang she actually felt and meant.

Fine music she knew nothing of ; she only admired sweet sounds, and the fashionable music of the present day, the only charm of which consists in its difficulty and unintelligibility, would have presented to her not one feature to admire.

> " She sang as sang the forest birds,
> For the pure love of melody·"

And had she been capable, which she was not, of saying anything to wound even the feelings or the vanity of any one, she would perhaps have made a similar reply to that attributed to Doctor Johnson, who, especially, detested fine music, and when once at a musical party, upon being asked by a lady at the conclusion of a wild piece of music, *a là* somebody, that nobody understood, what he thought of it, for it was *very difficult !* replied, with his usual pomposity,—"Madam, I wish it was *impossible !*"

Adeline sang the following words with exquisite feeling :—

AWAY SIR KNIGHT NOR LONGER WOO.

> " Hast, Sir Knight, to the battle plain,
> Loves wreath is not for you;
> You cannot sing of love and joy,
> Though you are brave and true.
> The fairest flowerets drooping die
> Hush'd is the minstrel's strain,
> Mute is love, as the breath of war
> Comes rushing o'er the plain.
> Away, Sir Knight, nor longer woo,
> For beauty's wreath is not for you.
>
> " Away, Sir Knight, a song of love
> Is floating in the air,
> The strains are those of hope and joy,
> My minstrel love is there;
> And ever as he sings and sighs
> Responsive to each strain,
> Till echo oft prolongs the strain,
> And sighs and sighs again.
> Away, Sir Knight, nor longer woo,
> For beauty's wreath is not for you."

The curate was very much delighted, and when the song ceased, he stood for a moment with a tear glistening in his eye.

"Adeline, Adeline," he repeated, with a sigh; "how happy will he be who succeeds in getting thee to grace his home!"

Mr. Endsleigh then knocked at the door, and was instantly admitted, for his knock was well known at Rose Villa, and he was ever a most welcome and honoured visiter to the inhabitants.

The unassuming kindness of the old curate had won much upon the gentle heart of Adeline, and she now as naturally looked to him for advice and kindness as if some natural tie had existed between them.

"Dear Mr. Endsleigh," she said, as he entered the parlour, "you have not been here for three days."

"And why is it, Adeline," he said, with a smile, "that you have not been to the parsonage for three days? Mrs. Plumpjoy is surprised! I am surprised! Nay, I believe the very cat and dog are uneasy, and miss your kind words, Adeline."

"I thought I would come to-day," said Adeline.

"Then do so," answered the curate. "My sister wants your advice about some of her flowers, and has been fretting about the house all day yesterday about your not coming; and you may guess, Adeline, how many times the horse has been shaved."

Adeline laughed, as she said with a slightly heightened colour:—

"I heard you had a sister, Mr. Endsleigh, and I feared to intrude upon you unasked."

"I suspected as much," said the curate. "I have a visiter, but the most welcome one must ever be yourself, Adeline."

"You are too kind to me," said Adeline.

"I might retort that," said Mr. Endsleigh, smiling.

No. 6

At this moment Mrs. Mourdant entered the room, and after the usual salutations, the curate said :—

"I trust you have no objection to Adeline continuing her visits at the parsonage, notwithstanding I have a young pupil with me at present?"

"None, certainly," said Mrs. Mourdant. "Your judgment is sufficient, Mr. Endsleigh, to make me easy upon that subject."

"The young gentleman I have staying with me," said the curate, "is the son of an early friend. He is young—tolerably good-looking—rather intolerably vain."

"It is sufficient," said Mrs. Mourdant, "that he is under your roof."

The curate looked rather grave at this remark for a moment, and then said :—

"I do not see any reason why my young friend Adeline should not visit as freely as ever at the parsonage."

"And should you see such reason, you would not hesitate," said Mrs. Mourdant, in a low voice, to the curate, "to—to ——"

"To say so," said Mr. Endsleigh, finishing the sentence. "I certainly would not hesitate for one moment, Mrs. Mourdant."

"I am grateful as well as satisfied," said the mother.

"Then, Adeline," cried Mr. Endsleigh, turning to her, "will you carry out your half-formed resolution, and really visit me to-day?"

"Yes," said Adeline ; "and I want you, dear Mr. Endsleigh, if you will, to tell the correct names of some flowers that we purchased of a wandering gardener yesterday."

"Bring some of them with you, Adeline," said the curate, "and we will see what we can do."

"Mr. Endsleigh," said Mrs. Mourdant, "will you excuse me for inviting myself to-day to the parsonage?"

"Excuse you, Mrs. Mourdant?" said the curate ; "I shall certainly not excuse you if you fail to come."

"Then I will come," said Mrs. Mourdant ; "and we will trespass upon you for tea, and an hour's pleasant conversation this afternoon."

"I need not say how much I shall be pleased," said Mr. Endsleigh.

He shortly afterwards took his leave, and immediately returned homewards to prepare Mrs. Plumpjoy to expect company.

"Mrs. Mourdant too?" cried Martha ; "well I never ! she who never will go anywhere. It's very odd !"

"Why, to tell the truth," said Mr. Endsleigh, "she has a mother's fears with regard to young Mandeville, and her daughter. Her object in coming here—and it is a justifiable and correct one—is to judge herself of the character of him who is now under my roof, and with whom Adeline, if she visit here as much as usual, must of necessity become acquainted. Do you not see, sister?"

"I am sure Mr. Mandeville is an uncommonly polite and handsome young man," said Mrs. Plumpjoy.

"Pho ! pho !" cried the curate.

"There you go again," screamed his sister. "Next comes a horse to be shaved, and a pig to have his corns cut."

CHAPTER XII.

"Oh, Love! how wondrous is the power,
Strengthening the weak and trampling on the strong."

PREPARATION AND EXPECTATION.—THE ARRIVAL.—FIRST IMPRESSIONS.—
LOVE.—LOVE !

THE news of the expected visit of Adeline to the parsonage was soon by Mrs. Plumpjoy communicated to Herbert Mandeville, who received the intelligence with evident satisfaction.

"Although," he thought to himself, " I shall see this beauty, this incomparable creature, who is so coolly set aside by my good friend Mr. Endsleigh, for that amazingly correct and proper young man with the horrible hair, and ill-fitting clothes, Charles Leslie."

As he spoke, he took a glance at himself in the glass, and was well pleased at the luxuriance of his own glossy ringlets, and the really noble profile which his countenance presented.

"Humph !" he said, half aloud ; " we shall see."

"See what, Mr. Mandeville?" said Mrs. Plumpjoy, who had overheard him.

"Eh ?" cried Herbert, starting, and the colour mounting to his cheeks.

"Why you said we should see something."

"Oh! I meant the peerless beauty—the creature without compare—the pure and admirable Adeline."

"Well, she is very pretty indeed," said Mrs. Plumpjoy, "and I shouldn't wonder if you were to fall desperately in love with her at first sight."

"But, my dear Madam," said Mandeville, with some degree of bitterness in his tone, which he could not disguise, " you know that would be very *malapropos* indeed."

"Why, I should like to know ?—I'm sure young, interesting, and handsome people ——"

Herbert bowed.

"Are always falling in love," continued Mrs. Plumpjoy. " There was myself, and poor dear Major Plumpjoy, for instance."

"A most striking instance, I admit," said Mandeville ; " always the major was as captivating for a man, as his bride was and is for a woman."

"What a sensible young man," thought Mrs. Plumpjoy.

"Of course," said Mandeville, continuing the conversation, " I dare not fall in love with Miss Mourdant."

"Dare not, Mr. Mandeville !" cried Mrs. Plumpjoy.

"Why, you know that Mr. Endsleigh has quite settled that his dear, and, I am sorry to hear, plain friend, Charles Leslie, is to possess such a rarity of nature ; and Adeline Mourdant, I presume, must become eventually Mrs. Leslie."

"Pho! pho! as my brother says," cried Mrs. Plumpjoy ; "I dare say there is no kind of engagement at all."

"You think not ?"

"Certainly not. Why, after all, Adeline is but a child, though she is full grown, and handsome, and sensible, and all that sort of thing."

"Of course I shall behave with the greatest circumspection," said Herbert " Not that I could ever hope to rival such a phœnix of perfection as Mr. Charles Leslie, if I wished."

"Oh! nonsense! nonsense!" cried Mrs. Plumpjoy. " Mr. Endsleigh has always got some crotchet or another in his head. He is quite mad now about

Adeline Mourdant some day marrying Charles Leslie ; but it's all moonshine, that's my opinion."

"Moonshine !" repeated Herbert ; "that is, fleeting, inconstant, and eva-nescent."

"Oh, yes, that's what I mean. You might as well expect next a horse to come and ——"

"Dear me," cried Herbert, "Mr. Endsleigh, I think, beckoned me from the garden. Pray excuse me, Madam."

He hastily left the room.

"A very nice young man indeed, is Mr. Mandeville," soliloquised Mrs. Plumpjoy ; "but he has a curious habit of running out of the room all of a sudden, sometimes, when one is speaking to him."

The afternoon at length arrived, the afternoon upon which Herbert Man-deville was to have an opportunity of judging from personal inspection of the rare charms of Adeline Mourdant.

Herbert, as far as he could venture to do so without exciting the observa-tions of the curate, had paid especial attention to his personal appearance, and the more particularly upon those points in which he had been told that Charles Leslie was so strikingly deficient.

He wore a coat, the fit of which was faultless, and a vest of a blue so pale, so delicately blue, that you could scarce pronounce it such. A rich scarf was negligently, yet artfully tied around his neck, so as to show, without obtruding upon notice, his exquisitely white and beautifully-shaped throat and neck to the greatest advantage.

The masses of his black hair hung admirably from his high classical fore-head, and his hands were so beautifully white, and the fingers so long and taper-ing that the highest court beauty might have envied them. Upon the whole, Herbert Mandeville was certainly a young man of uncommon personal attrac-tions, which, coupled with a mind of a rare order, could not fail to render him a dangerous companion to an unguarded female heart.

But did he pause to ask himself why he was so solicitous about his appear-ance to Adeline Mourdant, she whom he had never even seen ? Did he ask himself why he would have given a year or more from the scene of his exist-ance to be assured that he should, by the magic of appearance, and eloquence, and wit, and accomplishments, succeed in awakening a tender feeling in the breast of the fatherless girl to whom he was to be introduced for the first time ? No ! Had he asked that question, he must have answered that he was under the dominion of the master passion of his mind,—that passion which had already led him into every error or indiscretion that could be laid to his charge—jealousy !—a mad, insatiate jealousy of everything, and everybody.

Adeline might be beautiful, but it was of little consequence. She might be learned—virtuous—accomplished, but it was nothing to him. She was, however, admired—loved—adored by another, and that was everything to him : that Herbert Mandeville could not put up with for a moment. No, that other might have her—might wed ; but it must be after he, Herbert Man-deville, had had the refusal of her fair young hand himself. Had he been convinced that Adeline Mourdant was prepared to admire—to love him—he would probably have left the parsonage on a rural ramble, and scarce wished to return in time to see her. But such was not the case ; he had been told that she was not to be won, that she was already prepossessed in favor of one so very different from himself. Moreover, Herbert Mandeville hated Charles Leslie the more intensely for his very virtues. Every trait in his character which the good simple curate dwelt upon with artless eloquence to raise him in the esteem of all, was gall and wormwood to Herbert Mandeville.

He felt that he should not have acted as Charles Leslie had acted, and he hated him for his superior virtue.

And yet, notwithstanding all this, Herbert Mandeville was not a bad man. He had many virtues ; he was capable of the most generous actions. He worshipped truth in his heart ; and, in fact, had it not been for that peculiar bias of his mind which we have described, and which had been unhappily fostered in his early life, he might, and would have been, all that Charles Leslie, together with a host of glittering socialities and amenities of life which the other. in the calm serenity of his self-denying virtue was certainly deficient in.

It is a sad thing, but it is nevertheless a true one, that exalted virtue, truth, and high moral rectitude, is rarely found in combination with that charm of manner, which to use the glowing language of Burke,

> "Robs vice of half its deformity,
> By taking from it all its grossness."

But so it is ; we must in the majority of cases be content to admire and esteem where we cannot love ! and to love where we can neither admire nor esteem !

It was a glorious day, and the sun was still high in the heavens, when a knock at the parsonage door announced the arrival of the much expected Mourdants.

A flush, which Herbert Mandeville could not have banished, had he so wished, came across his cheek as he heard the summons for admission, and it gave the finishing touch to the really glorious face upon which it sat in so much dawning beauty.

Herbert Mandeville was usually rather pale, and he wanted but the slight tint which now glowed upon his cheek to render faultless the complexion which otherwise might have been possibly found fault with in a man for its feminine delicacy.

He rose from his chair, and fixed his eyes earnestly on the half-open door through which the curate had just passed to receive his guests, and the heart of the young man beat quickly in his breasts, as he said to himself as he there stood :—

"Now, we shall see the peerless form which is to be sacrificed at the shrine of the pattern man, the frigid, virtuous Leslie."

The curate appeared in the next moment with Adeline.

Herbert Mandeville was astonished. Such loveliness it had never even entered into his imagination to dream of. All his easy and polished manners,—all that self-possession, which was a great feature in his character, entirely for the moment forsook him ; and he, the gifted, the admired, the courted Herbert Mandeville, stood abashed, gazing upon the beautiful Adeline as if she had been a picture, or some fair statue, so entirely absorbed were all his senses.

"Mr. Herbert Mandeville—Miss Mourdant," said the curate.

Herbert started, and stammered something which was perfectly unintelligible to any one, and then, feeling that he must be looking rather ridiculous, he reddened, and made so great an effort to overcome the intense surprise which the wondrous beauty of Adeline Mourdant had occasioned, that he made matters ten time worse, by showing that it was an effort.

In fact, Herbert Mandeville's situation was to him galling in the extreme, and the recollection during the whole evening that followed was the more particularly painful, because his own bashfulness and nervousness were so strongly and strikingly contrasted with the innocent ease and self-possession of Adeline, who took the introduction, as a matter of course, so calmly and easily, that Herbert could have cursed himself for exhibiting the feeling which he wanted to see in her, and would have gloried in not exhibiting himself.

The fact was that Adeline had scarcely ever cast a thought upon the probability or possibility of the curate's pupil being a handsome and distinguished young gentleman, or the reverse ; nor did she conceive it to be to her a matter of the smallest importance who or what he was, or might become.

Before Herbert had recovered from his confusion, Adeline was at the window, deeply engaged in discussing with the curate the merits of the plants she had spoken of.

Herbert Mandeville leaned on the mantel-shelf, and contemplated the matchless form of Adeline Mourdant, and drank in the melody of her sweet voice, which was certainly rarely beautiful.

At that moment, while he there stood and gazed upon the fatherless girl, whose radiant beauty

> " Might have fired a world,
> And, like another Helen,
> Burnt another Troy,"

—at that moment Herbert Mandeville made a resolution which terminated in death, misery, horror !—a resolution to spare no pains—grudge no hardships, —to do all, to dare all, provided he could once win from Adeline Mourdant the words :—

" *I love you, Mandeville.*"

" I will win her !" he repeated to himself ; " I will win her, if I have to wade through deceit—difficulty—and—and even blood !"

" Why, Mr. Mandeville, what are you making such faces about ?" cried Mrs. Plumpjoy, as she entered the room with Mrs. Mourdant.

Mandeville started.

" Be still, my heart," he whispered to himself, and with a countenance radiant with smiles, he acknowledged the introduction to Mrs. Mourdant, and was soon engaged with her in a conversation which she evidently sought to have with him.

And now, lest any of our readers fair or unfair, should suppose for one moment that Mrs. Mourdant had any matrimonial design for her daughter, in her speculations concerning the rich and fascinating Herbert Mandeville, it is fit we should state at once that such was by no means the fact.

Mrs. Mourdant dreaded the loss of her daughter, even by a respectable and unexceptionable marriage ; but she dreaded still more the entanglement of her young heart at her early period of life by any one, and she was certainly most anxious, knowing her daughter to be a constant visitor at the curate's, to see and judge for herself, whether or not Herbert Mandeville was a young man likely to undertake the subjugation of Adeline's young and susceptible heart, as is too commonly the case,—namely, for the pleasure of conquest.

What was the result of the mother's scrutiny we shall see anon.

CHAPTER XIII.

> "The west wind dying on a sweet bank of violets,
> Mingling its sighs with odorous perfumes,
> Was not more beautiful than was her voice,
> Who gave such eloquence to music."

THE PARTY AT THE CURATE'S.—LOVE GLANCES AND SIGHS.—THE SONG.— PASSION.—RAPTURE.

THAT evening was, perhaps, the most delightful and yet the most tormenting that Herbert Mandeville had ever passed in his short life of enjoyment and luxury.

It was delightful, because he could look at Adeline Mourdant and never tire of her beauty. It was tormenting, because he was obliged to conceal his thoughts from every eye, and he dared not even cast one furtive glance of passion at the fair young creature who now filled his mind to the exclusion of all other objects.

The conversation soon became general, and Herbert Mandeville hastened to mix in it, to do away, if possible, by the varied charms of his conversational powers, with the impression to his prejudice which he could not help surmising his first awkwardness must have given rise to.

"I am sure," said Mrs. Plumpjoy, addressing Mrs. Mourdant, " 'tis quite a pleasure—indeed, I may say a very extraordinary pleasure, to see you at the parsonage, for my brother tells me you have not paid him a visit since your arrival here in Bracefield."

"You are very kind," replied Mrs. Mourdant ; "but my mind is so ill-attuned to company, that I remain at home from charity to others rather than to please myself."

"And so, Mr. Endsleigh," said Adeline, in her low, sweet voice, "you think the violet was not originally a native of England ?"

"No, my dear," replied the curate. "It was only brought into this country in the early part of the thirteenth century."

"My dear !" thought Mandeville. "What would I not give for the privilege of using, unrebuked, those words !"

"It is now," said Herbert, "the sweetest of our common English flowers. It has taken kindly to our land."

"Yes," said Adeline, "Shakspere meant the violet when he mentions—

> " 'The gentle blue-eyed flower that dies,
> Breathing sweet perfume in its sighs.' "

"That," said Mandeville, "is a beautiful description of the little modest flower, that when crushed breathes forth such delicious odours. How incomparable was the genius of that man ! The meanest incident became beautiful when wrapt up in the magic of his words."

"Dear me—you are talking of Shakespere, are you ?" cried Mrs. Plumpjoy.

"Yes," said the curate. "A book in which there is much true religion."

"Well, I never found the religion," said his sister ; "but I think Shakspere is very charming, nevertheless ; particularly where Julius Cæsar murders the children in the Tower, and the ghost of King Lear comes to somebody and says—'List! list! oh, list.' I am sure I saw it once, and all my flesh began to creep."

The curate smiled, Mandeville laughed outright, and Adeline smelt so energetically at a nosegay, that her face was quite hidden, and nobody could note its expression.

"Well, what's the matter now ?" cried Mrs. Plumpjoy. "Anybody would think you had never read Shakspere, any of you."

"Martha," said the curate, "you have a wonderful facility in confounding names and occurrences. You have mixed up in a few words the characters and incidents in two or three different plays."

"Well, it's all in Shakspere, I believe ?"

"Certainly it is," said Mandeville.

"Well, then," cried Mrs. Plumpjoy, with a triumphant look, "I suppose I may speak of what part of Shakspere's works I like ?"

"Oh, dear, yes, undoubtedly," cried Mr. Endsleigh ; "only Julius Cæsar did not murder the children in the Tower."

"How can you tell, at this distance of time, whether he did or not ?" said Mrs. Plumpjoy.

"I give in—I give in," said the curate.

"Oh, dear, yes, of course. That's always the way ; you catch me up and then make a merit of giving in."

"It's very wrong, indeed," said the curate.

"And enough," said Herbert, "to make a horse come to be shaved."

"I was just going to say so," cried Mrs. Plumpjoy.

"I knew it," said Mr. Endsleigh, "and a pig to have his corns cut."

"Well, how very odd," said Mrs. Plumpjoy ; "I was just going to say that too.   How very strange that you should think of it."

"Why, Martha," said the curate, drily, "I have heard you say it *once* before, and that put it into my head."

Herbert smiled, and turning to Adeline, he said, abruptly,—

"You love music?"

"Love music?" said Adeline, clasping her hands.

"Such as you, Adeline," said the curate, kindly, "ought to love music, for it is a pure pleasure—perhaps the purest that we are capable of enjoying in this world."

"You know I love it, Mr. Endsleigh," said Adeline.

"Yes, and with your rare power of producing sweet sounds," continued the curate, "it would be wonderful if it were not one of your greatest earthly pleasures, Adeline."

"May I hope," said Mandeville, in his most winning tones, "that this little conversation upon music may be but a prelude to a practical illustration of its charms."

He looked at Adeline as he spoke, and for the first time she dropped her eyes upon meeting the ardent gaze of admiration that was bent upon her by Herbert Mandeville.

"I never press anybody to sing in my own house," said the curate.

"But you will sing us a song, Miss Adeline?" said Mrs. Plumpjoy.

Adeline looked at her mother.

"Mr. Endsleigh, perhaps," said Mrs. Mourdant, "would rather not have singing just now?"

The curate smiled as he said,—

"Adeline knows how pleased I always am to hear her sing ; and if she will not think it rude to be asked—"

"I will sing, Mr. Endsleigh, of course, if you wish it," said Adeline, with enchanting sweetness and innocence.

The curate smiled and nodded.

"D—n it!" muttered Mandeville ; "I have been nicely put on the shelf in the matter.   Nobody ever appealed to me."

But soon all other feelings were absorbed in listening to the flood of pure harmony that flowed from the lips of Adeline Mourdant without effort or art.

While the following words were filling the air with music, he sat like one wrapt in some pleasing lethargy of thought.   Some dreamy, mental romance of bright colours and glorious images seemed to hold his soul in thraldom, and if anything was still wanting to sleep the senses of Herbert Mandeville in all the dear intoxication of a wild first passion, those heavenly sounds at once completed the delirium of the heart, and he loved—adored—worshipped Adeline Mourdant.

THE LAY OF THE NIGHT FLOWER,

"Who loves not the night flower ?
  Not I—not I !
When the red sun sets,
  A sigh—a sigh !
Bursts from the heart of the wild night flower.

"Who loves not the night flower?
Not I—not I!
When the birds sleep,
A sigh—a sigh!
Bursts from the heart of the wild night flower.

"Who loves not the night flower?
Not I—not I!
When the soft due falls,
A sigh—a sigh!
Bursts from the heart of the wild night flower."

A rapt silence succeeded the last note, and it was not until its faintest echoes had ceased to vibrate on his ears, that Herbert Mandeville, with a deep sigh, spoke.

"Beautiful! beautiful!" he cried. "I—I never before dreamt of such melody. Oh, how happy—how more than happy——"

He paused, and the varying colour in his cheek betrayed the feelings of his heart.

"What were you about to say, Herbert?" inquired Mr. Endsleigh.

"Why, really, sir," stammered Mandeville, "I—I——"

"Do not wish to say it?"

"I—I forget it."

"Humph!" said the curate.

There was a silence of a few moments, which was rather embarrassing to everybody, and it was a great relief even when Mrs. Plumpjoy cried, in her loudest tones—

"Well, that was a most beautiful song, Miss Adeline. It puts me in mind of poor dear Major Plumpjoy, who had a sweet voice——"

"Yes," said Mr. Endsleigh, drily.

Mrs. Plumpjoy looked exceedingly indignant at her brother, and contented herself by drawing her chair very close to Mrs. Mourdant's, and whispered in
No. 7.

her ear the whole particulars of her courtship and ultimate marriage to Major-General Plumpjoy.

The evident admiration of Herbert Mandeville for Adeline had awakened painful emotions in the hearts of two out of the small party assembled, and those two were the curate and Mrs. Mourdant.

Mr. Endsleigh felt vexed, and yet he scarcely knew why. It is probable that had he had leisure to have thoroughly examined his feelings, he would have found a latent suspicion lurking in his heart that Herbert Mandeville was not exactly the person to whom he would wish to see the happiness of Adeline Mourdant entrusted.

Mrs. Mourdant's feelings were, of course, much interested in any circumstance which could, nearly or remotely, have a tendency to affect the happiness of her darling child; and although she could find no specific fault with Herbert, still to her mind there seemed a kind of worldly-wise expression upon his face which she feared might have been required in company which London presents in great variety to a young man of wealth and fashion—company not of a low, or decidedly vicious grade, by any means, but still company in which a laxity of principle reigned, because any other class of opinions than those which set religion and the extreme niceties of morals at defiance would necessarily interfere largely with their enjoyments.

The party was broken up at a very early hour by Mrs. Mourdant rising, and pleading her early habits and delicate health as an excuse for returning home so soon.

The curate put on his hat to see his guests to their home, and Herbert Mandeville, as a thing of course, put on his.

The adieus between Mrs. Plumpjoy and her guests were spoken, and they proceeded across the little garden in front of the parsonage-house. The moon was shining with great beauty and splendour, and the whole of the surrounding landscape was as light as day with its soft silvery light.

"What a beautiful night!" exclaimed Adeline, who was ever keenly alive to the glories and beauties of nature.

She paused as she spoke, and her mother and Mr. Endsleigh were, in consequence, a few paces in advance.

"It is glorious," said Mandeville, who had left the house last of all, and now stopped because Adeline stopped.

Mrs. Mourdant spoke in a low tone to the curate.

"Will you let me see you as early as convenient to-morrow morning?" she said.

"Most certainly," he replied.

"At nine?"

"Yes—or earlier, if you wish it."

"No, my kind friend, that hour will do well. Forgive my troubling you, but I wish to ask your advice."

"I think," said the curate, "I can guess the subject," glancing back at Adeline and Mandeville.

"Yes, you are right," whispered Mrs. Mourdant. "Forgive a mother's perhaps foolish fears and scruples."

"I honour them," said the curate.

The short conversation we have recorded was over in a few moments—nay, it did not take half the time that it requires to write it. Herbert Mandeville, however, saw his opportunity, and he offered his arm to Adeline, who, without the slightest scruple, accepted it.

Mrs. Mourdant looked vexed; but without actual rudeness, and making a scene, nothing could be done, and she had no resource but to take the curate's arm in silence, and leave Mandeville to the fruits of his skill and diplomacy in securing to himself, for the short space between the parsonage and Rose Villa, the arm which he would not at that moment have resigned for the world's wealth.

CHAPTER XIV.

" Parting is such sweet sorrow."—SHAKSPERE.
" Oh, fly not yet, 'tis now the hour."

THE CHURCHYARD.—MOMENTS OF HAPPINESS.—THE GRAVESTONE.—A TALE OF WOE.—THE PARTING.

" Our nearest way will be through the churchyard," said Mr. Endsleigh; " and the moon is so bright, that I think we may walk down the narrow lane without any danger of straying into the ditch."

" The moon is, indeed, lovely," said Mrs. Mourdaunt.

" And yet," said Mandeville, in a low tone, to Adeline, " it borrows a new beauty from some of the forms it illuminates with its pale rays."

" I always loved the moonlight," replied Adeline.

" And I love this moonlight in particular," said Mandeville, with a sigh, which he intended should provoke inquiry; but he was disappointed, for Adeline made no reply whatever.

They had now passed through the wicket gate which opened upon the churchyard, and there, alike made beautiful by the moon's silver beams, was the humble grave of the peasant, and marble tombs of the magnates of the county. All there at least were equal.

" This is a dear spot," said Mrs. Mourdant. " This simple depository of the dead, with its long grass, wild flowers, and willows, always awakens in my mind feelings of peace and calmness, instead of the shuddering dread with which I have often regarded the last sad home of mortality in crowded cities and uncongenial situations."

" The contemplation of a place like this," said the curate, " ought to awaken feelings of calmness and peace."

" How clear the moonbeams fall upon these records of what has been," said Mandeville, indicating the gravestones as he spoke.

" Here is one directly in our path," said Adeline. " It seems to invite inspection. What says it?"

They paused a moment at the gravestone, which happened to be in such a position as to catch the full light of the moon as it rode, " Queen of the Night" in the clear azure vault of Heaven.

" 'Tis a sad inscription," said Mandeville.

Adeline leaned forward and read,—

J. M.,
ETAT 20.
" Of such is the kingdom of Heaven."

" So young?" said Mandeville.

" 'Twas soon to die," murmured Adeline.

" This may be the grave of some one who sued for death," said Herbert— " some one who, although young, had survived the extinction of the heart's best treasures. Death may have been a boon. Nay, it is a boon when———"

" When—what?" said Adeline.

" When we have no one to love—and when we love no one."

" Can that ever be?"

"The natural ties," said Herbert Mandeville, in low sensitive tones, "may become extinct by the course of time."

Adeline sighed.

"Then," he continued, "then the saddened heart, wrecked on the rock which was its beacon, should have some spirit, young as itself, upon the green earth to turn to—some hand to grasp that might——"

"Adeline!" cried Mrs. Mourdant.

Adeline started, and hurried forward.

"The night air is chilling, my love," said her mother.

"I stayed but a moment to read a grave-stone," said Adeline.

"Which was it?" asked the curate.

"It has the letters J. K. on," said Adeline.

"Ah!" said the curate, with a sigh; "some day when we are all in good spirits, and can bear a mournful tale, I will tell you the story of the young heart that sleeps in peace beneath that stone."

"I would fain hear it," said Adeline, mournfully. "How young to be placed in the cold grave."

"And yet, if we could but think so, such are the happiest," said Mr. Endsleigh, mildly.

"I believe it, and think it," cried Herbert. "There are many who struggle, as it were, with life, without finding pleasure in any of its gross and earthly enjoyments."

"That is true, sometimes," answered the curate, "and among that list may be found those of the most brilliant capacities; and yet, from want of interest in life, do nothing but exist and die."

"How beautifully has Byron versified that thought," exclaimed Herbert, in a tone of enthusiasm;—

> "Many are poets who have never penned their inspirations,
> Earth's mists with their pure 'pinions disagree,
> And they rejoin the stars; unlaurelled upon earth."

"There is Rose Villa," said Mrs. Mourdant; "and now good night, Mr. Endsleigh and Mr. Mandeville, for I cannot think of bringing either of you any further from home."

"As we are so close at hand," replied Mr. Endsleigh, "we may as well satisfy our consciences by seeing you to your door-step."

Herbert thought that was the most sensible speech the good curate had made all the evening, inasmuch as it implied that he was for a short time longer to have the enjoyment—and an exquisite one he thought it—of having the light fragile arm of Adeline reposing on his, and to feel that she was almost near enough to him to hear the beating of his heart.

Mrs. Mourdant made no further objection, and in five minutes more they did actually stand upon the door-step of Rose Villa.

"Now then, good night in earnest," said Mr. Endsleigh.

As Adeline's arm slipped from his, Mandeville continued for one fleeting moment to grasp her taper fingers in his. Oh, how exquisitely delightful was that gentle pressure!—A thrill of joy seemed to pervade his whole frame, and he felt as if he could have stood upon that spot for ever, with those small fingers resting in his hand.

"Good night!" said Adeline.

Herbert fancied there was a trembling softness in her voice, and the fancy was delightful.

"Good night," he said, "good night!"

He would have lingered on the spot, but he had just reflection enough left to feel the impropriety, as well as the indiscretion of any marked and observable manifestation of his feelings, and he reluctantly turned from the door of Rose Villa.

The curate and Mandeville walked for a few paces in silence, and then Mr. Endsleigh said, in a careless tone :—

"Well, Herbert, how do you like our friends?"

"How can I be otherwise than delighted?" said Mandeville.

"Delighted?" said the curate.

"Yes, sir," said Herbert, "I repeat, delighted. No one could fail of being so. I think Miss Adeline Mourdant the most perfect——"

"Oh," interrupted the curate, "I have no particular objection to your being delighted, only it appeared to me a strong term."

"But you must admit, sir, that Adeline Mourdant is in every way calculated to charm."

"She is rarely beautiful," said the curate, with a sigh ; "God help her !"

"You speak as if in pity," said Herbert.

"Beauty," replied the curate, "is a fatal gift, Herbert. How many has it lured to destruction ?"

"But Adeline——" said Herbert.

"Aye," cried the curate, "Adeline has a mind of as rare an order as her form and face. The false lights—the *ignes fatui* that would lead astray so many, has no charms for her."

"She ought to pass through life with some one of sense, and extreme probity and prudence," said Herbert.

"Indeed she ought, and I dare say will," answered the curate, without noticing the sneering tone in which Herbert Mandeville spoke, for he had Charles Leslie in his thoughts.

"She has the rarest musical power," said Herbert, "that ever I met with."

"Her voice is exquisite," answered Mr. Endsleigh. "I love her, Herbert, as I would a child of my own ; not for her beauty,—not for her accomplishments, natural or acquired,—but for the rare and high qualities of her heart, which I have had an opportunity of studying."

"The loss of her father must have been a sad blow," remarked Herbert.

"It was, no doubt," said the curate. "But as far as in me lies, that loss will I make up to her, by God's help."

"I must be cautious," thought Herbert, "or the second father will quarrel with the adopted daughter's lover."

"And Mrs. Mourdant seems a superior person."

"She is worthy to be the mother of Adeline," said the curate. "I have only one wish ungratified with regard to Adeline."

"May I presume to ask what that wish is ?" said Mandeville.

"It is," answered Mr. Endsleigh, "that a mutual affection may subsist between Charles Leslie and Adeline,—an affection which may terminate in their union through life."

"Mr. Leslie is happy," said Herbert, "in being the favoured lover of Miss Adeline Mourdant."

"Charles Leslie does love her," said the curate.

"And the feeling, I suppose, is a mutual one ?" inquired Mandeville.

"There may be—nay, I think there must be in Adeline's heart the germ of a love for Charles Leslie ;—a love that will ripen into health and most luxuriant beauty, for their mutual happiness."

They were now passing through the churchyard on their return homewards, and the curate paused by the grave-stone which had attracted Adeline's attention.

"The history," he said, "of the fair young being who now sleeps beneath this stone is neither uninteresting nor uninstructive."

"You are in possession of the particulars ?" said Herbert.

"I am," answered the curate ; "I have a manuscript which was drawn up by one who knew the circumstances therein recorded well. 'Tis a tale of wild ungovernable passion."

" Might I be permitted to see it ?"

" You shall have it this night, if you please."

" I thank you," said Mandeville.

They soon arrived at the parsonage, and shortly the small family separated for the night, but not before the curate had handed to Mandeville the manuscript concerning the young grave in the venerable churchyard.

CHAPTER XV.

' Art thou a spirit of health,
Or goblin damned ?''
HAMLET.

REFLECTIONS UPON THE PHANTOM OF THE NIGHT.—A RESOLVE.—A NEW CHARACTER.—CAPTAIN DUFOURS AND HIS PECULIARITIES, WHICH ARE NOT SO PECULIAR AFTER ALL.

HERBERT MANDEVILLE repaired with a quick step to his chamber, and bolting the door, he threw himself into a seat, exclaiming :—

" So, I have seen her !—At last her wondrous beauty has blessed my sight. I thought they must have painted her charms with partial eyes when they talked of her ; but how far—oh, how far does she transcend all possible description ?"

He rose and paced his room for some moments, apparently in deep thought. Then suddenly he exclaimed :—

" Adeline ! Adeline Mourdant !—henceforward you are the loadstone of my existence,—my haven of delight,—my pursuit in life. Henceforth the ties that bind me to existence shall be wound round thy young heart. Adeline ! Adeline ! I love !—I adore !"

He threw open the casement of his room, and the soft moonlight fell upon his pale and ample brow in a flood of glorious radiance.

" I will win Adeline," he cried, " despite them all. Not all the Leslies that ever were created shall stand between me and my first—my last—my only passion ! Am I not well born—rich—influential ?—Have I not personal advantages ?—Yes. Tremble, Charles Leslie !—The priceless jewel you covet never shall be yours. What man can do to win the heart, upon the possession of which he stakes his happiness here and hereafter, will I do to win Adeline Mourdant. Poetry, music, eloquence, the arts,—everything shall aid me. Like attendant sprites, I will summon round me all that can charm—all that can feed passion, and produce the delicious delirium of love !"

He stood proudly erect as he spoke, and his impassioned language imparted a fire to his eye, and an expression to his eloquent features, that might have became a fallen angel,—one who was

" Still beautiful in sin,
And not less than archangel ruined.''

For more than an hour he leant his elbow upon the window-sill, and with his brow resting upon his hand, he revolved in his mind all that he would do, —all that he could do, to win the innocent and guileless heart of her who was probably then sleeping the dear sleep of innocence, peace, and purity.

" Mine ! mine !" he cried ; " she shall be mine ! I defy all—everything

—everybody! The love of Adeline Mourdant is an engrossing passion ;—it overpowers everything. She shall be mine! She shall love me with a passion scarcely known in this cold clime. I will so turn her heart that it shal beat but for me. Our lives shall flow together like a stream, which, although it may arise from two sources, still bounds along in murmuring beauty in one channel. And now the mode of action—the first approaches. Let me think."

Again he remained for a long time wrapt in contemplation ; then rising and trimming his light, he said :—

"A good thought—a good thought ; I will write to Dufours. He is the man to aid me in such a matter. Moreover he will learn all particulars concerning Leslie. Yes, yes, a good thought,—I will write to Dufours."

It is necessary, and moreover convenient, while Herbert Mandeville is writing his letter, to give the reader some insight into the character of this Dufours, whose advice Herbert thought might be of such essential service to him in aiding him to supplant Charles Leslie, and win the innocent heart of Adeline Mourdant.

In a few words, then, this Dufours, or Captain Dufours, as he was usually called, was an unmitigated scoundrel ; he was one of those dangerous fascinating associates for a young man of wealth and prospects, with which all large cities abound.

No one knew how Captain Dufours lived ; in fact, no one knew where he lived, except that it was somewhere west of Temple Bar.

He was one of those indescribable rascals commonly called "men upon town," who dread nothing so much as getting a livelihood by honest industry ; and who, as far as regards their morals, are infinitely worse than the highwayman, who, with a pistol at your head, demands your purse or your life.

Captain Dufours was generally in the company of some young man of ample means, who, while they lasted, was kindly assisted in getting rid of his resources by the "gallant captain," as all captains are called in the public papers.

Herbert Mandeville had been initiated into a great deal of vice and immorality by this man while in London. But the kind of life into the vortex of which Captain Dufours succeeded easily in dragging the too susceptible Herbert Mandeville, was not called by such ugly names as vicious or immoral. Oh, dear, no. It was pleasure, gaiety, life, spirit ; and the persons who engaged in it were "fine fellows," and "choice spirits."

To this man it was, then, that Herbert Mandeville resolved to write concerning Adeline,—Adeline, the beautiful and innocent. It was a species of profanation to write her name upon the same page with Dufour's.

Herbert's main object in writing was to learn what he could of Charles Leslie, who ever rose up in his mind as a disagreeable encumbrance to the success of his suit with Adeline.

The letter was as follows :—

"Bracefield.

"MY DEAR DUFOUR,—I am located here, as I told you I should be, when I last saw you in the world, for this is certainly out of it. You know my resolution, when I first heard of my father's intention to send me here, was to make no opposition to the movement, but so to manage, when I did get here, as to get back again as quickly as possible. Now, however, I shall stay for ever!

"I fancy I see your look of surprise when you read this ; but, the fact is, there is an angel here, and so, you see, I am in good company.

"Now, Dufours, what I want you to do is this.—First, find out who Charles Leslie is, who is something odious in the odious city.

"Secondly,—find out who Captain Mourdant was. He was, I think, in the Indian Army; but gather all you can about him.

"Thirdly,—let me know by next post what you think the best plan of at once awakening an interest in the breast of a beautiful young girl, of about sixteen years of age, possessing wit, accomplishments, sense, discretion, &c., &c., far beyond her years. Nothing ordinary will do, so rack your fertile invention for something extraordinary.

"Let me hear from you as soon as possible, and should any money be wanted in the pursuit of your inquiries, just go to Downshot the attorney, and tell him to let you have it on my account.

"I am over head and ears in love. She is a divinity;—an essence of loveliness;—a concentration of beauty. She speaks music. Her slightest movement is a grace.

"Now, mind you write to-morrow evening.   Yours,
                                      "HERBERT MANDEVILLE."

"Dufour is a great rogue," was Herbert's reflection as he sealed his letter, "but he is a wondefully clever fellow, and of more use in an emergency than all your virtuous and moral people in a lump."

Herbert Mandeville felt in a somewhat calmer frame of mind after he had written and directed this letter to "Captain Dufour, Tenillade's Hotel, London." He had taken the first step in the business which was now next his heart, and he flattered himself that his success in winning the heart of Adeline Mourdant was certain.

The hour of twelve now struck from the church clock, and Herbert Mandeville still gazed from his open window.

He felt disinclined to sleep, and he would have amused himself, as was his frequent custom, by pacing his chamber, were it not that he feared to disturb the curate, and, moreover, it would be betraying the feverish and unsettled state of his mind; and Herbert had not yet resolved whether boldly to make Mr. Endsleigh a confidant of his passion, or work in secret upon the heart of Adeline, so that when it was discovered, he should have obtained too firm a hold upon her affections to be easily shaken off by the want of approval of others.

The moon was very high in the sky, and, if possible, more brilliant than at an earlier hour of the evening. There was a delicious cool air abroad, which just lightly stirred the leaves of the trees, and imparted an invigorating freshness to the air.

"I cannot sleep," thought Herbert; "the window is low, I can drop into the garden without disturbing the household, and take a moonlight walk, which may fatigue me sufficiently to induce a few hours healthy morning's sleep against I return."

He cautiously raised the window-sash to its utmost height as he spoke, and at the next moment alighted noiselessly upon the soft earth immediately below the casement of his chamber.

He soon passed through the little garden in front of the parsonage, and opening the gate which led from it, he passed out with a noiseless step into the bright moonlight, which, now that he was free from the shadow of the house, fell clear and brilliant upon his path.

"It is beautiful to walk in this moonlight," he said; "I like this better than the glaring light of day. And whither should I bend my footsteps but to Rose Villa? At least it will be some satisfaction to know that I am near thee, Adeline, and to please my fancy by supposing that I gaze upon the window of the room that enshrouds thy loveliness from the world during the dreamy hours of night."

With rapid steps he crossed the churchyard, and in one half the time that

the curate usually took to perform the distance, he stood by the garden gate of Rose Villa.

He paused, and ran his eye carefully from window to window, but all was darkness.

"Where does she sleep?" he said. "If I could but please myself by fancying that I knew her window. Let me consider. Have I any clue?"

After a few moments thought he said, hurriedly—

"Yes—yes; I recollect! In the course of conversation, she said she attributed the early blossoming of some flowers on her window-sill to their catching, for many days in succession, the morning sun, for that the days had been gloomy after an early hour. Her window looks, then, to the east, or nearly so. The house fronts the west. Adeline then sleeps not on this side."

This idea was no sooner formed in his mind than he acted upon it with all the impetuosity of his nature, and at once entering the garden by vaulting over the light paling, he made his way round towards the back of Rose Villa.

As Herbert Mandeville disregarded all obstacles in his path, he soon stood fairly at the back, which, as it was a detached residence, had been as carefully finished as the front.

He examined the various windows for some time without being satisfied that he could form any guess as to which was Adeline's, but finally he fixed his attentions upon one that was quite shrouded among roses and creeping plants. That he thought must be the window of Adeline's chamber.

To this window now he directed all his attention, that is the attention of his eyes merely, for although he might by a little climbing have easily attained its trifling height from the ground, he feared to risk such a proceeding.

Yet he did not like to leave the spot without some effort to let the gentle

No. 8

Adeline know that some one who loved her lingered near her even in the dead-hours of night.

He stood with his arms folded, in an attitude of deep thought as to what he should do, at the same time to manifest his passions and conceal his identity.

~~~~~~~~~~~~~~~~~~~~~~~~~~~~~

CHAPTER XVI.

" It stood pale and wan in the moonlight ;
My eyes were rooted on it, and the moonbeams
Looked by its side more ruddy than the western sun."
ANON.

A NIGHT ADVENTURE.—THE SERENADE.—THE APPARITION BY THE WICKET GATE.—REAL OR UNREAL.—A DISTURBED NIGHT.

"She love's music," said he, at length ; "what's so likely to charm her sensitive mind in the silence of the night as a serenade such as she has read of, but perchance never heard. Thank nature I have a good voice, and thank art it has been cultivated. The love of music is a sixth sense with many persons—it may be so with her. We will try. There may come some tender fitting moment when I can with effect own to being the midnight serenader. Now to conceal myself."

He looked warily about him, and saw by the moonlight that there was a tree, an elder he thought it was, growing so close to the house that he could well shade himself from any observation from the windows by standing close to its trunk, and should inquiry be pushed further, he might even escape entirely under its cover.

He took up his position, which was certainly a favourable one.

The air was still and serene. Nature herself seemed to be sleeping, and the effect amid the solemn silence that reigned around of Herbert Mandeville's really fine voice astonished himself, as he sung with plaintive earnestness the following—

SERENADE.

" Lady, lady, by the moon !
    I breathe a vow to thee !
Lady, lady, by the moon
    Give back a heart to me !

" Lady, lady, by the stars
    That gem the mild blue sky !
Lady, lady, by the stars,
    To thee I breathe love's sigh !

" Lady, lady, by the flowers
    That blossom in thy hair !
    Lady, lady, by the flowers
I vow that thine art fair.

" Lady, lady, by the stream
    That murmuring flows along ;
Lady, lady, by the stream,
    Oh, listen to love's song !"

He ceased, and the last words of his song died away in beautiful cadences upon the night air.

Attentively he listened, but for many minutes he could catch no sound, and a feeling of disappointment was growing up in his heart, when he heard or thought he heard a window raised.

He bent eagerly forward to listen, and heard with rapture a sweet voice say—

"Will it come again?"

It was the voice of Adeline,—that voice which was such dear music to his ears.

"It will—it will!" he cried, bursting from his place of concealment into the full glare of the moonlight.

A faint scream met his ears, and in the next moment a light flashed from the window which he had supposed to be Adeline's room.

It was not the object of Mandeville to be known, and he at once made a precipitate retreat from the garden of the Villa, quite satisfied that he had done enough for one night.

Herbert's object now was to get home to the parsonage as quickly as possible, and without exciting any observation from the curate's household.

He rapidly traversed the churchyard, and bounding along in all the buoyancy of health and youth, he was about to pass through the wicket gate, when he almost fell to the ground, so astonished was he at seeing a figure standing between him and the wicket.

For a moment Herbert Mandeville stood transfixed with surprise, and a variety of feelings began to take possession of his mind.

"Who," he said, "who are you?"

A deep groan burst from the figure.

Herbert felt the blood curdle round his heart at the supposition that now crossed his mind of the possibility of the form that arrested his progress in that receptacle for the dead being other than mortal.

"Speak!" he said. "Speak!"

The moonbeams fell clearly and brightly now upon the face of the figure; for the moment previous a passing cloud had obscured their radiance, and cast a shadowy gloom upon nature.

The face was very pale, and there was an expression of deep melancholy upon the features, which appeared to be those of a man past the prime of life.

Herbert Mandeville could say no more. His tongue clove to the roof of his mouth, and he could not utter the words that came gurgling to his throat.

For about three seconds the figure stood motionless by the little wicket gate, and then, with another deep groan—a groan of unutterable woe and anguish—it slowly glided from the spot, and was lost almost immediately to Herbert's sight.

It was some minutes before Mandeville could recover self-possession sufficient to pass through the wicket gate, and when he did so, his step was hurried and uncertain, and damp perspiration of deadly fear stood upon his brow.

He spoke not; nay, even he scarcely dared to think till he reached the parsonage house, and crossing the garden, with some difficulty scrambled in at the window of his own apartment.

The light that he had left burning was nearly expiring from want of attention, and his first care was to trim it; and then he closed the casement and threw himself into a chair, with a feeling of great relief that he was " home again."

He sat for a time involved in such a confusion of ideas that he was quite incapable of fixing his thoughts for one moment upon any particular object. After a time, however, his mind became more calm, and he was able to reason with some degree of clearness upon the singular appearance he had encountered in the churchyard, and which now occupied his mind almost to the temporary exclusion of the image of Adeline Mourdant.

"What could it be?" he exclaimed. "Was it natural or supernatural—or is what we call supernatural, after all, but in the proper order of nature?

I have hitherto been sceptical upon the subject of apparitions, but how to account for the feelings that came over me in the churchyard, I know not."

As he spoke to himself in a low tone he heard the church clock strike three, and he started at the sound as it broke upon the solemn stillness that reigned over the face of nature.

"I must endeavour," he said, "to seek some repose before morning, or my weary aspect may induce a suspicion that I have not slept."

Without undressing he threw himself upon his bed, and tried to close his eyes in sleep. It was long, however, before the gentle influence crept over him, and the sun was just gilding the topmost branches of the tallest trees before the wearied and perplexed Herbert Mandeville sunk into a profound and dreamless slumber upon his restless couch.

How long he slept he knew not, but he was awakened suddenly by a knocking at his chamber-door, and starting from his bed, he found himself in the full glare of a radiant sunshine.

"Herbert! Herbert!" cried the voice of the curate.

"Sir!" answered Herbert.

"Do you know the hour? You have over-slept yourself."

"I—I shall be down directly," cried Mandeville as he glanced at his watch.

It was half-past eleven.

He flew to the wash-hand basin and drenched his face and hands: then, hastily arranging his disordered apparel, he opened his door and descended to the parlour, where the morning meal had been long since partaken of.

"Why, dear me, Mr. Mandeville," cried Mrs. Plumpjoy, "you have taken a long sleep indeed."

"Yes," said Herbert. "I am rather subject to over-sleeping. I wish I had been called earlier."

"And so you would have been," replied Mrs. Plumpjoy; "but you see my brother went out quite early to call on the Mourdants."

"The Mourdants?" said Mandeville, "and I asleep!"

"Now," continued Mrs. Plumpjoy, "I thought to be sure you had gone with him, and he thought you were out for a morning's walk. So, till he came back again, we never thought, any of us, of going near your bed-room, because, you see, Mr. Mandeville——"

"Yes—yes," cried Herbert. "I—I thank you, madam. It was very foolish of me to over-sleep myself."

"Oh, it's nothing," said Mrs. Plumpjoy. "About seven or eight years ago, when I was quite a child almost, I used to sleep an astonishing number of hours—you wouldn't credit it."

"No," thought Herbert, "I wouldn't credit the fact of your being a child seven or eight years since."

Herbert rose now, and declared his intention of taking a walk.

"Why, you haven't had any breakfast," exclaimed Mrs. Plumpjoy. "Well, what can you be thinking of?"

"I—I—certainly forgot the breakfast," said Mandeville. "I think too much sleep confuses the mind."

"Oh, I believe you, it does," said Mrs. Plumpjoy. "Here, you idle slut, (to the servant,) bring Mr. Mandeville some breakfast directly."

The sight of a substantial country breakfast seemed to give Herbert an appetite; for in spite of his love and his last night's adventure in the church-yard, he contrived to make a very hearty meal.

He was still very much undecided how to act: whether to mention to Mr. Endsleigh all the occurrences of the night, or to keep them secret, still puzzled him. He felt conscious that he must very soon make up his mind upon the matter, because otherwise circumstances would decide themselves, and he would be left no choice; for if after one or two meetings with the curate he said nothing, he could not very well suddenly break out with a stale and tardy confidence, which, to have any grace at all, should have been immediate and ample upon the very first opportunity.

"I will take my letter," he thought—" my letter to Dufours, down to the village post-office, and I can consider on the road what I had better do in the matter. The walk will, perhaps, clear my faculties a little, and enable me to decide the point more satisfactorily."

With this determination he rose from the breakfast-table, well pleased that he had not encountered the curate, and securing his letter, he hurried from the parsonage-house towards the village, for the purpose of posting it to his quondum friend, and not very creditable adviser, the veracious and knowing Captain Dufours.

CHAPTER XVII.

" Music hath charms to soothe the savage breast."

THE MENTAL STRUGGLE.—HERBERT MANDEVILLE'S FAULTS AND QUALITIES.—THE CURATE.—A NOISE IN THE NIGHT.—MORTIFICATION AND INDIGNATION.

WHEN there is a struggle in the human mind between two particular courses of action, the one of which comprehends straightforward truth and candour, and the other duplicity and concealment, in nine cases out of ten the latter course will be ultimately decided upon; because the very fact that there is a mental struggle upon the occasion implies the predisposition to concealment and duplicty, which has but to overcome the lingering suggestions of truth and right to reign with undisputed triumph in the heart.

The reader will not be, therefore, surprised to hear that Herbert Mandeville decided, during his short walk to the village with his letter, to say nothing whatever of the preceding night's proceedings to the curate, and to follow up his course of secret wooing of the fair and gentle Adeline Mourdant at every available opportunity he could perceive.

Whether or not he would venture upon another midnight serenade to Adeline he could not fully make up his mind, and he left that part of the subject till the time for its execution or abandonment should arrive, when he could act according to the frame of mind in which he should find himself.

On his return to the parsonage, he could not resist the impulse to pass through the churchyard and examine the spot on which he had encountered the mysterious figure the preceding night.

He quickly stood by the little wicket, and it was with a feeling of interest and curiosity that he once more found himself alone upon that spot of ground which, had he been ready of belief, he would have at once dreaded as having been the scene of a supernatural visitation.

How different an aspect does a place assume at broad daylight, from that which it wears at the solemn hour of midnight!

The sunbeams were resting calmly and sweetly upon the silent graves. The little wicket gate, against which had stood the figure which had produced such an impression upon the mind of Mandeville, swung idly in the light breeze, that lent an agreeable freshness to the air, upon its rusty hinges.

The latticed windows of the ancient church shone in the sunbeams like pure burnished gold, and the birds sung sweetly as they hopped and fluttered among the grave-stones and the trees and shrubs that taste or affection had planted in that lone spot.

"Could my imagination have deceived me?" said Herbert, as he stood for a moment contemplating the quiet beauty of the scene around him. "Could the figure that I saw, or fancied I saw, have been merely the creation of an excited fancy? My mind was certainly in a state of exaltation. The hour was propitious for such a delusion. When I gaze around me upon this quiet scene, now so clear and distinct in the glorious sunbeams, I cannot but think I was deceived by heated fancy."

From the church porch there now came the curate, who had been within the sacred building performing some clerical duty.

Herbert Mandeville saw him, and as he approached, with the morning's salutation, he whispered to himself,—

"Caution !—caution !—not a word of last night's proceedings."

"Good morning," said the curate. "You were a late riser this morning."

"I was, indeed," replied Mandeville. "I certainly was surprised to find it so late when you called me."

"You have breakfasted?"

"I have. And you—you have been to the Mourdants'?"

"Yes," said the curate.

"They are well, I trust?"

"Quite well."

"I am glad to hear it. It would have given me great pleasure to have accompanied you on your visit."

"They do not receive company," answered the curate.

"I have no wish to intrude, of course," said Herbert, coldly.

"Certainly, Herbert. I am sure nothing could be further from your thoughts than obtruding yourself where you would not be welcome."

"Not welcome?" repeated Mandeville.

"Not welcome," said the curate, firmly.

They now walked on in silence for some minutes, for Mandeville was not very well pleased at the frankness of the curate ; and the curate, by some means, he could see, was not very well pleased with him."

"He has heard from the Mourdants of the serenade," thought Mandeville, "and he suspects me."

When they were close to the door of the parsonage-house, the old curate paused, and, turning fully round, he fixed his eyes upon Herbert Mandeville's face, as he said,—

"I am an old man, and plain spoken, Herbert. Will you answer me a plain question?"

The colour flew to Herbert's cheeks, as he answered,—

"Of course—I—I suppose so."

"It is answered," said the curate, mildly, but in a mournful tone of voice. "Herbert, your changing colour has answered me."

"To what do you allude?" said Mandeville.

"Some one trespassed last night upon the grounds of Rose Villa."

Herbert looked down, and said nothing.

"I exact no confidence," said the curate ; "but I wish to infer nothing. Were you that person?"

Herbert had sense and discretion sufficient to answer at once.

"I was," he said.

"You made a noise there, I understand," continued the curate, "and alarmed the little household."

"A noise?" said Herbert.

"Yes," said the curate. "A noise in the night-time, you must be aware, is very unpleasant."

Mandeville felt excessively mortified that his serenade should be called "a noise in the night."

"I did sing in the garden," he said.

"Well," said the curate, "Mrs. Mourdant will forego a prosecution for trespass this time; but she begs you will select some other place than her garden to practise your voice in for the future."

"Forego a prosecution?" said Herbert.

"Yes," said the curate, coldly.

"Absurd!" cried Mandeville.

"It's contrary to law to enter people's premises at night, trample down their flowers, and make a howling or a screeching, as the case may be," remarked Mr. Endsleigh, with great gravity.

"I am much obliged to Mrs. Mourdant," said Mandeville. "She is a most careful and discreet lady, no doubt."

"No doubt whatever," said the curate.

"She had better plant some spring-guns and man-traps, don't you think, sir?" continued Herbert, in a tone of irony.

"No, I don't think so," replied the curate.

"May I ask, sir," said Herbert, after a slight pause, "if Miss Adeline Mourdant was equally indignant?"

"I have the pleasure to say no," answered the curate.

"No?" cried Herbert, his eyes sparkling with pleasure.

"No," continued Mr. Endsleigh. "She slept soundly all the time; but her mother told her of the disturbance in the morning."

"Slept?" cried Herbert.

"Yes," said the curate, "the noise did not awaken her."

"Indeed!" said Herbert, incredulously.

No more conversation took place at that time upon the subject, and Mr. Endsleigh and his pupil parted, with a degree of coldness that did not augur well for the stability or pleasantness of their future connexion.

Herbert Mandeville betook himself to his own room; and when there, and alone, a very few moments' reflection convinced him that he had acted very foolishly in allowing his temper to overcome his judgment in his recent interview with the curate.

"Should he take sufficient umbrage at my conduct," thought Mandeville, "to write to my father to take me away, I have prettily mismanaged this business."

This thought was a most disagreeable one to Herbert, for he could not help feeling conscious that in Mr. Endsleigh he was dealing with a man of decisive and prompt habits, and that no considerations of a pecuniary nature, as regarded his (Mandeville's) sojourn at Bracefield, would have any effect upon his mind in the business.

The thought that he might already have done sufficient to induce such a result was alarming to Herbert in the extreme.

"I might be removed from here at a word," he said. "And what could I do at a distance of several hundreds of miles from Adeline?"

The mere imagining of such a thing was distracting, and Herbert paced his room in a most unenviable frame of mind.

The more he thought upon the subject, the more imminent did the danger of the curate acting precipitately in the matter appear to him; and so intolerable did his anxiety become, that he determined at length upon immediately seeking Mr. Endsleigh, and attempting to restore their intercourse to its former friendly footing.

With this view he descended from his room, and, upon arriving in the parlour, he looked eagerly around him for the curate.

"Dear me, Mr. Mandeville, what's the matter?" cried Mrs. Plumpjoy. "You look positively wild, I declare."

"I want Mr. Endsleigh," said Herbert.

"Well, let me see,' said Mrs. Plumpjoy, very calmly. "Where can he be?"

"Is he in the house?" said Herbert.

"Oh, dear, yes,—he's—"

Mandeville was off, and making the best of his way to the curate's study, before Mrs. Plumpjoy could finish her surmises.

"Well!" she exclaimed, "men are all alike—so impatient. It's really dreadful to have anything to say to them."

The curate was in his study, for he had flown there as to a place of refuge from Mrs. Plumpjoy.

Herbert knocked gently at the door.

"Come in," cried Mr. Endsleigh, in his usual mild, rich tone.

Mandeville immediately entered, and the glow upon his cheek at once told the curate that he came on some more than ordinary errand.

"Sit down, Herbert," he said, kindly.

"Sir," said Herbert, " I fear I have displeased you."

"As how—" said the curate.

"I own," said Mandeville, "my conduct last night was unjustifiable. This morning it was worse; and I can only say that Mrs. Mourdant shall not have again to complain of a similar annoyance. The serenade was thought of one moment, and executed the next."

"That is enough," said Mr. Endsleigh, with a gratified look.

"I will write an apology, if you please," continued Herbert.

"No," answered the curate, "that is not necessary. I will settle that part of the matter, Herbert."

"I sincerely thank you, sir," said Mandeville.

"The thing itself was trifling," remarked the curate.

"The 'noise in the night' you mean, sir?"

"Yes," answered Mr. Endsleigh, with a smile; "but Mrs. Mourdant has a right, in her peculiar situation, to take alarm, even at a trifle."

"I feel that you are quite right," said Mandeville. "It shall not be repeated, you may depend."

"I know it will not," said the curate, "when you say it will not."

Mr. Endsleigh was well aware of that most important fact in morals, that the surest way to induce a person to keep his word, is to place unlimited confidence in it.

Truth and honesty doubted, has frequently made a liar and a thief of one who might have been for ever free from either vice!

"Now, read this," added the curate, "and then throw it into the fire."

He handed to Mandeville a sheet of letter-paper, on which there were about three lines of writing, which the curate had been engaged upon at the moment of Mandeville's entrance into the room.

Herbert took it and read.

"Bracefield."

"My dear Friend,—I write to you in sorrow, genuine sorrow, to request you to remove your son from here. I have had a hard struggle with my heart to write this, for I think I could love him; but there is a duty which—"

The writing here abruptly terminated.

"This was to my father?" said Herbert.

"It was," replied the curate.

In a moment it was in the fire.

"You shall never have occasion, sir, to write such another note," said Mandeville, extending his hand.

The curate shook it warmly, as he said,—

"I don't think I shall, Herbert."

"Providence seemed to direct me here just in time."

"Providence, my dear Mandeville," said the curate, "is oftener directing us than we imagine. All is for the best, because all is from God."

CHAPTER XVIII.

> "Ah! who can tell how tenderly a mother feels
>   For the fair image that recalls
>   The scenes of youth, when hope was young,
>   And she herself was such a maid."
>   BEAUMONT.

THE MOTHER'S ALARM.—ADELINE'S INNOCENCE.—A LETTER OF A CONCISE AND BUSINESS-LIKE NATURE.—THE ANSWER.—NIGHT AGAIN.

It will be readily conjectured by the reader that the morning's conversation between the curate and Mrs. Mourdant turned chiefly upon the manifest passion which Herbert Mandeville had shewn for Adeline, a passion which, however well he, Herbert, imagined he had concealed, had by no means escaped the observant eye of Mrs. Mourdant, or, indeed, the remark of the curate.

Mrs. Mourdant likewise related how she had been awakened in the night by a serenade, which, the curate agreed with her, could have emanated from no other than Mandeville.

Mr. Endsleigh was much annoyed and disturbed at the information, and de-

No. 9

termined upon speaking to Herbert upon the subject the first opportunity that presented itself, and to be guided in his conduct, as to whether he should retain him at Bracefield or not, by the ingenuousness or non-ingenuousness of his replies.

The result of this determination we have seen; and the good curate, who was always ready to see goodness and candour in preference to lurking deceit, was completely imposed upon by Herbert's repentance, and, upon the whole, was rather pleased than otherwise at the whole affair, as he, in the kindness of his heart, fancied that it had given him a favourable insight into the heart of his young pupil.

There was, therefore, a better understanding, to all appearance, between the curate and Mandeville than before; and the old man felt his heart, for the first time, woven towards the son of his ancient friend.

"He is not," he thought, "possessed of that high moral sense that characterizes Charles Leslie; but time, while it ripens his judgment, will subdue the impetuosity of his temper, and he may become a man of rare qualities. Genius he has to a great extent, and his follies now are the follies of a boy, and will not adhere to the man."

Herbert in the meantime felt in a very dissatisfied and unsettled state of mind. He congratulated himself upon making his peace with Mr. Endsleigh, and thus warding off the greatest evil, namely, his departure from Bracefield, which would at once have crushed all his hopes with regard to the peerless beauty who now held his heart enchained.

Thus the day passed, and Herbert was afraid to make any allusion to Adeline, for fear of again exciting the suspicions he had only just succeeded in quelling.

One thought, however, sustained him, and that was, that despite of all the curate might say to the contrary, the lovely Adeline must have heard the strains that were offered up at the shrine of her beauty, and, hearing them, could not fail to feel some sensation of pleasure at the thought that she was beloved by some one who, in the silence of the night, thus poured forth his passion in song.

Under a plea of a headache, Mandeville retired early to his chamber, and and there he sat revolving over and over in his mind what should be his next attempt upon the heart of Adeline, and how he should ascertain what had been the result of his first effort.

He was absorbed in these reflections, when he heard a horseman gallop to the door of the parsonage.

A visiter was so rare an occurrence, that Herbert's anxiety was aroused to know who it could be, and he was upon the point of opening his window to ascertain, when some one knocked at his door.

His cry of " Come in," was immediately obeyed by the curate himself, who had a letter in his hand.

"The postboy has brought you a letter, Herbert," he said; "I suppose it is from your father."

Mandeville took it in his hand, and well he knew the writing. It was from the veritable Captain Dufours.

"No," said Herbert, with a slight confusion of manner. "I know the hand; it is from a friend in town."

"Well, I shall bid you good-night," said the curate, "for I am about retiring to rest, which I hope you will do likewise."

"There is no moonlight to-night," said Herbert; "the sky is black and cloudy."

"So you mean there is no temptation to a serenade."

"No," answered Herbert, laughing. "The weather is not sufficiently romantic; so good night, sir."

"Good night," replied the curate, and he left the room.

"Now, Dufours," cried Herbert, tearing open the letter, "we will see what you have to say and advise."

This was the letter :—

"D—n Downshot! he wont advance a penny without your note of hand. Curse him!

"Your's in the flesh,

"Herbert Mandeville, Esq.,   "Augustus Dufours."

"at Grass."

Herbert was both annoyed and amused at this epistle. He was annoyed because it gave no hint whatever to advance him in his present pursuit, and he could not but feel amused at the unblushing assurance of the captain, in only answering, without the least hypocrisy, that portion of the letter which was interesting to himself.

"There is a satisfaction to my mind," said Mandeville, as he threw down the letter, "in dealing with a man like this. There is no trouble about his honour and his delicacy ; he is to be purchased, and thus freely used. I must send a note of hand. It was foolish of me, for I ought to have guessed beforehand that a Jew attorney was not a man to make advances without tangible security."

He drew writing materials towards him, and drew in due form a note of hand upon the attorney for fifty pounds, which he knew well would be honoured, as he, Herbert, was the undoubted heir to immense property, which had been accumulated by his father and his uncle.

This he enclosed in another note to Captain Dufours, which ran thus :—

"Captain Dufours,—Enclosed is the note of hand you require. Read my first letter again and return me a proper answer, or you will hear no more from   "Herbert Mandeville."

This being done, Herbert once more resigned himself to reflection upon his situation and prospects as regarded Adeline, and he continued absorbed in unsatisfactory thought for above an hour.

"I will give the subject up for to-night," he said suddenly. "My brain is regularly fevered. I will think no more till morning. Yet I cannot sleep. I must do something to distract my thoughts from Adeline. From Adeline do I say? Can I ever forget her?"

He threw open the window and looked out upon the night. A south-west wind had sprung up and covered the fair vault of Heaven with massive clouds which effectually obscured the moon.

In fact, the night which Herbert Mandeville now gazed upon was as remarkable for its black darkness as the preceding one had been for its brilliant light.

"This is a night," he said, "upon which one might defy detection upon any expedition ; but I am in too ticklish a situation, just at present, with my very good friend, the curate, to run any risk ; so I must make myself contented, for to-night at least, in my chamber."

There was a chillness in the air, which did not induce Herbert to remain long at the window, and he soon closed it.

He smiled as he did so. "If," he thought, "the curate hears the window, he will make sure of another serenade. I wonder if he was ever in love himself. I should say decidedly not."

Mandeville felt that he could not sleep, and he looked round the room despairingly for something to engage his attention.

Suddenly a thought struck him.

"I have the curate's manuscript!" he exclaimed. "That will well pass away the hours."

He immediately produced it, and trimming his light carefully, he sat down opposite the window and opened the manuscript which Mr. Endsleigh had lent to him, and which related to the mysterious grave-stone, with the initials only, in the churchyard.

The manuscript was entitled

"WILD LOVE; OR, FATAL MISCONSTRUCTION!"

Mandeville was soon deeply immersed in its contents, which commenced as follows :—

"Two young men, of striking appearance, were, at the close of a serene and lovely day in autumn, some twelve years since, walking, apparently immersed in deep and interesting conversation, by the sea shore of a well-known fishing town on the coast of Kent.

"Their discourse seemed to be of beauty, for one suddenly exclaimed—

"'Still, Medwin, that undefinable quality which we call beauty, that harmonious association as you are pleased to term it, is not, I contend, so merely superficial as you would fain induce me to suppose; it is true that the heart of a Fantippe may find a home in a form of apparently surpassing loveliness; but will so keen an observer of human nature as I believe you to be assert that the fair features bear no impress of the mind within? You have prejudged this question, Medwin; you believed that personal beauty had, indeed, but a superficial claim to notice, and you look no further than to mere outline for its presence. Your philosophy is true, startling true, on many subjects; but believe me, my friend, that there is one in all the intricacies of which you believe yourself so great a proficient, but in which you are, in reality, but a tyro—it is the study of woman. Nay, nay, I know what you would say. You have studied woman,—studied her deeply too. But how? Not as you embark in any other investigation, by an intimate acquaintance with, and a careful examination of, the subject of your inquiry, but in your closet, from books, from history of actions, coloured according to the peculiar feelings of their authors, from the attempted records of that which never can be recorded—namely, the complex motives which give rise to human actions. Would you engage yourself in an investigation of the myriads of fair flowers which spring forth on the earth's surface by shutting yourself in a small boarded chamber, unvisited by even a ray of sunlight? Certainly you would not; and yet, most consistent wight! nature's fairest flower has received at thy hands no better treatment. Incline thine ear, my friend,—I will impart a secret.—If you would study woman, Medwin, seek her!'

"A pause of some moments ensued ere Medwin replied to his friend. He had been gazing abstractedly on the last ray of sunlight, as with golden beauty it lingered on the horizon; and when he did speak, it was with a tone and manner so different from that in which he usually expressed himself, that his friend turned in surprise to discover what new emotion had suddenly exercised so powerfully over him.

"'Frank Kennedy,' he said, 'I too have a secret, although now but a short time in which to impart it to you, for yon trembling line of lights on the still sea warns me to be gone. Forgive my tardy confidence, Frank; silence was forced upon me; but now listen, and I think you will own that I have approached the subject of our discussion somewhat more nearly than you had imagined. You have heard of Sir Richard Knightley's fair niece?'

"'I have. Her beauty is an universal theme!'

"'She is my betrothed, Frank.'

"'Can this be possible, Medwin? I always heard that she was watched by her uncle, who is likewise her guardian, with the most jealous care. She is likewise reported to be a being endowed with the most tender and romantic sensibilities, and——'

" ' Let me finish the sentence for you, Kennedy; you think your poor friend, Medwin, not the best qualified person of your acquaintance to awaken a tender sentiment in the breast of such a being. But are you sure you know me?—such men as I love but once, and that one passion, like a foaming torrent, is irresistible in its progress; but come, my friend, you shall see that to-night which shall rescue me, in your opinion, from the charge of shunning the beautiful and good—of being but a philosophical dreamer of woman.'

" He took the arm of Kennedy, and led him to a point of the sea-beaten coast which presented an easy ascent to the summit of the chalky cliffs, at the base of which the narrow strip of sand upon which our friends had been standing was rapidly contracting in size, as each succeeding wave of the advancing tide encroached upon its surface.

" Kennedy was silent. Medwin had given utterance, in impassionate language, to feelings to which he had believed him to be an utter stranger. He had spoken, for the first time, in the dreamy language of romance.

" Could he have been so much mistaken in the estimate of the character of his friend?—did he really possess a rich mine of feeling and imagination, the existence of which had escaped the penetration of his greatest intimates? It might be so, and Kennedy's self-pride felt hurt at the supposition: he felt that he had been superficial where he had imagined himself most profound. It had not occurred to him, that beneath á roughness of exterior, almost approaching to repulsive harshness, there might exist a heart attuned to the sweetest sympathies of human nature.

" Kennedy, in the self-condemnation, did not do himself justice. The feelings which Medwin had manifested, and which had so much surprised his friend, were new, at least in action. They had slumbered in his breast only to be awakened into life and energy by some overpowering influence; the spell which bound them was at length broken, and by one of the most humanising feelings which can find a home in the breast of man—the love of woman! His attachment to Marian Knightley, was the commencement to him of a new existence—the sun shone with brighter refulgence—the wild flowers bloomed in sweeter beauty in his path—the murmuring sea was more musical as it rippled over the sandy beach, and it seemed to him as if some mysterious veil had been withdrawn from his eyes, which had hitherto prevented him from enjoying the beauty and gladness of nature—

" ' Oh, love, how perfect is thy mystic art!'

" Of the character and feelings of Kennedy, the reader will find but little difficulty in forming a just estimate. With a mind possessing powers far above mediocrity, he was, nevertheless, so keenly alive to the opinions and prejudices of the society in which he moved, as to become the slave of habits and opinions which his own acute intellect would have at once condemned as artificial and mischievous.

" His lively imagination and eloquent address made his society sought after by all who knew him, and no scene of festivity in the rapidly increasing sea-port town, from whence our story dates its origin, was thought to be at all endurable, unless graced by the lively and mirth-inspiring presence of Frank Kennedy.

" He was sojourning in the town but for a few weeks, his ostensible object being the re-establishment of his health, which had been somewhat impaired by his too ardent devotion to the fine arts, in which he excelled. His friend, Medwin, held a commission in a regiment which was quartered in the immediate vicinity, which circumstance certainly materially assisted Kennedy to

the discovery that he required the salubrious breezes of the little town of
H—— for its recovery; for, although at first sight it would appear that no two
beings could be more dissimilar in habits and feelings than Medwin and
Kennedy, there had long subsisted between them one of those extraordinary
attachments which startle us as much by their frequency, as by the incon-
gruity of the materials of which they are composed.

"Medwin's principal mental characteristic appeared to be an indomitable
firmness and resolution, which, although it not unfrequently achieved important
results, and gave him the appearance of possessing a more vigorous intellect
than Kennedy, whose excursive imagination frequently produced a hesitation
of purpose, was likewise not unfrequently productive of mischievous results
from its very inflexibility.

"In his rambles along the coast, he had met with Marian Knightley. Accident had produced an acquaintanceship between them, and for the first time
he felt the influence of female loveliness, and with him it was intoxication of
the soul—he was like one under the influence of a sorceress, and so sweetly
beautiful were the chains which bound him, that each link had become entwined around his heart; she was his genius, the earthly deity which he
fondly worshipped.

"The friends had ascended the cliff, and proceeded at a rapid pace for a considerable distance. Medwin had become silent and contemplative, and Kennedy
chose not to interrupt his meditations. The moon was high in the heavens
ere they arrived at the borders of a thick wood, which apparently formed part
of an adjoining estate. Medwin paused, and enjoining silence and caution by
an expressive gesture, commenced rapidly, but lightly and noiselessly, threading
his way through the thick underwood which impeded his progress.

"Through the interstices of the majestic trees, with which they were surrounded, Kennedy obtained occasional glimpses of a mansion clearly defined
against the moonlit sky.

"Medwin paused at the termination of a low fence which enclosed a part of
the plantation, through which they had been directing their course. He hastily
unbuckled the sword-belt from his waist, and handed the weapon to Kennedy,
that it might not impede him in his progress, and then sprang over the slight
fence. He grasped Kennedy's hand as he addressed him in low quick accents,
in which there was much emotion.

"'Frank, I may trust you; follow me with your eyes, and, if possible,
warn me should any one approach. Does not nature smile upon my love?
How still is all around! Yon silver orb, sailing through the realms of
space, has been hitherto the only witness of that which thou shalt see to-
night. Farewell! Frank, for a short time, farewell! One moment's meeting
with those we love on such a night as this, is indeed worth a world of
sorrow.'

"Kennedy watched him, as with cautious steps he pursued a route which,
in a few moments, brought him to a rising spot of ground of but limited
extent, but free from the thick growth of trees and underwood with which the
rest of the scene was encumbered. The dilapidated remains of a small building, which retained but few traces of its former beauty, at once indicated that
art had been employed in clearing the beautifully verdant spot of earth.

"And there stood Melville, his not ungraceful figure in bold relief in the
moonlight, which shed a dazzling flood of brilliance upon every object. All
was still and calm, no sound disturbed the rapt repose of the scene, and, for
an instant, Medwin might have been mistaken for the statue of some sylvan
deity.

"The silence was broken, and Kennedy breathed more freely, for he had
feared to break the still repose of nature even by a sigh.

"Medwin had drawn from his bosom a flute, the plaintive and beautiful tones of which, as they stole upon the excited senses of Kennedy, appeared to posses a charm beyond their mere musical sweetness ; he knew the air well, ut never before had it fallen upon his ear with so much expressive beauty. In moments of joyous festivity he had often given utterance to the words which accompanied them, but now, as he mentally repeated them, he felt that with them would henceforward be for ever associated the events of that night.

THE SPIRIT'S SONG.

" Spirits of bliss, I see ye not,
    But I know that ye are there,
For music of another sphere
    Is floating in the air.
The strains ye sing are those of love,
    With hope around it clinging,
Sweet as the song of forest birds,
    Amid the wild woods singing.
Spirits of bliss I feel your sway,
I come, I come, I must obey!

" Spirits of joy, I greet ye well,
    I feel your blissful power,
'Tis welcome to my throbbing breast
    As dew-drops to the flower.
'Tis sweet as sunlight on the stream,
    When bounding to the billow;
Tis fair as moonbeams on the lake,
    Or tear-drops from the willow.
Spirits of joy, I feel your sway,
I come, I come, I must obey!"

" The strain ceased ; Medwin stood still as a statue, and Kennedy watched the spot with the closest attention. A slight rustling noise, indicative of the approach of some person, fell upon his attentive ear, and in the next instant Medwin was kneeling at the feet of a figure, the proportions of which could not be accurately distinguished, in consequence of it being enveloped in a military cloak of capacious dimensions, and a cap which completely enshrouded the face.

" Medwin arose, and gently removing the cap of the unknown, a profusion of fair ringlets escaped from their temporary confinement, and, as the unclasped cloak fell to the ground, Kennedy gazed with all the admiration of a highly sensitive imagination upon a young female of surpassing loveliness. The moonlight gave a spiritual expression to her beautifully regular and expressive features, and revealed to his fixed gaze a form of almost more than feminine sweetness.

" For a few moments Medwin and Marian,—for it was she who had stolen amid the stillness and beauty of nature, to meet her lover,—stood motionless and mute, gazing upon each other.

" It would seem as if the ordinary language of mortals was not sufficiently expressive to give utterance to the purity and intensity of their love. Medwin then placed the gentle girl's arm in his, and both left the spot, being quickly hidden amid the gigantic trees which spread their leafy canopies over their heads. Kennedy passed his hand rapidly across his eyes, as if to assure himself of his waking existence. It seemed as though some fair vision of a dream had fled, leaving him to awaken to reality and sigh for its departure. And yet he was nothing to the fair girl who had beamed but for a few short moments upon his bewildered senses, and a pang of envy shot across his mind as he crossed the fence to endeavour to trace the progress of his friend.

" Medwin's sword was at his side ; he had been enjoined to watch—to watch lest some wandering footstep should disturb his friend, while pouring into the ear of so beautiful a being the fervid and enthusiastic language of love—and he, the convenient friend, the sentinel, was rewarded by a momentary glimpse of the fair object of his friend's idolatry, and he there might probably wait until the east grew grey, ere one thought of him might cross the mind of the enraptured lover.

"The colour deepened on his cheek as he turned to retrace his steps, but his better judgment then asserted its supremacy, and he paused to reflect how far he was allowing a feeling of jealousy and envy to obscure his reason ; then forcing his way with some difficulty forwards, he gained the spot of ground from which his friend had so quickly disappeared. An instant's reflection now told him how futile would be any attempt to follow Medwin and Marian through the intricate mazes of the mimic forest which surrounded him on every side, and he was about to retire to his former post of observation, when he observed lying on the ground the flute, by the dulcet sounds of which Medwin had summoned to his side so fair a being. He placed it to his lips and breathed a few notes of the air which his friend had chosen as the signal of his presence, but ere the last lingering tones of the melody had subsided into silence, he felt himself seized from behind by an arm too powerful to render escape a matter of easy accomplishment. He, however, struggled with his assailant for some time, until they were face to face, vociferously demanding the cause of so unprovoked an attack. The person who had thus unceremoniously assaulted him was a hardy peasant of muscular proportions, and by his dress of faded green, was evidently in some manner connected with the preservation of the game on the estate. There was in his broad rubicund visage that expression of homely good nature, which is, or was, so much the characteristic of the English peasant. He preserved his grasp of Kennedy, although evidently somewhat reluctantly, and the latter, as the thought flashed across his mind that his temporary durance might be the consequence of a mistake, not at all detrimental to the interests of Medwin, avoided making any very violent efforts for his release.

"He, however, demanded his liberation, in tones of the greatest indignation, but the rustic was immoveable.

"'Noa, noa, zur,'' he cried, ' I bean't a-going to let 'e go. Mak 'e self easy loikes. Master Willum! Master Willum! I got un. Master Willum, where be thee? Doan't I tell 'e I got un.'

"'Remove your hands from me ; by what authority am I detained?'

"'Now doan't 'e tak on zo, zur ; I bean't a-going to let 'e go. Master Willum! danged if I doan't let un go. Doan't 'e pull about yo, zur, you'll do yourself a harm loike. Master Willum! I cotched 'un.'

"Master Willum now emerged from the surrounding obscurity. He was a tall, thin youth, sickly and effeminate in his general appearance, and his voice, as he urged the peasant, by the name of Ralph, to hold Kennedy firmly, was weak and tremulous. His dress bespoke his station in society to be among the wealthy.

"Kennedy, upon his appearance, instantly demanded to be released from the grasp of his servant, who he concluded the sturdy peasant, who had captured him to be.

"To this the young gentleman, who kept at a cautious distance from Kennedy, either could not find a ready reply, or disdained to parley with his prisoner, for after briefly commanding Ralph to follow, he commenced threading his way towards the antique mansion, before-mentioned.

"This cool insolence of Master William's deprived Kennedy of the small portion of patience which he had remaining, and he at once stated his determination not to proceed.

"'Now doan't 'e be crustaceous loike, zur ; I bean't a-going to let 'e go, danged if I am.'

"But Kennedy was spared from the consequences of the personal encoun-

ter into which he was preparing to engage, by the sight, through the interstices of the trees, of two figures slowly approaching the scene of action, that
they were Medwin and his Marian, he at once concluded. Ralph was in
such a position that he could not notice their approach, and Kennedy hastened to improve so desirable a state of things by removing him from the spot
as quickly as possible, entertaining as he did, no doubt, but that he was assailed under the supposition of his being Medwin, whose appointment with
Marian had by some accident come to the knowledge of Sir Richard Knightley,
he, therefore, suffered himself without opposition to be urged forward by
Ralph.

"'Now that be zenzible loike, zur, I said I wouldn't let 'e go. I am
bringing un, Master Willum. Didn't I catch 'un, he! he! he!' and the
delighted rustic laughed loudly at the recollection of his own prowess.

"They proceeded in silence for some time, Kennedy absorbed in reflections on the occurrences of the night, and in speculations with regard to the
probable termination of his own adventures.

"Ralph had relapsed into silence, after several fruitless attempts to engage
Kennedy in conversation ; he had relaxed his hold of the prisoner, who now
showed no disposition to escape. They skirted the edge of the plantation,
from which they had emerged for a considerable distance, and after traversing
several pieces of ground laid out with great taste, and presenting a pleasing
appearance of highly-wrought vegetation, they at length arrived at the boundary of a beautifully undulating lawn, through which a pathway led direct to
the mansion where Master William had preceeded them.

"Kennedy now thought that the time had arrived at which he might venture upon an explanation of the probable mistake which had arisen, without
injury to his friend's interest, or risking his capture. He was, therefore, about
to inform his trusty guard who, and what he was, when the silence was

No. 10

broken by the clear accents of a pleasing, though somewhat affected, and a
fresh female voice, in the rear of the party. Kennedy turned to observe the
speakers, but the darkness which reigned around, in consequence of their
proximity to the tall trees which sheltered the mansion, prevented him from
distinguishing the figure with accuracy.

" ' Well, Ralph, so I suppose you intend leaving me to find the way to the
village by myself at this time of the night too as you passed me, without so
much as a " How do ye do, Lucy." '

" Ralph paused and glanced at Kennedy, with an air of perplexed hesitation. ' Dang it, it bes Lucy, zurely. I say, doan't thee be in sich a hurry
loike, can't 'e stop, my gal ? danged if she wool ; I zay, Lucy ! Lucy ! doan't
'e be a fool loike. Come along, zur,' and he attempted to drag the now
much amused and laughing Kennedy in the opposite direction to that in
which they were before walking.

" ' Now, my good fellow, I think you may allow me to stand here on my
parole. Go and speak to your Lucy, and I give you my word, as a gentleman, you shall find me at your return.'

" ' Thank 'e zur, thank 'e koindly, thee may stand on what thee pleases. I
know who 'e be, Mister Medwin, a captain or a corporal loike ; now doan't 'e
go, zur.' And the anxious swain of Lucy hastened after to explain away, if
possible, his supposed want of gallantry.

" The pair returned to within a short distance of where Kennedy stood,
and he could overhear detached portions of their conversation.

" ' There, Ralph, you don't love me, at all ; I know you don't, I always
thought you didn't, so never speak to me again : I shan't break my heart, I
promise you.'

" ' Now, you be in one o' your passions loike, Lucy ; I can't, you zee I can't
let 'un go. I doan't know what to zay, loike ; doan't 'e look through one
zo, my gal.'

" ' Let Mr. Medwin go directly. Say anything, say—say—say,—you—you
—you couldn't hold him.'

" ' But, Lucy, my gal, you zee —'

" ' You must, Ralph, indeed, you must.'

" Lucy's voice decreased to a tearful broken tone, which must have had its
due effect upon Ralph. Tears are a woman's last and most powerful weapons,
and Lucy did not miscalculate their effect, even upon the lymphatic disposition of her ponderous lover.

" ' You—you—you cruel—good—for—nothing—I don't know—why—I
ever loved—such—a—a—a—a—'

" ' Muster Corporal Medwin ; dang it man, can't 'e run loike, doan't 'e stay
there loike a fool.'

" Kennedy now thought it time to interfere, which he did, by advancing,
and declaring that some mistake must have arisen, as his name was not Medwin.

" Lucy, to whom Medwin was well known, gazed with astonishment on
Kennedy, and immediately sought the protecting arm of Ralph.

" ' Who bee's thee, then, if thee bean't Muster Corporal Medwin ? why
didn't e zay zo afore, inztead o' ztanding on thy pole, as thee said thee would,
while I spoke to Lucy, loike.'

" At this moment, Master William approached, to discover the cause of the
delay in the supposed Medwin's arrival. A few words sufficed to assure him
of the mistake which had been committed. He clumsily apologised to Kennedy for the inconvenience to which he had been put ; and the latter, after
expressing his disgust at the whole proceeding, abruptly left the astonished
and disappointed group, and commenced retracing his steps to the plantation,
in the vicinity of which he hoped to find Medwin.

" The grey tints of morning were now rapidly advancing, and the eastern sky had become slightly streaked with red, ere Kennedy reached the low fence at which he had been left by his friend.

" Medwin was anxiously waiting his arrival, a part of his adventure he had been witness to, and he had remained on the spot, anticipating its probable result.

" Kennedy briefly related to him the night's proceedings, and on their return to the little village in which they resided, Medwin, in return, communicated to him some particulars of Marian and her guardian uncle, which, after the night's proceedings, possessed to him considerable interest.

" 'Marian is an orphan, Kennedy, but entitled to large estates upon the attainment of her majority, they being, in the meantime, held in trust for her by her uncle, Sir Richard Knightley, the great object of whose existence appears to be to promote an alliance between his fair niece and his son William, whom you have already seen.'

" By the accidental discovery of a note, our attachment has become known to him, and known but to be declaimed against as villany on my part, and heedless folly upon hers. I am without fortune, Frank, and that is the great secret of my disqualification. A few weeks will place Marian at her own disposal by the attainment of her majority, but to-morrow sees her on her route to the Continent, there to reside in strict seclusion, until the name of Medwin is for ever blotted from her memory, and had I been seized to-night, I make no doubt but that at any risk of future consequences I should have been detained until after her departure. But, Frank, she must not leave me thus. To avoid observation and remark she will travel to the port at which she is to embark, accompanied but by one female servant (Lucy) who is attached to my interests, as you have perceived, and Master William.'

" ' Can no plan be devised to arrest them, 'ere they reach their place of destination?'

" ' It can Frank. In a small village, near which their route will be, resides the nurse of Marian's childhood. If I can wrest the fair girl from the grasp of her tyrants, and place her under that well-known roof, she has consented to remain in seclusion for a few weeks, until she can bestow her hand where she has already given her heart. Will you assist me, Kennedy?'

" Kennedy grasped his friend's proffered hand, and long after the bright sun had tinged with golden radiance every object, they were still carefully and anxiously arranging the necessary steps for the completion of their enterprise ——."

Herbert Mandeville suddenly raised his head, for his candle, without his noticing it previously, had suddenly expired.

An exclamation came from his lips.

" God of Heaven!" he cried, " What is that?"

A dull red glare fell from the window upon every article in his room, and the sky was of a fiery glow.

In a moment he threw up his casement and looked out.

" There is a fire in the village by Heaven!" he exclaimed.

CHAPTER XIX.

" And still upon the midnight air,
    Arose that cry of horror.
  ' Fire !' ' fire !' burst from every tongue,
  And the vexed sleeper turned, and in his lethargy,
  Still muttered ' fire !' "

SHAKSPERE.

THE FIRE.—THE VILLAGE.—HERBERT'S FIRST ERROR.—ROSE VILLA.—DESPAIR.
  —CONFUSION.—THE BEREAVED MOTHER.—THE RESOLVE.—ADELINE'S FATE.
  —THE STAIRCASE.—THE CHAMBER.

As we have before remarked with regard to the character of Herbert Mandeville, he was by no means destitute of generous and noble emotions, nor incapable of purely disinterested actions. It was a vicious course of education which had engendered those feelings of jealousy and personal anxiety which, like the spots upon the sun, would occasionally obscure some portions of the radiant brilliancy of his character.

Without bestowing one thought as to whether the fire was at the cottage of one of the humblest of the inhabitants of Bracefield, or in the villa of one of "high and gentle seeming" as old Chaucer hath it, he bounded through his open window into the garden.

There for one moment did he pause ; but it was not a pause of doubt as to whether he should proceed in his purpose of rendering aid or not, but merely for one brief moment, to consider the shortest method of alarming the curate and his household.

He quickly decided that point, by throwing all the strength he could into his voice, and shouting till the air rang again with the sound.

"Fire ! fire ! fire !"

"Heartwell, rouse them," he said ; "they will look out assuredly, and the redness in the sky will tell them the whereabouts."

Clearing the garden gate at one spring, he flew, with great rapidity, towards the village.

Mandeville still kept his eyes fixed upon the sky, which was each instant growing redder and more glowing.

As he neared the village, he heard the hum of voices, and, occasionally, a wild cry of —

"Fire ! fire !" would break upon his ears.

Herbert needed not any excitement to speed ; but one cry that reached his ears, as he arrived at the outskirts of the village, almost, for a moment, turned his heart to stone. It was Rose Villa !

Mandeville absolutely reeled when he heard it, for it flashed across his mind then, for the first time, that the fire might be at Rose Villa, at the house of her whom he loved with such deep devotion, and that even now, she —the gentle Adeline, might require all his help to rescue her from a death of horror.

He stood for a moment bewildered. So great was the agony of his mind that he could scarcely stand.

"God of Heaven !" he exclaimed, clasping his hands. "Can it be possible ?—Adeline !—Adeline !"

The tumult of his mind was so great, that several moments elapsed before he could decide which way he was to turn to arrive at Rose Villa by the speediest route.

Some one at this moment he descried running at great speed within some dozen yards of him. With a bound, Mandeville overtook him, and cried in a voice of intense agony.

"The fire? Where?"

"At Rose Villa," said the man.

"Enough!" cried Mandeville, and with the speed of a maniac, he darted off in the direction of the house of the Mourdants.

In first proceeding to the village, Mandeville had unfortunately gone considerably out of his way, and it was full ten minutes before he came in sight of Rose Villa.

It was one mass of flames!

A cry, something between a sob and a scream, burst from the lips of Mandeville.

"Adeline! Adeline!" he cried. "Help—help—Adeline!"

Now he with frantic bounds rushed still onwards, and in a few moments more had gained the front of the villa.

There was a crowd assembled, but all seemed hurry and confusion, and it was evident that but little help was being rendered for the want of some one to direct properly the energies of the ignorant multitude who, as usual, only produced confusion and impeded each other.

With the strength of one possessed, Mandeville rushed into the thickest of the throng. To the right and to the left he thrust all that impeded his progress, and his cry was still—

"Adeline! Adeline!"

"My child!" cried a frantic voice. "My child! Save her—oh save her!"

Mandeville felt his knees clasped by some one, and looking down, he saw it was Mrs. Mourdant.

"My child! My Adeline!" she still screamed. "Save her! Save her—oh, save her!"

"Or die!" cried Mandeville, in a voice that rose high and clear above every other sound.

He disengaged himself from the grasp of the frantic and wildly despairing mother, and rushed, without hesitation, into the flaming building.

Then arose the cheer from the multitude, who are ever ready to applaud the generous act they none of them dared themselves to perform; but Mandeville heard it not. Still he cried, "Adeline! Adeline!"

On his first rush into Rose Villa, Mandeville fell, for he was half blinded and suffocated by the smoke.

In an instant, rising, he made a rush to the staircase, for although he had no directions as to where to find Adeline, he recollected, even amid the tumult of his thoughts, that the little window he had, upon the occasion of his serenade, supposed to belong to Adeline's room, was not upon the ground-floor.

The fire had evidently originated in the lower part of the building, for the smoke was rolling up the staircase in dense masses, and flames, like long fiery tongues, were curling round the bannisters, and hissing and cracking as they seized the dry wood-work.

Mandeville thought his voice might be heard by her who he sought, and that some answering cry might guide him where to find her.

"Adeline! Adeline!" he shrieked as he bounded up the staircase, despite of smoke and flames.

His voice was heard even by those without, and another cheer burst from every heart amid the awful grandeur of the scene.

Mandeville had reached but the middle of the staircase, when, by his weight, he felt it cracking and giving way under him. With a wild cry he threw himself forward, and just succeeded in gaining the landing-place, as the lower half of the staircase fell in with a loud crash, sending up a volley of sparks and a column of dense black smoke of fearful thickness.

For an instant Herbert paused. He tried to cry Adeline! but his voice failed him. He gasped for breath.

Dropping on his knees on the landing-place he had gained, he placed his mouth close to the floor.

The dense mass of smoke rolled over him, and he felt much revived by the purer air which was in immediate contact with the floor.

Now, as the flames gained power over the fallen staircase, the dense smoke somewhat decreased and Mandeville rose.

He stood for a moment upon the landing, and cried with all his power—

" Adeline ! Adeline !"

No answering cry gladdened his heart, and he burst into the first room that presented itself—it was empty.

In a moment he had left it and entered another—it was likewise untenanted. There were curling flames coming through the flooring, and the heat in that room was insupportable.

It would appear that the assembled multitude outside the building saw him, for a shout and a cheer burst from them.

Herbert felt his strength rapidly sinking. He could scarcely draw a breath, and although he still cried " Adeline ! Adeline !" his voice had lost its power, and the sound only echoed to his own sinking heart.

His brain reeled, and it was with tottering and uncertain steps that he strove to leave that room, the heat of which was awfully intense, and dreadful to bear.

For a few seconds he was obliged to support himself by a chair, and while he was so doing, a strange sound came upon his ears.

It was a burning regular heat—heat that he could not at all account for.

In a moment, however, he was made aware of the source from whence it proceeded, for a stream of water came into the room through one of the windows.

" They have a fire-engine," thought Mandeville.

He tottered forward as he spoke, and exposed himself freely to the dash of the water.

Oh how delicious were his feelings at that moment of refreshing coolness. His strength returned. He breathed freely, and once more, in a clear loud voice, that spoke to every heart, he shouted—

" Adeline ! Adeline !"

Another, and another cheer from those without burst upon Mandeville's ear, as he now rushed from the room to continue his search.

There was but another room. The smoke in the passage leading to it was thick and blinding. Herbert, however, rushed forward, heeding it not, and reached the door.

It was fast.

" Adeline !" he cried ; " Adeline !"

There was no answer.

CHAPTER XX.

"Who would not dare aught for the loved one?
She to whom the heart is knit in such close ties,
That souls seem one. Pain falls alike on both,
And the dear thrill of pleasure in each breast
Awakens tender throbbings."

THE SMALL CHAMBER.—THE DOOR.—THE FLAMING BED.—ADELINE.—THE LAND-
ING PLACE.—A FEARFUL LEAP.—THE FALL.—SAVED! SAVED!—THE MOTHER'S
JOY.—INSENSIBILITY.—ANXIETY AND HOPE.

MANDEVILLE hesitated not another moment, but making a rush at the door, he burst it from its hinges.

For an instant he recoiled from the entrance, for so dense a body of smoke rushed from it that he was nearly blinded, and could scarcely draw a breath.

It was but for a moment that natural instinct caused him to draw back. In the next, with the name of her he loved upon his lips, he rushed into the apartment.

He darted an anxious glance around the room. The flames were dancing and curling among the furniture of a small bed that was there.

"Adeline!" he shrieked, as he rushed towards the couch. It was empty. "Adeline!" he again cried with frantic eagerness.

A low sigh met his ears. He saw a white mass lying on the floor. He stooped—he raised it. It was—yes, it was Adeline! He said no more, but with a trembling eagerness folded her in his arms. Tears of joy rolled down his cheeks, and with one short prayer to God, he rushed from the room with his insensible burthen.

The flame curled round his head—burning wood fell about him—eddies of black smoke impeded his progress, but still he went on with a feeling of joy in his heart.

Now he came to the head of the stairs, and he remembered that they had fallen. Even the landing on which he stood he felt was trembling beneath his feet, and he heard, amid the hissing and roaring of the flames, the crack-ling of the dividing rafters.

He cast one look into the abyss before him; then, by the red unnatural light that glanced around, he looked upon the face of Adeline! She seemed as if asleep. A happy insensibility had come over her.

"God help us!" said Mandeville. "Adeline, I will save you, or perish with you?"

He pressed his lips to hers, and in one thrilling kiss of pure love and de-votion, he sealed his faith.

Then tightening his grasp of the inanimate form of the fair girl, who had no hope of life but from him, aided by Heaven, he took a fearful leap from the landing on which he stood, down into the passage of the villa, among the burning ruins of the fallen staircase that lay in a chaotic mass below.

He alighted among the burning fragments, and thus yielding nature proba-bly saved him from the severe concussion which a leap from such a height must otherwise have subjected him to.

He fell upon his side, but still he kept his grasp of Adeline. Although Mandeville felt himself much stunned by the fearful jump he had taken, he rose instantly, and struggling forward among the burning fragments, he in a moment was clear of the building.

A loud noise behind him, like the roar of artillery, made him turn for a moment. The roof had fallen in!

One moment later and he and Adeline must have perished together in the ruins of the Villa.

"Saved!" he shouted as he rushed forward. "Saved! Saved! Saved!" The multitude took up the joyous cry, and "Saved!" rung from every lip.

A hundred arms were stretched forward to relieve Herbert of his burthen, but he waved them off, and still rushed onward.

"My child! my Adeline!" cried a voice.

Herbert heard it. He pressed forward in the direction from whence it came.

"Saved! Saved!" he cried, as he placed Adeline in the arms of her mother, and then fainted at her feet.

Strange to say, Herbert Mandeville, save a few trifling bruises, was quite unhurt by all the danger he had gone through.

The curate was on the spot, for as Mandeville had anticipated, the cry of "Fire!" had aroused him immediately.

Rose Villa was burnt to the ground, and Adeline and her mother, as well as the old domestic, were conveyed by Mr. Endsleigh to his own house.

When Herbert recovered from his swoon, he found the curate leaning over him, and to his surprise he was in his own bed-room.

For a moment he thought it must have been all a dream, but when he was taken by the hand by the curate, he saw a tear glistening in the old man's eye as he said—

"God bless you, Herbert, my boy," he knew it was reality, and that, indeed, he had snatched Adeline Mourdant from death—a death too terrible to contemplate.

He pressed the curate's hand as he said—

"And—and she——"

"Is well, Herbert."

"Unhurt?"

"Quite. She is now, I hope, asleep."

"Thank God!" said Mandeville.

"Herbert," said Endsleigh, "you have this night done that which at once places you high in every heart: an act too, which must bring to you a lasting satisfaction through life."

"I—I am repaid," murmured Mandeville; "for I have saved Adeline. You are sure she is unhurt?"

"Quite sure. How do you feel yourself, Herbert?"

"A little tired," smiled Mandeville; "otherwise I am quite well. I think we both escaped wonderfully. I am sure I don't recollect half the danger."

"Now rest yourself," said the curate.

"What is the time?" inquired Mandeville.

"It is but two o'clock," answered Mr. Endsleigh; "and if you will now go to bed, we may all meet in health and spirits in the morning.

"I am very thankful," said Herbert.

"We ought all to be," said the curate. "Now, good-night, Herbert."

"Good-night, sir," said Mandeville.

The curate left the room, and Herbert Mandeville remained in a delicious train of thought, which effectually banished sleep.

"How can I sleep," he said, "when my mind is so full of the events of the night? Oh, Adeline! Adeline! Is it all a dream? or have I, indeed, snatched you from destruction?"

He would have paced his room till daybreak indulging in sweet meditation, but he feared to disturb Adeline, for she—even she, was under the same roof with him who loved her so devotedly, and who had so courageously proved the depth of that devotion.

Mandeville then passed another hour in thought. He could not sleep. He

felt he could not while his mind was occupied by Adeline alone, and still he felt weary.

A sudden thought struck him.

"I will finish the curate's manuscript," he said. "It may distract my thoughts from present objects, and even then, ere morning, I may snatch an hour's repose."

The manuscript lay open at the part he had been reading when he cast his eyes up and saw the glooming light in the sky which arose from the fire.

He sat down, and endeavouring to fix his mind as much as possible upon the narrative of the curate, he then proceeded :—

THE CURATE'S MANUSCRIPT CONTINUED.

"Medwin felt much happier when he had fully resolved upon a specific course of action, and although he hesitated long about inducing Marian to leave a home of comfort and luxury, to follow the fortunes of a soldier, still love at last prevailed, and he decided with his friend, Kennedy, upon the step.

"Medwin procured a short leave of absence from his military duties; a measure which he thought essentially necessary, as upon the sudden disappearance of Marian, he would naturally be suspected of being privy to her place of concealment. To avoid the embarrassment this might occasion, he purposed strictly to seclude himself from observation during the few weeks which interposed between the present time and that at which Marian was to attain her majority. This he was the more easily enabled to accomplish, as he had announced his intention of immediately visiting his friends, who resided in a distant part of the country.

"The day on which Marian departed from her uncle's gloomy mansion, under the care of Master William, Ralph, and the watchful Lucy, was one, which, for intense heat, could hardly be surpassed. A summer of unequalled

No. 11

splendour—although far advanced,—had not yet given place to health-inspiring and cheering autumnal breezes which are so truly grateful to the senses; the parched arid earth seemed gaping for moisture, and unparalleled numbers of the insect tribe had been called into existence in consequence of the unusual drought which had for many weeks prevailed. As the shades of evening approached the air became so thick and sultry as almost to impede respiration, and a moaning wind had occasionally swept down the sides of the verdant hills; in the horizon low black clouds had began to gather portentously; the birds flew timidly, as if uncertain of their course; the waves of the agitated sea washed heavily upon the beach, and far over the apparently boundless waters might be heard that low wailing sound, which is ever indicative of a coming strife of the elements. Along a road, which pursued a tortuous course around the base of a hill, a heavy carriage was slowly pursuing its route. The sun had sunk to rest, and the rapidly-advancing night had already involved distant objects in dim obscurity; occasionally a broad flash of lightning spread itself like a flaming banner in the sky, and the low murmuring of prolonged, although evidently distant thunder, proclaimed the commencement of the storm. The carriage had now begun to descend a gentle eminence, which although not of sufficient altitude to entitle it to the name of a hill, was still beset with difficulties sufficient to induce the driver of the cumbrous vehicle to bestow more than ordinary care upon the management of his steeds.

"'I'm dang'd if there woant be a storm, my gal. Put in e head, can't e? Dost thee want to be blinded loike?' exclaimed our acquaintance Ralph, who was the charioteer upon this occasion to Lucy, who had, in her anxiety to ascertain the state of things, externally thrust her head from the window of the carriage, in which she had been allowed to seat herself, at the earnest entreaty of Marian, although much to the dissatisfaction of Master William.

"'Why, Ralph, did you see that flash of lightning?—I declare I'm almost blinded.' Lucy was entrusted with a secret, and like many in a similar situation, could not help hinting at its existence. 'Ain't you afraid of being stopped, Ralph?'

"'Noa, I arnt; who's to stop un?'

"'Why, haven't you heard as there's two highwaymen on this road? Isn't it horrid?'

"'Noa it ain't, I never heard o' un afore; put in e head, can't e? Dang it, thee be'st a fool loike.'

"The voice of Master William now interrupted the colloquy, as a more vivid flash of lightning lit up the surrounding landscape, and the roar of thunder came booming on the ear like a distant cannonade.

"'Shut the window, Lucy; is Miss Marian to be subjected to inconvenience for your amusement?'

"A few heavy rain drops now announced the actual commencement of the storm, and Lucy, with a meaning glance, withdrew her head and closed the window of the carriage. The party proceeded for some distance in silence, uninterrupted save by Ralph's ejaculations and admonitions to his tired steeds, as, the difficulties in the road, in consequence of the violence of the storm, became momentarily greater. The coldness of Marian's manner had frozen Master William to silence, and he had thrown himself into a corner of the carriage, discontented with all around. But little prospect presented itself to his mind that he would ever be the possessor of the rich prize, on the fancied easy attainment of which he had so long counted. Marian and her fortune lost,—lost to him for ever. Occasionally he stole a glance at his fair companion, with the hope of gathering from the expression of some rebellious feature that his suit might not be altogether so hopeless, but all was still and calm, no dilating eye met his;—the sunshine of her

smile beamed not for him ;—the sweet music of her voice disturbed the stillness which reigned around ;—her thoughts were with another, and had she
been alone she would have breathed the name of Medwin to the wailing blast
as it swept past the carriage. Those who would have formed an estimate of
her character, as she there sat, from the almost girlish beauty of her countenance, would arrive at anything but a just conclusion with regard to ' the
mind which dwelt within.' Richly endowed as she was with all those rare
sensibilities of human nature which encompass the female character with an
atmosphere of so much romance and beauty, she likewise possessed an
energy of mind which placed her far above the ordinary weakness of her sex.
She had consented to place herself temporarily under the care of Medwin,—
she had consented to the means by which she was to be separated from her
present companions ;—she loved Medwin, and she trusted implicitly to his
directions. Calmly, therefore, she awaited the event which was to place her,
for a few weeks in, apparently, so ambiguous a situation.

" The carriage, which had been proceeding for some time at a slow uneven
pace along a narrow and unfrequented road, which, however, at its termination would have placed them considerably more forward on their journey than
the circuitous route of the high road, now suddenly stopped in its progress.
Marian's heart beat hurriedly, and the slight colour on her cheek deepened
to a roseate hue. Master William rose to discover the cause of the delay,
with a glance of suspicion at Marian's evident embarrassment.

" ' Ralph, what mean you by this delay?—Proceed, instantly.'

" ' What'll e do, Master Willum? Dang'd if some fool loike ain't ztopped
up the road with a ztump o' a tree, and it's zo dark. What'll he do zur?
I can't move un.'

" Ralph had dismounted from his elevated position, and was attempting
the removal of the obstruction, which presented itself in the shape of an
enormous mass of timber, occupying nearly the whole breadth of the road.
Master William hastily alighted, charging Lucy at the same time not to
leave her mistress. The storm had now considerably subsided, and the rain
had ceased, although massy dark clouds careering rapidly before the wind,
appeared ready to discharge their contents momentarily upon the heads of
the luckless party. Marian was now alone. With a smile of intelligent
meaning to the fair girl whose countenance betrayed her agitation, she
had sprang from the carriage to enact her part in the coming drama. To
Marian the most anxious moment had arrived ; action would have nerved her
to meet any exigency ; but to wait still and motionless, listening but to the
hurried throbbing of her own heart, with the knowledge that in a few short
moments an event was to take place which was to exercise so powerful an
influence over her future destiny, was indeed calculated to unnerve the
strongest mind.

" ' I'm dang'd if we musn't get a hold 'o this end, zur, and zwing un
round, loike,' exclaimed Ralph, as Master William approached. ' Zome fool
placed un here, zurely. Just hoist un up a bit, loike, and give un a zwing.'

" Master William glanced anxiously to the carriage which Ralph had drawn
off a few paces to afford room for their exertions. All was still, and he
stooped with Ralph to raise the heavy mass of timber from the ground. Their
utmost efforts were fruitless, it stirred not.

" ' What'll e do, zur, we can't move un.'

" ' Force yourself through the hedge, and call for assistance ; we will not retrace our steps. This is some vile scheme ; but it shall be frustrated.'

" The road was bounded on each side by thick hedges, from which tall
trees at intervals towered upwards, until their branches, from the narrowness
of the pathway, for road it could hardly be termed, became intermingled with

each other, forming a leafy canopy, and greatly increasing the obscurity of the scene.

"Master William kept his attention steadily to the carriage; he bent himself in a listening posture to catch the slightest sound, but all was tranquil stillness, with the exception of the occasional shout of Ralph from the adjoining field.

"'This is mere accident, after all,' he exclaimed, and as the night air imparted a chilly coldness to his frame, he prepared to return to Marian. 'Ah! you here, Lucy?—Return to your mistress immediately! Are you faithful——'

"He was about to fly to the carriage.

"'Oh, sir, don't be angry, and I will tell you all, indeed I will!'

"'All what?—Speak, or let me go directly. Are you mad?'

"She had grasped his arm, and he shook her violently to disengage himself.

"Two or three low notes from a flute now gently broke the stillness of the night, and as they slowly died away upon the gentle breeze which had succeeded the strife of the elements, they seemed to possess an almost unearthly sweetness. Master William paused until the last lingering tone expired upon his ear; then starting as if from a dream, endeavoured to force himself from the grasp of Lucy, who perseveringly clung to him.

"'By Heaven's! here is indeed some deep laid plot! Remove your hands from me, girl; I cannot hear you now!'

"'Oh, sir, you must! indeed you must! Did you say there was a plot, sir?—We shall be murdered!—You must not go, sir!—Think of your poor father, Master William!'

"'Do you wish to drive me distracted? Lucy, unloose your hands directly, or by Heavens I'll strike you!'

"Unwilling to use actual violence, he strove to disengage himself from her unwelcome embrace, but she clung to his garments with a pertinacity deserving of a greater object.

"'I shall die of fright, sir; indeed I shall. Do you see nothing, sir? Look! look!' and Lucy screamed with laudable energy—'Murder! murder! Ralph! Ralph!'

"Master William's stock of patience was exhausted; he threw her from him with violence, and turned to rush to the carriage; but here a new obstacle presented itself in the person of the indignant Ralph, who had returned in time to observe a struggle between his dulcinea and Master William; that the latter was the assaulted party he could not for a moment imagine; it was, therefore, with no small degree of indignation that he shook the fragile scion of nobility by the collar for his supposed gallantry.

"'You are mistaken, Ralph; for God's sake let me go.'

"'Noa mistake at all zur; dang'd if I let e go; I'll shake e life out o e. Cant e let a gal be? Looke, doant e be afeard, Lucy.' And the excited rustic shook Master William violently before he released him from his powerful grasp.

"Master William stayed not one moment either for revenge or expostulation. He flew to the carriage,—it was empty. For a moment he passed his hand across his brow to endeavour to connect the occurrences of the evening in such a manner as to direct his future steps. Pursuit, with the inefficient means then at his disposal, was, he felt convinced, fruitless. All around was impenetrable darkness; and not the slightest sound indicative of the proximity of any living beings, save his own servants, met his ear. He clenched his fist with rage, and with a bitter oath he cursed his own folly for leaving, even for an instant, the precious charge committed to his care.

"Ralph and Lucy now approached. Master William believed them both to have been accessories to the abduction of Marian. She pointed to the empty carriage ; Ralph's surprise was real, Lucy's affected ; Master William, therefore, gave the former credit for being the greatest adept at dissimulation.

" ' Ralph,' he said, ' you shall bitterly repent this night's work,' then flinging himself into a corner of the tenantless vehicle, he commanded an instant return to the house of his father.

" Marian had, in the confusion occasioned by the performance of Lucy's part of the plot, alighted from the carriage, and was instantly joined by Medwin and Kennedy. A few steps placed them in comparative safety from pursuit. Medwin tenderly supported the weeping girl until they arrived at a light carriage which he had prepared for her reception. Her heart was too full to speak, and but a few short words were interchanged between them in their progress.

" The carriage, to Kennedy's surprise, already contained one person, closely muffled up from the inclemency of the weather ; he glanced inquiringly at Medwin, for he had not heard that they were to have a companion in their enterprise, and that companion a young female too, as her voice denoted, for Marian was clasped in her arms, and with the most gentle accents of affection, she was endeavouring to calm the agitated spirits of the fair fugitive. Medwin smiled and replied—

" It is my sister, Frank ; my sister, Jessy, of whom you have heard me speak, she voluntarily offered to accompany me to meet Marian ; she will be the companion of her few weeks of seclusion; they were known to each other before this. But come, we are loosing time, we must begone ; you must make your bow to Jessy at some more fitting opportunity.'

" Medwin vaulted into the saddle of a led horse. Kennedy was already mounted, and in a few moments the party were proceeding at as rapid a pace as the difficulties of the road would permit.

" Medwin was silent and thoughtful, and Kennedy chose not to interrupt his meditation—he too was reflecting. He had often listened to Medwin's praises of his sister Jessy, and had ever considered it as the natural feelings of an affectionate brother towards a favourite sister, and she had always been so far removed from his personal observation, that he had never for one moment considered her as a being whom he could by any possibility encounter. The fond partiality of a brother might likewise have conjured up beauties of person, and excellencies of character, which might have no other existence than in the imagination of his friend ; but now that he was separated from but by a few feet of earth, a restless curiosity beset him to test, by occular demonstration, the accuracy of his friends description. Why had Medwin concealed her presence from him until the last moment ? Did he wish to surprise him into a sudden admiration of her attractions ? He had heard her voice, for a few short moments it had lingered in his ears, she had given utterance to feelings of kindness and sympathy, and in language glowing with tenderness and enthusiasm ; and then the voice was so musical, and appeared to harmonise so sweetly with the somewhat excited state of his imagination; and then a rapid succession of events, possible events, floated like the vision of a dream before his mind's eye. The dim veil of futurity appeared to be lifted from before his mental vision, and events and occurences of years to come were presented to him in the vivid colouring of reality. His friend Medwin and his gentle Marian, happy in each other's love, pure and exalted as it was above that of ordinary mortals. Himself, poor and dependant, alone too, a solitary being, no bright eye acquired additional brilliancy at his approach ; no cheering sounds of affection welcomed him home—home ! Where was his home ? nowhere fixedly, at least there were no home associations, and yet it was a brave thing to be so lonesome a being ; he would walk through the world as a being apart from, and possessing nothing in common with its myriads of inhabitants ; he

would note their follies, smile at their impotent graspings, the fleeting shadows
which constitute human greatness.   But would this bring happiness? was he
not mortal too? and might he not like them bring some fond conceit to his
heart, and fancy he grasped a tangible treasure?   And then a low sweet voice
seemed to breathe in his ear words of affection and truth, and the small taper
fingers of a being in whom were concentrated, all] the blissful associations
which might bind him to existence, were in imagination clasped in his;
and a face so fair, so exquisitely beautiful, was half hidden as it reposed upon
his bosom.   The light breath gently fumed his burning cheek, the waving
ringlets reposed in gentle luxuriance upon his shoulder, and the voice was so
like the voice of the occupant of the chaise, and the face was so like the face
which ought, nay, which must give expression to such a voice, and ——'

"'Kennedy, are you mad, or in the land of dreams?   Why, Frank, I have
been watching you with wonder for the last five minutes, and you have done
nothing but smile and sigh, without at all noticing that we have arrived at our
place of destination.'

"Kennedy started from his reverie, and glanced hurriedly around him.
The grey light of morning was rapidly acquiring power, and Medwin was
handing from the carriage the gentle girl, who for his love had done so much.
They were at the door of an irregularly built cottage, but which, by its exterior arrangements, betrayed the neatness and industry of its inmates.   The
good dame appeared to welcome her guests.   Kennedy threw himself from his
horse, and approached; he was to see the sister now.

"'Guard your heart, Frank, you don't know your own danger,' playfully
observed Medwin, as he made way for Kennedy to approach the carriage door.
Kennedy reddened, as if he had been detected in giving audible utterance to
his secret musings.

"'Jessy, my dear, this is my friend Mr. Kennedy.'

"Medwin passed into the cottage with Marian, and Kennedy was face to face
with his sister, the dearly loved Jessy.   She was certainly equal, more than
equal to his anticipations; but her beauty was of a different style completely,
without knowing why he had pictured her so fair and girlish in her appearance:
she was in reality neither the one nor the other.   Kennedy guessed her age to
be about nineteen years, she had not yet numbered seventeen summers; her
complexion was pale and delicate, beautifully contrasting with the dark ringlets which fell in great abundance over her shoulders.   Her eyes were un-
questionably fine, they were indeed eloquently beautiful.   Had she stood
still and motionless, and schooled her expressive features to calm repose, you
might have thought her an elaborately chisselled work of art; but it was because she did not stand thus, and because she allowed every noble feeling of
her mind to beam forth each speaking feature, that she was so truly beautiful.
It was this which enchanted Kennedy; it was the animated eloquence of her
unuttered thoughts, pure and beautiful as they were, which fixed his ardent
gaze upon her, until he was aroused to a sense of his rudeness by the slight
roseate tint which was slowly spreading itself over her face as she withdrew
her eyes from so searching a scrutiny.   He hastily and clumsily apologised,
but the words fell hesitatingly and disjointed from his lips, and after much
striving to amend them, which only rendered him still more unintelligible, he
found himself involved in a labyrinth from which he would have found it difficult to extricate himself had he not been relieved by the now laughing
Jessy, who presented her pretty hand to him, that he might assist her to
alight, and assured him of her pleasure to meet so valued a friend of her
brother's; and it was said with her sweet voice, that voice which had before
lingered in his ears like the last soft note of some sweet melody.   He silently
offered her his arm, and they entered the cottage.

"'And my first impression on the mind of this fair being has been any-thing but creditable to my gallantry or my eloquence,' sighed Kennedy, as he felt the slight pressure of her arm in his. He was mistaken.

"One week had elapsed since Marian's introduction to the cottage of her, who, with a mother's care, had tended her childhood. Her uncle had spared no pains to ascertain the place of her concealment; that Medwin was the companion of her elopement, he believed, although of him he could learn nothing more than that he had obtained leave of absence from his regiment, and was supposed to be in a distant part of the country, enjoying the society of friends, from whom he had been so long separated. Enraged as] was Sir Richard Knightely at being thus deprived of his charge, and of the prospect of retaining her fortune in his family, he yet abstained from giving publicity to the fact of her elopement. He, therefore, pursued his search silently, though dili-gently, but without the smallest success. Had she been elaborately hidden his numerous agents might have discovered and restored her to his power, but he never for one moment thought of looking for the heiress of a splendid for-tune by the fire-side of a peasant's humble dwelling.

"But one more week remained, during the progress of which concealment was necessary, when Medwin was hastily summoned to attend the death-bed of his father. To Marian, and to his friend Kennedy, he communicated the distressing cause of his sudden departure, but with srtict injunctions to keep the intelligence from the knowledge of the gentle Jessy. He knew that no consideration on earth would prevent her from accompanying him, and he feared the effect of a rapid journey, together with the distress occasioned by its melancholy object on her health, which he had fancied to be declining for some time past. To Kennedy he committed the care of the two beings so dear to his existence, during his temperary absence. He enjoined him frequently to call at the cottage, and after many adieus, he tore himself from the only spot of earth on which his wandering spirit would wish for ever to take up its abode. Jessy believed that business of importance called him away, and she cheerfully awaited his return.

"Kennedy was now a more frequent visitant at the cottage than he had been during Medwin's presence. But was it solely to cheer the drooping spirits of Marian in the absence of her lover? No; that fragile habitation was to his imagination a casket containing a jewel so rich and rare, that its possession became the all-absorbing object of his existence. The fair Jessy, so young, so beautiful, with a heart overflowing with all those romantic sym-pathies which ever find a home in the breasts of the young and beautiful.

"'To see her, is to love her,' sighed Kennedy, and his heart spoke from his eyes as he gazed on the fair girl. Nor was Jessy altogether indifferent to the tumult which she had evidently created in the heart of the young artist, for although he had not avowed an attachment, there exists a sort or freemasonry in affairs of the heart which communicates much more than the nimblest tongue can give utterance to. Jessy was one of the most unaffected of God's creatures, but as Kennedy's footstep on the trim gravelled walk of the garden surrounding the cottage, warned its inmates of his approach, she would occa-sionally be so very busy in sorting a work-box, or chirping to a canary, as to turn round with an appearance of great surprise on discovering his presence. We resume the thread of our narrative at a most poetic period, namely, on the evening of a summer's day; not that there existed on this particular even-ing any extraordinary circumstances calculated to impart to it an additional air of romantic beauty. The sun had sunk with the same gorgeous splendour for weeks previously, the same sighing breeze at close of day had borne on its wings the balmy breath of the same flowrets, and the same sea, which now shone like a lake of liquid gold, had borne upon its undulating bosom the same bright reflection on many thousands of previous occasions; but were we to judge from the apparently fixed attention which two individuals were bestowing upon the fair scene which spread itself before them in luxuriant beauty, as they stood upon the summit of a verdant hill, we might suppose That on this evening nature was attired in gayer garments than was her wont. they gazed in silence at the departing glory of the western sky, and it was not until the last lingering ray of sunlight had disappeared in the horizon, that the silence was broken by Jessy, for it was she and Kennedy who had strolled forth from the cottage to gaze on the departing glories of the setting sun. She had been looking on the fair scene before her with all the delight of an enthusiast, occasionally stealing a furtive glance at Kennedy to mark the influence for a moment so beautiful upon his manly brow. She gently touched his arm as the exclamation ' How beautiful !' burst from his lips. He turned from his silent contemplation of inanimate nature to the fair girl by his side. 'Beautiful !' he repeated, as if only giving utterance to an uninterrupted train of thoughts. ' Yes ! yes ! exceedingly beautiful.' Their, eyes met, and Jessy in her eloquent glance read a more extended appllication of his words than would have presented itself to a superficial observer.

" They were again silent, but it was a silence of eloquent meaning, and this time Kennedy broke it, although his voice trembled with emotion, and the anxious throbbing of his heart betrayed the importance of his words. That they were important, and possessed more than common interest, the pale cheek, now no longer pale of Jessy, sufficiently denoted. What he did say, and what the fair Jessy replied, we must leave to the imagination of our readers, contenting ourselves by informing them that it certainly was not an intimation that Marian would be surprised at their long absence, and that they had better quickly return to the cottage, although some grounds might exist for such a supposition, by the fact that in a few moments they were returning, Jessy with her arm locked in Kennedy's, and smiling through a tear, which, like a dew drop on a fair flower, hung upon her damask cheek. But still, as faithful chroniclers, we are bound in honor and conscience to record, for the special information of our fair readers, that some sort of agreement appeared to have been entered into, for the fast binding of which, it had been necessary that the lips of Kennedy should lightly visit the fair cheek of Jessy, imparting thereto an odour which would have gone far to contradict Medwin's assertion of her declining health.

" Jessy flew to Marian to impart to her her happiness, and in a short time the joyous party were assembled in the small, though neat apartment of the cottage, discoursing of future hopes and prospects. All before them appeared bright and unclouded, and they needed but the presence of Medwin to complete the happy circle. A military friend of Medwin's was the only ether person entrusted with the secret of Marian's place of concealment. Lieutenant Parbury was about the last person in the world whom any one would have pointed out as likely to become an associate of Medwin's, but an accidental service which he had rendered to him during an engagement, drew them together. The lieutenant possessed but a limited mental capacity, but he endeavoured to compensate by officious bustle, and an affectation of excessive discrimination, for what he wanted|in real judgment. Medwin laughed at his absurdities, respecting him solely for what he did possess, namely, a true heart, and a kind disposition. The discovery of a plot was to him the most delicious thing in the world, and he had occasionally called at the cottage ostensibly to inquire after the health of its inmates ; but really to ' see how matters stood,' as he expressed it. This individual now made his appearance on one of his formal visits, to the no small annoyance of the party. This visit was of short duration, and although he did not discover ' how mattres stood,' he fancied that they stood somewhat differently to what they did on his last visit. In fact, an appearance of mystery did present itself to

the plot-seeking lieutenant, for at his entrance various articles were hastily removed. Jessy, conscious of a secret, had left the room ;—the lieutenant was delighted—things looked strange—Marian blushed too. Kennedy was rather confused, and he departed with a firm conviction that things 'indeed stood very different.'

"The fact was simply this :—Marian wished to surprise Medwin by presenting him with her miniature likeness immediately upon his return, and had availed herself of Kennedy's professional assistance for its execution. Mr. Parbury's incapacity to keep a secret they well knew ; therefore was it that the half-finished portrait was hastily removed, together with the materials concerned in its execution, at his entrance. Jessy, with her love of mirth, enjoyed heartily the suspicious lieutenant's supposed discovery of some fearful plot.

"A few days thus elapsed, and Medwin's instant return was anxiously looked for.

"Jessy was happy—very happy ; her attachment to Kennedy was unbounded ; he was her world, and she was to him as the bright sun, without whose cheering influence all would be chaos and despair. She would sit by his side, watching the progress of Marian's miniature, for hours ; and when he arose to depart, it would seem as if the better part of her existence had departed with him.

"The miniature was finished, and as far as art could imitate nature, it was a faithful copy of the lovely original. Kennedy took it with him to the neighbouring village for the purpose of appending to it the necessary materials for its preservation. He sighed as he attached to the small gold frame in which it was deposited a chain of exquisite workmanship, which he purposed should be presented to Medwin with the miniature : and as he pursued his road through the verdant meadows which lay between the village and the cottage

No. 12

of Marian and Jessy, an unusual weight seemed pressing upon his heart. He strove, by thinking of Jessy—his Jessy—she who had plighted to him her love—who had given to him with confidence her young heart,—to regain the tone of his spirits. He had promised to return that evening, lest Marian should not be in possession of the miniature on Medwin's immediate arrival. For a moment he paused as he arrived at the low fence which surrounded the well-stored garden of the cottage ; the flutter of light drapery was discernible through the interstices of the trees, and the voice of Jessy met his ear as she gently pronounced his name.

"The moon was careering though a cloudless sky, and the balmy serenity of the air had induced Jessy and Marian to leave the cottage and walk in the garden until Kennedy's return. Jessy was leaning upon the arm of her friend, who was gazing with sisterly affection upon the animated face of the fair girl. The moon shone brightly upon her pale features, imparting to them an expression of almost more than mortal beauty. They had been talking of the absent, and as Jessy, with all the sincerity and happy enthusiasm of youth, poured into her friend's ear the ' story of her love,' an observer might have fancied that he was listening to the fervid eloquence, and gazing upon the fair form of a being of a brighter and a happier world than this. And so it is ever with young and innocent hearts like thine, Jessy, ere the contaminating influence of the world has dethroned the god-like spirit of innocence and truth from your breasts, to erect in in its place an artificial idol of deceit and dissimulation. And even you, Jessy, mentally devoted as you now are above the level of a heartless world, may yet attain so much of earthly wisdom that the cry of distress may plead to you in vain, and the pure and sincere impulses of your own heart will be suppressed as rebellious feelings, not in accordance with the acquired feelings and prejudices of a frivolous and heartless multitude of beings with whom you may be surrounded.

"Marian's heart beat responsive to every word uttered by Jessy ; her thoughts were with Medwin, and she exclaimed with fervour, as she drew the gentle girl to her heart,—

" ' How like is Kennedy to Medwin !'

"Kennedy attracted their attention before he sprang over the light fence, that his sudden presence might not occasion unnecessary alarm, and in an instant he was by the side of his Jessy.

"The portrait was produced ; it was executed with much taste and delicacy. Marian knew the pleasure Medwin would experience in receiving it, and she warmly thanked Kennedy for bestowing upon her so much happiness.

" ' But, indeed, Marian,' said the now smiling Jessy, ' you must not assume so serious an aspect when you present this miniature to my brother as you do now. I declare that the colours on the portrait, if one might judge from your appearance, must have been actually abstracted from your cheeks—it will be no parting gift, recollect."

" ' Forgive me, Jessy, if I possess not your buoyant spirits.'

" ' Well, well, Marian, say no more; I will be more serious ; but I see that you require a lesson—so give me the miniature.'

"She took the portrait from Marian's neck, who stood silently smiling at the vivacity of her friend, and approached Kennedy.

" ' Now kneel, Frank, like a true and gallant knight ; I declare this is quite romantic. Why don't you enjoy it, Marian ? And won't you kneel, Mr. Frank ? On your allegiance I command.'

" ' And I obey, fair despot. What feat of arms shall I achieve ?—what frowning fortress, guarded by malicious sprite or demon dread, shall I attack ?'

" ' Very well indeed. Now look, Marian, and listen.'

"She approached the kneeling Kennedy, with an assumed dignity of step and manner, to hang the portrait on his neck.

"'Now fancy, Frank,' continued Jessy, 'that this is my portrait, and that I very foolishly bestow it upon you.'

"'I may fancy so much, Jessy; although to waste one glance upon a copy when the orignal, glowing with——'

"'Stop! stop!—that's not in your part; you must not speak yet.'

"She stooped to hang the portrait on his breast till her light breath fanned his cheek; then rising with a brightened colour, while her voice slightly trembled, she repeated a few lines from a troubadoric romance which occurred to her memory,—

'When plumed heads lie low,
    In Judea's holy land,
This, then, shall guard thy life
    From every foeman's hand.
When on the raging flood,
    Where death awaits the brave,
This pledge of faithful love
    My own true knight shall save.
Then ever on thy noble breast,
    Oh, guard the treasure well;
Away—away, the trumpet calls,
    Farewell, my love, farewell!'

"He raised the portrait to his lips, then seizing the hand of Jessy, he imprinted on it a kiss.

"'How sweetly am I rewarded, dear Jessy.'

"'Now, Frank, you are making it serious. That's not what you ought to say, so let go my hand.'

"'Nor do I feel inclined to allow him to possess my portrait; so, Sir Knight, surrender it without delay;' and Marian advanced to take it from his neck.

"An exclamation from Jessy caused her to turn her eyes in the direction from whence it came, and she beheld Medwin. To fly to him with the words of welcome on her lips was her first impulse; but there was that in the expression of his countenance which fixed her to the spot. His lip was quivering with emotion, and his flashing eye denoted the tumult of his mind; he spoke not, but pointed to Kennedy, who still knelt on the green turf, with Marian's portrait on his breast.

"The distressed girl saw at once the situation in which she was placed, and her consciousness of innocence caused the blood indignantly to mantle in her cheeks, at what she considered the unworthy suspicion of Medwin, who still silently pointed to Kennedy, every limb quivering with emotion. She turned imploringly to Jessy, who broke the silence by walking up to her brother with more of real womanly dignity of manner than Marian before thought her capable of assuming. She touched his arm.

"'Richard, this is madness!'

"'Or truth, Jessy? Oh, Heavens! Parbury, you are no dreamer.'

"'Nay, indeed, Medwin,' exclaimed Kennedy, rising and advancing to his friend, 'here is some strange error; true, you saw me kneeling to Marian, but we did but jest.'

"'Jest! By what strange names do some call villany. Oh, man, who was my friend, thus I cast you from my heart!'

"With apparently superhuman force he struck Kennedy to the earth, and hastily darting through the hedge, disappeared from the astonished group.

"'Oh Heavens! my brother—my brother!' exclaimed Jessy; 'this must not be—you shall not leave us thus—I must and will explain away this madbrained jealousy.'

"She flew to overtake the rapidly-retreating Medwin; occasionally she could observe his figure in the interstices of the trees of a small woody spot of ground through which he directed his flight ; the briars and thick under-wood caught her attire as she rapidly pursued his steps, but she heeded them not ; one thought alone possessed her—that she had, by her heedless frivolity, produced all this misery, and she must see her brother to end it. He, how-ever quickened his pace, and was rapidly evading all pursuit, when she thought of an expedient which might induce him to retrace his steps. She screamed and called for help. The sounds fell upon his ear, and he paused. Misery had never called in vain on Richard Medwin for succour, and a few moments brought him to Jessy's side. She grasped him tightly by the arm.

"'Now, brother, you shall hear me. If you ever loved your sister Jessy, listen to her now. Kennedy is innocent—he is indeed :—you wrong him, brother.'

"Medwin replied in a low voice, evidently assumed to conceal the feelings which were struggling for mastery in his heart,—

"'First tell me, Jessy, whose portrait hung upon his breast.

"'Marian's. But, Richard——"

"'Hear me, Jessy,—at whose feet knelt he to receive it ?'

"'Mine, brother, mine !'

"'Your's, Jessy? Do I see visions, then, in my waking hours? Was I not hastening with all the speed of love to throw myself at her feet, when I saw my place usurped by another? There is a letter, Jessy ; I received it from Lieutenant Parbury during my absence ; it states that there existed evidently some secret intelligence between Marian and Kennedy, and once he overheard them conversing on the probable period of my return. They said that I should be surprised ; they likewise hoped their secret would be safely kept : but this—even this—I disregarded, strong in my confidence in Marian's love and Kennedy's friendship ; but now, alas ! I find it is but too true—there was a secret, and such an one—oh, God !'

"'Brother, there was a secret—nay, there were two."

"'If you still love me, my gentle Jessy, do not tell me more. They have deceived you too, my fair sister. By the care which I have always shown to you from your tenderest infancy to the present time, I conjure you to say no more of this. We will wander far hence, my Jessy ; to some other land we will bend our steps. Come, come, we are alone now, Jessy ; I will live but for you, my sweet sister.'

"He stooped and kissed her pale cheek, as, in accents scarcely above a whisper, he continued—

"'There exists now no other tie to bind me to a world I hate.'

"'Our father, Richard——'

"'Is in Heaven, Jessy.'

"As he spoke, he raised his eyes to the cloudless sky, and gazed with a mingled feeling of admiration and awe on the myriads of bright constellations which glittered in the vault of Heaven ; from one of them his father's spirit might even now be gazing on his children. When he again turned his eyes to Jessy, he held an inanimate burthen in his arms.

"'Jessy, Jessy—speak to me, Jessy—say what you will, so I but hear your voice again. Still silent ! Have you, too, left me, my gentle sister ?—Fortune, I defy thee now."

"He folded his military cloak around her fragile form, and raising her in his arms, rapidly pursued his route to the village. He committed Jessy to the care of the kind-hearted inhabitants of a farm-house in which he had be-fore taken up a temporary abode. Long and anxiously he watched over her couch for a sign of returning animation, when the colour again slowly revisited her cheeks. She awoke but to give utterance to the unconnected thoughts and delirious imaginings of a fever. Kennedy's name was ever on her lips, and Medwin heard, with agonized feelings, the secret of her love. He had addressed a note to Lieutenant Parbury, requesting his immediate presence. His arrival was now announced, and Medwin hastened to acquaint him with the events of the night, and to consult with him concerning the necessary steps to be adopted with reference to Kennedy. The lieutenant's advice was immediately given, to call him to the field.

" ' Then be it so, and instantly,' replied Medwin.

" ' That's as things ought to be,' exclaimed the officious friend, as he hurried off to seek Kennedy at his lodgings, the address of which Medwin had given him.

" Kennedy had arrived but a few moments before the lieutenant's arrival. He heard without surprise his message, and praying his patience for a short time, he despatched a messenger to the only acquaintance he possessed in the small village.

" Smarting under the disgrace of a blow, and indignant as he was at the unjust suspicions of Medwin, it is not a matter of surprise that he readily assented to Lieutenant Parbury's proposition. The night was now far advanced, and the events of the last three hours had produced in his mind an excitement which prompted him to acts of which his cooler judgment would have disapproved. He had pursued Jessy from the cottage, but mistaking his way, had arrived at the village by a circuitous route.

" Kennedy's friend Hortly now arrived ; he was a young medical student, who was sojourning in the village for the benefit of his health. Kennedy briefly related to him the events of the night, before he introduced him to the apartment in which Lieutenant Parbury was waiting. Hortly's advice was instantly given to defer all proceedings until the next day, and in the meantime to furnish Medwin with a statement in writing of the real facts of the case. To this Kennedy at once assented, but the lieutenant, in the name of his principal, refused to accede to such terms. Hortly, after an useless argument, returned to Kennedy with this information.

" ' Then be it to-morrow, Hortly : Medwin will repent too late. What is the time ?'

" ' It is now long past midnight ; you meet at six. I know the ground ; and now rest, Kennedy. I still hope to prevent this meeting ; morning will bring reflection, and let no false sense of honour blind you to the fearful consequences of an encounter with your friend. Farewell till six.'

" Hortly departed, and Kennedy retired to his chamber, but not to rest. The few hours which intervened before morning shone through the small window of his humble dwelling, he consumed in writing a full account of the whole transaction, together with his love for Jessy, to be delivered to Medwin in case he should fall in the encounter. To Jessy, likewise, he wrote ; and as he traced the lines tears fell over the blotted page. He begged her to forgive her brother, and assured her that his latest breath would be expended in a prayer for her happiness.

THE DUEL.

" The ground chosen for the hostile meeting of Medwin and Kennedy was a beautiful and romantic spot, and upon this occasion it would seem as if Nature had put on her most captivating smiles, that she might woo her wandering children to remain in love and peace in the fond embraces of so dear a mother. The sun was momentarily acquiring additional brilliancy, and as the dense white mists of morning which had enshrouded the beautiful valley, on the slope of which was to be enacted so fearful a drama, rose like a glossy curtain, gently rolling up the sides of the surrounding mountains, it revealed as fair a scene of beauty and harmony as the most ardent lover of nature, undefiled by the marring contrivances of man, could wish to look upon ; the glittering dew-drops hung trembling on every leaf, and the attentive ear might catch that too plaintive murmuring sound which is ever heard in the deepest solitudes of nature. Kennedy and Hortly were already on the ground ; they were silent and motionless. Hortly would not break the charm which the contemplation of so fair a scene appeared to have cast around the spirits of Kennedy, who gazed abstractedly on every point in the bright picture before him with evident delight ; and as the light and sighing wind which had chased the mists of morning from before a view of so much tranquil beauty reached the spot on which he stood, bearing on its gently-heaving bosom the fragrance of a thousand flowrets, his warm, ardent imagination, ever prone to discover sunlight even amid the deepest gloom, was excited even to the momentary forgetfulness of the work of death which had called him forth, and which was to dye, perhaps with his own blood, the waving grass and wild flowers which bloomed in luxuriant beauty at his feet. He had been accustomed to associate one sweet form with every blissful emotion of his heart, it was that of the gentle Jessy ; and the association did not now forsake him. Like the health-inspiring fragrance which played upon his cheek, it stole over his heart, and he smiled, aye, smiled as he was wont to smile but a few short hours since, while gazing into the depths of a pair of blue eyes, which beamed with love and intelligence for him alone. Jessy, his Jessy !—so beautiful, —she stood before his mental vision as upon that evening when blushingly she avowed her love, and he had claimed the troth kiss from her lips ; and then, as all the succeeding events rushed in tumultuous disorder across his brain, he covered his eyes with his hands, and tears—tears which the brave and good may shed at such moments—coursed each other down his checks. Jessy, his first and only love—her brother the friend of his heart, the companion of his boyhood, he whom he had pledged himself to meet for so fearful a purpose— Marian, the confiding and beautiful Marian, all passed before his mental vision with the vivid colouring of reality. But had he not received a blow ?— had he not been spurned, insulted, degraded ?—and should he, spaniel like, fawn upon his tyrant, calmly awaiting until he chose to listen to a tale of truth ? Never ! never ! Medwin was the author of his own misery ; he must abide the consequences ; and then, as his better nature asserted its supremacy, he fancied that a still small voice, but a voice so musical and sweet, that it insensibly entwined itself around his heart, was urging him to disregard the false sense of honour, which would compel him to the commission of acts to be repented of with tears of blood. And it suggested to him that to advance to Medwin with the open hand of conciliation and friendship, and the accents of truth upon his lips, would be preferable to grasping an instrument of death, the use of which might inflict so much misery, where happiness alone was due ; and Kennedy could hardly believe that it was the whisperings of his own heart to which he had been listening.

" ' Kennedy,' said Hortly as he touched his friend's arm slightly, ' they are here.'

" The dream was dispelled. Kennedy started as if a serpent had stung him ; the half-formed resolution of the moment vanished before the frowning glance of determination which he encountered from the advancing Medwin, who with his friend, Lieutenant Parbury, slowly emerged from the thick underwood skirting a plantation to the left of their position. The accommodating *friends*, whose duty it became on this occasion so to arrange that one or both of their principals should be shot according to the most approved method laid down in such cases, now advanced. But few preliminaries required to be arranged ; they slightly differed with regard to the position of the combatants. Lieutenant Parbury bowed low, and begged pardon in the blandest accents, and after many compliments, the point in dispute was satisfactorily arranged. Hortly returned to Kennedy, who had continued gazing at the parties with an abstracted air.

" ' Twelve paces, Kennedy ; when I drop my handkerchief, fire.'

"Kennedy grasped his hand, but spoke not.

" 'Hold your pistol tightly, and fire rather low than high. Now, keep your eye on me.'

"The obsequious lieutenant again advanced, and bowing low to Hortly, he begged to acknowledge his gentlemanly conduct as far as matters had as yet gone. Hortly slightly bowed.

" 'Frank, Frank, you are inattentive ; recollect this quarrel is forced upon you ; you are bound to attend to your own preservation. For Heaven's sake stand not thus listlessly ; be firm, my friend, and keep your eye on me.'

"Kennedy slightly smiled as his friend whispered in hurried accents his instructions in his ear.

" 'Thanks, Hortly, thanks ; I will be firm,—I am so. Does my pulse quicken ?'

"Hortly laid his hand upon his wrist, the pulsation was calm and regular. Medwin betrayed but little emotion ; an attentive observer might have seen that his mind was made up to some great purpose, and there it rested. Would Kennedy at that moment have cast the weapon of death from him and opened his arms to Medwin ?—had he observed in his face the slightest indication of a reciprocal feeling ? Yes, he would, and all might have been ' merry as a marriage bell ;' but he met with nothing but an expression of deep-set resolution. Medwin thought himself *right*, and that for him was sufficient ; his imagination opposed to him no obstacles to the execution of what he considered his just revenge. Hortly was rolling a handkerchief in his hands, and endeavouring, although in vain, to fix Kennedy's eye,—Medwin's never left him. He dropped the signal, and one sharp report struck upon his ear. A pheasant flew rustling and terrified from the neighbouring plantation. Kennedy's pistol was still undischarged ; he raised his hand, fired, and the gay-plumaged bird was at the next instant fluttering at his feet. Hortly had flown to his side—he was unhurt.

" 'By Heavens, Kennedy, this is bravely done ; but had I known of your intention, I would have dared anything rather than bring you here as a mark for that madman. But 'tis as well as it is. Thank God, this affair is over without bloodshed.'

"Mr. Parbury now advanced with many congratulations to Hortly, who at once proposed to remove his friend from the ground : this was agreed to by the diplomatic lieutenant, who declared that Medwin should be satisfied with what had been done. As they separated, Kennedy, with a firm step, advanced to Medwin, who stood still as a statue, on the spot where he had taken up his position ; he addressed him with a voice slightly tremulous, but clear and distinct.

" 'Medwin, I have been by you unjustly suspected of the blackest villany, insulted, degraded, nay, struck ; and finally, I have suffered you to aim a weapon at my life ; can you still believe that from you I have deserved so much ?'

" 'I can, Kennedy. We part not thus, magnanimous seducer ; this is no affair of honour, it is one of vengeance—just vengeance for deep injury ; and I here again denounce you as a villain, who, under the mask of honourable friendship, would rob from a trusting heart its choicest treasures, my sister Jessy.'

" 'Oh, tell me but of her, and I can forgive you all,' exclaimed Kennedy.

" 'Forgive me ! Oh, Kennedy, if there be a God above, may *he* forgive you, for I cannot,' and advancing to Kennedy, before the oscillating back of Mr. Parbury could recover its equilibrium from a bow of extreme and deferential respect to Hortly, or the latter guess his intention, he struck him with the discharged pistol, which was still in his grasp. The instant interposition of the seconds at once put an end to a species of conflict unsanctioned by the laws of honourable warfare, and a few moments more again saw the combatants placed in juxta-position, and the signal of strife, perhaps of death, in the hands of Hortly.

"Kennedy was now an altered man. In a few words he explained to Hortly how very different he felt his present position to be from that in which he stood before this new insult, and avowed his determination to fire at a foe who seemed resolved on the death of one or both. The handkerchief fell from Hortly's hand, and Medwin again fired alone. Kennedy was still erect, and a hasty ejaculation of thanks to Providence that he had again escaped unhurt, burst from Hortly's lips. He was in an instant at Kennedy's side, but was suddenly arrested in his hasty congratulation by the startling alteration in the voice of his friend, as, tightly grasping his arm, he addressed him—

"'Hortly, my dear friend Hortly, I could not fire, indeed I could not; she stood before him, Hortly—the fair Jessy, and smiled upon me through her tears. See—see—my friend she comes! Is she not fair, Hortly? I could not fire—no, no, no, no.'

"He fell heavily to the earth; the ball had indeed taken effect, and when Hortly, with the assistance of Parbury, raised him from the ground; the warm blood was trickling from his breast, and the breath of life seemed fast leaving the body of the brave, generous, gifted Frank Kennedy. He sighed, and slowly unclosed his eyes to look in Hortly's face, as the latter was gently unbuttoning his vest to discover the extent and nature of his wound. A written packet, carefully sealed and addressed to Medwin, fell to the ground—it had been perforated by the ball which had entered his breast. The dying Kennedy now signified to Hortly to listen to the few words he had to say ere death terminated the distressing scene. He spoke in a low voice, evidently struggling to overcome the anguish of his wound; and Hortly with glistening eyes,—for his medical judgment had at once assured him that Kennedy's wound was mortal,—knelt by his side, and inclined his ear to catch the low, broken, and almost inarticulate accents of his dying friend.

"'Tell Medwin—that—I forgive him, Hortly; and go—to Jessy—my own sweet Jessy.—Who will love thee now? Hortly, I could die without a pang—but that I am loving that fair girl—she must not know—by whose hand I fell. Medwin will see his error now.'

"'Alas! too late.'

"'True, Hortly, too late; I too might have done otherwise—but honour, forbade; reputation, alas! what art thou now?'

"He sunk exhausted in Hortly's arms, who gazed fixedly on his pale features, while the tear-drops fell slowly from his eyes, mingling on the breast of Kennedy with the life blood, which, despite Hortly's exertions, still flowed from his heart. A smile lit up his features, and he again spoke, but in firmer accents than before—

"'Jessy—Jessy, welcome, ever welcome; nay, do not weep—we shall be very happy. Kiss me, dearest: ah, gone! Where, where, Hortly! Hortly! Medwin! Jessy! Jess—'

"A convulsive shudder shook his frame, and the spirit of Frank Kennedy winged its way to another world.

"Hortly arose, and in a voice scarcely articulate from deep emotion, addressed himself to Medwin, who, with the letter in his hand, which had dropped from Kennedy's breast, was silently gazing on the face of the dead. Kennedy's fall had quenched his anger, and when he had perused the written statement which Kennedy had addressed to him, he passed his hand across his eyes, as if to assure himself of his waking existence.

"'Are you mad that you move not?—fly, and save yourself.'

"'Oh, Hortly, I have indeed done mad work; some demon has possessed me. Kennedy! Kennedy! shake off the sleep of death and kill me.'

" He dropped in a state of insensibility at the feet of the placid form, which now lay quiet and still on the green turf.

" But little now remains to be told. Jessy, the admired and beloved of all, became a heart-stricken maniac; her greatest delight was to wander by the verdant hill side, where, at sunset, Kennedy had first breathed in her ear the words of affection and truth.

" Some years after the events we have recorded, a traveller in Switzerland recognised, in a solitary being, inhabiting a wretched hut, and subsisting upon the charitable contribution of the surrounding peasantry, Medwin, his proud haughty spirit humbled to the dust, and prized for his meekness and devotion by all who visited in that sad seclusion.

" It is related, that during the severe winter which succeeded this accidental discovery, a stranger arrived in the neighbourhood and inquired for the recluse by his assumed name, and that being watched by the villagers, he sought the solitary hut of Medwin; they listened, and heard sobs and weeping, and to their surprise, a female voice praying fervently with the solitary man. In the morning, when they again sought the recluse, both he and the stranger had vanished. May Medwin and his Marian still be happy, for it was she who had wandered many a weary mile in search of the broken-hearted penitent."

THE END OF THE CURATE'S MANUSCRIPT.

Having now come to the conclusion of the curate's highly interesting narrative, and carefully deposited the manuscript in a drawer, Herbert Mandeville, after reflecting awhile upon the hapless fate of the noble Kennedy and his beloved Jessy, and offering up a prayer for Adeline, threw himself upon his couch, and the momentous events of the last few hours faded from his memory as mists before the morning sun.

No. 13

CHAPTER XXI.

' Who would exchange one generous feeling of the heart for wealth untold ?'"

THE MORNING.—ADELINE'S GRATITUDE.—A BREAKFAST CONVERSATION.—THE HAPPINESS OF HERBERT.—FLEETING PLEASURE.—A RIVAL.

How sweetly the morning broke upon the light slumbers of Herbert Mandeville ! The bright sun was shining in at the casement of his room ; the birds were singing in the garden beneath. A delicious dreamy langour hung upon his soul. He lay still and happy—incident after incident of the night slowly rose up before him like the clear phantasma of a waking vision. There was all the wild beauty of the day-dream along with the knowledge that all was real ! Oh, rare combination of mental luxuries !

He had saved Adeline from death. He had folded her in his arms. He had held her to his heart in the hour of danger, when each moment might have been his last. How he had bounded with her down the staircase, the blazing pile around him. How he had battled his way through the furious element that knows no pity. And it was all for her—for Adeline ; she who had lit the unquenchable flame of love in his young heart ; she, the beautiful ! the innocent ! the good !

How great was the change in Herbert's feelings ! At that hour yesterday all was doubt, uncertainty, and anxiety. But now—now he was her preserver ! He had a right to love her now—for had he not saved her ? He felt a kind of property in the fair faultless being he had snatched from the hot breath of the devouring flames.

Happy, happy Herbert ! In the wildest dream of his young warm imagination, he could not have placed himself in a position more enviable. That one night accomplished the work of years. What could he have done? What said or sworn would have placed him as he now was placed with regard to Adeline?

Gratitude, admiration—all would speak to her heart in his favour.

" Joy ! joy !" he cried. "She will love me ! Life is now before me like a gorgeous panorama. I stand upon the threshold of a thousand joys ! What shadow can now darken my heart that the sun of happiness will not gild to beauty? Adeline ! Adeline ! Dear—dear Adeline—you will be mine !"

And then came the sweet thought across his mind that she, the loved one of his heart, was under the same roof as himself—an inmate of the same house. He should meet her each hour. He would sing to her—gather flowers for her sunny hair ; he would talk to her of hope !—of love !—of joy !

Who could be happier than Herbert Mandeville?

Alas ! that when the bright genial happiness is in our grasp, we should ourselves do aught to dim its radiant lustre.'

Full of these delightful imaginings, Herbert Mandeville rose from his couch, and hurrying on his toilette, proposed to descend to the breakfast-parlour of the Parsonage.

With a beating heart he descended the stairs.

For a moment he stood at the door of the little parlour. The sound of voices met his ears.

" He must be fatigued," said the voice of the curate ; "I will not disturb him."

" And can it all have really happened ?" said a low silvery voice.

Oh, how these dear tones vibrated to the heart of Mandeville ; it was

Adeline who spoke, and she was speaking of him too. He understood it all in a moment. They had been telling her how he saved her.

He heard a sound as of some one weeping, after some low murmured words from the curate.

Herbert opened the door.

Suddenly some one uttered a cry of joyful recognition; it was Adeline. Her eyes were filled with tears. She placed both her hands in Herbert's, and looked in his face with deep thankfulness and interest.

He could not speak, or what he would have said he could not say before others. The shifting colour of his cheek, however, betrayed the feelings of his heart.

"Can I thank you?" said Adeline.

"Dear Adeline," replied Herbert, "if you knew——"

"Hem," said the curate.

"Dear me, know what?" cried Mrs. Plumpjoy.

"I was going to say," continued Herbert, "that the knowledge that I had been of service to Miss Mourdant brought with it its own reward."

"Very true," said Mr. Endsleigh."

"They have told me all," said Adeline, still looking in Herbert's face with confiding earnestness. "Mr. Mandeville, you have saved my life at the risk of your own."

"There was no risk," answered Herbert, "except that—that I—I—"

"In fact you acted nobly, Herbert," said the curate; "and Adeline, as well as every one of us, feels confident that you did so. Now, my boy, sit down to breakfast."

"Yes," cried Mrs. Plumpjoy, "I have heard all the particulars, Mr. Manville. You threw the staircase out of the window, I believe?"

"Not quite;" answered Herbert, with a smile.

"It puts me quite in mind of an incident that occurred to me at a county ball where——"

"Yes—a hem!" said the curate.

"Well, I'm sure, brother," cried Mrs. Plumpjoy; "I was not going to say anything so dreadful, that you need catch one up so."

The curate looked very hard at the ceiling.

"Well, as I was saying," continued Mrs. Plumpjoy, "at a county ball, the very one at which I first saw the poor dear major ——"

"You set your head alight, and Major Plumpjoy took off his wig, and clapped it on your flaming ringlets, by which means the conflagration was extinguished," said the curate.

"Well, I'm sure!" cried Mrs. Plumpjoy, tossing her head; "that's one way of catching the words out of folks mouth's. Next comes a horse——"

The curate groaned, and Herbert laughed outright.

"To be shaved," continued the indignant Mrs. Plumpjoy, "and a pig——"

"Enough—enough!" cried Mr. Endsleigh, good humouredly.

"To have his corns cut! if you please, brother," said Mrs. Martha, with great gravity.

"I am perfectly willing," said the curate.

"Mrs. Mourdant," said Mandeville, rising as Adeline's mother entered the room.

Mrs. Mourdant looked pale and harrassed, but she warmly and affectionately thanked Herbert for what he had done on the occasion of the fire.

"What have I now, Mr. Mandeville," she said, "to bind me to existence but Adeline? You have, by your noble gallantry, preserved her to me. If you will consent to hold a second place in my heart, be assured that in mine, next to my dear child, you will ever be a cherished guest."

"You have all made me very happy," said Herbert, in a tone of real feeling.

"And you have made us all very happy," said the curate; "so now let us to breakfast, dear friends."

The wide world might have been searched for a happier party than that which now partook of the social meal of breakfast in the good curate's parlour, but the search would have been a vain one.

We might truly paraphrase the words of Shakspere upon mercy, and say that

"A noble action is twice blessed!"

for Herbert Mandeville felt all the keen and heartfelt enjoyment of having behaved nobly and heroically, while those around him were filled with feelings of gratitude and admiration towards him.

The morning meal was soon over, and the curate then said that he had risen early, and had been to visit the ruins of Rose Villa, which, although not burnt to the ground, would be quite untenable for many weeks to come, even if it were repaired instantly.

"Then, dearest," said Mrs. Mourdant to Adeline, "we must seek another home."

"May I be permitted," said Mr. Endsleigh, "to indulge a hope that until the proprietor of Rose Villa rebuilds it, which he undoubtedly will, I may fancy you have found a home already."

Mrs. Mourdant shook her head.

"If," continued the curate, "you and Adeline will be our honoured guests, we shall all be inclined almost to forgive the fire for the fright it occasioned us."

Mrs. Mourdant hesitated, and glanced at Adeline. Herbert was afraid to breathe till he heard the answer, so deeply interested did he feel in the result.

"Mr. Endsleigh," at length said Mrs. Mourdant, "I will accept your proffered kindness as frankly as it is offered, but I will not—I cannot consent to be a burthen upon you, because ——"

"Oh, mother!" said Adeline, "how happy we shall be here!"

"Happy! happy!" responded the heart of Mandeville.

"We will, my dear madam, settle all preliminaries at another opportunity," said the curate. "Let it now suffice that we assure ourselves of the pleasure of having you and Adeline here with us."

"There is poor Mrs. Fellowes?" suggested Adeline.

"True," said her mother; "our old faithful domestic, Mr. Endsleigh. By miracle, she escaped the flames last night. She has followed us through varying fortunes, and ——"

"And shall follow you still," said the curate. "She shall find a welcome home here."

"You are so good," said Adeline, taking the curate by the hand, and looking up into the old man's face with bewitching sweetness.

"And you, my dear pupil," said Mr. Endsleigh, playfully, "are both good and beautiful. So you see you have the advantage of the old curate."

"Well I'm sure," said Mrs. Plumpjoy, "we shall make quite a family party. Don't you think, Mr. Mandeville, we ought to make ourselves uncommonly happy?"

"I do from my heart," said Herbert.

"Well I declare, now, brother," she then cried, "what do you think has just come across me?"

"Upon my word I don't know," answered the curate. "A wasp just flew in at the window—was it that?"

"Now, brother," exclaimed Mrs. Martha, "you are extra provoking to-day."

"Am I?" said the curate.

"Yes, indeed, you are. I was only going to say, if some one was just now to arrive at Bracefield——"

"Who, Martha?"

"Guess now."

"I am a bad guesser."

"Why, Charles, to be sure."

"Charles Leslie?"

"Ah!—there would be a surprise. Why, let me see, there would be then one, two, three, four, five, six of us, I declare! Well, I never!"

A cloud came across Herbert's brow.

"Curse Charles Leslie!" he muttered in his heart. "Is he to be the shadow on my sun of joy!"

~~~~~~~~~~~~~~~~~~~~~~~~~~~~~~~~~~

CHAPTER XXII.

"His love was like a gushing torrent,
It o'erwhelmed all sense—
He knew not how to be most blessed."—KNOWLES.

CORRESPONDENCE.—CAPTAIN DUFOURS AGAIN.—THE STRANGE SUGGESTION.—DANGER.—THE WALK TO THE RUINS.—HOPES.—DECEIT.—THE ASSIGNATION.

THE breakfast had scarcely concluded, when a letter was brought to Mandeville. He retired to his chamber to peruse it. It was from Captain Dufours.

Herbert smiled as he opened it. He felt curiosity only now—not interest in what Dufours should say.

The letter was as follows:—

"MY DEAR FELLOW,—Downshot has at last down with 'the shot,' so you may make your mind easy upon that score.

"I forgive your note; I dare say you were drunk when you wrote it, so never mind.

"You tell me there is a pretty girl in your neighbourhood? Very well. You want advice as to how to make yourself intimate? Very good. Now I'll just tell you what I would do in similar circumstances.

"*I'd set her house or cottage, or whatever it is, on fire in the night, and then drag her out of it!* That would be doing a bit of the heroic—you know, my boy. There will be no more reserve, no more distant young lady airs and fancies. Oh, dear, no.

"It's a good plan. Try it.

"Did you agree to allow Downshot twenty-five per cent. on your paper when you gave it to a gentleman, in addition to what he now charges you? D—n Downshot!   "Your's and the world's,
                                                "GEORGE DUFOURS."

"P.S.—Is the rustic beauty white and flabby, or red and hot-looking? You know all country girls are one or the other."

"How very singular!" cried Mandeville. "This rascal has advised a thing that has happened by accident. 'Tis strange, indeed! By Heavens!

what mischief this letter might do me were it seen. Innocent as I am, it would be my utter ruin with Adeline! Dufours, Dufours, you are a great scoundrel!"

As he spoke he heard the sound of voices beneath his window. One of those voices thrilled through his heart.

He flung open the casement. In the garden stood the curate, with Adeline and her mother. They were equipped for walking.

"Herbert," said Mr. Endsleigh, "we are going to see the remains of Rose Villa——"

"And—and you will allow me," cried Mandeville, "to accompany you?"

The speech was general, but his eyes were turned to Adeline's sweet face as it looked up with beaming innocence at his.

"We wait for you," said the curate.

Herbert immediately thrust the letter of Dufours into his pocket, and seizing his hat, he jumped from the window into the garden.

"You have grown expert at leaping from your window, Herbert," said the curate, in his dry manner.

"And yet," answered Mandeville, "this is but the third time I have done so. The first was——"

"To serenade," said the curate.

"No," said Herbert, laughing; "to make a noise upon other people's premises, you know, sir."

"Exactly," said the curate, drily.

An anxious expression came across the face of Mrs. Mourdant, and Adeline looked down, as if to hide the deepened glow upon her fair cheek.

There was a pause of a moment, and then Adeline looked up with a glowing cheek, as she said,—

"And the second time, Mr. Mandeville, was to save me from death."

"And to gild my own existence," said Herbert, "by the dear recollection of an act which I would not have had undone for worlds."

"Well, then," said the curate, "let the third jump be for the purpose of offering your arm to Miss Mourdant, and accompanying us to the ruins of Rose Villa."

Mandeville was not slow in offering his arm to the fair Adeline, who accepted it with a winning frankness that sunk deep into his heart.

Innocence! what a holy thing art thou. Herbert Mandeville had his faults, but the trusting simplicity of the gentle being who now leant upon his arm made a deep impression upon him, and he thought to himself—

"Now what a double villain should I be, to gain the young heart of this fair girl but to spurn it from me when possession had taken the gloss off its beauty."

"This is a dear place," said Adeline; "there is an air of peace and calm repose about Bracefield that I love much."

"Bracefield has a charm now," answered Mandeville, "that would make a desert beautiful."

Adeline looked in his face, but she said nothing.

"She is all beautiful simplicity," thought Herbert; "oh how dearly delightful will be the task of 'shaping her young thoughts to love.' Adeline, you shall be mine!"

"Yet, Adeline," he then said aloud, "one would think you had scarcely seen enough of life to be pleased with solitude."

"Solitude?" said Adeline, softly.

"Yes—a preference for the quiet scenes of rural life is generally the result of satiety in the bustle and amusements of a large city."

"Ah," said Adeline; "but not always. There is bustle and amusement enough for me here."

" Then you despise what is commonly called pleasure ?"

" Pleasure," said Adeline. " Despise pleasure ?—oh no. Have I not much pleasure ? Do I not love——"

" Love ?" cried Mandeville, starting.

" Yes," said Adeline, in her soft silvery tones. " I love books, birds, flowers, sunshine, music ; dearly I love them all."

" I should like," thought Herbert, " to add another item to the list of things loved."

" And there is Rose Villa !" suddenly cried Adeline, as they gained a rising spot of ground, which commanded a view of the smouldering of what had been her home but the day before.

" It is a complete wreck," said Herbert.

The curate and Mrs. Mourdant had likewise paused, and the little party were again together, and the conversation, as a matter of course, became more general.

" Let us," said the curate, " approach the ruins by the back of the house, and we shall escape the smoke which blows across the front."

They skirted along the hedge which Herbert had burst through on the night of the serenade, and entered the garden at the back of the Villa, through what had been a small gateway, but the gate had been torn from its hinges during the fire, for the sake of conveniently carrying out, in that direction, such articles as could be saved from the burning pile.

" My poor plants," said Adeline.

" Nay, Adeline," replied the curate, " I think they are but little injured."

" There are some that I would fain preserve."

" They shall be preserved," said Mandeville. " We will have them transplanted to the parsonage-house garden. I will see it done myself."

" Oh, thank you," said Adeline.

" But I shall not know your favourites," remarked Mandeville.

" But I will come and point them out," cried Adeline. " Let it be to-day."

" At sunset ?" said Herbert, in a low tone.

" Yes," answered Adeline.

" It would be a pleasant surprise to your mother."

" Surprise ?"

" Yes, Adeline. I should like your mother to see the flowers and plants in the curate's garden without knowing that they had been brought there, so——"

Adeline looked doubtful as Mandeville paused.

" You would not tell my mother ?" she said, softly.

Mandeville answered in a tone of slight confusion.

" Oh yes ; certainly, if you wish. But I thought she would feel a pleasureable surprise at seeing the plants——"

" Yes," said Adeline ; " I understand. How good and kind you are, Mr. Mandeville !"

Herbert's conscience smote him slightly, for he could not help feeling he was not quite entitled to unlimited admiration for his proposal, which regarded more the prospects of a tête-a-tête with Adeline at the witching hour of sunset in the Villa garden, than the pleasureable surprise of poor Mrs. Mourdant.

" You—you will come ?" he said.

" Yes," answered Adeline ; " and Mr. Endsleigh will help us."

This was a complete finishing-blow to Herbert, and with his usual unjust impetuosity of temper, he inwardly abused the innocent curate in the most unmeasured language. He dreaded, however, to show his disappointment, and he merely said—

" Certainly—as you please."

"I was beginning to love the Villa," sighed Adeline ; "and now it has passed away in a night, like a dream."

"But all, love," whispered Mandeville, "will not pass away like a dream, unless life itself be but a vision."

"At sunset," said Adeline, musingly.

They had wandered some distance from the curate and Mrs. Mourdant, who were conversing with some of the villagers, who had been stationed to guard the ruins.

"Yes," replied Mandeville ; "at sunset, Adeline—dear Adeline."

He pressed her hand as he spoke. She made a slight effort to withdraw it, but very slight.

"I will tell Mr. Endsleigh to meet us here," continued Mandeville.

"But we can all come together."

"Then your mother would know of the expedition ; and as well as removing the plants, I wish to search the ruins for anything that may be pleasing to her. If we find nothing sufficiently preserved from the flames, she will not be disappointed, not knowing of the search."

"True—true," said Adeline. "I thank you, Mr. Mandeville. Yes, I will come—I will be here."

"At sunset, Adeline ?"

"At sunset," she replied.

CHAPTER XXIII.

"There was a small speck in the sunny sky,
Not large enough to shade the sunlight from a rose ;
But still it grew, until it fell like death
On many hearts." ANON.

SELF-CONDEMNATION.—THE LAST LETTER.—THE ENVELOPE.—ALARM.—THE OLD SERVANT.—THE EVENING MEETING.—ADELINE DECEIVED.

IF Herbert Mandeville had had a bitter and irreconcilable enemy, one who would have gladly blighted both body and soul of his victim, he might well have said with a sneer of triumph—"Let him alone. He is doing more than I could."

And so in truth it was. Mandeville was his own worst foe ! With happiness within his reach—nay, almost in his grasp. What was he doing ? With golden opinions from all around him, as evidently awakening sentiment of love for him in the heart of the young, pure, and beautiful Adeline,—a glorious spark which might be formed into the flame of dear affection ; still, with all this, Herbert Mandeville, as if by some unhappy fatality, could not tread the beaten path before him, although it was the straightest and the most beautiful.

No ; he must equivocate—plan, and manoeuvre. He must be disingenuous, when candour and truth would have placed him on a height above the evil influence of busy tongues.

He must improve upon what was already at its best. He must tamper with that possession above all others that a man should hold as dearer than his life —his spotless reputation.

For the sake of a private interview with Adeline—opportunities for which, situated as they relatively were, must have sprung up in abundance—he started with a deception. He did not invite the curate to meet him and the gentle girl at the ruins of Rose Villa.

Mandeville passed the day in alternations of hope and anxiety. He sighed for the approach of evening, when he should have an opportunity of pouring his tale of love into the ear of Adeline.

There, upon the spot of the conflagration from which he had rescued her,—there, with every circumstance around speaking in his favour, he would tell her she was beautiful, and that he loved her. He would tell of his vow in the burning building, to save her or perish with her.

Could she be otherwise than deeply moved by such an appeal? Once, indeed, his heart told him it was not generous to call upon gratitude to assist love; but Herbert had a facility in silencing his own scruples of conscience.

The day wore on languidly to Mandeville. He saw but little of Adeline, for she and her mother were busy in arranging the rooms which had been ceded to them at the parsonage, which was a large building—at least, much larger than the good curate could himself occupy.

The evening at length gave notice of its approach. The lengthened shadows proclaimed that the sun was sinking to its rest.

Herbert's heart beat with anxious expectation. He was in a flutter of delight.

"Who would, who could have prophesied," he said, "that so soon I should have made such progress in my love as to be but waiting the hour of a blissful meeting with the fair Adeline alone?"

He forgot at the moment that he had made no such progress, and that the meeting alone with the innocent Adeline was based upon a falsehood.

He was now about to leave the parsonage, and make the best of his way to Rose Villa, when he suddenly paused, and exclaimed :—

"That confounded letter from Dufours! I had not time to destroy it this morning, but I will do so now. How innocently I might be involved in a sea of trouble if that infernal suggestion of his to set fire to the cottage of

No. 14

the Mourdants' were seen by any one. I begin to think you are rather a dangerous adviser, Captain Dufours."

While speaking, he was examining his pockets for the letter, but, to his surprise and consternation, he could find nothing but the envelope in which it had been contained.

"Surely," he exclaimed, "I put it in this pocket. By Heavens, it is lost!"

A cold sensation came over his heart as he thought of the possible if not the probable consequences of the letter falling into any one's hands who would be willing or able to do him an injury.

"Where could I have lost it?" he said. "I thrust it along with its envelope into this pocket before I jumped from the window; since then, I have forgotten its existence."

He searched his room narrowly. Again he carefully examined his pockets, but no letter. It was certainly gone.

When Herbert felt convinced that he had it not, he began to try to persuade himself that it was of no consequence; but he could not easily divest himself of the feeling of anxiety which the circumstance occasioned him.

"Pho, pho!" he suddenly exclaimed. "It's date will at once exonerate me. And the post-mark. Besides, there are plenty of witnesses to prove that it was delivered to me on the morning *after* the fire at Rose Villa."

A few minutes more, however, sufficed to convince Herbert that all these topics of consolation were fallacies.

In the first place, he began to suspect that the letter was not dated at all. And then how could he prove that the envelope he held in his hand ever belonged to that particular letter? And as to the date of his reception of the letter, had he not received another from Dufours some days previously, and how should he prove that that was not the one that contained the damning suggestion?

"What egregious folly I was guilty of," he exclaimed, "not to destoy that letter at once. It may yet be my ruin."

A low tap sounded at his room-door as he spoke.

He immediately opened it. The curate's serving-man stood on the threshold.

"Well, Andrew?" said Mandeville.

"Miss Adeline, sir," said Andrew, "wishes to know if you will need me to move some plants?"

"No, Andrew, no," replied Mandeville, "not to-day. To-morrow, if you please, Andrew, we shall be glad of your help—but not now."

Mandeville could not but observe that the old man hesitated for a moment, and he saw a look of uneasiness in his face.

A suspicion immediately darted across Herbert's mind that he, Andrew, had found Dufour's letter.

"Come in, Andrew," he said.

The old man entered the room.

"Close the door."

Andrew did so.

"I—I have lost a letter," said Mandeville reddening to his very temples.

"A letter, sir!"

"Yes! Tell me, Andrew, at once, have you found a letter addressed to me?"

"Indeed, sir, I have not," answered Andrew.

"Oh, very well," said Herbert; "'tis no matter—no matter. Thank you Andrew. I—I—thank you. That will do. 'Tis of no consequence."

The old man bowed and retired.

"I will torture myself no more about it," cried Mandeville. "It may have fallen somewhere and been destroyed. Pho, pho! I will banish it from my mind. And now Adeline, for thee I will think but of thy wondrous beauty!"

CHAPTER XXIV.

" He knew not how to frame the soft confession,
Yet it trembled on his lips, and oft
Revealed itself in sighs." ANON.

THE LOVER'S MEETING.—RECOLLECTIONS.—INNOCENCE ITS OWN SHIELD.—THE HALF DECLARATION.—NIGHT IS DEEPENING.—LET US HOME! LET US HOME!

THE sun had not yet sunk, but its golden disc was just dipping into the western horizon. A light balmy wind was stirring the young leaves upon the trees with a pleasant murmuring sound. In truth—

——————" It was a lovely hour,
An hour of golden beauty,
When heart to heart should breathe soft vows,
And call on smiling nature to record
The tender oaths of lovers."

"'Tis time," said Herbert; "'tis time. Adeline! Adeline! your pure young spirit seems to have lent a charm to this golden eve!"

He descended from his chamber, and succeeded, without exciting observation or inquiry, in quitting the parsonage. That Adeline would find a means of escaping to meet him he never doubted, and he hastened forward to the ruins of the villa.

He entered the gardens, and stood alone among the ruins.

There was now no one to guard the spoil from depredation, for all that was of any value had been carefully removed during the day, and there was nothing now presented to the eye but the walls which still stood, and the mass of ruins which had fallen within them, and to some extent into the front garden.

The western sky was glowing with radiant colours, the reflection from which tinged all things with gold. Gradually the lustre dimmed as the glorious luminary sunk to rest. The song of the birds became hushed. A cooler breeze gently swept among the ruins of the villa and fanned the glowing cheek of Herbert Mandeville. The faint yellow light had succeeded the deep red golden radiance of the western sky.

It was sunset!

Mandeville looked anxiously in the direction of the village.

"She comes not," he said. "Adeline! Adeline! 'tis sunset; why are you not here?"

E'en as he spoke, he saw her light agile form advancing.

He clasped his hands in an ecstasy of joy.

"She comes!" he cried. "Like music, she moves through the air but to bring joy! Adeline, if ever man loved woman, if ever a warm young heart beat madly for the object of its fond idolatry, I love thee, I adore thee!"

Nearer she came,—still nearer—and now Herbert sprung forward to meet her.

"Adeline—dear Adeline!" he cried, as he extended his hand.

She took it with artless innocence.

"Where is Mr. Endsleigh?" she said.

Herbert looked confused for a moment.   Then he said—

"He is not here, Adeline."

"I waited for him," said the gentle girl, "but I thought he had preceded me, as I saw him not at the parsonage."

"He may yet come," said Herbert, as he offered his arm and led Adeline into the garden.

The ruins now began to wear a cold and desolate aspect as the sunlight was gradually withdrawn from them; and the wind, light and warm as it was, moaned as it gently swept through the open windows and large breaches in the walls of the ruined dwelling.

Adeline paused, and looked up to the dismantled house in silence for some moments.

Mandeville followed the direction of her eyes.

"That was the window of your own room," he said.

"It was," answered Adeline, with a sigh.   "The fire was raging when I looked from it to see if I dared essay the fearful leap into the garden."

"The height is considerable," said Herbert.

"It is," continued Adeline. " I sickened at it, and turned from the window.   Then I think the smoke overpowered me, and I fell in a state of insensibility upon the floor.   Ah, Mr. Mandeville, can I ever forget your noble courage?   From what a fate you saved me?"

"I only remember," said Herbert, "two great sensations during the whole affair."

"And what were they?" said Adeline, looking in his face with ineffable sweetness.

"The one," said Herbert, "was my mortal agony as I flew from room to room and found you not."

There was a slightly increased glow upon the cheek of Adeline as he spoke.

"The other," he continued, "was of a different character.   It was when I felt my strength was giving way, and I was about to fall a victim to the heat and the suffocating vapour with which the rooms were filled, when suddenly there came through the window a dash of cold water in my face.   Oh! how welcome was that stream.   I gasped with pleasure as I stood in the full tide of its dashing progress, and then, Adeline, with renewed strength I sought, and, by the blessing of Heaven, found thee!"

"How much you suffered for my sake," answered Adeline.

"But how—how rich was my reward," said Herbert—"how rich is my reward now.   Do I not see you—do I not hear you speak?"

"Mr. Endsleigh does not come," said Adeline.

"It was surely," continued Mandeville, "some good angel kept me waking on that night, that I might add a charm to my existence by the consciousness of one act that would gild it to the latest period.   Methinks that in misfortune, should it overtake me, in pain—aye, even the bitterest moments of my life, and there are bitter moments in the sunniest existence—it will bring me joy to say—' I have saved Adeline Mourdant—I have snatched her from death!'"

Adeline seemed rather alarmed at the vehement warmth of his manner, but she did not withdraw her hand which he held clasped in his.

"The night is coming," she said, softly.

"But there is never-fading daylight in our hearts," said Herbert, in a tone of warm passion.

"Let us go home," said Adeline. "Mr. Endsleigh has forgotten us."

"And should all the world forget us, Adeline," replied Herbert, " we can smile while we—we remember each other."

"I never can forget my preserver," said Adeline.

"And I," said Herbert, "should forget Heaven ere I forget Adeline Mourdant."

"The evening is darkening," said Adeline, anxiously. "Let us return, Mr. Mandeville."

"Ah! Adeline," he said, half playfully, "those who know me call me Herbert."

Adeline was silent for a moment, and then she said softly,—

"I would fain go home."

"I have offended you, Adeline?" said Mandeville.

"Offended me! Oh, no—no."

"I—I thought I had, by asking you to call me Herbert ; but I am used to that name from those I esteem and—and love."

"If you wish," said Adeline, softly——

"You will call me Herbert?"

"Yes, Herbert!"

CHAPTER XXV.

"The spot he loved was desolate,
  No answering voice was there.
' Friends of my heart, oh, speak again!'
He cried, in wild despair."

A SURPRISE.—THE UNEXPECTED ARRIVAL.—CHARLES LESLIE'S FIRST APPEARANCE.—JEALOUSY.—DEFIANCE.—AN EXPLANATION.

THE night was striding on, and still Herbert detained the gentle Adeline by the ruins of the Villa.

"I am but young, Adeline," he said ; "yet I have, for some two years or more, been engaged in an anxious search."

"A search for what?" said Adeline.

"A heart," he replied.

"A heart?"

"Yes, Adeline. I felt in my own heart how I could love some dear kindred spirit—some being who would in herself concentrate all that should from thenceforth bind me to life—to love—to happiness."

"I am afraid," said Adeline, hesitating as she spoke——

"Afraid of what, Adeline?" cried Mandeville.

"I am afraid I should not hear you talk in such a strain. Oh, Mr. Mandeville, let us return!"

"Ah, Adeline, you call me Mr. still."

"Well, Herbert—Mandeville—anything you will, but let us go. Ah, we pretended to come here for the poor flowers ; we have not looked at one."

"It is my fault, Adeline," said Mandeville, determined to risk all, and make a declaration at once. "Hear me but for five minutes more, I implore——"

"No—no," said Adeline.

"I entreat!" cried Herbert.

"Let us go home," said Adeline. "Come—come."

"On my knees, dear—dear Adeline!" cried Herbert. "Here at your feet, fairest—best of beings——"

"God of Heaven!" suddenly exclaimed a manly voice from among the ruins of the Villa.

Mandeville started, and Adeline looked for a moment amazed and terrified.

"Speak!" cried some one advancing from the blackened pile. "Speak, whoever you be, I charge you speak! Tell me where is Adeline Mourdant, or—or tell me this is not—was not—Rose Villa!"

Adeline suddenly sprang forward, with a cry of joy, and was in the moment embraced by a stranger.

"Is it you, Adeline?" he cried. "Oh, Heavens! you do not know what a sickening sensation came over my heart when I saw the condition of this house. You are safe?"

"And well," said Adeline.

"Your mother?"

"Is well, too."

"And poor Mrs. Fellows?"

"All well."

"Thank God!" said the stranger, in a manly voice.

All this had passed so rapidly, that Mandeville had not time to think, much less act, upon the surprise and emergency of the moment, and he remained upon one knee on the ground, glaring upon the stranger with astonishment and rage.

He then suddenly sprung to his feet, and advanced towards him.

The light was fading quickly away, but Herbert could perceive that he confronted a tall man, who wore a travelling dress and an ample cloak.

Adeline's hands were both clasped in those of the stranger, and the sight inflamed Mandeville almost to a pitch of wild frenzy.

"Adeline!" he cried.

The girl started, for she seemed to have forgotten Mandeville for the moment.

"May I presume," continued Herbert, with difficulty conquering his rage sufficiently to speak with some degree of calmness—"may I presume, Adeline, to ask who this—person is?"

"Do you know this impertinent young man?" said the stranger, calmly, to Adeline.

"Villain!" cried Mandeville, his passion entirely overcoming his reason and sense of propriety.

"Nay, sir," said the stranger, calmly, "were I to retort 'fool' to your villain, I might be nearer the mark, for you don't know me, and you have exhibited your own folly."

Adeline clasped her hands as she cried,—

"Oh, do not quarrel. Why is this?—how is this? Charles—Mr. Mandeville!"

"Charles!" repeated Mandeville.

"Charles Leslie," said Adeline, "my mother's dear friend——"

"And your's, too, Adeline," said Charles Leslie—for it was, indeed, he.

"Yes, and mine, too, Charles."

"Charles Leslie!" repeated Mandeville.

"Yes, sir, Charles Leslie," said the object of his hatred. "Do you object to me or to my name?"

"To both!" cried Herbert.

"I beseech you both," said Adeline "to cease this strain. Strangers to each other, why should you encounter but as friends? You, Charles, the friend of my father—of my mother,—you who have done so much for us——"

"Hush! Adeline, hush!" said Leslie.

"And you, too, Mandeville," she continued—"you who, at the risk of your own life, saved me from death in these ruins! Oh! why should you two cause me the pang of seeing a quarrel between you? And for what?— oh, for what?"

The gentle girl burst into tears.

"Good Heavens! Adeline," said Charles Leslie. "Can this be possible? Saved your life, say you?"

"Even so, Charles. Mr. Mandeville snatched me from the burning ruins of this house, and bore me to safety."

Leslie was silent for a few moments, and then, advancing to Mandeville, with his hand outstretched, he said, in accents of much emotion,—

"Pardon me, sir. I—I could not, did not know you. Will you take my hand, and with it my heartfelt thanks and prayers?"

There was so much gentlemanly frankness in this offer, that had Herbert been ten times more self-willed and jealous than he was, he could not have resisted it.

He took Leslie's proffered hand.

"I—I thought you a stranger, sir," he said. "But I have heard before of Mr. Leslie."

"Nay, say no more," interrupted Charles. "Mutual error is frequently the growth of a moment. Now here are we two, Mr. ——"

"Mandeville," said Adeline.

"Mr. Mandeville," continued Charles, "who must and will be the best friends in the world, were just now ready to knock each other down. Mr. Mandeville, I envy you."

"Envy me!" said Charles.

"Yes," sighed Leslie; "I envy you for saving Adeline."

"I would not have exchanged that chance, sir, for a kingdom," said Herbert.

"You are right," said Charles. "I honour your feelings."

"D—n him, he won't even be jealous," thought Mandeville.

"Oh, Adeline," cried Leslie, "you can judge of my feelings when I saw this sight," pointing to the ruins of the Villa.

"I can, Charles," said Adeline.

"I came down here with a dear hope—the hope of finding you and your mother in comfort in this pretty rural abode, and I found it a ruin."

"And had you but just now arrived here?" said Adeline.

"But this hour," answered Leslie. "Various pressing matters have prevented me visiting Bracefield lately."

Mandeville stood sullenly by while this conversation was proceeding, and in his heart there was no living creature he nourished so deep a hatred for as Charles Leslie.

"I long to see Mr. Endsleigh," said Charles.

"Come, then, let us go gome," said Adeline. "Mr. Endsleigh's house is now mine and my mother's."

Charles Leslie placed Adeline's arm in his, and then, turning to Herbert, he said,—

"On some other opportunity, sir, may I hope that you will bestow upon me the favour and the honour of your acquaintance,—for it is both a favour and an honour to number in one's list of friends a brave and noble hero!"

"You are very good," said Mandeville, in a slightly sneering tone; "but I am going home likewise."

Charles Leslie looked inquiringly at Adeline, who immediately said,—

"This gentleman's home is the parsonage."

"The parsonage?"

"Yes, Charles; Mr. Mandeville is residing with Mr. Endsleigh."

"I have that honour," said Herbert.

"Then we can walk together," exclaimed Leslie.

"He won't be jealous yet," thought Herbert, as he offered his arm to Adeline, which she freely took, and walked onwards between two of the most opposed and opposite young men in all their tastes, habits, and feelings, that could well be imagined.

"He shall feel the canker worm of jealously in his heart before he sleeps this night," thought Herbert.

"I am still, Adeline," said Leslie, "in a maze of conjecture about this fire. I am only clear upon two points."

"And those—" said Adeline.

"Those are," continued Charles Leslie, "first, that you and all else in the Villa escaped, and secondly, in a feeling of deep gratitude to this gentleman."

"In such a cause," said Mandeville, "who could have done otherwise than I did?"

"Ah! who indeed?" said Charles.

"For Adeline Mourdant," continued Mandeville, "I would not merely have risked, but sacrificed life!"

"You see, my dear Adeline," said Charles Leslie, "that you win all hearts!"

"I'll make him jealous," muttered Herbert, "if I die for it."

CHAPTER XXVI.

" 'Tis hard to dissemble,
'Tis fearful to smile,
When the heart feels a passion
It cannot beguile."

THE WELCOME.—AN EVENING AT THE PARSONAGE.—THE RIVAL'S CONDUCT.—A MOTHER'S ANXIETY.—THE SONG.—GOOD-NIGHT.

CHARLES LESLIE was anxiously welcomed at the parsonage, and Mandeville felt that he now indeed had "a rival near his throne."

The dim twilight that had reigned in the garden of Rose Villa had not been favourable to a critical examination of Leslie's appearance, but now, in the curate's parlour, Herbert could make ample observations.

His first impression of Charles Leslie was fully in accordance with the report of Mrs. Plumpjoy. Charles was not handsome—decidedly not handsome.

But, by some unaccountable means, the more Mandeville looked at him, and listened to him, the more he began to doubt the correctness of his first impression.

There was an engaging frankness—a winning candour about the voice of Leslie, that had an indescribable charm. His conversation was rich and well stored with observation and research, without being pedantic. Charles Leslie never said a silly common-place thing, nor did he ever parade his aphorisms.

His hair was certainly of a wiry order; his mouth was rather wide; but then there was a redeeming expression of high intellect about his noble brow, a marked decision of character in his compressed lips, a world of kind good feeling in the rich tones of his voice. Over and over again Mandeville had to assure himself that Charles Leslie was, and ever would be, ordinary, for he was constantly forgetting it, and fancying him quite otherwise.

Herbert really possessed a mind himself of a high order, and he could not help fully appreciating Charles Leslie's conversation, in the course of which shone forth his varied information, and had his heart not been corroded by jealously, he would no more have thought of Leslie's wiry hair, or his mouth

that was too wide, or his ill-fitting and unfashionable apparel, than he would of his grandfather's shoe-buckles and bob-wig.

Mrs. Plumpjoy, who had very little mind indeed, was by no means turned aside from her critical researches with regard to appearance and costume, by any of the varied and glowing blandishments of a noble intellect; and if Charles Leslie had spoken like an angel,

"And whispered liquid sunshine to each heart,"

as Herrick has it, she would still have fixed her gaze upon his waistcoat, and regretted the set of the collar.

The evening passed rapidly, and, to some, delightfully. Leslie was evidently a very great favourite with the curate, and Mrs. Mourdant paid him the greatest respect, while Adeline treated him as she would a beloved relative who had cemented the loose ties of consanguinity by his actions.

All this was exceedingly bitter to Mandeville,—he who could not bear to shine as a luminary of the second class—he who would either be first or nothing. His vanity was inconceivably humbled, and yet every courteous attention was paid to him. When he spoke, he was listened to respectfully; his opinions were deferred to, or objected to, with courteous candour;—he had nothing to complain of, and that was the real reason he felt so unhappy! He wanted something hugely to justify him for being in a very bad humour.

The story of the fire at the Villa was recounted to Charles by the curate, and nothing was omitted which could in any way be gratifying to the vanity of Mandeville.

"Mr. Mandeville," said the curate, "has at once placed himself high in all our affections. I never shall forget my feelings when I saw him emerge from the door of the burning Villa, with our dear Adeline in his arms."

"A noble action," said Charles Leslie, warmly, "is a letter of introduction to every heart!"

No. 15

"I pray you to speak of it no more," said Herbert. "You will make me seem greedy of praise."

"Greedy of fiddlesticks!" cried Mrs. Plumpjoy. "I wonder how the Villa came to take fire at all."

"That is a complete mystery," answered the curate, "and seems likely to remain one."

"I am confident," remarked Mrs. Mourdant, "that there was no light or fire of any sort when we retired to rest."

"There is no accounting for many of these accidents," said Charles Leslie. "Our very precautions sometimes produce the catastrophe we most dread."

"It was a special providence," observed Mr. Endsleigh, "that Herbert should be up. We are all, my children, under the watchful eye of Him that sleepeth not."

Charles Leslie looked at Adeline with inexpressible tenderness, as he said,—

"How little did I guess last night that something was happening that touched me so nearly!"

"There was but little danger to Adeline," said Mandeville, "for I believe in all these cases the determination to save another, or—or——"

He paused, and there was a silence for a moment, which was broken by Charles saying,—

"You would have sacrificed your own life, Mr. Mandeville, to save Adeline!"

"I would," answered Herbert, in a tone almost amounting to defiance. "I hold all lives cheaply, in comparison with Adeline's,—my own included."

A slight flush passed over Leslie's brow, and was then directly succeeded by a death-like paleness.

"Ha!" thought Herbert, "he feels at last. The poison works. Now, Charles Leslie, peerless and virtuous as you are, to rest, to rest! but not to sleep!"

There was an awkward pause in the conversation, and the curate broke it by saying,—

"We will beg a song from Adeline, and then retire to rest, for our slumbers last night were not of long duration."

"Aye," said Leslie, starting, "a song, dear Adeline!—'tis long since I have heard your silver voice, except——"

"Except when? may I ask, sir," said Herbert.

"In my dreams," answered Leslie.

"Very like—very like," said Mandeville. "You can dream of Adeline, while I wake to watch over her safety."

"Herbert!" said the curate.

"Sir," replied Mandeville.

"Why, what's the matter now?" said Mrs. Plumpjoy. "Next comes a horse——"

"Hush! sister, hush!" said the curate. "If Adeline will favour us with the song, I think we had better separate."

"Yes, dear Adeline," said Mandeville. "Sing! sing!"

Mrs. Mourdant looked very much distressed, and Adeline glanced at her mother to know her wishes.

"Sing, my darling!" said her mother.

Adeline complied, and sang a favourite song of the curate's.

GOOD-NIGHT.

"Good-night—good-night—good-night!
The weary flowers are sleeping;
The moon, with silvery light,
It's midnight watch is keeping!
                    Good-night!

> " Good-night—good-night—good-night!
> The evening air is sighing;
> The sun has ta'en its flight,
> Its golden light is dying.
>   Good-night!"

The strain was now over, and Mr. Endsleigh rose and bowed Mrs. Mour-dant and Adeline to the door.

"Good-night all," said Mrs. Mourdant.

"Good-night, madam," cried Charles; "Adeline, good-night." He held forth his hand, which Adeline took as she said—

"Good-night, Charles; Mr. Mandeville, good-night."

"Charles and Mr. Mandeville," muttered Herbert; "we shall see, we shall see; it may be ere long, Mr. Leslie and Herbert."

The gentlemen still remained standing, and Herbert suspected he was ex-pected to go, but he still lingered.

"Before you retire to rest, my dear sir," said Leslie to Mr. Endsleigh; "I wish to have some private converse with you."

"Certainly, my dear boy," said the curate. "Good-night, Herbert."

Herbert had no resource but to leave the room.

CHAPTER XXVII.

> " It stood before him in the pale light,
> A form most like to mortal,
> Yet immortal."   SHELLEY.

HERBERT'S REFLECTIONS.—THE MYSTERIOUS LIGHT.—A NIGHT ADVENTURE.— THE PHANTOM OF THE WICKET-GATE AGAIN.—VAIN CONJECTURES.

HERBERT MANDEVILLE retired to his room, but not to sleep; his mind was agitated by many conflicting emotions; love, jealousy, hope, fear, hate, all in their turns held possession of his heart.

He threw himself into a chair, and covering his face with his hands, he strove to decide calmly upon some mode of action for the next day, which should most advance his views with regard to Adeline, who he now loved with a vehement and feverish passion that knew no bounds.

"She shall be mine," he repeated; "mine, mine! No power on earth shall wrest her from me. Not a thousand soldiers shall stand in the way of my love. She shall be mine. I swear it: mine! and mine only!"

He started from his seat and threw open the window of his room, and looked out in the direction of Rose Villa.

The night was very dark, and there was a cool fresh air blowing, which was exceedingly grateful to Herbert's heated frame and disturbed imagination.

Not a star twinkled in the Heavens. The sighing of the wind through the branches of the trees alone broke the silence of the night. Herbert Mande-ville leaned his face upon his hand, and again he strove to think calmly of some distinct mode of action as regarded Adeline.

"What can be the subject," he thought, "of this secret conference be-tween Leslie and the curate? By Heavens, it must be to plan how to rid themselves of me and my claims. Well they know that gratitude will speak trumpet-tongued for me in the heart of the fair Adeline. Perhaps I was wrong to awaken too soon the lazy jealousy of this virtuous Leslie. Well, well, 'tis no matter: I have planted a thorn in his heart—a cutting from that that even now agonises my own. Ha! ha! Master Charles Leslie, call upon your philosophy to aid you now!"

Something at this moment glanced across the darkness of the night like a meteor, and Mandeville, starting from his position of leaning on the window-sill, looked fixedly and curiously out into the intense darkness.

"That was surely," he said, "some light that crossed my eyes. It could not have been imagination? Ha! there again; it is a light."

A dim ray, evidently from a lantern carried by some one, was now visible; slowly it approached towards the parsonage, until it paused at the low fence which terminated the front garden.

The light was so feeble, that Herbert could not distinguish the least form or feature of its bearer; but it was evident that he who carried it was endeavouring, by its feeble rays, to acquire as accurate a knowledge of the place as possible, for the light was shifted about in various directions so as to throw its rays upon different parts of the building and garden.

"What can be the meaning of this?" thought Mandeville.

He debated with himself for a few moments, whether at once to leap from the window and satisfy himself of the intentions of the mysterious visiter, or await his further movements.

The light became now stationary for a time, and then Herbert could see that it was slowly receding from the spot.

Mandeville's love of adventure now got the better of every other consideration, and dropping from his window into the garden as quietly as possible, he determined to follow the bearer of the light, and endeavour to ascertain the motive of his visit.

His knowledge of the locality enabled him to clear the garden very quickly, and although he trod softly and cautiously, he found himself rapidly gaining on the dim light that but slowly preceded him.

Whoever the bearer of the light might be, he appeared to have taken alarm at something, for after a perceptible pause of a moment, it was suddenly extinguished, and Mandeville was left without the least idea of the direction in which the person he wished to overtake was proceeding.

Herbert was now very near the lane which led to the village church-yard, and he stood for several minutes listening to hear if the sound of a footstep should give him any clue to the person he had followed.

By placing his ear close to the ground, he fancied he heard a footstep slowly receding from him up the lane.

Mandeville hesitated not a moment, but as quickly as he could, consistently with caution, he bounded up the narrow pathway, convinced that now at least he must inevitably come up with the mysterious stranger, be he who he might, and discover his purpose by fair means or foul.

The eyes of Herbert had by that time become accustomed to the darkness that reigned around him, and he could better distinguish the various objects that surrounded him.

He advanced very rapidly until he came within sight of the little wicket-gate, of which such frequent mention has already been made.

Still he saw nothing of the form he supposed himself to be so closely following, and he came close to the gate, and was, in fact, in the act of placing his hand upon it to open it, when, with an uncomfortable thrill of alarm, he saw leaning upon it, in the same attitude as he had observed it in before, the identical pale and supernatural-looking form that had shaken his nerves upon a former occasion.

There was a pale sickly luminous appearance over the face, which, while it rendered it very visible, imparted to it at the same time an indescribable expression of horror.

"Good God!" exclaimed Herbert, in the first moment of his surprise, and he started back several paces.

When he recovered from the first shock the sudden and most unexpected appearance had given him, he felt ashamed of his weakness, but the figure was gone!

Mandeville darted forward and reached the gate again, for he had recoiled from it several paces. There was certainly no one there.

He tried to pierce with his eyes the darkness in the churchyard, but a moment's reflection convinced him how utterly futile would be any unaided attempt to search among the grave-stones and monuments for any one who chose to remain concealed.

"If this visitation," he thought, "be really supernatural, which I will not believe, a search is useless, an idle mockery; and if, as I strongly suspect, some scheme of plunder is on foot in Bracefield, more energetic measures must be taken than I at this moment have the power to undertake. So many events have passed upon my mind, that my imagination has hitherto not had time even to speculate upon the former appearance. I will return."

He walked slowly back to the parsonage, resolving on the morrow he would take an opportunity of calling the curate's attention to his night's adventure, and to the probability that some danger threatened the peaceful village from some quarter.

Still it was with rather an uneasy sensation that he walked along in the silence and solitude of the night, after what had seen, for that universal ingredient in all human compositions, superstition, was not entirely banished by philosophy from the mind of Herbert Mandeville.

"This village of Bracefield," he said, as he regained his chamber and provided himself with a light, "is a prolific region of romance. But I will think no more of what I have seen. Adeline! Adeline! it is of thee and thy matchless charms that I would meditate."

He remained some minutes in silent thought, then he suddenly exclaimed—

"To-morrow! aye, to-morrow! What is to be done to-morrow. Shall I declare my passion to them all, and boldly throw down the gauntlet of defiance to Charles Leslie; or—or, shall I win, beyond doubt or drawback, the heart of Adeline, and then enjoy my triumph? Yet why should I hesitate? I am more nobly born than he. Wealth is at my command. Honours await me. Shall I suffer myself to be disturbed by this base plodding plebeian? Never! Before his face I will commend my suit to the beautiful Adeline, and, with affected wonder, I will talk of his presumption in even daring to enter the lists with me."

He paced his room with rapid strides as he spoke, and his compressed lips and haughty brow might well have been the indices of nobler resolutions.

"I will speak to this old doting curate," he muttered; "I will tell him I love Adeline Mourdant, and he may, if it so please him, warn his pattern man—his philosophical friend, Leslie,—to beware of rousing the patrician blood that now boils through my veins as an impetuous torrent."

~~~~~~~~~~~~~~~~~~~~~~~~~~~

CHAPTER XXVIII.

"The love of a noble and true heart is a bright gift from Heaven."
GOLDSMITH.

THE INTERVIEW BETWEEN THE CURATE AND CHARLES LESLIE.—THE CONFESSION.—RESOLUTIONS.—A NOBLE MIND AND A SINCERE FRIEND.—WHO IS WORTHY OF ADELINE.

WE left the curate and Charles Leslie alone in the parlour of the parsonage. The door of the room was scarcely closed upon Herbert Mandeville, when

Charles Leslie laid his hand upon the arm of Mr. Endsleigh, saying, in a voice of considerable emotion,—

"My kind friend, I have a rival in this young man. I cannot be blind to his admiration of Adeline."

"Calm yourself, Charles," said Mr. Endsleigh; "you speak under excitement."

"No, no," said Leslie. "I see it all. He loves her."

"And should such be the case," said the curate, "Adeline has still her selection to make."

"Yes—yes," answered Charles; "she has. God knows I have but one thought, and that is for the happiness of Adeline. I love her, my good friend; and—and I would make her mine, because I think I could make her happy."

"Charles, Charles," cried the curate, "you torment yourself without reason. Is it to be believed that Adeline would prefer this comparative stranger to you, who she has known and treated, and——"

"Yes—oh yes," said Leslie. "Is it not often so? But let me free myself from one possible reproach."

"Reproach, Charles?"

"Yes, my dear friend; but not from you, for you would never dream of it. You know I have been of some assistance to the Mourdant's."

"Some assistance, Charles! Why, Mrs. Mourdant tells me it is through your unwearied perseverance only that she procured the pension she now enjoys, and without which she and Adeline would have been destitute."

"No, sir—no," said Charles; "Adeline nor her mother would never have known want while I had strength to toil for them. There was a difficulty in procuring the pension, because Captain Mourdant had actually sold out of the army one week before his decease, and was only with his regiment by accident at the engagement in which he fell."

"But you talked of some reproach, Charles?" said the curate.

"I did," answered Leslie. "I did not benefit the Mourdant's because I was struck with the graces of Adeline. I had done all before I saw her."

"No one that knows you, my dear boy," said Mr. Endsleigh, "would require such an assurance."

"Now," said Leslie, "you know not how dear she has become to me."

"You wrote to me of your sentiments in this particular," said the curate; "and believe me, it is now the first wish of my heart that you and Adeline, who are so rarely formed to make each other happy, should be united."

"But let me be just," said Charles. "This young man,—this Mandeville, I think you call him——"

"Yes," said the curate.

"He has saved her life?"

"He has."

"Oh! 'tis a great action," Mr. Endsleigh. "I—I must ascertain if he really loves her, and——"

"Now, Heaven forbid that he should ever think of love and Adeline," said the curate.

"Wherefore?" cried Leslie.

"Because, Charles," said the curate, "although Herbert Mandeville has many high and noble qualities, I do not think he is qualified to ensure the happiness of Adeline. He is fickle and inconstant in every thing,—a creature of impulse."

"Think you so?"

"I know him," answered Mr. Endsleigh; "I admire him while my heart bleeds for him, and I augur from his disposition a life of sighs and tears to himself and all closely connected with him."

"Yet he saved Adeline!"

"He did. He nobly saved her. He battled with the flames like one inspired by Heaven."

"And he loves her!" sighed Charles.

"I cannot say," replied Mr. Endsleigh. "I believe he is of that disposition that a thousand ephemeral passions will rise in his heart in the course of the few years that now divide him from middle age."

"His manner," said Charles, "his tone, his language, all told me I had a rival."

"I may not deny," said Mr. Endsleigh, "that I myself noted so much; but you must recollect, my dear Charles, that to admire is not to possess, and I have seen no symptoms of a corresponding feeling in the breast of Adeline."

"I—I came unawares," said Charles, "to the still smouldering ruins of Rose Villa. My heart was stricken at the sight, and I called loudly upon Adeline as I rushed through the deserted building."

"And you met her?"

"I did; she was there."

"There, at Rose Villa?"

"Even so; and—and this Mandeville was with her."

"Do not let that disturb you, Charles; it was a harmless strole."

"Listen to me," continued Leslie; "I heard some murmured words of passion."

"Indeed!" said the curate.

"Yes, my friend, and Mandeville was kneeling at her feet!'

"Kneeling, Charles?"

"Yes, at her feet,—at the feet of—of Adeline!"

The curate looked much disturbed for a few moments, and then he said—

"Charles, listen to me. I——"

"Pardon me, my honoured friend," cried Leslie. "First hear me. Should Adeline prefer him—should she bestow upon him the rich treasure of her young heart's love, I will pray for their happiness; but I will take upon myself one office."

"What office, Charles?"

"To see," exclaimed Leslie, rising and looking proudly at the curate, "to see that he prove not a villain!"

"A villain, Charles?"

"Yes. He may make vows, but he shall keep them! The love he proffers he shall give."

"Say no more, my boy, say no more," said Mr. Endsleigh, kindly; "I will take upon myself to ascertain the true state of this case. I will speak to Mandeville about it. I cannot say, Sir, you shall not love Adeline Mourdant, but I can and will say—Herbert Mandeville, you shall not trifle with the pure young heart of Adeline Mourdant."

"Enough, my dear friend, enough," said Leslie. "'Tis all I wish. She is all excellence, and why should I be surprised at any one loving her."

"This matter disturbs me much," said Mr. Endsleigh; "Herbert Mandeville belongs to a proud haughty family. There would be small chance of her happiness, even as the wife of this inconsistent young man."

"Alas! alas!" sighed Leslie.

"Be assured, however, of one thing," continued the curate. "Adeline shall know her real position. If this young man confesses to me his intention of endeavouring to gain her heart, I will take care there shall be no mystery, no sort of obscurity. She shall know all concerning him that is possible, and my position with regard to him makes it my duty to inform those who have a right to control his conduct in such a circumstance."

"We will both work for the happiness of Adeline," said Leslie.

"We will," answered the curate. "Of course you will remain here until all this affair is settled, and I sincerely hope to see my first wish gratified in beholding you the affianced husband of Adeline."

"My heart misgives me strangely," said Leslie ; "but I will endeavour to hope."

"Do so," replied the curate. "To-morrow morning shall end some of your anxieties, for if Herbert Mandeville disclaims all idea of pretending to the hand of Adeline, I shall be empowered to forbid any conduct upon his part that might imply that he had not spoken ingenuously."

"My kind best friend," said Charles, taking the curate's hand and pressing it warmly.

"Now to bed, Charles," said the kind-hearted clergyman. "At my time of life I ought to be free from lovers' squabbles ; but (with a smile) I must bring about a wedding between you and Adeline, in order that I may have the pleasure of officiating at the ceremony myself."

"Good-night, sir," said Leslie ; "I can never forget your great kindness."

CHAPTER XXIX.

"True love is ever silent,
'Tis meritricious passion, that can babble
Of its feelings, rant of its hopes, and
Number oath on oath!"   GARRICK.

CHARLES LESLIE AND HIS FEARS.—ADELINE'S INNOCENCE.—ALONE.—THE DOUBT.—WHERE ARE THEY GONE?

THE spirit of discord had, indeed, taken up its abode in the dwelling of the curate. It came, too, in the guise of love,—love, which should have brought peace and joy.

What a contrast does nature, in its unvarying beauty and serenity, present to the raging warring elements of which man's heart is composed.

The morning rose upon Bracefield in a world of beauty. The early birds skimmed the blue vault of Heaven in deep delight. The tenderest flowrets opened their shrinking buds to drink in the clear light from the eye of nature.

All was joy, animation, peace, love, and thankfulness, except where there ought to have been the most joy—the greatest animation—the serenest peace —the most fervid love—and the deepest thankfulness. The human heart was at war with its own happiness. The "trail of the serpent" was over its most glorious aspirations.

Of all who slept, or tried to sleep in the parsonage-house that night, there was not one, alas! not even one, who could lay his hand upon a peaceful breast.

The storm of wild ungovernable passion was raging in the heart of Herbert Mandeville, and rushing through his veins like liquid fire.

Charles Leslie's brave and noble spirit was subdued and chastened, for he fancied that he saw the day-dream of his joy fading away.

The good curate—the man of God—he who was not of earth earthly—he, too, was "weary with anxious thought," and in his "trouble of spirit" he could but say,—"God's will be done," and strive to be resigned. He dreaded an union between the fond, innocent, and gentle Adeline and the jealous, turbulent Mandeville. For both their sakes he dreaded ; but most for her's, for well he knew that where she loved she would stake all.

Nor was even the fair Adeline herself unmoved by the stormy moral at-

Death of Captain Mordaunt in the Mountain Pass.

mosphere around her. What were her feelings—what her hopes? What were her fears none could say ; but the pillow of the beautiful girl was wet with tears when the glorious sunshine of a summer's morn shone upon her slumbers.

It was rather later than usual when the party assembled at breakfast in the curate's parlour ; and when they did assemble, there was an air of restraint upon them, which, had they been asked singly to account for, would probably have given them some trouble.

The curate and Mrs. Mourdant looked anxious and uneasy. There was an appearance of suppressed grief upon the countenance of Charles Leslie ; and Herbert seemed, by his compressed lips and ever-changing colour, to be each moment expecting something to occur which would require resistance, fortitude, and great determination upon his part successfully to battle through.

Mrs. Plumpjoy was the only one who bore an unconcerned and easy aspect.

"I wonder," she said, "what ails you all? One would really think you were all in love."

"Yes," said the curate, abstractedly.

"Quite sweet enough," said Charles Leslie, with a sudden start, fancying she referred to his tea.

"Well, I never," cried Mrs. Plumpjoy. "What are you thinking of, Mr. Leslie?"

"Why, really," said Charles, conjuring up a smile, "I hardly know ; but I crave your pardon for my inattention."

The breakfast was over, and the ladies rose.

"Well, now, I think," cried Mrs. Plumpjoy, "we ought to arrange some little pleasure-party to-day, as it's so fine, and we are all here. We should be as happy as Grigs."

No. 16

" As who?" said the curate.

" As Grigs, to be sure, brother."

" And pray who is Grigs?"

" There you go again," screamed Mrs. Plumpjoy; " catching one up in your singular way. I am sure it's quite a common saying. I've heard it a thousand times, at least. How should I know who Grigs was?"

" Well, well," said Mr. Endsleigh, " we can talk of the pleasure-party after Mr. Mandeville and I have transacted some business that we have. Will you follow me, Herbert, to my study?"

" With pleasure, sir," answered Herbert. " I was about to request the favour of a quarter of an hour's conversation with you when you spoke."

A faint flush came over the face of Charles Leslie as Herbert spoke, but it was quickly gone again, and left a deadly paleness behind.

Upon the countenance of Mandeville there was a look of proud triumph, which did not escape the searching eye of the curate. It was a look which he did not like, for it spoke more of gratified vanity than heartfelt love; but he said nothing, merely bowing and quietly leaving the room, followed by Herbert Mandeville.

Charles Leslie stood by the open window in an attitude of deep abstraction. The gentle morning air was fanning his cheek, and the breath of a thousand delicious flowers was gently wafted into the room. But he saw not the beauty of nature; he breathed not with joy the soft perfume. Not for him did the songsters of the wood pour forth their tuneful lays. He had but one feeling—Mandeville, he felt assured, was about to adopt the course he had dreaded—a course with which he, Charles, in his deep sense of right and wrong, could not quarrel. He felt that even now his rival was declaring to the ear of Mr. Endsleigh his passion for Adeline.

Leslie's mind was one of rare justness and rectitude. Smitten as was his heart, almost to despair, at the thought of Adeline becoming another's, still his passion could not hurry him into one unjust thought.

In the midst of his agony he felt that Herbert Mandeville had a right to love Adeline if he chose—a right to adore her even as he, Charles Leslie, did.

" My interference," he thought, " is only justifiable in the event of this hot-brained young man behaving with fickleness or inconstancy to Adeline. Can I blame him for loving her? No—no. Do I not love her myself? Who could not—who would not love her? Yet she has called me by the name of friend. I knew her father, and he told me to protect his child. Yes, Herbert Mandeville may love her—he—he may ruin her heart; but woe—woe to him, having so won her gentle love, if he cast it then from him. I will hover around them as the guardian angel of Adeline."

A light touch upon his arm now aroused him from his reflections. He started. Adeline stood by his side, and her fairy finger rested upon his arm.

" Charles," she said, " you are unwell."

" Adeline—Adeline, I—I—"

" Good Heavens! Charles, you terrify me. Your looks are wild; you are not well."

" Yes, Adeline—yes, quite well," answered Charles Leslie. " I was only in deep thought. It was a gloomy thought, and my countenance may for a moment have borrowed the complexion of the fancies that were hurrying through my brain."

" Gloomy thought, Charles?" said Adeline, looking at him with sweet sympathy.

" Yes Adeline, the thoughts were gloomy; but—but you know that when I see you I am happy again."

"What a dear morning," said Adeline, looking from the window, and shading her eyes with her delicate transparent hand from the sun's rays.

"It is, indeed," answered Charles, "a dear morning for a ramble by lake and mountain."

He cast his eyes round as he spoke. He and Adeline were alone.

"They are gone," he said.

"Yes, they are all gone," laughed Adeline.

"And—and we are alone."

"Consequently," said Adeline, with a smile.

"Excuse me," said Charles ; "but my mind certainly wanders this morning, Adeline."

"Alone—alone with her now. Why not seize the opportunity of at once declaring the long pent-up passion of my heart? Before the sun has set again another may have poured a tale of love and joy in her ears. She knows not that I love her. 'Tis, perhaps, an opportunity presented to me by kind Providence. I cannot—must not reject it."

CHAPTER XXX.

"He told her that he loved;
And his rapt soul hung trembling on his lips.
Oh, Love! that thou should'st conquer thus
A noble heart!"

SHENSTONE.

CHARLES LESLIE'S DECLARATION.—TREMBLING HOPE.—THE REJECTION.—
DESPAIR.—THE PROMISE.—RESIGNATION OF A NOBLE HEART.

IT might be that too many words crowded to his lips for utterance, or it might be that no words were sufficiently fervid and expressive to portray the deep affections of his heart ; but certain it is, that Charles Leslie remained for some minutes silent, even after he had made his resolve then and there to tell Adeline that he loved her—that in secret he had long loved her—that she was the pure bright fatality—the light of his existence !

Adeline could not but see, by the agitation of his manner, that something strongly moved him.

"Charles Leslie," she said, "I know you are not well."

"Yes, Adeline," he replied, "I—I—will you promise me——"

"Promise what?" cried Adeline, alarmed at his manner.

"That—that you will not cease to think me a friend, even should I seek unavailingly for—for——"

Adeline clasped her hands, and the eloquent blood mantled in her cheeks.

"For a dearer title," continued Leslie.

"No more—no more! Oh, no more!" cried Adeline.

The spell was broken. The long pent-up feelings of the brave and noble heart of Charles Leslie now burst forth like an overwhelming torrent, and in all the eloquence—the natural eloquence of first and true love, he poured forth his tale of hopes and fears.

"Adeline !" he said, "I love you! There is no wish—no hope of happiness in my heart but what is associated with your dear image! You are the genius of my life! For you I live—breathe—hope! There is no joy—there can be none to me that is not associated with thy dear image. Pain even loses its power to wring the soul when the mind is so pre-occupied as mine is with thy great excellence and wondrous beauty! Oh! Adeline, I know not how to woo thee. My heart is all unused to beat to the soft cadences of love!

My imagination cannot so featly frame the language of adoration as many who will seek your hand. There may be voices more musical, and more used to the soft flattery of passion! but I, Adeline, love you in the deep enduring honesty of a heart that knows no guile.

"Distrust, if you will, the honied speech that comes upon the ear of beauty like a lisping echo! Distrust, if you will, the courtly phrase—the well digested rapture of the poetical gallant;—but, oh! distrust not the true homage of a heart that feels far more than tongue of mortal man can utter!"

"Charles, Charles!" cried Adeline; "Leslie, Mr. Leslie!—I——"

She sunk into a seat, and burst into tears.

"Speak, Adeline! oh, speak to me," cried Charles Leslie, bending over her in an agony of anxiety.

Adeline could not speak, her tears prevented utterance.

"Say, dear, dear girl," continued Leslie, fervently, "am I to be so blessed as——"

"Oh, cease, cease!" cried Adeline.

"You know not how often," he continued, "this confession has trembled upon my lips. You cannot guess, Adeline, how much the thoughts of that has stimulated me to exertion and nerved my mind to endurance. Oh, it was a delirious dream to think that in time to come you might love him who adored you. Perhaps I should not have striven as I now strive to invoke stern reality to break the spell of romance, which the secret love for thee had wrapped around my soul—"

"Charles," said Adeline, "when—when my poor father died I wept, but——"

"But what, dear Adeline?"

"Those tears were not so bitter as these that I now shed."

Leslie trembled. His voice was husky and low as he said,—

"I—I have no hope?"

"Charles, Charles," cried the fair girl, seizing his hand, "you are—you ever must be, the best, the——"

"Go on, go on," he cried.

"The truest friend of Adeline Mourdant."

"Friend?" repeated Leslie.

"Oh, yes, yes!" said Adeline; "'tis a dear title! It is happiness, Charles, without passion. The—the friend of Adeline."

"No more?" said Charles.

"No more," repeated Adeline. "I—I——"

"Say on, say on, Adeline; pause not."

"I dare not tamper with a heart like yours, Charles."

"You mean you cannot love?" said Leslie,

"Love is a wild word," cried Adeline; "let esteem, respect, dear friendship stand in place of it."

"Enough—enough!" cried Leslie, with a deep sigh.

Adeline's tears flowed freely as she looked in the despairing face of him who adored her.

"The morning has come," said Charles Leslie;—"the dream has passed away!"

"Oh, speak not thus!" cried Adeline. "Hear me now, Charles."

"I hear."

"You—you would not ask a heart that—that doubted?"

"'Tis true—true, Adeline. I—I think—I hope the bitterest pang is past?"

"The affection that you deserve, Charles," said Adeline, sobbing, "is not such as I could give. I would I could—I would I could!"

"Oh, Heavens!" cried Charles; "is it not most sad that at the mo-

ment of a loss we must feel assured of the value of the much coveted possession ?"

"Still, Charles, you will be my friend ?"

"As I hope Heaven will be my friend, I will be your's," replied Leslie.
"Adeline, 'tis true I have loved you—still love you, with a rare and holy
passion ; but in my dreams of joy—in my anticipations of the coming happiness that might be mine—in the airy pictures of events my fond imagination
drew, I ever loved to fancy myself as sacrificing something for you, or as enduring something for thy dear sake. I would have pictured my love as one
of self-exaction—a love that would have forsaken all—sacrificed all that men
esteem as the means of enjoyment and delight. Adeline, the love that still—
that ever will glow in my heart, is of that character! Your happiness is as
dear to me now as it was a short hour since, when hope was not—not—quite
dead."

"Charles, Charles," sobbed Adeline, "I am unworthy of a heart like
yours, most unworthy."

"No, no! Adeline ; say not that! What I would assure you of is this :
you need dread no passionate persecution on my part. No sighs, no weeping
supplications!—such were unworthy of you—unworthy of myself! From
this day you know my heart, and with that knowledge I would have you feel
that in care or misfortune, distress or danger, there is one who loves you so
well, so fondly, and so truly, that for your happiness, he—he——"

Charles paused a moment. His feelings almost mastered him, but in an
instant he resumed,—

"He could see you the happy wife of another!"

He took her hand and pressed it to his lips, saying,—

"The last time, dear Adeline, the last time !"

"You will still, Charles," she said, "be to me and to my dear mother
what you have been—our best friend ?"

"I will," cried Leslie. "Promise me, Adeline, that you will, should
(which Heaven forbid) doubt, difficulty, or distress assail you, apply freely
and at once to me."

"I do promise," said Adeline.

"Enough !" said Leslie. "I have still the same pursuit in life,—the happiness of Adeline Mourdant, although my own is not so mingled with it as I
had fondly hoped. Let me be in your thoughts as a dear brother."

"No, no," said Adeline, "I—I——"

"What would you say ?"

"Not that title," faltered Adeline, "not brother ; friend, friend, Charles—
a dear valued friend !"

"Be it so," replied Leslie. "And now, for a time, farewell, Adeline!
This has been an agitating interview for both of us. Such another cannot
occur."

"You—you will not leave Bracefield ?" said Adeline.

"No, not for a time ; a few days—perhaps longer."

"Thank you, Charles. Stay here as the friend and protector of Adeline."

Charles Leslie took her hand and led her to the door. Their hearts were
too full to speak, and in another moment she was gone. Charles closed the
door and sat down by the open window.

The birds were singing gaily upon every tree and shrub ; butterflies were
flitting from flower to flower ; the bright sun was gilding everything with
beauty. Universal joy seemed to pervade all nature.

For a time Charles Leslie gazed with an abstracted air upon the varied
beauties that lay before him. There was no answering music in his heart,
it beat not responsive to the joyous charms of nature.

Silently he there sat. His face was very pale : his lips were compressed and bloodless. There was a cold tremulous sensation at his heart ; an incessant whirl of ideas was searching his brain. A voice seemed to him to be wringing in his ears, the words—the words he had himself used,—

"The morning has arrived ; the dream has fled!"

How long he remained in this dreamy apathetic state he knew not, but nature at length gave way,—relief came. He rose from his seat, and with a gasping sob, he burst into tears ; such tears as are seldom shed above once in a human existence—tears that for ever leave their traces on the heart.

For a few fleeting moments Charles Leslie wept, and as he did so a feeling of inexpressible relief came across his heart. The confused whirl of images in his brain fled away ; calmness and peace crept over his saddened soul.

"The pang *is* now past," he said.

With a firm step, and a composed and tranquil mein, he left the apartment and retired to his own room.

CHAPTER XXXI.

"Vie you with him in nobleness,—
Let him not thus o'erreach you
With rare generosity. Be you
To him more noble!"

ANON.

THE CURATE AND HIS PUPIL.—AN UNEXPECTED CONFIDENCE.—MORE DIFFICULTY.—THE COMPACT.

The kind-hearted curate, when he found himself alone with Herbert Mandeville, felt very much at a loss how to commence the conversation with his pupil which he had promised Charles Leslie he would have with him.

After a somewhat embarrassing pause, he said,—

"Herbert, you may possibly take amiss what I feel it to be my duty to say to you, but nevertheless I must say it, and leave the question of offence to settle itself afterwards."

"My dear sir," replied Mandeville, with an assumption of great frankness, for he had resolved upon his course of action, "I cannot possibly feel offended at anything which you consider your duty."

"You are very good," said the curate, in his dry manner.

"In fact," continued Herbert, determined to take the initiation in the business, "in fact, my dear sir, I was most anxious for a private interview with you upon a subject most near and dear to my heart."

"Indeed," said Mr. Endsleigh. "I hope you have had no bad news from home?"

"No news whatever," replied Herbert, in a tone of slight vexation and impatience.

"I am all attention then," said the curate.

"I love Adeline Mourdant!" said Mandeville, suddenly and emphatically.

The curate looked at him across the table in surprise and consternation, for he had by no means anticipated so explicit a declaration.

"I repeat," said Herbert, who seemed to enjoy the perplexed look of the good curate. "I repeat that I love—adore—idolize Adeline Mourdant."

"That's a very frank and open confession," said Mr. Endsleigh, "and facilitates greatly what I came to talk about."

"I rejoice to hear it," said Herbert. "Frankness and candour I admire above all things."

"I am very glad to hear it," answered the curate, in his dry manner, that manner which was always so especially aggravating to Mrs. Plumpjoy.

"Our pleasure is quite mutual, sir," said Mandeville.

"I presume then," continued Mr. Endsleigh, "that you have no objection to a little candour on my part?"

"None on earth, sir," answered Herbert. "It is what I should expect from your high character, and—and——"

"Yes," said the curate, slightly coughing.

"I am all attention, sir," said Mandeville, with a slight accession of colour.

"Then, Herbert," began Mr. Endsleigh, "somebody else loves, adores, and, however I may disapprove of the term, idolizes Adeline Mourdant."

"I know it," said Herbert.

"Indeed!"

"Yes, sir. You mean Mr. Leslie?"

"I do, Herbert. Mr. Leslie some time since confided to me his feelings of affection for Adeline; with a delicacy which cannot be too much esteemed, he forbore to give speech to his heart's first affections, because he was at that time conferring benefits upon Mrs. Mourdant, who, you know, has not been long a widow, and who, but for Charles Leslie, would be now destitute."

Herbert merely inclined his head, but said nothing, and Mr. Endsleigh continued.

"I am convinced, Herbert, that the affection of Charles Leslie for Adeline is deep and enduring. It is not one of those ephemeral passions, born of love of novelty, and dying of satiety. No, Herbert! it is the honest love of a noble heart."

"Mr. Leslie is happy in your good opinion," said Mandeville.

"He has my good opinion," continued the curate, warmly. "He has the good opinion of all who know him. He has has high talents, and a rare rectitude of conduct."

"Yes," said Herbert, trying to imitate the curate's own dry manner of answering anything that he disapproved of.

"Charles is his own master," resumed Mr. Endsleigh. "By his industry and talent he has accumulated a competent independence. Mrs. Mourdant has the highest opinion of him. He *could*, and would, make Adeline happy!"

The curate paused, and looked earnestly at Herbert, who said in a tone of aggravation that belied his words :—

"I hope, sir, that in addition to his other virtues and rare excellences, Mr. Leslie has the patience that I have in hearing his rival praised and preferred."

"Charles Leslie will be no one's rival," said the curate; "it is beneath him."

"Indeed!" said Herbert.

"Yes," continued the curate. "And permit me to say, Mr. Mandeville, it is likewise far beneath you."

Herbert looked confused for a moment, and then said :—

"Tell me, sir, that Adeline has accepted the proffered love of Mr. Leslie, and I'll leave Bracefield within an hour."

"It has not been proferred."

"Adeline, then, knows nothing of it?"

"Nothing," said the curate."

"Then it is a mere dream?"

"Like your own passionate feelings, with this difference, that it has been tested by longer time."

"But at least we are equal in the respect of each loving the same object, and that object being in ignorance of our mutual passion."

"As I told you," said Mr. Endsleigh, "Charles felt a delicacy in declaring his affections under the peculiar circumstances in which he was placed, as the benefactor of the Mourdants."

" A very refined delicacy," said Herbert.

" Very," answered the curate, wilfully misunderstanding the sneer conveyed in the words of Herbert. " Charles Leslie is full of refined delicacies."

" But, sir," answered Herbert, " is nobody to presume to love Adeline Mourdant because Charles Leslie is full of refined and sensitive delicacies ?"

" He was fearful," said the curate, " that gratitude would speak so strangely for him in the breast of Adeline, that she might accept the tender of his hand, when under other circumstances it would have been refused."

" But how long was this refined feeling to last ?"

" Until she knew him so well, that she could decide upon the man, and not merely upon the friend and munificent patron."

" Still, sir, I love Adeline," said Herbert.

" You have saved her life."

" I rejoice to have had the opportunity."

" You are but an acquaintance of yesterday."

" True," said Herbert.

" Are you, then, not afraid that were you to declare a passion for the fair and gentle girl, that now, in the first flush of grateful feeling, her lips might sanction vows her heart might afterwards condemn ?"

Herbert reddened.

" Reflect !" said the curate. " Oh, reflect, Herbert ! Be not rash and headstrong in this business ! Let Adeline know you better ; let her forget you in some measure as the preserver of her life, and know you better as Herbert Mandeville."

Herbert looked confused at this direct appeal to his better feelings, and for a few moments he knew not what answer to make. At length, however, he said :—

" I will wait, Mr. Endsleigh. Let Mr. Leslie make his declaration ; until he is rejected, I will be silent with my tongue, although I cannot keep so strict a guard upon all my actions as not to betray, perchance, the secret of my heart."

" So far, then," said the curate, " I am satisfied. And now, Herbert, let us fairly understand each other. You will, for my sake, let Charles Leslie declare his love for Adeline unmolested by you ?"

" I will," answered Herbert.

" I will not insult you," continued the curate, " by asking you (assuming that you are preferred by Adeline) if your intentions be honourable, because I think you would not insult me by a contrary course of conduct."

" As Heaven is my judge," cried Herbert, " I would make Adeline Mourdant my wife."

" That is sufficient," answered the curate. " I trust if there must be disappointment somewhere, that at least we shall have no open rivalry or quarrelling."

" You may depend upon me, sir," said Mandeville.

" Leslie," resumed the curate, " came down here this time for the express purpose of laying his heart and fortune at the feet of Adeline. I shall, however, advise him to forego that purpose ; and as you are sufficiently generous to give him a first opportunity of declaring his passion, to give you and Adeline an extended opportunity of becoming better known to each other, relying meanwhile upon your honour."

" I quite agree to the arangement," said Herbert.

The curate rose immediately, and quitted the room much more satisfied than when he had entered it.

Herbert Mandeville carefully closed the door after him, and then folding his arms, while an air of satisfied triumph came across his face, he said :—

" So ! I am not to say, Adeline, I love you ! I am pledged so far, and so

far will I keep my oath. Humph!—How many methods are there of portraying the very ecstasy of passion without words? We shall see—we shall see. Ha! ha! what says the poet on the subject,—the gallant Raleigh?

> "'You hear me say it all in sighs,
>   And thus alone should love be said;
> You read it in my languid eyes,
>   And thus alone should love be said.'

Adeline, thus shall you see and read the passion of my heart; that passion which gathers strength with difficulty, and has grown gigantic in opposition. Adeline, you shall be mine!—mine! and mine only!"

CHAPTER XXXII.

"Why cannot we love those whom we admire?"

ADELINE'S TEARS.—THE MOTHER AND HER CHILD.—THE HEART'S CONFESSION.—POOR CHARLES.—AN EXPLANATION AND CONSTERNATION.

ADELINE, when she left Charles Leslie in the curate's parlour, sought her mother, and throwing herself into her arms, her feelings found vent in floods of tears and deep sobs.

Mrs. Mourdant was inexpressibly alarmed at the agitation of Adeline, and would have summoned immediately the curate, but the weeping girl laid her hand upon her arm, crying:—

"No, no, mother, call no one. I will tell you mother, and you only!"

No. 17

"My child!—my dear Adeline!" cried her mother, tenderly embracing her. "What has thus deeply affected you?"

"I have had an agitating interview, mother," sobbed Adeline ; "an interview I can never forget."

"With Herbert Mandeville?" cried Mrs. Mourdant, clasping her hands. "Alas! my poor Adeline!"

"No, mother," said Adeline. "No! no!"

"With whom, then?"

"Charles!"

"Charles Leslie?"

"Yes, mother ; it was with him!"

Mrs. Mourdant drew a long breath, as if inexpressibly relieved at this statement.

"Poor Charles!—Poor Charles!" sobbed Adeline. "Oh, how I wish—"

"Wish what?" said her mother.

"I could love him."

Mrs. Mourdant was silent for some moments, and then she said, kindly :—

"My Adeline, have you any objection to tell me what passed at your interview with Charles?"

"I will tell you, mother. He trembled, and while his quivering lips betrayed the anxious feelings of his heart, he told me that he loved me."

"And—and you, Adeline ——"

"Oh, mother! I thought my heart would break! for—for ——"

"For what, my child?"

"I felt that I did not love Charles as he wished me."

"And you told him so, Adeline?"

"I did! I did!"

A sigh of regret burst from Mrs. Mourdant's heart, and then she said, mildly, and kindly :—

"You were right, my darling—you were right. Now that this affair is past, I will tell you that I suspected Charles loved you before we came to Bracefield ; but I knew his noble nature well, and I was sure no word of hope or passion would pass his lips until he saw us in a position independent entirely of his own resources."

"Oh," cried Adeline, embracing her mother, "why cannot we love where we admire and respect?"

"'Tis better so, Adeline," said Mrs. Mourdant, "than to love where we can neither admire nor respect."

"Yes, mother! yes!" said Adeline. "If I thought I could love Leslie as he ought to be loved ——"

"Think no more about it, Adeline. There should be no doubt. Charles confided to Mr. Endsleigh his feelings towards you, who, in turn, let me know of them. My wishes, I confess, were warmly interested in his favour ; but never—never, my child, would I counsel you to give your hand where your heart went not freely with it."

"I know it, mother.—Well I know your kindness. Charles's kindness. I am surrounded by dear friends."

"Then dry your tears, my child, and be happy. Charles has too strong a mind to allow himself to be borne down completely by a disappointment of this nature."

"He said he would watch over my happiness," sobbed Adeline ; "and I promised ——"

"What have you promised?"

"I promised that in doubt, difficulty, or distress, I would apply to him."

"What rare nobleness?" cried Mrs. Mourdant. I—Adeline—Leave me now, dearest. Go to your own room, and strive to compose yourself. I will see Mr. Endsleigh."

Adeline retired to her own apartment, and Mrs. Mourdant, with a heavy heart, repaired to the curate's study, where she hoped to find him.

Mrs. Mourdant's opinion of Charles Leslie, and it was a well grounded one, was such that the first wish of her heart would have been gratified by confiding the happiness of her darling Adeline to his keeping. But although this structure of her imagination was thus suddenly overthrown, she had too much sense of right and love for her daughter, to dream for a moment of attempting to coerce or influence her actions in the matter. She had but one feeling, and that was deep regret.

She knocked at the door of the curate's study, but no answer was returned, and after waiting for some few moments, she entered the room, and sat down to wait Mr. Endsleigh's coming, for she knew it was the hour of the day he devoted to study. In a few moments Mr. Endsleigh made his appearance.

"Mrs. Mourdant," he said, "I have just had an interview with Herbert on the subject so near and interesting to you."

"Concerning Adeline?" said the anxious mother.

"Yes," answered the curate; "you will not be surprised to hear, after what we have both observed, that he declares, in the most enthusiastic terms, his admiration and love for Adeline?"

"Alas! alas!" cried Mrs. Mourdant. "I fear much."

"Do not alarm yourself, Mrs. Mourdant," said the curate; "from the conversation we have already had upon this most delicate subject, I was led to be a partaker of your fears, that the young and susceptible heart of Adeline might be ensnared suddenly by the singular beauty, the eloquence, the apparent high and noble qualities of this Herbert Mandeville."

"She thinks, too," said Mrs. Mourdant, "that his heroism in saving her life has something about it more than heroism."

"'Tis ever so with the young and enthusiastic," resumed Mr. Endsleigh. "I do not say that Adeline might not be happy as the wife of Herbert Mandeville; but I certainly feel that there would be the greatest imprudence, as well as the greatest danger, in allowing a hasty engagement to be entered into between them. Adeline is very young, and Mandeville himself is little better than a forward boy."

"I see it all," sighed Mrs. Mourdant. "A thousand evils present themselves to my imagination."

"Besides," continued Mr. Endsleigh; "Mandeville's father, is, I know, a proud man, — one who makes the world too much his thought and study——"

"I understand you," said Mrs. Mourdant: "my child would, without fortune, be ill received in such a family?"

"I cannot say so," answered the curate; "but Herbert, for years to come, must be dependent upon his friends, and I think premature engagements of a matrimonial nature rather injurious than otherwise."

"Heaven help my poor child!" said the weeping mother.

"Nay, nay," said the curate; "do not despair. We both feel convinced that Charles Leslie is eminently qualified to appreciate a disposition such as Adeline's, and to ensure for her as much happiness as this world can bestow."

"He is all that I could wish," said Mrs. Mourdant, "but——"

"Nay, Mrs. Mourdant, you must not take so gloomy a view of things. My own opinion is, that this flush of passion on the part of Herbert Mandeville will subside, and time, while it weakens the impression made upon the mind of Adeline by the events of the fire, will enable her to judge better of the man who aspires to her love than she can now."

"We will leave Bracefield," said Mrs. Mourdant.

"No," answered the curate. "If I thought separation would cure the evil that has arisen, Herbert Mandeville should leave this house to-day, for I confess to but little faith in his constancy of heart or purpose."

"No, no! We can go," said Mrs Mourdant.

"And, by so doing, add fuel to the flames," said the curate. "No, my dear madam; if familiarity will not cure love, absence will not.

"'Passion opposed is but passion accumulated.'

Let us give no excuse for desperation. Herbert stands upon his right to love Adeline, and it is difficult to say nay to that right in the present posture of affairs."

"What can be done?" cried Mrs. Mourdant.

"I have already gained time, answered the curate."

"Time, Mr. Endsleigh?"

"Yes. Herbert has promised me faithfully that he will take no steps to win the heart of Adeline until—when, think you, Mrs. Mourdant?"

"Alas! I know not."

"Until she has rejected Charles Leslie."

"Good Heavens!" cried Mrs. Mourdant.

"You alarm me," said the curate.

"That time has come."

"Come?"

"Yes!"

"Why—you—you—don't mean that——"

"Charles Leslie has been rejected!"

The curate sunk back in his seat in consternation.

"Rejected!" he exclaimed.

"Yes," sighed Mrs. Mourdant; "rejected."

"By Adeline?"

"By Adeline, this morning. Nay, not an hour since, he took some passing opportunity of declaring his love; and she has told him there is no hope."

This information was a great blow to Mr. Endsleigh, and for several minutes he was quite lost in distressing reflection.

"It may be," he then said, "that the hand of Heaven is manifested here. Alas! poor Charles; I must seek him instantly."

"Do so Mr. Endsleigh," said Mrs. Mourdant. "I will see him too, shortly, but not now."

"Nay, come with me, Mrs. Mourdant," said the curate. "We three—you and I, and Charles, I mean, are the best friends of Adeline. We will hold council together."

CHAPTER XXXIII.

"Fair maid, I seek thy happiness.
Find it with me, and I am happy
In myself. But as you find it
With another, thy reflected joy
Will shine upon my heart."   TERENCE.

CHARLES LESLIE'S GENEROSITY.—REAL LOVE CONTRASTED WITH PASSION.—ADELINE'S REPENTANCE.—THE REJECTION.—THE SUMMONS.—END OF THE FIRST EPOCH.

CHARLES LESLIE was sitting in the parlour reading when the curate and Mrs. Mourdant sought him. He started up at their entrance, and a transient flush of colour came across his face, for he saw in a moment by their countenances that they were aware of what had passed between him and Adeline.

"My dear Charles," said the curate, "we come to talk with you as friends to your wishes, and——"

"I know what you would say, sir," interrupted Leslie. "Well, I know I have your best wishes, and your's too, madam, I hope and trust."

"You have, indeed," said Mrs. Mourdant. "Do not despair, Mr. Leslie."

"Do not tell me to hope," answered Charles. "Let me ask one question. Has Adeline told you all?"

"She has," answered Mrs. Mourdant.

"I have then but one hope," continued Leslie, "and that is——"

His feelings choked his utterance, and he was silent for a moment, after which he resumed in a firmer tone.

"That hope is to forget."

"I have had the conversation with Mandeville," said the curate, "that I told you I would have."

"And he—he—" said Charles, anxiously.

"Avows a warm passion for Adeline."

"He is her preserver," said Leslie. "May they be happy."

"But my dear Charles," said the curate, "affairs have not yet came to that length. We still are ignorant of Adeline's feelings towards Herbert."

"No, no," said Charles, sadly. "Love is sharp-sighted. I saw it. His gallantry—his talent—his personal advantages—all have combined to win the truest heart in England. Adeline will be his! God send them happiness!"

The door at this moment opened, and Adeline stood upon the threshold.

She evidently had not expected to see Leslie, and she paused for an instant, while a rich crimson glow suffused her cheeks.

"Come in, Adeline," said the curate. "We are all friends here."

Adeline tremblingly advanced.

"I am glad you have come, Adeline," said Leslie; "for I made you a promise I fear I must break."

Adeline looked beseechingly in his face, and in a tremulous voice, he continued:—

"I promised to stay yet awhile here."

"And you will stay, Charles?" said Adeline.

"I—I cannot," he replied.

Tears came into Adeline's eyes, and there was a solemn silence for some moments. It was broken by the curate.

"I think," he said, "Charles is right. He should go."

"I am very unhappy," said Adeline, "that I should be the cause of parting dear friends."

"We will still be dear friends," said the curate, "although we may be far apart."

"Most dear friends!" cried Charles.

Adeline clasped her hands and wept.

"Now, farewell," said Leslie. "We will meet again when the fever of disappointed hope is past."

"Mother! mother! Mr. Eudsleigh!" cried Adeline; "tell me, oh, tell me what to do!"

"Be calm," said the curate.

Mrs. Mourdant was weeping.

"Charles! Charles!" cried Adeline. "Take me, if you will. I will be yours! Weep not, dear, dear friends. Take me, Charles, take me!"

A deep sob burst from Leslie's breast. Thrice he tried to speak, but his voice denied him utterance.

"No," he said at length, "no, Adeline, no! This scene was not contrived to prey upon your feelings. The words you have uttered thrill through my heart, but still I can be just."

"Let us end this painful scene," said Mr. Endsleigh.

"I think," said Leslie, "that before I go, I should strive to leave Adeline in a happier frame of mind."

"What do you mean, Charles?" said the curate.

"This," answered Leslie. "Adeline, Mr. Mandeville has declared a love for you."

Adeline started, and covered her face with her hands.

"He professes for you," continued Charles, "the warmest affection. He is your preserver, and is, upon that account, entitled to the warmest gratitude of all your friends ; but, nevertheless, that circumstance confers upon him no title to annoy you."

"Annoy?" said Adeline.

"Yes!" replied Charles Leslie. "Tell me that the projected attentions of Mr. Mandeville are disagreeable to you, and before I leave Bracefield, Mr. Endsleigh and myself will take measures to put an end to them."

Adeline was silent.

"Or should it be," continued Leslie, and his voice trembled slightly— "should it be that his vows find favour in your ears, I would fain, ere I leave, ear him repeat them, that I may know in after years Adeline is happy."

"I do not think I should consent to this," said the curate.

"No, no," cried Mrs. Mourdant. "It must not—cannot be."

"Pardon me, friends," said Leslie, "but I think it ought to be. If this young man proffers his heart's best love to Adeline, let him do so openly ; let him do so in the presence of those who will witness against him on earth and in Heaven if he be perjured."

"No, no, Charles!" cried Adeline. "I—I cannot consent to this. It must not be."

Charles Leslie had walked to the door.

"I will summon Mandeville," he said.

Herbert at the moment entered the house. He heard Leslie's words, and he stopped abruptly opposite the parlour door, saying,—

"Who summons Mandeville?"

"I," answered Charles. "Will you come in?"

Herbert was struck by the peculiar appearance of the party in the parlour. Adeline was weeping in her mother's arms, and the curate was standing anxiously and thoughtfully in the middle of the room.

"What is all this?" said Herbert.

"The condition has been fulfilled," said Mr. Endsleigh, in a low tone of much emotion.

Mandeville strode into the apartment, his face glowing with pleasurable excitement.

"Mr. Leslie, then, has——"

"Declared his love for Adeline Mourdant," said Charles.

"And—and——" gasped Herbert.

"He has been rejected," continued Leslie, firmly.

"Then here, in the presence of you all," cried Herbert, with enthusiasm— "here freely I declare my love—that love which, while life lasts, will form a part of my being—that heartfelt passion for Adeline which now consumes my heart, and fills my soul with hope and joy. Adeline—Adeline, I love you!"

"'Tis a frank avowal," said Charles Leslie.

"And shall be as frankly kept," answered Mandeville. "Adeline, speak to me. Fill my heart with joy, or kill me by one word of rejection."

Adeline sunk weeping into her mother's arms.

"It is enough," said Leslie. "My wish is accomplished."

"Your object accomplished?" ejaculated Herbert. "You loved Adeline, and——"

"And have been rejected," cried Charles. "Yet, sir, I love her still—love her as I did before. My love seeks the happiness of the loved object at all personal sacrifices."

Herbert was silent.

"Hear me, sir," continued Leslie, "and mark well my words. You have here openly professed an ardent attachment to this fair girl. May you be happy with her, sir, and may you make her happy; for I am not so unskilled in human hearts as not to see that you need not fear the pang of rejection."

"Charles—Charles!" sobbed Adeline.

"Pardon me," continued Leslie. "This is scarcely a time for idle forms. We have a higher stake—your happiness, Adeline."

"What more would you say?" asked Herbert.

"Thus much," cried Charles, with animation. "I wish you unbounded happiness with Adeline, because in that happiness must be found her's. But, mark me, if the vows you here have sworn with such high-sounding fervour be not fulfilled——"

Herbert reddened, and advanced a step.

"Aye, sir," continued Leslie, "fulfilled to the very letter, you have made a foe here who will exact a dire account from you."

"He will have made a greater foe there," said the curate, placing his hand upon Mandeville's breast.

"I forgive your words, sir," answered Herbert, glancing with bitter animosity at Leslie; "but recollect from this moment we know each other not."

Adeline looked up. Her eyes were swimming in pearly tears.

"Charles! Herbert!" she cried; "for my sake be friends. Oh, yes, be friends."

"I fear we never can," said Leslie. "An enemy I will never be to any man, for I do not call just retribution an act of enmity. Farewell—farewell, friends! In a week I will be here again, for I shall be mindful of my duty."

CHAPTER XXXIV.

"Ah! who can paint the pangs of blighted love—
Who tell the fretful anguish of heart,
When from the dearest image of our dreams,
By cruel fate, we cannot choose, but part?"—ANON.

THE DEPARTURE OF THE REJECTED ONE.—THE ROAD.—PASSION SUBDUED.— THE PURSUIT.—A COUNTRY INN.—OLD ANDREW.—THE COMMUNICATION.— A SURPRISE.—INDECISION.—THE RESOLVE.

WITHOUT another word Charles Leslie left the room.

"The struggle is over," he said. "They know not the bursting heart I strive to hide."

He made his way direct to the stables of the parsonage, and saddling hurriedly his own horse, he led it forth by the back of the house into a lane which communicated with the high road.

"I cannot, dare not stay now," he remarked. "In a short time I shall, perhaps, succeed in schooling my heart to greater calmness; but now—now I cannot look at Adeline. Without further adieu I will leave Bracefield. I could not, I feel I could not, trust myself even to speak to Mr. Endsleigh."

He sprang upon his horse, and giving the willing animal a free rein, he galloped up the verdant lane.

Once he paused to look back at the parsonage. Some one was at a window beckoning to him to return. He shook his head as he said,—

"It is old Andrew. I cannot go back—no, no."

Again he urged his steed to a gallop, and a sudden turn in the lane hid the parsonage from his sight.

The road by which Charles Leslie travelled was one of the most beautiful which the country of England could boast of. It wound among lofty trees, occasionally through the luxuriant branches of which could be caught views of a highhly cultivated country, extending far away to the blue horizon. Then it would sweep along open glades, finely contrasting with the wooded portions of the route.

By degrees, as Leslie pursued his way, his mind became more tranquil, and although a cloud still hung upon his spirit, the turbulence of his heart was passing away.

He slackened the speed of his horse to a walk, and gave himself up to reflections on his own and the position of the beautiful and trusting Adeline.

"Should he deceive her," he exclaimed ; "should he prove so base a villain, —and, Heaven forgive me, but I do strongly mistrust him,—he shall answer to me for his villany. He has torn from me the flower I would have cherished in my heart, and I will see he wears it nobly."

As he thus communed with himself, the distant clatter of a horse's hoofs came upon his ears. The sound came from the direction in which he had travelled.

Leslie involuntarily drew his rein and halted his steed as the sounds met his ears.

"That horseman must be from Bracefield," he said ; "for this lane is only used as a thoroughfare to the village. Who can it be? Pho! pho! it concerns me not."

Putting his horse to an easy canter, he pursued his way. The sounds of the approaching horseman momentarily increased upon Leslie's ear, and he felt sure that in a few minutes more his curiosity would be satisfied as to who it was who galloped from Bracefield at such headlong speed, for it was evident that the horse was at a full gallop.

A lengthened shout from behind him now once more induced Leslie to halt, and in the distance he saw a horse and rider rapidly approaching.

"Can it be he?" suddenly cried Leslie. "My eyes deceive me, or it is old Andrew, the curate's honest servant."

The horseman now was within but a short distance of him, and Charles saw that his supposition was a correct one. It was Andrew, mounted on a horse, which Leslie recognised as a fine animal belonging to Mandeville.

"Alas! alas!" said Leslie. "The old man comes with some kind message to lure me back. It cannot be—it cannot be. Be firm, Leslie ; 'tis but another trial."

The panting steed of the old servant now stood by the side of Leslie, who said kindly—

"Well, Andrew, is it me you seek?"

"Yes, Master Leslie," said the old man ; "I would have ridden a hundred miles to find you, sir."

"I thank you, Andrew ; my good friend, I thank you, for I know you mean me some kindness. You bring me a message from Mr. Endsleigh, I presume?"

"No, master Leslie," said the old man, shaking his head.

A slight flush of colour came across Charles's cheek, as he said—

"It is from—from—Adeline?"

"No," said the old man. "If you please, Mister Charles, it's from nobody."

"What do you mean, Andrew?"

"That's to say," continued the old servant, "it's only from me, Mister Charles; I didn't know you were going, as how should I, or else——"

"What, Andrew?"

"You wouldn't have gone at all."

"You speak in riddles, Andrew. I know you mean me well, but tell me at once wherefore you have followed me at such a headlong speed?"

"Just trot quietly back with me, Mister Charles," said the old servant; "and I can tell you as we go along."

Leslie shook his head and smiled faintly, as he said—

"The device is meant kindly, Andrew, but I cannot return to Bracefield yet."

"You will be in the old parlour again," said Andrew, "before the sun sets now."

"No, no," said Charles; "you are well mounted, Andrew, so ride with me a little way, and you can tell me what you have to say as we go on."

"It's going over the ground twice for both of us, Mister Charles, you may be assured," said Andrew; "but as you will, sir. Let us walk the horses."

"Agreed," said Leslie. "Now, Andrew, I am all attention."

"I meant to speak to you this very afternoon," said Andrew; "for I saw how things were going.

"What things?" said Leslie.

"Oh, between Miss Adeline and that young Mandeville."

"No more—no more, Andrew."

No. 18

"Oh, but I must say some more," persisted Andrew. "He has been a winding himself round the dear young thing's heart ever since he pulled her out of the fire."

Leslie sighed deeply.

"Well, Mister Charles, as I tell you, I saw how things were going. Poor Adeline was so grateful, and thought so much of him, and he is good-looking, Mister Charles—oh dear yes."

"Well, go on," said Leslie.

"But what's good looks?" continued Andrew. "What says the Psalm about that?

" ' The child of grace will always shun,
        The ——' "

"There, there!" interrupted Charles; "I know the rest, Andrew; come to the point at once. What have you to tell me?"

"That is the point," said Andrew.

"What?"

"Why, about Miss Adeline and the fire."

"Well, but you have told me nothing new upon that point, Andrew, that I am aware of."

"No, Mister Charles; but I'm preparing your mind."

"You are very considerate," said Leslie, smiling; "but, Andrew, my mind can bear to be told a thing all at once."

"But you wouldn't understand it, Mister Leslie, all at once, and you would blame me.'

"Blame you, Andrew?"

"Yes; because—because I hadn't told you sooner what I knew about—"

"About who?"

"Mr. Mandeville."

"Andrew," said Leslie; "be careful. I wish to hear nothing against that man but upon the fullest evidence."

"Well, sir, here we are just by the door of the Pig's Tail and Snuffer Tray, one of the best inns in the county. Come in, Mister Charles, and I warrant I can tell you something that will turn your horse's head the other way to what it is now, or my name aint Andrew."

"I care not if I make a halt here for a short time," said Leslie, as he dismounted at the door of the little inn.

~~~~~~~~~~~~~~~~~

CHAPTER XXXV.

Thrice is he armed who hath his quarrel just,
And he but naked, though locked up in steel,
Whose conscience with injustice is corrupted."
                                        SHAKSPERE.

THE ROOM AT THE OLD INN.—THE LETTER.—LESLIE'S SCRUPLES.—LOVE CONQUERS ALL.—THE PROOF OF GUILT.—A DETERMINATION.—THE PLOT THICKENS.

AT Leslie's request, he and his aged companion were shown into a private room, and when there, Charles repeated his desire to know at once whatever Andrew had to communicate to him.

"Mister Charles," said the old servant, "what I am now going to tell you, I have had upon my mind for some days, but I am an old man, sir, and—and I knew not what to do, so I beg you will forgive me. I fear I have done wrong in waiting so long, Mister Charles."

Leslie was very much surprised at this address, and his curiosity was greatly increased to know what Andrew could possibly have to communicate.

"Be assured Andrew," he said, "that whether this matter concerns me personally or—or those whom I love better than myself, I shall put the most favourable construction upon anything that you may have done. You may have erred in judgment, Andrew, but I am convinced not in heart."

"Thank you, Mr. Leslie; thank you," said the old man. "Oh, if I could but see you married to dear sweet Miss Adeline, then I should be happy."

Charles turned away his head, and motioned with his hand for the old man to cease.

"I was coming through the parsonage," continued Andrew, "when I heard my master say—'Charles is gone, peace go with him,' and you might have knocked me down with a feather, for I knew not then what had happened, and that if I had made up my mind an hour sooner, it might have been altogether so different."

"Go on, Andrew, go on," said Leslie, in a voice evidently struggling with his feelings.

"I went to the window, sir," continued Andrew, "the window of the hay-loft, and beckoned you, but you turned away; so I saddled Mr. Mandeville's hunter, and here you see I am."

Charles felt that if ever he was to learn why he had been followed by Andrew, and what he had to communicate, he must let him tell it his own way, and take his own time in the telling, so he merely inclined his head in token of assent.

"Well, sir," continued Andrew, "I was passing along the gravel-walk just under Mr. Mandeville's window——"

"To-day?" asked Charles.

"No, Mister Charles, a few days since; well, sir, I saw upon the ground a letter."

"A letter, Andrew?"

"Yes, Master Charles, a letter—and a letter to Mr. Mandeville."

"Andrew," said Leslie, "I sincerely hope you——"

"I didn't open it, Mister Charles."

"I scarcely could for one moment suspect you, Andrew, of such great meanness."

"It was open," said Andrew. "It had been in what you call a—a—dear me——"

"An envelope?"

"Yes, an envelope, Mister Charles; there it lay, half shut and half open."

"Consequently," said Leslie, with a smile, and rising from his seat, "you of course, Andrew, then returned it to its owner?"

"No, I didn't, sir."

"You left it, then, where you found it?"

"No, I didn't, sir."

Charles was silent, and the old servant inclining his mouth close to him, whispered—

"I have got it."

"Andrew!" cried Leslie, reddening with anger.

"Here it is," continued Andrew, taking from his pocket a rumpled piece of paper.

"Begone!" said Leslie. "Andrew, it grieves me much to be compelled to alter my opinion of you. From what portion of my conduct could you suppose that I could act so dishonourable a part as to pry into the secrets of of another in this debasing manner? Begone, sir, begone!"

"I knew it!" cried Andrew. "I knew you'd say that. Bless you, Mister Charles, I know you."

'In Heaven's name," cried Charles; "what do you mean?"

"He'll be hanged, Mister Charles, and you'll marry Miss Adeline, as sure as eggs are eggs."

"Who will be hanged?" cried Leslie, with some doubts of the old man's sanity crossing his mind.

"Mandeville," said Andrew.

"Mandeville hanged?"

"Yes, hanged."

"Are you mad?"

"No, Mister Charles; but I thought I should have gone mad when I came to know it."

"To know what?"

"Why, what he'd done, to be sure."

"But what has he done?"

"Dear—dear me, I forgot. You haven't seen the letter."

"The letter, Andrew? Nor will I see it."

"The letter will be his death-warrant," said the old servant, solemnly.

"Good Heavens, what has he done?" cried Leslie?"

The old servant shook his head deprecatingly.

"Is it murder?" whispered Leslie.

"Worse, worse!" said Andrew. "Oh, Mister Charles, he is young, and may repent. Let us save his life."

"His life, Andrew? Mandeville's life?"

"Yes, Mister Charles; this letter would take away his life. Now will you read it?"

"Yes," said Leslie; "to have a noble revenge, and save him, if possible."

He took the proffered letter. It was the same that Herbert had lost, and which contained the diabolical and singularly-timed suggestion from Captain Dufour's to fire Rose Villa.

Charles Leslie read the letter in silence, then it dropped from his hand and he staggered to a seat.

"God of Heaven?" he cried. "The villain himself set fire to the Villa!"

"Of course he did," said Andrew.

"What an awful discovery!" continued Charles. "Heaven help me now."

"You will come back now, Mister Charles?" said Andrew.

"My brain reels," said Leslie; "I know not what to do. And yet can I hesitate? The villain shall be unmasked."

"And hanged," said Andrew.

Leslie started.

"Yes!" he exclaimed; "they will take his life; nothing could save him. Oh, what a perspective of misery do I see before me. Adeline! Adeline! what will you suffer!"

"He might have sacrificed her life, poor thing, by his villanous scheme," remarked Andrew.

"He might," cried Leslie; "he might indeed, Andrew. 'Tis a heavy and a fearful crime. On his own head lie the consequences."

"Save his life, Mister Charles," said the old servant; "oh! save his life."

"How? how?" cried Charles Leslie.

"Come back to the parsonage, and charge him with the wickedness. Then tell him to go away for ever."

"This is a fearful secret," said Leslie. "Adeline, you must be rescued from this man. He who could stoop to so base and diabolical an act is no fit husband for thee."

"You will come back, then?" said Andrew, rising.

"I—I will," replied Leslie; "but not just now, Andrew. Leave me awhile. I would collect my thoughts, and thoroughly consider my course of action before I again visit Bracefield."

"But," said Andrew, "he—he—"

"He what?"

He is making all sorts of love to Adeline on the strength of dragging her out of the flames."

"Peace, old man! Peace!" cried Leslie. "Would you drive me mad?"

"No, Mister Charles," said Andrew. "I—I——"

"Go—go home, now," said Charles, "Say nothing of this. Before the family retire for the night, I will be at the parsonage. Leave me now, Andrew; leave me."

"I will, Mister Charles," said the old man; "but don't be rash; think well, sir."

"My old friend," said Leslie, "I will think, and, what is more, I will pray."

"That's right, Mister Charles."

"I thank you from my soul," Leslie continued, "for your good feeling towards me. Leave me this letter. We shall meet again at Bracefield."

"Before ten to-night, sir?"

"Yes, before ten."

The old servant left the room, and for several hours afterwards the people of the inn heard the steps of Leslie, as he paced in a disturbed manner the rooms, involved as he was in a chaos of conflicting emotions.

CHAPTER XXXVI.

" Must I be parted from my love
Ere yet the words of joy have passed my lips?
Ah, no! It cannot, must not be.
Come rack, come ruin, I will stay with thee."
FLETCHER.

THE CURATE'S PARLOUR.—THE LETTER.—MANDEVILLE'S FIRST SCHEME DEFEATED.—MR. DUFOURS AGAIN.—THE BAD MUST HAVE BAD AGENTS.—THE CURATE'S CAUTION.—DISSIMULATION AND ITS CONSEQUENCES.—THE FORGED REPLY.

FOR some minutes after the departure of Leslie from the parsonage, there was an embarrassing silence in the curate's parlour. Adeline still leant sobbing on her mother's breast, while Mrs. Mourdant herself was scarcely less disturbed. The curate looked anxious and unhappy; and the self-possession —that self possession upon which he so much prided himself, had deserted even Herbert Mandeville for a brief space.

The curate first spoke.

"I think, with Leslie," he said, "that this matter ought to be thoroughly and at once understood by all of us. I cannot allow persecution of any kind to go on in my house. If your proffered affection, Herbert, is agreeable to Mrs. Mourdant and Adeline, I can say nothing against it. My only duty will then be to acquaint your father with the whole of the circumstances."

"My father?" said Herbert, starting.

"Yes," replied the curate; "you cannot suppose me so neglectful, or so ignorant of my duty as your tutor, as to connive at an affair of this nature beneath my own roof, conducted in a clandestine manner."

"I—I have no objection," stammered Herbert.

"Of course not," said Mr. Endsleigh. "If, however, there is any objection on the part of my honoured guests to your presence or attentions, I beg that we may fully understand each other—that you depart from here within four-and-twenty hours."

"Oh! Mr. Endsleigh," said Mrs. Mourdant, "what can I say? You know the happiness of Adeline is my only wish on earth."

"Then, Adeline, you speak," said the curate.

"Yes, Adeline," cried Mandeville. "With your own lips pronounce my sentence. Tell me that henceforward life is to be a dreary waste to me, an inhabited wilderness, or lift me by one word to a happiness only dreamt of in a purer sphere!"

"Hem!" said the curate.

"A glance, a smile, the lightest sigh that ever fanned the gentle rose," said Herbert, "will tell me all the heart would say."

"Yes," said the curate, with additional caustic dryness.

"Will you not speak to me?" continued Mandeville. "One word, Adeline—but one word! Oh, let me hear the music of thy voice, even if it be to condemn as vain the dream of love that has, since I saw thee, haunted my brain."

Adeline spoke not. She still had her face in her mother's neck, and gently sobbed.

"Adeline," said the curate, mildly but firmly, "make your election. Is this young man to stay here or go?—fully understanding, mind you, that should he stay, it is entirely upon your account, solely."

"You are very kind, sir," said Herbert in a tone of sarcasm.

"I think I am," answered the curate; "I know I wish to be, Mr. Mandeville."

Herbert bowed.

"Shall he go?" said the curate, inclining his ear to Adeline.

A softly murmured, "No," came from her lips.

"Enough," said the curate. "I said I would have no persecutions in my house, and it would be a cruel persecution, Adeline, to force you to say more."

Herbert's face glowed with pleasure as he walked up to Adeline, and whispered some impassioned words to her ear.

"My preserver," answered Adeline; "he saved my life, mother."

"He did, my child," answered Mrs. Mourdant, and she took the proffered hand of Mandeville.

"Herbert," said the curate, "I write to your father by this night's post. You know the subject."

"All the world may know I love Adeline," replied Mandeville; "I shall write myself by the same opportunity. I will take your letter to the village, sir, with my own."

The curate looked full in the face of Herbert Mandeville, as he said :—

"I rather will spare you the trouble, and send yours with mine."

"As you please, sir," replied Mandeville. The tone was careless, but his face was crimson.

The curate turned aside with a deep sigh; he did not like that sudden flush of colour.

Adeline had risen, and was standing by the open window.

"Shall we walk down to the old Villa?" asked Herbert, with something of the air of an accepted lover.

Adeline consented, with a blush, and was soon arrayed for the walk.

"God bless you, Adeline," said the curate. "Do not stay till sunset, for a heavy dew falls at this season."

"I will be mindful, sir," said Adeline. She then kissed her mother, and taking Herbert's arm, passed out of the parsonage just as old Andrew entered it.

"Oh, Mr. Endsleigh," said Mrs. Mourdant, "advise me what to do."

"You can do nothing exactly now, my dear madam," said the curate.

"We can say nothing positively against this young man, except that we don't like him; and that would be rather absurd to say, and he might quote to us the old rhyme:—

> " ' I do not like thee Doctor Fell,
> The reason why, I cannot tell.
> But this I know, and know full well,
> I do not like thee, Doctor Fell.' "

"Alas! for my poor child," cried Mrs. Mourdant.

"I shall immediately write to Herbert's father," remarked the curate; "and I think, until we receive an answer from him, we should suspend our judgments altogether."

"I grieve, too, for Charles," said Mrs. Mourdant.

"And so do I," replied the curate, in a tone of deep emotion. "I know his noble nature well."

"He will suffer," said Mrs. Mourdant.

"He will," replied the curate. "But he will not complain. Let us now, my dear madam, leave this affair in the hands of an all-wise and merciful Providence, who will not suffer the weak to be trampled upon, nor the lowly-minded to perish."

Mrs. Plumpjoy, for a wonder, had remained for a whole half hour without speaking one word, so transfixed and interested an observer had she been of all that was passing. Now, however, her stagnant energies revived, and she suddenly burst out with an entirely novel ejaculation.

"I couldn't have dreamt it at all!" she exclaimed. "*It beats chimney-sweeping.* Well, I never! Only to think! Next comes——"

"A horse to be shaved," cried the curate, "and a pig to have his corns cut."

"Brother!" screamed Mrs. Plumpjoy, "you——"

The curate had left the room, and Mrs. Plumpjoy had no resource but to go the window and shake her head in a menacing manner at him as he crossed the little garden on his way to the church.

Another disappointment likewise awaited Mrs. Plumpjoy, for when she turned from the window, lo! she was alone, Mrs. Mourdant having taken the opportunity of stepping from the room unobserved by the pre-occupied widow.

"Well, I never!" cried Mrs. Plumpjoy. "The manners of some people! It shows their bringings up. It beats chimney-sweeping, and next, I suppose, will come a horse to be shaved, and Heaven knows how many pigs to have their corns cut."

So saying Mrs. Plumpjoy descended to the domestic regions of the parsonage, where she reigned supreme, and by numerous hints and innuendoes, soon made public all that had passed in the curate's parlour.

"Who's that galloping away?" she suddenly cried, as the sounds of a horse's hoofs receding from the parsonage struck upon her sensitive ears.

"Lor', mum!" cried the little untidy servant, "it's old Andrew on Mr. Mandeville's horse, and he's a galloping along like an old mad footman, mum."

"The impertinent old wretch!" cried Mr. Plumpjoy. "It beats chimney-sweeping!"

Old Andrew was starting on his errand after Charles Leslie, the result of which we have already become acquainted with.

CHAPTER XXXVII.

"There are things which a bold brain may conceive—
A bold hand execute,
Which to a tamer nature would be death."   ANON.

LOVE LAUGHS AT LETTERS. — MANDEVILLE DETERMINES TO ROB THE POST-OFFICE.—THE LEAP FROM THE WINDOW.—AN AWKWARD MEETING.—THE POST-HOUSE.

ONCE more the sun had sunk upon Bracefield, and the little party, as usual, assembled in the curate's parlour. It was evident that Herbert Mandeville had successfully pleaded his suit with Adeline during his walk to the ruins of the Villa, and now they sat side by side, looking more love than the most fluent tongue could utter in a summer's day.

"Have you written your letter?" said the curate.

Mandeville immediately rose, saying, with a glance at Adeline,—

"Indeed, sir, I forgot it ; but I will now write, and bring it to you in a few minutes."

"Do so," said the curate. "Andrew shall take them them both."

Herbert went to his own room, and when there, he stood for a few moments in deep thought.

"Yes, yes," he exclaimed, "it must be done. The letter of the meddling curate must not reach its destination. Let me consider. Should my father once know of this delicious love affair, the joys of which I have scarcely yet tasted, it would be nipped in the bud by my instant recal to London—a measure which I suspect would not be greatly afflicting to my kind friend Mr. Endsleigh. We shall see. If the fates are kind, I shall defeat them all. Dufours is a handy rascal."

So saying, Herbert Mandeville sat down, and indited the following letter, from which the nature of his scheme may be gathered :—

"Bracefield.

"DEAR DUFOURS,—Upon receipt of this, copy the enclosed paper, and address it to The Rev. Robert Endsleigh, Bracefield. Send it by next post. It is most important. Copy it in a small, light, running hand, which is the peculiar character of the governor's.

"Write to me by the same post.   "Your's,
"H. M."

(Enclosure.)

"MY OLD FRIEND,—So Herbert loves? Well, his heart is young, and I dare say the object of his choice is amiable and virtuous, or she would not be under your roof. We are both growing old, Endsleigh. Let it be our pleasure to encourage the warm feelings of the young. I am hurried, and can write no more at present, further than to say, let things take their course, old riend, till you see me, or hear further from

"Your's sincerely,

"The Rev. Robert Endsleigh,   "CUTHBERT MANDEVILLE."
"Bracefield."

Mandeville enclosed both these notes in an envelope, and then, with a smile of satisfaction and anticipated triumph, hurried down stairs to the curate's parlour.

"Here is my note, sir," he said. "I have addressed it to an old school-

fellow, who will forward the enclosed letter to my father. He lives, in fact, in the immedIate vicinity of my father's house in London."

"Would it not be better," said the curate, "to enclose the letter for your old schoolfellow in your father's, than your father's in his?"

"It may sound foolish to you, sir," said Mandeville; "but when we were playmates together, we made, perhaps, a silly promise to each other, and bound it by many boyish oaths, that the first who found the one being whom he could love should send word to the other before communicating the fact even to the dearest and nearest relative."

"Humph!" said the curate.

"Now, sir," continued Herbert, "you have my reason for writing to Captain Dufours first, and asking him to forward the note enclosed to my father. Nay, sir, if you please, I will put your's under the same envelope."

"No, I thank you," said the curate, drily. "I am not bound by any promises or oaths on the subject, so I shall send my letter, if you please, by itself."

"As you please, sir," answered Herbert.

"How unkind and harsh Mr. Endsleigh is," thought Adeline, "when Herbert only wants to do him a kindness."

The curate rung the bell for Andrew, who quickly appeared.

"Take these two letters," he said, "to Mrs. Green, at the post-office, and tell her to be sure to forward them."

Andrew respectfully took the curate's letter, together with Herbert's, and left the room.

"Now," said Mrs. Plumpjoy, "let us all sit down and be as comfortable as we can."

"Excuse me," said Mandeville; "I have, in hunting for some writing, so turned about all my private papers, that I must go for about ten minutes to put them to rights."

No. 19.

" Well, I never !" cried Mrs. Plumpjoy, with a glance at Adeline. " I'm sure, Mr. Mandeville, to-morrow would do just as well. The major—poor dear Major Plumpjoy I mean—would have seen all his papers in the fire rather than——"

" I am sure Adeline will excuse me," said Herbert, in a nervous manner.

" Oh, yes—yes," said Adeline.

Herbert immediately left the room.

" That beats chimney sweeping," cried Mrs. Plumpjoy.

Herbert's first action, when he reached his room, was to lock the door carefully in the inside ; then, slowly and cautiously lifting the window sash, he let himself drop lightly into the garden, among the soft mould.

" So far, so good," he said. " Now, Mercury aid me, for I must possess myself of the curate's letter by fair means or by foul ones !"

He darted through the garden, cleared the pailings at a spring, and hastened towards the village.

Suddenly he paused.

" A thought strikes me," he said ; " even if I succeed in abstracting the curate's letter from the little post-house, it will be missed, and another written. I have it ; a blank envelope must be substituted for the letter, with my father's address upon it. That will effectually lull suspicion. I will not return to my chamber, but will trust to good fortune and the credulity of the post-mistress."

The night was dark, and Mandeville walked rapidly and carefully towards the post-house, for he did not by any means wish to encounter old Andrew on his route.

He in a few moments was gratified by seeing the old servant pass him in the darkness, on his return to the parsonage. Herbert then redoubled his speed, and in five minutes stood at the door of the village post-office.

Mrs. Green, the village post-mistress, by no means allowed the government to occupy either the whole of her mind or the whole of her premises, for, in addition to having the charge of the correspondence of the district, she kept a shop, in which was sold so miscellaneous an assemblage of wares, that it would have puzzled any one to have decidedly said what she dealt in, or rather, we should say, what she did not deal in.

Mops and brooms, valentines and lollypops, snuff and Flander's brick, hearth-stones and lump sugar, stationery and cricket-balls, fiddle-strings and new-laid eggs ; in fact, nothing came amiss to Mrs. Green. She was a most comprehensive general dealer.

At the door of this comprehensive emporium Herbert Mandeville paused. He looked through the little door, which was one half of glass, and there sat no less a personage than Mrs. Green herself, looking over and actually sorting the letters for the post, which Herbert, with a pang, recollected would be called for by a boy on horseback very shortly, in order to be conveyed to the next market town.

Mandeville felt that there was now no time to lose, and placing his hand upon the latch of the door, he opened it, and entered the store-house of Mrs. Tabithia Green.

" Good evening, madam," said Herbert, with great suavity of manner.

Mrs. Green knew him by sight, and having a high opinion of his grandeur, in common with the villagers, she made her very best Sunday curtsey, and lisped a " Good-morning, sir."

Herbert Mandeville had a happy knack of making himself popular and familiar, in a very short time, with persons of any class of society, and he exerted all his tact to make a favourable impression upon Mrs. Green.

" I have called, Mrs. Green," he said, " to ask you a favour, my dear madam."

"Oh, lor! sir," said Mrs. Green, blushing till the unusual colour in her cheeks met the usual colour on her nose's tip, and then blushed with it in rosy unison.

"Yes, my dear madam," continued Herbert, "you can save me a walk to the parsonage."

A faint suspicion came across Mrs. Green's mind that he might expect her to carry him, so she only again repeated,—

"Lor! sir,"

"I wish, madam," continued Herbert, "to write a letter to London, and if you can furnish me with the necessary materials, and will allow me for five minutes to intrude upon you, I——"

"Oh, dear me! yes, sir," cried Mrs. Green; "in a moment, Mr. a—a——"

"Mandeville, my dear madam, at your service."

"Mr. Mandeville. Oh, yes," continued Mrs. Green. "A most sweet name."

"One sheet of paper," suggested Herbert.

"And pens and ink," remarked Mrs. Green, with a look of great sagacity.

"You are right, madam," cried Herbert, with extreme empressment of manner. "And pens and ink, Mrs. Green."

"A charming young gentleman!" thought the post-mistress. "Heigho!"

~~~~~~~~~~~~~~~~~~~~~~~~

CHAPTER XXXVIII.

"Lo! all's accomplished—I may sleep to-night
With an assurance of security."

BEAUMONT.

MRS. GREEN'S GREENNESS.—VANITY THE SOFT SIDE OF HUMAN NATURE.—THE STOLEN LETTER.—THE BLANKS.—A HOLE IN A DOOR OUTWITS HERBERT.—THE RETURN.—THE SPY.

MRS. GREEN soon placed before Herbert Mandeville a quire of the best gilt-edged post, and the necessary materials for writing.

"I am giving you a great deal of trouble, my dear madam," said Herbert. "Really, I am quite ashamed."

"Oh, dear, sir," cried Mrs. Green, "it's no trouble at all. I'll just move all these letters out of your way, and——"

"No, no, my dear madam," interrupted Mandeville, as Mrs. Green was gathering up the letters; "I cannot consent to your putting yourself to any inconvenience upon my account. Pray let the letters be, I can make quite room enough."

"Oh, sir," cried Mrs. Green, "you are too good! I'll move them all in a minute."

"Not on any account, my dear madam."

"But——"

"No, no! I cannot consent to give so much trouble."

"But——"

"You will quite distress me, Mrs. Green, now, if you move any of those letters."

"But——"

"My dear madam, say no more, let me entreat you."

"What a sweet young man!" thought Mrs. Green.

Herbert took the pen in his hand and commenced operations.

He was sorely puzzled what to write, for he felt that Mrs. Green's eye was upon him.

"I am quite incommoding you, Mrs. Green," he said.

"Not at all," answered Mrs. Green.

"You are too good," said Herbert.

"Oh, lor!" answered Mrs. Green.

"Pray sit down, my dear madam."

"Oh, sir! I couldn't think——"

"Nay, my dear Mrs. Green, you must oblige me by being seated."

"What a love he is!" thought Mrs. Green, as she sat herself down exactly opposite to Mandeville.

This close proximity of Mrs. Green did not at all suit Herbert, for it inferred too close a watch upon the letters.

"Now really," he said, "it quite distresses me to think that I am intruding upon your valuable time, madam. When you do everything so well, Mrs. Green, it is quite a shame for me to keep you here doing nothing."

"Oh, sir, you are very good," simpered the buxom post-mistress; "all I have to do to-night is to sort the letters."

"It's foolish of me," said Herbert, with a laugh, "but would you believe it, Mrs. Green, I never can write a letter when—when—a—a——"

"What, sir?"

"When a lady is setting opposite to me, possessed of the attractions of yourself," said Mandeville.

Mrs. Green was immediately in a state of the most happy confusion; her nose assumed a redder tint, as with a mincing voice she replied,—

"Mr. Mandeville, you are a—a—perfect gentleman. I—I—really,—heigho!"

Mrs. Green then ensconced herself in the parlour, remarking to her inmost soul,—

"What a dear, delightful, beautiful, lovely creature he is! and what a beast Mr. Green is, in comparison with him!"

Thus was the correspondence of one third of the county left at the mercy of Herbert Mandeville. Hastily turning over the letters, he soon found his own addressed to Captain Dufours, and the curate's to his father. This latter he at once secured and slipped into his pocket.

He then folded a blank sheet of paper, sealed it, and on the outside wrote the name and address of his father.

"All is right," he muttered. "Mrs. Green will miss no letter; and I have attained my object."

Let not the reader imagine that Herbert Mandeville perpetrated this act unblushingly. He felt an intensity of shame while abstracting the letter addressed to his father, that ought to have warned him that he was far from the right path to happiness; but he was blinded by passion, and the thought of being withdrawn from the society of Adeline at the moment when he was begining to taste its greatest charms was too agonising.

He thrust among the letters which lay before him the blank envelope with his father's address, and was about to rise from his seat, when he recollected that he had sat down upon pretence of writing a letter, and that he must, to avoid suspicion of some other object, produce one, or at least the semblance of one. What a maze of deceit does one crime lead the unfortunate perpetrator into!

Herbert hastily made up and sealed another blank half sheet of paper which he addressed to the first name that came to his mind.

Then he hastily rose and summoned Mrs. Green, who immediately emerged from the parlour.

"You will have the kindness, madam," said Herbert, "to let this letter go with the others."

"Oh, dear, sir, certainly," replied the post-mistress, taking the blank letter in her hand. "Mr. John Brown, King-street, London. Certainly, Mr. Mandeville."

"What am I indebted to you, Mrs. Green?" said Herbert, producing his purse.

"A mere trifle," replied the post-mistress. "Really sir, I—I cannot make any charge."

"Oh," cried Herbert, placing half a crown upon the counter, and making for the door, "I cannot consent to use your paper and give you so much trouble for nothing."

"The trouble, sir, is a pleasure," remarked Mrs. Green.

"Good evening, madam," said Mandeville, in his most insinuating tone.

"Good evening, sir," answered Mrs. Green. "Heigho!"

Herbert left the little shop, and hurried towards the parsonage.

"How very odd," said Mrs. Green, when Mandeville was fairly gone. "How very odd!—He took away a letter!—I saw him through a hole in the door. Oh, lor! oh, lor! what shall I do? He's such a love, too."

While Mrs. Green is struggling with her tender feelings, we will follow Herbert Mandeville, who flew, rather than walked, to the parsonage, for he felt he had been a considerable time absent.

Panting and fatigued, he reached the garden gate. It was locked, but he climbed it in a moment, and rushed across the small space towards his window.

Suddenly he paused. A figure seemed to be gliding away from beneath the window. His first impulse was to hide himself; his next to dart forward and ascertain who was the spy, who he doubted not had ascertained that he (Herbert) was not in his chamber.

Mandeville did make a rush in the direction the figure had taken, but he was unsuccessful, it had disappeared, and he felt that time was just then too valuable to waste in searching for the intruder.

Herbert now approached his window, and making a spring, he caught by the sill, and drew himself into his own room. One glance at the door assured him that all remained as he had left it, and it was with a feeling of great relief that he sat about procuring a light, in order to peruse the letter which the curate had sent to his father.

With trembling hands, and a beating heart, he broke the seal, and read as follows:—

"Bracefield.

"MY DEAR FRIEND.—You intimated an intention of coming here shortly; will you carry that intention into effect within as short a time as possible, for something has occured of great consequence to Herbert's future happiness and prospects, which I could explain to you more fully in ten minutes consultation, than by a volume of correspondence.

"Hoping to see you soon,—I am, my dear friend,

"Yours sincerely,

"ROBERT ENDSLEIGH."

"Cuthbert Mandeville, Esq."

"More trouble! more trouble!" ejaculated Herbert, as he finished this most unexpected epistle. "What a maze of difficulties I have involved myself in! My note to Dufour's will be a strange answer to this letter, which names nothing of Adeline! Yet it may do! The curate must be led to suppose that my father founds his answer upon the contents of my letter as well as his. Yes ; that will do. Courage, Herbert ! all is well ! Hark ! the village clock strikes.—Nine ! I thought not so late by an hour !"

"Who's there ?" cried Herbert, hastily snatching up the curate's letter from the table, and crumpling it up in his hand, while a guilty flush came across his countenance, and his heart beat with alarm !

"Who's there ?" again he cried.

"Me, sir," said some one.

"Oh ! Andrew ?"

"Yes, sir. Please, sir, supper's on the table."

"I'm coming—coming directly."

Herbert heard the old servant go down stairs.

"Now to destroy this letter !" he exclaimed.

He lit it by the taper he had burning, and in a few moment's reduced it to white ash.

"Now ! now !" he cried, with an air of exultation for Adeline. "Adeline, the beautiful !—My Adeline !"

He unlocked his door, and hastened down stairs to the curate's parlour.

CHAPTER XXXIX.

"How many a man has been ruined by his company. There is a reflected vice, as well as a reflected virtue, always cast upon us by those with whom we associate." FRANKLIN.

THE CURATE'S PARLOUR.—AN UNEXPECTED ARRIVAL.—THE CHARGE OF FELONY. THE PROOF.—HERBERT'S DESIGN.

"BLESS me, Mr. Mandeville," cried Mrs. Plumpjoy, "where have you been all this time ?"

"I—I," stammered Herbert, "think I must have fallen asleep."

"Asleep, Herbert?" said the curate.

"Well I never," ejaculated Mrs. Plumpjoy. "Why, the major never slept ——"

"After his marriage," said the curate, drily.

"No, nor before, either, brother, when he could see me."

"I am sure Adeline will pardon me," said Mandeville. "I really was —"

A beaming glance from the eyes of Adeline was sufficient. She knew no guilt, and suspected none.

"Well," said the curate, "let us to supper."

"But then it's so very odd," persisted Mrs. Plumpjoy. "Here's Mr. Mandeville, and ——"

A startling knock at the door of the parsonage at this moment produced a general feeling of alarm in the breasts of the little household.

"Next comes a horse to be shaved," cried Mrs. Plumpjoy. "Who can that be at this time of night?"

"I dare say I am wanted by some of my poor parishioners," said the curate.

The parlour door was suddenly flung wide open, and old Andrew announced in a loud voice :—

"Mr. Leslie."

"Leslie !" cried the curate, rising in surprise.

"Leslie !" screamed Mr. Plumpjoy. "Well, next comes a pig to have his corns cut."

A slight flush came across Adeline's face, and Mandeville rose, and stood gazing at the door-way in surprise.

In a moment Charles Leslie entered the room. He was very pale, and his lips were compressed together, as if he had wound up his mind to some purpose that required all his mental fortitude.

"Charles," said the curate, advancing, "I am glad you have come back to us."

"It is my duty!" said Leslie, solemnly.

"Your duty?"

"Aye," repeated Leslie. "My duty, Mr. Endsleigh!"

He raised his hand as he spoke, and pointed to Herbert.

"What is the meaning of this?" cried the curate.

"He can guess," said Charles, still pointing at Mandeville.

"He can," cried Herbert, vehemently. "He does guess!—He guessed before that the affected high-mindedness of the most correct Charles Leslie was but a cloak to cover some scheme of revenge!"

"Hold!" cried Charles. "You speak in vain. You cannot move me."

"Charles! Charles!" sobbed Adeline; "why do you look thus horribly?"

"Speak, Charles, I conjure you!" cried the curate. "You have some fearful errand here this night, I can tell, by your blanched cheeks and quivering lips."

"His errand here is to insult me, of course," said Herbert. "My course will be to resent it properly. Charles Leslie, beware!—You may raise a spirit you cannot quell! Beware! I say! and break not the truce between us, hollow though it be!"

"You have raised a spirit you cannot quell!" said Leslie.

"The spirit of a rejected rival," sneered Herbert.

"Herbert Mandeville," said Leslie, "the bitterest taunt you can cast upon me could not give me half the pain that what I must say to thee will give me!"

"What in the name of Heaven is this?" said Mrs. Mourdant.

"I come with a name upon my lips, to call this young man," said Charles, pointing to Mandeville.

"A name?" cried the curate.

"Beware!" said Herbert, his face flushing with passion.

"Speak! Leslie, speak!" sobbed Adeline. "What name! oh, what name?"

"*Felon!*" said Leslie, solemnly.

"*Liar!*" shouted Mandeville, making a spring forward, but he was arrested by the curate, who cried,—

"Hush—hush!—Would you make my house the scene of a brawl?"

"Felon!" again repeated Leslie.

"There will come a time," cried Mandeville, "when I will force you on your knees to retract that word."

"Or boldly prove its truth," said Charles, calmly.

Adeline sunk sobbing on her mother's breast.

"Charles Leslie," said the curate, "you know my friendship—my affection for you; but this is an occasion upon which I must discard all personal feeling, and see justice done, as between man and man."

"So I wish you should," answered Leslie.

"You come here," continued the curate, "at a strange hour to make a strange accusation. Charles Leslie, you will prove your words true before you leave this room, or I mistake you much."

"I will prove them," said Leslie.

"Shallow schemer," cried Mandeville, "you cannot. You have succeeded but in one thing, in alarming, by a malignant falsehood, the innocent heart of Adeline, whom you affected to love."

"I would give my right hand," said Leslie, "if Adeline's heart had no greater alarm to suffer than that which I have just now caused it."

"Herbert," said the curate, "give me your word as a gentleman, that you will hold my house sacred from unseemly strife."

"I will, sir," answered Mandeville, "if you will give me yours that this false charge against me shall be now on this spot investigated."

"It shall," said the curate, as he released Herbert from the hold he had kept upon him.

"To the proof, then," cried Herbert, springing forward, and locking the door. "Now, sir, (to Leslie,) your proofs! your proofs!"

Leslie looked at the countenance of Mandeville for a few moments in silence.

"You really dare me," he said, "to the proof?"

"Dare you?" cried Mandeville. "Were it not for the presence of those I love and respect, I would ——"

"Hush—hush!" interrupted the curate. "Come, Charles, to the point."

"Herbert Mandeville," said Leslie, solemnly, "there is the door. You hold the key in your hand. Understand me, I charge you with a crime affecting your life! Will you go now in peace?"

"Go!" cried Mandeville, half choked with rage "Ha! ha! ha! By Heavens this is too shallow! Will I be scared away by a word? Ha! ha! ha!"

"Tell him to go!—oh, implore him to go!" said Leslie to the curate.

"You amaze me, Charles," said Mr. Endsleigh.

"The proof!" cried Herbert.

"Oh, Mr. Leslie," said Adeline. "This from you?"

"Enough—enough," said Charles; "I will do my duty."

There was a pause of a few moments, and expectation was painted upon every countenance. Leslie began, and it was evident that he was struggling with his feelings, for his voice faltered, and he drew his breath heavily at every word.

"*I—I charge Herbert Mandeville with setting fire to Rose Villa!*"

Mr. Endsleigh absolutely staggered and sunk into a chair with a deep groan.

A scream burst from Adeline, and she sprung forward and clung to Leslie's arm.

"No, no, Leslie," she cried, "no, no! He did not—he could not. No, no, Charles ; say it is no true!"

"I charge Herbert Mandeville with setting fire to Rose Villa!" repeated Leslie, solemnly.

Herbert himself looked aghast. In a moment he comprehended his situation. The letter from Captain Dufours, containing the singularly timed suggestions, at once recurred to his mind. He recollected losing it, and now he felt sure that Charles Leslie had it. He felt perfectly bewildered. The blood rushed to his cheeks for a moment, and then retreated to his heart, leaving his face as pale as ashes. In vain he tried to speak ; his tongue clove to the roof of his mouth, and he could only glare upon the startled group around him in speechless dismay.

"Is he guilty?" said Leslie, pointing to Herbert.

Adeline cast one glance at the pale face of her lover, and fainted at Leslie's feet. The curate lifted her from the floor, and consigned her in silence to the care of her weeping mother.

"Will you go?" said Leslie to Herbert. "The door is before you. You are free! Will you go?"

"No," cried Herbert, recovering from his momentary stupefaction; "no, I am innocent!"

Leslie shook his head.

"Mr. Leslie," said Herbert, "you believe me guilty——"

"I have good reasons," answered Leslie.

"I know you have—unexplained."

"There can be no explanation."

"There can, and ample. My feelings towards you are now very different to what they were five minutes since."

"How can that be?"

"Because I now know how you have been misled. I in your situation should most probably have not acted so temperately. You have the strongest reasons for believing me guilty of the crimes you charge me with."

"Indeed!" said the curate.

"He speaks truth there," remarked Leslie.

Adeline had recovered from her temporary insensibility, and was now with clasped hands gazing on the face of Herbert Mandeville.

CHAPTER XL.

"They stood apart——
  Like rocks that had been rent asunder;
A dreary sea now flows between,—
  But neither heat, nor frost, nor thunder
Shall wholly do away, I ween,
The works of that which once hath been."—COLERIDGE.

THE CURATE'S DECISION.—ADELINE'S DISTRESS.—THE DEPARTURE.—THE RIVALS.—CHARLES LESLIE'S GENEROSITY.

"You speak, Charles," said the curate, "and let us know your grounds for bringing this terrible charge."

No. 20.

"I have a letter," said Leslie.

"I know it," said Mandeville. "'Tis addressed to me by one Dufours."

"Read it, sir," said Leslie, handing the letter to the curate.

"Before you do read it," cried Herbert, "allow me to confess that I have been foolish—very foolish, but not criminal. I can explain that letter."

The curate took the document, which had caused so much mischief, in his hand, and read it silently.

When he had finished he raised his eyes from the paper, and fixed them with a sorrowful expression upon Herbert's face.

"Young man," he said, "you have heaped bitterness upon your own head. God help you!"

"I am innocent of the crime imputed to me," said Mandeville, "most innocent."

The curate pointed to the letter, and shook his head.

"I know what you mean," continued Herbert; "but I am the victim of coincidences."

"Are you aware," said the curate, "that this letter would go far to take your life?"

"His life!" shrieked Adeline. "Oh, Heavens! Let me see it. Herbert, Herbert, can it be true?"

"By Heavens, I am innocent," cried Herbert. "Here, before God I swear——"

"Hold! hold!" cried the curate; "I cannot listen to such asseverations."

"We want proofs," remarked Leslie.

The curate still held the letter in his hand.

"Give me the letter," said Leslie.

"Nay, it is mine," cried Herbert.

"Fear not," said Leslie. "It is too dangerous a document to exist. Herbert Mandeville, you think me your enemy. I will take a noble revenge!"

As he spake he cast the letter into the fire, where it was in a few seconds consumed.

"Now," continued Leslie, "you are safe. If you have one particle of shame remaining you will leave this place for ever. Your life is saved!"

"God of Heaven!" cried Mandeville; "this is past human patience. I never saw that letter until Rose Villa was a mass of ruins."

"You admit it was genuine?" said the curate.

"I do, but——"

"Hear me out. Was it addressed to you in answer, as it seemed, to your application to the bad man who wrote it for advice?"

"It was. But I never saw it until the day after Rose Villa was burnt."

"God forgive me, Herbert Mandeville," said the curate, "if I judge you wrongfully, but an assertion of that nature is not sufficient to counterbalance the proof of crime which was contained in that most wicked letter. The fact of your being in correspondence with such a man is greatly against you. Herbert, I pity your poor father."

The curate's feelings overcame him, and he sat down to weep.

"This is maddening," said Herbert. "Adeline, you at least will believe me. I am innocent of the frightful crime I am here charged with. As for you, sir," turning to Leslie, "there may come a time when I shall call you to account for your base meanness in prying into my private letters. Such an act was worthy of the high-minded Charles Leslie."

"I am willing now," answered Leslie, "to account for my having that letter in my possession. It was found by old Andrew, and handed to me."

"Indeed?" sneered Mandeville. "So old Andrew has been the spy upon my actions?"

"No, sir," said the curate, "he has not. There is no spy in my house. However, you will be no more subjected to any disagreeables here."

"No more?"

"No, sir. The presumption of your guilt is so strong that I cannot sleep under this roof with you again."

"Oh, sir!—Mr. Endsleigh," cried Adeline, throwing herself at the curate's feet. "He says he is innocent—did you not hear him declare his innocence?"

"I did," answered the curate; "but I likewise heard another voice, supported by testimony, cry 'guilty!'"

"I scorn to remain where I am unwelcome," said Herbert. "Adeline, for a brief space, farewell! In a few days we shall meet again, when I will bring ample evidence that the letter was written and posted to me after the fire at the Villa!"

"You can accommodate yourself in the village till morning," said the curate. "Then let me advise you to proceed to London, and in a spirit of truth acquaint your father with what has happened."

"I shall be here again shortly," said Herbert.

"No, Mr. Mandeville," answered the curate. "I am bitterly disappointed; I thought you weak, and perhaps, in some respects, selfish—but not criminal. Let me see you no more, unless——"

"Unless what?"

"Unless in a spirit of such repentance that it would become my duty as a christian minister to pray with you and comfort you."

"Let the guilty repent," said Herbert. "I am innocent. Adeline, farewell!"

"Farewell!" sobbed Adeline.

"You believe me innocent?"

"'Tis ungenerous to ask the question," said the curate. "Prove yourself innocent if you can—then ask for belief."

"I am aware that I leave enemies behind me," said Mandeville, glancing at Leslie.

"You do not leave me behind you," said Charles, "for I shall not sit down in this house. I had a duty to perform—to rescue the innocent and guileless from a villain, and I have done it."

Herbert glanced fiercely at Leslie, and seemed about to give utterance to some passionate speech, but he suppressed it, and merely said,—

"Enough; I see I am now an intruder here. In five minutes I shall leave the house."

"Herbert Mandeville," said the old curate, "have you no shame?—no remorse?"

Herbert did not reply to the curate, but as he passed Leslie, and unlocked the door, he whispered,—

"We shall meet again, slanderer."

"Slanderer in thy teeth," said Leslie. "We shall not, I hope, meet again. Wretched man, thank Heaven you are not delivered over to that justice you have outraged by a crime justly considered as one of the greatest magnitude."

Herbert smiled contemptuously, and passed from the room.

There was a dead silence in the curate's parlour for many minutes, and then a step was heard descending the stairs; the front door opened, and was then closed with a sound that went to the hearts of all.

"He is gone," said Leslie.

"Heaven grant him grace!" said Mr. Endsleigh.

Adeline slowly rose, and with an unsteady step left the room, leaning upon her mother's arm.

The door closed upon them, and a deep sigh burst from the heart of Charles Leslie.

"I foresaw all this," he said ; "but it was my duty."

"It was, Charles," said the curate, taking his hand. "You have nothing to reproach yourself with in this matter. Be of good cheer."

"Heaven knows I struggled with my convictions to avoid all this," said Charles ; "but Adeline could not be left in the hands of such a man."

"She could not," said the curate.

"Better one bitter pang than a life of misery."

"Come, Charles, sit down with me."

"No, no, my dear friend ; as I came, let me go. I—I could not bear to meet her now. 'Tis better, my dear friend, that I should go."

"You are right," said the curate, after a pause,—" you are right, Charles. Leave Adeline for a time ; her feelings now conquer her reason. This is her first trial in life, but I misjudge her much if she will not in time be thankful for it, and then——"

"Hush—hush!" cried Leslie ; "I know what you would say. I have done with hope. Do not—oh, do not strive to awaken feelings that are partially deadened in my heart. Adeline and I are for ever apart."

"I have better hopes," said the curate.

"Now, farewell !" cried Charles. "I perceive Mrs. Plumpjoy has left the room ; make my apologies to her, and—and likewise, when time is fitting, say something for me to—to——"

"Adeline."

"Yes, to Adeline. To Mrs. Mourdant I will write. Now once more, dear friend, farewell."

"But where do you go?"

"My horse is at the door."

"Farewell, then, my boy ! and let me hear from you soon."

"I will—I will."

"This has been a sad evening."

"It has—it has. Once more, farewell !"

Leslie pressed the hand of the curate, and in a few minutes afterwards was rapidly galloping from the peaceful and slumbering village.

<hr />

CHAPTER XLI.

"I'll not fight with thee."

MACBETH.

THE RUINS OF THE VILLA.—LESLIE'S REFLECTIONS.—A MEETING.—THE CHALLENGE.—THE STRUGGLE, AND THE CAPTURE.

Leslie paused as he came within sight of Rose Villa ; drawing in his horse, he gazed upon the blackened ruins with a variety of feelings.

"The villain !" he cried, as the thought crossed him that Adeline might have been sacrificed in the burning house. "The villain ! to take so desperate a means of winding himself round the heart of the young and beautiful."

He slowly paced his horse past the ruins, and was upon the point of urging the animal again to its speed, when a figure started out from the shadow of the wall, and stood full in his path.

The moon was young, but the night was clear, and there was sufficient light for Leslie to be certain, after a moment's examination, that it was Herbert Mandeville who stood before him.

"Well met, sir," cried Herbert.

"Ill met, incendiary," replied Leslie. "Give way; I will not be stayed by thee."

"We shall see," replied Mandeville. "We have an account to settle, and by the Heavens above us it shall be settled here in sight of these ruins."

"We have no account, misguided man," said Leslie. "We might have had, or, rather, I might have been an instrument in the hands of Providence to bring you to a fearful account before the outraged laws of your country. I have spared your life. What now would you have?"

"I wish to know if the philosophical Mr. Charles Leslie can stand fire?"

"Be more explicit, for I consider I waste time and demean myself by holding converse with you."

"I will be more explicit. We are alone."

"Well?"

"Here are pistols. Take your choice, and give me the satisfaction of a gentleman, if you have any claim to be called one."

"Madman!" replied Leslie; "do you fancy I am so besotted as to allow myself to be stopped on the highway by such as thee, and forced into a conflict which from my heart I condemn and despise?"

"Coward!" cried Mandeville.

"That shall not move me," answered Leslie; "I have no need to fight with you to convince you of my courage, because I hold your opinion as of no moment. I will not fight with you."

"By Heavens you shall."

"In self-defence, of course, I shall resist a ruffianly attack on the highway. I do not thirst for your life, young man; if I did, I should have left you to the law. My own existence I will not place at your disposal."

"You cannot pass me," said Herbert; "I am armed."

"You may add a murder to your other crimes," calmly observed Leslie.

"Coward! Calculating cold blooded man! Will nothing move thee?"

"Nothing from you. Out of my path."

"These weapons," said Herbert, holding up a brace of pistols, "are unfit for you, it seems. Honourable contest you affect to despise, but really dread. Be it so. I will adopt a course that will better suit your plebeian nature. This horsewhip may, perhaps, cure your slanderous tongue for a while. There is no clergyman now to step between me and my just resentment."

"Herbert Mandeville, beware," said Leslie, calmly. "I am, I think, the stronger of the two. It is rarely I am roused to passion, but I never received a blow yet, and I know not to what it might move me. Be warned, rash man. Out of my path!"

"Will you dismount?" said Herbert.

"Wherefore should I at your bidding," replied Leslie.

"Then we can try conclusions as we are," said Herbert, at the same moment he made a spring towards Leslie.

Charles Leslie was an admirable horseman, and by a touch of the rein he made the noble animal he bestrode swerve sufficiently on one side to avoid Mandeville completely.

"Beware again," cried Leslie. "You know not the possible consequences of your folly."

With an infuriated gesture, Herbert again rushed at Leslie, and this time the latter made no effort to avoid him.

In an instant Herbert felt himself seized by the collar with a grasp of iron. At the same moment Leslie gave the spur to his horse, and turning its head back again to the village, he dragged Herbert along with a speed and strength that set all resistance at defiance.

Not a word was spoke upon either side, and three or four minutes brought them into the middle of the village.

Charles Leslie then drew in his horse, and shouted loudly—

"Halloo! a constable here!"

Mandeville writhed and twisted in the nervous grasp that held him in vain. His passion seemed almost to choke him, for although his lips moved, he spoke not.

Numerous windows were now thrown open, and night-caped heads popped out, eagerly inquiring what was the matter.

"Where is the constable?" shouted Leslie.

"The constable! the constable!" cried many voices. One old lady leaned out of window and sprung a large rattle, which effectually alarmed the whole village, and reached the ear of the official personage for whom all were calling.

"A highwayman! a highwayman!" cried several, and the news spread like lightning over the village. Men half dressed rushed from their houses, and Leslie and his prisoner were soon surrounded by a throng of persons.

The constable, a stout burly man, who likewise officiated as parish beadle, now pushed his way through the crowd with his staff of office in his hand.

"There is your prisoner," said Leslie, casting from him the exhausted Herbert, with a fling that sent him full into the constable's arms, who immediately twined his arms round him, and shook his staff over his shoulders, in a manner that produced a roar of laughter from the assembled villagers.

Herbert recovered himself in a moment, and made an attempt to spring at Leslie, but he was too much encompassed by the crowd to render it effectual, and the constable the next moment fixed a hold upon him which he could not easily shake off.

Several persons had now brought lights from the houses, and half a dozen lanterns and candles were held up to Herbert's face at once, to ascertain if he was known.

A cry of astonishment burst from the villagers, as they recognised in the prisoner their respected pastor's pupil, and they could scarcely believe the evidence of their own senses.

"'Tis Master Mandeville," they cried. "What has he done? What has he done?"

"Master Mandeville?" said the constable, involuntarily letting go his hold.

"I warn you," said Leslie, "to take care of your prisoner. I charge this young man with an assault upon the highway. Let him go at your peril, officer."

"Cowardly libeller," cried Herbert, fixing his flashing eyes upon Leslie. "There will come a time when you shall pay dearly for this night's proceedings."

"You will get into trouble, Master Mandeville," said the constable. "Here's a load o' witnesses."

"I defy you all," cried Herbert.

"Send for Mr. Endsleigh," suggested a voice.

The constable seized upon the idea instantly.

"Come," he said, "let us go all of us to the parsonage, and hear what Mr. Endsleigh says."

"Mr. Endsleigh has nothing whatever to do with it," said Leslie; "but if the prisoner wishes for the advice of that gentleman, I have no objection."

"Oh, come on, come on," cried the constable, who was quite willing to shift the responsibility of any course of action from his own shoulders to those of the curate.

Charles Leslie said no more, but wheeling round his horse, he preceded the whole male population of the village towards the parsonage-house.

They soon arrived at the garden-gate, and Leslie, casting his eyes to the house, observed that lights were still burning in the parlour he had so recently quitted, he thought, for a long time. "It is strange," he thought, "that by some fatality I am brought always back here, when I imagine I have left it for so long a period."

The throng of persons paused at the garden-gate, and one of them stepped forward and knocked loudly at the curate's door.

Charles Leslie now threw himself from his horse, and gave the animal in charge to one of the villagers. His face was very pale, and it was evident that, although he preserved an appearance of outward composure, his heart was ill at ease.

There was a flush upon the countenance of Herbert Mandeville, and the excitement of his feelings betrayed itself in every movement. His eyes wandered incessantly from one to the other of the group by which he was surrounded, and his torn apparel and general disordered condition, gave him a wild and singular appearance.

CHAPTER XLII.

"How darkly may suspicion point
To a fair name, aided by time,
And most propitious circumstance.'—ANON.

A SCENE AT THE PARSONAGE.—THE OLD SERVANT.—UNEXPECTED CONFESSION.—HERBERT'S INNOCENCE.—THE CURATE'S JOY, AND ADELINE'S THANKFULNESS.

WE must leave the assembled throng at the curate's door for a short time, in order to possess the reader with what had taken place in the parsonage after the departure of Mandeville and Leslie.

The curate sat alone in his parlour, and as he thought over the occurrences of the last few weeks, bitter and painful were his reflections. For some time he sat thus absorbed in thought, and then with a deep sigh he rose, and was about to leave the room to betake himself to his chamber for the night, when a low timid knock upon the parlour door met his ears.

At first he thought it must be fancy, but in a moment the knock was repeated.

"Come in," he cried.

The door opened, and with a slow step, the old confidential servant of Mrs. Mourdant entered the room.

"What is the matter, Mrs. Fleming?" said the curate, much alarmed, for he saw that she had been weeping.

The old servant only sobbed in reply, and a dreadful thought crossed the curate's mind that something serious must have happened to Adeline.

"For Heaven's sake speak," he cried. "Is Adeline ill?"

"No, sir—no, sir—not that."

"Mrs. Mourdant?"

The old servant shook her head.

"Sit down, then," said the curate, much relieved, "and tell me the cause of this emotion. I presume you wish to do so by coming here?"

"Yes, sir, I do wish," said Mrs. Fleming. "You are a clergyman, sir, and will intercede for me to——"

"To whom!"

"My mistress—my dear kind mistress."

"Tell me calmly," said Mr. Endsleigh, "what you wish me to do, and be assured I will advise you, if not wisely, at least sincerely."

"My mistress tells me, sir, that Mr. Mandeville is gone."

"He has gone."

"And that he is suspected of having set fire to the Villa; I could not tell my kind good mistress, sir, but—but——"

"But what?"

"Mr. Mandeville is innocent."

"Innocent?"

"Indeed he is, sir."

"Can you—have you any proof of what you say?"

"I have, sir."

"Thank God!" cried Mr. Endsleigh, fervently.

"I will tell you all, sir," continued the old servant; "and beg of you to intercede with my mistress for me."

"Say on, say on," said the curate.

"On the night of the fire, I sat up to read in the parlour after Mrs. Mourdant and Miss Adeline had gone to rest."

"Well, proceed."

"I don't know how it was, but I fell asleep, and when I awoke, I found the candle had fallen on to the floor, and the window-curtains were in flames. I was so much alarmed that for some minutes I could not move. Then I rushed to the back of the house for some water from the well, for I thought I could, perhaps, put out the flames before alarming my mistress. In my fright and hurry, however, I fell down and struck my head against the stone steps leading to the little green-house. I think then, sir, I must have fainted, for I knew no more till I found myself in the midst of the crowd, and heard the people saying that Mr. Mandeville had saved Miss Adeline."

The curate was silent for some minutes, then he said—

"You feel certain that the fire originated from the candle falling against the window-curtains?"

"Yes, sir, quite certain. When I fell asleep, I must have shaken the table, which was small and unsteady, and that caused the accident."

The old servant now covered her face with her hands, and wept bitterly.

"Be of good cheer," said the curate, kindly. "This communication you have made to me will lighten other hearts as well as mine. I will undertake to say that Mrs. Mourdant will look over the accident."

"Thank you, sir; oh, thank you. It has been upon my mind ever since, and when I heard that Mr. Mandeville was falsely charged, I could not keep the secret any longer."

"You were quite right," replied Mr. Endsleigh. "To have delayed an hour would have been criminal and wicked in the highest degree."

"I do not like Mr. Mandeville," continued the old servant; "but then——"

"Never mind," interrupted Mr. Endsleigh. "This is a matter in which likes and dislikes have no account. He is innocent, and we must do him justice."

"But he is gone, sir."

"No further than the village, I dare say. I will take measures to find him. Is your mistress still up?"

"Yes, sir."

"And Adeline?"

"Yes, sir, they are both up."

"Then go and say that I have something important to say to them before they retire for the night. I will await them here."

Mrs. Fleming immediately departed upon her errand, and before five minutes had elapsed, she returned, ushering in Adeline and her mother.

"This is an evening of disturbances," said the curate; "but I hope this last one will compensate for some of the disagreeables that have already occurred."

"Oh, sir, keep us not in suspense," said Mrs. Mourdant.

"I will not," answered the curate; "in one word then, I am convinced of Mr. Mandeville's innocence of the crime laid to his charge."

"Innocent!" cried Adeline, joyfully. "Oh, Mr. Endsleigh, say so again. Is he indeed innocent?"

"From my heart I believe him innocent of setting fire to Rose Villa; as innocent of that crime as I believe him guilty of the greatest indiscretion in choosing his advisers. This circumstance ought to be a lesson to him through life."

The curate then related to the delighted Adeline what had been told him by the old servant.

"Then he is innocent," said Adeline. "Mr. Endsleigh—mother—you—you will now——"

"Reinstate him in his former position of course," said the curate; "at the same time I must state, that although he may be, and I doubt not is, innocent of setting fire to Rose Villa, it is a fact that the suggestion was made to him by a scoundrel, who addresses him with the greatest ease and familiarity, and to whom Herbert admits he applied for advice as to how to create a favourable impression in your breast, Adeline. It is my duty to tell you thus much. You and your mother can act upon the knowledge as you think proper."

"He is innocent," said Adeline.

"Of setting fire to the Villa, certainly," said the curate.

"But not of other things," said Mrs. Mourdant. "Oh, Adeline, think again, my child, before you give your affections into the keeping of this man."

No. 21

"You tell me he is innocent," said Adeline.

"Of the one specific crime, my dear child," said Mrs. Mourdant ; "but think what an awful trust you place in his hands when you confide to him your happiness."

"What noise is that?" suddenly exclaimed the curate ; "I hear a confused murmuring as of many voices. Pray Heaven some calamity may not have happened in the village !"

The noise rapidly increased, and now the hum of many voices came from outside the parsonage. Suddenly the sounds ceased, and then a heavy blow was struck upon the door, which reverberated through the curate's dwelling.

CHAPTER XLIII.

"Oh, then, what joy was her's !
She never thought him guilty,
And her trusting heart
Still clung the fonder in adversity.'—CLARE.

THE ARRIVAL.—HERBERT'S WELCOME.— EXPLANATIONS.—THE RENEWED CHALLENGE.—WAIT TILL TO-MORROW.

OUR readers are aware that it was Leslie's knock at the curate's door, which alarmed the inmates of the parsonage-house. The curate had himself opened the parlour door to anwer the unusually late summons ; but old Andrew had already admitted Leslie, who now stood pale and composed upon the threshold.

"Leslie !" cried the curate.

"Aye, my old friend, you see me back once more."

"And—and——"

"Wherefore, you would ask. I have been assaulted on the highway, and the prisoner desired, as I understand, to be brought hither."

"Is it possible ?"

"It is true."

"Where is the wretched man ?"

"The man is here !" cried Herbert Mandeville ; "but not a wretched man, Mr. Endsleigh."

"Oh ! Herbert, Herbert !" cried the curate, "why will you be your own greatest enemy ? Even now I was about to repair to the village to seek you."

"To seek me ?" said Mandeville.

"Yes. But come in, both of you—come in."

"Pardon me, sir," replied Leslie. "This young man (pointing to Mandeville) is a prisoner."

"Take my word for his safe custody," said the curate ; "and you, Herbert, give me your promise not to leave here without my permission."

There was something in the curate's voice and manner that convinced Mandeville some favourable change had taken place for him since his departure, and he readily replied,—

"I promise all that you require, Mr. Endsleigh."

"Do you consent?" cried the curate to Leslie.

"I do," answered Leslie, rather surprised at the curate's manner towards Mandeville.

"Then, friends, good night," said the pastor to the villagers ; "go to your homes—good night."

The crowd of villagers departed slowly, very much dissatisfied that their curiosity was not further gratified ; and on old Andrew closing the door, the rivals once more found themselves together under the hospitable roof of the curate.

Adeline started when she saw Leslie enter the parlour; but when she caught a glance of the form of Mandeville, the blood rushed to her cheeks, and she sprang forward, exclaiming,—

"Herbert—Herbert!—you are innocent!"

"As Heaven is my judge I am innocent," said Mandeville.

"You are innocent," said the curate. "Circumstances have transpired within the last hour to prove that you were not guilty of the act imputed to you."

Herbert's colour forsook his cheeks, and he clasped his hands in deep thankfulness.

"Is it possible?" he cried. "I—I thought fate had so hemmed me in by unfortunate circumstances of suspicion that escape was impossible."

"Your observation is true," replied the curate; "but there is one thing, Herbert, that I pray you to recollect——"

"What is that, sir?" asked Herbert.

"It is this," said the curate. "You must recollect that the circumstances of which you complain were created by yourself."

Herbert looked down abashed. Then, as he looked up again, his eyes encountered those of Adeline, and a radiant flush come over his countenance.

"Adeline—Adeline," he cried, "you, at least, thought me innocent?"

"I did," said Adeline—"I did Herbert—believe me I did."

"My own Adeline, your heart spoke in my favour."

Charles Leslie now advanced, and, in a voice of emotion, said, addressing himself more particularly to Adeline and the curate,—

"I doubt if any one here present is more rejoiced than I at the change which has taken place in the position of Mr. Mandeville. At the same time I cannot but doubt that by some present I shall not be so implicitly believed as I would wish."

"By me, Charles," said the curate, "you are justly estimated."

"I know it," said Charles.

"And by me, too," cried Adeline. "Believe me, Charles—Mr. Leslie, believe, I honour if——"

"If you cannot love," said Charles Leslie, gloomily.

"In making excuses to you, Mr. Mandeville," said the curate, "permit me to add, that the suspicion against you was so strong, and so built up by your discretion, that a verdict of guilty was a necessary consequence in the minds of all."

"I acknowledge," said Herbert, "to the great indiscretion; but—but—"

"But you are innocent," sobbed Adeline.

"I need not say that under these circumstances I at once abandon all charge against Mr. Mandeville," remarked Charles Leslie.

Herbert glanced at Leslie with a meaning look.

"I should like at the same time," continued Charles, "to be possessed of the exact circumstances which have proved the innocence of Mr. Mandeville."

"That I will soon detail to you," said the curate, "and I beg you all to give me your most serious attention, for it is a tale which proves how much we may be misled by circumstantial evidence, and likewise how very careful all persons should be that they should not associate themselves with the vicious, in case they themselves acquire the taint of vice."

Mr. Endsleigh then briefly related the circumstances connected with the fire at Rose Villa as they had been detailed to him by Mr. Fleming.

Herbert listened with the most rapt attention, and he felt a sensation of pleasure, such as he had never before experienced, at his rescue from a mass of circumstances from which he had but a short hour since seen no probable means of extrication.

"You will stay with us this night, Charles?" said the curate, addressing Leslie.

"No—no." answered Leslie. "Once more I will attempt to leave Brace-field."

"Since you have returned," remarked the curate, "do not go again until the morrow."

"Stay Mr. Leslie," said Mrs. Mourdant; "I wish for your advice and assistance."

"That is sufficient," said Charles. "Until to-morrow, then, Mr. Ends-leigh, permit me to be your guest."

"My ever welcome guest," replied the curate.

"Come, Adeline," said her mother, "the night is wearing on—let us retire, my dear."

Adeline rose to leave the room.

"Good night all," she said, in her usual soft, silvery tone.

But Herbert Mandeville felt satisfied that there was a special "good night" whispered to him from the heart of the fair girl, whose best affections he gloried in the consciousness of possessing.

"Let us have no more discussion now," said Mr. Endsleigh. "We all require rest."

Herbert bowed, and walked to the door. There he lingered for a moment, as if waiting for Leslie to pass out.

Charles saw the hesitation, and bowing to the curate, who did not see it, he left the room.

For a moment he and Mandeville stood confronting each other in silence in the dim light that came from a lamp which was always kept burning at night in the passage.

"We are once more equals," said Herbert. "The shadow of suspicion is removed from my name."

"You are acquitted," said Charles, coldly, "of setting fire to Rose Villa."

"May I, then, now presume upon that acquittal so far," said Herbert, in a sneering tone, "as to suppose that Mr. Charles Leslie will accord to me the satisfaction of a gentleman?"

"For what?" said Charles.

"Numerous insults," replied Herbert. "And if they will not suffice, I must add something on my own part which may stir the sluggish nature of Mr. Charles Leslie."

"Young man," answered Leslie, "I have several times had occasion to warn you not to stir the sluggish nature of one of whom you know so little as you do of me. Once more I say, Herbert Mandeville, beware."

"Will you give me an answer?" cried Herbert.

Charles seemed to reflect a moment, and then he said,—

"I hold duelling as absurd as it is unchristian."

"Will you fight?" reiterated Mandeville.

A hectic flush came across the cheek of Leslie, and he replied, in a low tone,—

"To-morrow."

"Enough," said Mandeville—"to-morrow be it."

"To-morrow," again repeated Leslie, and he ascended the stairs leading to the chamber he usually occupied when he chanced to sleep at the parsonage.

CHAPTER XLIV.

"Sir, you are no gentleman.
Sir, you are no judge." OLD PLAY.

THE MORNING. — THE MEETING OF THE RIVALS. — THE PROPOSAL. — A DIFFI-
CULTY. — THE SUDDEN ARRIVAL OF TWO NEW CHARACTERS. — MANDEVILLE'S
IMPETUOSITY.

SWEETLY the morning shone upon the little village of Bracefield. It was
yet early, and the slanting beams of the god of day were gilding with beauty
the humble roofs of the cottages, when, after a fevered and anxious night,
Charles Leslie arose, and endeavoured by a morning's walk to cool the fever of
his blood.

He took the direction towards the village church, and standing by the
wicket-gate in deep meditation, he mentally ran over the proceedings of the
last few days. Something seemed to whisper him that Adeline could not be
happy with such a man as Herbert Mandeville ; for although in the eyes of
the gentle girl herself his acquittal of the great crime laid to his charge ab-
solved him from all lesser ones, Leslie was too clear-headed to be so carried away by his imagination. He felt that the friend and correspondent of
such men as Captain Dufours was not one calculated to ensure the happiness
of Adeline Mourdant.

He had remained some twenty minutes thus "chewing the cud of sweet
and bitter fancy," when he heard a voice suddenly behind him exclaim,—

"I am glad, sir, you have accepted my invitation."

Charles Leslie started, and turning hastily, he saw Herbert Mandeville
standing close to him.

Charles had quite forgotten what had taken place between himself and
Mandeville when they parted the preceding evening, and he replied, with some
degree of hauteur and coldness,—

"What mean you, sir ? You speak in riddles."

"In riddles ?" sneered Mandeville. "Has the fit of valour gone off ?"

"If you have followed me here to insult me," said Leslie, his face slightly
flushing as he spoke, "you will find that I have both power and will to resent it."

" 'Tis you have insulted me," said Herbert.

"How ?"

"Methinks the events of last night cannot have escaped your memory."

"I apprehended you for an assault on the highway, and you are indebted to
my clemency for not pressing the charge."

"Your clemency ?"

"Aye," repeated Charles Leslie. "My clemency !"

"Now this passes all patience," said Mandeville. "Will you fight, sir ?"

"My answer to that question," replied Leslie, "must be borrowed from the
occasion."

"You are a coward !"

Charles Leslie smiled.

"You are no gentleman, sir."

"You are no judge," replied Charles, calmly.

"Will nothing goad you ?"

"Do not tempt me too far. You have already felt what I can do."

"Indeed !"

"Aye, indeed. Do not, I say, tempt me again to lay hands upon you! Beware, Herbert Mandeville, beware!"

"The curate tells me," said Herbert, "that your father was a soldier."

"He was," said Leslie, reddening as he spoke.

"I demand satisfaction of you, according to the usuages of gentlemen."

For a moment Charles Leslie was silent; then some powerful feeling seemed to cross his mind, and he said in a low tone :—

"You shall have it."

"'Tis well," answered Mandeville. "I have pistols with me: you shall take your choice."

"You demand of me," said Leslie, "satisfaction, according to the usages of gentlemen. Surely you cannot be so ignorant of those usages, as to suppose for moment that I would, without witnesses, engage in such a conflict?"

"Oh, that is easily arranged," said Herbert. "I will to the village and procure some one to second me, and you can do the same."

"I beg you will give yourselves no such trouble, gentlemen," said a person at this moment emerging from behind a monument, just within the verge of the churchyard.

Both Leslie and Mandeville stared in amazement at the stranger. He was a young man of faded fashionable appearance. He wore moustachoes; and altogether there was an air of recklessness about his appearance which Charles Leslie held in contempt, but which was rather admired than otherwise by Herbert.

"Who are you?" said Mandeville.

"A jolly dog," replied the stranger. "A friend to the distressed who want seconds, and a particular acquaintance of Cornelius Beercroft, Esq."

"And, pray, sir," said Charles, "who is Cornelius Beercroft, Esq?"

"Your humble servant," replied the stranger.

"That he may be," said Leslie. "But I ask who is he?"

"I myself, of course. None but myself can be my parrallel."

Mandeville looked at Cornelius Beercroft, Esq. with a puzzled expression, and Leslie was silent.

"You want seconds, gentlemen," said the stranger. "You shall not be baulked. Only tell me what is the subject of the little disagreement; I don't want the particulars, only the subject matter."

"You are a stranger, sir," said Leslie, "and I am not in the habit of answering questions."

"Exactly," said Cornelius Beercroft, Esq. "Just answer me one question."

"What is it?"

"Is your quarrel about a petticoat?"

"A what?"

"A petticoat."

"It is," answered Mandeville, with a smile.

"Then I'm your man," cried Cornelius Beercroft, Esq. "You want seconds. Here I am."

"You talk of yourself in the plural number," remarked Herbert Mandeville.

"Certainly," said Cornelius. "My Pylades is at hand. Halloo! halloo!"

"Who do you call?" asked Herbert.

"My very particular friend, Lieutenant Smallacre. Halloo! Smallacre! Smallacre!"

An individual was now observed approaching through the churchyard, making his way carefully among the grave-stones. He soon reached the wicket-gate, and presented to the eyes of Leslie and Mandeville a stout square-built man, apparently about forty years of age; his aspect was unprepossessing in the extreme. He wore a black patch over one eye, and altogether there was a bull-dog-looking ferocity about the man which was exceedingly disagreeable to Charles Leslie.

"Gentlemen," said Mr. Cornelius Beercroft, Esq., "allow me to introduce to your kind notice my esteemed friend and chum, Lieutenant Smallacre."

The problematical lieutenant growled out something unintelligibly, which Cornelius translated, by exclaiming :—

"The lieutenant says he is proud and happy."

"You may, or you may not be what you represent yourselves," said Leslie, "but ——"

"Ha ! what ?" cried the lieutenant interrupting him ; "are we doubted ?"

"Yes," answered Leslie.

"Cornelius," cried the lieutenant, "shall we put up with this ? Death and the devil !"

"'Pon my soul, it's too bad," said Cornelius Beercroft, Esq.

"You may do as you please about putting up with it," continued Charles Leslie, "but I decline accepting either of you as a second."

"An insult, by Jove !" cried the lieutenant.

"Oh, certainly," said Cornelius.

"Shall I elongate his proboscis, my dear Cornelius, or what ?"

"Oh, I'm not particular," said Cornelius.

"You can say what you please," said Charles, "for I mind it no more than the yelping of a strange cur."

"Cur !" cried the lieutenant.

"Yes, cur," repeated Leslie. "But do not come within reach of my arm."

"There are three of us," said the lieutenant, glancing at Mandeville, as if he expected him to join in an attack upon Leslie.

"No," cried Herbert "there are two to two."

"Eh ?—What ?" said the lieutenant.

"You are evidently a great scoundrel."

"Death and the devil !" cried the lieutenant.

"Very true," remarked Cornelius Beercroft, Esq. "That will be in the natural order of events ; death and the devil ! Uncommonly true, Smallacre."

"Herbert Mandeville," said Charles ; "hear me for once and for all ; I will not fight a duel with you."

"You will not ?"

"I will not."

"Then you must take the consequences."

"I defy the consequences."

"He defies the consequences !" cried the lieutenant.

"Yes ; very good," remarked Cornelius Beercroft, Esq.

"Lend me that switch you have in your hand," said Herbert to the lieutenant.

"You are welcome. Take it."

Herbert Mandeville took the small cane which was handed to him, and approached Charles Leslie in a threatening manner.

CHAPTER XLV.

THE CONFLICT.—MANDEVILLE'S DEFEAT.—CHARLES LESLIE'S CONDUCT TO LIEU-
TENANT SMALLACRE.—THE ROBBERY.—CONSOLATION.—THE CURATE AND
THE OLD SERVANT.

> "There are many kicks and cuffs in the world,
> And he is a wise man who gets the best paid."
>
> ANON.

"HOLD!" cried Leslie, as Mandeville was advancing towards him, evidently with an hostile intention. "Pause, Herbert Mandeville, if not for your own sake, for the sake of her whom you affect to love."

Herbert, however, was blinded by passion, and he said,—

"No consideration on earth shall stay me. These persons, be they who they may, shall see that I can and will chastise meddling insolence."

"The consequences, then, be upon your own head," said Charles.

"Capital sport," remarked Cornelius Beercroft.

"Go it, gentlemen," said the lieutenant.

Herbert still advanced.

"Beware!" said Leslie.

"Beware thyself!" cried Herbert.

He raised the lieutenant's switch as he spoke; Charles Leslie made one step in advance, and seizing Herbert's light form in his powerful grasp, he lifted him fairly off the ground for a moment. That moment Herbert was in eminent danger; but Charles Leslie's better feelings overcome his passion, and he contented himself by snatching the switch from Herbert's hand, and giving him a fall upon the grass. The consequences of the fall, however, were more serious than Leslie wished; for Mandeville's head coming in contact with a stone, he was for a few minutes stunned, and lay motionless at his conqueror's feet.

"Sir," said Leslie, turning to Lieutenant Smallacre, "a man of your age and probable experience, ought to know that it is dangerous to lend a weapon."

"Well, sir?" blustered the lieutenant. "Death and the devil, sir! what do you mean?"

"You are in for it, Smallacre," remarked his friend.

"Your switch has not been used," continued Charles; "and before I return it to you, I am anxious to make trial of its merits."

So saying, to the utter surprise of the lieutenant, Leslie grasped him with one hand by the collar, while, with the switch in the other, he raised a cloud of dust from his back.

"Death and the devil!" roared the lieutenant.

"Fine sport! capital sport!" said Cornelius Beercroft, Esq., quite calmly.

Leslie, after bestowing some score of blows upon the writhing lieutenant, snapped the switch in two, threw the pieces in his face, and walked slowly towards the parsonage, without even looking behind him.

For a few moments after Charles Leslie's departure the discomfited Small-acre looked with a rueful countenance at his friend Cornelius.

"Curse that fellow," he said; "who'd a thought he'd have come out in such style."

"Oh, you are used to it," sneered Mr. Beercroft.

"Am I?" replied Smallacre. "I shall know my man again, he may depend."

"Well, I've nothing to do with it," remarked his friend. "You must

arrange your own little private affairs, but that must not interfere with our business. Come away ; we have no time to lose."

"And what's to become of this cove ?" said the lieutenant, indicating the insensible Mandeville with the point of his toe.

"Pho ! pho !" said the other ; "there is no harm done there. Come on, come on."

Lieutenant Smallacre followed his companion through the wicket-gate into the churchyard.

They had not, however, proceeded far, when the lieutenant paused, and striking his breast, said :—

"No, d— it, I can't leave him."

"Leave who, you infernal humbug ?"

"That young fellow. I'll just run back and prop up his head."

"You infernal, cursed liar !" remarked Cornelius Beercroft ; "you want to rob him. Well, it's no business of mine, only don't stick a knife in him, or anything of that sort—it's foolish."

"Ah," cried Smallacre, "you have no feeling—none at all, and you don't believe anybody else has any."

So saying he walked quickly back to where Herbert was lying.

"There you are, my young bantum," he exclaimed. "We'll see if you are worth plucking."

The conscientious lieutenant then secured Mandeville's purse and watch, consoling himself at the same time with the remark that they paid him indifferently well for the bruises he had received through lending his switch.

"Death and the devil !" he muttered ; "I'd lend it once a day on the same terms. Let me see, a gold watch and chain, two seals, a key, and a split ring, twelve sovereigns, eight shillings, and sixpence. Death and the devil ! that's not so bad."

No. 22

Smallacre made all speed now to join his companion, and without further remark or adventure of consequence to aid our story, they proceeded on their way.

Charles Leslie's heart smote him when he got half way to the parsonage for leaving Herbert Mandeville insensible, and at the mercy of two such suspicious characters as Cornelius Beercroft, Esq. and his friend.

" Yet, why should I return," he thought. " If he be recovered, I shall be subjected to fresh insults, and if he still remain insensible, I had better proceed on to the curate's, and send him more ample assistance than I can give him."

Acting upon this detertmination, Leslie quickened his speed, and soon arrived at the parsonage. He was fortunate enough to meet Mr. Endsleigh upon the very threshold of the house.

The curate saw by Charles's countenance that something had occurred to distress him.

" Charles," he said, " you have some bad news to tell me !"

" I hope not very bad," answered Leslie. " But Herbert Mandeville pursued me some half hour since ——"

" Alas! alas!" cried the curate ; "he will be his own utter destruction."

" He was resolved to quarrel with me," continued Charles, " and after in vain trying to taunt me into fighting a duel with him, which I steadily refused, he was imprudent enough to attack me."

The curate sighed.

" In self-defence," resumed Leslie, " I was compelled to use what strength I am possessed of—and I fear he is hurt."

" Hurt !"

" Yes ; but not seriously."

" Good Heavens, Charles!—you—you ——"

" What, my good friend ?"

" You are sure ——"

" Sure of what ?"

" You have not killed the boy ?"

" God forbid ! I but threw him gently upon the grass."

" But where is he ?"

" He was lying where I laid him when I came away. I will accompany you and Andrew to the spot, if you please. He cannot be hurt."

" We will go directly," cried Mr. Endsleigh. " Alas! alas! what trouble is coming upon me in my old age? Here, Andrew! Andrew !"

The old man soon made his appearance.

" Come with us," cried the curate. " Quick, Andrew, quick !"

Mr. Endsleigh then took Charles's arm, and the two, closely followed by the astonished Andrew, left the parsonage and hastened towards the spot of the recent encounter between Leslie and Mandeville."

" Well, I'm sure," cried Mrs. Plumpjoy as she saw them from the window of the breakfast-room hurrying from the house. " What now, I wonder ? Here we shall have the breakfast spoiled. Well, I never. Next comes a horse to be shaved, and a pig to have its corns cut. Why, they are running, I declare. It beats chimney-sweeping, it does, indeed."

CHAPTER XLV.

"Parting is such sweet sorrow."—SHAKSPERE.

"The heart that loved me is away,
And I am desolate."—ANON.

MANDEVILLE RECOVERED.—LESLIE'S DETERMINATION.—THE GALLANT STEED.
—AN UNEXPECTED MEETING.—FAREWELL.—ADELINE'S HEART.—INDECISION.
—HE IS GONE.

THE curate and Leslie walked rapidly, so they were not long in arriving at the spot of the encounter.

Leslie paused, for, as he neared the wicket-gate, he saw Mandeville standing in the pathway.

"He has recovered, Mr. Endsleigh," he said. "I do not wish to provoke further quarrel. Allow me here to bid you farewell."

"You will not leave us so suddenly, Charles?" remarked the curate.

"Believe me, it is better that I should. My presence will be a constant source of discord."

"You may be right."

"I feel that I am. Farewell!—It may be long before we meet again."

"If it be very long, Charles, we shall not meet again in this world at all. I am an old man."

"And yet may wear out many a young one," said Leslie.

"As Heaven wills it,—as Heaven wills it, Charles," replied the curate.

"Farewell then, sir! My best friend, farewell!"

"Farewell, Charles."

The curate pressed his young friend's hand, and Leslie then hurried back to the parsonage, in order to procure his horse and make another effort to leave Bracefield. He walked to the back of the house, and, entering the stable, himself saddled his faithful steed, and led him out into the lane, which has been already mentioned as leading to the high road.

He was arranging some of the head-gear of the animal, when a hand was laid upon his shoulder. He turned sharply round, and beheld Adeline.

For two or three seconds neither spoke. Then Adeline said, in a low voice,—

"Charles!—I—I mean, Mr, Leslie. You are going?"

"I am," answered Charles.

"But not for—for long?"

"Perhaps, Adeline, for ever."

"For ever?"

"Aye, for ever."

Adeline was silent for a few moments, then she said,—

"You are still my friend?"

"If you will permit me to return the title, Adeline, I will gladly call myself such."

Adeline held out her hand, and Charles clasped it in his with deep emotion.

"May you be happy," he said.

"And—and —"

"And what, Adeline?"

"Should I not ——"

"Should a cloud ever cross your heart, Adeline, that can be dissipated by a devoted friend, then send for me. Let me be where I may, a summons from you shall be attended to."

"Thank you, Mr. Leslie.   Thank you."

Charles Leslie felt that the interview was distressing to both, and he wished to terminate it.

"Once more farewell!" he cried ; and, throwing the horse's rein over his arm, he led the animal slowly away from Adeline.

The beautiful girl still stood by the hedge-side silent and irresolute. Charles looked back once, and he saw that her eyes were filled with tears.

"I must be firm," he thought.

He sprang upon his horse.

"Charles," said Adeline, in a low tone.

Leslie heard her, but he dared not again look back.   He moved his hand, as he said,—

"Farewell !—Farewell !"

Then, giving his horse the rein, he galloped from he spot with a heavy heart.

Adeline walked slowly back to the house, and it is doubtful if, at that moment, Charles Leslie did not occupy a greater share of her thoughts than Herbert Mandeville.

All other considerations were, however, absorbed in the sight that presented itself to her in the curate's parlour.   Herbert Mandeville was there, pale and sickly-looking, and Mrs. Plumpjoy was administering a cordial of her own manufacture.

"What has happened?" cried Adeline, clasping her hands in dismay.

"Do not be alarmed, Adeline," said Herbert, faintly.   "'Tis nothng—nothing, I assure you."

"Nothing, indeed !" cried Mrs. Plumpjoy.   "I've no patience with young men now-a-days : they go fighting always.   Now, the poor dear major never did anything of the kind ; and, when a passionate and most disagreeable man trod on his toes quite on purpose, at the county ball, he whispered to me that he thought it a most rude thing, but he wouldn't notice it on account of my delicate nerves.   Now that was consideration !"

During this speech from the volatile Mrs. Plumpjoy, Adeline was gazing, full of apprehension, into the pale face of Herbert, and vainly conjecturing what had happened to him.

"Who has been fighting?" she said.   "Ah ! Herbert, surely ——"

"Surely what, Adeline?" said Mandeville, not a little pleased to see the interest he created.

"Leslie and you have not ——"

"Been fighting?   Why, to tell the truth, we had a little *fracas.*   In an accidental fall, I struck my head, it seems, against a stone.   The blow produced insensibility, and the high-minded Charles Leslie left me."

"Left you?"

"Yes ; and some person or persons have robbed me likewise."

"Robbed you, Herbert?"

"Yes, Adeline.   I can guess who the depredators were ; but just at present I am more anxious to ——"

Herbert paused, and Adeline said,—

"Leslie is gone, if you mean that you would renew these quarrels."

"Gone?" cried Herbert, starting up.

"Yes ; and, by so doing," said Mr. Eudsleigh, "he has shown his judgment."

"And his discretion," said Mandeville.   "That discretion which, in the opinion of some, is the better part of valour."

"I may likewise add," said the curate, mildly, "that he has shown his forbearance to a beaten foe."

Herbert bit his lip at this retort ; but he controlled his feelings, for he was far from wishing to create a rupture with Mr. Eudsleigh.

An awkward pause ensued, which was interrupted by Mrs. Plumpjoy exclaiming,—

" Well, I'm sure you had better go to bed at once, Mr. Mandeville ; and the only thing that surprises me, is about your having been robbed, for this is considered a very honest place indeed."

" I should know the men again," said Herbert.

At this moment old Andrew put his head in at the door, and looked doubtful whether to come quite in or not.

" What is it, Andrew ?" said Mr. Endsleigh.

" A letter, sir."

" For me ?"

" No, sir."

" 'Tis for me, then," said Mandeville.

" No, sir, it's for Miss Adeline."

" For me ?" cried Adeline. " I have no correspondents."

" It's for you, Miss."

" My mother, most probably."

" No, Miss. Here it is. A man looked over the garden-rail, and, says he, ' Halloo !—do you live here ?' 'Yes,' says I. ' Give Miss Mourdant that letter, then,' says he, and he threw it over the rails, and then made off himself very quick."

Adeline took the letter in her hand. It was addressed to her. With a trembling hand she unsealed it, and a deathly paleness came over her, as she read its brief contents.

" Adeline !" cried Herbert. " What ——"

" You are ill, Adeline," said the curate.

" Well, I never !" cried Mrs. Plumpjoy.

" No—no," gasped Adeline. " 'Tis nothing—nothing—a—a little faintness merely."

" That letter distresses you ?" said Mandeville.

" No—no," answered Adeline ; " that is, I —"

She crushed the letter up in her hand, and rose to quit the apartment. She tottered to the door, and, without another word, passed from the room, leaving Herbert and the curate in the greatest astonishment and alarm at her singular emotion.

CHAPTER XLVI.

" Secrets are the graces of love."—SHENSTONE.

" Suspicion is the grave of love."—RALEIGH.

THE MYSTERIOUS COMMUNICATION.—ADELINE'S EMOTION.—SILENT COUNSEL.—
THE CURATE'S STUDY.—HERBERT'S ANXIETY.—THE SECRET.

ADELINE did not seek her mother. She wished to take secret counsel of her own heart ; and, pushing open the door of the curate's study, she entered it, and sat down in his chair to think alone.

For a time the young and guileless girl sat silent. Then her heart found relief in tears ; after which, feeling more composed, she re-read the letter, which ran thus,—

" ADELINE,—I must have money. When I say I must, you know I mean it ; so no excuses. Meet me this evening, with all the cash you can muster, at the wicket-gate, by the burying-ground. This comes from you know who. *GEORGE."

" P.S.—I shall expect you at eight."

"Alas!—alas!" cried Adeline. "What can I do? Where fly for counsel? It would break my mother's heart to know what has lain heavy at mine own for some weeks past. Why should I be thus tortured? Yet I must meet him."

A knock sounded on the door of the study ; and Adeline, starting suddenly, placed the mysterious note in her bosom, and said, in a trembling voice,—

"Come in."

The door opened, and Herbert Mandeville stood in the entrance.

"Herbert!" exclaimed Adeline, starting.

"Adeline!" was Herbert's exclamation, for it was the curate he had expected to find.

"Oh! Herbert," said the confiding girl. "You require rest : you were much hurt."

"My bodily hurt, dearest Adeline," replied Mandeville, "has turned out trifling, and of no importance whatever ; but—but ——"

"But what ?"

"I have a mental source of disquietude."

"You have, Herbert ?"

"I have, Adeline."

"Confide it, then, to me."

"I will do so. I rejoice at this opportunity to seek an explanation which at the same time I scarcely know how to ask."

"Speak freely, Herbert."

"Between those whose hearts are united there should occur nothing which, by any means, could be construed into a want of that full trusting confidence which must ever form the greatest charm of mutual affection."

"Yes, Herbert,—oh! yes," said Adeline, for the moment totally forgetful of her own situation.

"Then you will ease even the momentary pang that shot across my heart, Adeline, when I first saw your deep emotion."

Adeline turned very pale, and sunk into a seat.

"My emotion, Herbert ?" she said. "When ——"

"When you received a letter some short time since."

"The letter?—the fatal letter?" said Adeline, with a deep-drawn sigh.

"A fatal letter?" cried Herbert.

"Fatal, I fear, to the peace even of the innocent. Oh! Herbert, ask me nothing."

"Ask nothing, Adeline ?"

"Nothing, Herbert—nothing! Trust freely, but ask, in this case, no explanation."

"You have, then, a secret, Adeline ?" said Mandeville, in rather a tone of pique.

"I have," answered Adeline.

"Which may not even be confided to me ?"

Adeline shook her head and sighed.

"Oh! Adeline," cried Mandeville, passionately. "Secrets are the graces of love."

"Then love must die," answered Adeline. "I have likewise heard that suspicion is the grave of love."

Mandeville felt for the moment rebuked ; but his vanity was terribly wounded at not receiving the unlimited confidence of Adeline.

She was silent, and Herbert felt completely at a loss what to say next.

Adeline looked in his face, and, while a smile struggled with the tears that stood in her eyes, she said in her own dear gentle voice,—

"You will trust me, Herbert ?"

To this Mandeville could not make a harsh reply, and he said,—

"Trust you Adeline? Can I do otherwise? I certainly hoped that—that ——"

"That what, Herbert?"

"Oh! no matter. Let us talk of something. There may come a time when you will tell me all about your secrets."

"Alas! Herbert, I have but this one; and, Heaven knows how cruelly it has forced itself upon me."

"Cruelly, Adeline?"

"Yes; it is enough to break my heart."

"Indeed!"

"Yes—yes, Herbert. It is a cruel persecution."

"A persecution?"

"A most cruel one."

"Then, Adeline, give me the right to end. Can you imagine for a moment that I would suffer the mightiest on earth to persecute you? Oh! Adeline, dearest Adeline, you should have said less, or you should now say more. You have given a theme of disquietude, which you cannot blame me for pressing you to remove. Do not leave my mind to form vague conjectures alike unworthy of us both."

"Unworthy? That is impossible, Herbert!"

Mandeville felt that he had gone a little too far.

"I meant not that, Adeline, he said; "but my anxiety will now be so great, until I am aware of the secret, that I shall, I am convinced, know no peace."

"I cannot tell it," answered Adeline. "It involves a life—perhaps more than one."

"Is it possible?"

"Alas!—it is true!"

"And you, so young, Adeline—so innocent, so guileless, to be involved in a mystery of life and death!"

"Even so, Herbert. You see I have cause to ask you to trust me—and you will."

"I must, Adeline."

"No," answered Adeline, with a slight flush of wounded feeling, "there is no compulsion. Say that you do not implicitly —"

"Adeline!—Adeline!" interrupted Herbert, "say no more. My vexation at your distress spake, and not my heart: I know you to be all purity, all goodness. Adeline, I trust you as I trust Heaven."

Once more a smile irradiated the countenance of the beautiful girl, and she extended her hand to Herbert, who pressed it to his lips.

Mandeville was beginning to have a new insight into the character of Adeline Mourdant. He began to suspect that beneath the charming innocence of manner which so won upon all hearts, there was likewise a strength of character, and a firmness of disposition, that he would do well not to arouse.

"These things," said Herbert, alluding to the recent little misunderstanding, if it could be called such, "are but fleeting clouds in the fair summer-sky of young love, dearest Adeline—a breath creates them."

"And they vanish," said Adeline, with a sigh.

"They do, dearest, and the sigh, I hope, vanishes with them."

"The time will not be long," said Adeline, with a touch of melancholy in her voice, "when the only subject which should call forth a sigh will have passed away."

"I rejoice to hear you say so, Adeline. And now, dearest, let me make an appointment with you. Suppose this evening, at sunset, we take a delicious stroll by the ruins of the old Villa, which has cost me so many sighs, and yet bestowed upon me so much happiness."

"At sunset?"

"Yes, dearest. I always think the hour after sunset is the most delightful of all: it is acknowledged as the fittest for lovers' converse. Do you not recollect the lines,—

> "'When the sun's last ray is streaming
> In a flood of golden light,
> And the first dim star is gleaming
> Before the coming night.
> Then, by every dearest token,
> Should young love's first words be spoken.'"

Adeline replied faintly,—

"Herbert!—I—I—"

"What would you say, Adeline? You hesitate."

"Let it be to-morrow."

"Ah!—why not to-night?—or, rather, that sweet hour between the day and night, when —"

"Urge me no more, Herbert. I cannot come to-night."

"To-morrow? Let it be to-morrow."

CHAPTER XLVII.

> " The Heavens darkened,
> And the sighing wind,
> Betokened a fierce contest
> Of those wild elements of nature.
> The wind, the sky, and the electric blaze."
>
> DARWIN.

THE COUNTRY WALK.—REFLECTIONS.— THE STORM.—A STRANGE SHELTER.— HURRAH FOR BRACEFIELD.—NIGHT IS COMING, AND FOUR MILES TO GO!

HERBERT MANDEVILLE was far from satisfied with his morning's interview with Adeline. He had failed in two objects, and those the only two that he attempted to succeed in. He was not told the cause of Adeline's emotion upon receipt of the letter, and, for some inexplicable reason, she refused accompanying him for an evening walk, upon which he had quite set his mind.

Our readers are sufficiently acquainted with the character of Herbert Mandeville to form a tolerably correct notion of what would be his state of mind under such circumstances.

The whole of the day he was fretful and uneasy. He could not read—he could not study; nay, he could scarcely make himself tolerable company to the inhabitants of the parsonage.

He saw but little of Adeline, and he had not another opportunity of speaking to her alone; in fact, for a successful lover, Herbert Mandeville found his situation as uncomfortable as possible.

Adeline's mind was evidently very much occupied with something, and Herbert guessed that that something was the provoking secret which she so firmly persisted in not confiding to him.

The curate evidently avoided Herbert, and when the latter made an effort after dinner to engage him in conversation concerning Adeline, he said, in his plain, straightforward manner,—

"Mr. Mandeville, until I hear from your father I would rather decline saying anything further upon this matter."

Mrs. Mourdant kept her chamber the whole day, and Mrs. Plumpjoy was

the only one who seemed disposed to enter into fluent conversation with Herbert, and she favoured him with a minute account of the whole progress of Major Plumpjoy's courtship, including a full and particular account of the county ball at which he was first smitten with her maiden charms, and which ultimately led to the union of their congenial hearts.

To all this Herbert occasionally replied—" Yes—indeed—dear me—of course—and such like phrases, which were quite sufficient for Mrs. Plumpjoy.

The evening at length came. The long shadows proclaimed that the sun was near its sinking, and the incessant singing of the birds in the trees fronting the parsonage sufficiently assured the lover of nature that the day was at its close.

"She will not walk out with me," said Mandeville to himself, " so I must e'en stroll by myself, and endeavour to rid myself of the disagreeable feelings that have been oppressing me all day."

He accordingly sallied forth, and walked at a brisk pace through the village, and some mile or two on the London road.

Mandeville's mind had been so much occupied with Adeline all the day, that he had scarcely bestowed a thought upon his adventure of the morning. He had been told of Charles Leslie's departure, and notwithstanding Herbert was constitutionally brave, he felt a secret satisfaction at the absence of a man with whom he evidently stood no chance in a personal encounter, and who obstinately persisted in not using those weapons which place the dwarf upon an equality with the giant.

Now, however, Herbert's thoughts reverted to the morning's disagreeable adventure—disagreeable in every respect, for he had not only been worsted by Charles Leslie, but robbed likewise by, he doubted not, the two amiable

No. 23.

gentlemen who had so kindly volunteered to act as seconds in the projected duel.

Who and what those men could be, and upon what enterprise they had come to the quiet village of Bracefield, he could not conjecture.

We are sorry to say that Herbert Mandeville had seen enough of a peculiar kind of London society, to be perfectly sure that Cornelius Beercroft, Esq., and the lieutenant, his friend, belonged to a very questionable, but not at all equivocal class. That they were gentlemen who made their wits stand in the place of settled incomes he had not the smallest doubt, and he felt quite certain that some object of moment to them could only be their inducement to visit so retired a village as Bracefield.

So intent was Herbert Mandeville in pursuing this subject in his mind, that he extended his walk much further than he had intended, and it was only the rapidly darkening landscape that warned him to turn back towards Bracefield.

As he did so, a large drop of rain fell upon his face, and looking up to the sky, he observed that the clouds were gathering portentously, and that there was every indication of a coming storm.

Long streaks of lurid light appeared in the horizon, and the wind swept by him with that low moaning sound which is generally indicative of an approaching strife with the elements.

"I am, at least, four miles from Bracefield," thought Herbert.

He quickened his pace as he spoke, and although the dust blew in dense masses in his face, he made great speed towards the village.

Dull, heavy splashes of rain now began to fall at intervals, and a low muttering of distant thunder came upon his ears.

"A storm is evidently approaching, and there is no shelter between here and Bracefield," said Herbert. "I had better have gone on further, for there is an inn some mile or so in advance."

For a moment he stood irresolute whether to persevere in returning to the village, or continue on the road till he came to the inn. He, however, determined upon the former course, and pressing his hat firmly on his head, he again started for Bracefield with a hasty step.

Another peal of thunder now smote his ears, and it was evident that the storm, although yet some miles distant, was rapidly approaching that part of the country.

Blinding masses of dust obstructed his progress for a time, but the heavy rain drops, which came dashing from the black clouds over head at intervals, soon dissipated that evil, and Mandeville urged his way onward for above a mile, rather amused than annoyed at being caught in the storm.

Suddenly, however, and without the smallest previous indication, there came down a shower of hail of such thickness, and the hail-stones of such unusual size, that Herbert was for a moment completely staggered by its violence.

The hail-stones struck him severely in the face and on the hands, and he looked about him for some time through the blinding shower in vain for some temporary shelter.

There were some trees a few furlongs in advance of him, and to these Herbert ran as fast as he could, and in a few moments gained this shelter—a shelter, however from which he was glad quickly to emerge again, for the hail-stones broke off so many small branches from the trees in their descent, that he found himself more assaulted and incommoded than before. Moreover, Herbert Mandeville had all a Londoner's horror of insects, and so many of the spider tribe were stricken from the trees, that he found himself in much too close connection with the "long-legged spinners."

Brushing these unwelcome guests from his person, as best he might in the hurry of the moment, Herbert left the deceptive shelter of the trees, and preferred encountering the worst fury of the storm upon the open road, which now wound through a sandy common.

He found that the worst of the hail-storm was past, for although hail still fell in abundance, the frozen pieces were not so large, and a considerable admixture of rain fell with them.

Wet and miserable Herbert Mandeville set his teeth against the wind, and pushed on towards Bracefield.

CHAPTER XLVIII.

" It cannot be that she is guilty,
So fair—so innocent—so beautiful;
Ah, no; I will not—cannot think
Her aught but a pure model of
High virtue."   ANON.

THE STORM CONTINUES.—THE RUINS.—A SHELTER.—A SURPRISE—THE CONSEQUENCES.—MYSTERY AND UNHAPPINESS—THE TRUST.

THE evening was now rapidly advancing, and huge masses of black clouds were rolling up from the east as Herbert Mandeville came in sight of the spire of the little church at Bracefield.

Although the fury of the storm had somewhat abated, the rain still fell in abundance, and the wind had settled down into a steady gale, which promised to be of some duration.

The ruins of the burnt villa lay directly in Mandeville's way, and he paused a moment as he arrived by the blackened walls, irresolute whether to take shelter there or not from the fury of the storm.

" I am wet through as it is," he thought, " and I had better continue in action until I can rid myself of these uncomfortable, clinging garments."

The nearest way to the parsonage was to cross the garden of Rose Villa—and, in fact, now there was a thoroughfare quite through the house, for some of the walls that were considered dangerous had been pulled down, and little remained of the once pretty suburban village but the lower story or ground floor, which was not very greatly injured by the fire.

Herbert entered by the front door, and rapidly took his way along the passage, intending to emerge into the back garden, and so cross the fields to the parsonage.

As he was passing the door of the back parlour, however, his steps were arrested by hearing the sound of voices within the room.

Herbert paused in surprise, for he little expected to find any one in the ruins of Rose Villa. His second thought, however, was that some of the villagers had been surprised by the hail-storm, and sought the tempory shelter of the ruins, and he was about to pass into the parlour, when a voice struck his ear that at once transfixed him with astonishment and passion. It was the voice of Adeline Mourdant, and the words fell like molten lead upon the brain of Mandeville. They were these :—

"Dear George, spare me—I cannot—Indeed, I dare not. You know I have always loved you. Oh, spare me !"

Some reply was made in a man's voice, but Herbert could not understand its purport. He was so overcome by a variety of conflicting emotions, that he ruins of Rose Villa seemed to swim round him like the hideous phantasma of some frightful dream. He leaned upon the blackened wall for support, and it was some minutes before his senses returned to him sufficiently for him to comprehend what followed.

His first impulse was to rush into the room ; but he controlled that feeling, and with a quickened pulse, and a brain full of excitement, he stood still as a marble statue to hear what next would be said.

"I tell you, Adeline, I must," said a man's voice.

"Oh, George— George !" said Adeline, in a tone of much grief.

"Come, now," replied the man—"come, come—don't put yourself out of the way about it ; get me, by hook or by crook, fifty pounds, and I'm off to America."

"America ?"

"Aye, America," replied the man. "You know that's the place for me. England has grown too hot for George ———"

"Oh, hush ! hush !" cried Adeline. "Breathe not the name even here."

"Well, I don't want to—to disgrace you, I suppose is the word."

Adeline sighed deeply.

"You know, George," she said—"you must know———"

"Oh, never mind what I know," was the reply. "Don't let's have any snivelling. Can you by any means get me the money ?"

"Alas ! it is impossible."

"Nonsense—nonsense. It can be raised, you know as well as I."

"Raised !—how ?"

"Why, on the pension, to be sure."

"But———"

"No buts for me. You must set about it. Tell the old lady to draw bills on the army agent. I'll get cash for them."

"Oh, George—George, you know not what you say."

"Yes I do, Adeline. I'll be off, I tell you—off to America. But I can't fly there."

"I cannot help you," said Adeline.

"Then beware !"

"Oh, mercy—mercy !"

"Mercy be hanged. I must have money, I say. Now I tell you what, Adeline, if I don't have it, I'll spoil your sport."

"My sport !—what mean you ?"

"Why, there's a young fellow here, I understand, who would marry you."

Adeline was silent.

"Oh, I know all about it," continued the man. "Now, you know, a word from me———"

"Oh, horror ! horror !" said Adeline.

"Oh, that's horror, is it ? The money, then."

"You may destroy my happiness, George—you may take my life—but I cannot do as you require."

"Then I'll just see this young Mandeville, I think they told me his name was, and tell him that his beautiful Adeline Mourdant is———"

"Hush ! hush !" cried Adeline.

"But I won't hush. I'll seek him out."

"No—no—no."

"Yes—yes—yes, I say."

"What can I do ?"

"A great deal. Get me the money."

"George," said Adeline, "you can do as you please ; I will not be the means of persuading my poor mother to part with her only means of sub-sistence. I will not, I repeat."

"You will not ?"

"I will not."

"Then—yet, stay ; I'll give you another kick."

"A what ?"

"A chance, I mean."

"What chance ?"

"Why, this young man,—this Mandeville is rich, I hear, is he not ?

"Well ?"

"Well, then, get it of him."

"Get what of him ?"

"Why, the money, to be sure."

"Money ?"

"Yes, money. The circulating medium,—tin—blunt."

"I ask money of Herbert Mandeville !"

"Yes, to be sure. He's rich, and in love. Come, you will get off easy now. Ask him for fifty pounds, Adeline."

Adeline was silent for a few moments, then she said, in a firm tone,—

"Farewell for ever."

"Oh, dear, no—you must promise."

"George, would you distract me ?"

"Money !"

"Would you drive me mad ?"

"Money !" repeated the man.

"Unhand me. I—I must—I will go."

"Money !"

"I will cry for help."

"You dare not."

"'Tis too true !" said Adeline, bursting into tears.

"Now, hear me," cried the man, raising his voice. "By ——"

"Villain !" cried Herbert Mandeville, in a voice that rung the blackened ruins. In another instant he was by the side of Adeline.

"Damnation !" cried the man.

Adeline, with a scream, fell insensible on the arm of Herbert Mandeville.

CHAPTER XLIX.

"Who is this man ?
Ask me not.
He has power
Over me, yes—oh, such power." BEAUMONT.

INSENSIBILITY.—THE CONVERSATION OF THE LOVERS.—THE SUM OF MONEY.—
THE PROMISE.—HERBERT'S TRIUMPH AND DISAPPOINTMENT.—THE RETURN.

HERBERT was too much alarmed by the condition of Adeline to attend for a few minutes to any other consideration. He called her frantically by her name, and in vain looked around him for some means of recovering her from her death-like swoon.

"Adeline ! Adeline !" he cried, "look up ; oh, smile again. Tell me that you live, and all is well. Speak to me, Adeline !—oh, speak !"

Adeline, with a deep sigh unclosed her eyes, and fixed them upon Herbert with an expression of unutterable sorrow and distress.

"You are better ?" said Mandeville. "Dearest Adeline, tell me you are well again."

"Well !" said Adeline. "Oh, Herbert !"

"What would you say ?"

" Where—where?"

" Where what?"

" Where is he?"

Herbert groaned. In the anxiety of the moment he had quite forgotten the circumstance that had led to the present distressing scene.

" The—the person who was here," he answered, in choking accents, " is gone."

" Gone?"

" Yes ; he fled the instant I appeared."

" Thank Heaven !" said Adeline.

" Could I have stayed his flight, I would have made him dearly repent his insolence."

" Oh, no—no—no," sobbed Adeline.

" No, Adeline?"

" No, Herbert ; you must not imagine aught against him."

" Adeline," said Mandeville, " there is some fearful mystery in this business."

" There is—there is."

" Confide it to me, then."

" I—I dare not."

" Dare not?"

" No ; lives hang upon the disclosure."

" What am I to think, Adeline?"

" At present, Herbert, you can take one of two courses."

" What are they?"

" Leave me for ever."

" Leave you, Adeline !"

" Aye, Herbert, for ever."

" No, no—the very thought is madness."

" Then you have the other resourse."

" And that, Adeline?"

" Is to trust me."

Herbert Mandeville was silent for a moment, then he said,—

" Adeline, can you love me, and yet not trust me "

" With my life I would trust you, Herbert."

" Then why not end my distress, by at once confiding to me this secret."

" Because it is another's secret as well as mine."

" And you will allow me to be tortured by doubts and fears——"

" No, no !"

" How can it be otherwise, Adeline?"

" If you have doubts, Herbert, let me again repeat, we part for ever."

" Adeline ! Adeline !"

" Make me a promise, that even what you do know you will keep a secret, and seek to know no more."

" But, Adeline, knowing that I love you with my whole heart and soul, can you not imagine what agony it must have been to me to overhear words of such strange import between you and a man who even dared to threaten?"

" Words of strange import, Herbert?"

" Yes, Adeline. I heard him demand money of you, and threaten you with the consequences of a non-compliance with his wishes. I heard you weep, and evidently dread those consequences."

" You heard this, Herbert?"

" By Heavens I did."

" Then—then——"

" Then what, Adeline?—you pause."

" Herbert, it was unworthy of you to listen," said Adeline.

Mandeville was rather confounded at this mode of meeting the question, and after a moment's pause he said,—

"We expect confidence and trust from those we love, Adeline."

"We do," said Adeline.

"Then give me confidence and trust."

"Give them to me, Herbert."

"But they should be reciprocal."

"They should," answered Adeline,—"they should, Herbert, I know. I feel they should; but in this case they cannot. You must trust me or forget me."

"Is there no other alternative?"

"None."

"I will trust you then, Adeline."

The fair girl's eyes sparkled with pleasure as she held out her hand to Mandeville.

"There will come a time," she said, "and I will pray that it may be soon, when I can explain all this mystery."

"I have but one fear," said Herbert.

"And what is that?"

"It is, that you have allowed yourself, in your innocence, to be imposed upon by some fancied claim urged by this man.

Adeline shook her head and sighed, as she replied:—

"No, Herbert, it is not so; you are mistaken."

"Then you cannot resist his importunities?"

"I can, and must."

"He has no real claim upon you for—for money?"

"None. But—but——"

"But what, Adeline?"

"If I thought—if I was sure that the sum he mentioned would really be devoted to the purpose he promised, I would do as he bade me."

"Procure it of your mother?"

"Yes, and she would gladly give it."

"Is it possible?"

"It is too true."

"Adeline, now hear me. I have said I would trust you, and you know I love you. Do not distress yourself or your mother. Be this man who he may, let the foundation of his claims be what it may, it is sufficient for me to meet your wishes. By the next post from London I will place the sum required in your hands."

"Herbert!" said Adeline.

"You do not doubt me?"

"Could you think—could you believe for one moment that I listened to the—the proposal that was made to me by him you saw me with. Oh, Herbert, Herbert. This is the unkindest of all."

Adeline burst into tears, and leaning on the blackened window-sill, sobbed as if her heart would break.

"Adeline," cried Mandeville, "I swear, by my hopes of Heaven, I never wronged you by such a thought. Let me do as I propose: I implore you, if you would compensate me in any manner for the anxiety I have suffered, to permit me to do so trifling a service."

Adeline still wept.

"Speak to me, dearest," continued Herbert; "say, you will permit me. You think it much. You think it a favour, perhaps, of magnitude. Believe me, Adeline, it is not. It will cost no more trouble, if so much, as to stoop for your glove or handkerchief; it is no obligation whatever."

"Oh! Herbert! I dare not. My mother."

" Your mother need not be distressed upon the subject ; she is getting now in years, and her health does not seem all that those who love her would wish."

"Alas ! alas !" cried Adeline.

"For her sake, then," said Herbert.

"For her sake ?" sobbed Adeline.

" Yes! In your mother's name, I urge you," said Herbert, who at once perceived that that was the point upon which Adeline would give way, if she gave way at all upon the subject.

"Herbert," said Adeline, covering her face with her hands, " I—I———"

"Speak, Adeline, speak !"

"I dare not refuse."

CHAPTER L.

" And then he told his love
With all the eloquence of a first
High passion."   BAYLEY.

THE MORNING.—A LOVERS' MEETING.—THE ELOQUENCE OF THE HEART.— SUNSHINE AND JOY.—A CLOUD IS GATHERING.

HERBERT MANDEVILLE was completely lost in a maze of endless conjecture with regard to the stranger who seemed to exercise so great an influence over Adeline, and at length, from from pure uneasiness of thought, he gave up the subject, and endeavoured to seek the repose he stood so much in need of.

The morning broke, stormy and tempestuous, and it was decided at the curate's breakfast-table that it would be impossible to venture from the house while the weather continued to be so unfavourable. Herbert was not sorry for this, and he only requested the curate to forward a letter to the post-office. It was the letter he had written which would procure him the money he had so urged Adeline's acceptance of.

The curate, after the morning's meal, told Mandeville that he had read a letter from his father, and upon shewing it to him, Herbert saw it was the one he had requested Captain Dufours to write.

"I can have no further objection," said the curate, "since your father writes in this style. I certainly think it a most extraordinary answer to my letter."

"But you must recollect sir," said Herbert, "that I wrote to my father by the same post, and what he did not gather from your epistle, he took amply from mine, and hence his answer."

"I view it in that light," said Mr. Endsleigh. "If I did not, I should pronounce this letter a forgery."

"A forgery ?" said Herbert, the colour deepening in his face as he spoke.

"Yes," said the curate. "But that is grossly improbable. I only hope we shall see your father down here as early as possible."

"And until then, sir———"

" Why, until then, things must just go on as they are, I suppose," said Mr. Endsleigh.

Herbert was very much pleased with this declaration from the curate, and determined to keep his father from Bracefield as long as possible, and in ignorance of what was proceeding there. He made an excuse to leave the curate, and hastened to seek Adeline.

He found her alone in the parlour, for Mrs. Mourdant was indisposed, and Mrs. Plumpjoy was in the lower regions, superintending various domestic arrangements.

And there sat Herbert Mandeville, heedless of the mass of difficulties he had accumulated around him by his foolish duplicity, in earnest and delighted converse with the beautiful and trusting Adeline.

Mandeville at that time really loved her, and he poured forth, with all the eloquence of fervent passion, the feelings of his heart,—

"   While she, delighted, listened to the sounds
      So sweetly pleasing to a youthful heart."

"Ah! Adeline," he cried, "what a delicious thing is young love, unalloyed by any of those feelings which destroy the dear romance of affection."

For a few moments the fair and beautiful girl remained, her head pillowed upon his breast. And was she not happy? Yes, it was one of those moments of pure joy, unalloyed by care, which rarely falls to human lot above once in life, and when it does, it must be when the heart is young, and all ideas are in the spring of beauty.

"True happiness is, indeed, my Adeline, only to be found in pure love: 'tis the light of the soul, dearest."

"It is; oh! it is, Herbert,—'tis a new existence. Before I knew you, Herbert, I know not what I was; I appear since then to have started into a new being since love took up its abode in my heart."

"'Tis a gift from Heaven, dear Adeline, is pure and holy love; pure, because it is innocent and holy—and holy because it is so pure."

"Oh, Herbert, talk on, 'tis music to hear you speak. Let me listen to every word you utter as upon inspiration. Say on, dearest, you love your Adeline with that pure holy love. Oh! 'tis indeed a Heavenly gift from God."

"I do, sweet Adeline, but I cannot tell you how much I love you, for words cannot translate hearts."

No. 24

"Oh, tell me, Herbert, while thus I feel the beating of your noble heart, how you have loved your Adeline."

"The sun, dearest, would set and rise again ere I could tell the tale of my love. The day would depart, and to-morrow's sun would gild the earth with beauty, ere now I could whisper to your ears the feelings that, crowd upon heart."

"But begin, Herbert, I will attend."

"Then, sweet Adeline, I saw thee, and Heaven's own sunlight broke into my inmost soul ; life became joyous ; the barren plain became rich with flowers, that breathed forth their sweet incense to the sun. Dear Adeline ! all was lovely for you were there ; it seemed to me as if some mysterious veil had been suddenly withdrawn from the face of nature, for I had never before beheld objects as I then did. But, dearest, it was my love for thee that made the most desolate of spots appear beautiful. It was that new and delightful feeling which made the wild flowers appear clothed in more luxuriant beauty at my feet. It was, my Adeline, the sweet sunshine of the heart that lent the rich gilding to all things."

"Dear Herbert, I love to listen to thee."

"I lived, dear one, in a land of sweet romance ; I thought but of thee. My whole life was like a summer's cloud, bright and joyous to look upon."

"Go on, dear love, 'tis music."

"Sometimes, my Adeline, the bright sun would cast a streak of dazzling light across my path, a light which cast a reflected beauty on the shade ; and that, dear Adeline, was when I saw thee, and thy wondrous beauty came across my path of life. Then, as the hours rolled by, I could wander in the shade of some gigantic trees, while the soft wind would sigh among the leaves for the absence of the glorious luminary. And then, again, the golden radiance would flit before me, and all was bright and lovely. Thus, sweet Adeline, was it with your Herbert. When I saw you the sun shone upon my way ; when you were gone, the shadow fell upon heart, and all was darkness and gloom. This, dearest, was then my happy life, like a sweet stream, with the bright sun shining on its glassy surface."

"Oh, Herbert, how different do all things appear to me, with you by my side to admire and to love."

"Dear Adeline, the world to me is changed ; I could almost fancy myself in a new world, so bright and joyous does nature seem with thy bright image to reflect upon its beauty. The birds seem more beautiful ; flowers appear clad in gayer colours ; all things look more bright and cheerful ; nature herself seems smiling upon our love. Dear Adeline, may we ever be thus ; may we pass through life without one care to annoy or destroy our happiness."

"My Herbert, with thee I could pass through life, and think myself blessed in having thee to love. If anything annoyed your Adeline, she would think of thee, Herbert, and all would be sunshine."

"Sweet Adeline, thy dear presence lends to all objects a new charm ; the light from thy dear eye sheds a lustre upon all things ; even vice would turn abashed away from thy heavenly beauty."

"Dear Herbert, I love to hear thee speak ; thy voice is like the gentle lute, so soft and beautiful does it fall upon my enchanted ear. In pain or sickness, one dear word of thine would act like a charm upon me, and drive all things away, save the tones of thy melodious voice."

Thus passed the happy fleeting hours to the young lovers. They dreamt not of care or woe ; life seemed to them a garden of delight, in which they might wander freely, and pluck the fairest flowers as they wandered in the sunny light of a never-ending summer. And thus another day passed away at the parsonage—another day of deceptive joys and fleeting happiness. Truly might Adeline, in after reflections, have said in the words of the poet,—

> "Alas! such fleeting pleasure,
> 'Tis all too dearly bought;"

for that conversation rivetted the charms of young affection so firmly around her heart, that in the effort to wear them away, that young and trusting heart was broken.

CHAPTER LI.

"Music is the food of love; it steals young hearts, and changes coldness to the warmth of passion."—ANON:

ANOTHER DAY.—ALL JOY.—THE BRIGHT MORNING.—THE GARDEN.—A SERENADE·
—THE CURATE AND HIS PUPIL.—AN ARRIVAL.

ANOTHER day day dawned upon Bracefield—a day of sweet redeeming beauty. The sun shone brilliantly from a cloudless sky; the winds were hushed down to the softest murmur, and there was a beautiful aspect of repose upon the face of nature, as if the elements tried if contention had sunk to rest upon the green fields, gentle slopes, and smiling valleys.

Herbert Mandeville opened his window to inhale the pure air that wantoned among the sweet summer flowers. There was a delicious freshness in everything, for although the storm of the day before had seemed terrible in its effects, still nature, now that it was over, seemed to wear gayer garments than was her wont. The grass was greener and fresher, the leaves upon the trees had a richer colour, and there was a balmy serenity in the air that amply compensated for all the violence of elemental strife of the day which had passed into the tomb of time.

"I should be happy," said Herbert Mandeville, as he looked from his window. "I have been tolerably successful. Let me see, I have accomplished a great deal lately. First gained the love of Adeline; then silenced and got rid of my only rival; hoodwinked the curate; kept my secret from my father, who would at once have put his veto upon the whole proceeding, and established myself past all retraction in the heart of the beautiful girl, whom I certainly love to—to—distraction. All's right; I can now abandon myself to enjoyment and the delight of summer rambles with Adeline. I will talk to her of love, and she shall sing to me of love; so we will pass the happy hours, gilding each with beauty."

Herbert completed his toilet while he was engaged in these self-congratulatory and pleasant reflections. He then repaired to the curate's parlour, but finding no one up, as the hour was very early, he strolled into the garden, not without a hope of getting a glimpse of Adeline at her window.

"I suppose," thought Mandeville, "I might almost venture upon a serenade now, without being told that I made a disagreeable noise. I thank Mr. Endsleigh for that phrase, and will not forget it. He and I will cry quits some of these days for various little particular favours."

So saying, Herbert Mandeville arrived under the window of the room in which he knew Adeline slept. All was still, however, and it was evident she was not stirring.

"She sleeps," said Herbert. "I will try to wake her thoughts. I will have another serenade, if it is but to provoke Mr. Endsleigh."

So saying, with a few preliminary "hems!" Herbert Mandeville, who really had a fine voice, commenced singing.

HERBERT'S SONG.

" My Adeline,—I see ye not,
    But I know that ye are there,
For music of another sphere
    Is floating in the air.—
The strains are those of love and joy,
    With hope around it clinging,
Sweet as the song of forest birds
    Amid the wild woods singing.

                                My Adeline.

" My Adeline,—I greet ye well—
    I feel your blessed power,
'Tis welcome to my throbbing heart
    As dew-drops to the flower,—
'Tis sweet as sunlight on the stream,
    When bounding to the billow,—
'Tis fair as moonbeams on the lake,
    Or tear-drops from the willow.

                                My Adeline."

He ceased ; and scarcely had he done so, when he saw the white muslin curtain of Adeline's window gently moved, more, it appeared, to let him know she was listening, than for any other purpose. Then again all was still, and Mandeville despaired of receiving any further indication of her presence, when he was delighted by hearing her sing, in a low tone, but sufficiently loud to reach his attentive ear, the following lines :—

ADELINE'S SONG.

" Sweet melody is breathing
    Love and joy to every heart,
And tears are gently flowing
    As the happy sounds depart.

" Oh ! would that they could linger
    Till life had pass'd away,
But all things that are fairest
    Are soonest to decay.

" And even at the moment
    A glimpse of joy appears,
Ere we've smiled upon its pleasure,
    We mourn it with our tears.

" Thus is it with the young and true,
    O'er whom the gentle spell
Of Love is thrown ;—they weep to say
    That fearful word--Farewell !"

" Dear Adeline !" cried Herbert, when the strain ceased ; " my own dear Adeline, I——"

" Hem !" said the curate, suddenly appearing in the garden.

" You here, sir ?" said Herbert.

" Yes," said the curate, drily.

" I—I thought——"

" I had no right to be so impertinent as to intrude into my own garden ?"

" No, not that. But——"

" You wish me anywhere else," said the curate, with a smile. " I can't help it, however. I have got my dahlias to look to, Herbert."

" And I," said Mandeville, trying to appear composed and do away with the ill-natured tone in which he first spoke, " I have my fair flower to look to, —the fairest of all, Mr. Endsleigh, I think you will admit."

" Yes," said the curate.

" So I made bold to make a noise, you see."

" So I heard."

" And Adeline made another noise."

"Adeline?"

"Yes."

"Well, well, Herbert, I don't exactly like this serenading. There is more of show, methinks, than of sincerity in the custom. I don't mean in your case. But it is a foreign fashion, and, I think, an indifferent one."

"I am sorry to differ from you, sir."

"When do you think we shall see your father?" said Mr. Endsleigh, suddenly changing the discourse.

"Very soon, I dare say," replied Herbert, slightly reddening as he spoke.

"He has never seen Adeline?"

"Not to my knowledge."

"Nor knows he anything of her?"

"He knows I love her."

"That seldom suffices."

"But you had his letter, sir."

"I had, and a strange letter it was."

"He—he—you know, sir. That is—my father——"

"What do you mean, Herbert?"

"My father may have been ill when he wrote it."

"I hope not," said the curate, gravely.

At this moment the sound of horse's feet at a hard gallop came across their ears, and Herbert and the curate, by one common impulse, cast their eyes in the direction from whence the sounds proceeded.

CHAPTER LII.

CLEON.	How fares your noble master?
BIDUS.	Alas! sir, he is——
CLEON.	You pause!
BIDUS.	He has paused, sir—he is dead.

OLD PLAY.

THE HORSEMAN'S ARRIVAL.—GOOD NEWS SELDOM TRAVELS SO QUICK.—A DEATH.—GRIEF AND REMORSE.—CONSOLATION AND A RESOLVE.

"Good news," said the curate, "seldom travels so fast as yon horseman.—I hope he is bound for somewhere else than Bracefield, Herbert."

"I hope so too, sir," answered Mandeville, who did not feel sorry for an excuse to change the conversation, which was becoming rather embarrassing.

"He pauses at the entrance of the village," said Mr. Endsleigh; "I begin to fear that his visit may be for some of us."

"Still," remarked Mandeville, "his errand may be a pleasant one, Mr. Endsleigh. Couriers of good news sometimes spare neither whip nor spur."

The curate shook his head, as he said,—

"They should spare both, Herbert, and not sully good tidings by cruelty to a poor beast."

"He seems to be coming this way."

"Do you recognise him, Herbert?"

"No; he is a stranger to me. And yet he is so enveloped in dust that I would not swear he was not my most intimate friend."

"He has travelled far," said the curate.

"Evidently," replied Mandeville, "His horse is jaded and worn."

"He comes this way."

"In truth he does, and fixes his eyes on us."

"Herbert," said the curate, solemnly ; "I feel a presentiment of some evil tidings."

"Evil tidings, sir ?"

"Yes, Herbert ; I pray I may be mistaken ; but still I fear."

"He evidently is making towards us. Do you know him, Mr. Endsleigh ?"

"No Herbert, I do not."

"Nor I, sir, so he cannot come to us ; at least it is unlikely."

The man was now rapidly approaching, but still it was difficult to say if he meant to pause or pass on.

Mandeville's curiosity was very greatly excited to know upon what errand a stranger could, at such headlong speed, approach the usually quiet village.

Nearer and nearer came the horseman, and as the morning sun glanced on his dusty apparel and jaded steed, Mandeville could see that his ride must have been a long and rapid one. The man was so begrimed with dust and perspiration, that his features could scarcely be distinguished, and it was only with a feeling of general curiosity that Herbert watched his approach.

Now he paused a moment, and partially reining in his tottering steed, he wiped the moisture from his brow, and glanced around him as if in quest of some one to whom he could put an inquiry. In a moment he saw the curate and Mandeville in the garden, and moving his hand to them, as if bespeaking their attention, he urged forward his horse, and in a moment stood by the garden-gate of the curate's house.

The words, "Can you tell me, gentlemen—" had scarcely passed his lips, when clasping his hands together, he suddenly exclaimed :—

"Good Heaven's, Master Herbert, is it really you ?"

Herbert sprang to the man's side, and looking him fixedly in the face, he said—

"It is Green ; my father's confidential domestic."

"It is, Master Herbert," replied the man ; "and——"

"And what ?" cried Herbert. "Speak ; you have ridden hard to bring me some tidings ?"

The man shook his head mournfully as he replied—

"Yes, Master Herbert, I have ridden hard. Ill news, sir."

"Always travels fast," said Mandeville ; "tell me the worst, Green."

"Your father—" said the man.

"My father ?"

"Yes, Master Herbert ; my poor master——"

"Is ill ?"

The man shook his head.

"My old friend has departed ?" said the curate to the servant.

"Dead ?" shrieked Mandeville. "Dead ? my—my father dead ? You—you can't mean——"

"He is dead, Master Herbert," said the man, in a solemn tone.

"God's will be done," said the curate. "Herbert, bear up against this visitation as a man and a Christian."

"My father dead ?" ejaculated Herbert, as if he could not convince himself of the possibility of such an event.

How hard it is for us to convince ourselves that those whom we love and respect, can thus pass away like a summer's cloud,

"And leave not a rack behind."

Natural as was the event, for Mr. Cuthbert Mandeville was a man in years, and of a worn constitution, still the actual assurance of it came across the mind of Herbert as if he had been suddenly assured of the occurrence of some phenomenon of nature which set at defiance all her ascertained laws.

"My father dead?" was all he could repeat in tones between doubt and dread.

"Come into the house, Herbert," said Mr. Endsleigh, "and we will together consult upon what had best be done."

Herbert allowed himself mechanically to be led into the parsonage by the curate, and the latter, calling to his old domestic, ordered that every attention should be paid to the messenger, and refreshment given to him and his steed.

"Come with me to my study, Herbert," continued the curate, kindly. "Come, come, rouse yourself, Herbert. Rouse yourself from this lethargy."

"I—I will," said Herbert. But it was evident that, for the moment, his mind was stunned by the blow it had received by the sudden tidings of his father's death.

The curate was one of the most kind-hearted of men, and in Herbert's evident sorrow for his father's death he forgot everything but the necessity and the wish to console him, and bring that comfort to his wounded heart which he would wish administered to his own under similar calamitous circumstances, for he, too, had known what it was to be told that those we love had passed away for ever from mortal sight, leaving

" Not a rack behind.''

Herbert allowed the curate to lead him to a seat without an effort to speak, either in a tone of consolation or complaint.

"My dear Herbert," began the curate, "this is a great misfortune ; but the circumstances attendant upon it, while they should not suffice, perhaps, entirely to dry our tears and stop the lachrymary fountains, yet should disarm grief of some portion of its agony."

"Circumstances?" said Herbert.

"Yes, Herbert ; in all misfortunes we shall find, if we examine them carefully, there is something which should be to us, if not a consolation, a reason for bowing in meekness to the decree of Heaven."

"Alas! alas!" said Herbert Mandeville ; "what consolation can I find?"

"Much—much, Herbert."

"Much! Oh, sir, my poor father is dead."

"He is, Herbert. But——"

"And I was far away," added Herbert, in a tone of agony. "There was no one to smooth his dying pillow, to listen to his last words, and see him to the confines of that better world—that awful bourne

" From whence no traveller returns.''

Herbert's feelings quite overcame him here, and he burst into a flood of tears.

Well the curate knew the solemn efficacy of those tears, and he strove not to hinder their flowing. Mandeville wept on for some time. The fountains of his heart were unsealed, and as his tears flowed, a feeling of calmness, hope, and resignation, crept across his mind.

The curate saw that the storm of passion was slowly subsiding.

"Herbert," he said, "now look up and speak to me."

"I will attend to you, sir," answered Mandeville.

"It is probable," continued Mr. Endsleigh, "that under these circumstances some responsibility of action at once devolves upon you."

"Action, sir?"

"Yes, Herbert. Your father was a widower?"

"Alas! that word *was* !" sighed Mandeville.

"But such was the fact?"

"It was."

"And you an only child?"

"True."

"Then your presence must be required in London immediately; both for your own sake, Herbert, and for the sakes of those who may have been dependant upon your father."

"Yes," answered Herbert, rising ; "I see the truth of what you say, sir ; I must go."

"You must, Herbert ; and you should lose not a moment."

"I will return with the man who brought this melancholy intelligence."

"Do so, and by the way he will doubtless inform you of all those particulars which your affection for your father will naturally make you anxious to know."

"Yet, before I leave Bracefield—" said Mandeville, with an air of hesitation.

"You would wish to bid all friends a brief good-bye, Herbert?"

"I would, sir. And Adeline——"

"Adeline, of course. Remain here ; I will send her to you."

"Nay, sir, I fancied, as we ascended the stairs, I heard her voice in the parlour ; I will seek her."

"As you please, Herbert ; but remember your duty calls you quickly hence."

Herbert assented, and immediately left the room.

CHAPTER LIII.

" At lovers' vows they say Jove laughs."

THE FAREWELL.—THE LOCK OF HAIR, AND THE LOCKET.—LOVERS' VOWS.—
ADELINE'S HEART.—THE DEPARTURE.—FAREWELL BRACEFIELD.

WITH a beating heart Mandeville hurried down the staircase near the foot of which was the parlour-door. There he paused to endeavour to still, for a moment, the wild tremulous beating of his heart ere he entered the room to bid farewell to her whom he had fondly hoped to linger with so long in uninterrupted felicity. All was silent within the room, but his heart told him she was there. He placed his hand on the lock of the door, and was about to enter, when he heard the sweet voice of Adeline singing. He could not lose sounds so dear to every feeling, and he lingered to drink in the Heavenly music of the voice of her he loved. It was a happy strain that flowed from the lips of the young and beautiful Adeline.

LOVES SIMILES.

" Love, like a shadow,
    Love, like a shadow,
        Oft haunts a sunny heart ;
    Life's clouds recurring,
    Life's clouds recurring,
        Tell lovers they must part.
                    Ah, part !

" Love's like the ocean,
    Love's like the ocean,
        Never, never quite at rest ;
    Winter's winds blowing,
    Winter's winds blowing,
        Oft shake its happy breast.
                    Ah, happy !

" Love's like the sunshine,
Love's like the sunshine,
   So bright the least cloud shows ;
The fond heart beating,
The fond heart beating,
   From slight cause sorrow knows.
      Ah, sorrow !"

The strain ceased, and for a few moments Herbert stood irresolute by the chamber-door.

"Shall I," he thought, "by a tale of distress and woe, dim the brightness of her joy? Alas! it must be done. Better that I should tell her I am going than some ruder tongue tell her I am gone."

He softly opened the door and entered the room. Adeline was looking from the window, and was not conscious of his presence. He heard her whisper a name—it was his own.

"Adeline! my Adeline!" he cried.

She started from her reclining position on the flower-decked window-sill, and while a radiant blush suffused her cheeks, she said—

"Herbert—ah, Herbert—I knew not you were here."

"Nor have I, dearest, been here a moment. Adeline, I—I have come to—to——"

"Herbert !" cried Adeline, looking anxiously in his face. "Oh tell me what has happened. You are pale as death—I know it—I see it. Something dreadful has occured."

"Calm yourself, Adeline ; calm yourself."

"Are you calm, Herbert ?"

"Do not ask me."

"Herbert, suspense is terrible. Tell me the worst."

"The worst, Adeline, is, after all, but what might have been expected, and must have been anticipated."

No. 25

"Speak on! Speak on."

"My father, Adeline, is dead."

"Dead?"

"Aye, dead, Adeline."

Adeline's tears flowed sympathetically for Herbert's grief.

"I have no father now," he added.

"I have no father," sobbed Adeline.

"And yet—yet I have seen you smile, Adeline, like the soft sunlight peeping through a cloud."

"Yes, Herbert. The shock of losing those we love is very great, but time will dull the keen edge of sorrow, and although we may still cherish fondly in our inmost hearts the memory of those that are gone, it is with a calm and chastened sorrow that we do so."

"True, Adeline, true," said Mandeville. "Time, however, is now but young with me, and the wounded heart has not had leisure to heal."

"Herbert—dear Herbert," said Adeline. "I feel for you. From my heart I feel for you."

"I know it, Adeline. Well I know it, my own dearest girl, but——"

"But what?"

"There are other griefs."

"Other griefs, Herbert?"

"Yes, Adeline."

"None, surely, to compare with this?"

"I came, Adeline, to bid you farewell."

"Farewell?"

"Yes, dear Adeline, I must leave you now."

"Leave me, Herbert? Oh—no—no——"

"My father, Adeline, was a lone man. The dear partner of his life and love has long slept in the silent grave."

Adeline sunk on a chair, overpowered by her feelings.

"I am now the only one of the name of Mandeville," continued Herbert. "Judge then, dearest Adeline, how much my presence must be required, even if it were only to see that due honour was paid to my poor father's sad remains."

"You are right, Herbert," said Adeline, making an effort to control her feelings. "Go, Herbert, go."

"It is a sad necessity."

"We may perchance meet again."

"May meet again, Adeline? Do you doubt me?"

"No—no. But——"

"Oh, Adeline, hear me even now in the moment of my heart's agony. I will fly back to thee as a tired wanderer to his happy home, whenever I am released from the mournful duties that await me in London."

"Till then, Herbert, farewell."

"My thoughts, Adeline, will be ever with you, although I am absent. The visions of my slumber will carry me to Bracefield, and indulge my dreaming fancy with a glance at thee."

"I believe you, Herbert. You cannot forget your Adeline."

"Forget! Sooner might I forget Heaven."

"Then I will live on hope."

"'Tis sweet food, dearest. And you know that hope may in this case, perchance, be deferred; but in the end, it will—it must be fulfilled, and the happy day will come when we shall part no more."

Adeline smiled through her tears as she said;—

"With such words, Herbert, let us for a time say farewell."

"We must breathe that word, Adeline. But, dearest, although your image in my heart will always present you to the imagination in the brightest colours of reality, I would fain carry with me something upon which I could gaze with pleasure as a remembrance of my Adeline until the happy time when we shall meet again."

"What can I give you, Herbert?"

"Sever one of these fair locks for my sake," said Herbert, drawing Adeline towards him, and laying his hand gently upon her luxuriant curls.

"That is a poor gift, Herbert."

"The giver makes it rich."

Adeline took from a work-box on the table a pair of scissors, and severed a long, sparkling tress of hair.

"Take it, Herbert," she said. "If it be but half so much prized as it is freely given——"

She paused, and Herbert exclaimed with animation,—

"The wealth of worlds, Adeline, should not purchase from me this little memorial of your love and beauty. In sickness and in sorrow I will gaze on this, and smile at fate."

He carefully placed the lock of hair in his bosom, and then, taking from his neck a gold locket and chain, he placed them in Adeline's hands, saying,—

"Let us exchange gifts, my Adeline, although yours so far outvies mine."

"I could retaliate your words upon you," said Adeline, with a smile. "The giver gives a value to the gift."

"You will keep this locket for my sake?"

"To my latest breath, Herbert."

"Now then, Adeline, we must utter that fearful word ——"

"Farewell!" said Adeline.

"Aye, farewell!"

For one moment Herbert Mandeville clasped the blushing girl in his arms, and imprinted a burning kiss upon her lips.

Adeline's heart was too full to speak, and Mandeville feared his own firmness would forsake him if he lingered longer.

"Again, farewell!" he said, and rushed from the room.

Adeline sunk upon a couch, and burst into a flood of tears.

CHAPTER LIV.

"How soon the mind borrows a new complexion from new scenes."
GODWIN.

LONDON.—A MANSION IN A FASHIONABBLE SQUARE.—A MEDITATION ON NEW PROSPECTS.—THE LETTERS AND THE FIFTY POUND NOTE.

WE will pass over the details of Herbert Mandeville's journey to London, which presented nothing worthy of note, and at once conduct our readers to a mansion in Portman-square, the residence of the late father of our young hero.

The mansion was one of the highest class, and replete with all the elegances and conveniences of social life. The saloons were strewed with works of worth and vertu, and the indications of wealth and taste abounded in the building.

The walls were hung with pictures, and costly draperies hung in massive folds from every window. Servants in gorgeous liveries glided from room to room, obedient to the slightest mandate, and altogether the establishment was a specimen of refined luxury.

In a small apartment, the contents of which were rich and dazzling in the extreme, sat Herbert Mandeville, now the sole owner of a large fortune, and all the collected riches and luxuries he saw around him.

An open writing-desk was before him, and a quantity of papers were strewed over the table. Herbert was writing a letter: it was to Adeline. It ran thus:

"**Portman-square.**

"DEAREST, EVER-DEAREST ADELINE.—I am at length in the house that was my father's, but which, I grieve to say, is now my own. How hateful it seems to me to be master here now. I feel as if I were constantly doing my poor father some injustice, by ordering his household. Time, however, dearest Adeline, will accustom me to all this; and when this mansion has a mistress, how different will all things appear! Dear Adeline, how I look forward to that happy time when I can welcome you here, and tell you it is your home! I will write to you by every post, and shall expect, dearest, to hear from you as frequently. Indulge me so far, Adeline. I am wearied and annoyed by business of all kinds. My father's affairs seem dreadfully complicated; and, what with lawyers, tradesmen, servants, legatees, and others, I am worried from morning till night. All this, however, will pass away like a cloudy day, and the sun of my happiness will rise more serenely beautiful by contrast.

"Ah! Adeline, here I sigh for Bracefield and thee!

"I enclose fifty pounds for "the stranger," because the letter, which will come to the parsonage for me, with the necessary amount, will be returned now that I am not there.

"With best love to all, but to thee, Adeline, a whole heart's gushing fondness. "Believe me, dearest, your own,

"HERBERT MANDEVILLE."

This letter Herbert carefully sealed with its enclosure, and then wrote the following note to Mr. Endsleigh, in which he enclosed Adeline's:—

"MY DEAR SIR,—Will you hand the enclosed to Adeline? By the suddenness of my father's decease everything is left in much confusion here; but I hope to reduce the chaos to something like order in a short time, and then you will see me at Bracefield. Till when,

"My dear sir,

"I am your friend,

"HERBERT MANDEVILLE."

Herbert rang for an attendant, and despatched these epistles, after which he leaned his head upon his hand, and gave himself up to contemplation of his future prospects.

"I am now," he thought, "the possessor of a large fortune. The means of unbounded enjoyment are at my disposal. Shall I cast them from me, or use them? I have youth, health, energy, everything that can enable me to enjoy life to its greatest possible extent. Would it not be wilful folly to cast from me such advantages? It would, indeed. Henceforth pleasure shall be mine. I will revel in refined enjoyments, and Adeline—ha! I had forgotten Adeline!"

He rose, and paced the apartment with hasty steps, and the troubled cloud that for a moment had rested on his brow was soon dissipated in the vision of coming pleasures which his warm, ardent imagination pictured.

"Who shall say me nay now?" he cried. "Who control a single wish of my heart? Who tell me, thus much shalt thou enjoy, and no more! No one! Let me consider. My fortune, I am told, exceeds eighteen thousand pounds per annum. By Heaven a goodly sum! What a wide field of pleasure does it not open to my enraptured gaze!"

A servant now noiselessly opened the door, and presented, upon a richly-chased salver, a card to Herbert.

He took it, and read—"Captain Dufours."

For a moment Mandeville hesitated, and he said, mentally,—

"Shall I see that rascal, or have my door shut in his face?"

The voice of pleasure, however, prevailed, and Herbert's next thought was—"After all, rascal as Dufours is, he is a first-rate caterer of enjoyment. He knows everything and everybody in London. Show him in."

The man bowed, and retired.

"Dufours is certainly a great rogue," soliloquised Mandeville; "but what matters that to me. I may as well make him useful, and, at least, he is an accomplished and gentlemanly villain. There can be no harm in seeing him."

The door now again opened, and the servant announced Captain Dufours.

It will not be amiss here to give some brief description of the gallant captain. He was a man of about forty years of age, and had all the appearance of having at one time been finely and elegantly formed. Dissipation had, however, done its full work, and Captain Dufours presented to the eye but the ruins of his former self.

There was, however, an air of high breeding in his manner, which carried with it an irresistible charm to those who, like Herbert Mandeville, looked no deeper than the surface of a character.

His dress was half military and half civil, and he wore black mustachoes, which well became his still handsome olive complexion.

"Well, Dufours," said Mandeville. "So you have found me out, have you?"

"Exactly," answered Dufours. "What's the state of things here? Shall I congratulate or condole?—or what? I am obliging, you know, Mandeville. Just give me my cue, and make it worth my while."

"Pho!—pho! Dufours. A truce with nonsense."

"You might have said take a seat, old friend, and taste a bottle of champaigne," remarked the captain, as he threw himself upon the ample yielding cushions of an ottoman that was in the room.

"Confound your impertinence!" said Herbert. "Don't you know that this house is mine?"

"Certainly. That is the very fact that enables me to do what I like in it. I like the house extremely."

"Well, upon my honour, Dufours, your impudence would quite overcome some people."

"Yes," remarked Dufours.

"But you know I am above it," continued Herbert. "It has no effect upon me, so you may as well try to be respectful, if you want anything."

"Want anything?"

"Yes. You come here as if the house were your own, and talk of champaigne as if you had a reversionary interest in my wine cellar."

"I have a direct personal interest in it," exclaimed Dufours; "that is to say, as long as there is anything drinkable in it. D— your cellar! When it's empty, you may go and live in it, and study philosophy."

"Where I should never see you," remarked Herbert.

"Certainly not," said the captain.

"' God bless every one who's aught to give.'

is my motto."

"It's a great many peoples' motto," said Herbert, laughing; "but they have not the impertinence to avow it."

"Not the candour, you mean."

"Well, it may be so. But candour is very often impertinence."

"Very true," said Dufours, rising, and ringing the bell furiously. "How idle you have grown, Mandeville."

"Idle?"

"Yes; I told you to order wine."

"Now, upon my word, Dufours ——"

"You forgot. Well, never mind, it's done now."

"Really your im ——"

"Oh! no excuses. I don't require them from friends."

Herbert burst into a laugh, during which the door was opened by a servent, in answer to the bell.

"Champaigne!" cried Captain Dufours.

The man looked amazed for the moment; and then, seeing that Mandeville did not contradict the order, he merely bowed and retired.

"This won't do, Dufours," said Herbert, striving to look offended, bt completely failing.

"Pho, pho?" cried Dufours. "You can order the ice yourself; I certainly did forget it."

"Your impertinence is beyond belief, Dufours."

"Yes."

"You are the most consummate rascal ever I encountered."

"Yes."

"Your assurance would be disbelieved in a romance."

"Yes."

"Will nothing move you?"

"Yes."

"What, then?"

"The champaigne, for I'm hardly going to drink on the flat of my back on this ottoman."

Herbert bit his lip to try and appear much displeased, as he repeated,—

"I tell you it will not do, Dufours."

"But I tell you what will do."

"What?"

"There is an assembly to night."

"An assembly?—where? But what is it to me?"

"A great deal—everything."

"Where is it?"

"At Clara Seagrave's."

"Clara's?"

"Exactly."

"Yes; and you will go, of course."

"No, no, no."

"I say yes, yes, yes."

"I cannot."

"You must."

"I will consider, Dufours. Do not press me."

"You don't want pressing. You must, and will go. But here's the champaigne."

CHAPTER LV.

"With accents gentle as the zephyr's sigh,
She strove to woo him back to honour."—ANON.

A PEEP AT THE STATE OF AFFAIRS AT BRACEFIELD.—THE FIRST LOVE-LETTER.—
A STRANGE ASSIGNATION.—ADELINE'S SINGULAR ACQUAINTANCE.—THE MONEY.

WHEN Herbert Mandeville left Bracefield, how desolate was the heart of the young and beautiful Adeline. She had but one source of consolation, and that consisted in constantly repeating, "He will come again! he will come again!" She wandered about the whole of that day in listless inaction. She could not read. She could not work or draw. She could find no pleasure in any of her usual dear occupations, for her heart was far away.

It was the second morning after his departure that the curate presented her a letter, saying :—

"This came enclosed to me, Adeline, with a request that I would lose no time in delivering it to you. It is, as you may guess, from ——"

"From Herbert! from Herbert!"

"It is," answered the curate.

Adeline flew to her own room to peruse the epistle, the first she had ever received from her lover. Oh, with what delight she lingered over every word! What commentaries did her young heart make upon each sentence.

A blush of wounded sensibility suffused her cheeks as the fifty pound note fell from its enclosure ; but then she thought of her mother, and the pangs she could save her through its instrumentality, and she fervently and from her heart thanked Herbert Mandeville for bestowing upon her so much pleasure.

That evening, just as the golden orb of day was sinking in the glowing west, Adeline hurried from the curate's house, and taking her route through the churchyard, she paused not till, with beating heart, she stood among the blackened ruins of Rose Villa.

Adeline then, with a heightened colour, reclined against a charred window-sill, and as the shadows of evening gradually deepened around her, she sighing, said :—

"He comes not! he comes not!"

Hardly had the words escaped her lips, when she heard a heavy tread among the blackened ruins, and withdrawing into the shadow of the walls, awaited in breathless suspense the approach of the intruder.

A man quickly appeared ; it was he who had been surprised by Herbert Mandeville with Adeline.

"Adeline!" he cried, in a coarse voice. "Adeline, I say, are you here?"

"Yes, George," said Adeline, stepping forward ; "I am here. I have been waiting ——"

"Well, where's the odds."

"But the place is lonely."

"Psha! Lonely!—nonsense! All the better! But to business. Have you the money?"

"I have, George ; but ——"

"You have?"

"Yes."

"All's right, then. None of your buts for me! Come, hand it out! By Jove, Adeline, you are a cleverer girl than I thought you."

"Oh, George! George! before I give you this money, hear me."

"No, thank you. The money first ; then prate as long as you like."

"But, George."

"The money!"

"George—George!"

"The money, I say! Damnation! give me the money!"

Adeline tremblingly produced the fifty pound note, and handed it to her brutal companion.

"Humph!" he said. "This will do for the present."

"For the present, George!"

"Yes, for the present."

"But I thought—"

"Who cares what you thought. I suppose, in your simplicity, you thought fifty pounds would last a gentleman for life."

"But, George, you promised —"

"Well?"

"You assured me —"

"What?"

"That if I would by any means procure you this amount of money, you would leave England for ever."

"Did I?"

"You know you did, George."

"England is a very comfortable place, at least that part of it lying between Temple Bar and Hyde Park Corner; as for the rest, why its uncommonly dull."

"But you will go?"

"To town, certainly."

"Your life, George, you know, is in danger!"

"Pho! pho! Nothing is so uncertain as human life! There's a piece of moral philosophy for you."

"You will break my heart, George."

"You must get it mended again, then, my dear."

Adeline burst into tears.

"Well," cried the man, "if there's anything I dislike above another, it's snivelling. So, good-bye."

"Stay," cried Adeline; "stay yet a moment, and tell me what you really mean to do?"

"It's difficult to say; and, you see, I can't do much with a beggarly fifty pounds."

"You will, as you promised, go to America?"

"America?"

"Yes, you said you would, if you had the means."

"But I hadn't the means then."

"You have now, though, George."

"Exactly. And that's what alters the case."

"How alters it?"

"Why, this way. When a man hasn't a penny, he would be glad to go to America; but when he has fifty pounds, America may be d—d!"

"You have deceived me, George."

"Young women are always deceived."

"Oh, do not turn my lingering affections to—to —"

"To what?"

"Contempt!"

"It's all one to me. If you are going to be disagreeable, I'm off. So good evening, at once."

"Oh, think again—think again," sobbed Adeline.

"So I will when this money is spent. I will then think how to replenish an exhausted exchequer."

"George—George, you are resolved on self-destruction!"

"Quite the reverse, Adeline. I am resolved on self-preservation. I am resolved on enjoyment."

"You mistake the road to it."

"Curse all preaching! If you have anything else to say, say it at once, for I hate this dull country place. If it hadn't been for some fun I and some others have had, which I must not mention, I should have died of ennui here among the fields and flowers, and such like vapid trash."

"Lost! lost!" cried Adeline, wringing her hands.

"What's lost?"

"You are lost."

"Am I?"

"Yes, George. Quite lost."

' You can advertise me, then, if you like; and now, once more, good-night! I shall see you again."

"Never, George, never!"

"Never?"

"No—we never meet again."

"I say we shall, though."

"I am firm, George; this is our last meeting. You have deceived me; I trust you no more."

"Hark you, Adeline: I will see you when I like, and where I like. Aye, and sooner, perhaps, than you expect."

"No, no," said Adeline.

"You cannot escape me."

"I can and will."

"Pho—pho! you rave. Who can step between us? who prevent me from hunting you out whenever I like? Tell me that. Who can baulk me?"

"There is one who will try," said the curate, suddenly stepping between Adeline and her unprincipled companion.

"Damnation!" cried the man.

Adeline clung to Mr. Endsleigh's arm, as she cried,—

"Go—go! Fly, George, fly."

The man hesitated a minute, and then, with a brutal oath, rushed from the ruins.

CHAPTER LVI.

"It is a secret ;
And I must bear your hard construction
Till you know me better."
OLD PLAY.

THE CURATE'S FAITH.—THE DREAD SECRET.—ADELINE'S REQUEST.—A LOVE-
LETTER.—A YOUNG HEART'S PURITY.

FOR a short time the curate stood by Adeline in silence. He seemed at a loss to know what he could say further, and Adeline herself only hung down her head, and wept bitterly.

"Adeline," at length said the curate, mildly, "from whence spring those tears?"

"From an oppressed heart," replied Adeline.

"But not a guilty one?"

"Oh! no, no. As Heaven is my judge, no!"

"Come with me home, then," said Mr. Endsleigh, cheerfully. "Do not weep, Adeline. Tell me, if you will, on our road, how it happened that I found you in such strange and unseemly company."

Adeline took the curate's arm in silence, and together they left the ruins of Rose Villa.

Adeline was silent, and the curate could not but perceive that there existed a disinclination to speak concerning the recent singular encounter.

"Understand me, Adeline," he said, "I do not ask for your confidence, or press you to disclose anything to me that you would rather keep locked in your own breast; but I am an old man, and know some little of the world and its ways, notwithstanding we are so near parting company ; and if you are imposed upon, or persecuted by any one, I can and will protect you."

"Alas !" said Adeline, "I am indeed persecuted."

"Endure it then no longer. Let those friends, Adeline, who esteem you protect you."

Adeline was silent for a few minutes ; then she said,—

"There is a secret."

"Secrets are bad things," replied Mr. Endsleigh.

"I know they are—well, I know they are. But oh, sir, this is one that is forced upon me."

"Forced upon you, Adeline?"

"Yes ; forced most unwillingly upon me. Mr. Endsleigh, a human life hangs upon it."

"A life?"

"Yes, a life ; and that life—but I must say no more. Let me only implore you, whatever you may see, whatever you may hear, to believe me innocent."

"I do believe you innocent, Adeline. I have seen in my life quite enough to convince me of the fallacy of judging by appearances."

"Thank you, sir—oh, thank you," cried Adeline. "There will come a day soon, I expect and—and hope, when I can explain all, but—but——"

"But what, Adeline? Speak freely."

"Will you promise me——"

"Promise you what? You are agitated."

"Promise me you will say nothing to my mother of this circumstance?"
The curate considered a moment, and then replied,—

"I do promise, for I have no right whatever to interfere in the matter further than I am requested. But let me, as an old man, Adeline, beg of you, and sincerely advise you, to discard from your mind all concealment and mystery; keep nothing, Adeline, from your mother."

"Oh, if I could—if I dared explain!" said Adeline.

"Nay, do not torment yourself further," remarked Mr. Endsleigh. "I know your purity of thought and action, Adeline. Consult only your own mind, and you cannot go far wrong. You may err in judgment, but not in principle."

"Thank you, thank you, Mr. Endsleigh; you are very kind to me,—kinder than I deserve."

"Say no more about it, Adeline. Here we are at home."

The curate shook hands with the fair girl and retired to his own room, while she sought her chamber to weep.

After a time Adeline became more composed, and she again and again perused Herbert Mandeville's letter, which in her too partial eyes was a perfect specimen of the truest affection.

"He does love me!" she said, half aloud. "Yes, Herbert loves me, and I should be happy. How they belied him who said that he was wayward in his fancies, and fickle as the winds. But the old ever judge harshly of the young in matters of the heart. Herbert unfaithful!—How ridiculous is the thought. In the midst of all his new occupations, mournful and gay, troublesome or delightful, he still thinks of me—his own Adeline. Shall—shall I write to him? No, no; and yet why should I hesitate?—he trusts me with his young heart, and why should I not trust him? There should be no reserves in honest love. Herbert, it will give thee pleasure to read—and—me—ah, what pleasure it will give me to write."

Adeline blushed to herself as she drew towards her writing materials, and for the first time thought to indite a page of real feeling. She felt the full force of the proverb, that the first step is the greatest difficulty in everything; for how to begin was to the gentle and shrinking Adeline a tremendous task indeed.

Twenty times she essayed a commencement of her letter, and as often crossed what she had written. "Herbert" merely at the begining was too cold;—"Dear Herbert" she shrunk from with alarm, and at length she determined to write no superscription at all, but commence her letter abruptly; and thus the gentlest, fairest, and most innocent of all creatures, wrote to him who held the sacred trust of her young heart's dearest love in his soul keeping :—

"You still think of Bracefield, Herbert, and Adeline. Will you be pleased to receive these lines? My heart tells me you will, for I judge of you, Herbert, by my own feelings, and I have treasured your brief note. What mournful duties must have awaited you in London. Ah, Herbert, did they not strangely contrast with *our* happiness in this quiet scene of sylvan beauty? You will come to Bracefield again soon, Herbert. Then—but till then, the flowers will be beautiful, and the birds will sing with rich music from the trees. It is love that alters all tastes—governs all feelings. Come back, Herbert, to dear Bracefield. "Your own,

"ADELINE."

With trembling hands Adeline folded and sealed her note, and addresse to Herbert, in London. Then she thought she would not— could not send but love was the conqueror, and Adeline stole gently down the stairs to find old Andrew to take her letter to the village post-house.

The old man was working in the garden, and Adeline approached him with as much agitation as if she were some great criminal.

" You are busy, Andrew," she said.

" Yes, Miss," said the old man, " we always find something to do."

" Doubtless," answered Adeline. " I—only thought you might spare time, Andrew, to take a letter for me to the post."

" It's my duty, Miss, to take it," said Andrew.

" Here it is," said Adeline, handing the note to old Andrew.

" Humph!" said the old man, glancing at the direction. " To Herbert Mandeville, *Eskevire*."

" Yes," said Adeline, hurriedly ; " It's—it's, as you see, to Mr. Mandeville."

" Ah, I see," replied the old man. " Him as was going to burn Rose Villa—oh, I know."

" Andrew !" said Adeline.

" Miss Mourdant ?" said the old domestic, who was in the habit of doing just what he liked in the household.

" You know Mr. Mandeville's innocence was satisfactorily proved, and it is ungenerous as well as unjust to make such remarks of the absent."

" I believe, Miss, he didn't burn down the Villa, but ——"

" But what, Andrew ?"

" The letter, Miss—the letter."

" What letter ?"

" The letter as comed here a advising of him to do it."

" That is all arranged," said Adeline, looking down.

" God bless you, Miss Adeline," said the old servant. " You be kind, and good, and beautiful, and God bless you, I say, from my heart. For your dear sake, Miss, I do hope all be arranged, and that this young man may turn out a better article than I, old Andrew, do think him to be."

" You are prejudiced, Andrew, against Mr. Mandeville."

" Mayhap I be,—mayhap I be," said Andrew. " I dare say I'm an old fool —oh, no doubt."

" Andrew, I said no such thing."

" Oh, never mind, Miss, never mind. I'll take the letter. It's no matter what I think."

Vexed as Adeline was, she could not help smiling at what she considered the dogged obstinacy of the old man in his bad opinion of Herbert Mandeville.

" Thank you, Andrew," she said. " I wish the letter to go early."

" Oh, it shall go now," said old Andrew, throwing down his spade, and holding the letter between his finger and thumb, as if it contained some deadly poison. " I don't want to keep it longer than I can help, Miss."

Adeline turned and entered the house with a half sigh.

" Ah," she thought, " how poorly can such persons judge of a true and noble heart. And that letter the old man mentions. How could Herbert prevent a bad man from sending him a letter ?"

How fertile is love in excuses ! and how little Adeline suspected that Herbert and the bad man were at that moment laughing over their champaigne.

CHAPTER LVII.

"Now, sir, take warning,
Whatever you do,
Read this short letter
Quite through and through,
If it grill you, and fret you,
Why, take to your bed,
Or get in a passion,
And peg at your head."

PETER PINDAR.

THE OLD SERVANT.—A RESOLUTION.—MRS. GREEN AND LITTLE CUPID.—
THE WARNING.

OLD Andrew thought himself specially ill-used in having even to convey to the village post-house a letter with the, to him, highly obnoxious name of Mandeville upon it.

"So, she's a writing to him, is she?" he muttered. "Well, now, I don't like that at all. Poor young thing, it's very foolish of her; but young women are just like young mares; they are always getting over the traces, or bolting off when one least expects it. Now what a elegant Mrs. Charles Leslie she'd a made, to be sure! There would have been a match! I'll just write to Mr. Leslie, I'm hanged if I don't, and tell him as Miss Adeline's actually sending *Billy Doos* to that Mandeville. It'll be a sort o' great satisfaction to him to know the length things is a going."

Full of these reflections, old Andrew arrived at Mrs. Green's shop, and walking in, he threw the letter down on the counter with a look of extreme contempt, exclaiming:—

"There, Mrs. Young, what do you think o' that?"

"Lor, what can I think?" said Mrs. Green. "It's no use thinking about letters in envelopies!"

"In what?"

"Pasted up kivers, Mr. Andrew. They are called envelopies."

"Oh, are they. You mean there's no such thing as getting a peep inside 'em?"

"A peep?"

"Yes, a sort o' twist o' the eyes into the interior."

"Lor, Mr. Andrew, how can you suspect me for a instant of peeping into nobody's letter. All I means to say is this,—if so be as any one was dying to know what was in a letter they couldn't, when it's done up in one o' these here disagreeable new-fangled thingumties."

"That's very true, Mrs. Green."

"Who's this from, did you say, Mr. Andrew?"

"Why, from that foolish young thing, Miss Adeline, to be sure. Mrs. Green, Mrs. Green, you may take my word for it as he doesn't mean no good at all."

"Goodness gracious, Mr. Andrew, you don't say so!"

"Yes, but I do say so, Mrs. Green. Now, what would you think if I was to say to you——"

"Lor, what, Mr. Andrew?"

"Oh, how beautiful you is. What a charmer!—What a duck!"

"Lor!"

"Well, I says, what would you think?"

"Think, Mr. Andrew? I shouldn't know what to think."

"Well, but you'd think I meant it, maybe."

"Well, and if so be as you did—what then?"

"Why, supposing it was all a do?"

"A do?"

"Yes; all broad-wheeled gammon."

"But——"

"No buts. Supposing as it was all my eye."

"Then, Mr. Andrew, you'd be a wretch."

"Exactly; and that's what makes this young Mandeville a wretch."

"Lor!" cried Mrs. Green, "how one lives and learns."

"There's more folks, Mrs. Green," remarked Andrew, tapping the side of his nose with his finger, "as lives and learns, than as learns to live, I can tell you."

"How very true," sighed Mrs. Green.

"And now, mum," said Andrew, "I want a halfpenny sheet o' the best writing-paper."

"And a pen, Mr. Andrew?"

"And a pen, mum."

"And ink, I s'poses?"

"You are a witch, Mrs. Green. I do want ink. The truth is, I've got a letter to write, mum."

"A—a—a love-letter, Mr. Andrew?"

"A what?"

"A tender epistle."

"What, me write a Billy Doo! Me—me, Andrew!"

"Well, I'm sure, Mr. Andrew, you needn't be offended. Here's the pens and ink, and here's the paper."

"Mrs. Green," said Andrew, "what I am going to write is a moral."

"A moral?"

"Yes, mum, a act o' morality, mum."

"Dear me."

"Thank you, Mrs. Green. I'll begin now, if you pleases."

"Oh, dear, yes," said Mrs. Green, vanishing into the back parlour, and leaving Andrew to his meditations.

First of all, Andrew, with his rough hand, smoothened the virgin paper, and then, taking a pen full of ink, he cast his eyes in a maniacal manner up to the ceiling, apparently lost in deep thought as to how he should begin his epistle to Charles Leslie.

"That'll do," at length exclaimed Andrew. "It'll be a good beginning."

He then commenced writing, and with various interruptions of deep cogitation, succeeded in producing the following specimen of epistolary correspondence.

"Onhaired Challs Lesli,

"Deer Sir,

"Shes a kumin it broun unkimhon—Shes a rite in toe im i sawed the lettr its a Billy Doo and noe miss tak yow must hintherfeare I re peets shes a kumin it broun—Adhelean i meens—This cums hoppin yew ar wel as like-wyze his ewer umbel sarvant,   "Andrew."

Having completed this highly original and satisfactory epistle, the composition and orthography of which had put old Andrew into a perspiration, he called to Mrs. Green for a wafer, and that exemplary lady made her appearance forthwith.

"Here's a letter, Mrs. Green," said Andrew, with an air of great exultation, "as will do wonders, Mrs. Green."

"You don't say so!" exclaimed Mrs. Green.

"Yes, I do. A wafer, if you please."

Andrew was accommodated with a large red wafer, which having well moistened, he applied to his letter, and than sat down to write the address, which he thus accomplished,—

> " Mr. Challs Lesli
> " hat Lesli hand trumans
> " cannon lane
> " City."

Andrew then consigned his epistle, along with Adeline's, to the letter-box, and having made his adieu to Mrs. Green, he walked homewards with a firm conviction that he had accomplished some very clever act.

Adeline felt by turns satisfied and dissatisfied with herself for writing to Mandeville. One moment she would accuse herself of indiscretion and blush for her own forwardness in writing at all. Then love—resistless love—would take possession of her heart, and she would whisper to herself,—

" Can it be wrong to give so simple a pleasure to one who loves me so truly as Herbert does? Ah, no. The motive sanctifies the act. My short letter will be to him a solace in the midst of care and anxiety. I *am* glad that I sent it."

After arriving at this resolution, Adeline would take up her guitar, and strive to wean her mind from fond regrets in the witchery of music's tones. The following ballad was her favourite, as it spoke truly the feeling of her own young and innocent heart :—

I WILL NOT DOUBT—I WILL NOT DOUBT.

" I will not doubt—I will not cast
  A shadow on my heart;
Young Love is ever shining there—
  I cannot say depart.

" I will not doubt. My trusting love
  Is life and joy to me ;
'Twere death to doubt—'twere death to doubt
  His plighted constancy.

" I will not doubt—his gallant soul,
  Though he is far away,
Knows no deceit—knows no deceit,
  'Tis true as is the day.

" He loves me well—he loves me well ;
  His image at my heart
Oft whispers to my throbbing brain,
  'Twere death to make us part."

CHAPTER LVIII.

"When the dread whirlpool of vice is once entered, how swift is the career to destruction in the yawning vortex."

THE LONDON SALOON.—A FINE LADY.—HERBERT'S INFATUATION.—PLAY.— FASHION AND FRIVOLITY.

WE left Herbert Mandeville in the hands of his arch enemy, the self-styled Captain Dufours. If at this period of his young life Herbert Mandeville had been so fortunate as to have fallen among the good and just, how different might have been the tenor of his after existence.

The great fault of his character consisted in that easy ductility of mind, which made him the slave of any one who would take the trouble to assume a command over him by flattery or satire.

That evening saw him in the gay and not very creditable saloon of what was called " a woman of fashion," but who the curate, in the innocent simplicity of his heart, might have called by some name less pleasing to " ears polite."

The scene was one of gaiety and splendour.   Everything that could please the fancy, and captivate the most fastidious imagination, was there to be found ; and the splendid mistress of the equally splendid mansion was all " smiles and honied sweetness."   To look at her, one might well imagine that her breast was at least serene and happy.   There was no gall in the radiant smile with which she welcomed her guests.   She was a part and parcel of the universal glitter that prevailed around.

It was not to be supposed that Lady Clara Seagrave, the mistress of the revels, was unheedful of so important a personage as a young man just entering into life as the possessor of a splendid, unencumbered fortune, and she had accordingly her blandest smile and sweetest welcome ready for Herbert Mandeville, whose sojourn in the country seemed only to have sharpened his appetite for the refined pleasures of a London life.   The gay music inspired him with delight.   The sparkling lights—the varied dresses—the sallies of wit without good nature—all seemed to Herbert perfect and delightful.   He forgot the curate—he forgot his poor father, so lately a tenant of the silent tomb—he forgot even Adeline, the beautiful girl whose young heart he had won so entirely and prized at the winning so highly.

" Mr. Mandeville," said Lady Clara Seagrave, with one of her blandest smiles, " you spend the season of course in town ?"

" Yes," answered Mandeville.   " I—that is—oh, certainly."

One thought of Adeline had swept across his mind, but the disposition of Herbert Mandeville was

> " When away from the lips that we love,
>   To make love to the lips that are near."

" I am so glad to hear it," continued Lady Clara.

" You flatter me," said Herbert.

" Alas ! no—perhaps I flatter myself."

" Nay, now——"

" You know my mind is susceptible, painfully susceptible of melancholy impressions."

" Yes," said Herbert ; although he knew no such thing.

" It is only thus," continued the lady, " by plunging myself into the vortex of society that I can banish gloomy images from my mind."

" Exactly," said Herbert.   " I have heard of people living in such a crowd that the demon of melancholy could not push his way towards them."

" Oh, dear ! a most felicitous idea."

Herbert bowed, and Lady Clara continued,—

" I purpose giving a series of *petit soupers* all the season."

" Delightful !" exclaimed Mandeville.

" Select, of course."

" Oh, of course."

" Mrs. Delancey !" announced a servant, at this moment.

" Oh, the delightful Mrs. Delancey," cried Lady Clara Seagrave, and she sprung forward to embrace her guest.

Herbert looked at the new comer, and was not long in coming to the conclusion that she was a most charming woman, although a more critical eye would have detected an air and manner about her which spoke of low breeding.

Mrs. Delancey remained in earnest conversation with Lady Clara for a few moments, and then the latter, taking her hand, advanced to Mandeville, and said,—

"Mr. Mandeville, you must not be astonished, but Mrs. Delancey is all nature."

Herbert did look a little astonished, but he merely bowed and muttered something about the beauties of nature.

"Mrs. Delancey," continued Lady Clara, "positively insists upon being introduced to you."

"She does me too much honour," said Herbert, very much flattered, nevertheless.

Mrs. Delancey advanced, and laying her hand upon his arm, gazed in his face, saying,—

"And you are Mr. Herbert Mandeville? At length I meet you of whom I have heard so much."

"Really, madam," said Herbert, "you will make me too vain."

Mrs. Delancey shook her head and sighed deeply; then, with a faint smile, she said,—

"No, no. There are some minds—but no matter."

"She is certainly a very beautiful creature," thought Mandeville. "She seems unhappy. Some brute of a husband, I presume——"

"Mr. Delancey!" announced the footman.

A perceptible shiver ran through Mrs. Delancey's frame, and she grasped Herbert's arm, as, advancing her face so close to his that their cheeks just touched, she whispered,—

"Do not know me—or speak—or even look at me. Hush! he comes."

Before Herbert could reply to this singular piece of confidence and familiarity on the part of Mrs. Delancey, she had walked away, and he lost her in the throng.

"I should like to see what sort of person is this Mr. Delancey," thought Herbert, and he gently pushed his way towards the door.

No. 27

Mr. Delancey was a tall, sinister looking man, with but one eye, and Herbert was not a little amazed that he and the delicately beautiful Mrs. Delancey should ever have come together.

"She is evidently unhappy," he thought, "and I don't wonder at it, for a more unloveable man I never saw."

It was the dawning of morning when the party broke up, and although Herbert had traversed the splendid suite of rooms repeatedly, he had not seen anything more of Mrs. Delancey.

On the steps of the mansion he was joined by Captain Dufours, who said,—

"Why, Mandeville, what's this I hear about love charms?"

"Love charms?"

"Yes. It's in everybody's mouth that the moment a certain fair lady saw you she was captivated."

"Who do you mean?" said Herbert. "Come, come, no nonsensical jesting, Dufours. You know I don't like it."

But Captain Dufours saw by the sparkling of Herbert's eyes, and the half smile that he strove to conceal, that he did like it, and he continued,—

"It's very odd, Mandeville, but wherever you go you do something to make a sensation. Now poor Mrs. Delancey, whose heart——"

"Mrs. Delancey?"

"Yes."

"What the—the rather pale——"

"But decidedly interesting young lady."

"Whose husband——"

"We call the Cyclops. Exactly. Your motto, Mandeville, should be—'I came—I saw—I conquered.'"

"So there has been some gossip about it, has there?"

"Gossip? To be sure. It was *the* feature of the evening. Come, now, Mandeville, send your carriage home, and stroll onwards with me. It's delightfully cool. I can tell you all about the Delancey's as we go along."

Herbert allowed himself to be led, or rather misled, by the "gallant captain," and before he got to his home it was mid-day, and he had lost nearly six hundred pounds "en route" at a gambling-house, which had been highly recommended by the gallant and most disinterested captain.

CHAPTER LIX.

"Then to cheat the tedious hours
Of weariness, she'd dip into the pages
Of some ancient history—of love—
Of war—and of the heart's deep grief
From over trusting fondness."

THE TRIALS OF A YOUNG HEART.—ADELINE'S HOPES AND FEARS.—WEARY TIME.—NO NEWS OF HERBERT.—THE ROMANCE.

DAY succeeded day at Bracefield, and still Adeline heard no tidings of Herbert Mandeville. No answer came to the fond out-pourings of her young affection. The good curate looked grave as each morning the post came not to the parsonage. Mrs. Plumpjoy looked fidgetty and vexed, and proclaimed the arrival of so many horses to be shaved, and pigs to have their corns cut, that the curate was continually leaving the room in despair.

Adeline, however, complained not. Now more than a week had passed away, and Herbert had not written; but still she strove

"To wear her old accustomed smile,"

although pain and sorrow were in her heart.

The curate was greatly distressed, however, at the growing paleness of her face, and after a few days' more delay he determined upon writing to Mandeville himself, to know the cause of such unwarrantable fickleness.

"If," thought Mr. Mourdant, "he has really forsaken the young heart that repaid his vows with such trusting affection, then God forgive him and comfort Adeline, for she is better to be forsaken as she is than as his wife."

Before writing to Herbert the kind old man sought an interview with Adeline. He found her weeping in a little summer-house in the garden.

"Adeline," he said, softly.

His voice startled her, for she had not seen him approach, and she hastily rose, brushing away the tears that hung upon her long silken eye lashes. She strove to smile,—but oh! how faint and unlike was that smile to the smile of happier days, when

"The young heart sat lightly
On its bosom's throne."

"Adeline," he continued, "be of better cheer. Our happiness is mostly in our own keeping."

"I will—I will," said Adeline.

"I sought you, my child, because I intended to-day to write to Herbert Mandeville."

A flush of colour came over Adeline's face as she repeated the words,—

"Herbert Mandeville?"

"Yes, Adeline, and I thought you might have something to say."

Adeline shook her head.

"Have you no word?"

"None."

"Nothing to send, or——"

"Nothing, nothing!" said Adeline.

There was a silence of a few moments, and the curate felt that he had said enough upon the subject, and he likewise felt that Adeline was right in her resolve.

"You must amuse your mind Adeline," he said; "you will find in the drawers of my private cabinet, a record of suffering and oppression. 'Tis a strange thing in human nature, but I have ever found that nothing so much reconciles us to our own griefs as hearing of the griefs of others."

"Yes, yes," said Adeline, eagerly; "I would withdraw myself from the actual to plunge into the unreal. If I could not read, I—I think I should die a martyr to my own imagination."

"Go, my child, go," said the curate.

Adeline left him, and with tearful eyes sought the cabinet he mentioned.

She knew the curate had a store of legends and moving histories, and she felt that if there were any escape from the deep depression of her own thoughts, it was to be found in books.

Oh, how many have found a solace from the same blessed fount? How often has the breast of care been soothed, the tears of despair quenched, the couch of pain robbed of some of its misery, nay, even death itself robbed of some of its gloom, by books!

Adeline found a small roll of papers, and striving to give all her attention to the characters written upon them, she commenced an eventful narrative, which spoke of suffering, despair, hope, and final triumph in the dear reward of innocence.

The manuscript was called,

THE PERSECUTORS; OR, THE LAST INQUISITOR.

And commenced thus :—

"Soon after the commencement of the eighteenth century, when the powers of the inquisition were still exerted with unwearied force to extirpate heresy and dissent from the soil of Spain, Alvarez di Narvaes came to reside within a few miles of the city of Cadiz.

" Alvarez had been studying at the University of Salamanca, where he had acquired such a reputation for profound learning and extensive knowledge, that he bade fair to become one of the first scholars of Spain.

" Neither had Alvarez confined his studies to the dry pursuit of theology, or to the mere acquisition of languages ; the belles lettres in general, and the sciences in particular, had also been made the companion of his midnight hours. Newton and Leibnitz were his instructors in science, and his acquaintance with those celebrated men was not merely confined to their works, but being treated by them as a friend, a correspondence was carried on between them.

" Alvarez was about thirty years of age, and being active, clever, and persevering, almost everything that he undertook turned out successful.

" Chemistry and astronomy were his favourite sciences, and nearly the whole of the night was devoted by him either to the one or the other. These were at that time dangerous pursuits in the country of his birth, and few of his countrymen ever ventured to undertake their study, as these sciences brought upon their professors the ill-will of the priesthood, and the suspicion of the inquisition.

" The people, too, were so superstitious and ignorant, that the light of science being imperceptible to their narrow comprehension, they foolishly believed that no one ever studied the position of the stars in the Heavens, except for the purposes of astrology. And as to the study of chemistry, it was a prevalent belief in Spain, that the professors of that science followed their avocations merely to make the powers of evil subservient to their will, which, though for a time successful, would sooner or later bring down upon them the vengeance of the Prince of Darkness, who would carry them away with him to his domains of everlasting fire.

" Such being the creed of the people, the astronomer and the chemist were looked upon with suspicion and dislike ; and, therefore, those who delighted to revel in the mysteries of these sciences, pursued their study in secrecy and silence.

" It was late on the evening of a celebrated festival which had been held in honour of one of the numerous saints that adorn the Spanish Calendar, that as Alvarez was pursuing his favourite study of astronomy on the flat roof of his neat compact residence in the neighbourhood of Cadiz, that the silence of the night was suddenly broken into by the shrill shriek of a female voice.

" It was heard but for an instant ; but Alvarez immediately looked in the direction from whence the shriek had proceeded, and as the evening was clear, he perceived what appeared to him to be a female in a light-coloured dress struggling with two dark figures, who were endeavouring, to the utmost of their power, to hurry her away.

" The house of Alvarez was lonely and solitary, and he was therefore unable to seek for assistance to attempt her rescue.

" This was, however, but a secondary consideration with him, for seizing his sword and stiletto, he hurried to the spot where he had last seen the three figures, fully determined to rescue the lady or die in the attempt.

" It was not long before Alvarez came up to the persons whom he sought. Two men had hold of a lady who was muffled up in a cloak, and they were dragging and carrying her between them, but as the lady resisted to the utmost of her power, the men could not proceed very fast.

" Alvarez called out to the men to stop, and insisted upon knowing why they compelled the lady to go with them against her will.

"One of the men told him to mind his own affairs, or it would be worse for him, while the lady earnestly entreated his interference in her behalf.

"Alvarez repeated his question, and declared that they should not drag the lady any further, and drawing his sword and stiletto, he prepared to attack them.

"One of the men immediately loosened his hold of the lady, and drawing his sword, suddenly rushed upon Alvarez, as if expecting that the suddenness of his assault would take him by surprise, when he could easily despatch him. But Alvarez was a wary and excellent swordsman, and prepared for all comers, and though his opponent was a powerful fellow, he quickly wounded and disarmed him.

"The other ruffian, seeing the fate of his companion, would not venture to try a bout with Alvarez, but quitting his hold of the lady, he made his escape as fast as possible, and the wounded man was not long in following his example.

"Alvarez did not attempt to prevent the escape of either of the ruffians, but devoted his sole attention to the lady, who was now offering up to him a thousand thanks for her rescue and preservation.

"Alvarez assured her of the gratification it afforded him in having rescued her from the men who had recently fled, and as the gates of Cadiz were by that time closed, and she would not be able that night to enter the city, he invited her to his residence, and early the next morning he said he would conduct her to her friends.

"The lady accepted his invitation, and Alvarez called up the old woman who waited upon him, (and who was the only member of his establishment), to attend upon the lady and assist her to retire to rest after the fright and fatigue which she had recently undergone.

"While the old woman was busy in her preparations, Alvarez, for the first time, began to examine the countenance of his guest, and such was her extraordinary beauty, although somewhat pale in consequence of the danger from which he had rescued her, that he inwardly thought he never before had looked upon features of such exquisite loveliness. He could have gazed at her for ever, but as this would not have been quite correct, besides creating some little confusion in the lady, Alvarez contented himself with a stolen glance now and then, when he thought himself unobserved.

"The lady, however, though not completely recovered from the alarm consequent upon her recent danger was agreeable and affable in conversation. She said she was the daughter of the Marquis di Carena, and Alvarez also ascertained from her that her name was Inez.

"On Alvarez requesting to know how she had been inveigled into the situation from which he had rescued her, she answered,—

"'I was walking on the Prado rather late this evening, with one or two of my female companions, when a note was put into my hand, which informed me that my father was taken suddenly ill, and requested my instant attendance upon him.

"'As my father was staying at his residence a few miles in the country, and the note, it was said, was written at his request by the surgeon who attended him, I requested the messenger to wait while I went home to apprise my family of my father's illness.

"'This, the messenger observed, was unnecessary, as he himself had apprised my family of the circumstance, and they had sent him to the Prado in search of me; and as my father would probably be dead before I arrived, unless I started instantaneously, no time ought to be lost.

"'The person then led me to a carriage in waiting, and believing the statement of the man to be true, I stept into the carriage, and he quickly followed me.

" ' We had not, however, proceeded above a few miles, when, in conse-quence of its ricketty state, the carriage broke down, and we were obliged to alight.

" ' It had now become very late, and as no passengers were upon the road, we could procure no assistance, and my companion was determined to proceed to the next village and get another carriage.

" ' The man, therefore, who had inveigled me away, and also another, pro-ceeded with me to the village, while a third was left in care of the carriage.

" ' It suddenly struck me, while proceeding with the men, that the road we were pursuing was strange to me, and that it was not the one which led to my father's residence. I mentioned this to the men, and they replied that they had come a nearer way, and had chosen a bye-road to reach my father's the quicker, and they requested me to make haste on with them, or we should be too late to see my father alive.

" ' My suspicions, however, were not allayed by their reply, and the conduct of the men in keeping such a watchful eye upon me rather tended to confirm them. But when I heard the ringing of the distant bells of the convent of Saint Mary, where I had been educated, and whose sounds were so familiar to me, I became instantly convinced of the treachery of my conductors.

" ' This convent I knew to be standing in quite an opposite direction to that where my father's mansion was situated.

" ' I mentioned to the men the discovery which I had now made, and after censuring them for their treachery towards me, I insisted that we should retrace our steps and return to Cadiz.

" ' This they refused to do, and immediately attempted to muffle me in a cloak, but before they could effectually do so, I had uttered the shriek which brought you to my assistance.'

" ' But do you not know the men?' said Alvarez.

" ' I never saw them before,' replied Inez.

" ' Have you no suspicion, then,' rejoined Alvarez, ' why the men attempted to decoy you away, or who employed them?''

" ' Yes, I have a suspicion as to their employer,' resumed Inez. ' The Senor Gonzalo, one of the chief inquisitors of Cadiz, a few months since, made overtures of love to me, which, as I disliked the man, I instantly re-jected, and he has frequently renewed his advances, but with the same suc-cess. Gonzalo is said to be violent and treacherous; and I believe him base and villanous enough to be concerned in a disgraceful affair like the present; and having been heard to mutter revenge against me, I suspect that the men from whom you rescued me were in his service.'

" Inez again renewed her protestations of gratitude for her deliverance, and she looked so lovely and fascinating while making them, that Alvarez longed to kiss the sweet lips from whence they proceeded; but at that moment the old woman came into the room, to inform Inez that every thing was ready for her reception; and Inez, after wishing Alvarez a good-night, retired to bed.

" The next morning Alvarez conveyed Inez to her friends in Cadiz, and directly afterwards the Marquis di Carena arrived.

" The friends of Inez had been all night in the greatest anxiety respecting her, and though they heard of her going away in a carriage, they were unable to ascertain in what direction or with whom she had gone.

" Inez informed her father of the deception which had been practised upon her, and mentioned her suspicion of the inquisitor Gonzalo. But when Gon-zalo was charged with the abduction, he denied all knowledge of it, and as the men employed in the affair could not be discovered, no tangible charge could be made against him, and consequently the matter was allowed to drop.

" Alvarez, however, was received by the whole of the family of Carena with the greatest favour, and an intimacy was established between them of the closest description. When Alvarez came to Cadiz, he made the Palace di Carena his home, and the marquis frequently condescended to honour the abode of Alvarez with his company ; for, unlike the majority of his countrymen, the marquis could derive a pleasure from the attractions of science ; and the chemical apparatus of Alvarez often conferred upon him both amusement and instruction.

" But it was the favour and esteem of Donna Inez which Alvarez was the most ambitious of acquiring, and he lost no opportunity of letting her know how much she had gained his admiration, and the deep impression she had made upon his heart.

" Neither was he suffered to sigh hopelessly and unrequited. His passion did not long remain unreturned. With the characteristic generosity of her sex, Inez allowed her love to follow close upon her gratitude, and her affection for Alvarez was as fervent and sincere as that of Alvarez for herself.

" Weeks and months passed away in all the bliss of unopposed and joyful love. Parents and friends all united to sanction the marriage of Alvarez with Inez, and the lovers would have smiled at the words of the poet, when he sang—

> " ' Oh, love, what is it in this world of ours
> Which makes it fatal to be loved ? Ah, why
> With cypress branches hast thou wreathed thy bowers,
> And made thy best interpreter a sigh ?'

But the sad reality of the poet's lines burst with sudden force upon the lovers, and they too soon discovered that happiness and love were not twin sisters."

" The inquisitor Gonzalo had watched, with the malignity of a fiend, the happiness of the lovers, and he determined to annihilate joys which he could never experience.

" It was this man, as Inez had suspected, who had planned and procured her abduction from her home, and though foiled in his attempt, yet, as his treachery remained undiscovered, he resolved that as Inez would not accept him for a lover, she should not wed another.

" The office of inquisitor which he held, he knew would enable him to procure the death of any person obnoxious to him, upon the vague charge of heresy ; and he determined to enter a charge of this description against Alvarez, and thus ensure his destruction.

" ' The lover removed,' exclaimed Gonzalo to himself, ' who knows but that the proud beauty may be glad to be the bride of the inquisitor.'

" As Alvarez was returning one beautiful evening to his residence, thinking upon the enjoyments of the next day, when he was to accompany his beloved Inez to the country residence of her father, where everything was to be settled preparatory to their union, he found himself surrounded and arrested by the alguazils of the inquisition.

" The alguazils took him first to his own residence, where they seized upon his papers and books, and also upon his chemical apparatus and astronomical instruments, and they safely lodged him in one of the dungeons of the inquisition.

" Alvarez was paralyzed by the suddenness of his seizure, and it was not till after he had been some time in his dungeon that he could bring his mind to reflect upon the occurrences which had recently befallen him, and the cause of his being arrested.

" He knew that the officers of the holy office never assigned a reason for the arrests which they made, and till his hearing he should not be made acquainted with the nature of his crime. He knew, too, that where the power of the accuser was great, the accused, whether innocent or guilty, possessed but a slight chance to escape. Mercy, or the tender feeling of pity, was seldom to be met with in the breast of an inquisitor.

" Why he was arrested Alvarez could not imagine, but at length he recollected that Gonzalo, having placed his affections upon Inez, had always scowled upon him with a malignant eye, and he at once conjectured that the inquisitor was the person who had caused his apprehension.   And when Alvarez thought of the power and hatred of his accuser, and his own utter helplessness, he felt that his last hour was not far distant.

" After Alvarez had been confined a few days in his dungeon, his stern-looking but silent gaoler came to tell him that he must follow him to the the judgment-hall, 'where your fate,' said the man, 'will shortly be decided.'

" As they walked along the dusky gloomy passages, the gaoler pointed with a grim look of pleasure at the dreadful instruments of torture which lay in their path, and which also hung up in the rooms through which they had to pass.   At length Alvarez entered the hall where the judges were seated.

" This room was wholly hung with black cloth, and contained no aperture through which to admit the light of day, and the proceedings of the judges were conducted by the light of torches, which cast their lurid glare upon the black cloth walls, with the design, apparently, of leading the poor prisoner to believe that he had passed the portals of death, and had arrived at the place which religion assigns to the condemned souls of the wicked.   Neither did the instruments of torture, which were thrown carelessly about in all directions assist to improve the appearance of the hall of judgment.

" The judges were three in number, and they had a secretary, and two or three attendants to wait upon them, all of whom were dressed in deep black.

" The heads and faces of the judges and attendants were covered with black cloth, so that only their fierce and glaring eyes were visible ; but Alvarez fancied that in the contour and voice of one of the judges he recognized the inquisitor Gonzalo.

" The chief inquisitor opened the proceedings, by abruptly demanding of Alvarez, ' if he were guilty.'

" ' Of what am I charged,' said Alvarez.

" ' Examine your conscience,' was the reply.

" ' I have, my lord,' rejoined Alvarez, ' most searchingly, and can discover nothing to bring upon me the vengeance of the holy office.'

" ' Beware !   Speak not lightly,' exclaimed the inquisitor, ' or torture may extract a confession from you.'

" ' Torture cannot make me confess that of which I am ignorant,' observed Alvarez. ' I again say, that I can recollect nothing which I have done heinous enough to bring upon me the displeasure of the inquisition.'

" ' What are your pursuits ?'

" My life has been devoted to study ; my wish has been to acquire knowledge, and in the exercise of that wish I believe my actions to be blameless.'

" ' What are your chief and favourite studies,' questioned the inquisitor.

" ' Astronomy and chemistry,' replied Alvarez.

" ' Which,' rejoined the inquisitor, ' which you use for the purposes of astrology and necromancy, both of which our holy religion strongly forbids.'

" ' Pardon me, my lord,' said Alvarez, ' my studies have never been devoted to such unworthy pursuits. I despise and abhor them as much as yourselves.'

" ' Do you not maintain a correspondence with heretics,' observed the inquisitor.

" ' I confess I have done so, but——'

" ' Hold,' interrupted the inquisitor ; ' that is enough. Is not that contrary to your creed as a true Catholic?'

" ' But, my lord,' resumed Alvarez, ' I have not corresponded with heretics on theological subjects, but simply on those of a scientific nature.'

" ' No matter,' answered the inquisitor ; ' our holy religion forbids you to

hold any communication with heretics, and expressly declares that all those who communicate with them are to be considered as guilty of heresy; and the documents found in your possession sufficiently testify to your having corresponded with both English and German heretics. Do you admit your guilt?'

" 'If such is the true definition of heresy,' replied Alvarez, 'the proofs in your possession are conclusive against me, and I cannot deny the charge. But——'

" 'That is enough,' interrupted the inquisitor. 'We now allow you to return to your dungeon without resorting to the torture, but unless at your next hearing you are more explicit in your replies, and at once confess yourself guilty of the crime of necromancy, with which you will then be charged, torture must be used, and the rack put in force, to compel your confession. Gaoler, take away the prisoner.'

" Alvarez was then hurried from the judgment hall, and as he was returning to his dungeon, the gaoler informed him that it was fortunate for him there was such an immense number of trials for heresy to come on that day, or he would never have escaped the first hearing without a taste of the torture.

" When Alvarez returned to his prison, he perceived at once that he was a doomed man. Already had the inquisitors so wrested the meaning of heresy to their purpose, that they had obliged him to confess himself guilty of it, and there was no doubt they would pursue the same system with respect to the other charges.

" He felt that he was placed in the midst of two dangers. If he avowed his guilt, he would be consigned to the executioner to be publicly burnt; and if he declared his innocence, he would be condemned to endure the most excruciating torments, and probably expire upon the rack.

" His judges, he saw, had in their own minds predetermined upon his guilt, and from the documents and philosophical instruments found at his residence,

No. 28

they had drawn as a positive conclusion that heresy and necromancy were thus satisfactorily proved against him. Their bigotry and ignorance disqualified them from seeing the utility of the chemical apparatus, and their superstition could only attach to them the powers of devilry and magic, with which, at his next hearing, they intended to charge him.

"As Alvarez, too, was unable to teach the inquisitors the wonders of science, because their prejudice and superstition taught them to despise the teacher, he saw the utter impossibility of escaping from the dreadful doom which awaited him.

"Gloomy, therefore, were the days, and sleepless were the nights of Alvarez in his damp and miserable dungeon, and hope almost fled from his bosom, and yielded him up a victim to despair.

"While pondering one evening over his impending fate, and pacing to and fro along the pavement of his dreary cell, Alvarez accidentally struck his foot against a stone in the wall, which, to his surprise, appeared to be loose. He stooped down to examine the stone more minutely, and feeling about it with his hands, he unintentionally pressed upon a secret spring which was fixed in a groove in the stone, and as the spring yielded to his pressure, the stone immediately flew open.

"An aperture presented itself large enough to permit Alvarez to escape, but as everything beyond was as dark as the grave, he felt some hesitation in leaving his gloomy, but still lighter dungeon.

"But his next examination before the inquisitors presented itself to his thoughts, and as the doom which then awaited him was certain, Alvarez was determined to nerve his courage to the task, and explore the path which accident had discovered to him.

"'If the passage leads to my death,' he inwardly exclaimed, 'my life will only be shorter by a few hours;' while love and hope sweetly whispered to him, 'that though dark, the path might ultimately lead to liberty and to Inez.'

"Fortunately, the gaoler had some time previously brought him his evening meal, so that he had the remainder of the afternoon before him. Alvarez, therefore, availed himself of the aperture, and closing the stone after him to prevent any pursuit, he carefully and slowly groped his way along the damp walls of the dark passage for a considerable distance, when he came to a door, once apparently very thick and heavily studded with nails.

"The door was closed, and would have bade defiance to the utmost exertions of Alvarez to open it, had not time and the damp stood his friends, which, having decayed the wood and corroded the iron, the door made but a slight resistance to his struggles for freedom, and he soon made an opening in it large enough to enable him to escape.

"Having obtained a clear passage, no further obstacle presented itself to his regaining his liberty, and as Alvarez then caught sight of a glimmering of light, which appeared at a great distance, he followed in that direction till he found himself standing at the mouth of a cave by the sea side, congratulating himself upon his fortunate deliverance.

"The prison of the inquisition had been a Moorish castle, and when that enlightened and ingenious people were driven from Spain, the wonders and mysteries of their architecture remained undiscovered, so that the passage by which Alvarez had escaped was totally unknown to the officers of the inquisition. When, therefore his cell was found to be empty, the ignorant inquisitors actually believed that either the Prince of Darkness had claimed him for his own, or that Alvarez had availed himself of his powers as a necromancer, and, by assuming the body of a bird or an insect, had escaped through the narrow aperture which gave light and air to his dungeon

"In the meantime Inez and her friends were surprised that Alvarez did not keep his appointment for the next day, and fearing some accident might have caused him to break his engagement, a messenger was sent to his house to ascertain the cause of his absence.

"It was not long before the messenger returned with the unwelcome intelligence that Alvarez had been arrested by the alguazils of the inquisition, and that his books, papers, and chemical instruments, had been seized at the same time.

"To what place he had been carried, his old housekeeper could not say; but, by dint of persevering inquiry, the marquis at length ascertained that a stranger had been seized by alguazils on the night in question, and brought in a carriage to the prison of the inquisition at Cadiz; and the marquis had no doubt, from the description he had received, that Alvarez was the stranger alluded to.

"He therefore used every exertion to obtain the immediate discharge of Alvarez, but in vain. The inquisition was a tribunal of so sacred a character, and so completely independent of all others, that the Ministers of Spain declined to interfere in behalf of the prisoner, and even the king refused to exert his authority to restrain the proceedings of the inquisition.

"The marquis, though vexed at the failure of his exertions, resolved not to relax them, or leave a stone unturned to procure the liberation of the prisoner. He therefore applied to Gonzalo, as a friend, to use his influence with his brother inquisitors, in favour of the unfortunate Alvarez. But Gonzalo professed his inability to save him, as in consequence, he said, of the documents and things found at the residence of Alvarez, there could be no doubt of his guilt.

"'Besides,' continued Gonzalo, 'the prisoner has confessed himself guilty of heresy, and the proof of his being a necromancer is in our hands, and were I even possessed of the power to save him, my oath of office would forbid me to interfere.'

"As the marquis ultimately found that every avenue of mercy was closed against his solicitations, he was reluctantly obliged to leave Alvarez to his fate. Several days thus passed away, and Alvarez still continued a prisoner.

"Inez was not to be daunted in her resolute determination to preserve the life of her lover. She, too, applied to the powerful officers of the court to intercede for Alvarez, and she even in person presented a petition to the king, but in vain; the cold answer was invariably returned, that the inquisition would be sure to administer strict justice.

"'If Alvarez is innocent,' said the king, 'he will shortly be set free, but if he is guilty, I cannot interfere with a religious tribunal, expressly established for the extirpation of heresy; and it would be contrary to the title of Catholic King, bestowed upon my ancestors by the Pope, were I to succour or intercede for a heretic.'

"Thus thwarted in her endeavours to obtain the freedom of her lover, Inez attempted to bribe the fidelity of one of the officers of the inquisition, but the man refused to assist her.

"'The penalty consequent upon discovery,' he observed, 'was a violent and lingering death, and the oath which he took when appointed to the office was too awful and solemn to be broken.'

"Driven almost frantic by her want of success, and at the impending fate of Alvarez, as a last resource Inez sought an interview with Gonzalo, hoping that the regard which he had so often expressed for her would aid her to procure her lover's preservation.

"But whether the inquisitor could not, or would not, interfere in behalf of Alvarez, certain it was to all her earnest entreaties to allow the prisoner to escape, Gonzalo returned the cold answer, that he could not intercede in favour of a heretic.

"'Believe me, lovely Inez,' he said, 'that though one of the chief officers of the inquisition, my power is too limited to be made available to save Alvarez. Were I to attempt his liberation, I should be suspected of heresy. Consider, therefore, your late lover as already dead, and allow me, adorable Inez, to supply his place in your affections. Surely a union with Gonzalo is far preferable to a marriage with the necromancer Alvarez.'

"Inez was wounded to the soul at the heartless and unfeeling conduct of the man, who could talk of love while announcing to her the impending death of her lover,—who, at such an unseasonable time, could press a suit, which, at all times disagreeable, was now doubly so in consequence of her suspecting him to be the murderer of Alvarez, by betraying him into the hands of the inquisition.

"Vexed and irritated at the villany of Gonzalo, Inez allowed her passion to get the better of her discretion, and forgetting the cause which brought her to the inquisitor, she vehemently upbraided him with his treachery to Alvarez, and taunted him with being a cowardly blood-thirsty hypocrite, fit only to do the cruel and dirty work of the inquisition.

"Gonzalo was exasperated at the taunts of Inez, and casting aside his usual coolness of temper, he passionately exclaimed :—

"'Yes, yes, I admit the deed. It *was* me who betrayed the heretic Alvarez, and I glory in the act. Nay, more; to show you that I am not a person to be provoked, or slighted with impunity, I throw off all disguise, and tell you (what before I would not, because I thought the intelligence would wound your feelings,) that your Alvarez, your lover of a star-gazer, heretic, and necromancer, expired but yesterday upon the rack !'

"'It was my voice that condemned him to his doom ; it was I that gloried in his torments ; and when I saw him enduring tortures upon the rack to the very utmost of human endurance, it was I that ordered the dreadful machine to be still more distended, and your lover—your Alvarez, was pulled joint from joint, and expired in excruciating agony upon the instrument of torture !'

"Gonzalo, after giving utterance to this false inhuman speech, sneeringly demanded of the pale and horror-stricken Inez how it was that she could not command a few tears at the untimely and piteous fate of her lover.

"Inez deigned no reply to the cruel question of the cold unfeeling monster. The passions which oppressed her brain were too varied and violent to allow them to give utterance in words. Her lover she felt was dead, for she implicitly believed the statements of the inquisitor, and his murderer stood before her.

"Unlike the colder beauties of the north, who love fervently, but not so wildly as those of the south; and had such a catastrophe happened to them, would meekly and quietly have let

> "Concealment, like a worm in the bud,
> Feed on their damask cheek."

brooding over the happiness of by-gone days, and ultimately yielding themselves victims to insidious advances of consumption.

"Not so with Inez ; the passions in her bosom were as fierce as her own meridian sun. The Spanish and Oriental maidens love more warmly than the maidens of colder climes. But then the wild feeling of vengeance for thwarted passion, burns in their bosoms equally furious with that of love. In the words of the poet, who knew them well :—

> "'Their revenge is as the tiger's spring,
> Deadly, and quick, and crushing.'

It was thus with Inez,—

> "'Her love was Heaven! but her revenge was hell!'

"She returned not the taunts of Gonzalo, for they were beneath her notice.

She viewed him only as the murderer of her lover, and the time to act, and not to talk, had now arrived.

"Acting, therefore, from the impulse of the moment, while yet Gonzalo was triumphing in his own heart at the agony he had created in her's, Inez cautiously drew a dagger from her bosom, (a not unfrequent appendage to the toilet of a Spanish maiden,) and as Gonzalo approached unsuspectingly within a few yards of her, she bounded upon him with the fury of a tigress, and buried the dagger in his breast.

"Gonzalo cried out loudly for assistance, and attempted to seize her, but Inez eluded his grasp, and finding himself growing more faint in consequence of the excessive hemorrhage, he fell to the ground, and in a few minutes he was a corpse.

"In the meantime Inez made the best of her way to her father's palace, whither the officers of the inquisition pursued her, and she had scarcely time to inform her friends of the deed which she had committed, when the alguazils arrived at the Palace di Carena.

"The marquis, however, determined to protect his daughter to the utmost of his power, and he armed his servants in her defence; and when the people of Cadiz saw the number of alguazils which surrounded the palace of Carena, and ascertained the cause of their arrival, they resolved to make common cause with the marquis, and aid him in protecting his lovely daughter.

"Hundreds of the people congregated together for that purpose, and they only wanted a leader to commence their attack upon the alguazils,—and a leader soon presented himself.

"A man in the garb of a fisherman suddenly made his appearance, and seizing a sword from one of the officers of the inquisition, he took upon himself the command of the people. He led them to the attack, and in a short time the whole of the alguazils and their supporters were completely routed. Several were slain, and many were wounded.

"Neither the marquis or his servants had taken any part in the fray, but as it had happened in the defence of his daughter, he was fearful of incurring the king's displeasure, and he therefore determined to make a journey to Madrid (where the king resided) to procure his majesty's pardon both for himself and the people.

"But he determined to conceal his daughter in the meantime, that if he should be called upon to deliver her up to the holy office, he might excuse himself by declaring that she had made her escape, and he knew not where to find her.

"The marquis therefore sought out his beloved Inez to advise with her as to the future course she had better adopt, but on entering her apartment, what was his astonishment at seeing his daughter in the arms of the fisherman who had acted as leader of the people.

"Surprised and angry, the marquis was about to rebuke her for her conduct, when the fisherman, suddenly turning himself round, revealed to his view the features of Alvarez.

"Pleased and delighted at the unexpected meeting, the marquis was anxious to know how Alverez had obtained his liberation from the dungeons of the inquisition.

"The manner of his escape Alvarez quickly explained, and he told the marquis that having reached the sea-shore, he disguised himself in the habit of a fisherman, determined to see his beloved Inez once more previous to embarking for a foreign country, as his residence in Spain would no longer be safe, and he fortunately arrived at the palace of Carena just time enough to preserve his beloved from becoming the victim of the inquisition.

"The marquis was highly gratified at the narrative of Alvarez, and informed him of his intended journey to Madrid.

"'But,' said the marquis, 'my daughter must in the meantime be sent abroad, or placed in a convent, as the holy office will never submit to be deprived of their victim. Whither, Alvarez, do you intend going?'

"'To England,' replied Alvarez. 'I have ascertained that a vessel will leave this port for England in two hours. I have secured my passage, and shall go on board within that time.'

"'Would to God,' rejoined the marquis, 'that Inez could accompany you, for I know not how to preserve her in Spain. An English vessel would prove a better protection than a convent.'

"'If such is your wish,' observed Alvarez, 'nothing is more easy than to allow Inez to go with me. You have already been pleased to give your consent to our union, and had I not been arrested by the alguazils, the day for our wedding would have been settled at your country residence.'

"'True,' said the marquis, 'it would have been.'

"'Then,' rejoined Alvarez, 'if you have not withdrawn your consent ——'

"'Certainly not,' interrupted the marquis.

"'Or,' continued Alvarez, 'if my dear Inez still retains the love for me which so often she has expressed!'

"'Still retains her love'—repeated Inez. 'Have I not embrued my hands in blood for your sake, and yet, Alvarez, you can speak so doubtingly of my love. Love you!—my love is unalterable—is the same as ever.'

"'Beloved Inez,' resumed Alvarez, 'pardon me,—I know your love is unchangeable. Well, then, my lord, such being the case, this affair can be easily settled. Your chaplain, at your request, will unite us in the course of a few minutes, and within two hours Inez and myself will have sailed for England.'

"'Be it so,' said the marquis; 'I approve of your plan, and the property which Inez possesses in her own right, and also a handsome annual provision from me, I will instruct my agent to invest in the English funds for your benefit; and may you continue to love each other and be happy.'

"Accordingly the marriage ceremony was instantly celebrated between the lovers, and after providing themselves with a few necessaries for their voyage, Alvarez and Inez embarked on board an English ship, and in a few hours were far from the city of Cadiz, and beyond the vengeance of the inquisition.

"As the passage was a pleasant and quick one, the new married couple arrived safely in England, and took up their residence in the neighbourhood of London.

"In the meantime the Marquis di Carena hurried to Madrid, and having procured his own pardon, and that of the people, he returned to Cadiz, where the late fray and the murder of the alguazils were quickly forgotten.

"A few years afterwards the marquis was appointed to the office of Grand Inquisitor of Cadiz, and the king, having granted a free pardon to Inez for the assassination of Gonzalo, and consented to allow the withdrawal of the charge of heresy and necromancy against Alvarez, Inez and Alvarez returned to Cadiz, where the remainder of their days were peaceful, happy, and prosperous; and they continued through life to love each other with a fervour of affection which time could neither lessen or destroy.

"Alvarez amused himself with the study of his favourite sciences, without again incurring the displeasure of the Inquisition. The light of science had now dawned upon Spain, and instead of being scouted as an astrologer and necromancer, Alvarez found himself admired and respected by the most learned of his countrymen, and his levees were attended by the literati of all nations, who vied with each other in doing honour to the first and greatest philosopher that Spain had ever produced."

The tale was over, and Adeline looked up from the curate's manuscript with a mind more at ease than she had commenced it.

"I must be patient," she said; and she sought her own chamber with a happier mind.

CHAPTER LX.

"Oh, Love! how perfect is thy mystic art!
Strengthening the weak, and trampling on the strong."

THE CURATE'S LETTER.—MANDEVILLE'S COMPUNCTIONS OF CONSCIENCE.—A SUDDEN RESOLUTION.—THE JOURNEY.—EXPLANATION AND RECONCILIATION.

THE curate's letter to Herbert Mandeville ran thus:—

"Bracefield.

"HERBERT MANDEVILLE,—If you are ill, forgive me for addressing you as I now do, and at the same time blame yourself for not letting us know of it, that we might not misconstrue your silence.

"You have said to us all that you love Adeline Mourdant; but you must likewise recollect that we all here love her likewise, and the fact of your love for her was only grateful to our feelings so long as it contributed to her happiness.

"Herbert Mandeville, Adeline is not happy!—Ask your own heart the reason!   "Your friend,
                                                  "ROBERT ENDSLEIGH."

The curate felt his mind now at ease, when he had written and sent the above letter to Herbert, for the good old man had still sufficient confidence in humanity to believe that if Herbert even had strayed for a moment from his pledged devotion to Adeline, he would return again the moment the chord of awakening feeling was touched.

The day passed away more calmly and serenely than usual, and even Adeline seemed to reflect some of the renewed hope and confidence which animated the breast of the curate. It would be the third day before an answer from London could arrive, and Mr. Endsleigh armed himself with all the patience he could muster to calmly wait the result, and in the meantime he determined, by keeping Adeline occupied and her mind always in action, to prevent, if possible, the brooding of uneasy thoughts.

On the second morning, therefore, he proposed a day's tour round the neighbouring country, and as the weather was serene and beautiful, all gladly assented to the proposition.

Mrs. Mourdant even smiled upon the proposal, and languidly gave her consent. For some weeks Adeline's mother had appeared to be sinking into an apathetic state, which at any other period would have attracted Adeline's attention; but her own mind was so engrossed with anxieties that she failed to observe the saddened appearance of her mother.

The little party consisted of Adeline and Mrs. Mourdant, the curate, and Mrs. Plumpjoy, and lastly, old Andrew, loaded with a basket of cold provisions, which had been prepared by the provident foresight of Mrs. Plumpjoy, who remarked, that if it was not for her she did believe nobody would think of anything, and that if Mr. Endsleigh's head was moveable, she was quite sure, that she was, that he would be continually leaving it at home.

The curate gave his arm to Mrs. Mourdant, and Adeline walked by his other side, while Mrs. Plumpjoy followed, engaged in an earnest discourse with old Andrew, concerning the depredations that had been recently committed in the dairy by some strange cat, who had dipped his or her whiskers in all the cream regularly every night for a week past, and never been caught yet.

"The weather is always more delightful after rain," said the curate; "it beats down all vapours that encumber the pure air."

"The country does indeed look beautiful," said Adeline, with a sigh.

"How far do you think of going?" said Mrs. Mourdant, in the weak, querelous tone of an invalid.

"About a mile and a half from here," said the curate, "is a magnificent old ruin, standing most singularly in a valley. It is sheltered from every wind, and will afford us a place of rest, as well as ample food for reflection and conversation."

"It must be a black cat, Andrew, I tell you," screamed Mrs. Plumpjoy. "Black cats always go from one cream pail to another, while *torture shells* always——"

"Tortoise—tortoise shells!" cried the curate.

"There you are again, brother," replied Mrs. Plumpjoy, "snapping one's nose off as usual, if one don't say things your way."

"But is there not a right way and a wrong, sister?"

"Oh, fiddle-de-dee! I have got my way and you've got yours."

"And next comes a horse to be shaved and a pig to have its corns cut!" said the curate, with a smile. "Now you see, Martha, I've adopted your old saying, so you had better give it up."

"My saying?"

"Yes. You know——"

"I don't know any such thing, Mr. Endsleigh. When did you ever hear me—— My saying, indeed! Well, I never. Next comes a horse—— a hem!"

None of the party could refrain from laughter at Mrs. Plumpjoy, and that lady, in great indignation, drew herself up very stiffly, muttering something about the deceased Major Plumpjoy.

"There is the ruin," exclaimed Mr. Endsleigh, as they arrived at the brow of a little hillock, which communicated a tolerably extensive view of the surrounding richly cultivated country.

In the distance could be seen the ruin mentioned by the curate, looking grey and venerable with the marks of age and decay.

"The distance appears great," remarked Mrs. Mourdant.

"But it is not so in reality," replied the curate; "less than half an hour's ordinary walking will place us within the shadows of yon ruined pile."

They quickened their steps, and before the sun had climbed the meridian they stood within the crumbling walls of what had once been a feudal residence of repute and power.

The most perfect spot about the building was a spacious court-yard, which had been paved with some durable species of stone, and which was to all appearance in an admirable state of preservation.

Here our party paused, and seated themselves on the shafts of some fallen pillars which had once lent a grace to a handsome portico conducting to the principal apartments of the building.

Andrew spread a cloth on the cool flagstones, and produced, under the superintendance of Mrs. Plumpjoy, the cold provisions which that energetic lady had so carefully selected for the entertainment of the little company.

Adeline felt her spirits revived by the genial exercise of the walk, and the solemn grandeur of the ruins imparted a serenity to her mind which it had, unhappily for some time been a stranger to.

With an increased glow upon her cheek she partook of the repast, and the conversation began to flow easily and pleasantly from one to another of the attached friends who were there assembled.

"I wonder," said Mrs. Plumpjoy, "who used to live here?"

"Some ancestors, doubtless," replied the curate, "of the family who now own the ruins."

"It's enough to give anybody the horrors, it is, to come here," continued

Mrs. Plumpjoy, who had no eye for the picturesque. "As for sleeping in such a place, I wonder anybody ever could."

"You forget," said the curate, "that these mouldering walls were once new—that these deserted halls were once, doubtless, redolent of substantial comfort and brilliant with decorations."

"And yet," said Adeline, "these ruins have a charm for me which the finished and perfect mansion would have wanted."

"A melancholy charm?"

"It is a melancholy one, but not, therefore, unpleasing."

"Melancholy pleasure !" cried Mrs. Plumpjoy. "Well, I never."

"There is a charm in melancholy," said the curate—"a luxury in grief ; but its indulgence is both dangerous and enervating."

"Well," cried Mrs. Plumpjoy, "let those be miserable that like. Give me a good laugh, and plenty to eat and drink."

"You are dreadfully unromantic," said the curate, laughing.

"To be sure I am. Rheumatic, indeed ; I'm not so old as to be——"

"Romantic !" cried the curate. "I did not say rheumatic, Martha."

"Well, I suppose it's much the same thing."

"Why, one is a disease of the mind, and the other of the body," said the curate ; "but you know you are fond of similes, sister."

"Fond of what?"

"Similies."

"Indeed, then, I ain't. Give me good English fare, roast-beef and plumb-pudding, before all the foreign dishes."

Here there was a general laugh, and Mrs. Plumpjoy looked from one to the other in deep indignation of spirit."

"Now, brother, I know you've been holding me out," she cried.

"Holding you out?"

No. 29

"Yes, to be sure."

"I should say," remarked the curate, with great gravity, "that your weight, Martha, would effectually screen you from any such proceeding."

"There you go again! Snapping me up?"

"Nay, nay!"

"But I say yes."

"As how?"

"Oh, you all know well enough. All I have got to say is——"

"Next comes a horse," interrupted the curate.

"To be shaved," roared Mrs. Plumpjoy, laughing herself.

"Now I'm defeated by good humour," said the curate; "the most powerful weapon in the world, if people did but know how to use it."

"The clouds seem gathering," said Adeline.

Mr. Endsleigh looked up at the sky rather anxiously, as he replied :—

"They are, but not heavily, Adeline. We have ample time to get home."

Even as he spoke the murmur of thunder afar off came dully upon the ear.

"A storm!" cried Mrs. Mourdant.

"'Tis many miles distant," remarked Mr. Endsleigh.

Suddenly a scream burst from Adeline.

All eyes were immediately turned towards her in alarm. Her face was ashy pale, and her eyes were fixed upon an open door-way immediately opposite to her.

"What alarms you?" said the curate.

"Speak, Adeline, speak," cried the curate.

"Goodness gracious," screamed Mrs. Plumpjoy.

"It—it—was—" faltered Adeline.

"What?—what?" asked Mr. Endsleigh and Mrs. Mourdant in a breath.

"I—I—. Nothing—nothing. It was—nothing."

"Nothing?"

"No—no."

"But, Adeline."—

"No—no," she repeated. "It was nothing. Only a sudden impulse—nothing—nothing."

CHAPTER LXI.

"I have a grief I may not tell,
A harbouring sorrow, which may haply
Hurry me to death!"—OLD PLAY.

THE MYSTERIOUS INTERRUPTION.—ADELINE'S GRIEF.—CONJECTURES AND FEARS.—WHO IS HE?

THE surprise of the curate at Adeline's singular emotion was not unmixed with serious alarm lest there should be really some cause more than mere nervousness for her sudden exclamation.

The whole party was very much discomposed by the alarm, and as the clouds were still gathering portentously in the horizon, Mrs. Mourdant proposed their immediate departure for home.

"We shall be wise, I think," said Mr. Endsleigh, "to follow your advice. Without being very weather-wise, I think the aspect of the sky warrants me in predicting a storm."

They all rose, and Andrew having packed the remnants of the repast, the little party was ready to commence its homeward march.

Just, however, as they were on the verge of the ruins, and when a few steps would have carried them beyond its shelter, a deluge of rain came down, which compelled them to shrink back, and find what refuge they might among the time-worn halls of the ancient building.

"We are fairly caught," said the curate ; then, as he observed Adeline shudder, as if with some secret dread upon again entering the gloomy precincts of the ruins, he added :—

"Such storms as these cannot last long, and we shall soon again be on our homeward hack.

"Yes, yes," said Adeline. "Would we were home, indeed."

"Are you not well, Adeline," said her mother, with affectionate earnestness."

"Yes—yes, mother. Quite well now."

Her looks, however, belied her words, for she was very pale, and her eyes wandered incessantly in all directions, as if she momentarily feared that some horrible sight would blast their vision.

The curate took an opportunity of approaching Adeline unobserved by her mother and Mrs. Plumpjoy, and said,—

"Adeline !"

She started, and a flush of colour came across her pale cheek, as he continued,—

"Can you confide to me what has really alarmed you?"

For a moment she was silent, then, with an effort, she said,—

"I—I can."

"And will you?"

"I will."

"I am glad to hear it, for there is a chance I may relieve you."

Adeline whispered in the curate's ear,—

"*He* is here."

"Who?"

"Oh, do not ask me."

"He whom I once saw you with in the ruins of Rose Villa, Adeline?"

"Yes."

"That man who——"

"Hush! hush!"

"Adeline, how can you suffer yourself to be thus persecuted?"

"Do not—oh, do not ask me."

"Whatever this man may be, he cannot wish or mean you well."

"Alas! I know it."

"Then throw off the weakness which makes you dread him."

"I cannot."

"Adeline, the innocent can always, if they will, resist such oppression."

"You think—" gasped Adeline.

"What?"

"Me guilty?"

"No—Heaven is my judge, no. But——"

"But what?"

"I do think you——"

"What, oh, what?"

"Weak, Adeline."

"I am—I am," she cried ; "and yet—oh, what other can I do? You cannot judge, Mr. Endsleigh, because you know not my mystery."

"True," said the curate ; "but take care of one thing, my dear girl."

"And what is that?"

"That you are not giving way to some false feeling, and doing really more harm by your fancied suffering than would result from the most unguarded candour."

"I have thought of that," said Adeline.   "Such an idea has crossed my mind."

"I rejoice that it has."

A peal of thunder at this moment echoed through the mouldering ruins, and for a moment afterwards an awful silence reigned over the face of nature, and the little party looked at each other in unconcealed apprehension.

"Well, I never !" ejaculated Mrs. Plumpjoy. "We shall all be buried alive and ruinated."

"We had better endure the rain," said Mrs. Mourdant, " than trust to the fragile walls of this ruin."

"These walls," said the curate, "are far from fragile.   What now remains of this once splendid feudal abode consists of that portion which has most successfully battled with the assaults of time and tempests."

"Yes—yes," said Adeline, "let us stay. See, the storm is passing off ; there is light in the sky."

"I think so too," said Mr. Endsleigh.

Adeline plucked his sleeve, saying,—

"Sir, will you——"

"Will I what ?"

"Do me one favour ?"

"A hundred if you wish."

"I—I—must see the—the person."

The curate looked grave, as he said,—

"Alone, do you mean ?"

"Alone."

"You think him still here ?"

"I do."

"And wish me to seek him ?"

"No, no—I will seek him.   Will you engage my mother's attention while I leave you for a few minutes ?"

"I fear," said the curate, "I ought not."

Adeline looked in his face with an expression of such mute suffering that the good old man's heart relented, and he said,—

"Adeline, I believe you all honour, truth, and innocence ; be it as you wish."

Adeline looked her thanks.

"Go," said the curate—"go now."

"As he spoke he advanced to Mrs. Mourdant, and said to her,—

"Suppose we look out at yonder window, and observe the aspect of the sky ? Come, Martha."

He walked towards the window, and was followed by Mrs. Mourdant and Mrs. Plumpjoy, while Adeline silently left the spot she had been standing upon, and passed through an arched doorway which led more into the interior of the ruin.

With a quick step and a beating heart Adeline took her way from room to room of the dilapidated edifice, without meeting the object at once of her search and dread.

At length she paused on the landing of a crazy-looking staircase, and raising her voice, she cried as loudly as she was able,—

"Adeline is here."

"Here—here," repeated the echoes in the crumbling building, and then died away in low muttering sounds.

"Thank Heaven !" said Adeline, clasping her hands—"thank Heaven he has gone !"

"Don't make too sure of that," said a voice, which Adeline knew too well, and at the instant, from a small room which opened on to the landing, the man appeared, with whom the reader has already been made acquainted as the companion of the veritable Captain Dufours and the persecutor of Adeline.

"Well," he said, as Adeline remained silent, "you don't ask me me how I am."

"Do you expect me to welcome you?" said Adeline.

"Yes, to be sure," replied the man.

"Then I cannot."

"Oh, very well. It's much the same."

"What do you want with me?" said Adeline, the tears starting to her eyes as she spoke. "Why do you persecute me thus?"

"My want," replied the man, "is a very common one."

"Cruel—cruel," sobbed Adeline.

"Yes, a cruel want, if you please, Adeline. The short and the long of it is, I want money."

"And you come to me for it—to me, a poor, penniless girl. Oh, shame shame!"

"None of your nonsense and heroics for me," cried the fellow, although his flushed cheek and slightly faltering tone showed that he was cut to the soul by Adeline's reproof.

"Heroics?" said Adeline. "Ah, if you——"

"If I what?"

"If you had the heroism to be virtuous."

"Well, what then?"

"You might be happy."

"But I am happy, I tell you. Ha! ha!—who is happier, I wonder?'

"You happy?"

"Yes, I."

"No, no—you are wretched."

The man bit his lips and stamped, with a bitter execration, as he said,—

"Adeline, I don't come here to hear a sermon."

"I know it."

"Well, then, don't treat me to one. I want money."

"For what end?"

"To leave England."

"No, no—that was the former pretence. You know I cannot trust you most solemn words."

"Yes, you may; I'll leave this confounded country altogether; but I can't go without means."

"You had ample."

"Yes, I had."

"Where is the large sum you had of—of—me?"

"Gone, to be sure."

"Then there is no more."

"Nonsense."

"Can you tell me where?"

"From the same quarter."

"No," said Adeline, firmly. "I would see you given up to the laws you have offended rather than that."

"You would?"

"I would."

"Well, then, you shall see it. I'll give myself up to-morrow—aye, to-day."

Adeline shook her head.

"You doubt me?"

"No."

"Why do you pretend you do then?"

"I have no doubts; you will *not* do what you threaten. 'Tis a weak device. George, you have taught me distrust and caution."

" And why will I not ?"

" Because——"

" What ?"

" You must have become a coward."

" A coward ! Damnation !"

" Yes, or you would protect, not persecute me."

" Protect you !"

" Yes, protect me, George."

" Ha ! ha ! and why, I should like to know ?"

" Because you happen to be my most unworthy——"

" Well. go on."

" BROTHER !"

" Ha ! ha ! Well, that's the very reason I came to you for money, you little jade. Where have you plucked up so much spirit, I wonder ? Not from old square-toes, I should think."

" Who ?"

" Why, that old canting curate, to be sure."

CHAPTER LXII.

"One's relations fancy that such a connexion gives them a license to behave as badly as they like without fear of consequences."—SWIFT.

THE BROTHER.—THE BLESSING OF RELATIONS.—LIGHT AND DARKNESS.—THE ARREST.—AN EXPLANATION AND A DEFIANCE.

IT is strange how, under peculiar circumstances, the weak and timid can and do exercise a power over the strong and wicked at which they tremble, while they affect to despise it.

George Mourdant—for that indeed was his name—quailed and shrunk like a guilty thing, as he was, before the indignant glance of purity and innocence which darted from the eyes of Adeline when he spoke thus slightingly of the curate, who she considered as her best and most disinterested friend.

" George," she said calmly, " you know, while even your tongue speaks lightly of that good old man, that in your heart you own his excellence and envy his happiness."

" Envy him ? Ha ! ha !—that is good. It will be some time before I envy a country curate, I think."

" Oh, George, if you——"

" If what—if I what ?"

" If you, however far from approaching his true excellence, would endeavour only to imitate any one of his virtues——"

" Pshaw !—don't preach. I suppose when he pops off the hook you expect to be made curate yourself, and are practising beforehand. But a truce to nonsense. I have but one word on my lips."

" And that, George ?"

" Is money."

Adeline shook her head.

" Money I will, and money I must have," cried the brother. " Now, once for all, Adeline, I tell you what I intend to do."

" Say on—say on," sobbed Adeline.

" I'll go to this young fellow—this Mandeville."

" To him ?

" Yes ; why not ? I'll tell him I came from you to borrow a little of hi superfluous cash."

" You do not—you cannot mean it."

" Don't I ? You will hear."

" Then, George, hear me. It is time that I declare what I will do."

" You do !"

" Yes, weak girl as I am, you shall find that I can put a stop to your most——"

" Well, say on ; never stop at an ugly word."

" I will not. Your most infamous career."

" Good—very good. What then ?"

" I will endeavour, through my friends, to take such measures that, although your life may be safe, you shall leave England, and permit our poor heart-broken mother to—to die, at least, in peaceful ignorance of what would strike her to the earth."

" Oh, indeed. You'd give me up, would you ?"

" I would. George, I could succour you in distress ; I would beg for you. Even in crime I would aid you if I saw contrition, but——"

" But what ?"

" But I cannot aid you with the means, not of flying from criminality, but evidently for the purpose of prosecuting a life of infamy, which must end——"

" Where ?"

" I shudder to think."

" Why don't you say gallows ? But you'd be wrong if you did. They sha'n't make a show of me. No, no."

" Torture me no more," said Adeline. " Away, away !"

" Away, be d——d !" cried George. " Give me a note to this—Mandeville, for a hundred pounds."

" I ?"

" Yes, you."

" Never !"

" You won't ?"

" As Heaven hears me, I will not !"

For a few moments George Mourdant was unable to speak from excess of rage, and then, dashing forward, he seized Adeline's arm with violence, exclaiming,—

" Say you won't again, and——"

" You'll murder me ?" said Adeline.

" Write me the note."

" Not for my life's sake !"

" Are you mad, girl ?"

" George, George, you are."

" Once for all, now. I have writing implements with me, purposely,—you use them ?"

" I will not."

" Furies—you—you dare not refuse me."

" You see I dare."

" Curses——"

" Hold !" cried the voice of the curate, and he suddenly appeared before the eyes of the infuriated George.

" Adeline, what is all this ?"

Adeline flew to the curate's side, and grasping his protecting arm, burst into tears.

George's first impulse seemed to be to fly, but after glancing round him, he stood doggedly facing the curate, who looked sternly at him as he said,—

"Who you are, and what may be your business with, or claims upon this young lady, I know not; but this I do know, that no possible circumstances can excuse a man for behaving with violence to a woman.

"Who are you," cried George, "that dare question my conduct, I should like to know?"

"My name," said the curate, calmly, "is Robert Endsleigh. I am the curate of Bracefield. Will you be equally candid, young man?"

"That's as it suits me. I don't tell my name and pursuits to every idle inquirer."

"I don't wish to know who you are," said the curate. "I believe that you are a bad man, whatever name you bear."

"You do, do you?"

"Certainly I do."

"Well, what then?".

"That opinion is the worst conclusion I can come to," replied Mr. Endsleigh. "There is no climax worse than that in my mind."

"Well then, old big wig, now you've had your say, perhaps you'll have the kindness to take yourself off, for I and that ' young lady' have got some business to settle before we part."

The curate turned an inquiring glance to Adeline, and she continued,—;

"No! oh no! It is not so. Do not leave me, Mr. Endsleigh."

"I certainly will not," he replied.

"Oh, you won't go," sneered George.

"This young lady is under my protection," said the curate; "and I will not betray my trust."

"What if I throw you out of yonder window?" said George to the old man.

"I am an aged man," said Mr. Endsleigh, "but I could answer your supposition with another."

"And pray what may that be?" jeered George.

"What if I were to resist such treatment, and——"

"And what? Don't be afraid. Go on. Ha! ha!"

"And call for the assistance of those below."

"Those below!" cried George. "Ha! ha! That is good. Those below. Ho! ho!"

"Yes," said the curate, mildly; "those below."

"Two old women."

"Nay more, that they——"

"Yes. Ha! ha! A superannuated old gardener. Ho! ho! Why, old gentleman, your whole party ain't a match for me."

"I doubt that," said the curate.

"You do?"

"I do."

"And wherefore?"

"Because we have had a little addition."

"An addition?"

"Yes, since the rain set in."

"Well?"

"Others have taken refuge in these ruins."

A dark scowl passed over George's brow as he said, in a tone of suppressed bitterness,—

"Speak, old man; who are they? But I don't believe it at all."

"You may be convinced."

"Then who are they, I say? Speak, or——

"Hold, young man. I have no disinclination to tell you we have protectors here."

"Well?"

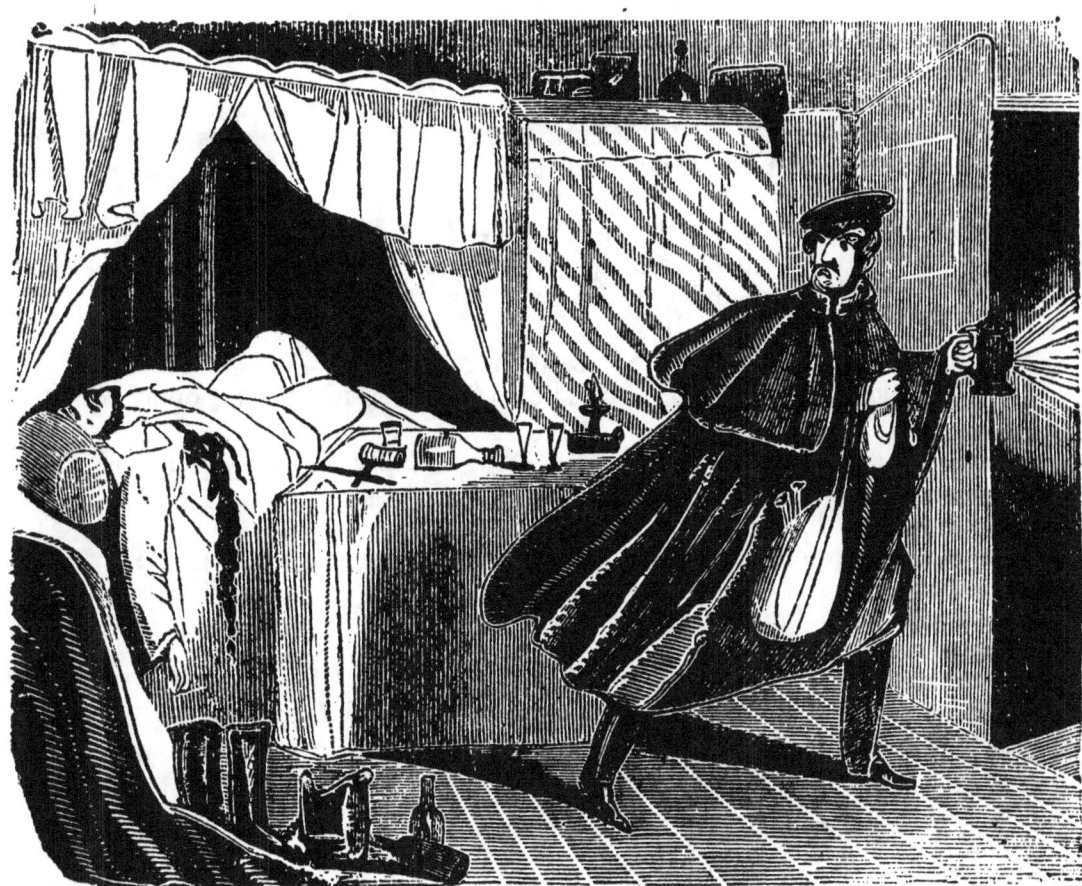

"A party of soldiers has taken refuge in the ruins."

"Soldiers?" gasped George.

"Yes, soldiers."

"And—and—did——"

"Did what?"

"Did they say—their errand—in—in this part of the country?"

"Yes."

"And—and—it was? Speak old man!"

"To apprehend a deserter from Gibraltar, who had committed robbery and——"

"And—well—well——"

"Murder!"

George Mourdant clutched by the crazy bannisters of the mouldering staircase, and the big drops of fearful perspiration burst out upon his brow, while his face became ashy pale.

CHAPTER LXII

"Oh votaries of crime—thy footing is unstable,
And in every breath thou hearest a cry
Which warns thee of pursuit." ANON.

THE MURDERER.—THE ESCAPE.—AN EXPLANATION.—THE FAITH OF RUFFIANS.
—ADELINE'S GRIEF.

An utter prostration of both mental and physical power seemed to come over George Mourdant, and with one arm twined round the bannisters of the stairs, he stood in an attitude of breathless attention, to the slightest sounds which might reach him from below.

No. 30

Adeline too was thunderstricken by the curate's information, and clasping her hands, she said,—

"George ! fly—fly !"

"Do they seek him ?" said the curate.

"Yes—yes," said Adeline ; "they do."

"Indeed ?"

"Hush—hush," whispered George ; "I—I am lost."

"Unhappy man," said the curate. "It is not my province to deliver you to justice. Fly, and repent ye of that ye have done."

"How ? Where ? Which way ?"

"No, no," said Adeline ; "he is safer here."

"I am," said George, faintly. "They would see me in the open country. I shall be lost—lost."

"Adeline," said the curate ; "is not this a fitting time to tell me who I am screening from justice ?"

"It is," said Adeline.

"I will spare you the trouble," interrupted George ; "my name is Mourdant."

"Mourdant ?"

"Yes."

"Then you are Adeline's brother ?"

"I am."

The curate shook his head as he said,—

"Young man, young man. You should have been far different from what you are."

"Will you aid me ?" said George.

"I will not send your captors to you," replied the curate.

"Hark !" whispered George ; "hark."

"Order, arms !" cried a voice from the ground floor of the ruins, and it was succeeded by the rattle of the soldiers' muskets.

"Ground arms," was then cried, and the old ruins echoed with the clang of the firelocks on the stone flooring of the dilapidated hall.

"Pile arms," was the next order, and then ensued a rattling noise for a few seconds, succeeded by the sound of feet, as the little military party strolled about among the ruins.

"By Heavens !" said George, "they contemplate some stay here."

"The storm still continues," said the curate ; "they will not leave until it has abated."

"And I am cooped up here like a bird in a cage, confound them."

"Hush, hush, young man," said the curate. "They are doing their duty. Are you doing yours ?"

George's lips curled into a sneer, and under any other circumstances than those of his present danger, he would have made some angry reply to the curate's admonition, but as it was he merely said,—

"Well, sir, I must even do the best I can. You will not betray me ?"

"Betray," replied Mr. Endsleigh, "would be scarcely the proper word to apply to the action, even if I were to call upon those men below to come and apprehend you ; but I am one that thinks the conscience of a criminal is his worst punishment. I shall not direct your pursuers to you."

"We had better descend," said Adeline. "We shall be missed, and possibly sought for."

"True," replied the curate. "Come, Adeline."

"So," said George, "you are walking off, Adeline, without saying good-bye or good luck to your own brother."

"George," said Adeline, "how long is it since you recollected you were my brother ?"

"How long?"

"Yes; how long since was it that you sneered at that title, when I reminded you of it to save me from—from——"

"From what, Adeline?" interposed the curate.

"Personal violence!"

"Did you dare, sir, to be so wicked?" cried Mr. Endsleigh, turning to George, who shrunk beneath the old man's earnest gaze.

"I—I only asked her a favour," stammered George.

"A favour?" said the curate.

"To procure money," faltered Adeline; "you would have forced me to stoop to beg of—of——"

"I see, I see," said the curate. "Come away, Adeline, come away."

Adeline turned to the head of the stairs, then she paused a moment, and every feeling of deep resentment that had momentarily found a place in her innocent breast gave way, and bursting into tears, she turned round and extending her hand, said—

"George, how gladly would I forget all that is painful, if you——"

The ruffian seemed a little touched, and he said in a husky tone,—

"If—if what, Adeline?"

"If you would be what you once were—the dear son and much loved brother; oh, George, try to win back your better nature."

"It is too late," said he.

"No," said the curate; "it is not too late."

"It is—it is," said George. "You do not know all. It is too late."

"You are wrong, young man. Thank Heaven it is never too late to repent and reform."

"Leave me now; leave me now. I—I will think on what you have said."

"Come then, Adeline," said the curate; "let us go with the comforting belief that we may have done some good."

Adeline and the curate slowly descended the crazy staircase, and it was not without a shudder that the gentle and affectionate girl cast her eyes upon the soldiers who were carelessly grouped about, and whose errand she so well knew and so much dreaded.

The officer commanding the party advanced and courteously bowed to Adeline.

"I trust," he said, "our presence here does not disturb any festive preparations. The storm forced us here."

Adeline bowed and the curate replied,—

"You are very polite, sir; but we are not so churlish as to feel otherwise than pleased with the company of a gentleman."

"Adeline, my dear," said Mrs. Mourdant; "where have you been?"

"With me, Mrs. Mourdant," said the curate. "We have been exploring a little this old house."

"It seems very old indeed,"

"I wonder," said Mrs. Plumpjoy, "the parish don't look to it, and at least have it whitewashed. Don't you, sir?" to the officer.

"Certainly I do, madam," he replied, with a smile. "It's quite scandalous."

Mrs. Plumpjoy did not at all perceive the smile that was lurking at the corner of the young man's mouth, nor had she the remotest idea that he was indulging in the fashionable amusement called quizzing.

"An exceedingly sensible young man that," she whispered to Mrs. Mourdant; "and as like poor dear Major Plumpjoy as two peas."

"Indeed," said Mrs. Mourdant.

"Yes," sighed Mrs. Plumpjoy; "only the major was a little stouter."

"Stouter?"

"Yes; and—and not quite so tall."

The curate here laughed, which put Mrs. Plumpjoy in so great a rage that she gave up instituting any more comparisons between the deceased major and the young and really good looking officer who was "as like him as two peas."

The rain still continued to descend in a complete deluge, and not the smallest opening now appeared in the sky to predict that the shower would soon be over.

"I am afraid, ladies," said the officer, "that our stay here is likely to last some time, if we wait for the subsidence of the shower."

"It looks unpromising," said the curate. "May I ask, sir, whither you are proceeding?"

"On one of the most disagreeable errands, sir," replied the officer, "that a soldier is sent upon."

"Indeed?"

"Yes; to make an arrest, if possible, of one who has committed several military and civil crimes."

"An arrest?" said Mrs. Mourdant.

"Yes, madam; we are bound for the village of Bracefield."

Adeline was in an agony of apprehension lest the name of her brother should pass the officer's lips, but she dared not, for his safety's sake, interfere, and she could only clasp her hands and inwardly pray that her mother might be spared the knowledge of George's delinquencies, of which, as yet, she was happily ignorant, for she supposed him with his regiment at Gibraltar.

CHAPTER LXIV.

"It was too much for the o'ercharged heart,
And with one sigh of bitterest anguish,
The imprisoned spirit flew to brighter realms."
ANON.

THE DISCLOSURE.—A MOTHER'S GRIEF.—CONSOLATION.—ADELINE AN ORPHAN. —THE CURATE'S OFFER.

THE curate was beginning to share Adeline's uneasiness, and was bethinking himself of some mode of putting an end to the conversation between the officer and Mrs. Mourdant, when that lady said,

"May I ask, sir, to what regiment you belong?"

"Certainly, madam," he courteously replied; "I am an ensign in the ninety-third."

"The ninety-third?"

"Yes, madam."

"Good Heavens! You—you were at Gibraltar, were you not?"

"Recently, madam, we were. The regiment, however, has been at Chatham for some months now. From there we go to India."

"Oh, sir," exclaimed Mrs. Mourdant; "I rejoice to have met with you. I have a son in your regiment, sir, an only son."

"Indeed, madam?"

"Yes; he holds the same rank as yourself. You must know him."

"Of course, madam. May I ask——"

"His name?"

"Yes."

"His name is Mourdant."

"Mourdant?" exclaimed the officer, starting back a pace or two.

Adeline clasped her hands and whispered,—

"God's will be done."

"Perhaps 'tis better as it is," whispered the curate to her. "Bear up, Adeline, against this shock. Be calm, my child, be calm."

"Mourdant?" again repeated the young officer, as if still doubting that he had heard aright.

"Yes," said the mother; "my son, George Mourdant, ensign in the ninety-third."

"You are sure, madam?"

"Quite sure."

"George Mourdant?"

"Yes. Why do you look so surprised, sir?"

"May I ask, madam, when you heard from—from your son?"

"Heavens!" exclaimed Mrs. Mourdant. "Tell me, is he dead?"

"Not that I know off," replied the officer.

"We have not heard from him for more than ten months."

"Humph!" said the officer. "Nor heard anything concerning him?"

"Nothing."

"Then, madam, I—I——"

"Why do you hesitate? Good Heavens! some misfortune has happened to my poor boy."

"Your poor boy?" echoed the officer.

"Yes, sir. Why that sneer?"

"Nay, madam, I meant it not for a sneer. Are you willing to hear all that it is in my power to communicate?"

"Hold, sir," said Adeline, stepping forward; "spare a mother's feelings." The officer bowed.

"Feelings!" cried Mrs. Mourdant. "What—what am I to hear? He is dead—dead."

She burst into tears and sobbed aloud in a paroxysm of grief.

"Mother," said Adeline, "you had better hear the truth than be suffered to indulge in these vague conjectures."

"He is dead! he is dead."

"Mother, George is not dead."

"He—he lives?"

"He does."

"Thank Heaven!"

"But mother——"

"But what, Adeline? What is misfortune—illness, to death? He lives and all is well."

"No," said Adeline.

"No?"

"I would it were all well."

"Wherefore do you look thus at me, Adeline?"

"George is quite well, mother."

"Well, and yet you sigh."

"I cannot tell you. Sir," turning to the ensign; "I am that young man's sister."

"I am sorry to hear it," replied the officer.

"Will you oblige me," continued Adeline; "by telling us all you know of —of the unhappy, and I fear criminal, George Mourdant."

"Criminal?" cried Mrs. Mourdant.

The officer nodded.

"No, no—it cannot be. He is falsely accused. He cannot be criminal."

"Speak, sir," said the curate. "It were mercy to tell us the worst."

"I grieve to say," replied the officer, "that what I have to tell is no secret."

"Say on, sir," interposed Mrs. Mourdant, making a great effort to listen with composure.

The officer continued.

"Ensign Mourdant was addicted to gaming."

"The parent of all vices," said the curate.

"Having lost a large sum of money to a brother officer——"

"Well, sir, proceed," gasped Mrs. Mourdant.

"He sought his quarters in the early morning, and——"

"And what ?   They—they quarrelled?"

"No.   Mourdant robbed his room of everything of value."

"Robbed him ?"

"Yes, and then fled."

"My son ?"

"Yes, madam ; leaving his victim——"

"Victim, sir ?   The term is strong."

"Leaving his victim weltering in his blood."

"His blood ?"

"Yes.   A ghastly corpse only was found in the morning.   An investigation was immediately instituted, and Ensign Mourdant was declared guilty of robbery and murder !"

With a deep groan, Mrs. Mourdant fainted in the arms of the curate.

"You would have the tale," said the young officer.   "I have rather softened the truth than coloured.   My errand here is to search the whole neighbourhood for the very man we are speaking of.   We had private information he had been seen lurking about the village of Bracefield within the last month."

"Sir, you are not to blame," said the curate.   "You have been as courteous as possible.   Here, Andrew, Andrew !"

The old servant made his appearance.

"Go to the village," said the curate, "and procure any conveyance you can in which Mrs. Mourdant may be taken home."

"Ah, poor lady," remarked Andrew ; "I knew how it would be.   Ever since that young Mandeville comed among us, we have been main unlucky surely !"

"As quick as you can, Andrew," said Adeline.

"Ah, Miss, I be going—and now I be gone."

So saying, the old domestic, with many oracular shakes of the head, departed for the village.

Mrs. Mourdant still remained perfectly insensible, notwithstanding all the means which the real sympathy of Mrs. Martha Plumpjoy prompted her to use towards the recovery of the heart-stricken mother.

The rain was evidently abating, and now and then a gleam of sunshine would for a moment light up the old ruins, and then be as quickly withdrawn again, as some dense cloud sweeping across the sky would intercept its cheering and delightful ray.

There was a dead silence in the ruins, for the young officer had retired to a window, and Adeline's tears were coursing each other down her cheeks, too quickly for utterance.

Suddenly the officer sprung from his listless attitude by the window, and called out in a voice that echoed through the old building,—

"Guard !"

The soldiers were on the alert in a moment, and looking enquiringly about them.

"Unpile arms !" was the command.

"Fall in."

The men were in rank in an instant.

"Order—arms ! trail arms !—Bring in that man," were the rapid commands issued all in a breath.

The officer pointed from the window, and the little company immediately sprung from the ruins, headed by their sergeant.

The curate advanced to the window, and to his grief and dismay he saw George Mourdant crossing a field at some distance off.

CHAPTER LXV.

" They said she died of age and slow disease;
But, ah! how quickly when the heart decays
Will all the springs of life dry up!"

ANON.

THE RACE.—THE FUGITIVE.—A PLACE OF REFUGE.—A SUDDEN ARRIVAL.—THE DEATH.—NEW VOWS, ALAS! TO BE BROKEN.

ADELINE for one moment left her mother in the care of Mrs. Plumpjoy, and followed the curate to the window, too well guessing the purport of what had occurred.

She just caught a glimpse of her fugitive brother as he plunged among some trees, which were clustered thickly together about a quarter of a mile from the ruins.

The officer was pointing with his sheathed sword to the spot, and she saw the soldiers making towards it with great speed.

Then turning from the window, she thanked Heaven for her mother's insensibility, which saved her from the agony of such a scene.

"He is lost!" she said; "he is lost!"

The curate shook his head, as he replied,—

"I fear he must be taken. How could he be so mad as to leave the ruins?"

"I cannot look," said Adeline, after endeavouring again to force herself to the window.

"Go to your mother," said the curate. "I will remain here and tell you faithfully what occurs. Go, Adeline, go."

Adeline returned, and the curate continued to watch the progress of the chase from the window.

"They have not got him yet," he said.

"Can you see him?"

"No, he is hidden in the wood."

"Alas—alas! how frail a chance."

"Now they seem at fault. Ha! the officer points again with his sword."

"They see him?"

"I fear they do. Yet, no—the men return; at least some of them. Now they skirt the wood."

"Is it possible he can have escaped them?"

"It would seem so. Now I can only see the officers. Yet, no. They are planting sentries all round the plantation."

"Then his doom is sealed."

"The officer, the sergeant, and two men only are left idle."

"And—and they——"

"They enter the wood."

Adeline covered her face with her hands, and said no more. Of the result, she felt too certain.

"It's very strange," remarked the curate, "they do not return. The wood might be well searched in two or three minutes."

"What noise is that?" said Mrs. Plumpjoy. "Lauks! I shall die of fright. What a millintery adventure, to be sure."

"I hear the sound of carriage wheels," said Adeline.

"'Tis Andrew, then," remarked the curate, "returning from the village."

"Oh, sir," cried Adeline, "look again."

"The officer and sergeant return with the two soldiers. They have not found him yet."

"Is it possible he can have escaped?"

"Hark!—that bugle sound. The pursuit is given up."

"Then—then he is saved. God help him! He is yet, with all his enemies, my brother."

Adeline burst into tears, as again the wind of the bugle blast penetrated the ruins.

"A shay!" said old Andrew, suddenly entering the old hall.

"Oh, a chaise. Well, Andrew, bring it as close as you can to the building."

"Oh, this is frightful insensibility," cried Adeline, still regarding the inanimate form of her mother. "It may be mercy in an all-wise Providence to cast, as it were, this shadow of death over the heart's bursting feelings, but 'tis terrible to those that can see, and think, and feel."

"Repine not, my child," said Mr. Endsleigh; "all is for the best. You go on before, and take your place in the chaise, while Martha and I assist your poor mother into it."

"And must we leave, sir, these ruins while still so much doubt hangs over the fate of—of——"

"Of your brother, you would say?"

"I would."

"I fear we must, Adeline. Your mother, just now, must be your chief care."

"True, most true. Come, dear friend, I am ready."

The curate, assisted by Mrs. Plumpjoy, carefully lifted Mrs. Mourdant from the recumbent position in which she lay, and conveyed her to the chaise, which old Andrew had brought from the village with so much, for him, extraordinary expedition.

Adeline saw her mother safely laid upon the cushions, and then she entered the vehicle herself, with tears streaming from her eyes.

"Now, Andrew," said the curate, "drive home as quickly as you can, and we will follow on foot. Come, Martha."

"And a pretty mess I shall be in to be sure, when I does get home," exclaimed Mrs. Plumpjoy, carefully gathering up her gown, and placing its skirts over her head like a friar's hood. "Here's my second best poplin a-going to be ruinated. Well, I never. Next comes a horse to be shaved. People call this a pleasure party, do they?—and a pig to have his corns cut. Well, I never in all my blessed days. If poor dear departed Major Plumpjoy was here——"

"Why, he would have to go through the wet, to be sure," said the curate. "So come along, sister, and be less loquacious and more considerate of other people's feelings."

The chaise was upon the point of starting, when Adeline, casting her eyes in the direction of the little wood, in which her brother had taken refuge, and so singularly baffled his pursuers, she saw the officer returning towards the ruins, accompanied by some of his men.

"Stay one moment, Andrew," she said; "but one moment."

The young ensign saw her eager and interested look, and he advanced to the side of the humble little vehicle.

"He—he is not taken?" she gasped.

"No, madam, he is not," replied the officer, in a tone of slight disappointment.

The words, "Thank Heaven," were on Adeline's lips, but she suppressed them, and said,—

"You—you have lost him?"

"For the moment, madam."

"In the wood?"

"Assuredly, in the wood. My duty is not a pleasant one, but I must do it."

"Yes, yes. But he has escaped?"

"Certainly not, madam."

"Not?"

"No. He must fall into our hands. I grieve to distress you, but——"

"Enough, sir. For your courtesy I thank you."

The officer bowed.

"And should you——"

"I attend, madam."

"Should you capture him, may I beg——"

"Anything consistent with my duty you may rely upon my freely granting."

"You will treat him—kindly——"

"Madam, it were far beneath the honour and dignity of a British officer to ill-use a prisoner, be he who he may."

"I thank you, sir. And one more request——"

"Name it."

"Will you promise me in such an event to let me know?"

"I will. If you will favour me with your address, I shall, be assured, not neglect your natural request."

"My name is Adeline Mourdant, and my address—the Parsonage, Brace-field."

"Your wishes shall be attended to," said the officer.

Adeline bowed, and the young man gracefully lifted his cap.

Old Andrew impatiently smacked his whip, and the chaise was soon in rapid motion for home.

No. 31

The curate and Mrs. Plumpjoy followed on foot, and the latter kept up a running conversation, which she had all to herself, about the extreme barbarity of her brother in "snapping her up" always, and otherwise betraying a want of consideration for her, while he well knew she kept a home over his head, and that it was a wonder to all the parish what he would or could do without her, Mrs. Plumpjoy, and her superintending care and extraordinary watchfulness over all his temporal affairs.

CHAPTER LXVI.

"I see a hand thou cannot see,
　Which beckons me away;
I hear a voice thou cannot hear,
　Which bids me not to stay."

　　　　　　　　　　　　TICKELL.

THE COUCH OF DEATH.—MANDEVILLE'S RETURN.—SUNSHINE AMID GLOOM.

IN the due course of time the little party reached the Parsonage, and Mrs. Mourdant, still insensible, was immediately conducted to her chamber, that chamber which she was never again to leave in life.

The only medical man in the village was immediately sent for, and he—although from regard to the feelings of Adeline, he suppressed the truth in her presence—candidly informed the curate that the hours of Mrs. Mourdant were numbered.

"Is it indeed so ?" remarked Mr. Endsleigh.

"I can give no hope," said the medical man.

"Heaven's will be done !"

"There seems so complete a prostration of all energy in the system that I doubt if the lady will ever come out of her present deep swoon."

"How long," said the curate, "do you think she will be spared ?"

"It is difficult to say ; but my opinion is, that twelve hours, at the latest, must so exhaust the resources of life that she cannot live beyond that time."

"You can do nothing ?"

"Nothing."

"I thank you, sir, for your candour."

The surgeon bowed.

"Should she, however, awaken——"

The medical man shook his head.

"You think it very improbable ?"

"Very."

"But 'tis just possible ?"

"Certainly."

"In that case, what shall we do ?"

"Give her some warm wine immediately, and send for me."

"It shall be done."

"You will find, most probably," continued the surgeon, "that about two or three minutes before death she will recover consciousness."

"I have heard," said Mr. Endsleigh, "that such is not unfrequently the case."

The surgeon then bowed himself out, evidently considering the case as perfectly hopeless.

The curate then sat down to consult with his own mind whether or not he should inform Adeline of the true state of her mother. After some reflection he considered that it was his duty to do so, however hard might be the trial to her affections and his feelings.

Slowly the good old man sought the chamber of death, and there he found Adeline sitting by the bedside of her still inanimate mother, in an attitude of great grief.

Mrs. Plumpjoy too was there ; and the curate, approaching Adeline, said to her in a low tone,—

"Adeline, allow my sister to take your place for a few moments ; I wish to speak to you."

"Alas! sir," said Adeline, "I have now but one all-absorbing thought, and that concerns my mother."

"It is concerning her that I wish to speak to you," replied Mr. Endsleigh.

Adeline looked in his face a moment as if she would read his thoughts, and then gently rising, she, without another word, left the little chamber, and followed the curate in silence to his study.

"Be seated, my dear child," he said, kindly, "and arm yourself with fortitude and resignation to the decrees of Heaven."

"It is so!" cried Adeline, clasping her hands ; "my worst fears are true."

"Hush—hush! Be calm. Your mother——"

"Yes, yes ; my mother——"

"Is in some danger."

"Danger?"

"Yes. I think it ought not to be disguised from you, Adeline."

"Danger?" repeated Adeline. "Oh, sir, I read the fatal truth in your face. She is——"

"Nay, Adeline, nay!"

"She is—I know she is——"

"Hush, hush!"

"Dying—she is dying!"

Overpowered by her feelings, Adeline dropped her head upon the table and wept bitterly.

The curate for a few moments allowed the full tide of feeling to have its way, and then gently laying his hand upon Adeline's arm, he said,—

"My child, think for a moment. We have in this world even higher duties to perform than to give way to excessive grief, when those whom we love are taken from us to be happy with God."

"Thank you, Mr. Endsleigh," cried Adeline, "thank you, for reminding me of that. But it is so hard to part with——"

"It is," said the curate ; "I *know* it is, Adeline. I am an old man now, but I have not passed through life unscathed by sorrow."

"You are very good to me," sobbed Adeline.

"Go now back to your mother," said the curate ; "and, without anticipating or dreading the worst, prepare your mind if you can to resign your mother for a brief space to the care of Heaven."

The curate's quiet and calm impressive manner was admirably calculated to soothe sorrow. He was not one of those divines (?) who strive to surround a death bed with gross and vulgar terrors. His religion was one of love, resignation, and cheerful hope. How different were his mild admonitions to Adeline from those of some evangelical alarmists, who crowd like vultures around the dying, and

"Ring the gospel gong in both their ears,
If they feared not—filling them with fears."

When Adeline reached her mother's chamber she found her in the same deathlike trance, in which she had now lain so long.

"It's getting dark," said Mrs. Plumpjoy, "we'd better have a light."

Adeline assented, and Mrs. Plumpjoy departed to procure a light.

The weather had cleared up after the showers, and the sun had just sunk in the glowing west, leaving behind it a tinge of its mid-day glory.

The birds were twittering, and calling each other from branch to branch of the trees that grew close to the window, and as the waning light from the god-like luminary streamed into that little chamber, and lit up the face of her mother with a fictitious glow, a pang of agony shook through the breast of Adeline, as she bent over the still form of her only parent, and thought,—

"This is the last sun that will shine on her in life. It will rise again, and——"

Suddenly Mrs. Mourdant unclosed her eyes.

"Mother—mother!" cried Adeline.

The dying mother sat up in the bed as strongly as if in perfect health

"Adeline!" she said.

"Here, mother, here—I am here," said Adeline.

"Is it morning?"

"No, mother—no."

"Night?"

"The sun is sinking."

"Who is that singing, my Adeline, so sweetly?"

"Singing?"

"Yes, my child. Hark!"

Adeline could hear nothing.

Her mother turned to her and kissed her cheek, saying cheerfully.

"I am weary. Bless you, Adeline, and when you hear from your father ——"

"My father?"

"Yes, Adeline ; and little George. Bless you all—all."

She slowly sunk on the pillow.

"Mother !" said Adeline ; "mother, speak !"

She faintly smiled.

Adeline flew to the door.

"Help—help !" she cried ; "Mr. Endsleigh—help !"

The curate and his sister entered the room together.

The smile was still upon the face of Mrs. Mourdant, but it was the face of a corpse.

With a loud cry Adeline fell to the ground in insensibility.

At that moment the heavy sounds of a horse's feet sounded at the Parsonage gate, and the voice of Herbert Mandeville called loudly,—

"Adeline, Adeline !"

"Good Heavens !" cried the curate ; "it is Herbert !"

Mrs. Plumpjoy lifted up her hands in amazement, and, for once, could not speak.

"At such a time, too !" said the curate.

"Adeline, Adeline !" again cried the voice of Mandeville.

The curate left the room, and Mrs. Plumpjoy busied herself in endeavouring to restore Adeline to consciousness.

<hr />

CHAPTER LXVII.

" Oh, true love's the light that illumines the world."

THE LOVER RETURNED.—THE SOLEMNITY OF DEATH.—EXPLANATIONS.—RENEWED VOWS.—OLD ANDREW'S OPINION.—THE CURATE'S DOUBTS.

No one could be more surprised than was the curate at the sudden and most unexpected arrival of Herbert Mandeville. He almost doubted the evidence of his own senses, when he heard the voice calling upon Adeline, and it was not until he reached his garden gate, and actually saw Herbert standing with the reins of his horse in his hand, that he felt sure of his actual presence.

"Herbert?" he said.

"Yes; Herbert!" replied Mandeville.

"Is it possible?"

"Quite," replied Mandeville, smiling. "Where is old Andrew, to take my horse!"

"He comes," said the curate, as the old servant sulkily approached.

"Am I welcome?" said Herbert, as they entered the curate's parlour.

"In what spirit do you come, Herbert?"

"A repentant one."

"Then, indeed, you are welcome. Sit you down."

"I received your note," said Mandeville, "and—and—you see, sir, I have nswered it myself, by coming here to crave forgiveness."

"Which you will have, Herbert, as we ourselves hope to be forgiven."

"You look unusually solemn, my dear sir."

"I am unusually solemn."

"Mr. Endsleigh—sir—nothing has happened?"

"Something *has* happened, Herbert."

"Good God!"

"A solemn event——"

"Solemn?"

"Yes."

"Speak, sir. This suspense——"

"We have had a solemn visitor here."

"A visitor?"

"Yes; an unwelcome one."

"Who?"

"Death!"

"Death? death?"

"Yes, Herbert; death has invaded this peaceful home."

"Gracious Heavens!" cried Herbert, clasping his hands. "Speak, Mr Endsleigh, or I shall go mad! Adeline—Adeline!—speak of her!"

"Adeline is——"

"God help me!" cried Herbert.

"Hear me out," said the curate.

"I—I will."

"Adeline is well."

"Well? Say that again—again and again."

"Well in body, but——"

"But what, sir?"

"But in deep grief."

"For whom?"

"Her mother."

"Oh," said Herbert. "Well, I'm really very sorry."

"Mrs. Mourdant is no more."

"Dear me!"

"She expired but ten minutes since."

"Indeed!"

"Nay, even on the moment almost of your arrival."

"How very singular!"

"Singular and afflicting both to Adeline, Herbert."

"Oh, yes, most afflicting. Ah! Mr. Endsleigh, we all live in the—the shadow, as it were, of death."

"We do," said the curate.

"And we should study to be resigned to the dispensations of Providence.

" Which is the more easy," said the curate, who was disgusted with Herbert's sudden change of manner, " which is the more easy when death comes not between us and our passions or objects. Then when it does, so we rave.''

Herbert looked abashed for a moment, and then said,—

" This event was sudden ?"

" It was.   And Adeline's afflictions is great."

" Assuredly.   She was tenderly attached to her mother, I well knew."

" Most tenderly, Herbert.   Her nature is one to cherish deep affection. I trust you will see the propriety at such a time as this of departing again."

" Departing, sir ?"

" Yes, immediately."

" Why—I ——''

" This is no time for you to see Adeline.   You have come unfortunately. In a few weeks her mind will be calm, and she can then see you."

" But, sir, I stand in her mind as—as —''

" As one who made light of his word, and the young and guileless heart he had won," said the curate.

Herbert looked at the ceiling.

" You shall see her to explain yourself, and then begone," continued the curate.

" You are very kind," said Herbert.

" I mean to be so," replied the curate. " Stay here a moment, and I will see if Adeline be well enough to see you, and likewise willing."

The curate left the room.

" How troublesome the old man is," said Herbert to himself. " Ah, well, never mind ; Adeline loves me, and all will be right again."

In a few moments the curate returned, but alone.

" We cannot get her to leave her mother's room," he said. " You had better go there and say what you wish, Mandeville."

" Would not that be a most unwarrantable intrusion, sir ?"

" As you think —''

" Well, I will go."

" Andrew," said the curate, as they passed the open door leading to the garden.

" Yes," said Andrew.

" Bring Mr. Mandeville's horse round ; he will want it almost immediately.''

Herbert bit his lips, and ascended the staircase after the curate, who he thought was using him very badly, after he, the great, handsome, and rich Herbert Mandeville, had actually condescended to ride down to Bracefield, and say he had been in the wrong, and came all that way on purpose to repent.

Adeline's mind was too much engrossed by the calamity which had just befallen her to feel all that she could have done upon the occasion of so unexpected a visit from Herbert under other and happier circumstances.

" She could not," she thought, " see him at such a moment, and yet to send him away without a word—could she do that ?"

She told Mrs. Plumpjoy that she would be in the parlour in half an hour, and Herbert Mandeville felt some degree of petty triumph over the curate, as he said :—

" I am sorry, sir, that Adeline thus forces me to remain longer under your roof than to you seemed necessary or agreeable."

The curate merely inclined his head, and left Herbert alone in the parlour.

The half hour passed tediously away, and as Herbert for the twentieth time examined his watch, the door slowly opened, and pale and wan Adeline entered the room.

Herbert sprang forward to meet her, and took her hand, which he pressed to his lips.

Neither spoke for a moment, the heart of Adeline was too much oppressed for words, and even Herbert, really indifferent as he was to the death of Mrs. Mourdant, could not but respect the silent sorrow in Adeline's countenance.

"Adeline," he at length said, "can you forgive me?"

She looked in his face for a moment, and burst into tears.

Freely the tears of the orphan girl fell, and Herbert Mandeville thought she had never looked so truly beautiful as in that deep grief.

"Dear Adeline," he said, "I sympathise with your sorrow ; but can nothing heal the wound which your heart has received?"

"Nothing," she replied.

"Not the devotion of my life to your happiness?"

"Herbert !"

"Hear me," Adeline. "I may have seemed neglectful, but in thought I never forgot or wronged you. Is all forgiven me, Adeline?"

"All," she replied. "I never yet could bear resentment, and least of all at such a time as this."

"Then think of happier days," interposed Herbert.

"I cannot so soon forget."

"Certainly not forget, Adeline ; but remember with calmness."

"Yes, Herbert, I will try."

"And let me hear from your own lips that you are still mine."

Her glistening eyes met his for one moment, and told more eloquently than words could speak how truly and entirely she was all his own.

On the impulse of the moment, Herbert kissed her pale cheek, and for the time was sincere, when he said :—

"The time, Adeline, shall not be far distant when I can again hope to repeat my question at the altar's foot."

"Leave me now," said Adeline. "This is a house of mourning."

"But can I not stay to charm away some of its gloom, Adeline ?"

"No, Herbert. Return when all is over, and then I will strive to meet you with a happier welcome."

"Your wishes are sacred commands, Adeline. I will set off immediately for London, and until I hear from you, think of nothing but of the weary space that separates us."

"Farewell," said Adeline.

"You will write ?"

"I will."

"Then farewell, dear girl, and remember there lives still a heart in which you are enshrined."

He led her to the door, and they parted.

Herbert had no longer a motive to remain at Bracefield, and he at once made for the front of the house, where old Andrew stood holding his horse.

Herbert sprang upon the animal's back, and turning to Andrew as he threw him half a crown, he said :—

"Tell your master that I shall trouble him with another visit soon."

"I don't want your money," said Andrew.

Herbert frowned.

"What do you mean, old man?"

"I never takes money of them as I don't like."

"So I have the honour of being disliked by you?" answered Mandeville.

"Yes," said Andrew, calmly.

"Idiot !" muttered Herbert, as he clapped his spurs to his horse, and rode away.

"Rascal !" growled Andrew, slowly walking back to the house.

CHAPTER LXVIII.

" With a name upon his lips, he came,
. Which had a charm—though he was hateful.''

ANON.

MANDEVILLE IN LONDON.—AN INVITATION.—REFLECTIONS AND RESOLVES.—A SURPRISE AND A CURIOUS MEETING.

THE first thing that interested Herbert when he arrived in town was a note lying upon his study table, which ran thus :—

"LADY CLARA SEAGRAVE presents compliments to Herbert Mandeville, Esq., and begs the honour of his company to a *petite soiree* and *fête musicale* this evening.   (" Yours,

"C. S."

" N. B.—Dear Herbert, be sure to come."

" This evening ?" said Herbert, looking at the date. " By the lucky fates it's to-night. And yet—ought I really to go ? Why not ?—Adeline !—Psha ! because I've won the heart of a pretty girl, am I to deny myself all pleasure ? Besides, Lady Clara will think it so very odd, and—and in fact I don't see why I shouldn't go."

" Captain Dufours, sir," announced a servant.

" Dufours ? Oh, tell him I'm busy."

" Yes, sir."

In a few moments the servant came back to say the captain was in no hurry, and would amuse himself with a cigar and some champaigne till Mr. Mandeville was quite at leisure, and upon no account was Mr. Mandeville to hurry himself for him.

" Confound his impertinence," said Herbert. " Show him in to me."

In a few moments the captain appeared.

" Well, sir ?" said Herbert.

" Well, sir ?" echoed Dufours ; " is that the way to greet your best friend ? Oh !"

" Really, Dufours, your impudence is only equalled—by—by —"

" Your admiration and appreciation of it," said the captain. " Come, come, no nonsense. I say, what a sensation you did make, to be sure."

" Sensation ?—Where ?"

" Why, at Lady Clara's, to be sure. Everybody was saying where is he ? Is that him ?—That handsome young man with the eye-glass ? Is he Mr. Mandeville ? Then the young girls blushed, and the old girls stared, and tried to blush."

" Psha !"

" Upon my soul, Mandeville, I wish I was in half such luck."

" Nonsense !"

" Fact, on honour."

" More romance."

" Stern reality."

" Well, well ; I don't want to hear such gossip."

" You do though," thought Dufours.

" Will you take anything ?" said the much pleased Herbert.

" Yes, if you have anything of that real stuff—that out of the way magnificent claret left ?"

Herbert rang the bell, and ordered claret.

The wine was brought, and the captain filling a bumper, said :—

" Mandeville, I'll give you a toast."

"Well, what is it?"

"Here's a wet blanket, and a north-east wind to the fool who has a brimming cup of pleasure held to his lips, and won't taste it."

"You don't mean me?"

"You?"

"Yes, me."

" Psha!—You don't mean to push the cup of pleasure on one side?"

" No; but ——"

" But what?"

"I don't mean to drink the dregs."

"Dregs?—Ha! ha! ha!"

"Yes; a good draught at the said brimming cup is all very well; but woe be to him who drinks too deep."

" Capital!" roared Dufours. " He is beginning to moralise. Now confess, Mandeville, you learnt that of the old parson, down at what's the name of the place?"

" Bracefield."

" Ah, Bracefield. By the by, how is the milk of roses?"

" The what?"

" The hawthorn bud. The hedge lily. The little bit of pretty rurality. —Eh?"

" I tell you what, Dufours, if you let your tongue run so much, I'll try the strength of this claret-jug on your head."

A footman at this moment appeared at the door.

" What is it?" said Herbert.

" A person, sir, wishes to see you."

" A person?"

No. 32

"Yes, sir. He—he—isn't a gentleman, sir."

"Kick him out, then," said Dufours.

"Did he give his name?" inquired Herbert.

"No, sir; but he said it was particular business; and when I told him as you were engaged, sir, with Captain Dufours, he—he——"

"Well?"

"He—he—said, sir, he ——"

"Speak out! What did he say?"

"Beg pardon, sir ——"

"Speak, fool!"

"Well, sir, he said as he'd pull—pull —"

"Pull what?"

"Captain Dufours' nose, sir, if so be he didn't take himself off, sir, in a minute or two."

Mandeville leaned back in his chair and roared with laughter.

Captain Dufours bit his lips, and said :—

"Give him into custody, the scoundrel!"

"No, no," said Herbert; "it's capital. You must go, Dufours—or—stay—get behind the curtain. Shew the fellow in here."

"Curse it, do you think I—"

"Come, come," cried Mandeville; "behind the curtain with you."

Dufours was just concealed as the footman ushered in a man with a cloak closely wrapped round him, and a hat drawn far over his forehead.

Mandeville rose and confronted the stranger.

"Well, sir," he said, "your business with me?"

"We are alone?" said the stranger.

"Go on," said Herbert, certainly not saying yes to the stranger's question, but implying as much.

The stranger took off his hat, and allowed the cloak to fall at his feet.

"Do you know me?" he said.

"I have seen you."

"Where?"

"At Bracefield, as you know."

"Do you know who I am?"

"I do not; but I believe you to be a bad character."

"Ha! ha! you do?"

"I do. And it is probable I may think it necessary to send for a constable to remove you."

"Hold, Herbert Mandeville. You will do no such thing."

"Will I not?"

"You will not."

"Wherefore?"

"Because I bear a charmed name."

"Nonsense, man."

"Sit down, sir, and listen to me."

"I shall do no such thing."

"Hold! Ring that bell, and I will stand in your hall and say something you will wish unsaid when it is too late."

"Who are you?" cried Herbert.

"When did you last see Adeline?" said the man.

"Adeline?"

"Aye, Adeline Mourdant'"

"You do not know ought of—of her?"

"Don't I!"

"What?"

"You will not betray me?"

"What on earth do you mean?"

"A price is on my head, Mr. Mandeville."

"A criminal?"

"Yes, if you like the title. But the fact is I must leave England now. It's too hot to hold me any longer, I see."

"Well, sir."

"Well, I want money."

"And you come to rob me?"

"No, only to borrow a trifle."

"Insolence!"

"Nay, not so fast. Mind you don't know me yet. I ask again when did you see Adeline?"

"If that name is again polluted by passing your lips," cried Herbert, "I will give you into instant custody, you rascal."

"Rascal!"

"Yes."

"No matter. There may come a time. Now I want money."

"Money of me?"

"Yes."

"On what pretence?"

"Oh, Adeline will thank you."

"Again her name?"

"Yes, to be sure. Come, I want a hundred pounds on Adeline's account."

"This insolence passes endurance. I ——"

"Stay a moment. My name is ——"

"What?"

The man looked cautiously round him, and then whispered in Herbert's ear :—

"Mourdant!"

"Mourdant?"

"Yes."

"Who in Heaven's name are you?"

"A very poor fellow just now, who hopes notwithstanding to be your respected brother-in-law."

Herbert sunk into a chair, as he said :—

"You are surely no brother of Adeline's?"

"I am."

"Then that accounts ——"

"Yes," interrupted the man; "that accounts for a great deal. Ha! ha! Come, will you hand out the money?"

"Is it possible that the gentle and sensitive Adeline can have such a brother as thou art?"

"Perhaps it ain't," replied George Mourdant, for it was he; "but it's true nevertheless."

"And yet," cried Herbert, "I'll not believe it."

"You won't?"

"I will not."

"And you refuse to assist me?"

"I do."

"Then I will go back to her."

"To—to Adeline?"

"Yes."

"No—no!"

"Oh, that touches you, does it? Oh! oh! oh!"

The brutal George Mourdant threw himself on a chair, and laughed discordantly.

CHAPTER LXIX.

" I may not stir,
A price is on my head."

MALONE.

FILIAL AFFECTION.—CAPTAIN DUFOURS' CHARACTER.—THE PROPOSAL.—GOOD BYE AND A BUMPER OF CLARET.—MANDEVILLE'S SELF-CONCEIT.

HERBERT MANDEVILLE gazed at his visitor with conflicting emotions; he could scarcely bring himself to believe that the man before him could be in any way related to Adeline; but when he came to consider that there was by Adeline's own confession, a mystery of a painful nature connected with her, and that this explained it in the most natural manner, he reluctantly believed that he indeed looked upon the brother of his virtually betrothed bride, Adeline Mourdant."

"Come," said George, " you love Adeline?"

Herbert frowned.

"Oh, well," continued George, "I don't want to press you, but I tell you what I will do:—Give me, or lend me just what you like—a hundred pounds, and you shall have my free consent to marry her to-morrow."

"Your consent? Absurd."

"Yes, my consent. And what's more, I really will be off to America, that last retreat of all rogues and vagabonds."

"Are you aware," said Herbert, " that Mrs. Mourdant is dead?"

"Dead!" echoed George.

"Yes."

"When?"

"But yesterday."

"Indeed? I—I—Well, I can't help it."

"But you can regret it?"

"Well I do feel a little. But you know the old must die to make room for the young."

"Your heart is indeed callous," said Mandeville.

"And why not?" cried George, fiercely. "Am not I hunted like a wild beast?"

"Because you have acted like one. The most savage have some tenderness for their parents. Have you quite forgotten the divine commandment, to honour thy father and mother that thy days may be long in the land?"

"I don't want my days to be long in the land. D—n the land, so that job's jobbed."

"You are past all hope," said Herbert, who with all his faults, was inconceivably shocked at the unblushing wickedness of George Mourdant.

"Come," said George, " am I to have the money, or am I not?"

"You bear a name," replied Herbert, "which is your protection."

"Exactly."

"To spare Adeline pain ——"

"You will give me the money?"

"Yes, but ——"

"Psha!—No buts —"

"I mean—I must be assured that you will leave the country."

"How?—I give you my word."

"I fear your word is of small value."

"Do you?"

"Indeed I do. I will pay for your passage to America, and through some banker in New York you shall be paid fifty pounds."

"You are very cautious, Mr. Mandeville," sneered George.

"I am," answered Herbert, "when I deal with such men as you."

"And complimentary too."

Herbert was silent.

"And what am I to do till the ship sails?" added George, after a pause.

"I will give you a small sum for present exigencies."

"What do you call a small sum?"

"Five pounds is all you shall have."

"Five pounds?"

"Yes."

"What the deuce is the use of five pounds to me?"

"Don't take them then."

"Well, if I can't do better, I must. And now I'll give you a bit of advice, which is worth ten times the money."

"What is that?"

"Why, you know Dufours?"

"Yes."

"Well, he's the greatest scoundrel unhung, and if you don't look sharp, he'll play you a slippery trick some day."

"I know him pretty well," said Mandeville, secretly enjoying the confusion which Dufours must feel at having himself thus spoken of.

"You can't know him," added George. "He is the greatest swindler in London."

"With one exception," thought Herbert.

"Well you have me in your power now, Master Mandeville, and I must take your offer."

"Hear then is five pounds," said Herbert. "Leave me some means of finding you, and I will take immediate steps for your leaving the country. But mind it must be for ever."

"Well, for ever be it. One country is as good as another to me now."

He walked to the door as he spoke, and would have passed out, but Herbert called to him.

"You have not told me how to communicate with you."

"True," he replied. "Give me a slip of paper."

Herbert did so, and he wrote on it :—

"Mr. Smith,—No. 3, Meard's Court, Soho."

"You shall hear from me," said Herbert. "And now get away with you as quickly as you can."

George lingered and glanced at the table.

"Mr. Mandeville," he said.

"Well."

"I have not tasted wine for a long time."

"Drink, then," said Herbert.

George Mourdant took up the claret-jug, and emptied it at a draught.

"Very good for claret," he muttered as he left the room ; "but I shall have to drink a bottle of brandy to correct it."

The moment he was gone, Dufours stepped out from his place of concealment.

"Well, Dufours," said Herbert, "you seem to be well known."

"The lying scoundrel!" said Dufours.

Herbert laughed as he said :—

"Why I fancy it's something like the dispute between the pot and the kettle."

"Upon my honour," said Dufours, "I believe that George Mourdant to be a most atrocious villain."

"Ah! ah! Capital," said Herbert.

"You perceive," continued Dufours, "that he has no sense of religion or morality?"

"Why, you hypocritical rascal," cried Mandeville. "Your notions of morality must indeed be exalted."

"Well, I must go, Mandeville. That fellow has kept me longer than I intended."

"And drunk up all the claret into the bargain."

"By Jove, yes ; and done you out of five pounds."

"If he leave the country, I don't mind what it costs me," said Herbert.

"Hem !"

"Besides, I got value for my money."

"Value ?"

"Yes."

"What value ?"

"Why the advice concerning you."

"Psha !—The rascal !—But—hem !"

"What do you mean, Dufours ?"

"Oh, nothing—nothing."

"Well, good-day to you."

"We meet to-night ?"

"At Lady Clara's ?"

"Yes."

"I shall be there. But positively, Dufours, I will not play high."

"As you please."

"I am determined."

"Well, adieu till night."

Dufour departed, and Mandeville laughed in his own conceit as he said,—

"Dufour is a rogue I believe, but he won't succeed in swindling me,—no —no."

Herbert looked about on his table for George Mourdant's address, but *it was gone.*

CHAPTER LXX.

"Let the wondering world then say,
A month he lived, but that was May."
                                    O'KEEFE.

A LETTER TO ADELINE.—THE SOIREE MUSICALE.—THE ILL-USED YOUNG LADY. —PLEASURE BEAMING.

HERBERT MANDEVILLE was one of those persons who seldom resist temptation if it came in the garb of pleasure ; but he always liked to have some excuse to make to his own conscience for his weakness in yielding to impulses which he more than suspected he ought to resist.

Thus, before dressing, to proceed to the very questionable, and far from select, evening party of Lady Clara Seagrave, he quieted his conscience by writing the following letter to Adeline :—

"London.

"DEAREST ADELINE,—I am at home again, but it is not the dear home it once was, because it is not the dear home of my heart—that is at Bracefield. Ah, dearest Adeline, how I long for the time when I may welcome you to the ancient house of my regretted father. We are both orphans, Adeline. We have lost those whom we loved so long, and that consideration should bind us closer together in the happy bonds of pure affection. We must be all the world to each other, because without each other now the world to us can be nothing.

"Write to me, dearest, and abridge as much as possible the dreary distance between us, by allowing me to converse with you in thought, if not by speech.

"And dearest, when the mournful duties are over, which you would not permit me to be a partaker in, or a spectator of—then tell me that your heart turns to me, and write, if it be but one line, to say—'Herbert, come for me, I am thine now.'

"Ever, dearest Adeline, your own

"HERBERT MANDEVILLE."

"What more can I do?" thought Herbert, as he folded the above letter. "I may as well see a little pleasure while I can; besides, I am not so weak as to fall into every snare that is spread to catch the unwary. I will visit Lady Clara Seagrave, and laugh at her machinations."

So saying, Herbert, with great self-satisfaction, dressed himself for the *Soirée Musicale*, and departed strong in his own conceit to resist all kinds and descriptions of temptation.

It was past ten o'clock when Herbert Mandeville entered the saloons of Lady Clara Seagrave.

A showy assemblage of a certain class were there already, and Herbert was received with marked distinction by the hostess.

"My dear Mr. Mandeville," said Lady Clara; "you are really in astonishing request."

"Indeed!" said Herbert. "You flatter me, Lady Clara."

"No I do not. A certain person would have been in despair if you had not graced our poor saloons with your presence."

"A certain person, madam?"

"Yes."

"Who do you mean?"

"Cannot you guess?"

"Indeed no!"

"Oh, false one. You know too well."

"Indeed, Lady Clara, you give me credit for a degree of duplicity that I have no pretentions to on any account."

"Do I?" said Lady Clara, archly.

"On my honour you do."

"Then I will whisper a name."

"Thank you, I am all attention."

"Mrs. Churchill," whispered Lady Clara.

"Oh, the—the lady—who——"

"Who you so much admired, and who has such a churl for a husband."

"She is certainly handsome," said Herbert; "but I never for a moment imagined that—that——"

"That she thought you the handsomest and most agreeable gentleman she ever had seen," interposed Lady Clara.

Herbert actually perpetrated a blush, as he said in a deprecating tone,—

"Really, madam, you do your fair friend but small service."

"Hush! hush!" said Lady Clara. "She comes—she comes—hem—"

Herbert looked in the direction indicated by Lady Clara, and he saw approaching the young, and really beautiful, Mrs. Churchill.

She stopped as if doubtful whether to proceed or not when she saw Mandeville, and then, as if hastily summoning courage, she advanced and bowed coldly to him.

He eagerly returned the salutation, and Mrs. Churchill then immediately turned to Lady Clara, and made some casual remark upon the heat of the rooms.

Mandeville felt rather piqued at this well acted indifference, and forgetting all his prudent and careful resolutions, he advanced and said,—

"I trust, madam, it is not ill health that has robbed your cheek of some of its bloom?"

"You are pale," said Lady Clara. "I am sure you fret."

"I?" exclaimed Mrs. Churchill. "No—no—why should I?"

"She is an angel," whispered Lady Clara to Herbert. "She never will blame that wretch of a husband of hers."

"What a rascal he must be," thought Herbert, "to neglect so charming a woman."

A strain of music at this moment broke upon Herbert's ears, and a movement among the brilliant throng by which he was surrounded, for the movement separated him from Lady Clara Seagrave and her fair friend.

A general cry of "Hush! hush!" now ensued, and Herbert was obliged to remain quiet where he was, until a song, which had just commenced, was finished.

The voice of the singer was an unquestionable good one, and Mandeville's taste for music almost consoled him for the temporary deprivation of the company of Mrs. Churchill.

The song was this :—

PLEASURE BEAMING !

" Pleasure beaming—pleasure beaming,
    From a thousand sparkling eyes,
Ever seeming—ever seeming,
    Greatest bliss beneath the skies.
Who shall say discord a treasure,
    Lest it e'er should give us pain,
Then fill high a sparkling measure,
    Drink to rosy joy again.
        Pleasure beaming—pleasure beaming
        From a thousand sparkling eyes,
        Ever seeming—ever seeming,
        Greatest bliss beneath the skies.

" Who shall tell us to be gloomy,
    When the fancy sports in bliss,
Who shall tell us to throw from us,
    Panting lips we love to kiss.
Let the sage grow old and rusty,
    In his academic lore ;
We are sons of joy and freedom,
    Then welcome pleasure o'er and o'er.
        Pleasure beaming—pleasure beaming,
        From a thousand sparkling eyes,
        Ever seeming—ever seeming,
        Greatest bliss beneath the skies.'

This song, which was well adapted to the tastes and feelings of those for whose special edification it was sung was rapturously applauded, an applause in which Herbert, in the enthusiasm of the moment, joined most heartily.

CHAPTER LXII.

" And shall I see his face again,
    And shall I hear him speak.''—Old Song.

THE CONSERVATORY.—A CURIOUS CONVERSATION.—ALL FOR LOVE.—
MANDEVILLE DECEIVED.

THE heat of the rooms now became excessive, and Herbert Mandeville traversed them with a hope of discovering some cool ante-room, in which he

could take his stand for a short time, to get rid of the overpowering sensation of heat that oppressed him.

He was delighted to see through a glass door a conservatory of choice plants, in the centre of which a jet of water was splashing merrily. He placed his hand upon the handle of the door; it was not locked, and he entered with pleasant and grateful feelings the delicious cool air of the conservatory.

He sat down on a rustic seat and watched the dashing spray of the waters for some moments, as it glanced brightly in the rays of light which came from the brilliant saloons.

Suddenly he heard the handle of the conservatory-door turned, and the voice of Mrs. Delancey met his ear, saying—

"My dear Lady Clara I will not delay you from your guests, but, believe me, the sweet beauty and company of these plants, is more pleasant to me, and more consonant to my feelings than your crowded rooms."

The voice in which she spoke was so soft and musical that Herbert listened in spite of himself, and after delaying for a few moments to make his presence known, he withdrew still more into the deep shadow of an aloe tree, expecting that Mrs. Delancey would soon leave the place and free him from his predicament of being an eaves dropper.

"You indulge in too much melancholy," said Lady Clara; "and yet why should I wonder at that."

"Ah, why?" interpolated Mrs. Delancey, with a deep sigh which seemed to come from the bottom of her heart.

"Why, indeed," continued Lady Clara. "Mated as you are to one whom you cannot love."

Mrs. Delancey sighed again, and Lady Clara Seagrave continued—

"And loving one who——"

"Hush! hush!" cried Mrs. Delancey. "Breathe it not even in this solitude."

No. 33

"Nay," said Lady Seagrave, "you must not fear."

"Oh yes; I fear the slightest air that blows. You know not the horror that would await me did he but suspect——"

"Delancey you mean?"

"Yes."

"He is a——"

"Hush! say nothing of him for or against, my dear friend; you know I was forced into his arms without a particle of affection, and now——"

"Now when your heart is really touched you are unhappy."

"Truly unhappy!"

"Well—it may be criminal to entertain the thought of love for another in your case, but while I buried it in my heart, if I were you, I should still hug it as a dear fond feeling."

"No, no,"

"Besides you are more than excused."

"Excused?"

"Yes."

"Why? wherefore?"

"Because, my dear friend, the temptation is great."

Mrs. Delancey again sighed."

"You know," continued Lady Clara Seagrave; "that your idol——"

"My idol? oh, Lady Clara!"

"Well, I wont call him so, but you know he is handsome?"

"Too well I know it."

"Intelligent?"

"Yes."

"A charm of manner which could win any woman?"

"Ah, yes."

"A tongue which would woo an angel from Heaven to earth?"

"Oh yes—how true you paint him."

"Well then, my dear friend, by all those things you stand much excused."

"Do you really think I do?"

"I do."

"Truly?"

"Most truly."

"Then—then you think I may venture to—to——"

"To love him?"

"Yes."

"Indeed I think you may. Were I in your case I would not hesitate to snatch the only pleasurable feeling the world could afford me."

"Oh, if I were free as I was once."

"Well," interrupted Lady Clara, "as you are not free, you must endeavour to gild your chains and make your captivity as agreeable as possible."

"But dare I?"

"That's as you have courage."

"And I am timid."

"True, but you know love strengthens the weak and tramples on the strong."

"I do know it. You have changed the current of my gloomy thoughts. Oh, if I could——"

"Could what?"

"Venture to cherish the passion that now consumes my very heart."

"Indeed you may."

"But he—if he should suspect——"

"Your husband?"

"No, no."

"Oh, the fond object of your heart's desire. The young Herbert Mandeville."

"Even so."

Herbert was thunderstricken.

"But enough of this," cried Mrs. Delancey, "I have kept you too long already.. Go, my kind friend; I will but calm my feelings and join you."

"So soon then," said Lady Clara, going.

How little Herbert Mandeville imagined that the foregoing conversation was got up expressly for his hearing.

CHAPTER LXXI.

HERBERT'S REFLECTIONS.—MRS. DELANCEY'S SOFT CONFESSIONS CONTINUED.— A SURPRISE.—A SCREAM AND A CROWD.

> "She told her love
> And would not let concealment
> Feed on her painted cheek."
>
> SHAKSPERE (new reading.)

HERBERT MANDEVILLE had been attacked at his weakest point. He really, in his heart, thought himself handsome and accomplished, and so he was, but it was to be regretted, that along with those advantages, he did not possess a small portion of discreet modesty.

As it was, he felt quite in a flutter of delight at what he had overheard, and for the moment he quite forgot the beautiful and confiding Adeline.

Scarcely daring to breathe for fear of alarming Mrs. Delancey, he bent all his attention to listen if she should burst into any soliloquy about his attractions.

He was not disappointed.

"I do—yes—I do love him," murmured Mrs. Delancey. "He is the personification of my earliest dreams of romance; yes, I must ever love him, and his dear image will lie enshrined in the inmost recesses of my heart."

"She is a beautiful creature," thought Herbert.

"Ah! unhappy me!" sighed Mrs. Delancey.

"What a delicate and sensitive mind," thought Herbert.

"My absence," said Mrs. Delancey, "will be noted—I—must calm my feelings and return."

"Shall I shew myself," thought Herbert—or—or shall I let her go. I—I think I may as well tell her I'm here. She evidently adores me. It would, perhaps, sooth her feelings to tell her I think her a fine woman."

Mrs. Delancey paced with agitated steps the conservatory. "I cannot venture yet," she murmured "into those brilliant saloons. I feel as if every eye could read my secret. No—no—I must pause; yet a brief space, and learn to conquer the feelings I cannot smother."

"What a dear sensitive mind, she has," thought Herbert. "Upon my soul that husband of her's must be a great brute."

It is probable that Mrs. Delancey, who knew very well that Mandeville was in the conservatory, began to loose patience, for she increased the rapidity of her walk, and finally sat down on a garden seat, with a deep sigh.

"I'm in rather an awkward position," reasoned Herbert, with himself. "Poor thing, how shocked she would be to find I, of all persons, had overheard her tender confessions."

Another sigh came from the depths of Mrs. Delancey's heart.

"She don't seem disposed to go away either. What shall I do? I fear I must declare myself, and heavens know what may then ensue."

Mrs. Delancey now began to sob audibly.

"Her feelings overpower her," thought Herbert.

Again she sobbed.

"Poor thing," he thought.

"Mandeville ! Mandeville !" she murmured.

"I can stand this no longer," said Herbert, and he suddenly rushed forward, and stood before Mrs. Delancey.

"'Tis he ! 'tis he !" she cried, and with a piercing scream that echoed through the whole house, she threw herself into his arms and fainted clean away in the most natural and off hand manner that can be conceived.

Herbert Mandeville was certainly taken by surprise at the extraordinary effect that his sudden appearance produced upon Mrs. Delancey, and notwithstanding the loud scream of the lady, was far from being unflattering to his personal vanity, he would certainly, at the precise moment, have preferred that the charming Mrs. Delancey had chosen some quieter method of testifying her admiration and love.

"Hush ! for God's sake, madam, hush ; you will alarm the house."

The mischief was already done, for the scream had been loud enough, not only to alarm the house, but the whole street likewise.

Before Herbert could command himself sufficiently to determine upon any course of action which presented a chance of escape from his present disagreeable situation, the door of the conservatory was thrown open, and a general rush of guests took place. In a moment, Herbert was surrounded by twenty eager questioners.

Everybody spoke at once, and nobody seemed inclined to listen.

"What's the matter?" cried one.

"Who screamed?" cried the second.

"Anybody dead?" shouted another.

"For Heaven's sake," cried Herbert, who stood in the middle of the curious throng, still supporting the insensible Mrs. Delancey in his arms. "For Heaven's sake, will no lady assist Mrs. Delancey?"

A general titter ran through the assemblage, but no one seemed inclined to relieve Herbert of his fair burthen.

"This lady," he added, "has unfortunately fainted."

The titter now became a general laugh, and Herbert was rapidly losing both temper and patience.

A gentleman in advance of the throng put an eye-glass to his eye, and added to the mirth of the company by repeating, in an affected, drawling voice,—

"So the lady has unfortunately fainted, has she? Dear me !"

Herbert turned angrily, and said,—

"Sir, if you were not a puppy, and beneath my contempt, I would kick you down-stairs for a glass of water."

"Poor young man," said the gentleman with the eye-glass, at the time prudently getting quite out of Herbert's reach. "Poor young man, his wits are evidently effected."

"Good Heavens !" cried Lady Clara Seagrave, suddenly advancing from among the throng. "Can it be possible that I see Mrs. Delancey in the arms of Herbert Mandeville?"

"It is quite possible, madam," said Herbert. "Surely it is possible for a lady to faint, and for a gentleman to save her from falling on the floor."

Mrs. Delancey at this moment thought proper to recover a little, which she effected in the most admirable manner, by opening her eyes half way, and heaving a first-rate sigh.

"Gracious powers," she said, faintly, "where am I ?"

"Here's Mr. Delancey," cried several, and at the moment, apparently foaming with rage, he appeared, and confronted Herbert Mandeville.

With a violent pull he took Mrs. Delancey from Herbert's arms, who was not sorry, under existing circumstances, to be rid of his fair charge.

The enraged husband, after handing his wife to the care of Lady Seagrave, turned again to Mandeville, and exclaimed,—

"Sir, you have outraged my honour."

"Certainly he has," cried several voices.

"You must fight him, Delancey," cried one, in a loud voice.

"Fight?" exclaimed Delancey, "my revenge must be terrible!"

"What do you mean?" said Herbert.

"Blood!—blood!" cried Delancey.

"Don't make yourself ridiculous," said Herbert. "There's my—my card. If you want me, you can send for me."

So saying, Herbert threw the card at the feet of Mr. Delancey, and turning on his heel, left the house.

CHAPTER LXXII.

" When bad men disagree,
The honest prosper."
OLD PROVERB.

AN OLD FRIEND.—THE FATE OF GEORGE MOURDANT.—THE TEMPORARY TRIUMPH OF VILLANY.

WE will leave Herbert Mandeville, for a very brief space, to follow the wily Captain Dufours, when he left Herbert's mansion.

He had possessed himself of the card of the unfortunate George Mourdant, and revenge as well as cupidity, for he thirsted for the reward offered for George's arrest, alike urged him to lose no time in betraying to justice his former friend and boon companion, whom he had mainly helped to reduce to his present state of degradation.

Well the wily Captain knew that, in order to procure the whole of the reward offered for the apprehension of George Mourdant, he should have to wait for his conviction, which might be a tedious process. He therefore adopted a shorter, although not quite so profitable a course.

He called upon an ex-Bow Street officer, who still, however, carried on his profession as an amateur, and the following edifying conversation took place between the worthies.

"What's the row now?" cried the officer, who was not altogether ignorant of Captain Dufours or his peculiarities.

"Nothing particular," replied Dufours. "By the by, what is the total amount of reward offered for the apprehension of George Mourdant?"

"Oh!" cried the officer. "You know where he is, of course?"

"That's neither here nor there," said Dufours. "I merely ask from curiosity."

"Of course."

"Well, do you know?"

"In course."

"What is it, then?"

"Two-hundred-and-fifty."

"And the evidence?"

"Is good."

"The conviction, then —"

"Is certain."

"So I thought. Then to those that can wait, the money is certain."

"Safe as a trivet with an extra leg."

"Good."

" Very good. What then?"

" Why, I rather think I know where there is a chance—"

" To pitch upon him?"

" Yes."

" Dufours, you know exactly where he is?"

" Well, if I do?"

" Why you have come to tell me, to be sure."

" On conditions."

" In course."

" Shall we say halves?"

" Halves be it."

" And my share down."

" Half down."

" And the other half on conviction?"

" Yes."

" Agreed, then."

" You do know where he is?"

" I do."

" That's your sort. Just wait a moment till I put my little barkers in order."

" Now, before we go," said Dufours, " the cash, if you please."

" The cash?"

" Certainly."

" Do you doubt my honour?"

" Oh, dear, no ; but —"

" Well, I'll down with twenty yellow un's, but no more."

" Give me them," said Dufours.

The officer handed him twenty sovereigns, and the worthy pair set out on their mission.

When they neared the court, in Soho, in which the wretched George sojourned, Dufours paused, saying,—

" Now you must go alone."

" Alone?"

" Yes. He would know me and take the alarm instantly."

" Very well, as you please. I shall take him direct to Bow-street, swear to his identity, and have him locked up till to-morrow."

" You are sure you know him?"

" Quite."

" Then I will wait here at the corner of Charles-street."

" Do so."

The gallant captain lingered behind, and the officer walked briskly across Soho-square.

He soon arrived at the place of his destination, and being provided with the card which George had left at Herbert Mandeville's, he was enabled to ask for the unhappy young man by his assumed name.

The woman of the house, who was aware that George had some reason for remaining in concealment, gave a very common answer at lodging-houses, saying,—

" I don't know whether he is at home or not."

" Will you see," said the officer.

" Yes ; I'll run up to his room and see," she replied, which meant, I'll go and ask him.

The officer, however, was an experienced hand, and allowing the woman to get some distance up the staircase, he followed her two stairs at a time, and sufficiently quick to see her enter a small room on the second floor.

He paused on the landing, and heard all that passed within the room.

"There's a person as wants you, sir," said the woman.

"Did he say who he came from?" asked George.

"No, sir."

"You are sure?"

"Oh, quite sure."

"Then, my good lady, you must understand I'm in debt a little, and don't want to see anybody unless—unless——"

"Unless what, sir?"

"Unless he says he comes from a Mr. Mandeville."

"Mandeville?"

"Yes; now, mind the name—Mandeville."

"Then you ain't at home now?"

"Certainly not."

"Very good, sir."

The woman turned from the room, and seeing the officer, uttered a loud scream.

"Who's there?" cried George.

"You are my prisoner," cried the officer, darting forward.

"You are a meddling fool," said George, snatching a pistol from his breast.

"Fire away," said the officer, springing forward.

"Now you've got it," said George, as he shot him dead upon the spot.

He then darted over the body, and was gone before his landlady could even scream.

Scrambling over a large assortment of children that crowded the step of the street door, George Mourdant darted across Soho-square, and arrived nearly breathless with speed at Charles-street.

Captain Dufours never made more sure of anything in his life than of George's capture, and he was strutting about with considerable self-satisfaction, hugging himself upon his own cleverness in pocketing a sum of money of no inconsiderable amount to a gentleman in his circumstances, at the same time that he gratified his revengeful feelings against George for speaking of him as he (George) had done to Herbert Mandeville, when he suddenly saw his supposed victim within three paces of him, and staring him full in the face.

For a moment the gallant captain was paralysed with astonishment and dismay. Then he at once turned and made a rush into an old china shop, the door of which stood invitingly open.

George surmised in a moment that this attempted capture had emanated from the veracious captain, and springing forward, he materially accelerated his progress into the old china shop by a tremendous kick, which projected him among a mass of old teacups, jars, and superannuated saucers.

Having accomplished this feat, George Mourdant darted into Oxford-street, and, turning to his right, in a few minutes sought refuge in the sacred and odorous precincts of St. Giles's.

The discomfitted captain was immediately fastened upon with the fury of a tigress by a lady with large mosiac ear-rings, and three rings of questionable metal upon each of her fingers.

A crowd collected in a few moments, and the gallant captain, after demuring loudly at the demand of seven pounds sixteen and threepence for broken china, was compelled to pay the same rather than be walked off to a station-house.

Thus terminated the vigorous and well-arranged plan of the capture of George Mourdant.

CHAPTER LXXIV.

" Murder most foul as at the best it is."—SHAKSPERE,

SOME LETTERS.—THE CURATE REMONSTRATING AGAIN.—ADELINE'S ILLNESS.—
A PUBLIC CHARACTER.—THE MURDER.

ON the morning after the *Soirée Musicale* at Lady Clara Seagrave's, Herbert found two letters upon his table. The first he opened was from Mr. Endsleigh, and ran thus :—

"DEAR SIR,—However troublesome you may think me in thus addressing you, I must be consoled by the reflection, that to the best of my ability I am endeavouring to do my duty.

"I look upon Adeline Mourdant as left by Providence in my care, and her happiness is as dear to me as if she were a child of my own.

"Herbert, her heart is full of grief. The death of her mother has preyed heavily upon her spirits. Her bright eyes are dimmer than they were. The colour is fast leaving her delicate cheek. You have sworn to love her—you have asked her to be your wife, and she has consented. She has given you her young heart's best love. Why do you not fulfil your vows?

"Make her your wife if you love her; if you do not love her, do not trifle with a heart which knows too much pain already.

"Trust me, Herbert, I make this appeal to you in no bitterness of spirit. I admire your many good qualities, and I believe your bad ones (you see I am candid) are more the results of youth and inexperience than anything else. For your father's sake I love you, Herbert. Let me likewise do so for your own.   "Believe me to be
                                        "Your sincere friend,
                                                "ROBERT ENDSLEIGH."

"Make her my wife?" said Herbert, when he had perused this letter; "of course I shall marry her—I mean to do so; but there's no particular hurry that I see. Besides, I hate to be dictated to. That Mr. Endsleigh is decidedly the most troublesome and fidgetty man I ever knew."

He walked up and down the room for some minutes in a decidedly bad temper; for if there was any one thing which annoyed Herbert Mandeville above another, it was to be told something condemnatory of his own conduct, which his own heart told him at the same time was strictly true.

"Of course I will marry her he repeated. But surely I am the best judge of the when. Besides, I think it's uncommonly foolish of Adeline to make so great a tumult, and injure her health, and—and spoil her beauty, because in the natural course of events her mother died."

He then sat down and opened the other letter. It was from Adeline.

With a flushed cheek he read as follows :—

"DEAR HERBERT.—I fear I am ill; but I dare say it will pass away. My poor mother is consigned to the tomb. Oh! Herbert, but for you I should be alone. Alone—how dreadful a word!

"I dare say—nay, I know you must be occupied on most important matters in London, so that, although I now say come to me, I will not expect you very soon. I will only hope.

"This place has now become lonesome and dreary to me. The good curate is very kind, and all are considerate and watchful of my happiness.

Still I am not happy here. My accustomed walks are no longer agreeable, for they are crowded with associations now which give me pain.

"They say I am looking pale and ill, but I shall be well again.

"Adieu, dear Herbert.   "ADELINE MOURDANT."

"I—I must go to Bracefield soon," said Herbert, "and—and marry her out of hand, and bring her home. I wish she would wait a year or two though, for I really don't like the idea of matrimony just yet. The worst of girls is, that they are always in such a hurry to get married. She loves me, that's quite clear, and I took her away from that cursed cold-hearted wretch, Leslie. Upon my word I did that rather well. How that poor Mrs. Delancey doats on me too, and she is a charming woman."

The bawling voice of a man in the street now arrested Herbert's attention, and with an impatient gesture he went to close the window.

"Here you have it!" bawled the man. "Here you have the full and interesting account for the small charge of one halfpenny!"

He then, seeing Herbert at the window, pertinaciously stopped before it and shouted,—

"Here you have it for one halfpenny. This most atrocious, most singular, and most——"

Herbert was rather amused at the fellow, and he continued,—

"This most atrocious murder! Committed for the small charge of one halfpenny."

"Murder!" exclaimed Herbert.

"Here you have the full, true, and particular account, along with a copy of verses, which is supposed to be wrote by the murderer to the ghost of his mother, for one halfpenny."

"Ridiculous," cried Herbert. "Upon my word the fellow has some humour."

No. 34

" Here you have a *re*presentation **of** the murder, and the ghosteses *a*-looking on.   Here you have a most sanguine*hairy* murder for one halfpenny."

Herbert was about to retire from the window, when he was suddenly shocked by hearing the man bawl out, at the top of his lungs,—

" The murder of Mr. Jonas Slickery, the officer, by the notorious George Mourdant for one halfpenny.   Only a blessed halfpenny.   Now's your time."

" George Mourdant !" gasped Mandeville.

" And here's the copy of verses," continued the man, " and they begins in this here affecting vay,—

> " ' Come, all ye tender mothers dear,
>   What hugs a precious babby,
>   To this here murder give a ear,
>   And feel with horror flabby !'

" Here you have it for one halfpenny."

Herbert rung the bell violently.

In a moment a servant appeared.

" Go," gasped Herbert, and—and buy one of that man's papers."

" About the murder, sir ?"

" Yes.   Quick—quick."

" Yes, sir."

The man withdrew, and Herbert waited in an agony of impatience and curiosity for his return.

In a few moments the servant appeared, and handed to Herbert, on a silver waiter, the bill.

It gave a detailed account of the attempted arrest of George Mourdant, and the murder of the officer, who, it appeared, had lived about an hour, and his deposition of the circumstances of the case had been taken on oath by a magistrate.

" Poor Adeline," thought Herbert, " what would be her feelings if she were to hear of this circumstance ?   I must write to her immediately."

CHAPTER LXXV.

CLEON.—An assignation say you ?
METAS.—Aye—a dear, delightful, secret assignation.
                                        OLD PLAY.

A FEW REFLECTIONS.—A LETTER.—AN ASSIGNATION.

HERBERT's feelings, with regard to Adeline, were more common under similar circumstances than is generally imagined.   There are very many minds, and those of a high order, too, that cannot stand under success.   When a *pursuit* is over they lose all energy, and whether it be in love, or distinction, or wealth, the possession of the heart, the long coveted title, or the glittering gold, robs each and every of them of their dearest value.

While the heart of Adeline Mourdant was *to be* gained, who so ardent in the pursuit of that inestimable treasure as Herbert Mandeville?   When he *had* gained it, who so careless of its possession?

Herbert was one of those who needed the constant stimulus of difficulty to be overcome, and something to be conquered.

He felt the necessity, however, of answering Adeline's letter, as well as the curate's, and he wrote as follows to the tender-hearted girl, who was so anxiously waiting the joy of his presence :—

"DEAREST ADELINE,—You are quite right when you suppose that business of grave import detains me in London. My father's affairs are very complicated indeed. Still I hope the time may not be far distant when you will see me at Bracefield.

"In the meantime believe me to be

"Your constant lover,
"HERBERT MANDEVILLE."

"There," exclaimed Herbert, as he folded and sealed this short and cold epistle, "I am sure that ought to suffice. In fact, if Adeline be the sensible girl I took her for, she will easily imagine the difficulties in the way of our immediate union."

To the good curate, who he felt some degree of anger with, he wrote in the following Jesuitical style :—

"MY DEAR SIR,—Your sacred office and rare piety I have no doubt enables you to comfort the bruised heart of Adeline. Particularly I consider it your duty to drive from her mind vain regrets for her departed mother.

"With regard to my immediate marriage, there are a variety of circumstances which prevent me from rushing to the altar as you kindly suggest.

"Wishing you every success in your pious exertions for everybody's good, "I am, my dear sir,

"Yours, very truly,
"HERBERT MANDEVILLE."

Herbert quite laughed at what he considered his own cleverness in writing the above insulting letter, and considered that he was justly rebuking the curate for meddling with other people's affairs.

He then debated with himself for some time upon the necessity or otherwise of taking some steps in the affair of George Mourdant. After some consideration on the subject, he came to the conclusion, which was certainly both justifiable and reasonable, that should the brother of Adeline favour him again with a visit, stained as he was with a new crime of such magnitude as murder, his only course would be to warn him never again to cross the threshold of his door, upon pain of being delivered up to the justly offended laws of his country.

It cannot be denied, likewise, although Herbert would have been slow to admit the fact, that the gentle and confiding Adeline had fallen considerably in his estimation on account of the crimes of her brother.

Thus, then, it appeared that there were two reasons, if reasons they could be called, which struck deep at the very root of the happiness of Adeline Mourdant.

In the first place, she had too easily surrendered her heart's best affections to one who never valued that which he possessed.

In the next, she had the misfortune to be disagreeably connected with a bad man, and Herbert, instead of contrasting, as he ought to have done, the many virtues and excellencies of the sister with the vices of the brother, allowed the black shadow, as it were, of the criminality of the latter to dive in his estimation some of the brightness and the beauty of the former.

He paced the room with agitated steps ; as he did so, the idea, for the first time, shaped itself into words of casting Adeline Mourdant from his heart.

"Shall I," he cried, "be firm, and rid myself of a passion which has now lost half its charms?"

He spoke half aloud, and his consciousness of how dishonourable was the suggestion, caused the blood to flush to his cheeks, even although he was alone.

One of our poets as truly said that—

> " Love once doubted
> Is already flown."

And it is more than probable that already in Herbert's mind the excitement of pursuit had indeed given way to the listlessness and ennui of possession.

Another rival in the affections of Adeline would most probably have renewed all Herbert's affection in its former vigour.

But such was not to be.

He was fast reasoning himself into a belief that to wed with Adeline would be to make some tremendous personal sacrifice, quite forgetting that had he never sought her with vows and protestations in her quiet solitude, she would most probably have been the contented wife of Charles Leslie, instead of being so indiscreet as to prefer Herbert's fleeting vows to the quiet constancy of his rival.

Alas! how bitterly did Adeline suffer for that indiscretion.

Herbert Mandeville was absorbed in these not very pleasant reflections for a considerable period of time, and as he had risen but late in the day, the lengthened shadows of evening were slowly creeping over the face of nature before he had settled upon any decided course of action.

He was, at length, interrupted in his meditations by the entrance of a servant.

Herbert started from the back of a chair upon which he had been leaning, and cried hastily,—

" Do you want me?"

" A letter, sir," replied the servant.

" A letter?"

" Yes, sir."

" From whom?"

" The messenger only stayed, sir, to deliver it."

" Give it to me."

The man handed his master the letter, and then left the room.

Herbert tore open the envelope. The hand-writing was evidently that of a female, and the contents were as follows :—

" One who has but lately learnt to know that there is one form she could worship in this world—one heart she could cling to under all circumstances—all afflictions, will wait Mr. Herbert Mandeville's presence at the corner of Park Lane, this evening, at eight.

" By the memory of one whose feelings were too much for her discretion within the last twenty-four hours you are begged to come."

" By Heavens!" cried Herbert, " this note must be from the charming Mrs. Delancey. Lights there!—lights—lights!"

CHAPTER LXXVI.

> " I have not shut her from my heart,
> But she can ne'er be mine."   OLD PLAY.

BRACEFIELD AGAIN.—THE CURATE'S HOPES AND FEARS.—A MOST UNEXPECTED ARRIVAL.

IT is a relief to the mind to turn from the gaieties and the frivolities which marked the career of Herbert Mandeville in London, to the quiet seclusion of Bracefield and its parsonage.

It was evening, and the setting sun was gilding with beauty every object. A gentle sighing wind was wafting sweet odours from flower to flower, and as it rustled among the leaves of the trees, it just sufficed to give them a trembling action, which made them in the golden sunlight look like the leaves of burnished gold, which, we are told in the Georgian's fanaticism of the east, hangs upon the trees in the Mahomedan paradise.

The birds were hieing to rest, and the air was filled with sweet and grateful perfumes from the roses which bloomed in the curate's delightful garden.

Alone in his study sat Mr. Endsleigh, and, from his attitude, he was evidently in deep thought. His head was resting upon his hand, and ever and anon he sighed, as if the complexion of his meditations was of a mournful character.

At length he spoke.

"I pray to Heaven I may be wrong," he said ; "but I cannot divest myself of the notion that unhappiness and misery must result from Adeline's acquaintance with this young man—this Mandeville. He has not a bad but a *weak* heart ; and, after all, what is wickedness but weakness, for who that had sense and courage to be virtuous could make so dreadful a mistake as to seek for happiness amidst the turbulence of vice?"

Then he rose and paced the room with nervous and uneven steps, for the old man's life of kindness and benevolence was drawing to its close.

"Poor Adeline," he said, "when I am gone what will become of thee ? without father, mother, or friend in the wide world. Alas! for thee, Adeline —alas! for thee."

He walked to the window as he spoke, and looked out upon the glowing landscape that spread far and wide before him, in all the radiant beauty of a glorious sunset.

"No," he suddenly cried—"no, she will not be alone—she will not be unprotected. *He*, who has given life and beauty to all this animated scene that my old eyes gaze at with such pleasure, will protect the innocent and the guileless. Has He not said that the orphan should be his care ? Yes—yes— and I repined—I repined !"

For a few moments the old curate was engaged in silent prayer. It was a prayer for Heaven's blessing on the head of the orphan girl, who seemed to have been by Providence committed to his care. Then the old man smiled, as he said,—

"If an earthly protector be necessary for the gentle girl, Heaven will send her one when I am gone."

He looked with fervour and pleasure up to the glowing sky, and peace was in the curate's heart, for his hope was not of this world, but lasting as eternity.

The sound of the latch of his wicket-gate struck his ears at that moment, and casting his eyes in that direction, he suddenly clasped his hands and cried in a voice of joy,—

"Welcome! welcome !"

Charles Leslie was tying the bridle of his horse to the gate-post.

The curate immediately left his room, and hastened to meet his esteemed young friend. They were soon hand in hand.

"My dear Charles," said Mr. Endsleigh, "I am so delighted to see you."

"The feeling is mutual," said Charles. "You know, my dear sir, that I look upon you as a second father."

"Come in," cried the curate—"come in, Charles."

"Stay yet one moment," said Leslie.

The curate paused.

" Is she———"

" Adeline ?"

" Yes ; is she his wife?"

" No, Charles."

" Then she is still here ?"

" She is, and alone."

" Alone ?"

" Yes ; Mrs. Mourdant is no more."

" I grieve to hear it," answered Charles. " I have been too short a time in England to learn any news. I have but returned from Lisbon yesterday, and you may be sure I have thought of nothing but the shortest way to Bracefield."

" Adeline is in her chamber, Charles," said the curate, " and Martha is at the village, so come with me to my study, and while you refresh yourself after your journey, I will tell you all that has happened, since you were last among us."

The old man took the arm of his young friend, and led him to his study; there with his own hands he laid before him refreshments, and pressed him so affectionately to partake of them, that the tears stood in Charles Leslie's eyes, for he was one to be always touched by kindness.

" Now, dear Mr. Endsleigh, tell me all the news," said Charles.

" I will," answered the curate. " Herbert Mandeville is now, as you know, his own master."

" I am aware he is, and likewise master of a very large fortune, I understand."

" That is true, I believe, Charles. But———"

" But what, sir ?"

" He does not ask our Adeline to come and share his possessions. He contents himself with letters, breathing alternately raptures and coldness."

" Indeed !"

" It is too true, Charles. He has won the heart of Adeline, but there he has paused."

" Alas !" cried Charles Leslie; " have I indeed read this young man's character aright ?"

" You have, Charles—you have. He is now trifling with the fondest, purest heart that ever beat in mortal bosom."

" Are— are you sure ?"

" He knows that Adeline is now an orphan. He is his own master ; he affects to love her—has taken pains, Charles, to win her. What should follow ?"

" Marriage."

" So I have told him."

" And what said he, sir ?"

" He rebuked me for my busy meddling, Charles."

" Dare he———"

" Nay, Charles, heed not that. I am an old man, and may, perhaps, have laid myself open in some measure to such a reproach, and even if not, it is not hard to bear. Heed that not, Charles."

" Does he visit here ?"

" But once for a long time."

" You remember, Mr. Endsleigh," said Charles, in a voice of deep emotion —" you remember, my dear friend, when I gave up to this young man freely the young heart that I would fain have cherished as my own, that I did it on conditions."

" I do remember," said the curate.

"And these conditions were," continued Charles, "that he was to love and cherish that dear possession which he had wrested from me who would have held it as a sacred trust from Heaven."

"True, most true, Charles."

"Then, sir, has he failed in the compact?"

"He has."

"It is my duty, then, to exact from him an account of his trust. Mrs. Mourdant's often expressed wishes—Adeline's own consent—the feelings of my own heart—all—all have delegated to me the task of watching over the happiness of the young heart that first taught me what it was to love, and then a bitterer lesson."

"Charles, Charles," said the curate. "Do nothing rashly."

"Depend upon my discretion," replied Charles. "I wish to be clear only upon one point. Is Adeline happy and satisfied with **Mr. Mandeville's** conduct?"

"She will not tell me, Charles, that her heart is wrung, but I can see it in her fading cheeks."

"Her fading cheeks?" replied Charles, with emotion.

"Yes, and her wasted form."

"Good Heavens! Has it come to that?"

"It has."

"Oh! Adeline, Adeline," he groaned. "I—I think I could have made you happy."

"My dear Charles," said the curate, "controul your feelings; all may yet be well. You shall see Adeline yourself, and—and ——"

"And what, sir? What would you say?"

"Forgive me, Charles. It was but a stray thought; but—but ——"

"Keep me not in suspense."

"Should she, then, even now, with a better judgment, cast from her the wild and feverish dream of love, which this Mandeville possessed her mind with ——"

"Hold, my friend!—hold!" cried Charles. "I know what you would say. Indulge not in such a dream: the time has now passed. Adeline can never now be my wife!"

"You say so solemnly, Charles?"

"I do—most solemnly."

A low tap sounded now on the study-door, and the curate rose to see who knocked.

CHAPTER LXXVII.

" ——Paler ever grew her cheek,
And yet she murmured not."
ANON.

A PAINFUL INTERVIEW.—THE FAINTING.—LESLIE'S DETERMINATION.

It was Adeline herself who stood on the threshold of the door of the curate's study.

Charles Leslie's back was turned towards her, and she did not at first perceive that there was another person in the little room.

"May I intrude upon you, Mr. Endsleigh, for a short time?" she said.

Charles started at the voice which he knew so well, and, rising, he ejaculated,—

"Adeline!"

"Charles!" she cried. "I—I—Mr. Leslie, I mean."

He advanced, and took her hand kindly.

"Adeline, I am glad to see you," he said.

His voice faltered as he spoke, and the flush of colour which had given a temporary glow to Adeline's cheek, slowly died away, leaving her very pale.

"You know," she said, in her old sweet tones, "I am very glad always to see you."

"Sit down, both of you," said the curate.

"Nay," said Adeline, "I fear I am an intruder."

"That, Adeline, you can never be to your friends," replied the curate.

Adeline smiled faintly, and sat down.

Charles Leslie was very much shocked at the excessive paleness of her face.

"I fear you are not so well, Adeline," he said, "as you used to be."

"No, no," she said faintly; "not quite so well. Do not be alarmed; but any sudden surprise affects me now, and your unexpected arrival—Charles, Charles!"

"Good Heavens!" cried Leslie, starting from his seat; "she is fainting, Mr. Endsleigh."

"Fainting ?" cried the curate.

"Oh, Adeline! Adeline!" said Charles Leslie, in a voice of deep anguish, as he supported her in his arms. "Has it come to this?"

Adeline had fainted, and now, as her head lay upon the breast of him who loved her so fondly and sincerely, she was scarcely paler than usual, and who can describe the pangs that wrung the manly heart of the noble and gallant-minded Leslie in that moment.

The curate had left the room for restoratives; but, before he could return, Adeline seemed to be recovering.

She spoke faintly.

"So you have come to me at last, Herbert," she said. "You have come to your Adeline?"

Leslie groaned.

"It was cruel," she continued, as she burst into tears upon his breast. "It was cruel to leave me in my sorrow; but you have come now. You have come now—and all is forgotten, all is forgiven!"

"Adeline, Adeline," cried Leslie, "you mistake."

"Ha!" she cried, starting up; "Mr. Leslie."

"Nay, Adeline, be not confused, nor shrink from —. The breast you reposed on was one that loved you, that still loves you as a dear friend."

"Oh, Charles!—Charles!" sobbed Adeline, as she sunk into a chair, "what has happened?"

"'Twas nothing, Adeline," he said. "You fainted, and a friend's arm saved you from falling."

"Fainted?"

"Even so, Adeline."

"I am very weak, Charles—Mr. Leslie. I know I am very weak."

"Tell me truly, Adeline. Is it illness or sorrow that affects you thus?"

"Charles," she said, "I will not conceal from you that—that ——"

"That what, Adeline? Why do you gaze at me thus strangely?"

"I am dying, Charles."

"Dying?"

"Yes; I know it. My heart is broken!"

Charles was inexpressibly shocked. He could not speak, and it was a great relief to him when Mr. Endsleigh opened the door, and appeared accompanied by Mrs. Plumpjoy, who had just returned from the village.

"Goodness gracious, my dear!" she exclaimed upon seeing Adeline; "and so you fainted?"

"Well, never mind that now," said the curate. "You see, Martha, she has recovered."

"Of course I see," cried Mrs. Plumpjoy, "and you are here, too, Mr. Leslie. Well, I never."

"I hope you are quite well," said Charles.

"Tolerable," sighed Mrs. Plumpjoy. "I've so much to do that it's killing me by inches."

"Adeline," said the curate. "I would advise you to take some rest."

"And some Plumpjoy cordial," added the curate's sister. "It's a beautiful drink: the poor dear major told me how to make it, and he had the **proscription** from his great aunt."

"Thank you all," said Adeline. "Rest will do more for me, I think, Mrs. Plumpjoy, than the cordial."

She rose, and, leaning on the arm of Mrs. Plumpjoy, walked to the door.

"We shall meet again," she said, turning to Charles Leslie.

"Assuredly," he said.

With a faint smile she left the room.

Charles Leslie gazed after her for a few moments in silence, then evidently making a great effort to master his emotion, he said,—

"My dear friend, tell me candidly what is your opinion of Adeline's present state?"

"Charles, Charles," said the curate. "I knew she was weakly; but she has not fainted thus before."

"And now?"

"I do, indeed, fear."

"The worst?"

"Nay, not so, Charles; but I think her sensitive heart feels dreadfully the slighting conduct of Mandeville."

"I know it," groaned Leslie.

"This," continued the curate, "is one of those natures that require kind

No. 35

ness and tenderness. Harshness and neglect would soon destroy her delicate frame."

" What can be done ?" exclaimed Leslie.

" That I have asked myself over and over again," said the curate, " and found no answer."

Charles appeared in deep thought for some moments, then he said,—

" I will not waste time in idle regrets. My heart is very heavy, and I—I could sit down and weep, were it not that a sense of duty bids me battle with my sorrow."

" My noble young friend," cried the curate, " what can you do ?"

" I will do two things immediately," said Leslie.

" Two things ?"

" Yes."

" And they ?"

" I will repair to London to-night, and the first thing in the morning I will bring with me a physician, who will satisfy us with regard to the state of health of Adeline."

" And what next, Charles ?"

" Then I will call on Mandeville."

" Call on Mandeville, Charles ?"

" Yes ; trust me, I will not quarrel. He cannot be quite heartless. I will endeavour to awaken his slumbering feelings : I will strive to give life to those dormant sensibilities which he cannot be wholly destitute of. I will paint to him the happiness that he may bestow, and with it the happiness that he may receive. By every appeal I will move him to do right."

" Oh! Charles," cried the curate ; " if he was but like you."

" Say no more, my kind and partial friend," interposed Charles. " Say no more. Is my horse still at the wicket-gate ?"

" No ; I beckoned old Andrew to take it to the stable."

" Then let me here, until to-morrow morning, bid you a kind farewell. I will myself get the horse. Say nothing of my errand. Early in the morning you shall see me again at your hospitable gate."

The curate's heart was too full too speak, and he could only grasp Charles's hand.

Leslie said no more, but, immediately quitting the room, hurried by the back way to the stable, where he found old Andrew busily rubbing down his horse.

" How be ye, Master Leslie ?" said the old man.

" Well, Andrew, well," said Leslie. " I want the horse again directly."

" Why ye beant a-going."

" Yes ; but I shall be back in the morning."

The old man saddled the horse, and then he said,—

" I—I—wrote a bit of—letter ——"

" And I received it," said Charles. " I know you meant well, Andrew ; but do not write to me again."

" Not again ?"

" No ; I never meant such a thing. Folks would misconstrue your honest intentions ; besides, Andrew, I shall not again go far away. Good-bye."

So saying Leslie mounted his horse, and, with a smile to the old servant, and half-a-crown, he galloped away.

" Bless him !" said old Andrew. " That gal must be mad not to a jumped at he !"

CHAPTER LXXVIII.

"—— He's quite a man of the world, sir,
Games, swears, drinks, like a hero!"
MASSINGER.

HERBERT AGAIN.—THE APPOINTMENT.—A GREAT DEAL OF SELF-SATISFACTION
AND SENTIMENT.

WE will leave now Charles Leslie to commune with his own heart, as he urges his steed over the winding country between London and Bracefield, and again convey the reader to the great metropolis, and open to him the proceedings of Herbert Mandeville, who, while the purest, dearest possession which Heaven can bestow—a faithful heart was breaking at Bracefield, was plotting and planning in London how best he could engage his time in heartless frivolity and profitless gaiety.

He determined to keep the mysterious appointment with the very flattering author of the anonymous note, which has already been presented to the reader, and he was not a little impatient at the slow progress of time which, had he spoken candidly, he would have said that the thought ought **to be** accelerated speedily upon his account.

At length the hour came sufficiently near to warrant him in sallying forth to meet his fair incognita, who, however, he never for a moment doubted, he would find to be no other than the charming and ill-matched Mrs. Delancey.

Herbert Mandeville was boyish enough to fancy that there must be some degree of personal credit attached to an intrigue ; thus, the impression which he believed he had made upon the far too perceptible heart of Mrs. Delancey, flattered him extremely, and there was only one drawback just then to his satisfaction, and that was that there was no one to whom he could narrate his *bon fortune,* and from whom he could derive that gratifying blame which is usually lavished on such occasions, and which generally consists in such expressions as,—

"Ah! you are a wild dog! Can't you leave the woman's heart alone, &c."

It was with no small exultation, therefore, that Herbert walked up Oxford Street, to the place appointed in the note of his fair incognita. The hour of meeting peeled from several steeples, as he reached the end of Park Lane, and when upon the first glance round him, he saw no one, it for the second time faintly crossed his mind that the whole affair might be a hoax. Such was not however the fact, for scarcely had a muttered sound of impatience passed his lips, when a female figure, closely veiled, brushed so nearly by him, that he felt convinced that design, and not accident, actuated her movements.

Fearful, however, of a mistake, Herbert remained passive for a few moments, and his heart fluttered as he saw the figure turn when about ten or twelve paces from him, and again approach the spot on which he stood.

"It must be the authoress of the billet," thought Herbert. "Her figure is good ;—her hair and manner decidedly superior. I will speak."

He was spared that trouble, for upon the veiled lady passing him again, she mentioned his name in an exceedingly sentimental tone.

"Yes," he replied eagerly ; "I am Mr. Mandeville."

"Follow!" said the unknown ; and then gliding onwards towards Grosvenor Gate, rather taxed Herbert's speed to keep up with her.

When a short distance past the gate, the figure paused, and leant upon some rails. Herbert was in a moment by its side, and to his surprise, heard the sounds of weeping, and deep sobs of grief, proceeding from the unknown.

"Why do you weep?" he cried. "Good Heavens, are you ill?"

"Alas ! alas !" was all the reply.

"Tell me at least who you are," said Herbert, passionately, "that I may know what name to associate with her who has confessed a favourable opinion of one so unworthy as myself."

"No—no—not unworthy !" said the lady.

"This is some very superior person," thought Herbert. "Do not grieve," he said aloud, "that you have confided so dear a secret to me."

"Does not your own heart," faltered the lady, "tell you who I am ?"

"Mrs. Delancey ?" said Herbert ; for now he recognised the voice, as the lady, no doubt, intended he should.

"Oh, call me not by that name," cried the lady. "Call me anything but that."

"Not for worlds would I annoy you," said Herbert.

"Oh, Heavens !" cried Mrs. Delancey, throwing aside her veil, and casting up her really fine eyes. "Oh, Heavens, what must you think of me ? But I will tell you all—I will confide the inmost secrets of my heart to you."

"Believe me," said Herbert, "I sensibly feel the debt of gratitude I owe you for your kind opinion, and if the devotion of my heart——"

"Oh, talk not thus," interrupted Mrs. Delancey. "Do not let me dream even of—of—so much bliss. There was a time—but that is past ! Gone for ever ! and I—I am another's now. Oh, how I tremble !"

She laid her small beautiful hand upon Herbert's arm, and it certainly shook.

"Dear madam, calm yourself," said Herbert.

"Tell me one thing," she whispered ; "do you despise me ?"

"Despise you ?"

"Yes. Do you not think me weak—too—too fond ?"

"The feelings you have expressed towards me, my dear Mrs.—a—a— De——"

"Call me Marian," she said, faintly.

"My dear Marian," continued Herbert, "are of that nature, that my heart overflows with joy."

"Then I will tell you all," she said. "My husband is jealous—of you. He has threatened my very life, and you he has marked for vengeance !"

"Indeed !" said Herbert.

"Yes ; he said your life only would satisfy his rage, and then—I—I forgot everything in anxiety to warn you. I thought not what construction you might put upon my conduct ; I only knew you were in danger, and I flew to beg—to entreat—to implore you to be careful of a life that is—alas ! too dear to her, who now with tears addresses you !"

"Most generous of women," cried Herbert.

"Nay, thank me not."

"How can I do otherwise? I were insensible indeed not to feel the delight of having inspired an interest in such a breast as yours."

"I know not what my fate may be," continued Mrs. Delancey ; "in this world—we may never—never—meet again."

"Not meet again ?—Oh, yes. Can you think for one moment that after the generous step you have taken to warn me, that I could abandon you? Oh, no, dear Marian, since you permit me to call you such, do not think me so cold-hearted."

"I may fall a sacrifice to the blind fury of a husband I cannot love ; but I shall be content if I have saved you," she whispered.

"No !" cried Herbert, in the excitement of the moment. "Leave the heart that cannot appreciate you, and—and ——"

"And what ?" she gently whispered, placing her soft cheek so close to his that he felt the down-like pressure of her lips.

"Cling to the heart that adores you!" he cried. "Fly with me to some secure retreat, and—let love, eternal love light our path with the brilliancy of extatic joy!"

"Oh, tempter! tempter!" cried the lady.

Now, of all things, Herbert Mandeville was most flattered by being called a tempter, so he continued:—

"Marian, say you will let love alone be your guide. Oh, say you will be mine!"

"My heart drinks in the sweet passion," said Mrs. Delancey, languidly. "I cannot think—when with you—we—we will meet again."

"To-morrow?" cried Herbert.

"Be it so," murmured 'dear Marian.'

"On this spot to-morrow, then, at the same hour, let me hope!"

"I must away!" said the lady, affecting sudden alarm. "Till to-morrow, adieu!"

CHAPTER LXXIX.

"His very name is like a breath from hell!"
BEAUMONT.

THE NEXT MORNING.—HERBERT'S PLEASANT REFLECTIONS.—A MOST UNEXPECTED AND UNWELCOME VISITOR.—A PECULIAR CONVERSATION.

HERBERT's self love was not a little gratified by the result of his interview with Mrs. Delancey. The gentle and timid affection of Adeline, sanctioned as it was by virtue and high principle, was for a time forgotten in the tumult of gratified vanity, which the intriguing Mrs. Delancey had awakened.

Herbert was not, however, without some misgivings as to the consequences which might eventually arise from his acquaintance with the wife of another, and he could not conceal from himself that, although he might in a certain class of society enhance a worthless reputation, yet that an elopement under such circumstances, might by some remote possibility be bitterly repented of, when repentance would be too late. But when did sober reason ever stand a chance when struggling against excited passion? Such thoughts as these would occasionally obtrude themselves, but they came as unwelcome visitors, and were banished as quickly as possible. They were blemishes upon the surface of his gratified and self-elated vanity, and the conviction that he had inspired a tender passion almost at sight, in the heart of a beautiful, accomplished, and as he considered, highly sensitive female, was too delightful to be got rid of by any suggestion of consequences.

Upon a review of all the circumstances, Herbert fancied himself not only a most insinuating and agreeable person, but especially fortunate in all at once attracting so delightful a person as Mrs. Delancey. His slumbers were haunted with agreeable visions, and he rose in the morning on as excellent terms with himself as any young gentleman need wish to be.

"Yes," he thought, "I will meet again this charming creature, who has singled me out from the mass of mankind, in so distinguished a manner. She shall not 'waste her sweetness on the desert air,' and as for her wretch of a husband, I dare say the truth is, he has not courage to resent anything, and if he has, I have courage to meet him in any way he chooses. Let me see, here am I—a young fellow, of tolerable good looks—some thousands a year—my own master—the adored of the most fascinating woman in London, and likely to fight a duel, which I know very well does a man no harm among fellows of any pretentions to spirit."

A servant now appeared, and laid a card before Mandeville, saying, respectfully :—

"The gentleman, sir, is waiting in the library."

"Mr. Charles Leslie!" exclaimed Herbert, reading the card with unaffected surprise. "What on earth could induce him to cross my threshold. Such insolence is unparalleled. Tell him to leave the house immediately, for I decline seeing him!" There was an angry flush upon Herbert's brow, and a flutter at his heart, as he gave this message to the servant, which was sadly at variance with the feelings of self-congratulation which had filled his breast some few minutes only before. The name of Charles Leslie was to Herbert Mandeville the most hateful that could be presented to him. If there were any circumstances in his life which he would have given anything to blot from his memory, they were all connected with Charles Leslie, and now as everything that had occurred in which he and Leslie had been joint actors, flashed across his mind, he rose from his chair, and paced the room with agitated steps, and a countenance indicative of shame and rage.

"Curses on Leslie !" he muttered. "The serpent in my path—the poison in my goblet of pleasure. His very name comes across my heart like a chilling deadening shadow! I will not see him. See him, indeed! How dared he come to a house of mine? Such vulgar assurance is beyond all conjecture. Am I to be thus annoyed?"

The door was opened, and the footman said, mildly—

"Sir, Mr. Leslie won't go away."

"Won't go away? cried Herbert.

"No sir. If you please he says his business is too important to stand upon ceremony, and he hopes you will think better of it and see him, sir."

"I will *not* see him," roared Herbert, in a voice that made the man jump again. "Tell him to begone from my house. I can have no business, important or otherwise, with him. Tell—tell him. By Heavens! I never heard of such impertinence."

The footman, with a look of dismay, left the room, and Herbert, trembling with rage, stood gazing at the door. In another moment it opened and Charles Leslie stood upon the threshold.

For a moment neither spoke, for Mandeville's rage deprived him of the power of utterance, and Charles Leslie seemed desirous of being accosted first.

Seeing that such, however, was not to be the case, he said, in a firm low voice,—

"Mr. Mandeville, any other business than that which I come about, would render my presence here a most unwarrantable intrusion, painful to me, and doubtless disagreeable to you."

Herbert did not speak, and Leslie continued.

"I come to you, Mr. Mandeville, with a name in my mouth which should command your respect—that name is Adeline !"

Mandeville started, and then replied—

"You have rightly named your presence here an unwarrantable intrusion. I will hold no conversation with you. I know your disappointment with regard to Adeline Mourdant is bitter. Let it rankle in your heart."

"*You* cannot insult *me*," said Leslie ; "I have a duty to perform, and so help me, Heaven, I will perform it. Listen to me you shall, Herbert Mandeville."

"Ah—shall ?"

"Yes, that is the word ; you shall hear me. After you have done so you can take what course you like, but till then I am a rock !"

"My servants shall spurn you from my door," cried Herbert, furiously.

"No, sir ; they dare not. Summon them, and see if one dare lay a finger on me. Young man, put aside for a moment all personal feelings towards me

—think of your own happiness, not my griefs. You wrested from me the young heart that I adored, what would you more? You rudely awakened me from a dream of joy, and stepped between me and my happiness in this world, what then would you more? 'Tis you have triumphed, not I. Oh, Herbert Mandeville, you totter upon a precipice, a false step and you are lost for ever."

There was an impressive earnestness about the manner of Leslie, which, in spite of him, powerfully affected Mandeville. In vain he struggled against it; he could not look Leslie in the face, and he only said,

"What does all this lead to?"

"My errand is simple," replied Leslie; "but first hear my authority for interference."

"Go on, sir."

"When Adeline's father, as gallant a soldier as ever lived, went to India, from whence he never returned, he said to me—' Charles Leslie, should I fall, will you look to my wife and child?' After Mr. Mourdant's death, a letter was found addressed to me; it contained but these words—' Charles Leslie, watch over my child.' When I surrendered to you the heart of Adeline, I did it on condition that you should prize it. What *have* you done?"

"Is that *all?*" said Herbert.

"Not quite."

"Go on. Go on!"

"Adeline is dying!"

"Dying?"

"Yes. From my heart I do believe what I say; the canker-worm is at her heart."

"No—no—no," gasped Mandeville.

"Have you, or have you not, broken faith with her?" said Leslie, firmly.

"She—she did not complain to you?"

"Complain to me? No, she complains to no one, not even to her God. She only suffers."

"What—what can I do?"

"Now mistake me not, Mr. Mandeville, I do not come here to urge you to make Adeline Mourdant your wife, far from it. Do not go unwillingly to the altar—do not go from principle even—do not go because a feeling of tardy justice is awakened in your heart. No! If you cannot go as a lover, go not at all."

"What would you have?" faltered Herbert.

"A decision."

"What decision? what do you mean?"

"Renounce at once the heart that trusted you, or let it feel cause to trust you still."

"Renounce?"

"Aye, renounce. Tell Adeline your passion was a fleeting fancy, fastened by opposition, born in vanity. Tell her it has died in success."

Herbert Mandeville shrunk before the glance of Charles Leslie, for true he felt these last words to be.

"I understand you," he said. "Will you come here again to-morrow?"

"For an answer?"

"Yes."

"At what hour?"

"The same hour."

"Enough," said Leslie; "I will be here."

So saying, without another word, he left the room, and Herbert sunk upon a couch a prey to not the most pleasant reflections.

CHAPTER LXXX.

' Sir, I am hunted,
I pray you lend me wings to fly.''—TERENCE.

A RE-ACTION OF IDEAS.—THE VIRTUES OF CHAMPAIGNE.—AN INSTRUCTIVE
CONVERSATION.—THE CRIMINAL.—A BIT OF REVENGE.—HUE AND CRY.

For nearly half an hour Herbert remained absorbed in uneasy thought. At one moment he thought of ordering post horses and repairing to Bracefield without delay, then again his mind vascilated to the appointment with Mrs. Delancey.

"Am I," he cried, "to be betrothed by Charles Leslie? Fool that I was to allow him to move me as I did. No, I will not be made the tool of his hypocritical cant; he wants me to resign Adeline to him. Ha! ha! good faith. By Heaven I should have told him that before he went, but somehow there was a chill upon my spirits. Curse him, that voice of his is enough to damp any one; I am cold to my very heart even now."

He rung the bell violently, and when the servant appeared he said loudly—

"A bottle of champaigne!"

"Captain Dufours waits your leisure, sir," said the man.

"Show him up, anybody is welcome now except that preaching Leslie. By the gods! I'll give him a different reception to-morrow. A bottle of champaigne, I say, quick."

"Make it two, my man," said Captain Dufours, as he passed the servant and ntered the room.

"Ha! Dufours, my boy, how are you?" cried Mandeville.

"Well, damme!" cried Dufours; "this is like old times again. Why Mandeville, what's put you in such spirits, eh? Upon my soul I don't care though, I look to effects, not causes, and an infernal good philosophy it is too."

"Then don't ask me," replied Mandeville, laughing in a forced and unnatural manner. "Let's have a carouse, Dufours. Wine, wine!"

"Oh, I've no objection in life," said the complaisant captain. "Wine, wine, say I too."

"Let's enjoy life while we can," cried Herbert; "hang care."

"By the by, talking of hanging," remarked Dufours, "don't you think my d—d good-natured friend, George Mourdant, stands a chance?

"Is he taken?"

"Not that I know of."

"I trust he will come here no more."

"I hope he may when I am here," muttered Dufours.

The wine was now placed upon the table, and Herbert immediately poured himself a bumper, which he drank off at a draught.

"Example is better than precept, as the copy-books at school say," remarked the captain, as he finished the bottle and sent the cork of the second one spinning up to the ceiling.

"There is nothing like wine," said Herbert.

"And after that sentiment, nothing like champaigne," suggested the captain.

"It's rather too early to drink, Dufours, but I've been devilishly annoyed."

"Exactly; take another bumper. By the by, was not that sanctimonious fellow I saw leave your door a little while ago, someway mixed up with that little rural affair of yours at the village, with a green and a duck pond, and daisies and buttercups, and all that sort of thing, eh?"

"Yes. Ha! ha! Upon my soul, Dufours, your description is graphic. He—he was a little mixed up in it. That is, I took the girl from him, that's all."

"Oh!" said the captain, looking at his wine critically.

"Yes," continued Herbert, drinking rapidly. "That was it, and now—Ha! ha! he wants me to waive my pretensions in his favour."

"A good joke truly."

"Ah! very good."

"By the by, Mandeville, couldn't we have a quiet game at vingt-un? eh?"

"We could."

"You have cards, of course?"

"Yes, and upon my word, Dufours, I think gaming is next to woman."

"And wine," said Dufours.

"Aye, and wine. Those are the three rocks that a young fellow may split upon."

"Yes; but you should recollect, my dear Mandeville, how short life is, as the saints tell us; so I say there is the more need of making haste to enjoy it. Time, as the song says;

"Inspires us and fires us."

And women—dear delightful women, are like rare and piquant sauces to the plain dish of existence. Then gaming, when all things pall upon the senses, when a fellow is ready to cut his throat from downright ennui, what revives him but gaming; if he win, what so delightful? if he lose, why he can curse himself into good humour again!"

"Ha! ha! ha!" laughed Herbert. "Upon my word, Dufours, you are quite a philosopher."

"The cards—the cards then; and I say, while you are up, tell your fellow to bring some more wine." Herbert produced cards, and having ordered more wine, he sat down with his worst enemy to endeavour to banish care by heaping up ample food for future uneasiness.

They played at first for but comparatively small sums. These were, how-

No. 36

ever, increased to large ones, under the skilful and stimulating taunting of Captain Dufours, aided too, as he was, by the quantity of wine which Herbert kept drinking.

The mid-day was past, and yet Herbert, although he knew himself a great loser, recklessly played on.

The wily captain congratulated himself mightily upon his good fortune in calling upon Mandeville when his mind was in so admirable a state to be played upon by such a sharper as he, the "gallant captain" was. He never allowed the conversation to flag for one moment, and by the time they had sat some three hours, Herbert found himself a loser of three thousand pounds to his extremely entertaining and facetious companion.

The copious draughts of wine the inconsiderate young man had taken now began to exercise their influence over him. He wept, raved, and swore by turns ; then he began to get drowsy, and would have fallen from his chair in a deep sleep had not his unprincipled companion done all he could to keep him up, as it was no part of his plan to allow his dupe to fall asleep three thousand pounds in his debt, and possibly forget all about it by the time he awakened again.

"Hilloa! Mandeville, my boy," he cried, shaking him roughly. "Don't let a few glasses of Champaigne get the better of you."

"No—no—certainly not," said Herbert. "I am—very well, thank you. How's the game?"

"Why, if you will just give me a cheque for what's coming to me, we can go on again."

"A—a cheque?"

"Yes ; come, come, I thought you had a better head than this."

"What have I won?" said Mandeville.

"Tush ! 'tis I have won."

A servant at this moment appeared at the door with a little scrap of paper in his hand.

"What do you want?" said Dufours.

"My master, sir," replied the man. "He is wanted."

"By whom ?"

"A Mr. Johnston —"

"Ah ! let me see that paper. Humph. Tell the person who brought this to wait in the library ; and, I say, go quickly and send some one else for a constable."

"A constable, sir ?"

"Yes ; this Johnston is a criminal. Quick—quick, I say ; a ten pound note shall be yours if he is caught in the house."

The servant looked irresolute for a moment, and then left the room.

"It's George Mourdant, by all that's lucky !" cried Captain Dufours. "I have him now safe."

CHAPTER LXXXI.

" Now all may know him.
Truly is he branded."
                    SHAKSPERE.

THE CAPTAIN OUTWITTED AT LAST.—A REFUNDING PROCESS.—A CURIOUS OPERATION AND A LITTLE GUNPOWDER.

SCARCELY had these words of triumph passed the lips of Captain Dufours, when George Mourdant himself walked into the room and confronted him.

The captain could not have looked more scared had an apparition suddenly stood before him, he turned as pale as ashes and trembled in every limb.

The first act of George, after casting a withering look at the captain, was to lock the door and put the key in his pocket.

"George; my good fellow," stammered Dufours; "w—what do you want? I—I shall be glad to assist you."

"Do you imagine I don't know your abominable treachery?" cried George Mourdant. "Scoundrel! we have robbed together—crime was familiar to us both, but we trusted each other, and you—you Dufours, of all people, set the fool on me who has lost his life for his pains."

"You—you don't believe what you say, I'm sure," faltered the captain. "You can't think me capable of anything of the kind."

"Not capable?" answered George. "Dufours, who murdered his own child —"

"Hush—hush," cried Dufours.

"I waste time," said George. "I came here for money, but I see you have drugged this dupe till he can neither see nor hear."

"I can let you have a trifle," said the captain, catching at any chance of a reconciliation with the man he had betrayed.

"You have been playing?" said George, pointing to the cards.

"Yes," replied Dufours. "Just to pass a tedious half hour."

"What have you won?"

"I won, George? Why should I win?"

"Don't trifle with me," cried George. "My time is precious, and so is yours."

"Mine?"

"Yes; you have desired the servant to fetch the police. I am in hopes of leaving here before he can execute his errand. If, however, he *should* come back too soon, I intend to blow out your brains, and then my own. You see I have the means."

As he spoke, he took from between his waistcoat and his under clothing, a pair of pistols.

A cry of terror burst involuntarily from the captain as he heard this uncomfortable explanation.

"Silence!" said George. "Such another outcry as that and I will anticipate my intentions."

"For God's sake go!" gasped Dufours. "Here—take all—all I have—but go!—go!"

"Ha! ha!" laughed George, as his alarmed quondam associate emptied his pockets of all the ready money he had won of Mandeville. "Ha! ha! why, Dufours, you are quite flurried."

"There! there!" cried Dufours. "On my soul, that is all. Take it and go. Fly and save yourself."

"How careful you are of me;" remarked George.

"Yes—yes—oh, George, you are wasting precious time—most precious time."

"I know it," replied Mourdant, rapidly collecting the money. "How much is here?"

"Above three hundred pounds."

"Then you had made a good morning's work out of my respected and simple brother-in-law, that is to be."

"Anything you like, but go. For Heaven's sake go!"

"What a hurry you are in," said George, calmly. "Do you imagine now, I'm going without leaving a little remembrance behind me to my old friend, confidante, and companion, the gallant Captain Dufours?"

"What—what *do* you mean?"

"No—no," continued George; "I am not so ungrateful for past favours.

We may not meet again at all, and if we do, it may not be in half so convenient a place as this."

"Are you mad?" cried Dufours, "that you thus trifle with your safety?"

"Gratitude, gratitude, you know," said George, taking from his pocket a piece of rope.

"W—w—what do you want with that?"

"Do you think it's to hang you with?" said George, with perfect *sang froid.*

"Hang *me?*"

"Yes."

"You—you don't consider. Hilloa! help!"

"Another cry," said George, ferociously stepping up to him and placing the cold barrel of the pistol against the captain's chattering teeth. "Another sound above your breath, and I'll scatter your brains on yonder wall."

"Mercy!" groaned the captain.

"Wine—more wine;" muttered Herbert, in his sleep.

"Contemptible villain;" said George, "know that I am safe here. The servant will not obey your orders in fetching the police. I *am* safe here—safer than anywhere else, probably throughout this great city; but mind ye, I know your treachery."

"You have taken all from me," said Dufours; "what would you more?"

"Give you something in return."

"Give me something?"

"Yes, and now fully understand me. If you so much as wince or struggle at what I am about to do, I will shoot you as surely as you are a sneaking villain."

The miserable captain saw there was no hope, and with bitter groans and anticipations of some horrible fate, he submitted to be bound down with the rope George had produced in a massive arm chair.

"Good God," he said, "what are you going to do?"

"Cut your throat if the humour takes me," replied George Mourdant.

The captain groaned and gave himself up for lost.

George now busily searched among the gold that Dufours had emptied from his pocket till he found an exceedingly sharp-edged half sovereign, and with that in his hand he approached the bewildered and alarmed captain.

"I'll put society on their guards against you," said George, calmly. "You know you are a rogue. Come, confess you are a rogue."

Again the barrel of the pistol rattled against his teeth, and the captain, with a groan, murmured,

"Yes—yes—anything you like."

"Very good," said George. "Then you shall carry the first letter of your name about with you till you are hung. Now one cry, a shriek, or a scream, even a groan too loud, and it's your death."

So saying, with the sharp-milled edge of the coin, George cut a large R upon the gallant captain's forehead.

The perspiration of intense agony and dread rolled down the face of the discomfited villain, and when the operation was concluded, George took some loose gunpowder from his pocket and rubbed it well into the wound.

With clenched teeth and hair bristling with rage, pain, and terror, the captain bore all this, and at its conclusion, George remarked;

"You will find that mark indelible;" and flinging the half sovereign in his face, he turned with a laugh of scorn and unlocked the door of the room. "Adieu, Captain Dufours," he cried. "You will now remember George Mourdant. I have the means of flying to a foreign land, and when people ask you what is the meaning of that letter on your forehead, you can tell them Rogue or Rascal, as best suits your humour."

CHAPTER LXXXII.

[" Hope smiled and shook her golden hair."—COLLINS.

A TRIP TO BRACEFIELD.—ADELINE'S HOPES.—THE CURATE AND HIS ANTICI-
PATIONS.—TWO LETTERS.

WE will leave Captain Dufours to recover from his shame and indignation, and Herbert Mandeville to sleep off the fumes of his Champaigne, while we again beg the reader's company to Bracefield and its inhabitants.

The tenderest father watching over the health and happiness of his dearest child, could not have shewn more solicitude and anxious care than did the good curate of Endsleigh, as he dwelt upon the evidently decreasing health and strength of the gentle Adeline. The old man looked upon her as a trust reposed in him by the bounty of Heaven, and the duty as he conceived it, of watching over her welfare and happiness was rendered a pleasure, although an anxious one, by his high appreciation of the many amiable qualities of the orphan girl.

After the last departure of Charles Leslie, her spirits seemed partially to revive, and a deeper bloom visited her velvet cheeks. That hope

" Which springs eternal in the human breast,"

had again made known its flattering presence in her heart. Herbert would come to her again she thought. He would explain to Leslie the causes of his seeming coldness, and all would be once more happiness and love.

With these blissful imaginations crowding round her mind, Adeline again smiled, although the curate thought the smile not so radiant as it used to be.

Again she tended her flowers, and music opened for her once more its varied charms and treasures. All the songs that Herbert had admired, she sang to herself again and again, and strove to recollect the various circumstances under which she had last sang them to him, when at the end of each verse, he had in all the rapturous poetry of love, poured forth to her wonder-stricken but delighted ear the fervour of his passion.

Ah, how sweetly passed the hours in such dear recollections, and how grateful to heaven was the old curate when he saw his child, as he called her, smile again when she met him.

But Mr. Endsleigh's satisfaction would not stand the test of solitary thought. When in the silence of his own chamber he reasoned calmly on all that had happened with regard to Adeline and Mandeville, he became more and more convinced that the character of the young man was not such as could ensure the happiness of the gentle girl, whose heart was a mine of such rich affections that it must meet with a return in kind, or sink deeper into gloom for ever.

Still he could not find in his heart to breathe the doubts and fears he felt in the ears of Adeline. He saw in the future unhappiness and grief, but he was not one of those who would dim the present by the shadow of what was to come unless he saw that by such warning he could accomplish more happiness in the end to those he loved, and when the old man wept, for weep he did, when oppressed by painful anticipations of the future, it was in secret, and he would rise, saying " God's will be done," to meet Adeline with a smile as she returned from a ramble among the old tombs in the churchyard, or from plucking wild flowers, which else had bloomed unseen, in the hedge rows and green lanes which in their shady solitude had such a charm for her.

She was beginning to recollect her mother with a more chastened sorrow. The violence of grief for the dead was calming down into a serener feeling of resignation to the inevitable lot of all humanity, and had but he, to whom she had given all the love which father, mother, and lover could possibly possess, from one lone heart, been one who could have properly prized the rare treasure he had found in the wilderness of the selfish world, how happy might they both have been. But alas! too truly may it be said that we live in the shadow of a valley of tears. The kindred spirit that would have loved and cherished Adeline, as she wished to be loved and cherished, had not the charm to fix the devotion of heart, and he who had the wizard power used that heart but as a toy to be the pastime of a moment and then neglected, leaving upon his own mind a feeling of disagreeable consciousness, only because while he resigned that love he had striven so hard to gain, he could not likewise forget it.

And now that a day had passed away, and Adeline felt sure that Leslie had had time to see Herbert, she became restless and uneasy. She would start at every distant sound of a horse's feet, and the colour would mantle her cheek as she told herself,—

"Now he comes!"

Toward the close of the day, although Charles Leslie came not himself, he wrote two letters, one to the curate, and one to Adeline, and sent them by a messenger on horseback, for well he knew that sickening of the heart which arises from "hope deferred," and he would fain spare Adeline the slightest pang.

Adeline's feelings would not permit her to speak as she heard the horseman stop at the parsonage gate. She looked only imploringly at the curate, and he well understood that speaking glance, for, laying his hand gently upon her's, he said,—

"I will bring you word who it is, my child. Sit ye still and wait for my return."

Adeline had not voice to thank him, and he rose and left the room.

"If," thought Adeline, "it should even be Herbert himself."

"It is a messenger from Charles," said the curate, returning quickly. "He brings a note for you, Adeline, and one for me likewise."

Adeline's hand trembled as she extended it to take the small note.

"I—I will read it in my chamber," she said, as she rose to quit the room.

"Do so," said the curate, "and come to me, Adeline, when you have done so, and we will consult, my child, if you do not think the old man's advice is troublesome."

Adeline answered him by an appealing look and a forced smile as she left the room.

The curate then opened his letter, which ran as follows :—

"MY DEAR FRIEND,—I have seen Herbert Mandeville, and during our short and unpleasant interview, I succeeded in awakening in his mind some sense of shame; but oh, my friend, if *that* is all upon which Adeline has to depend, how sad and frail is the foundation upon which she wields her happiness. Besides, does it not speak volumes on the subject, when we consider that the once ardent, anxious lover, who lived but in the light of the eyes he adored, should require awakening from a dream of indifference to a consciousness not that he loves still—not that he worships with his heart, but that his *honour* is disagreeably compromised in an affair which he blushes to think of, and of which he sickens like a child who is tired in an hour of the toy he thought it such joy to possess.

"You know, my dear friend, that I think and speak dispassionately upon this subject. Disappointed love does not warp my reason. True, I loved Adeline, and my dream of airy joy was to make her my happy wife—*that* dream is dispelled. I am jealous of my love. No divided heart would do for me. I have but one wish—one object in this, I fear unhappy business, and

that is to secure to Adeline serenity, if not happiness; and now for my deliberate opinion. The worst evil that could happen to Adeline would be Herbert Mandeville, in a fit of repentant passion, coming post to Bracefield and marrying her!   " Believe me, my best friend,
" Yours in truth,
" CHARLES LESLIE."

The curate gave a deep sigh as he finished this letter, and continued in thought for several moments.

" I feel," he said faintly, " the truth of this. If Adeline is to be awakened from her dream of love, let it, for God's sake, be now that she is surrounded by those that love her, and will soothe her wounded spirit. A neglected wife she must not be."

CHAPTER LXXXIII.

" She saw it in the moonlight,
When the sun had gone to rest."—ANON.

ADELINE'S LETTER.—YOUNG LOVE'S PHILOSOPHY.—A SUNSET, A WALK, AND AN ADVENTURE.

ALTHOUGH Charles Leslie had written thus freely to the curate, he could not bring his pen to shape such words to Adeline. The struggle in his mind was between sympathy and duty. His sense of rectitude told him that Adeline ought to know fully her situation with respect to Herbert Mandeville, yet he shrunk from the self-imposed task of inflicting the pang which he knew, sooner or later, must reach the pure heart of the gentle girl.

" By sickening and slow degrees she will find it out," he thought, " and is it not far better to inflict at once a wound than, fibre by fibre, inflict tenfold misery in its completion?" His reason told him yes; but still he could not write the words that he spoke to his own heart, and which would have been—" Adeline, forget Herbert Mandeville, he has forgotten you."

" The good curate," he thought, " may find some fitting opportunity to tell her this, but I cannot."

With these feelings, therefore, did Charles Leslie write the full and clear letter we have perused to Mr. Endsleigh, and with these feelings he likewise wrote the following cautious note to Adeline,—

" DEAR MISS MOURDANT,—I have seen Mr. Mandeville, and am to see him again on the morrow. I will then return to Bracefield, and, Adeline, if an old friend might give you a piece of worldly wisdom he has picked up in his travels, it would be to look for your greatest and purest happiness in the integrity and truth of your own heart.
" Believe me, dear Miss Mourdant,
" Your friend,
" CHARLES LESLIE."

Adeline read and re-read this epistle several times, then a death-like paleness came over her face, and she gasped,—

" It is true, then—inclination, and not necessity keeps Herbert Mandeville from Bracefield; and yet I will not judge too hastily. ' Look for your greatest and purest happiness in the truth and integrity of your own heart.' 'Tis good advice. I—I will do so, and—and I will not judge Herbert yet. This note is ambiguous; it seems to wish to convey, and yet conceal some dreadful truth, like—like poison skilfully given in a cup of nectar. I will speak to Mr. Endsleigh; he will resolve my doubts. Yet why should I doubt? No, it is beneath me—beneath Herbert. I will still dream that I am beloved. Oh, may I never awaken."

She looked from her casement as she spoke, and her mind became tranquillized as she gazed on the glories of the setting sun.

The glowing west was "crowded with bright colours," a crimson tint of beauty was cast over all things, and the meanest shrubs looked like the golden vegetation of another and more glorious world than this.

Adeline put on the rustic hat she usually wore, and placing Leslie's note in her bosom, she walked quietly down the staircase, and left the parsonage by the garden gate without meeting any of the family, intending to take a lonesome stroll among the old elms of the churchyard until the red disc of the sun had fairly dipped below—

"The extremest verge of the bright western sky."

The evening was full of beauty, the air was musical with the songs of many birds, who were seeking their various homes until the light of morning should call them again to life and joy. A quiet, soft air was creeping over the face of nature, just gently ruffling the flowers and forcing from them with loving violence their sweetest perfumes. The rustling of the leaves on the old trees made a pleasant murmuring sound, and when Adeline reached the wicket-gate of the churchyard, she leant upon it for a moment and forgot all her cares and sorrows, hopes and fears in a dreamy, delicious contemplation of the beautiful landscape that lay stretched before her in all the diversity of hill and dale, lit too, as it was, by such a radiant light, that heightened the greatest charms to something more than earthly, and gave to the lesser beauties a glow of loveliness that made them—

"Full of gloriou wonders."

And now the brightness began slowly to fade away, and with a deep sigh Adeline whispered to her heart,—

"Thus fade the glories of the imagination, thus fade all that we would render immortal. The chill uncertainty of night does not, with more exactness, succeed such glorious tints as those that now streak the western sky, than the gloomy midnight of the mind follows the airy phantoms of young love and hope."

A tear trickled down her cheek, and she started as she felt it fall like the first presage of a thunder shower on her hand.

"I must not," she said, hurriedly, "give way to these wayward fancies. I would yet fain catch one more glimpse of the bright orb of beauty sinking from the world."

She remembered, that quite through the churchyard, there was a hillock which commanded a more extensive view than she could obtain from the spot on which she was then standing, and opening the little wicket-gate, she walked quickly past the quiet lambs, and soon reached the small eminence which permitted her a wider range of vision.

Now she saw the rim of the sun again, but it was only for a moment, and then it dipped from her sight, leaving long streaks of purple and crimson light to mark the spot where it once had been.

Adeline became intensely absorbed in watching the gradual fading of the bright colours that the setting luminary left in its wake. Fainter and fainter they grew, until nothing of them was left but a pale yellow radiance tinting far and wide the whole western horizon. Then one by one the stars peeped forth, and as is ever the case with nature, when one object of beauty fades away another succeeds it.

So wrapt in contemplation was Adeline of the scene before her, that it was

not until she felt a perceptible coldness pervade her frame from the night wind that was beginning to sigh among the trees, and moan round the spire of the old church, that she started and recollected that the shadows of evening were rapidly gathering around her, and she was yet far from home, at least far for her to be after sun-set and quite alone.

Adeline might have chosen a winding green lane as her road back, but however beautiful it was when making its own shadow by its luxuriant vegetation from the mid-day sun, it was at night particularly black and gloomy; moreover, through the old churchyard was the shortest route, and notwithstanding a saddened feeling possessed the mind of the gentle girl when she passed through, because her mother slept beneath its holy sod, she descended rapidly from the hillock on which she had been standing, and determined to take her road homewards through the silent and humble tombs.

The moon was faintly gleaming in the south-east, and when Adeline turned from her contemplation of the western sky, she saw that the gentle light of the luminary of the night had lighted up the churchyard, and her way lay clear before her.

With a hurried step she passed onwards. Her mother's grave lay at some distance from the pathway, and for a moment Adeline paused and thought she would visit it by that chastened light, but then she knew the curate would be anxious if she remained longer from the parsonage, and she hurried onwards.

What was her horror and astonishment as she approached the wicket-gate, to behold standing by it, in the pale moonbeams, a figure similar to what she had once seen before and thought but the creation of a disordered fancy.

Her heart beat wildly in her bosom, and she paused with her eyes fixed upon what she at that moment firmly believed to be an inhabitant of another world.

The figure slowly moved from the gate, and walked with a stately step past her. She could have touched the flowing white garment it wore, had she but

No. 37

stretched out her hand, but terror froze her faculties, and she neither spoke nor moved.

"Adeline! Adeline!" said the figure, in mournful accents as it passed her.

A cloud came over the moon and all was dark. Adeline darted forward, and in five minutes was in her own chamber at the parsonage, in a confusion of thought which defies description.

CHAPTER LXXXIV.

" His words were full of passion ;
Wild and wayward as his nature."—BYRON.

LONDON AGAIN.—HERBERT AND HIS DEAR FRIEND.—A CONSULTATION.—A NOTE.

WE left Herbert Mandeville, and his dear friend, the gallant Captain Dufours, in no very agreeable situation. The captain was muttering all sorts of imaginable and unimaginable oaths, and Mandeville was sleeping on the Turkey carpet which adorned his room.

Dufours tried in vain to twist himself clear of the cords that bound him. He stamped with rage and pain, for the smarting of his wound was intolerable. He wished to awaken Mandeville if possible, for he dreaded any of the servants seeing him in his present predicament, for well he knew that his disgrace would be the town's talk, if once it got to the ears of servants, whose tongues he had not the power to silence, while Herbert he thought, for his own sake, would keep his secret.

"Mandeville," he cried; "curses! can you not hear me? Herbert! Herbert!"

No reply followed such speeches, and the gallant captain was afraid to raise his voice very high for fear of alarming the house, and bringing in a troop of servants, which was just what he most dreaded.

Despairing, therefore, after a time of arousing Herbert, whose faculties were too deeply steeped in his own champaigne, the captain made a desperate effort to free himself from his bondage, which, although unsuccessful in the manner he meant, most certainly had the effect of expediting his release, for in his struggle he upset the chair to which he was tied, and he and it came to the ground together, with so much noise, that Mandeville not only immediately started awake, but several servants came into the room in great haste, thinking their master and his guest were varying their amusements by a personal encounter.

A few minutes served to release Dufours, who was nearly choking with rage, pain, and shame.

Mandeville rubbed his eyes and looked on the scene in utter amazement.

"Tell them to leave the room, for God's sake, Herbert," cried Dufours, keeping his hand on his forehead.

"What is the matter?" said Mandeville, looking all astonishment around him.

"I will tell you," said Dufours; "but let them go."

"Go all of you," said Herbert. "I feel quite giddy and confused. Bring me some soda water some of you. By Heaven, Dufours, I begin to think I took a glass too much of the champaigne."

"I know you did," growled Dufours, as the servants closed the door after them.

"What's the matter with your head?" said Herbert.

"It—it aches."

" Have you been bleeding yourself for it ?"

" Bleeding myself?"

" Yes, your face is all over blood and some black stuff, that looks as if you had been up the chimney."

" Mandeville," cried Dufours, striking the table with his first violently ; " I am nearly mad."

" Mad ?"

" Yes ; but I will have revenge. Revenge I say—a deep and bitter revenge."

" Against whom ?"

" George Mourdant."

" Has he been here then ?"

" He has, and by an accident overpowered me, and would have taken my life."

" Can this be possible, Dufours, and I not know it ?"

" You were sleeping off the fumes of your champaigne on the carpet. Revenge ! revenge !"

" What has he done to you?"

" Look !"

Dufours took away his hand from his forehead, and exhibited the letter R stamped thereon, and what with the blood and gunpowder, and the working of his own face from intense passion, he looked altogether so singular and inhuman, that for a few seconds Herbert could do nothing but stare at him without speaking. At length an irresistible desire to laugh came over him, and just as the servant brought in some soda water, and the captain popped his hand across his forehead again, he burst into a roar of laughter.

" Yes, you may laugh," writhed Dufours ; " but comic as you think it, it's only the beginning of a tragedy."

" Why, in Heaven's name, Dufours, what possessed you to let the fellow mark you in that way ?"

" He was armed and I was not."

" But I would have lost my life ten times over before I would have submitted to such an awful degradation."

" Would you ?"

" By my faith would I."

" I wait for revenge."

" Revenge or not, Dufours, you are out of society. Why, man, you can never show yourself with that upon your forehead."

" I—I can cover it," said Dufours.

" Which will be nearly as bad. How on earth did he contrive to do it ?"

" Don't question me, Mandeville, or you will drive me mad," cried Dufours. " Suffice it, it is done, and I have but to wait for vengeance, ample and complete."

" Dufours," said Mandeville ; " I know you to be an unscrupulous man, but I begin to suspect that you are not a courageous one."

" What could I do ? A man with a pistol in his hand, and the barrel of it in my mouth."

" That was going to extremes," remarked Herbert.

" Yes, and I will go to extremes with him," cried Dufours. " Let me wash off these stains from my face."

" Now, Dufours," said Mandeville ; " let us clearly understand each other. After this I don't want to see you any more here. I cannot look at you again."

" You—you cannot ?" stammered Dufours. " By——"

" Nay," said Mandeville, " 'tis of no use your vapouring here—you are a coward !"

" A coward ? I a coward ?"

" Yes," said Herbert, calmly.

"Pay me what I won of you."

"While I was not in my senses?"

"Senses be hanged; you played and lost."

"How much?"

"Eight hundred pounds."

"And can you suppose I am so besotted an idiot as to allow you to come here as my guest—ply me with my own wine, and then rob me wholesale in this way?"

"The debt is one of honour."

"One of dishonour you mean. Dufours, I have done with you."

"But the money?"

"What you won of me in cash you can keep; I find my purse empty, and I know that before I sat down to-day to play with you it was tolerably well lined, Master Dufours. You have made no bad day's work."

"Bad day's work? By Heaven and earth I have not a sixpence."

"Absurd!"

"'Tis true I say; I have been deprived of all."

"Then what have you done with it?"

"The villain George Mourdant——"

"He took it?"

"Yes."

"Well, Master Dufours, if you let yourself be robbed as well as stamped, I cannot help it."

"Now, Mandeville; come, come, no nonsense. Don't make a jest of a fellow because he has met with a mishap. Come, come."

"I assure you," said Herbert, "I am perfectly serious."

"Why, you don't mean to say that you—you——"

"Go on—that I what?"

"That you wont pay me?"

"You acknowledge to stripping me of all the money I had, and then you tell me you was robbed of it. Surely that is no concern of mine?"

"But for old acquaintance sake."

"Our acquaintance is over."

"Then hear me," said Dufours, rising from the table with a glance of hatred and defiance. "Hear me I say, Herbert Mandeville; treat me as you threaten and I will denounce you as harbouring a murderer. I will send the police to your splendid mansion, and not all your wealth shall save you from a criminal prosecution."

"Have you done?" said Herbert, coldly.

"No I have not," continued Dufours. "I will likewise avow *who* this George Mourdant is. The brother of the dear, sweet creature who holds the heart of young Master Mandeville in such delicate and tender bondage. Do not provoke, or you see I *can* be dangerous."

"Can you indeed," said Herbert, rising and proceeding to a closet adjoining the room from whence he immediately returned with a formidable horse-whip.

Captain Dufours no sooner saw how Mandeville was armed, than, without another word, he made a dart to the door with terror depicted on his countenance.

"You infernal scoundrel!" said Herbert, just reaching him in time to give him three or four hearty lashes as he fumbled with the lock of the door; then with a bawl of rage, and pain, he rushed from the house, and so Herbert Mandeville and his dear friend and counsellor, the gallant Captain Dufours, parted.

CHAPTER LXXXV.

————" These letters, sir, are full of strife.
They will breed broils—dissensions—murders."
SHAKSPERE.

HERBERT ALONE.—WHO IS RIGHT.—A RESOLVE.—THE APPOINTMENT AND THE
LETTER.

WHEN Herbert found himself alone, he sat down in no very enviable frame
of mind to review his present situation as regarded several persons, the most
troublesome of whom, to his mind, was undoubtedly Charles Leslie, whose
promised visit on the morrow rose up before the thoughts of Herbert, with
all the aggravation of conscious wrong.

"Yet," he cried, "why should I fear this man?—Why allow him to become a bugbear to my imagination? Has he any power over me, save what I
have been so foolishly pleased to invest him with? His interference in my
affairs, appears to me, upon reflection, to be the most unwarrantable piece of
insolence that ever I was subjected to. I cannot—I will not suffer it. My
door shall be to-morrow slammed in his face!"

In vain by lashing himself into a rage, Herbert tried to stifle the still small
voice of conscience which told him that Charles Leslie was right, and that he,
Herbert Mandeville, it was whose conduct was unwarrantable, and it was
great relief to him when he recollected his appointment with the charming and
delightful Mrs. Delancey.

"I will go," he cried; "of course I will. There, at least, I am appreciated
properly. What's the time?" He hastily consulted his watch, and seeing
that the hour of meeting was fast approaching, he retired to his dressing-room,
and completing a hasty toilette, hurried from his house towards Park Lane,
full of enamoured thoughts of the woman, who by skilfully flattering his
vanity, had established for himself an empire over his fickle and most ca-
pricious heart.

The evening was cool, and Herbert walked quickly through the squares,
which lie northward of Oxford Street, towards the place of meeting. To say
that he was entirely free from any misgivings with regard to Captain Dufours,
and what he might do, would be to give Herbert a degree of stoical firmness of
mind, to which he was not entitled, and now, as with rapid steps he hastened
to keep an appointment which ought to have cast dishonour upon him, he fell
into a train of thought with regard to how very unpleasant it would be to have
his name coupled with Adeline's brother's as intending, or wishing to form a
family connexion in such a quarter.

Again by a system of false reasoning, he seemed to think that because
Adeline had the misfortune to be sister to a bad man, she was somehow herself culpable.

"If," he said to himself, "the sacrifice was ever so great to my feelings, I
fear I should be obliged to surrender any claim upon Adeline's hand, on account of her brother's character, and I am sure she is not half so sensible as I
thought her, if she does not see the matter in that light."

So poor Adeline, with a heart pure as unsullied snow, was to be punished
because the accident of birth had given her a wicked relation! Alas! alas!
the mind that could compass such reasoning, was no longer worthy of
meeting with the fair orphan of Bracefield.

The clocks in the vicinity were chiming the appointed hour as Herbert
reached the corner of Park Lane. He cast an anxious glance round him, but

could not see his fair acquaintance, and he walked with a slow step and sauntering air towards Grosvenor Gate.

We are aware that Herbert was not blessed with a great deal of patience, and after wandering to and fro for about a quarter of an hour, and seeing nothing of Mrs. Delancey, he began to get into an exceedingly fretful state of mind, and to contemplate giving up an intrigue which cost him the enormous sacrifice of waiting in Park Lane twenty minutes beyond an appointed hour, when a young-looking female stepped up to him, and said :—

"Sir,—I beg your pardon, but is your name Mandeville?"

"Yes," said Herbert.

"Oh, then, I am right—that is if you are the same gentleman who was to have met Mrs. Delancey?"

"I am," replied Herbert. "Do you come from her?"

"Yes, sir. Here is a note. My mistress is very unwell. Ah, poor lady!"

"Nothing has happened?" said Herbert, anxiously.

"Oh, nothing uncommon, sir; but all I say is, that master is to be sure one of the greatest brutes as ever was. Oh, I could tear his eyes out."

"He certainly does not appear the most amiable of gentlemen," said Herbert. "If you will wait a moment, I will read the note by the light of this lamp. It may require some answer."

"Thank you, sir," said the confidante, with a demure look, and Mandeville stepping towards a lamp, that cast a full glare upon the epistle of love, read hastily as follows :—

"I need subscribe no name, dear Herbert, to this imperfect scrawl. I write to say that I cannot meet you to-night. I am a prisoner in my own house. Some sigh—or smile—or tear—has awakened all the jealousy in *his* nature. You know *who* I mean; and I am under lock and key. She who brings you this is a faithful friend to her poor mistress. Trust her, dear Herbert, with a note in reply to this, to cheer me in my worse than solitude, and oh, is it asking too much for you to be at Park Street to-morrow evening, at the same hour, in case I should escape?"

"What a scoundrel that Delancey must be," thought Herbert. "Really his conduct is shocking!"

While Mandeville made this reflection, he never considered what *he* would do in the shocking Mr. Delancey's situation, or that he, Herbert, was endeavouring to blast for ever the domestic felicity of the scoundrel, always presuming that Mr. Delancey had any domestic felicity to blast, and that Mrs. Delancey was the dear, sweet, sensitive creature, she appeared to Herbert's simplicity, and we are compelled to add—vanity.

Herbert walked up to "the faithful creature," who had brought the note, and said :—

"My good girl, tell your mistress that my feelings when I received her note, were ——"

"Oh, sir," said the girl, wiping her eyes with the sleeve of her dress, "I am sure my poor mistress will die if she hasn't a dear sweet letter from you to hide in her bosom, and kiss and cry over."

"Poor thing!" said Herbert.

"And I'm sure I can't blame her, that I can't," resumed the 'faithful creature,' "for you are to be sure the very handsomest —— Oh, dear, what am I saying?"

"Never mind," said Herbert, greatly gratified. "You are a very good and— and clever girl, and I have no doubt quite a treasure to your mistress."

"No, sir; it's you is the treasure," said the girl.

"Well, well, don't say any more about that. Just follow me home, and I'll write a note to your poor mistress."

"Oh, thank you, sir," said the girl ; "I know it will be all the world to her."

"Keep me in sight then," said Herbert ; "and I will go direct home and write the note."

With a full conviction of the entire truth of all that the girl said, and more particularly that part of it which related to his, Herbert's, fascinations ; he walked towards his own house, never once reflecting upon the extreme danger of writing to Mrs. Delancey.

He arrived in due time at his own door, and making a sign to the confidential domestic, who had closely followed him, to wait, he knocked and entered his domicile.

Repairing then at once to his library, he sat down to what he considered the gratifying task of inditing a note for the charming and ill-used Mrs. Delancey to cry over and wear in her bosom.

The note ran as follows :—

"MY DEAR MRS. DELANCEY,—My grief at your detention from our appointment, was only to be equalled by my pleasure at receiving, under your own hand, a confirmation of my dearest hopes. Will I be at the appointed spot to-morrow, you ask ? Most charming of women, can you doubt ? How cold and miserable must be the man who does not appreciate your charms ? Such am not I, and if I have one hope dearer to my heart than another in this world, it is, that some day you may be emancipated from care and indifference, to taste all the joy of love and the most ardent attachment.

"Believe me to be ever,

"My dearest charmer, your own,

"HERBERT MANDEVILLE."

"I think," said Herbert to himself, with a self-congratulatory smile, "that I have hit off a very tolerable love-letter. You are, without doubt, a beautiful and discerning woman, Mrs. Delancey, and deserve all my attention. In fact, I should be a brute to treat such extraordinary affection with indifference."

So saying, Herbert impressed the letter with a seal, on which were two doves looking as amiable as possible, with the motto, "constant ever," and ringing for a servant, he told him to call the young woman he would see waiting near the door, into the hall.

Mandeville then descended, and himself gave the precious note into the hands of the female Mercury along with a sovereign, and saw her depart, fancying himself a man of the world! a gallant! a fine fellow! and all that sort of thing.

CHAPTER LXXXVI.

" And all were gone,
She was alone—with none to love her,
No kindred heart in the wide world!"

ADELINE'S REPOSE.—THE VISIONS OF THE YOUNG.—MORNING IS COMING.—
THE FIRST BLOW IS STRUCK.

ADELINE'S nerves had received a greater shock by the singular appearance in the churchyard, than was at first apparent. After she had been at home for some time a cold shivering seized her, and she was conveyed to her bed with all the symptoms of a serious illness.

In the deep silence of the night that followed, Adeline communed sadly with her own heart, and the suspicion which had been hovering over it so long—that she had bestowed her young affections where they were not suitably prized, crept over her weakened spirit, and she wept long and bitterly. Then the idea came across her mind that what she had seen in the churchyard was a visible warning of her own approaching death, and although she shuddered at the thought of

> "———— That bourne
> From whence no traveller returns,"

she did not view death as armed with so many terrors, as he would have brought in his train, had Herbert Mandeville been all that her radiant fancy dreamt he was when first she whispered to her throbbing heart,—" I love him !"

He had been tried and found wanting, and Adeline was content to die. Her's was one of those pure spirits that wish not to outlive the dearest affections. Her father was gone ; her mother, too, slept in the quiet churchyard ; and last of all, Herbert Mandeville, he, who she had set up as an idol in her heart of hearts—he who was to be to her father, mother, husband—he, too, was as dead, for the pure and holy love that made him what he was no longer, like a halo from Heaven, encircled him.

The tears of the gentle girl fell fast upon her pillow, and at length tired nature relapsed into a troubled slumber, and she closed her eyes, saying faintly,—

" Take me, oh, Heaven—I am content to die !"

How strangely do circumstances coincide to produce certain results. At the moment that the gentle Adeline was shedding tears of bitter feeling, Herbert Mandeville was congratulating himself upon his progress in life in an intrigue which could end in nothing but misery to all and probably destruction to some.

The sleep of Adeline was haunted by many visions, and, among the rest, one strange shadowy scene was twice presented to her mental vision.

She saw the churchyard of Braccfield, and a small white stone, on which was inscribed her own name, and Charles Leslie was standing by it, weeping.

Then, towards morning, the visions of the night passed away, and a deep calm sleep came over the mind of the gentle girl, and for a time Adeline was happy.

The gentle sunlight gilded the windows of the parsonage ; the shades of evening passed away, and another day shone upon Braccfield.

Mrs. Martha Plumpjoy was early in the chamber of Adeline, and she was shocked at the change which the night of restless suffering had produced upon the countenance of the beautiful girl.

" My dear Adeline," she said, with much real feeling in her tone, " you look unwell. What is the matter, my dear?"

Adeline smiled faintly as she said,—

" I am only weak, Mrs. Plumpjoy. I will rise, however, and then I shall be better."

" Do so, my dear," said the good lady, who, notwithstanding all her eccentricities, had a really kind heart. " You will be better after your breakfast."

Adeline, although scarcely equal to the exertion, did rise, and she strove to smile and look cheerful as she entered the breakfast-room, where were seated the curate and his sister.

" Adeline," said Mr. Endsleigh, kindly, " we must not have you look so pale. Folks will say we starve you."

" No, sir," replied Adeline, " folks know you too well."

In vain she tried to rally her sinking spirits during the meal, which had once been the most cheerful one of the whole day. There was a deep depression at her heart which she could not remove, and she was grateful when

the breakfast equipage was removed, and there was no longer a necessity to seem to eat. How strange and sudden are our resolves sometimes; in the few moments that were occupied in removing the breakfast, Adeline determined to tell the curate of the strange vision that had crossed her in the churchyard, although till then she had shrunk from such a resolve, because, palpable as it appeared to her, she still thought it might possibly be but the creation of her own excited imagination. No sooner had she determined to tell Mr. Endsleigh, than she felt something like a sensation of relief, and she said :—

"May I intrude upon your time, sir, for a few minutes?"

"You know you may," replied the curate, assuming a tone of gaiety very foreign to his feelings. "Come to my room, and we will have a talk."

Adeline followed him, and when there she related to him how her path had been suddenly crossed by the unearthly-looking visiter of the churchyard, and in conclusion, she said :—

"I will not—I cannot deny but this appearance has given me a shock, and preyed upon my spirits. Tell me, Mr. Endsleigh, what is your opinion of it?"

"My opinion," said the curate, "is this, Adeline :—such things are not impossible, but they are very, very improbable, and if it be really true that supernatural appearances have presented themselves to the eyes of mortals, I have no doubt that such instances are as one to a million of cases in which the imagination has created its own spectre."

"Then you think, sir, this appearance [was merely a creation of my own fancy?"

"I certainly do, and would advise you to dismiss the recollection of it from your mind."

"But if I cannot?"

"If you cannot, then reason yourself into a belief of its harmlessness, for

No. 38

never believe, Adeline, for one fleeting moment, that the great God ever made one class of creatures merely for the torment and apprehension of another. Such a belief would be incompatible with every other notion we can have of a just and beneficent Deity, as you must feel, if you think at all."

"I know you are right, sir," said Adeline; "and now tell me, is—is Mr. Leslie coming here to-day?"

"I expect him, Adeline."

"Then before he comes, I wish a letter to be posted to London."

"It shall be done, Adeline, as you desire."

"It is," she added, "to Mandeville."

The curate was silent for a few moments, then he said, gravely :—

"Adeline, I would not write to him."

"I must, I must; I feel, sir, that I ought to do so."

"His own heart should dictate to him, Adeline, what course he ought to pursue; not an appeal from you."

"An appeal, sir?—No, I send no appeal."

"What then, Adeline?"

"A release from every promise—every vow."

Adeline had no sooner uttered these words than a death-like paleness came across her face, and she fainted at the curate's feet.

Inexpressibly shocked at the extreme weakness which these fainting fits— to which Adeline was becoming subject,—betrayed, Mr. Endsleigh rung for assistance, and the pale and insensible girl was conveyed to her own room, amid the tears and heartfelt lamentations of the little household, for all loved Adeline Mourdant. Her gentle temper and unvarying kindness had attracted every heart, and none were insensible to her many excellencies but he who ought to have known them best of all, and admired them the most of all.

It was nearly half an hour before Adeline recovered to consciousness, and then it was to awaken to greater weakness than before.

The curate had been much alarmed at her protracted insensibility, and had sent to the only medical man which the village possessed, but he was from home, for he was a man of great humanity, and his presence was never refused far or near, even in the habitations of the humblest and the poorest, where remuneration was not expected at ever so distant a date.

Adeline, therefore, had recovered when Mr. Arundel arrived at the Parsonage, and he was shewn into the parlour where sat the curate. His first question to Mr. Endsleigh was :—

"Am I called to Adeline Mourdant?"

"Yes," said the curate. "Why do you ask that?"

"My good friend," said Mr. Arundel, feelingly, "I have noticed that young fragile creature in her lonely walks, and spoken to her once or twice. Any serious shock would, I am convinced, be fatal to her."

"Fatal!" gasped Mr. Endsleigh, for an idea of Adeline really dying had never taken firm possession of his mind.

"Yes," said Mr. Arundel, "I speak advisedly. With care and a serene and happy mind, she would, without doubt, overcome her constitutional delicacy; but otherwise, such is the slight hold which life has in airy beautiful structures like hers, that they never can contend against mental suffering successfully. They feel too keenly."

"Come with me, and see her," said the curate, with much emotion; "then, Mr. Arundel, I shall beg of you, without reserve, to give me your genuine opinion."

"You are greatly interested, my good sir, in this young lady's happiness."

"I am. Were she a dear child of my own I could not love her more than I do. Come, sir, come."

The curate took the arm of Mr. Arundel, and with a tottering step—for the surgeon's opinion of Adeline seemed to have added twenty years to Mr. Endsleigh's age,—they together sought the chamber of sickness.

CHAPTER LXXXVII.

" And wilt thou leave us, beauteous girl?
Thou the beloved—the beautiful and good.''
ANON.

A PROFESSIONAL VISIT.—THE LETTER.—A CANDID OPINION.—THE CURATE'S DISTRESS.

WHEN Mr. Endsleigh and the medical man entered the chamber in which was Adeline, she was seated by a small table writing, and by the heightened colour that glowed upon her cheeks, no one would have for a moment imagined that her health was in the precarious state which it really was.

She looked up at their entrance, and smiled faintly as she recognized Mr. Arundel, whom she knew.

"Adeline," said the curate, " I have brought Mr. Arundel to see you, and to assure me if he can, that you are not really ill."

The medical man stretched out his hand and took Adeline's in a friendly grasp, as he said :—

"Miss Mourdant, I don't want you for a patient. How do you feel now?"

"Better—much better," replied Adeline.

Mr. Arundel led the conversation to general topics, and after about a quarter of an hour's conversation, he rose, and with the curate left the room.

When they reached Mr. Endsleigh's study, whither he conducted Mr. Arundel, the feelings of the kind-hearted old man were so much interested in what might be the opinion of the medical man, that he could only motion him to a seat, and wait for him to begin the conversation.

"Your young friend," said Mr. Arundel, " is exceedingly delicate, but I can see nothing from which to anticipate immediate danger."

The curate hung on every word he uttered, and after a slight pause, Mr. Arundel continued :—

"I cannot, however, conceal from you my conviction, for it amounts to this—that this young creature, beautiful and interesting as she is, will droop into an early grave."

The curate clasped his hands and sighed deeply.

"If," continued Mr. Arundel, " her mind could be amused, and her feelings kept quite free from excitement, there might be hopes of her remaining yet a long time among us ; but excitement, grief, or any intense feeling will destroy her."

"Alas! alas!" cried Mr. Endsleigh. " My poor Adeline, how am I to bring serenity and peace to thee?"

"She should certainly not be left to the solitude of a sick chamber," said Mr. Arundel. " You may believe me when I tell you, that in her case cheerful society and pleasurable bustle will do her more good than any medicine which I or any other medical man could possibly prescribe for her."

"Sir, I sincerely thank you," said the curate. " You have been candid, as I asked you to be, and with that candour you have been kind likewise. You do not know, and I—I cannot tell you, sir, how much my affections are wrapped up in that young creature. I know her worth, sir, and she has twined herself round the old man's heart so closely that—that should I lose her, I lose all on this side of Heaven. Oh, Mr. Arundel, can nothing positively be done to snatch so fair a flower from an early blight?"

"My dear friend," replied Arundel, "I might, as medical men usually do in these cases, amuse you with a thousand false hopes. I could tell you that Italian air would revive her, that the fertile and beautiful climate of Madeira would bring again the bloom to her cheeks, but such advice, however kind it may be as nourishing the sweet delusion of hope in some cases, it is not my duty to give you. Such remedies are all so many delusions, and they are expensive ones too. All that can be done for this poor girl can be done here. She shall have my unremitting attention; but as you are a minister of God, let me beg of you to prepare yourself for the worst."

Mr. Arundel rose and grasped his friend's hand in a cordial shake, and then without another word, for he was one who respected the sanctity of feeling, he left the Parsonage.

The curate sat for many minutes in the deep solitude of his own thoughts, then suddenly his aged head bowed upon his breast and he wept aloud. For several minutes the long pent up agony of grief found at length a vent in tears. Deep sobs shook the old man's breast, and then when the sobs had subsided into sighs, and the overcharged heart was in some measure relieved, he rose, and with a calmer expression of countenance and a firmer voice, he said :—

"If it be Thy will to take her, oh, God—Thy will be done. I weep, but I do not murmur. Take her, all beauteous Heaven, and in thy good tent, let again the old man who loved her, see her in a better and a happier world than this."

He then knelt by the open window, through which the glorious sunlight streamed upon his venerable brow, and prayed long and earnestly. Then he arose, and with a firm step and a serene aspect, he descended the little staircase to the common-room where his sister was wont to sit.

Mrs. Plumpjoy was sitting very intently stiching some interminable borders, about which she had been for upwards of a year.

"Martha," said the curate, "Mr. Arundel thinks poor Adeline in a very precarious state."

Mrs. Plumpjoy laid down her work, and while a tear glistened in her eye, she said :—

"Brother—if poor Adeline Mourdant is—is really taken from us, then all I've got to say is, that that young Mandeville is no better than a murderer."

"Hush Martha, hush," said the curate ; "we must not talk so. All we have to do is, to the utmost of our abilities to be kind and attentive to her while—while she is with us."

"And that I will be, brother," said Mrs. Plumpjoy ; "for as poor dear Major Plumpjoy used to say, kindness costs nobody anything, and if it did, it's sure to be cheap at any price."

"The major was right there, at all events," said the curate. "I suspect, now, Martha, that Adeline is writing to that—that—no, I will call him nothing but his own name—to Mandeville. I wish you would go to her, and try to persuade her not to do so ; I know it is a task which can do her no good."

"To be sure I will, brother," cried Mrs. Plumpjoy ; "and you may depend, if ever I do see that fellow again—that Mandeville, with his smooth tongue, and his smiles, and all that nonsense, I'll tell him such a piece of my mind as will astonish him. What next, I wonder? Is a fellow to come here and make love to a beautiful creatuie, and then walk off in that way? Well, I never. I should like to have seen the poor dear departed major serve me so ; I'd have taken his two eyes out of their sockets, I would. Oh, the wretch ! Next comes a horse——"

The curate ran out of the room, and left his eccentric sister to "shave the horse," and "cut off the pigs corns" by herself.

The day was wearing on apace, and it was with the first feeling anything akin to pleasure that he had felt for many weary hours, that the curate recollected that Charles Leslie would soon be at Bracefield.

Further appeal to Mandeville he determined not to make. He felt that his duty now was to assist Adeline in forgetting that she had ever loved, and he trusted greatly to the manly eloquence, and good sense of Charles Leslie to aid him in the task, provided he could induce him to take up his abode for a time with Adeline.

Alas! how little the old man guessed the sacrifices of feeling, which Leslie had already made, and was still making for the sake of Adeline! What a precious heart she had lost when she refused his! and now that he had renounced all hope, and his day dream of happiness was scattered to the winds, with what a persevering constancy he still strove for the happiness of her who he loved so purely; and who, but for the sudden wild and wayward passions which had possessed her heart for the more accomplished, but oh, how much less sincere Mandeville, might have been the happy wife of one she must have honoured and respected as well as fondly loved.

The sun was now nearly at its meridian, and Charles Leslie, the curate knew must arrive soon. He took his hat and walking stick, and left the Parsonage, determining to walk down the London-road and meet his dear young friend, by which arrangement he could gently, and in his own manner, be the first to explain to him the state of affairs at Bracefield, as well as receiving his account of his projected interview that morning with Herbert Mandeville, the result of which, however, had scarcely continued to arrest his attention, so greatly absorbed was he in what regarded the health of Adeline.

He had not proceeded far when the distant sound of a horse's foot met his ears, and he doubted not that it was Charles Leslie. In a few minutes more, by a turn of the road he could see him. He moved his hand, the signal was answered, and shortly Charles reined up his panting steed by the side of his old friend.

"Well, Charles," said the old man.

"My dear old friend," said Leslie, with emotion. "Adeline's first lesson in life has been to love."

"Go on, Charles, go on."

"Her second must be *to forget!*"

"It is as I expected," said the curate, clasping his hands; "tell me all at home, but first listen to me."

Leslie dismounted from his horse, and hanging the bridle over his arm, the two proceeded together in earnest discourse towards the Parsonage.

CHAPTER LXXXVIII.

"'Tis ever the privilege of him who is most in the wrong to be the most violent."
GOLDSMITH.

THE INTERVIEW IN LONDON.—HERBERT'S VIOLENCE.—AN AFFRAY.—ALL IS LOST.

HERBERT had scarcely the next morning risen from a luxurious breakfast, when the most unwelcome name of Charles Leslie was announced to him.

Herbert hesitated for a few moments whether to admit him or be denied to his call. He could not conceal from himself that a visit from Leslie was about the most annoying circumstance which could possibly affect him, and what was more he could not conceal from his own heart that such annoyance proceeded from a conviction whispered to him by the still small voice of conscience, that he, Charles Leslie, was right, while his opponent was so very wrong.

Herbert's pride, however, decided the question of the admission or non-admission of Charles Leslie to his presence.

"He will go to Bracefield," he thought, "and say I was afraid to see him. Shew Mr. Leslie up."

In a few moments Charles entered the luxurious breakfast parlour, in which Herbert, with a flushed and anxious countenance, was seated.

"Will you be seated?" said Herbert.

"I mean you no discourtesy, Mr. Mandeville," said Leslie, "by remaining standing. You know the subject upon which I come. Are you prepared with an answer?"

Herbert felt nearly overcome by the calm and steady tone and manner of Leslie, and after a violent struggle to command his feelings, he did what people very commonly do, when they are in the wrong ; namely, make up by noise and insolence what they want in argument.

"I am always ready," he replied, "to answer an impertinent question in a proper manner."

"Sir," said Leslie. "It is beneath me to wrangle with you about words. I was present, as you know, in that peaceful house into which you introduced confusion and unhappiness, when you called upon Heaven to witness the sincerity of your attachment to Adeline Mourdant. Will you now ask your own heart if you have acted up to the spirit of your most solemn vow?"

"Have you finished?" sneered Herbert.

"I have, until your answer, as regards your intentions."

"Then, sir, I decline informing you of my intentions."

"You cannot," said Leslie. "Your acts speak for themselves. Young man, you are too stultified by your own vanity to know your position in this, to me, most painful business."

"This language to me? and in my own house!" cried Herbert passionately.

"Cease, cease," cried Leslie. "Whose house it is can make no difference in fact. Hear me out, and then take what course your nature may suggest. I tell you, you do not understand your situation."

"And may I then presume so far as to indulge a hope that Mr. Leslie will explain to me my precise situation?" said Herbert, in a mocking tone.

"You may presume so, for" answered Leslie, with great calmness, "it does not require that you should make any declaration of your intentions towards Adeline Mourdant."

"Indeed, sir."

"Aye, sir, indeed. Your conduct has sufficiently declared for you. You are only called upon for a defence. If you can excuse the palpable neglect with which you have treated the—the young heart that too readily submitted to be yours—now is your time. Your acts make you guilty. Explain those acts and prove them inevitable or accidental, and I will be the first to say, 'Adeline, he loves you still.' Your refusal of an explanation only confirms the suspicion of your desertion from her you have sworn to love. Do you understand your position, now, sir?"

"This insolence is not to be borne," cried Herbert. "If you are an emissary from Adeline, go back to her and tell her, her advocate has ruined her cause."

"How ruined it?" cried Leslie.

"I will not be dictated to. I know not that I shall ever visit that detestable Bracefield again. Adeline's weakness is unpardonable in talking, either to you, or that meddling dotard, Endsleigh, about her affairs."

Charles Leslie was silent for a moment or two, then he said,

"I will not leave under a misconstruction, although I am fully answered now, and, I thank God, you have taken the course you have. The only hope of happiness for Adeline in this world, was for you to have the candour to deceive her no longer. Free from you she has a chance of serenity and happiness. The only thing I dreaded was a renewal of your vows and protestations. Mr. Endsleigh and myself both dreaded that result ; we dreaded it because we have no faith in you. Nay, if you had carried a fit of repentance, so far as to have married Adeline, we both felt that that would have been the greatest misfortune that could have befallen her, because we have no faith in you. Our most sanguine hopes hardly reached so far as to think that you would show yourself in your true colours. I thank you. Adeline, thank God, is free."

Herbert listened to this speech in an agony of rage, and when Charles Leslie had finished, he sprung from his seat, exclaiming :

" The time has now come when we two must settle accounts. I have a long arrear of vengeance to wipe out, and blood alone can efface the memory of the insults I have received from you."

" Will you name one ?" said Leslie.

" Coward !" cried Mandeville.

" Brave blusterer ;" said Leslie, with a smile.

" You shall not—you cannot escape me," roared Mandeville. " Fight you shall."

" Certainly, if occasion offers," replied Leslie.

" Choose your weapons, and name your own time and place, to give me that satisfaction which a gentleman can have."

" Once before," said Charles, " I told you I would not fight a duel with you."

" You will not ?"

" Certainly not. Do you imagine, that because you have behaved badly and discreditably, I am going to allow you to endeavour to take my life ?"

" I will have revenge !" cried Herbert.

" Beware ! beware ! said Leslie. " I will not fight a duel with you, as you hear. You can tell the story when you like, but tell it truly, and add to it, that Charles Leslie holds you in contempt."

" Contempt ?"

" Aye, that was the word. Be discreet in your anger, and tempt not your own fate. Henceforth, sir, we are strangers. Never presume to address me again."

" By Heaven !" cried Herbert, you shall not carry it off thus bravely. I will pass you as a coward in every public place in London."

" Folks will not believe you," said Leslie.

As he spoke he walked to the door, but Herbert sprung to it, and placed his back against it.

" Herbert Mandeville," said Leslie, calmly, " are you mad ? You know nature has gifted me with more strength than she has you. Why should you tempt me, perhaps, in the heat of a moment to do you a serious injury ? Let me pass, young man. Let me pass, I say."

" I may not have strength," cried Herbert, " but I have that which gives a dwarf a giant's power."

" Indeed !"

" Yes— courage !"

" Temper it with discretion," said Leslie, " and 'tis a rare quality. Give way, sir ; give way."

" Never," cried Herbert, who was worked to a state of furious passion, incapable of controul.

Without another word Leslie flung his arms round Mandeville, and, despite his resistance, lifted him off his feet.

What might then have ensued, it is hard to say, had not the door suddenly opened, and disclosed the form of Mandeville's portly butler.

"Take care of your master," said Leslie, flinging Hubert completely into the arms of the butler with so much force, that, in order to preserve his own equilibrium, the man was forced to twine his arms round Mandeville.

With a hasty stride, Charles Leslie then passed from the room, and before Herbert and the stout butler could recover themselves, he had left the house.

CHAPTER LXXXIX.

" If you have ceased to love,
'Tis greatest love to tell me so.'"   OLD PLAY.

ADELINE'S LETTER TO MANDEVILLE.—A SHOCK.—THE HORSEMAN.—ALL IS LOST !

THE letter which Adeline considered it her duty to write to Herbert Mandeville was a heavy trial to her feelings and fond trusting heart. She was not one of those persons who can resent injury and find a consolation in anger. She could only suffer, and complain not. She could weep, but she could not reproach. Still, however, she felt that Herbert ought to be explicit, and although gentleness itself, the fair girl had an intuitive comprehension of right and wrong, which could not be overcome even by her love, deep rooted as it was, for Herbert Mandeville.

Her letter was as follows :—

"HERBERT,—I am surrounded by friends whose opinions |I value, because I know they are dictated by honesty and good feeling. These friends, Herbert, think that you have ceased to remember Adeline, or if remembering, ceased to love. The changes and alterations which the feelings undergo, even against our wills, may have blotted me from your heart ; but, Herbert, there are immutable principles of right and wrong which know no change, because they are dependant upon reason and owe nothing to passion. In our case, Herbert, one of those principles of right is that we should be sincere, candid, and open as the day. Do you, Herbert, fancy I can hear unmoved the whispered suspicion of your constancy ? Ah ! no. Vindicate yourself, Herbert ; you have two modes of doing so. The one is to come to Bracefield, and be to me all that you once were ; the other, is not to temporise or play with the feelings of her whom you professed to love, but to have the generosity, if not the justice, to proclaim the change, and leave her to seek serenity free from the storm of sickening hope and endless mortification.

"Herbert, do not imagine that this is an appeal to your slumbering affection. I here renounce all claims—I here give you back all vows. I ask but one thing—release me from doubt.   "ADELINE MOURDANT."

Without daring to trust her feelings to read this note after she had written it, Adeline hastily folded and sealed it.

"Uncertainty," she whispered to herself, " is the worst agony a heart can feel. Let him renounce the love he strove so hard to gain, and pride, my wounded feelings, all will conspire to—to support me."

Even as she spoke, it was evident how deeply the barbed arrow of disappointed love had sunk into her heart, for she reclined her head upon her hand, and wept bitterly.

While the tears were still trickling between her delicate fingers, Mrs. Plumpjoy came into the room with a newspaper in her hand, exclaiming,—

"Dear me, Adeline, here's such a horrid murdering man in the paper."

Adeline looked up, with her eyes swimming in tears.

"What is the matter?" cried Mrs. Plumpjoy. "Well, I never. My dear, you'll cry your poor eyes out. Now just listen to this. It will amuse you, I'll warrant. Here's a murderer of the same name as yourself."

Adeline started.

"The—the same name?" she gasped.

"Yes; George Mourdant. There's a hundred pounds reward for him, as I'm a sinner. He's been a killing some low person or other. Only to think now that he should be the same name as you, and a murderer too. It quite beats chimney sweeping, it does. Do you spell your name with a ——"

Mrs. Plumpjoy here looked from the paper at Adeline, and to her dismay, she saw that she had again fainted.

It was longer this time than before ere Adeline recovered consciousness, and when she did so, her first words were,—

"Have you sent my letter—addressed to—to *him*?"

"To Mr. Mandeville?" said Mrs. Plumpjoy.

Adeline inclined her head in acquiescence.

"No, I haven't, my dear; I thought it better to wait till you got better, and ——"

"Let it, if you please, go now," said Adeline. "Oh, Mrs. Plumpjoy, I— I am a great trouble to you."

"Indeed you are no such thing," cried Mrs. Plumpjoy. "You can't think how grieved I am about you being so weak."

"Never mind it," sobbed Adeline, "I shall be better."

The curate now tapped at the chamber door, to inquire if Adeline was better. She heard his voice, and said faintly,—

"Come in, my dear friend, come in."

No. 39

"Adeline," said the old man, "tell me you are better."

"Yes, much better," she said. "Do not weep for me, Mr. Endsleigh; I shall yet live to thank you for all your kindness to the poor orphan Adeline, the deserted by all but Heaven and—and you, dear friends."

"Heaven will never desert you, Adeline," said the curate. "The blessing of God will be upon your pure young heart for ever."

"Hark—hark!" suddenly cried Adeline.

"What do you hear?" said the curate.

"The tramp of horses' feet. Who—who can it be?"

"If it is any one for us," replied the curate, "it is Charles Leslie."

"If it be he, let him come here and speak to me."

"He shall. Calm yourself, my dear child; all here love you. You are with dear friends who will do their utmost for your happiness."

She stretched out her arm and grasped the curate's hand, while a gentle smile crossed her melancholy and pale face.

"I know it well," she said. "God will reward you, for I cannot."

"The clatter of the horses' hoofs now sounded closely and distinctly upon the roadway leading to the parsonage, and then the sounds ceased, as the horseman paused at the door.

"Is it Charles?" said Adeline.

The curate immediately left the room to inquire, and Adeline conversed in a low broken tone with Mrs. Plumpjoy.

In a few moments a low tap at the door announced his return, and he entered the room.

"Is it Charles?" said Adeline.

"It is. Shall he come in?"

"Oh, yes, yes. Bring him to me."

The curate went to the door, and beckoned to Charles Letlie, who was standing upon the staircase, and he walked with a slow step into the apartment.

"Charles," said Adeline, stretching out her hand to him.

"Adeline!" he cried, in a faltering voice, taking, at the same time, the taper fingers in his, and pressing them to his lips.

"You have seen—*him?*" said Adeline, after a pause.

"I have."

"And—and—he— Tell me all, Charles. Truth is never so dreadful as conjecture. Speak, Charles! speak!"

"He refused all explanation," said Leslie, "and denied my right to ask it."

"Enough," said Adeline. I have written a letter which will remove all his difficulties."

"But are you sure," suggested Mrs. Plumpjoy. "Are you quite sure that Mandeville *is* a horrid villain? Now, I recollect, perfectly, once the poor dear major, who is dead and gone, had a regular tiff with me, all about whether the drugget should be put down over the best carpet,—and a beautiful carpet it was—on a Sunday or not; but we made it all right again, by having the drugget down all the morning, and taken up after dinner. The carpet was all yellow sprigs, and—"

"Sister, sister," said the curate. "How can you fatigue Adeline with such nonsense?"

"Nonsense, indeed," cried Mrs. Plumpjoy. "Next comes a—hem!"

"There is one thing I wish," said Adeline.

"Your wishes shall be obeyed," said Charles, "like behests from Heaven!"

"*He*—you know who I mean—gave me a locket,—I wish it returned."

"It shall," said Charles.

"Yes," said Mr. Endsleigh; "I will return it myself."

"You, sir?" said Charles.

"Yes," continued the curate. "I owe it to myself to see this young man once again. I will go to London, where I have not been for many years, and give him back that locket. Do not mistake my notions, my friends. I do *not* go to supplicate, or to reproach ; I will merely give him the locket, and if he can let me go again without one word of regret or repentance, I shall think worse of human nature than ever I did in my life before."

Adeline looked up in the old man's face as he spoke, and when he had finished, she whispered to him, while a radiant blush mantled her cheeks.

" If, Mr. Endsleigh, you do go, ask him for my gift back again. 'Tis but a lock of hair—and—and you keep it to remind you of Adeline, when she is gone !"

The curate pressed her hand in silence. She took the locket from her neck, and gave it him, and without another word, he took Charles Leslie by the arm and led him from the room.

CHAPTER XC.

" Should any cares assail us, boys,
We'll drown them in the bowl !"

POPULAR PHILOSOPHY.

LONDON AGAIN.—HOW TO DROWN CARE.—THE PROJECTED ELOPEMENT.—THE ROAD TO RUIN.—AND BOULOGNE.

FOR some time after his agitating and extraordinary interview with Charles Leslie, Herbert was so convulsed with passion, that it was fearful to behold him. He would have flown in pursuit of Leslie, but no one knew, or would tell if they did know, whether, when he left the door of Mandeville's house, he had turned to the right or to the left. Herbert then locked himself in his room, and for more than an hour, walked to and fro with agitated and unequal steps. Then suddenly seizing the bell, violently he flung open the door again, and when a trembling servant appeared, he shouted " Wine ! wine !" in a tone which echoed through the entire house.

Wine was immediately brought him, and he tossed off several brimming bumpers, as if they had been water. Then as the intoxicating fumes mounted to his brain, a wild exhilaration of spirits came over him, and he laughed long and loudly to himself.

" 'Tis all a farce," he cried. " A hideous farce, to fancy that I, Herbert Mandeville, was to be led for life by the apron string of a feeling sentimental girl ! Ridiculous, Ha! ha! ha! A rare escape. I, Herbert Mandeville, the young, the handsome—the rich—the courted, admired, and feted. By my soul 'tis rich. They would have liked me to live at Bracefield, I suppose— attend the parish church, and—ho ! ho ! I might have come to the dignity of being churchwarden in time."

Then again he rung the bell furiously, and when it was answered, he cried :—

" What's the time ?"

" Twelve, sir," replied the terrified man, who really thought his master was mad.

" Twelve—only twelve ?"

" No more, sir. I am very sorry, sir, but it is only twelve, and there's M'Daunshot been waiting, sir, an hour."

" Let him wait another, then," said Herbert.

" Yes, sir. Certainly, sir."

" I'm sorry," muttered Herbert, " that I sent off that rascal Dufours as I did. 'Twas an useful knave. By Heaven I could have better spared a better man. No matter, though, Mrs. Delancey and a glorious intrigue, will keep me alive. Perhaps I may contrive a duel with the husband, who knows. Ha! ha! ha! But how to kill time till night? Aye, that's the question. Humph! gaming! yes, gaming! gaming! There's wild flashing excitement in that. Hurrah for the rattle of the dice! Hurrah!—This is life."

He seized his hat, and hurried from the house to a noted gaming table, where he was welcomed with enthusiasm, for well they knew that "he was a young pigeon that would well repay the trouble of plucking."

He played with a desperation that was particularly delightful to the "gentlemen," who honoured that brilliant saloon of iniquity with their presence, and how delicate were their attentions to him. How readily were his written acknowledgments taken in lieu of cash. What rare and costly wines were placed within his reach. Hour after hour rolled away in a delicious dream of excitement, and when Herbert at length, with some shadow of consciousness, started from his seat, he found that the sunshine was exchanged for the brilliant glare of the chandaliers. It was past seven o'clock!

"So late," cried Mandeville.

"Yes, sir," replied one of the *employe's* of the house, which was one of the highest of its class. "I beg to state, sir, that we ourselves hold all your papers."

"Ah, my acknowledgments?"

"Yes, sir; we have paid in cash every one to whom you lost anything."

"Very well."

"At what hour in the morning shall we have the honour of waiting upon you to take your cheque for the amount?"

"When you please—when you please."

"At twelve, sir?"

"That will do."

Dizzy with wine and excitement of high play, Herbert left the place, and just retaining recollection enough to take his right road, he hastened to keep his evening appointment with Mrs. Delancey.

His rate of walking sobered him considerably by the time he reached Park Lane, and as he was a little before the specified hour, he strolled into the park to enjoy the delicious cool air that was gently blowing along its wide expanse.

But little time, however, had he for the busy reflections that were crowding, like so many hideous spectres across his brain, for he heard the hour of eight given forth by several clocks, and hastening through Grosvenor Gate, he strolled leisurely up Park Lane towards Oxford Street.

He had not proceeded far, when, through the dim twilight, he saw a figure pause as if expecting some one. He hastened forward.

"Herbert?" said the voice of Mrs. Delancey.

"Yes—yes," he said eagerly; "'tis I."

"Oh, Herbert! Herbert!" she said in a voice of great grief and tenderness. "What have I not endured to see you once again."

"Endured? Mrs. Delancey, is it possible that you have been subjected to ill-usage?"

"Oh yes—yes. I tremble even now to think of the violence of him with whom I am forced to associate, but who, in comparison with thee, Herbert, is something comparing a grovelling mortal to a God!"

"Then why—oh, why, most charming Mrs. Delancey, why do you not fly?"

"Fly? Alas! alas!"

"Yes, adored woman. Fly from the wretch whose cold heart cannot appreciate your charms."

"Oh, Herbert," she replied; "dear Herbert, I am a woman, and have not the resources of one of your nobler sex. Tell me, Herbert, whither, oh whither could I fly?"

"Whither, Mrs. Delancey?"

"Aye, where could I find a heart to love me?"

"That heart is here!" cried Herbert.

"Where," continued Mrs. Delancey; "where could I, Herbert, find a home to welcome me?"

"If," said Herbert, "I could be so blessed as to think for one moment you would condescend to accept a refuge from the storms of fate in—in——"

"Where, oh, where?"

"In the arms of him who loves—who adores you!"

"Ah!"

"Let me urge you, dearest, fly from the arms of him you cannot love, to him whose heart is filled only by your bright image."

"Oh, tempter! tempter!"

"Nay, 'tis thou art the tempter," cried Mandeville, with enthusiasm. "Thy charms would tempt the coldest heart to love."

"What can I say?"

"Say yes; say you will live for love alone. We will fly far from here. My fortune is ample. We will scorn those whom we leave behind, and in some beauteous spot—

> " '—— The world forgetting,
> And by the world forgot,'

we will speak, think, dream, but of love!"

"Herbert!" cried Mrs. Delancey; "you would woo an angel from its starry sphere! Where got you that rare gift of more than mortal eloquence?"

"'Tis the heart speaks."

"You urge me to—to—elope."

"And you consent. You will consent?"

"When, oh, when?"

"Let it be to-morrow, dearest. I cannot brook delay."

"Be still, my heart," said Mrs. Delancey, laying her hand upon her breast.

"Free me," cried Herbert, "from this agony of suspense. Oh, say you will be mine."

"Herbert; I—I—dear Herbert."

"Speak. Say on."

"Can I live and refuse *you*?"

"Then all is settled," cried Mandeville. "Believe me, I fully appreciate an attachment like yours."

"'Tis a passion," said the lady, "which fills my soul."

"And so it should, dearest," replied Herbert. "Ah! how long will seem the time till to-morrow."

"I—I suppose," faltered Mrs. Delancey; "that at this same hour, dear Herbert, you—you——"

"Say on. Oh, what Heavenly music is the voice of her we fondly, dearly love."

"You will be on the road to somewhere, with—with post-horses."

"Of course," cried Herbert. "Where shall we go?"

"With you anywhere."

"But we should decide."

"Well—well, Brighton."

"It's rather a public place," said Herbert.

"You shall choose then, my Herbert."

"Suppose we go to Dover. No one would dream of looking for us there, and in the event of—of anything unpleasant, we could cross to Calais."

"A charming thought," cried Mrs. Delancey; "oh, how fertile in resources is a mind like your's."

"Oh, flatterer!" cried Herbert.

"Nay, that is impossible."

"Remember then the hour. At eight to-morrow evening I will have a post-chaise and four waiting in the Kent Road."

"Oh, how my heart beats, Herbert."

"'Tis with delight then?"

"It is! It is!"

"Let us," continued Herbert, "meet here on this spot. A hackney coach will convey us to the post-chaise, and then for Dover."

"And—and—joy!"

"A foretaste of Heaven!"

"Now then, Herbert, let us part. I will be punctual, no power on earth shall keep me from you."

"I am happy in that dear belief. Remember eight."

"Think you I *could* forget?"

"No—no. Pardon love's anxious fears."

"Love's fears are ever graceful!" exclaimed the lady. "And now, till to-morrow, adieu!"

"Adieu," said Herbert, and favoured by the darkness, he snatched a kiss from the really beautiful lips of the charming Mrs. Delancey.

They then parted, and Herbert, calling a coach, directed the man to drive him home, and on the way he congratulated himself not a little upon his own tact and personal recommendations, that had in so short a space of time won the unlimited affections of so delightful a woman as Mrs. Delancey, who he apostrophised in his own mind, as a creature all innocence and affectionate feelings.—We shall see!

CHAPTER XCI.

"When the wine is in, the wit is out."

THE NEXT MORNING WITH HERBERT.—A VISITER.—A LITTLE ACCOUNT.

HERBERT'S mind was now in a complete fever of wild excitement. There were times when, do what he would, he could not stifle the feelings of self reproach which assailed him with regard to Adeline. His judgment, however he might try to stifle it upon that point, was too good not to let him know and feel that he had acted an unworthy part with regard to the beautiful and amiable being who had loved him, and who still loved him with such pure devotion and singular constancy. In vain he strove to reason himself into good terms with his conscience. He had tact enough himself to see and detect the hollow sophistry with which he strove to blind his own judgment; and yet feeling and knowing all this, he had not courage sufficient to do what he knew was right, but got angry and irritable because he could not convince himself that he was perfectly qualified in all his proceedings.

Herbert's state of mind, singular as it may appear, was no means so uncommon a one as might at first be supposed. People frequently persevere in a course of action which is directly contrary to their own reason and conviction merely from the petty dread of retracing a few wrong steps, and raising a laugh from vacant minds, or a remark from those around them upon the subject. If there be one principle in human nature stronger than another, it is that which induces the majority of mankind to shrink from a confession of error. Not one person in a million possesses moral courage sufficient to say,—"I am wrong." No, they will endeavour to cheat themselves, as Herbert was endeavouring to do, into a belief in the justification of their acts ; and, if they cannot succeed in smothering a consciousness of wrong doing by sophistry and erroneous argument, they will, as Herbert was likewise doing, fly to stimulants and excitement, in order to crush reflection entirely, and give the mind no time to look back upon itself, and to reason upon its acts.

This was Mandeville's position precisely. He sought the oblivion of wine, gaming, and intrigue. In the brimming cup he thought to find forgetfulness ; in the wild excitement of the gaming-table he sought his recreation, and in the vice of intrigue he vainly imagined he should find that inimitable charm which virtuous affection only can bestow.

Whenever reflection now intruded upon him, he called for wine ; and, no sooner had he returned from his interview with Mrs. Delancey, than he sat down, and consumed a quantity of champaigne, which a few months before that time would have heated his imagination to a pitch of insanity.

Then, under the stupifying effect of the reaction of the wild excitement of his nervous system, he sought repose, vainly fancying that the torpidity induced by drink, would stand in place of the healthful sleep, which alike refreshes both body and mind.

The sun was high in the Heavens before Herbert awoke the next morning, and his first exclamation was in the shape of a deep groan, for his tongue was parched, and his temples throbbed with agonising pains.

He rang his chamber-bell furiously, as if it was some one else's fault instead of his own that he was suffering from his preceding night's potations.

Such men as Herbert Mandeville are always most excessively indignant at the consequences of their own excesses, and seem to consider themselves most especially ill-used because they are not, as it were, protected by nature from the inevitable consequences of every sort of debauch.

"Coffee ! coffee !" he cried, the moment a servant made his appearance. "Black and strong ;—do you hear ?—and—Oh ! curse this head-ache, drop some ammonia in it. Quick—quick !"

His orders were promptly obeyed, and he swallowed huge draughts of that delightful beverage, coffee, in which, according to his directions, a few drops of pure ammonia had been placed. Then, reclining back upon his pillow, he again dropped into a slumber, having given orders to be awakened at three o'clock in the afternoon.

Three o'clock came, and he was gently aroused by his valet, who told him, in a sycophantic whisper, that a gentleman had been waiting to see him for two hours.

"Who is he ?" said Herbert, with a little better temper, for he found himself much better.

"He gave the name of Muggs, sir."

"Muggs ?—Muggs ? I know no one with such a hideous appellation. Tell him he must state to you the nature of his business."

The valet retired, and Herbert proceeded to dress himself, feeling, at the same time, that his mind was still in a state of great bewilderment.

In a few moments the valet returned to say that Mr. Muggs had called, pursuant to an appointment with Mr. Mandeville, for the settlement of a small account which Mr. Mandeville might recollect it was arranged should be paid by twelve o'clock.

"What on earth does he allude to ?" thought Mandeville. "An account at twelve o'clock ? Let me think. Where was I yesterday ?"

Then by degrees the events of the preceding day came to his bewildered recollection, and he became tolerably sure that Mr. Muggs came from the highly respectable saloon at which he, Herbert, had took a sum of money, the precise amount of which he had not the remotest recollection of.

"Show Mr. Muggs into my private room," he said, "and tell him I am dressing, but will be with him soon. Then Herbert set about trying to think how much he had really lost, but he was completely baffled in that inquiry, and he reluctantly came to the conclusion that he must trust to the honesty or the mercy of Mr. Muggs as to the amount; but that, at the same time, he must be particularly careful not to let the aforesaid Muggs into the secret of his, Mandeville's, lack of memory on the occasion.

Mr. Muggs, when Herbert walked into the room in which he was waiting, bowed very low, and hoped Mr. Mandeville was well.

"Pretty well," said Herbert. "You have some I O U's of mine, I believe, Mr.—Mr.—Slugs."

"Muggs, or Slugs, just as you please, sir," replied the other, quite calmly.

"What is the amount?" said Herbert.

"You have a memorandum, I presume, sir?"

"Oh, yes; but it is in my dressing-room. You can tell me."

Mr. Muggs cast a keen, knowing look from out of his little greenish-looking eyes at Mandeville, as he at once concluded in his own mind that "the young pigeon knew about as well as the leg of the table how much he owed."

"The amount, sir," said Muggs, "is a mere trifle."

"Very well," said Herbert, sitting down, and unlocking a desk, in which was his cheque-book. "Just tell me how much?"

"Eleven hundred and forty pounds," said Muggs, with the greatest calmness.

"What?" cried Mandeville.

"Eleven hundred and forty pounds," again said Muggs, looking all the while intently at a bronze lamp that hung from the ceiling.

"Nonsense," said Mandeville, "you are joking."

"Never made a joke in my life, sir," replied Muggs.

"I cannot have lost such a sum."

"Here's your paper, sir. Gentlemen generally have short memories about these things, and that's why our house always takes paper, and if they let a gentleman go without leaving his I O U, and he says next day he don't recollect it, we never ask again for the money, because we consider it our own fault in having no voucher."

So saying, Mr. Muggs laid before Herbert, very calmly and collectedly, six or eight little scraps of paper, each of which was adorned with the magical, but disagreeable letters I O U, and referred to certain amounts, being likewise signed "Herbert Mandeville."

Now Herbert more than suspected that several of these documents were forgeries, and, pointing to one for two hundred pounds, he said,—

"Really, Mr. Muggs, that don't look like my writing."

"You are quite right, sir," replied Muggs, with a smile. "It don't look like your writing; but you know, sir, when a gentleman drinks freely, and we don't charge for wine, his hand is not quite so steady; you understand, sir."

Mandeville had a confused notion that he had certainly been a great deal overcome by wine at the house to which the polite Mr. Muggs belonged, and he could not very well dispute the line of argument adopted by that gentleman. Moreover, he well knew that if he did not honour his I O U in this instance, he would at once lose all credit upon town as a man of spirit— a fine young fellow, &c., so he took up his pen, and wrote a cheque for the amount, which Mr. Muggs received very coolly and politely, and, hoping to have the pleasure of seeing him again shortly, he took his leave.

"Humph!" thought Herbert, "this is rather an expensive enjoyment; and, after all, did I enjoy it? Well, it's no use thinking about it. Let me see: there's all the elopement business to arrange with the charming Mrs. Delancey; that can't be so expensive as gaming, at any rate. I certainly miss Dufours; he was a clever rascal, and tormented with no scruples. I

verily believe Dufours had his price for anything. Let me recollect. A post chaise at eight—yes, that was it. By Heavens! this affair will make a sensation in the saloons. They will say I have began early, and certainly Mrs. Delancey is a most beautiful and loveable creature—such mind, such discrimination, such enthusiasm. Let me see ; my valet had better see to all the minor arrangements. He is clever in his way, although certainly not equal to Dufours."

Herbert then rung for his confidential servant, and gave him a sum of money and ample instruction what to do, after which he sat down to breakfast as the clocks were striking four in the afternoon.

CHAPTER LXCII.

"———— Oh, my good angel !
Step between me and my warring passions.
Save me—oh, save me from myself !"   OTWAY.

ANOTHER VISITER TO HERBERT.—THE LOCKET.—AN OLD MAN'S COUNSEL.—HE IS NOT QUITE LOST.

WITH that elasticity of mind which generally characterises the young, and which was particularly manifested in the character of Herbert Mandeville, he soon forgot the disagreeable impression which had been left upon his mind by the visit of the gentleman with the I O Us, and he turned now his attention completely to the consideration of the successful issue of his intrigue with Mrs. Delancey, and the species of eclat that it would give him in the fashionable world.

No. 40

He sat at his breakfast absorbed in these vain glorious speculations, when the name of a visiter was announced to him, which was as unexpected as unwelcome. In fact, had a thunder-bolt suddenly fallen at his feet, Herbert could not have been more astounded than he was at the announcement that the Rev. Robert Endsleigh requested to see him.

For a few moments he was not in a state of mind to give any directions to the servant; then his first idea was positively to decline seeing the curate, but his pride stepped to his aid, and he thought—"They will say I was afraid to face the old man! I will, I must see him," and turning to the servant, he cried in a tone of desperate resolve,

"Shew Mr. Endsleigh up here, and give him, at the same time, my compliments, and I am very glad to see him."

The servant thought this a very odd message, but he delivered it, and in a few moments the old curate was ushered with great ceremony into the presence of Herbert.

Now, during the brief period that the servant had been gone, Mandeville had made up his mind to a stroke of policy which he thought must at once silence Mr. Endsleigh and place him in an awkward position; that is to say, providing he came to find fault and remonstrate, as Herbert did not for a moment doubt he had; and that was so to overwhelm him with civilities and hospitality, that he should hardly be able to get in a word of reproof edgeways.

This was a plan of operations which would have succeeded with a vast number of persons, but Mr. Endsleigh was about the very last to be turned from a purpose by such means, and it completely failed, as will be seen.

In pursuance of his plan, the moment Mr. Endsleigh appeared, Herbert sprung from his seat, and extending his hand, exclaimed—

"My dear sir, I am quite delighted to see you. Really I take this friendly visit as a great kindness indeed. Pray be seated. How do you do? What will you take?"

The curate looked very hard at Herbert, and quietly put his hands behind him, waiting with the greatest calmness until Herbert was done, and without so much as interposing a single word. Now, nothing is so extremely difficult as to go on being excessively friendly and enthusiastic all alone, and after a vain struggle to keep up the tone in which he had commenced, Herbert was forced to give it up in despair, and a dead silence all at once ensued. Then the curate spoke mildly and earnestly.

"I would rather decline sitting down in your house, Herbert Mandeville," he said, "because I could not conscientiously make you welcome to a seat in mine."

Herbert bit his lips with vexation, and all his good humour, real and pretended, at once deserting him, he said in a tone of anger,—

"Then what brings you here at all, sir, if you come in so unfriendly a spirit? A spirit, I must say, which reflects no credit on you or your sacred calling."

"If," said Mr. Endsleigh, "I thought your reproof a just one, I should thank you for it; but while my sacred calling teaches me charity and love, it teaches me another virtue."

"May I ask its name, sir?" sneered Herbert.

"Certainly—sincerity."

"Indeed?"

"Yes, Herbert Mandeville, I cannot clasp your hand, because, where I give my hand, I am accustomed to give my heart."

"May I ask your business with me?" cried Herbert, striking the table passionately.

"Adeline wished a locket to be returned to you, which she says you gave her in happier times, and I am merely her humble messenger."

A paleness came over Herbert's face, as he replied, "I—I cannot take it."

"And wherefore not?" said the curate. "She sends it back to you, because the circumstances under which she received it are so strangely altered. That poet in whose writings there is much pure religion, says :—

" Rich gifts wax poor when givers prove unkind,"

and this, it is needless to deny, is returned to you because the giver has proved unkind, but it is returned without reproach, without remonstrance."

The curate as he spoke took the locket from his pocket and laid it upon the table before Mandeville.

"Adeline," gasped Herbert, "sent this to me?"

"She did, and I offered to be its bearer, because I had another object in seeing you."

"She sent no message?"

"Yes; she forgives you for nourishing in her breast a delusion which is now dispelled."

"She forgets me?"

"I hope she does."

"Is—is—her health. Tell me, sir. What is her true condition?"

"'Tis said she is dying."

Herbert sank upon a chair, with a deep groan.

"But life and death," continued the curate, "are in the hands of the Almighty. Herbert Mandeville, now hear me, and discard from your heart all vain anger against an old man who strives but to do his duty. I loved your father—we were playmates together, and we confided each to each the inmost secrets of our hearts; so, knowing and esteeming him as I did, my old heart yearned towards you, Herbert, and I loved you because you were the son of my old familiar friend, my fellow-student, the partner of my cares and joys, when I was but upon the threshold of existence. Herbert you have many virtues, you have great capacity, a mind of a high order, and all the power to be what you are not—a great because a good man. Can you bear to hear your faults? If so, hear them from me. You are misled by a false light, an *Ignis fatuus,* which will lead you to destruction. Herbert, you love fame better than you love virtue; you love conquest better than you love constancy; you love the wild applause of the selfish and the wicked better than you love the quiet approval of the good and virtuous. Oh, Herbert! child of my old and best friend; it is not now too late. Rouse the godlike spirit of truth and justice within you, and secure a happiness as enduring and firm as your present pursuits are fleeting and unstable. Herbert—Herbert, I beg of you, I implore you to rouse your better nature, and think upon my words."

"It—it—is too late;" gasped Herbert.

"No," cried the curate, in a firm voice. "It is never too late. Turn from evil at the eleventh hour, and there is much joy still to come; it is not too late, Herbert."

"But—but—Adeline?"

"Nay, do not mistake my meaning, Herbert. Adeline and you are for ever asunder."

"What mean you?"

"The grave will soon close over the broken heart."

"No—no!" cried Herbert. "Oh, God! no—no!"

"My object is to beg you to let the remainder of your life atone for the wild delusion which you created in the breast of that young thing who is now hovering on the brink of eternity."

"But—if—even now I fly to her."

"No, no, Mandeville. That dream has passed away. What is done is done. Let Adeline die in peace."

"Die! die!" repeated Herbert. "She must be saved. What can be done?"

"Be content," said the curate. "She is with those who love her. Tell me, Herbert, have I awakened one chord of better feeling in your breast?"

" What would you have me do?"

" What you think right."

" Mr. Endsleigh, I believe you mean me well. But, I am in a vortex from which there is no escape."

" That vortex is but an image of speech and has no reality. Have but the will to escape, and you are at the moment free."

A French clock on the mantel shelf now sounded six o'clock, and at the same time played a lively French waltz.

By what trifles human nature is influenced! The air reminded Herbert of the gay and voluptuous saloons of Lady Clara Seagrave, and of the luxurious beauties who therein swam

"The mazes of the giddy dance,"

then he thought of his engagement to Mrs. Delancey, and he sprang from his chair.

"I thank you, Mr. Endsleigh," he said, "for all you have said and done. Your good feeling I cannot for a moment doubt—but——"

"But what, Herbert?"

"The time is past, I must pursue my course, I am too deeply pledged."

With a deep sigh the curate gazed for a moment in Herbert's face, then he said—

"A few moments more and my errand is done. In confidence Adeline has confided to me that you lent her fifty pounds."

"No, no," cried Herbert; "it was for George Mourdant."

"But, nevertheless, a loan to her," added Mr. Endsleigh; "there is the amount," laying some notes upon the table before Mandeville.

"I cannot, will not take it," he cried. "How can she pay such a sum?"

"It is enough," replied the curate; "that it is repaid to you. I pay it."

"You, sir?"

"Yes, Herbert; and I thank God I have the means."

So saying, without another word, Mr. Endsleigh walked from the room, leaving Herbert in no very enviable state of mind.

And what did Herbert do then? He wept a little—then laughed bitterly—called loudly for wine, and before another hour had once more succeeded in partially drowning reflection. Well, indeed, might the maddened young man declare that he was in the vortex of a whirlpool, from which he could not escape.

He then commanded the attendance of his valet to report progress concerning the elopement, and being told that all was arranged according to his orders, he put a quantity of money in his pockets, and sallied out upon his enterprise of intrigue and shame.

CHAPTER XCVIII.

" —— He spoke to her of hope,
And the wild radiance of her joy
Shone from her eyes, as smilingly
She pointed to the sky and whispered,
It is there!"

THE CURATE'S RETURN.—ADELINE'S CHAMBER.

Mr. Endsleigh remained in London that night; but by the earliest conveyance, which passed near Bracefield, he started for his humble home.

It was mid-day, therefore, on the morrow after his interview with Herbert Mandeville, before he once more stood upon the threshold of the Parsonage. Old Andrew had been watching for his master and met him at the garden-gate, where the curate's first question was after Adeline.

"Missis Martha do say," replied the old man, "that she be much of a muchness, poor thing."

"Then she is no worse, thank Heaven," said Mr. Endsleigh, entering the house, where he was immediately met by Mrs. Plumpjoy, with the following question—

"Well, brother, did you see him?"

"I did, Martha," said the curate, "and I strove to convince him that he was not in the road to happiness, but he would not be turned aside from the path he was pursuing, which I fear is one that leads to utter destruction. But how is Adeline?"

"Still the same, brother; but perhaps weaker."

It is the will of Heaven," said Mr. Endsleigh. "If she is not sleeping, Martha, will you tell her quietly that I have returned; and if she then expresses a wish to see me, I will come to her immediately."

Mrs. Plumpjoy went on this message, and presently returned to say that Adeline was awake and wished to see the curate.

"Is Charles in the house?" asked Mr. Endsleigh.

"He's moping about somewhere," replied Mrs. Plumpjoy. "I think he said he would go for a walk. Oh, brother, I was very wrong when I said Charles Leslie was not so good looking as Herbert Mandeville."

"Indeed, Martha?"

"Yes. For nothing makes people so beautiful as acting right, and nothing so ugly as wickedness."

"You never were more correct, Martha," said the curate; "and with all your eccentricities, I know you have a good heart."

So saying, the curate left the room to proceed to Adeline's chamber.

"What does he mean by my 'eccentricities' I wonder?" thought Mrs. Plumpjoy. "He's a great deal more odd and out of the way than I am, I'm sure. Eccentricities indeed! Next comes a Turkey cock to have his nails pared!"

With a slow step and a heavy heart, Mr. Endsleigh ascended the staircase leading to Adeline's chamber. He tapped gently at the door, and then immediately heard her soft low musical voice, the sweet tones of which even illness had not destroyed, say—"Come in, Mr. Endsleigh."

He opened the door and entered the room, then drawing a chair to the bedside of the beautiful sufferer, he said—

"My dear Adeline, are you not better?"

She shook her head, and a faint smile for one fleeting moment lit up her pale face.

"You see I have soon returned," added the curate, kindly.

"Thank you, thank you, sir," said Adeline. "And you gave him the locket?"

"I did, Adeline."

She raised her head slightly from the pillow, and looked anxiously in the countenance of the curate, as if she would there read all that had passed between him and Herbert.

Mr. Endsleigh guessed what was passing in her mind, and he said—

"I spoke as kindly as I could to him, Adeline, and I am not altogether without hope that he may benefit by my counsel."

"I cannot thank you, sir," said Adeline, "for my heart is too full of gratitude for words to express its feelings. I think, nay, I am sure, that I am dying, and yet, even yet, I am so weak that I cannot altogether forget that— that——"

She here burst into a hysterical passion of weeping, and the curate, after a moment's pause, said kindly—

"Adeline, if there is anything that I, or any one in this house, can do to bring you serenity of mind, it shall be done."

"No, no," she said faintly; "no more. Too much has been done for me and for my sake already. I thought that I had schooled my heart to think no more of him; but oh, Mr. Endsleigh, I can speak to you as I would confess to Heaven. I still love Herbert Mandeville."

The old man sighed deeply as he replied—

"This clinging of your affections to him, Adeline, is to me only another proof of their constancy and purity."

"Tell me," she added, after a pause; "did he not say he would come, if it were but to bid me farewell?"

The curate shook his head.

"He sent no word of love?"

"I cannot say that he was indifferent altogether, Adeline," said the curate; "but as if I were answering to the judgment seat of God, I will answer you. My conviction was, and is, that his passion has subsided, and that he is only tormented by the annoyance that his conscience, which is not quite callous, gives him, for having fostered a passion in your breast; the promises connected with which, he intended not to fulfil."

"That is enough," said Adeline. "My dear friend, I thank you. Your candour I can appreciate. It is a kindness. Now, I—I will speak of him no more."

"There are still, my dear girl, many who love you," said Mr. Endsleigh; "and that with an enduring love too, which knows no change. Let us hope then that you will be long with us in your purity and beauty, to bless those who really look upon you with an affection that is lasting, because it is based upon firmer principles than vanity or passion."

"I would fain stay with you all," sobbed Adeline; "but my heart is broken."

"Nay, Adeline, say not so. Time may, and will obliterate the ravages of the deepest griefs."

"'Tis too late," said Adeline. "Mr. Endsleigh, I see my error now. I was deceived by the glitter of false lights, and now I am their victim."

"We will think no more of the past," said the curate; "we will speak no more of it. Think not of those events which pain you, but as the varied chimera of some troubled dream. All of us here in this house will work together to bring you comfort and joy again: I—my sister—Charles Leslie—all love you."

"Ah!" said Adeline, "Charles Leslie, too. How little have I deserved the kindness of such a heart as his!"

"He esteems you, Adeline, from conviction of your innocence and worth."

"You are all too partial in your judgments of me," said Adeline. "I feel I have been weak, foolish—most vainly presumptuous in my own opinion."

"But your motives have all been pure and good," interrupted the curate. "There is great distinction, Adeline, between errors of judgment, and crimes of reflection and anticipation. You are still to all of us here, Adeline, as when first we knew you, and can appreciate your singleness of purpose and gentle heart. Again, I say, forget, if possible, the past, and strive to live for a happier future."

"My future is there," said Adeline, pointing to the blue sky which shone in beauty through the little casement of her chamber.

"True, Adeline," said the curate; "but we have duties to perform here, as well as hopes of joy hereafter."

"We have," said Adeline, "and my duty is, and shall be, while I live, to love and pray for blessings on those who have succoured and spoken words of hope and kindness to the orphan, broken-hearted Adeline."

Her voice was faint as she spoke, and the curate began to fear that he had already prolonged the conversation beyond the limits of her failing strength.

"You are tired, Adeline," he said, "and I will leave you."

"I think I could sleep," she said.

"Do so, and the blessing of God be upon your slumbers," said Mr. Endsleigh, as he rose quietly, and closed the blinds of the window. Then, as he again approached, the deep, regular breathings of Adeline showed that she had dropped, even in that moment, into a quiet slumber.

With his hands clasped, and his aged eyes fixed upon the calm, pale face of the sleeping girl, the man of God stood for many minutes. Then, as he thought how soon it was probable she would pass away from him, and how desolate would be then his home without the young guileless heart he had attached to himself so closely, and to which he was attached with a love which surpassed description, the tears coursed each other down his furrowed cheeks, and again the old man would have wept aloud in the anguish of his feelings, but that he feared to awaken the gentle slumberer before him.

Then he knelt by the bed-side, and, with his heart and his mind, he prayed, although he uttered no sound ; and, if ever prayer ascended to the throne of Heaven, that silent heartfelt aspiration of the old curate did so, and peace was sent down upon his heart from God like a sweet flood of gentle sunshine, for once more he was enabled to rise with calmness, and, in a firm voice, to say,—

"God's will be done! I mourn, but I do not repine."

He then, with a noiseless step, left the room, and repaired to his own study, for he wished to be alone with his own thoughts.

CHAPTER XCIV.

"In every bush the thief sees an officer,
How timid is guilt!"

EIGHT O'CLOCK IN LONDON.—PARK LANE AND THE ELOPEMENT.—THE FALSE ALARM.—DOVER.

FAIN would we linger in the quiet village of Bracefield, by the couch of the gentle, the beautiful and the suffering girl, whose young heart had received so severe a shock by the faithlessness of him who they loved

"Next unto Heaven."

We love to record the simple, earnest piety of the old curate, as he talks in his pure simplicity of mind to the young girl who has wound herself so around his aged heart that it would go near to break it, were those tendrils of clinging affection to be rudely unclasped. But, alas! such may not be. We are recording a series of occurrences, no one of which must be omitted in its proper place, and here we must shift the scene again to London, and to Herbert Mandeville.

Eight o'clock was sounding from the many steeples of London, when Herbert turned from Oxford Street into Park Lane, on his expectation to meet Mrs. Delancey. The moon was obscured, and there was a dampness in the air, which showed some predisposition to rain ; but Herbert was in too excited a state of mind, from wine, and the peculiar step he was about to take, to notice the signs and portents of the weather.

He walked rapidly on towards Grosvenor Gate, and, punctual to her appointed time was Mrs. Delancey. The moment he came up to her, she clung to his arm, and burst into an admirably-acted passion of tears.

"My dear creature," said Herbert, "take courage. Recollect that we have before us a life of love, and that is a life of enchantment."

"Oh! Herbert, Herbert," she cried ; "you speak of enchantment. Where did you procure that magic power which attracts to you all hearts ?"

"Nay, you are quite a flatterer," said Herbert. "Come, let us move forward. A cold air blows across the park."

"Ah!" said Mrs. Delancey, "when absent from you, Herbert, a thousand fears and scruples assail my shrinking heart ; but, when with you, there is a magic in your very voice which is more powerful than all the reasoning and reflection in the world."

"There is always a magic in love," said Herbert. "What care we for the world and all its musty precepts ? We will found a new sect of philosophy— the philosophy of love, and none shall be admitted within the circle of our intimacy but those who, like ourselves, have forsaken all the grovelling, mean notions of society, to luxuriate in the only one passion which lifts humanity above the earth."

"What eloquence !" sighed Mrs. Delancey.

"She's right," thought Herbert, whose vanity was at its height. "Methinks now I could woo an angel from its starry sphere !"

He drew the seemingly half-reluctant arm of Mrs. Delancey within his own, and they walked together up Park Lane towards Oxford Street."

"Do you know those impertinent people ?" said Herbert, as their path was twice crossed by two men arm-in-arm.

"Know them, Herbert ? Good Heavens ! how should I know them ?" ejaculated the lady.

"How, indeed ?" said Herbert with a smile. "Forgive the foolish question. 'Tis your beauty is the attraction, and, like moths, they flutter round the blaze of your unequalled charms."

By the time this pretty compliment was concluded, and Mrs. Delancey had gently breathed a deprecatory sigh, they had reached Oxford Street.

"I have made every requisite arrangement," said Herbert, in a low tone. "We will take a hackney coach here, which will convey us to the Old Kent Road, where my confidential valet is waiting by this time with a post-chaise."

"I tremble !" said Mrs. Delancey.

"Nay, courage ! courage !" cried Herbert. But Mrs. Delancey—sweet, delicate creature, still trembled violently, and it required all Herbert's eloquence and encouraging speeches to induce her to step into a hackeney coach, which he beckoned off the stand, and when they were in, it required all Herbert's philosophy to prevent him from jumping out to inflict instant punishment upon some impertinent man, who, before he, Herbert, could raise the glasses, placed his face close to the coach window, and deliberately looked in, while a broad grin sat upon his insolent-looking countenance. In fact, Herbert would have got out, had not Mrs. Delancey laid her hand upon his arm, and declared herself to be very faint.

"Really such impertinence," he exclaimed, "is beyond comprehension."

"It is so rare," faltered Mrs. Delancey, "to see a gentleman of your—I must say it—distinguished appearance, in a common hackney coach, that it excites the curiosity of the vulgar."

"That must be it," said Mandeville, putting up the glasses, greatly mollified by Mrs. Delancey's flattering and delicate explanation of a circumstance, that had she chosen, she could have explained in quite a different manner, but as it was, Herbert was so besotted by personal vanity, that her remark acted like oil on the troubled waters, and at once restored his good humour.

Herbert gave the requisite direction to the coachman, and the elopement with the charming Mrs. Delancey was fairly begun.

The lady shed tears all the way to the Old Kent Road, and in intervals, said something implying the extraordinary fascinations of Herbert, so that to him the time passed very delightfully, and when the coach stopped with a jerk, he was startled from an agreeable reverie upon the subject of his own irresistible attractions, and the " sensation" that the news of his elopement with Mrs. Delancey would make in the "*beau monde*."

The confidential valet was there, and the post-chaise was there, so that everything proceeded quite smoothly as yet.

Herbert whispered a few words in his valet's ear, containing directions what to do till he wrote to town, and then handed Mrs. Delancey into the chaise.

"Dover, sir?" said the post-boy, touching the rim of his perfectly round white hat.

"Yes," said Herbert, "and the quicker you get over the stages the more money for yourself."

Crack went the whip, and away flew the chaise at a good pace, but not before another piece of impertinence had been perpetrated by some one as before, looking in at the window of the chaise with a knowing grin. Before, however, Herbert could say an angry word upon the subject, or adopt any course of resentment, Mrs. Delancey leaned so heavily upon his arm, and trembled so violently, that had he not enshrined her for the time being in his heart as his "lady love," common courtesy would have compelled him to have turned his attention at once to her.

"Timid again?" he said. "How you tremble."

"'Tis rather with love than fear," replied Mrs. Delancey. "Oh, Herbert! All sacrifices are light, when made for you."

"We shall in a few hours reach Dover," said Herbert, "for we are going at

No. 41

a slashing pace ; then should the slightest difficulty or disagreeable occur, we can, as I before remarked, cross to Calais, and if needs be extend our tour of love and romance to that most delightful of all countries, Italy."

"Ah !—with thee, Herbert, a desert would be a paradise."

In such delightful converse stage after stage was passed. The chaise rattled through Rochester, and was fast decreasing the distance between that place and Maidstone, when Herbert thought he could hear occasionally the heavy tread of horses' feet behind on the road, at a furious gallop. Sometimes he thought his imagination had deceived him ; then again, he would hear the sounds so clearly and distinctly, that he could not doubt their reality.

"My dearest, do not be alarmed," said Herbert to his fair and frail companion, "but it appears to me that we are pursued."

"Pursued ?" cried Mrs. Delancey, clasping her hands. "Gracious powers! —Oh, Heavens !"

"Be not alarmed," said Herbert ; "such may not be the case, and if it be, depend upon it, let our pursuers be who they may, they shall meet a reception that may induce them to think they had better have remained in London."

"Oh, what do you mean?" cried the lady. "Your life to me is too precious."

"And to myself likewise," said Herbert, with a smile ; "so I took care to provide myself with arms ; I have a brace of pistols in my pocket."

"Pistols !" shrieked Mrs. Delancey.

"Yes—for your defence."

Mrs. Delancey's alarm was probably now quite serious, and she put her pretty head from the chaise-window, despite of Herbert's remonstrances, to see if she could if they were pursued.

"The noise of the chaise," said Herbert, "confuses every other sound. I will make the post-boy pull up a moment, that we may listen."

He then shouted to the post-boy, who immediately pulled up his horses.

"Do you hear anything on the road?" said Herbert.

"Yes," said the post-boy, who, by the by, was a man of forty years of age. "What do you make of it?"

"Osses at a hard gallop," replied the boy.

"They must overtake us," said Herbert. "Hark! how rapidly the sounds approach. You could not distance them ?" said he, to the boy.

"In course not. We has a shay, you see, and they has not, you sees."

"Most conclusive," said Herbert. "But I wont be hunted by any one. Let them come up when and how they like. Drive on at a quiet pace."

Off started the chaise again, and now the loud sound of the horses' hoofs upon the ground proclaimed that in a very few minutes the chaise must be overtaken.

Herbert took his pistols from his pocket, for now that he had embarked in the hazardous adventure of carrying away another person's wife, he was determined to go through with it with eclat, if it cost him his life, or involved the necessity of taking somebody else's.

"Whatever you do," said Mrs. Delancey, "be careful of your own safety. Think of me, Herbert, and expose yourself to no risks."

"Believe me, I will not," said Herbert. "Hark! they are close at hand. Sit as far back as you can in the chaise, and leave me to settle this matter."

He had scarcely ceased speaking when several horsemen drew up their foaming steeds close to the chaise.

"Hush ! hush !" whispered Herbert, as Mrs. Delancey was about to utter an exclamation of fear. "Hush ! don't speak. Leave them to begin hostilities."

"Halloo !" cried one of the horsemen, in a bantering tone ; "is this the road to Maidstone, old fellow ?"

"Perhaps it is, if you follow your nose and don't squint," replied the post-boy.

"How long will it take us to get there?" said the same voice, amid laughter from his companions.

"That depends on the pace," said the post-boy.

"Then good night to you, old crusty," cried the man. "We'll be there in time, now."

So saying, with a loud laugh, the party started forward at a smart trot.

"'Twas a false alarm," said Herbert.

"Oh, thank Heaven!" ejaculated Mrs. Delancey.

By grey morning the chaise rattled into Dover, and drew up at the best inn, by Mandeville's direction to the driver.

CHAPTER XCV.

"The storm of passion briefly ended,
And the bitter consequence was all
That of its presence then was left."

THE PLOT THICKENS.—BREAKFAST AT DOVER.—A DAY PASSED.—A SUDDEN ARRIVAL.—THE RESULT.

MRS. DELANCEY and Herbert were seated at breakfast at their inn at Dover, on the morning after that which had witnessed their hasty arrival, when there came a waiter into the room to say that two gentlemen wished to see Mandeville.

"To see me?" cried Herbert. "Who can have found me out here? There must be some mistake."

"No, sir," said the waiter. "Mr. Mandeville, they said."

"Tell them, then, that I am busy, and can see no one here on any pretence whatever."

The waiter departed on his errand, but returned almost instanter to say that the gentlemen would not go away, but were even then upon the stairs.

Herbert sprang from his seat, and Mrs. Delancey gave a slight scream as the cadaverous face of Mr. Delancey protruded itself into the room.

"Wretch!" cried the awful-looking husband, rushing into the room, and making towards his wife.

"Hold, sir!" cried Herbert. "If you have anything to say, say it to me, and not to a woman."

"Villain!" shrieked Mr. Delancey.

Herbert smiled.

"You may indulge your temper by calling me just whatever you please," said Herbert; "only when I think you have said enough, I shall assuredly take the liberty of kicking you down stairs."

"Do you hear that?" cried Mr. Delancey. "He talks of kicking me. Come in—come in."

A tall, ferocious-looking man now skulked into the room, and said:—

"Oh, oh,—they are here, are they?"

"That's my wife," cried Delancey; "and that's her seducer."

"Oh, oh,—I shall die!" cried Mrs. Delancey, and she forthwith fainted away.

The heads of one half the household now appeared at the door, and so singularly placed was Herbert in the whole transaction, that he stood irresolute, and not knowing what to say or do.

"Sir," suddenly cried Mr. Delancey; "you shall hear from my solicitor."

"As you please, and when you please," replied Herbert, with a sneer.

"Lots of witnesses," remarked the coarse tall man, who had entered the room along with Mr. Delancey.

"I beg that some of you," said Mandeville, addressing several female attendants who stood in the doorway, "will render assistance to this lady. I will soon settle matters with these persons."

So saying, Herbert advanced to Mr. Delancey, and said, in a calm, determined tone :—

"Are you aware, sir, of where you are?"

"A—a—where I am?" stammered the heroic husband.

"Yes, sir; because if you do not know, I can tell you that this is my private apartment."

"Well sir!" said Delancey, glancing at his big companion, to see that he was close at hand, in case of an emergency.

"I order you to leave it then, immediately," said Mandeville.

"But suppose he wont?" said the tall man.

"Then I shall be under the necessity of making him," said Herbert, "while you wait your turn for undergoing the same operation."

The tall man burst into a loud laugh, which was so peculiarly provoking to Herbert, that leaving Mr. Delancey, he made but one stride up to him and seizing him suddenly by the collar, the tall man being just in the doorway, lost his footing, and disappeared headlong down the staircase, as quickly as if he had suddenly vanished through a trap-door.

With his eyes flashing with excitement, Herbert now turned to the astonished Mr. Delancey, and impeded that gentleman's retreat, which he was endeavouring to effect unaided.

"Now, sir," cried Herbert, "you can follow the scoundrel who has just made so rapid a descent down stairs."

"Murder!" cried Delancey, as he twined his arms round the balustrade at the top of the staircase. "Murder! help! murder!"

In vain Herbert strove to disengage the nervous grasp of Mr. Dalancey. The "injured husband" only held the firmer, and at last, with one desperate pull, Herbert tore down the rails to which he clung, and together with Delancey and the railing rolled to the bottom of the stairs amid the screams, shrieks, and general outcries of the whole household.

Falls, which in cool blood would break every bone in a man's body, seldom do much mischief under excitement, and Herbert sprung to his feet the moment he reached the landing place at the bottom of the stairs perfectly unhurt. He had no sooner, however, done so, when a constable's staff was held within half an inch of his nose, the owner of the said staff vociferating :—

"No resistance! Holloa! Holloa! You are my prisoner. Come, no resistance!"

"Nonsense," said Mandeville; "what have you to do with this business?"

"I give him in charge for a desperate assault," said the tall man, who stood rubbing his head at a cautious distance from Herbert."

"So—so do I," groaned Mr. Delancey, gathering himself up from the passage. "A murderous assault, he tried to take my life."

"These men would not leave my apartment by fair means," said Herbert, "and consequently I was forced to use foul ones."

"Come on all of you!" cried the constable, who was evidently in a great state of trepidation, and had a dread of some violence on the part of Mandeville. "Come on! The mayor is sitting—no resistance—mind. Hilloa! you young fellow; mind, I'm a constable."

"Take me wherever you like," said Herbert, "but do it quickly."

"To the mayor! to the mayor!" cried the constable, as he laid his hand upon Mandeville's arm, who immediately shook him off, saying,—

"Hark you, friend—I will follow you to the mayor on this charge of assault, for I am not so foolish as to resist the constituted authorities of my country; but if you so much as lay a finger upon me, I'll cram that staff of yours down your throat as you are a living man."

The constable gave a great jump of alarm at this speech, and the mob that had rapidly collected round the inn door, cheered Herbert lustily, for mobs always enjoy greatly any defiance of the civil authorities.

The constable evidently thought that discretion was the better part of valour, and after cuffing a little boy who stood on the door-step, he cried:—"Come on, come on," and marched before, followed by Herbert, who, now that his blood was cooling a little, began to be heartily sick of his adventure, and to surmise that it was neither pleasant nor reputable to be escorted through the streets of Dover by a constable and a great crowd, however admiring and complimentary the latter might be.

When the party arrived at the mayor's, Herbert looked in vain for Mr. Delancey. He was no where visible, and the only charge of assault that was preferred against Herbert was by the tall man he had tumbled down stairs, and who gave the name of James Lee.

He swore to the assault, and as there was a host of witnesses, the charge was very easily proved, in fact Herbert never denied it, but based his defence upon the legality of his conduct in turning Mr. James Lee or Mr. Anybody out of his room if he choose.

The mayor, after patiently listening to both sides, got out of the difficulty of adjudicating, by making Herbert enter into his own recognizances in five hundred pounds, to answer any charge that might be brought against him at the ensuing sessions. This was done, and Herbert finding himself free, as in duty bound, hurried back to the hotel, to attend upon the alarmed and forlorn Mrs. Delancey.

"How is the lady?" was his first question.

"Gone away, sir," replied a waiter.

"Gone away?—Where?"

"Don't know, sir. But a gentleman with yellow-looking face and shocking bad whiskers, him as you left on the mat, got up when you were gone, and ordered a chaise."

"And took the lady with him?"

"Yes sir."

"Was she better?"

"No sir—carried into chaise."

"Humph!" thought Herbert. "Here is an end to my adventure, with a vengeance. Get me a chaise and four for London, as soon as possible, and bring me a bill of all damage."

CHAPTER XCVI.

" Then was the stinging agony of guilt,
The guilt of blood upon his soul!"—ANON.

TO TOWN AGAIN.—HERBERT IS STILL UNHAPPY.—THE REACTION OF EXCITEMENT.—A QUARREL AND ITS CONSEQUENCES.

IT may be readily imagined that Herbert was in no very enviable frame of mind as he rattled along the country roads towards London, which he thought he had bidden adieu to for some time, when he started on his tour of guilty pleasure.

For the first time it began to strike him that he was not on the right road to happiness or even serenity, and he arrived at his own house tired and disgusted with himself, everything, and everybody.

The reaction from intense excitement Herbert understood well, but he had not the mental courage to allow that again to subside, and leave behind it the calm serenity of mind which mankind took such opposite methods of attaining.

After an hour's listlessness at home, he could bear his own thoughts no longer, and he resorted to his usual fatal source of, not enjoyment, but temporary oblivion of fearful thought—and hastily calling for wine, he found in the excitement of his physical system a fragile and fleeting set off against the anguish of thought.

More excitement, however, than even sparkling wine could afford, was necessary to Herbert Mandeville now; and he asked himself where he could find that but at the gaming-table? He then immediately left his house, and repairing to the same place at which he had already been so large a loser, he was soon lost in the wild delirium of play!

Reckless whether he won or lost, but playing on with a desperation that must soon have reduced him to beggery, Herbert shouted, drunk, and laughed, and staked large sums one after another, with a desperation which surprised even the oldest frequenters of the place.

Men of honour, as the world goes, were occasionally to be found in that haunt of iniquity, and one of these, a naval officer, touched Herbert slightly on the shoulder, saying—

"My dear friend, you are playing a random game."

"Well, sir?" cried Herbert, not in the politest tone.

The other smiled as he replied,

"Your object is to drown some disagreeable thoughts I can easily see. Do you really know what it is costing you?"

"Your impertinent interference will cost you something," said Herbert, in reply to this civility, but his mind was in no state to enable him to act rationally.

The gentleman slightly smiled, and with a scarcely perceptible shrug of the shoulders, turned upon his heels; and there the matter would have ended, had not Mandeville, in the wild excitement of the moment, caught up a glass of wine and thrown it full in the face of his kind monitor.

The reply to this consisted in a knock down blow, which upset Herbert, chair and all.

Further conflict was of course instantly prevented by the proprietors of the house and the company, who were equally interested in the suppression of any brawls in the establishment.

This little interlude had the effect only of sobering Herbert, so far as to make him more rationally, or rather more determinedly obstinate, and he loudly exclaimed—

"Your card, sir—your card. Let me know that I am quarrelling with a gentleman."

"Everybody here but yourself, I dare say, knows me well enough," said his opponent, "and you shall not be long without that information if you are worth powder and shot. I am Captain Meriton, of his Majesty's navy. Now, sir, who may you be?"

Herbert threw down his card.

"Humph!" said Captain Meriton; "the son, I presume, of Mr. Cuthbert Mandeville? Young man, I have heard something of your mode of life. Let me advise you, as one who knew your father slightly, to avoid your own temper."

"You shall hear from me in an hour,' said Mandeville, haughtily.

"No—no," said Captain Meriton. "Nonsense—no challenge need come of this."

"You are a coward, sir!" cried Herbert.

Captain Meriton put on his hat, and turning to Herbert, he said calmly,—

"Young man, I am now going home ; there is my address."

So saying, he flung his card in Mandeville's face, and left the room instantly.

Few persons in the rank of life of Herbert Mandeville are without those convenient friends who are ever ready to see their dearest intimates shot according to rule, and one of these the headstrong and excited Herbert found to carry a hostile message to Captain Meriton. By some strange process of mind Herbert concentrated all his hoarded up dislikes, hatred, and revenge against everybody upon this gentleman, Captain Meriton, who had only offended him by endeavouring to do him a kindness.

He waited most impatiently for the return of his good friend who carried the message, and when he came back, to say that everything was arranged for a meeting at seven o'clock the next morning, Mandeville felt a degree of excited pleasure that even gaming had failed to give him.

The probability that in the coming encounter he might lose his life, never occurred to him. He kept only repeating to himself, "how dared he interfere with me?"

Nor did another circumstance which occurred in the course of the day affect him greatly, for his mind was in such a whirl of excitement, that it could scarcely be considered that the events of existence made this due impression upon his mind.

That circumstance consisted in the receipt of the following polite epistle :—

"Lincoln's Inn.

"Sir,—We are instructed by our client, Mr. Peter Augustus Delancey, to proceed forthwith against you for criminal conversation with his, the aforesaid Mr. Peter Augustus Delancey, our client's wife, and we hereby give you notice in due course of proceeding, that the said action at law, for the recovery of certain damages, estimated at eight thousand pounds sterling, on and for the aforesaid crim. con. will be commenced, and *de facto* is commenced, and herewith we, on behalf of our client, mentioned in these presents, do hereby serve you with notice *pro forma*, of the said action, and request the name and residence of your legal adviser or legal advisers, as the case may be.

"We are, Sir,
"Your most obedient servants,
"SNAFFLE and SQUASHTOTTLE.
"Attornies."

"To Herbert Mandeville, Esq."

"Snaffle and Squashtottle be ——!" was Herbert's polite and expressive ejaculation, as he finished this epistle. "I must try and get some sleep now before morning."

So saying, without undressing, he threw himself on a couch, and from pure exhaustion of mind and body, he fell into a sound sleep, which lasted until six o'clock the following morning, at which hour he was roused by a servant who told him that the Honourable George Fungi insisted upon seeing him.

"Tell him to go to the devil," said Herbert.

The servant went with the message, which the Honourable George Fungi considered a very extraordinary one, seeing that he was the obliging friend who had arranged the duel, and was to stand second to Herbert on the occasion, all of which for the moment Mandeville had entirely forgotten.

"Is your master awake?" was the question of the honourable.

"Scarcely, sir," replied the servant.

"Oh, very well; I must see him, so I wont trouble you again. Where is he?"

Herbert's voice at this moment was heard on the staircase, shouting :—

"Fungi, I beg your pardon ;—walk up."

The honourable gentleman accordingly did walk up, and was quite satisfied with Herbert's explanation that he was half asleep when the servant first announced him.

There was no time to lose, and in about ten minutes more Herbert and his obliging friend started for the scene of a deadly encounter, which could not possibly have arisen in a more frivolous manner.

The captain and a friend were there already; the ground was measured with all due formality, but few words were spoken. The pistols were loaded and handed to the principals. A handkerchief was dropped as the signal to fire.

The report echoed among the trees that grew close about the spot. The slight puff of smoke cleared away.

"Are you touched?" cried the Honourable George Fungi to Herbert.

"No," he replied. "I am unhurt."

"Captain Meriton is dead !" said his second, advancing.

"Dead?" cried Mandeville.

"Quite dead! Your pistol ball is in his brain." Every object seemed to swim before Herbert. While a film was suddenly lifted from before his mental vision, his physical one could descry nothing, and with a groan of deep anguish, he dropped insensible upon the green turf at his feet.

CHAPTER XCVII.

"They said she of consumption died,
But there was one who knelt
Her weary couch of pain beside,
A darker influence felt."

BAYLEY.

THE CHAMBER OF THE DYING GIRL.—THE REQUEST.—LESLIE'S GRIEF.—EFFORTS
TO AMUSE AND SOOTHE THE SUFFERER.

ADELINE'S strength was decreasing day by day, although the bright colour was deepening upon her cheeks. Alas! how deceptive was that fleeting glow which settled on the fair face of the young and beautiful. The curate saw it with anguish, and except when in the company of Adeline, the noble heart of Leslie gave way to the deep emotions which wrung it to its inmost core, and he would weep tears of such intense agony and frantic grief, that in a few short days it seemed as if ten years at least had been added to his age.

He was sitting alone and sorrowful one evening, in the curate's study, when Mrs. Plumpjoy came to tell him that Adeline wished to see him.

He started up, and calming his feelings as he was wont to do when about to see Adeline, he sought the chamber from which she had not now stirred for some time.

"Charles," she said, "I am so troublesome to you, that—that—"

"You are not, Adeline," he replied. "Could I but see you as—as I fondly hope to see you—once more well—"

His voice faltered as he gave utterance to the delusive hope, and he was compelled to pause, in order to conquer the agitation of his feelings.

Adeline shook her head mournfully, as she said :—

"Alas, Charles! it was not of living that I begged for you to come to speak to me about, but—but—of dying !"

Nay, Adeline, indulge not in such gloomy fancies."

"Do not strive to cheat me with a false hope," said Adeline. "I have a request to make to you, Charles."

"Dear Adeline, make no requests which tend to indulge a thought but of your health and happiness. Rather let me amuse your mind by reading to you some romance of love and joy, based upon principles and rectitude, or some tale of unmerited suffering, ending at last in the poetical justice which is ever so pleasing to the feelings."

"Your reading to me, Charles," said Adeline, "is now the last charm which binds me to life; but hear me first. Will you promise me—when—I am gone—to—let *him* know?"

"Herbert Mandeville?"

"Yes; take him the news that I am no more, and with it some kind words in case he should feel more keenly than I wish."

"No more, Adeline, no more," cried Leslie. "Each word you speak wrings my heart."

"You will promise me, Charles?"

"As Heaven is my judge, I will do your bidding."

She stretched out her wasted hand and clasped his with the long taper fingers, while a grateful smile lit up her angel's face. For a short time then there was a silence, which, however, was broken by Adeline, saying, in a low voice,—

"Will you read me a tale, Charles, that the curate has borrowed to amuse me?"

"With pleasure, Adeline."

She pointed to a manuscript which lay on a small table, and Leslie read in his rich musical voice the following brief tale :—

"On the border of a wild heath, where the furze, with its ever-lively blossoms and bright green thorns gives a cheerfulness to   otherwise desolate

No. 42

and solitary aspect, stood, some years since, a house long celebrated as the residence of Ralph Downing.

"Behind the cottage rose a solemn forest of pines, whose peculiarly mournful moan as the wind passed over them, rendered the gloom, which ever prevailed within the wood, at once awful and melancholy. In the minds of the people for miles around, it had gained a reputation which heightened its naturally gloomy aspect in no ordinary degree; it was associated in their imagination with many a horrible tale of departed spirits, still at certain times doomed to expiate their crimes, or sooth their sorrows, by a visitation to the scene of their wicked or unhappy fates.

" Doubtless some real event had been the source of these imaginary terrors; some dreadful tragedy in ages long since passed away, of which the tradition, altered, exaggerated, and combined with these supernatural horrors, was all the history remaining.

" Perhaps these dismal traditions had their origin within the walls of a priory, whose ruins still sufficed as a monument of one of those magnificent sources of crime and devotion, of charity and oppression. This building had no doubt been originally situated at the border of the wood, but two or three thick chumps of oak and other forest trees and underwood, had almost concealed the ruins from observation. Thus this place was rendered a most fitting scene of the event which, as we shall have occasion to show, soon after occurred.

" The house we have alluded to had been the farm-house, but every vestige of such a mode of employing it had ceased to exist, and it merely appeared from the outside a large, old-fashioned, though very neat residence, fit for a gentleman of moderate income. The woodbine strewing its sweet leaves over the trellis which formed a porch; the carefully-tended little garden in the front, a few choice flowers in the windows, all indicated the abode of some one besides the stern, plain man who was its ostensible tenant. This being, whose presence threw such a grace into the aspect of this gloomy residence, was Catherine, the daughter of the recluse, eccentric Ralph Downing.

" She was about nineteen, and to the naturally sweet expression of her brilliant countenance, was added such a look of intelligence as would surprise those who found such a being in such a solitary wilderness.

" Ralph Downing was apparently about middle age, his aspect was cold, stern, and repulsive, yet those who occasionally met him in his rambles, always found him obliging as far as their need required. This civility was sometimes tested by a stray traveller who missed his way in the wild neighbourhood around, and his readiness to show the right path, might be called courteous, yet his manner was evidently intended to check all intrusion into the privacy of his life. All that was known of him was the uniform pattern of his dress, and the manner of a man whose mind was cultivated. When he saw a stranger he always endeavoured to avoid him.

" Many and various were the causes assigned by the rustics around for this singular disposition. Some supposed that nothing but an early sorrow could prevail upon a man to give up the world as he did, others more gravely, stated their belief that his conscience must have been troubled by some shocking crime, but the real truth was known only to few.

" Ralph Downing was the son of a gentleman who had a small landed estate, and died soon after Ralph came of age, leaving him and one daughter only; his wife died some years before. Ralph looked upon his sister with such affection, as they only, who are happy enough to feel, will generally believe. Every arrangement that could be made to please his younger sister was made, and no pleasure was equal to the delight he felt in her society. But his sister, Matilda, unhappily for Ralph, saw a young lieutenant, who was shortly to sail for India. They became passionately attached, and in spite of Ralph's remonstrances, Matilda eloped with Lieutenant Henry Trevor just as the ship was about to sail. Ralph's anger and sorrow at the discovery were unbounded, he immediately set out for the coast where the ship was lying, but only arrived in time to see her sails upon the horizon. He returned to his solitary home sad and dejected with melancholy forebodings that he should see his beloved Matilda no more.

"But grief is generally alleviated by the soothing wing of time. Ralph found another affection occupying the void occasioned by his sister's departure, in a lovely young being, who, softened by his sorrows, loved him deeply. His affection for her was deep and manly, and in a short time they were married.

"Their married life surpassed, in its enjoyments, all that he had anticipated, but alas! sorrow was his lot, for in giving birth to her first-born, his beloved Catherine, the wife of his bosom, was taken from him.

"Soon after this heavy stroke, tidings arrived of the total wreck of the ship which conveyed his sister Matilda.

"These were the causes of his solitary life. His feelings were not so much of disgust with the world as of fear of it. He dared not run the risk of a continuation of such bereavements. His affections were blighted hopelessly. He sold his paternal estate and left it, to take up his abode in the place we have described, intending to devote his whole care upon the cultivation of his beloved infant's heart and mind, and, we have seen, that so far his desire was accomplished.

"His own stores of knowledge were laid out before Catherine at a very early age, and seeing little to distract her from these subjects, her progress was rapid. Her father had also instilled into her mind th rudiments of music, and taking deep delight in this beyond all her other amusements, she became a very excellent player. But the great charm of her performance was the exquisite feeling which prevaded all. Her father would listen for hours buried in thought, only giving way to an irresistible flood of tears, as some sweet melody would recal the memory of some past scene of elevated enjoyment.

"Thus their lives glided on without any desire or any prospect of alteration. The rich and varied conversation of Ralph was change enough for Catherine, while attendance upon him, soothing his melancholy, and delighting him with her accomplishments, afforded sufficient play for her affections.

"But while all was so peaceful and virtuous here, the town about three miles distant, was the scene of a dreadful commotion. A young woman had been missed from her home, and hitherto all search for her had proved ineffectual. She had been attached to a young man of respectable connexions but of loose character, but he was taken very ill on the night when she was missed, so that no suspicion fell on him; and in further confirmation of his innocence, he had been away from the town for some time, and did not return until the next morning.

"The sufferer was young and a general favourite, and consequently public sympathy was highly excited, and great was the popular indignation against the unknown murderer, for it was at once concluded that such was her end.

"She had been seen alone on the night when she was missed, in the road between the town and the wood, but although diligent search was made, no trace could be discovered. At length a deputation of officers and others waited upon Ralph to request his guidance among the intricacies of the wood. He consented with the utmost readiness, and led them along paths, perhaps unknown to any but himself and his dogs. They wandered among the gloomy ruins in every conceivable direction, but without success, and were on the point of relinquishing their search, imagining that some other fate had befallen her, when a sudden bark of one of Ralph's dogs indicated some discovery.

"All hastened to the spot, and there, concealed by the luxuriant foliage of the overshadowing ivy, lay the mangled remains of the unhappy woman.

" Her death had evidently been occasioned by heavy blows, and the bruises and torn garments, and disordered hair, all told that a fearful struggle had taken place ere she gave up her life.

" A jury was instantly summoned, who immediately gave an unanimous verdict of wilful murder against some person unknown.

" Who could be the wretch to attack *her?* what could be the motive, being poor, having, as far as the world knew, no enemies? It must have been some stranger who imagined that she had wealth, or mistook her for some other person.

" But the minds of the excited townspeople were soon relieved of their surprise, for a stranger, dressed in sailor's clothing, resting at an inn, the next day was observed to be in possession of a handkerchief marked with her name, for he had just gone from the house and left the handkerchief behind him, when the name was instantly discovered and recognised, and a body of constables and others were immediately sent in quest of him. He had not proceeded far along the road, when he was overtaken and assailed with the most violent imprecations.

" He was a handsome young man. His face showed plainly that he had been in other climes ; but the open manly countenance could scarcely be supposed by any but those whose discernment was blinded by their eagerness to punish, to be that of a murderer.

" Besides, there was in his behaviour a certain degree of refinement which showed that he was a gentleman, while frankness and benevolence were beyond dispute essentials of his character.

" But the excited eager crowd had their minds so prepossessed with the idea of his having the handkerchief, that they hesitated not one moment to take him before a magistrate, with the full assurance of his guilt.

" The general panic had extended even to this solemn dispenser of law and justice. After hastily congratulating the officers upon their success, he turned to the young man :—

" ' Well, prisoner,' said he, very gravely, ' this very dark evidence of your concern in this awful matter, has in the minds of those who are now assembled, stamped you as the destroyer. How come you into possession of this handkerchief?'

" ' I found it in the road about a mile from the wood.'

" ' Did any one see you pick it up?'

" ' No, I was alone.'

" The magistrate looked towards the constables, whose countenances reflected the incredulity of the crowd, who only cried out :—

" ' Oh ! the outlandish liar !'

" The prisoner was requested to give some account of his purpose in coming to this part of the country, his name and station. To this he replied in an indignant proud tone, evidently astonished at the cause which had brought him hither :—

" ' My name, sir, is Richard Trevor.' (Ralph had in this instance thrown off his usual reserve, and was present. At the mention of the name of Trevor he started.)

" ' I am now in search of a relation of my late father, who was an indigo planter in Bengal. The ship in which I have just arrived from India is now in the Downs, and my mother is now at Portsmouth awaiting my inquiries. She once had a brother living in these parts, but he has been dead some years.'

" ' At what time of the day did you find this handkerchief?'

" ' About four in the morning.'

" The deceased was missed in the course of that night.

" ' No honest gentleman, as you profess yourself to be, would be walking at that hour.'

" A murmur of applause from the crowd signified their assent to this assertion.

" ' I always rise with the sun, in order to walk in the cool morning.'

" ' These are very pretty excuses, young man, but I am afraid a jury will not consider you justified by them ; the whole tale is very improbable, and I must commit you for trial.   Constable, take care of the prisoner.'

" ' But will you not send to my ship to know the truth of what I state ?'

" ' No, no, we have heard quite enough.'

" Trevor here became very angry, but seeing no effect likely to arise from resistance, at length quietly submitted.

" He was accordingly thrust ignominiously into the gaol, there to await his trial.

" The emotion which Ralph felt at the mention of his sister's name, almost subsided at the recital of the farther particulars which he mentioned, and he reasoned within himself that the young man would have uttered something respecting him, if he had been any descendant of his lost sister.   Yet he could not entirely shake off the impression the name had made upon his mind, and thinking that the evidence against the prisoner was forced, he felt some interest in his case.   Ralph was much pleased with his manner too ; to his calm and discerning scrutiny he presented none of the appearances of a guilty man ; yet he saw the dangerous position in which he was placed.   His passing the border of the wood within so short a time of the murder, and at such an un-usual hour, and the very handkerchief in his possession.

" All these things Ralph saw were, as the law was then administered, quite enough to convince a jury that it was their duty to inflict the punishment of death.

" To the prisoner's urgent request to the magistrate to send to the coast to ascertain the truth of his statements, no reply was deigned, further than that the matter must be considered by the jury.

" When Ralph returned home he related the examination to Catherine, who deeply sympathised with Trevor, but she scarcely dared to urge her father to seek an interview with him, knowing how greatly anything relative to his lost sister agitated her father, even at this great distance of time.   Yet her heart glowed with the idea of the rapture he would feel were he only to discover some authentic account of Matilda's end.

" ' Perhaps, dear father, you might prevail upon the squire to consent to send a messenger to the place where the young man wishes, and if you were to save an innocent man, how delightful a reward for your efforts.'

" ' I know the squire better than you do, love,' said he ; ' when he de-termines, neither reason nor anything short of truth, will alter his intention.'

" ' But they will not allow him to hold any intercourse with those whom he says he is seeking.   This seems very hard.   Do go to him, father, and at least your opinion would have weight with the jury.   Besides, such a person as you say the prisoner is, cannot be a murderer.'

" ' Well, my dear Catherine, it does appear almost a duty at least to let him be heard.   But bless your innocent charitable heart, you forget that

" **Man when smoothest he appears,**
Is most to be suspected."

" ' But, dear father, whether he be innocent or not, you say he aught not to be committed on such slight evidence.'

" Thus they argued, until at length Ralph overcome his repugnance to move forward, and resolved to visit the prisoner in the morning.

" Accordingly he set off, and having gained the magistrate's consent, was introduced to Trevor, who, deeply dejected, sat overwhelmed with sorrow, pre-senting a painful contrast to his appearance when Ralph first saw him.

"Ralph's heart was touched, and he addressed the young man in a cautious tone.

"Hearing a voice, which seemed to speak sympathy, he looked up with a momentary flush of pleasure across his sorrowful countenance.

"'Young man,' said Downing, 'I do not presume to pass a judgment upon your guilt or innocence, but I deem it right that you should have a full hearing, and that no feelings should warp the opinions of those men who will shortly be your judges. If you think proper to confide in me, I will undertake that your case shall be properly heard.'

"'Generous man!' exclaimed Trevor; 'would that the magistrate who has thus degraded me, had your sentiments. I am a stranger,—I was never in this country before—I know nothing of your manners, and because I happen to be in the immediate scene of a crime so horrible, as scarcely to be thought of, am charged with it. But,' said he, checking his feelings, 'I will not intrude upon your patience, yet to make you acquainted with the reason of my being in these parts, I must acquaint you with my history. My father was an indigo planter, and died a few months before I left India. Some property which he has bequeathed, has been for many years unduly withheld by some distant relatives named Norman, living, as my mother informed me, near this place, and in hopes of discovering these who so wronged my father, I am come over. My profession, as you may perceive by my dress, is that of a sailor; but now, as my dear mother is alone, I intend to settle on land, and take care of the estates that she will come into possession of. I travelled post until I arrived within about twenty miles of this, when the loveliness of the scenery induced me to proceed on foot. Wayworn, dusty, and with very little in my pocket, it was quite natural that I should be taken as a vagabond. Oh! could I but see my poor mother!—What will be her feelings at my continued absence?'

"'I must confess that such a tale has the appearance of an invention, although God forbid that I should judge you. You say you are wealthy, but here you are found with all outward semblance of a poor wanderer. You state yourself to be in search of people who nobody knows anything of, yet I have reason to believe you, and I will personally make the necessary inquiries. For the present, farewell. You shall see me on my return.'

"Ralph left the prisoner, overwhelmed with gratitude at the generous offer he had made to assist him.

"When he arrived at home, Catherine observed an unusual animation about her father's behaviour. Why should he take so warm an interest in this young man's case? many instances of oppression had occurred under the jurisdiction of the same magistrate, which he had taken no notice of. Surely the mere name, without any connexion with them, could not be the cause? yet this was the secret of his enthusiasm, and although he was quite satisfied that his sister had been lost in the wreck, his energies had been aroused, and he would go through the whole matter.

"'Should you not like to see our sea coast, Catherine?' said he to her. 'I think a little journey would be very beneficial to you.'

"'If you go, father, I should like it dearly.'

"It was soon arranged, and Catherine, with all diligence, prepared for departure on the morrow. They set off in a post-chaise, expecting to reach Portsmouth that evening.

"Meanwhile we will return to Trevor in prison. The distant relative of his father was in existence, but the name of Norman was extinct. The last of the name was a female, who had married the father of William Hartwood, the young man who was the professed lover of the young woman who had just been murdered. Yet he had always lived on the same property, and his father before him, as long as any one in the town could remember. But

Hartwood was too ill to have any communication, and the selection of such a person only seemed to throw more suspicion upon the prisoner that his tale was a false one.

" The time for the return of the travellers had now arrived, yet they came not. Judge of the miserable Trevor's horror when day after day passed on, and no tidings arrived. He was quite altered in appearance ; he had become thin, pale, and weak, and lamented incessantly his separation from his mother. His importunity that inquiry should be made respecting his ship, and the truth of his story, made the authorities at length consent to send a messenger to Portsmouth. The messenger returned, and said the ship had sailed the day before, on a cruise. His misery now was unbounded, for although a lady had been at the inn, no such person could now be found.

" The time for the trial had now arrived. These repeated assertions of Trevor all having been groundless, had exasperated the popular indignation against him still more. No other murderer was discovered ; no suspicion fell on any one else ; and it was tolerably certain what would be the verdict of the jury. The atrocity of the case, sympathy with the deceased, who was generally beloved, the recent occurrence of the sad event, all conspired to render the trial one of surpassing interest.

" The unhappy prisoner had calmly resigned himself to the strange concurrence of circumstances. He looked intensely dejected, but still his noble, manly figure, though somewhat attenuated, commanded great admiration as he walked solemnly towards that part of the court appropriated to him. ' How sad to think that *he* should be a murderer !' said some. ' See how remorse has prayed upon his countenance !' said others. While some gravely moralised upon giving way to unlawful passion.

" The evidence was little more than that given before the magistrate, yet to the jury that was convincing. Poor Trevor was called upon for his defence, but he had nothing now to offer. When it was mentioned that Ralph Downing had taken a journey for the very purpose of investigating the affair, some of the jury thought it of very little consequence to regard the opinions of so whimsical a person as he was declared to be, and further, why did he not come back ? Doubtless something had shewn him that the whole defence was a fabrication, and disgusted with the affair, he had determined to have no more to do with it. Whatever might be the cause, he came not.

" The trial was a short one ;—Trevor had no witnesses, and the jury soon agreed upon a verdict of ' Guilty.'

" The last awful sentence was passed, and scarcely believing that he existed, the prisoner was taken back to his dungeon, with feelings such as no language can paint. He had left his mother alone at Portsmouth,—she must be distracted at his absence, and with her weak frame, how dreadful would be the effect of the tidings upon her. Oh, that Ralph Downing would return to relieve the suspense which well nigh drove him to despair. Not even the consciousness of his innocence could support him against the distressing tumult of his emotions.

" The long-continued absence of Downing and Catherine had by this time excited surprise among those who knew the object of his journey, for although his behaviour could not frequently be understood, no one doubted that whatever he took in hand he would persevere in to the end ; no obstacle ever hindered him from doing what he had determined. Four days had now elapsed beyond the period when they should have returned. They had travelled post haste to Portsmouth, when they found that Mrs. Trevor was at the inn her son had mentioned, but not expecting her son to return for a few days, had determined to make an excursion round the Isle of Wight, in hopes of deriving benefit to her health, and she had given no direction which route she would take.

" Ralph and his daughter immediately crossed to the lovely little island, where their anxiety to discover Mrs. Trevor could not render them insensible to its romantic beauties. They sought in vain for the lady for two days, when they discovered that she had gone to Southampton; here they arrived just in time to discover that she had returned to Portsmouth. Catherine then greatly needing rest, they stayed here one night, and arriving at Portsmouth, their disappointment was excessive to find that she had left finally; the waiter did not know whither. But upon close inquiry of the other servants, they were informed that the lady in looking over the newspaper was suddenly taken ill; no one could tell why; and as soon as she was a very little recovered, she determined to leave the inn in a moment by the London coach, which had not long gone.

"It seemed as if Downing's benevolent purpose was to be defeated. Yet he felt some gratification at finding such a lady as Trevor had described. He begged to see the newspaper which had so powerfully affected her, when he was almost as much agitated to see an account of the trial and dreadful sentence of the young man for whom he felt so strong an interest. This seemed, however, to Ralph to establish the truth of Trevor's description, that the lady was his mother. He immediately ordered a post-chaise and four, offering the men a reward for their efforts to make all possible speed.

" Travelling as they did, they overtook the heavy coach at about three stages on the road, and among the passengers who had just alighted, they found a lady whose grief and agitation appeared to have reduced her to the utmost state of debility. Two maid-servants were supporting her, while the hostess was entreating her not to proceed until she had taken some rest, and had medical attendance; but the lady appeared regardless of all their prudential remonstrances, and only desired to be so far strengthened as to pursue her journey. Ralph did not see her face, but desired Catherine to offer the post-chaise, saying that he would ride on the box, for the lady would not listen to any proposal for delay.

" The coach accordingly went on, and the lady was assisted into the chaise, and Ralph seeing that it was impossible to have any conversation at present, took his station outside, while Catherine supported the invalid. A few hours brought them to the end of their journey, when the invalid was thoroughly exhausted, and swooned away so often and so long that her life was despaired of. Ralph was immediately setting out to make inquiries at the prison, when a tremendous uproar was heard in the street. Looking out, he saw a great crowd coming with branches and flags, surrounding several gentlemen in an open carriage. Ralph wished that they had chosen some other scene for their rejoicing, for they blocked up the road in which was his way to the prison, and in his anxious frame of mind, sympathising with the suffering mother and the melancholy prisoner, he was little disposed for noisy mirth.

" He thought, as the carriage drew nearer, he recognised in one gentleman a form which he had seen before; but judge of his astonishment when he plainly saw that Trevor was the object of all this outrageous joy. Their eyes met, and in a moment Trevor was embracing him who singly had been his friend, and the means of his deliverance.

" But before we inform the reader of what took place upon the meeting of the mother and son, we must explain how this sudden reverse originated.

Ralph had previously to his departure induced a party of men, by liberal promises, to overcome their horror of the haunted wood (rendered doubly horrible in their imaginations by the melancholy murder which had just occurred), and to examine every part of the awful ruins for some farther clue to the perpetrator of the dreadful deed. Some of his own servants accompanied the party, and it was not long before they picked up a pocket-book, containing some memorandums dated the evening of the day on which the poor girl was murdered. A waste leaf or two of other books and some fragments of cloth-

ing were all found together, which seemed to indicate that the memorandum-book had fallen from the pocket of the murderer during the struggle. But there was no name on any of the things. The writing did not correspond at all with that of Trevor. It was a peculiar hand, and was soon identified with that of Hartwood, the man who had pretended to love the deceased. He was still very ill, but the book was identified by his servant. The vengeance of the populace seemed now likely to be directed to him. He was told of the discovery, when assuming a look of the utmost horror his troubled conscience could not withhold a full confession, even to the most minute circumstances. The handkerchief which Trevor had so unfortunately picked up, Hartwood had purposely dropped, hoping that it would be found, and thus divert suspicion from him. Having made this confession, he fell back quite exhausted. As he could not be removed, he was watched at home until he should be so far recovered as to occupy Trevor's place.

"At the moment when Ralph encountered Trevor's triumphal procession he had just been liberated, and when it was discovered that he was what he professed, high and low, rich and poor, endeavoured to do him honour.

"Let us now return to the inn where we left our invalid Mrs. Trevor and the happy party. In a short time she recovered sufficiently to receive her son, who then introduced Ralph as his preserver from death and infamy.

"'And I should certainly never have sustained the journey but for my dear young friend here,' said Mrs. Trevor, pointing to Catherine.

"Trevor's gratitude was too strong for utterance. All this time Ralph stared at the face of Mrs. Trevor, as though he saw one who had risen from the tomb, too agitated to express his thoughts. Mrs. T. had not yet heard his name, but a servant coming with a message, mentioned it.

"'My lost brother,' said she, overcome by the discovery.

"Poor Ralph could only reply by wild caresses; it was his long lost sister

No. 43

—she in whom he once found all his pleasure, and for whom his heart had so many years retained the energy of his love. The vessel in which Matilda embarked with her husband was indeed wrecked; but they were saved on some logs. By degrees Mr. Trevor attained a large estate, and dying, left it to his son and widow. As the health of the latter was failing, she had determined to spend the remainder of her days in England. She had been informed of her brother's death, and as he had so completely hidden himself, it was not known where to send letters which she wrote to him, and, therefore, receiving no reply, believed the report, and considered him for ever lost.

"As might naturally be expected, the introduction of Catherine and Trevor under such circumstances, with hearts warm with mutual gratitude, and uncorrupted by the contamination of the world, soon rendered their hearts still warmer with another feeling. When Trevor visited the romantic abode of his uncle, Ralph Downing, he found everywhere traces of the elegance of Catherine's pursuits and the elevation of her soul, and as they were immediately one in heart and mind, before many months had elapsed they were in name also.

"But we are anticipating. The poor unhappy wretch Hartwood, was taken to the prison where Trevor was liberated, and then appeared his motive for the dreadful deed. The poor girl's master had been employed to nurse the elder Hartwood, during his last illness. He had said something about the destruction of a deed which was the only means Trevor's family had to prove their right to a certain estate. This estate it was which Trevor had come to England to seek at her master's death, the poor girl was the only one who knew of the elder Hartwood's villainy. His son came into possession of the estate, refusing his penitent dying father's request to restore it to the rightful owner. The deceased had often urged him to relinquish it, she said she could live happy with him in a cottage, but never in possession of that. At length, fear of disgrace from her betrayal of the secret, exasperated him to determine upon her destruction. How awfully was this crime avenged. After he had gone through the few necessary formalities to put Trevor in possession of the property, he became frantic with despair and remorse. By turns he cursed, he shrieked and wept, as if suffering a foretaste of his eternal doom. The man employed in his cell to watch that he did not commit self-destruction, hearing a longer pause between his imprecations and groans, looked round and beheld his eyes starting from their orbits, and his face of a livid hue, his hand clenched with convulsive force upon his throat, told how the murderer had died.

"Ralph was never weary of listening to his sister's adventures, and she found her health and energy rapidly return in the pure air of that lovely retreat. By and by, as little ones began to gambol around, he became quite an altered man, and his memory is now held in veneration, as one of the most tender-hearted and social, as well as the most inflexibly just of men."

*   *   *   *   *   *

Leslie ceased reading, and Adeline thanked him with a quiet, beaming smile.

"Sleep now, dear Adeline," he said. "Let imagination exert her most benificent sway over your mind, and lose, in a world of dreamy romance, the remembrance of sorrow."

"I will, Charles, I will," she said, faintly.

Leslie took up the small, delicate hand that lay upon the table, and pressed it to his lips; then, suddenly starting, as if he had allowed himself too much happiness, he left the room, and Adeline closed her beautiful eyes in sleep.

May the angels of peace and love watch over and guard her slumbers!

CHAPTER XCVIII.

"The law is like a homely gentlewoman,
Better to follow than to meet."

HERBERT IN A SEA OF TROUBLES.—A CONSULTATION WITH A LEGAL ADVISER.
—CANDID ADVICE, AND A TRIP TO THE CONTINENT.

WE left Herbert Mandeville in no very enviable frame of mind; and when, after all that had occurred, he shut himself up in his study, and felt the necessity of a little thought upon his situation and prospects, he could not but tremble at the possible, if not probable, consequences of his acts for the last month. All thoughts of Adeline were agonising in the extreme, and his great effort, in his mental ruminations, was to banish her constantly-recurring visage from his mind. Oh! what an agony is thought, when there is no one point in all our mental retrospections upon which the mind can rest with pleasure. If Herbert could have called to mind any one circumstance within the last few fleeting weeks concerning which he could conscientiously say,—'There at least I was right!' it would have been a gleam of moral sunshine amid the awful gloom in which his mind was steeped—a bright green spot

" In memory's waste."

But, alas! there was no such circumstance: all was wild passion—headstrong folly and vice.

"I cannot, dare not think!" he cried, or, rather, shrieked as he struck his forehead with his clenched hand. "What have I done, that fate should thus make a wreck of me in the early season of my life? Oh! God, what have I not done? What opportunities wasted! What dear happiness have I not cast from me! The curse of blood even is upon my soul! It wanted but that to make me all the wretch I am; and Adeline! Adeline! No—no —I cannot think of her. Let me consider. Is—is—suicide an easy way to oblivion? Is the grave the place of rest that, in its quiet beauty and solemnity, it seems?—or—or—is there really that something after death which paralysed the hand of Hamlet when he would have drunk of the sweet cup of oblivion? Yes—there is—I feel there is. I—I dare not die!—at least, not that way. I will seek some spot, now, on the face of the habitable world, where some contest is going on for justice and freedom. There I will die; and, if my life has been ignoble and bad, my death shall be glorious, and my name shall borrow a lustre from the cause in which I died! It shall be so."

After making this resolution, which, like all the other resolutions of Herbert Mandeville, was doomed to melt away again into thin air, and be no more remembered, he rose with an intention of proceeding to put his affairs in order, for the purpose of carrying out, without delay, what he considered the result of his meditations.

He felt conscious that it might be necessary, and, in fact, highly advantageous, to conceal himself from the consequences of the duel which had terminated so fatally, and the affair in which he was involved with Mr. Delancey likewise required some sort of settlement. All this occurring rapidly to him, he, after some consideration, came to a most erroneous and foolish decision concerning both of them,—that is, he made up his mind not to go and seek the advice of the really respectable firm of solicitors who had been in the confidence of his father, and who were really conscientious persons; but, considering neither of the affairs very creditable, he decided upon seeking the advice of the attorney who, during his minority, had supplied his extravagancies at the trifling interest of one-hundred-and-sixty per cent., and of whom the reader has already heard something, and will probably recollect was named Downshot.

Pulling his hat close over his eyes, and disguising his appearance as much as possible, Herbert accordingly left his house to seek that legal gentleman in his chambers in New Inn.

The chambers of Mr. Downshot were exceedingly dingy and anti-respectable, if we may be allowed to coin such a term. They were situated on the third floor of a very dirty and time-worn house, and altogether presented anything but an appearance of comfort or respectability; but then Mr. Downshot consoled himself every evening, and all day on Sunday, at a country house near Streatham, where he certainly had every luxury, his only drawback being an excessive nervous fear that anybody should find it out, and thence conclude what an enormous rogue he, Downshot, must be to get the means necessary to support it, as the amount of his legitimate legal business was well known to be very small.

Herbert was tolerably well acquainted with the locality of Mr. Downshot's chambers, and, without hesitation, he ascended the ricketty staircase, and knocked at the legal gentleman's door, which was immediately opened by the unhappy boy, whose lot it was to be the fag of Downshot.

"Is Downshot within?" asked Herbert.

"Yes, sir, to you," replied the boy. "Please to walk in, sir; we will attend to you directly."

The fag then proceeded to an inner room, where, after in a confidential whisper, announcing Mandeville's presence, he returned, and requested him to "walk in to Mr. Downshot's private room," which Herbert accordingly did with very little ceremony.

"My dear sir!" exclaimed Downshot. "This most unexpected honour —is—a—a really—it is indeed!"

"Downshot," said Herbert, throwing himself into a chair, "I want advice, not compliments. No nonsense now. I have two very ugly affairs on hand."

"Ugly affairs?" repeated Downshot. "Really—dear me! Are—are they —civil, or—or—a little in the criminal line—eh?"

"A little of both," replied Herbert, "although I am only sure of one."

"Dear me!" ejaculated Downshot. "Jacob!" calling to the fag, "Jacob! I ain't at home, do you hear?"

"Very well, sir," said Jacob.

"Now, my dear sir, go on," said Downshot. "I am all attention to you, and I have only to remark at the offset, that it's a disgrace to a civilized country that a gentleman of your fine property should not be allowed to do just as he likes—I mean without trouble, because we know such is the case in reality. There is a price for everything in this truly great and happy country, Mr. Mandeville, and it's a great comfort there is, or else, my dear sir, what would become of the little recreations of the rich? I see by this morning's paper that our excellent police-magistrate, Timgus, has announced that five pounds is the price of a brutal assault on a female."

"Confound you," cried Herbert, "I never know whether you are in jest or earnest. Hold your tongue, and listen to me."

"My dear sir, go on."

"Firstly, then, I am threatened with an action for running off with a man's wife."

"You—don't—say—so?" remarked Downshot, with great coolness.

"I do say so, though," replied Herbert. "They want eight thousand pounds damages of me."

"Is it—a—hem—a very clear case?"

"Why, I should rather say it was."

"That's the civil business, then?"

"Exactly; and the criminal one is this. I've killed a man."

"In—deed!"

"Yes; l've shot a fellow in a duel."

"That's all, just at present, I presume?" remarked Mr. Downshot, delibe-rately mending a pen.

"And enough too, I think," replied Herbert.

"What's the name in the civil case?"

"Delancey."

"Humph! Delancey v. Mandeville. Damages, eight thousand pounds. Verdict, four thousand. Costs, seven hundred and fifty. Humph."

"Upon my word you settle it remarkably easy, my friend," said Herbert.

"Yes," replied the legal gentleman. "Use is everything."

"Well, then, what do you prognosticate of the criminal case?"

"Coroner's inquest. Verdict, manslaughter—bail—trial put off two or three sessions till nobody cares a bit about it. Verdict, guilty—twelve months imprisonment—application to Secretary of State, representing prisoner to be a gentleman. Fifty pounds to a charity, and a free pardon."

"Oh, that's the way, is it?" said Herbert.

"Precisely. Now what I advise is this. You go to the Continent at once and don't come back till I send for you, and tell you yeu must come. Leave me a cheque for a few hundreds, say six, and I'll manage the whole affair nicely for you, of course, not including the damages in the civil action."

"Your advice," said Herbert, after a few moments' pause, "coincides with my own wishes. I will go to Rome."

"Go to the—a-hem! if you please," said Mr. Downshot, "but your policy I assure you is to go somewhere for a time."

"I have no doubt of it," remarked Mandeville. "I will be off to-day, or to-morrow at the latest."

He then wrote a cheque for six hundred pounds, and handing it to the legal gentleman, added ;—

"I rely upon you, Downshot, altogether in this business. Do your best and you will not find me illiberal."

"Stay a moment," cried Downshot. "Who are the legal advisers of this Delancey?"

"I really forget," said Herbert, "but I will send you their notice of action, together with every particular."

Mr. Downshot bowed very low, and Herbert left the old chambers, certainly somewhat lighter of heart, from the assurances of the attorney (which he ought to have known before) that in England *every crime has its price.*

CHAPTER XCIX.

"A word will make us,
As a word hath marred."

A REVULSION OF FEELING.—A SUDDEN JOURNEY.—DISAPPOINTMENT.

How strange it was that now, when Herbert contemplated leaving his native land for a considerable time, the mere extra condition that he was about to place a large portion of the world between him and Adeline, should wring his half repentant heart in the manner it did ; and it was so, for when after re-turning to his home, he made every domestic arrangement for an immediate departure, he sat down and burst into tears, exclaiming :—

"Adeline! Adeline! I shall never now see you more."

For some time he gave way to the violence of his feelings and wept bitterly; then suddenly he rose and said—

"If I could see her but for a moment, ere I go for ever, perhaps, for something tells me I shall see England no more, it would heal somewhat the wound which now rankles at my heart. Is it yet too late ?" he repeated to himself. "No ; I may still leave to-morrow my native shores, and have time in the interim to visit the spot which contains her, whom I think I really loved, if ever the real passion of love warmed my heart."

He walked to the window, and gazed musingly out for some time. The day was gloomy and overcast. A hollow moaning south wind was gathering up the clouds from the distant horizon in dense masses, and then with furious gusts sweeping them across the Heavens, like dark battalions ready to do battle in some awful strife of nature.

"Nature is congenial to my feelings," said Herbert ; "all is tumult and strife without, and all is agony and indecision here within." He struck his breast as he spoke, and sighed deeply. Then, after a few moments more thought, he turned suddenly from the window, and hastily summoning a servant, he cried,

"My horse ! quick ! my horse."

The domestic, terrified by his master's violence, hastily communicated his orders, and ere five minutes had elapsed, a favourite hunter was ready saddled at the door.

Herbert sprang into the saddle, and just as the first indications of a heavy shower began to show themselves, he gave the rein to the noble steed, and at a gallop started for — Bracefield.

He heeded not the lowering aspect of the Heavens—he heeded not the looks of surprise, with which his headlong speed was regarded. Soon he cleared the city, and its gigantic suburbs, and the hedges began to appear on each side of his road. He relaxed not, however, in his speed, but urging on his horse by voice and action, determined not to pause until he saw the spire of the village church at Bracefield.

The day was now far spent, but Herbert heeded not the rapidly gathering shades of evening, which cast a gloom across his mind. On—on he dashed as if it were for life and death, and but one all engrossing idea possessed his brain ; that being, that by some fatality, he was forced not to relax speed or draw rein till he reached Bracefield. Villages were passed through. Two post towns he galloped recklessly past, and the wide open tract of country which lay between the last collections of houses, worthy the name and the picturesque valley in which Bracefield was situated, lay before him. Still he paused not. The annihilation of the distance between him and the village seemed the sole object that actuated him, and on he dashed, although his panting steed began to show some symptoms of distress at the hard pace he had been kept at since his starting. Herbert's mind was in that state that he heeded nothing but his own sudden and wild desire to proceed at a headlong pace to Bracefield. Hills, or level roads made no difference to him ; still he urged the noble, but wearied animal onwards.

Now they arrived at a turn of the road, which when once passed, would command a distant view of the picturesque ruin where Mrs. Mourdant had received such a shock by the account of her son's crimes—a shock which had sapped the remainder of her feeble existence, and hurried her to the grave.

Mandeville cast his eyes in the direction of the mouldering ruin as a landmark, and he saw it standing out in the black sky, still blacker than the massive clouds, which nearly assimilated with it. He knew now that he had but a few miles to ride, but at the moment he was congratulating himself upon that fact, his horse stumbled, and fell with him to the ground with great violence.

Herbert was fortunate enough to release his hold of the rein, and without pausing to reflect upon any injury he might have sustained, he sprung to his feet and assisted the animal to rise.

It struck him then, for the first time since his starting, that the speed at which he had ridden was more than sufficient to account for the exhaustion of his steed, and notwithstanding the excited state of his own feelings, he patted and caressed for a moment the generous and grateful creature that had brought him so far upon his journey, and after a moment's thought he resolved to proceed the remainder of his way on foot.

With this determination he carefully tied the horse's bridle to a gate-post which stood near, and then started forward by himself a near cut across the fields where there was no bridle path, but which saved a considerable round in the approach to the village.

The rain was falling heavily, and had collected in little pools made by the feet of the cattle in the open fields, so that Herbert's progress across the damp meadows was anything but quick or agreeable. At any other time he would have felt considerable annoyance from his feet continually slipping into holes filled with muddy water, but now he said nothing, no sounds of impatience escaped his lips. He was thinking of Adeline, and what he should say to her should he be enabled to see her.

The fields were at length crossed, and the spire of the church came in sight. Then in a few more anxious moments he reached the humble grave-yard, through which lay his nearest path to the parsonage.

He paused not, but hurrying along the narrow pathway which wound among the rounded mounds of earth marking the last resting-place of many a once warm and glowing heart, he reached the wicket-gate, at which in the young spring-tide of his passion for Adeline, he had once paused to pour into her ears the fond tale of his devotion and his love. The spot recalled the scene too well to his remembrance. Even then, in fancy, he would see the upturned face of the gentle girl as half confidingly, half timidly, she listened to his glowing words. These and other thoughts combined were too agonising, and with a groan of mental anguish, Herbert dashed through the wicket-gate, and made his way direct to the parsonage.

The hour was not late, but the simple habits of the peaceful inhabitants of Bracefield led them to rest at a period of the evening, which in London would but have constituted the selected hour for some appointment of pleasure. Peace was therefore in the village, and it would appear as if the stormy state of the weather which had been so conspicuous in London and its immediate neighbourhood had either greatly subsided or was of a mere local character, extending not so far from the metropolis as Bracefield.

Masses of clouds were certainly drifting across the sky with more than usual speed, but the blue vault of Heaven, sprinkled with its myriads of sparkling stars, could occasionally be seen between the interstices of the moving vapours which were between Heaven and earth. A great deal of rain had evidently fallen, and there was in consequence a cold freshness in the air, which to Herbert's excited and fevered frame was rather welcome than otherwise.

It was not until he came very close to his journey's end that he paused for a moment to try to consider in what precise manner he should make his approach. Well he knew the little chamber in which Adeline usually slept the sleep of guiltless innocence and peace, and after some brief moments' anxious consideration, he resolved to proceed to the back of the house, to which the window of Adeline's room looked, and see if there was or was not a light in her chamber.

He was, of course, well acquainted with the premises, and with a quiet stealthy step he moved around the house until he came to a part of the paling, which he knew was sufficiently low to allow him to pass over without creating any disturbance.

He quickly reached the spot, and vaulting lightly over on to the soft mould of the garden, he once again stood within the premises in which was Adeline!

His heart beat wildly as he cast an anxious and scrutinizing glance up to the house.   There was a light in Adeline's chamber.

With noiseless steps he crossed the garden and stood beneath the little casement.   A low murmuring sound met his ears as if some persons were in anxious conversation.

He listened attentively, and he could after a time detect the voice of Mrs. Plumpjoy.   She was evidently speaking to Adeline, and he heard her say :—

"Now, my dear, it was quite against my brother's advice that I brought you this——"

A deep drawn sigh was Adeline's only reply, and Mrs. Plumpjoy continued :—

" This is an evening paper, you see, my dear, which has been brought us by the mail that passed through the village, and I think, my dear, that such news ought to comfort you in one way, because it ought, you see, to make you rather rejoice at escaping from any permanent connexion with that bad young man."

"Who does she mean?" thought Herbert. "Not me, surely?"

" I will hear it," he heard Adeline say faintly, and the voice thrilled through his veins like an electric shock.

Mrs. Plumpjoy began to read as follows :—

" We present our readers with the authentic and carefully-collected particulars of two events in which one person has been the principal and infamous actor.   That person is a Mr. Herbert Mandeville, a young man of family and fortune."

"Stop, stop," said Adeline ; " I will—hear no more.   Herbert has—not been kind to me—but—I do not wish to hear anything to his prejudice."

To his intense agony Mandeville heard her weeping bitterly.

"Well, my love," said Mrs. Plumpjoy, " I won't read it to you any more. It's all about his killing a man, and running away with somebody's wife. Shocking !—Next comes a horse to be shaved."

" It is not—cannot be true," said Adeline.   " Herbert Mandeville, with all his faults, is not so bad as that.   If he were here, he would say,—'Adeline, that at least is not true.' "

A cold shiver ran through Herbert's frame as he heard these words of trusting confidence from her whose innocent heart he had so cruelly betrayed.

" No—no—no," he gasped.   " I—I could not say that.   No—no—God help me ! I could not!"

With an unsteady gait he slowly retraced his steps across the garden ; then he paused, and turning a last gaze at Adeline's window, he said, with a voice of awful anguish :—

" Farewell, Adeline, for ever ! I dare not look upon your face again !"

In another hour he was galloping to London.

CHAPTER C.

"When the heart knows no joy—no sunshine,
It loves better to look upon nature in strife,
Than decked with loving smiles !"   ANON.

THE ARREST.—AN ESCAPE.—DOVER.—THE PACKET.—A STORM AT DIEPPE AND MANDEVILLE'S MISFORTUNES.

SAD and dispirited, Herbert reached London again.   He threw himself off his tired steed, rather than dismounted, when he gained his own door.   He

knocked for admittance in a listless and dispirited manner, and when the door was opened to him, he staggered rather than walked, into the hall of his stately home.

It was with a feeling of bewilderment that he heard some one address him, and he scarcely caught, or if he did, the meaning of the words did not reach his understanding, and it was not until the person who spoke to him laid a firm grasp upon his arm that he felt himself compelled to pay some degree of attention. Then when he looked at the man, he saw he was a stranger, and he suspected something uncommon had occurred, or was about to occur, by their peculiar and alarmed looks.

"What is the matter?" he then said.

"I beg your pardon, sir," said the strange man, "but I have my duty to do."

"And what is your duty?" said Mandeville. "What have I do with your duty?"

"I have a warrant against you, sir."

"A warrant!"

"Yes, sir. It's quite regular. You are accused of murder, sir, though from all as I hears, it will only turn out a manslaughtering business."

"You are a police officer, then?" said Herbert.

"In course," replied the man; "and humbugging stuff as I think all these here manslaughtering cases, I must take you, you see, sir."

"Take me where?"

"Why, I shall have to lock you up till morning, when in course you'll be committed."

"You have no objection to my sending for my legal adviser?" remarked Herbert.

"I haven't no objection to nothing in a gentlemanly way," said the man

No. 44

looking earnestly into the palm of his own hand, while he held it very close to Mandeville.

"Oh, I understand," said Herbert, and taking several sovereigns from his purse, he placed them in the expectant palm, saying,—

" You can remain here, if you please, while I send a note to my solicitor."

Herbert was then about to ascend the staircase, when the officer interposed, and laying his finger on the side of his nose, he said,—" No, thank ye. Oh, dear no. We never lets prisoners go up stairs. There's so many atties, and attic windows, you see. I ain't no ways in a hurry oh, no. Just write yer note on the ground floor, if you please, sir."

" I presume I must do as you please," said Herbert, as he walked into the room on the ground floor, which was usually devoted to the reception of chance visiters on business.

When Herbert was fairly alone, he threw himself into a chair in an agony of fretful thought.

" So," he thought, " this is to be the end of my career, is it? Adeline, you may hear some day that Herbert Mandeville was arrested in consequence of wasting time which would have placed him in safety, in an attempt to implore your pity and forgiveness! Alas! alas! what can I do now to save myself from disgrace and a prison?"

" Now, sir, if you please!" said the officer, protruding his head within the door.

" In a few moments I shall be ready," cried Herbert. " After all, I cannot do better then send for Downshot; he will do more for me in this most unfortunate dilemma than any one else can."

Mandeville then hastily drew writing materials towards him, and penned a note to the attorney, requesting him to come immediately.

He then rung the bell, and a footman immediately answered the summons.

" Charles," said Herbert, " take this note to——"

A thought came across Herbert's mind like a flash of ligthning at this moment, and he paused a short time, before he added in a low tone :—

" Charles—close the door."

The footman obeyed.

" I believe," continued Herbert, in the same cautious low tone of voice, " you would have no objection to assist me to escape from yon man in the passage?"

" Certainly not, sir," replied the footman, " please to command me, sir."

" First, then," said Herbert, hastily writing a few lines on a slip of paper ; " in case your kindness to your master should involve you in any trouble, here is some recompense."

The footman took the paper, and started with surprise, as he said :—

" Bless us, sir. This is a cheque for a hundred pounds."

" I know it," said Mandeville ; " and now, my good fellow, all I want of you in exchange, are your coat, waistcoat, and cravat. Your shoes too, by the way, I shall require."

The footman looked for a moment astonished, then all at once comprehending his master's meaning, he divested himself in a twinkling of the articles Herbert mentioned.

Rolling up his trousers then, so as very closely to imitate the knee breeches of the man, Mandeville took off his own coat, waistcoat, boots, and cravat, and in a few seconds looked a very smart footman, albeit as he then was in Charles's clothes."

" Now, Charles," said Herbert, " put on my coat and sit down at the table, with your back to the door, and by no means stir or speak till you are forced to do so."

The man did all he was required, and Herbert, taking his own letter in his hand, passed boldly out into the hall.

The officer immediately jumped up from a chair in which he was sitting, but he resumed it again instantly, saying :—

"Oh, it's you, John, is it?"

Herbert made no reply, but walking leisurely to the street door, calmly opened it, stepped across the threshold, and closed it behind him.

Then he felt a flush of pleasure glow in his cheeks at the thought that he had so well and so easily escaped. He walked at a tremendous pace till he came to a wardrobe shop, which he recollected to have noticed in his walks and drives, and entering, he soon equipped himself in less remarkable clothes than a showy livery coat and waistcoat. Then calling a coach, he jumped into it, and told the driver to take him to London Bridge ; when there, he embarked in a wherry to Blackwall, from whence he immediately procured a conveyance to Dover, and by the morning's light, although dreadfully fatigued, he felt delighted at rattling with a good pace into the streets of Dover.

His first question was concerning a packet to the Continent, and he was told, to his great satisfaction, that one was just upon the point of starting for Dieppe. He then lost not a moment, but hurrying down to the pier, got on board as the boat was getting under weigh, and thus, by a train of lucky circumstances, he had not only escaped his captors, but left the shores of England behind him.

There was a peculiar sultriness in the air, which was remarked by all on board, and the captain shewed by his countenance how anxious he was to cross the channel before the storm which he declared to be brewing should burst forth in its fury.

Fortunately the wind was favourable, and the packet ran into Dieppe, after an unprecedently quick passage, just as a few heavy drops of rain began to fall in a menacing manner on her deck.

Herbert was among the first that stepped on shore, and hastily entering the nearest hotel, he inquired if he could have some immediate means of transit to Paris.

"Monsieur might have a horse," he was told, and exchange it *en route* at the places they would name to him.

"Instantly, then, let me have it," said Herbert.

The Frenchman shrugged his shoulders.

"Monsieur might go if he like, but there would be a storm."

Herbert heeded not this prophecy, but mounting the horse that was brought him, and which he was glad to see was a much better animal than he expected, he set off at a round trot through Dieppe.

A rattling peal of thunder smote his ears as he started, but the reader has known Herbert Mandeville long enough to be well aware of that peculiar perseverance which he had upon small occasions, and the only notice that he took of this signal to stop, was to urge his horse to still greater speed.

A storm of no common magnitude was evidently coming on, and if there had been no other indications of its approach than the extreme timidity which began to affect his steed, Herbert should have been warned to seek some shelter from the approaching strife of the elements. He heeded not these indications, however, but pushed recklessly on.

His road wound for a little way along the rugged coast, and then struck inland ; but soon even he, with all his tenacity of purpose, became rather alarmed at the aspect of nature.

In the deep valleys and caverns of the earth a kind of rumbling noise, resembling the continued progression of heavily-laden waggons over a wooden bridge, and acccompanied with sounds of a rushing wind. The cattle on the mountain sides, before so quietly grazing in full security, now began to low and bleat, making the woods resound with plaintive cries, while their restless motions and the trembling of their limbs seemed to convey to them a sense of some unknown pending calamity. The sun, as he sunk into the western sky and took his leave of the closing day, assumed a dark and bloody aspect, while the moon and stars, which now succeeded, shone forth with increased brilliancy, and seemed of more than ordinary size. The wind, which for some time previous had been due east, now shifted suddenly due west; the sky became overcast, and the luminaries of Heaven, before so bright, became enveloped in a halo of mist, and fiery meteors shot with wild impetuosity across the gloom. Again the wind shifted towards the east, and drove before it dense volumes of cloud and vapour, and as it rushed past, encountered another current in the opposite direction, when a violent conflict ensued. The murky clouds were rent by incessant flashes of vivid lightning, which followed in such quick succession, that before the impression of the former had left the eye, its successor met the sight, and caused the scene to appear one sheet of liquid fire; then the clouds, driven by a furious blast, would seem high piled in heavy masses, and then descending to the earth, filled the air with a darkness more impenetrable than the obscurity of midnight. As the demon of the storm expended his awful powers whole tracts of forests were shivered and stripped of their foliage and branches, which were carried forward with the rapidity of the driving blast, while trees of gigantic size were torn up by the roots, and hurled to a great distance. The groves that had so long shaded the mountain precipices were whirled from their natural stations, and large masses of earth and rock were precipitated into the valleys, and choked the rivers in their course.

The storm was now at its height. There were fearful noises in the air and earth; the thunder pealed in awful rounds, rolling from cloud to cloud with majestic grandeur, or suddenly bursting with a violent expression, appeared as though the dissolution of nature were at hand. Whole streams of fire ran along the ground, blasting every vestige of animation in its track, while the howling of the wind might resemble the rolling and screaming of ten thousand demons and beasts of prey, and this mingled with the crash of falling rocks and trees, whirled with distracting fury, rendered the scene a chaos that the highest flight of imagination can scarcely conceive or picture.

The wretched inhabitants, overwhelmed with fear, fled to the caverns for safety, from the devastating scene, for their homes had been carried far distant by the raging blast, and not a vestige of a house remained; or they huddled together in wild dismay beneath some rugged cliff that broke the fury of the tempest, and afforded a temporary shelter. When the hurricane reached the harbour, the vessels that had been for some time at anchor, riding smoothly on the glassy surface of the wave, were now whirled and torn from their moorings; some were driven high and dry upon the land, and their yards and spars borne far away upon the wings of the tempest; others before they could close their ports and hatches, were overwhelmed by the rising surge, and were seen no more, or driven about, dashing upon each other, became mere wrecks upon the shore, while the raging billows rose to an unprecedented height, and rolled with their crested and foaming heads for some miles inland, sweeping and washing away what the fury of the wind had left.

At length the tempest began to moderate, the waters reverted to their former boundary, carrying the wreck of ships, houses, trees, and whole plantations, upon its surface: the wind began to lull, and subsided from a roar to a gentle whistle. In the distance might be heard a confused murmur, which marked the course of the storm; and, as the morn began to break, and the sun to shine upon the devastated scene, no trace of its former appearance met the eye. Where before had been houses, woods, and groves, now were mud, shells, slime, and seaweed interspersed with planks and cordage, and the bodies of those who had been killed in endeavouring to seek a place of shelter. The inhabitants, palsied with fear and horror, regarded each other in mute dismay, as they gazed around, and the mothers clasped their children more closely to their breasts.

Herbert's horse trembled, and then fell with him, [partially stunning his rider, and the first words which the wounded and bewildered fugitive heard when he partially recovered, were,—

"Your passport, Monsieur."

"Passport?" he repeated. "I—I have none."

"Then you are a prisoner."

~~~~~~~~~~~~~~~~~~~~

CHAPTER CI.

"How harsh and full of discords are the tones of love,
When the dear passion lives no more for us."

KNOWLES.

ADELINE'S LAST SIGHS.—THE FORSAKEN HEART TOUCHED DEEPLY.—LESLIE'S FAREWELL.

COULD Adeline have been aware that Herbert Mandeville had heard her trusting words spoken of him in the fullness of her heart, she would have wept for joy to think that he had carried with him to a distant land so pure and unexpected an evidence of that clinging faithfulness, which never leaves such hearts as Adeline's; but such was not to be. Herbert came, and was gone again with an additional wound to his conscience, which, had that mysterious principle of mind been ever so deeply slumbering, must have raised it to all the agony of self-reproach.

She could some time before leave her chamber—now her bed was never deserted. Sometimes the curate would pray with her, and then retire to silence and solitude to shed the tears which he would not let her see dimmed his aged eyes, and belied the patience and resignation which, by precept, he strove to inculcate, but which are, alas! so hard to practise in reality.

There was as much cheerfulness as possible kept around the couch of the dying girl, although almost every heart was bleeding with sorrow that so fair a flower should be so early plucked by the grim and awful destroyer of the young and beautiful.

At least once each day Charles Leslie saw and conversed in gentle and cheerful strains with Adeline; and, although grief was making fearful ravages upon his manly form, and his heart was nearly broken, he suffered no sigh to escape him when with Adeline; but ever addressed her in the calm accents of serious but cheerful hope.

Thus affairs went gloomily and drearily on for some weeks, and Adeline's health, like a waning star, was gradually declining, and sometimes the gentle girl herself would seem, by some mysterious means, to be aware of her approaching departure from the life which is, to that which is to come, and she would point to the silver crescent of the moon as it rose in the calm serenity sometimes of a cloudless sky, and predict that she would never again see it at its full.

Charles Leslie would reason with her on these fancies, and the curate would tell her that life and death were in the hands of God alone, and that it was not for mortals to know or judge of his times and seasons for gathering to himself the pure spirits of the young and innocent.

Adeline then would gently shake her head, and smiling faintly, bid them not to mourn for her when she was gone, but to let her live in their hearts and remembrances as one whom they loved, and who had tasted of the bitter cup of sorrow, until she left a world of woe for one of peace and joy, where she would wait the coming of those she loved to meet by the throne of God, where there would be no tears and no bitter partings.

She would then, with a quiet smile, such as might illumine the face of a slumbering angel, murmur a gentle blessing upon them, and slept for many hours with such sweet calmness and serenity, that no one could have imagined, who was uninformed of her state, that she was so near the portals of death, and that the shadow of the tomb was upon the form of the beautiful girl.

Charles Leslie had now passed a considerable time at the Parsonage, and at length he, with a mournful tone, said to the curate,—

"My dear and best friend, tell me what I ought to do. You know how my heart has ever clung to the spot on which was Adeline ; and—now—when—when——"

He burst into tears, and for some time could not proceed from excess of emotion.

"Charles ; my dear Charles," said the curate in a faltering voice ; " what would you say, that thus blanches your cheek and stirs your feelings ?"

"I was going to say—when she is going from us, but the words nearly choked me. I—I am better now, dear friend, and I can proceed. Pray pardon me this childish grief. There was a time when I did not think it possible that anything could have thus wrung the heart of Charles Leslie, but lately my spirits have flagged, and my heart has become as heavy as stone in my breast, while I, who used to boast of my philosophy, weep like a girl."

"Charles," said the curate ; " your feelings do you honour instead of discredit. In the pride of my heart I thought I had outlived the vehemence of human feelings and passions, and that I had succeeded in schooling my mind to the practice of the patience and resignation it has been my duty for so many years to preach ; but alas ! Charles, I well remember the frantic words of a broken-hearted mother, who was shrieking and wailing for the death of her child, once in the village. When I tried to comfort her and preached to her patience, she turned to me and said,—

"'Mr. Endsleigh, we know you are kind and good to us all and mean us well, but oh, sir, wait till grief crosses your own threshold, and death snatches from you the object you love best on earth, then, sir, preach patience and resignation.'"

The old curate paused, and Charles could see that the tears were in his eyes, for truly had sorrow stopped at his door, and death was tearing from him the young innocent being who had wound herself by truth and gentleness around his heart.

"There is a bitter truth in your words," replied Charles.

"Go on, my dear boy, go on," faltered the old man ; " I am sure you were about to say something of moment when I interrupted you."

"I was about to say," replied Charles Leslie, " that although my feelings were all centered on this spot, there were many circumstances demanding my occasional presence elsewhere."

"Are they duties, Charles ?"

"They are."

"Then they must be fulfilled."

"But how to tear myself from Adeline," cried Leslie ; " I know not."

"My dear Charles," said the curate ; " our greatest difficulty in life is to sacrifice our feelings to our duties. If you feel, which I am sure from your manner you do, that there are things which you ought to be attending to elsewhere, you should go at once and I am sure you will go."

"I have been struggling," said Charles, " with the conviction that I must leave Bracefield for a few days. There are others whose means of existence depend upon me."

"Then go, Charles," said the curate, earnestly. "You know you leave Adeline with those who love her, and will attend to her slightest wish."

"Well I know it, my dear friend," said Leslie; "and now may I ask you if you will tell Adeline, that for three, or it may be four days, I am compelled to leave her?"

"Certainly," said the curate. "When would you wish to go, Charles?"

"Early—very early in the morning."

"Then you had better quietly and calmly, Charles, bid Adeline adieu for a short time. I will go now and break the matter to her."

Charles Leslie looked his thanks more eloquently than he could have spoken them, and the curate, after having left the room for a few moments, returned to say that Adeline would be glad to see him then.

They together repaired to the chamber, and as they were ascending the staircase, Mr. Endsleigh turned and whispered to Charles,

"Let me advise you to be brief. Farewell is ever a mournful sound, Charles, and Adeline is too weak at present to bear an affecting adieu."

"I will subdue my heart," replied Charles.

In another moment they entered the chamber. Mrs. Plumpjoy was sitting by the bed-side of the beautiful and gentle sufferer, and when the curate and Leslie entered the room, Adeline turned her eyes upon the latter and said,—

"Charles, you are going to leave me?"

"For a very brief space, Adeline," he replied.

"God bless you for all your kindness to the poor orphan girl," she said fervently. "Charles, wherever you go, the blessings of those you have been good to, will cling to you."

"Adeline! dear Adeline," said Charles; "I only go now for a few short days, that I may return to you again with greater freedom of mind, because there will be no other duty but that of attending upon you pressing on my mind."

Adeline took his hand, and he saw by the slight quivering of the lips that she was endeavouring to command her feelings sufficiently to speak to him. He did not interrupt her, for he scarcely dared even to trust his own voice. At length she spoke in a low soft voice.

"Charles," she said. "If—if we should never meet again——"

Leslie turned away his head to hide his deep emotion, and the tears that rushed unbidden to his eyes.

"If such," continued Adeline, "should be the will of Heaven, receive here and now my last blessing."

She took the hand she held, and pressed it to her lips, then sinking ck upon the pillow, she could but just say "go," and burst into tears.

The curate laid his hand upon Leslie's arm, and said:—

"Charles—you had better go, now."

Leslie clasped his hands in deep grief, then bending over the pale form of Adeline, he imprinted one soft kiss upon her marble brow, and hurried from the room.

He then shut himself in his own chamber, and when the curate went to him, he said,—

"Leave me to myself, and I shall be better, my dear sir; I am weaker than I thought."

By the earliest dawn, or rather before it, he rose, and without disturbing any of the household, he repaired to the stable, and saddled his trusty steed which had had a long rest, and welcomed its master now with affectionate neighings, for Leslie was kind to everything.

Then without daring to trust himself even to look round upon the house he was leaving, he led the animal into the high road, and mounting, turned his course to London.

The last glimmering star was fast disappearing from the concave arch of Heaven, and the waning moon in the west, was about to hide her broad disk beneath the horizon, to yield her sway to the chariot of Apollo, whose approach the goddess Aurora now hailed, enveloped in her mantle of sober grey, sparkling with drops of dew. As the god appeared, a thousand warblers filled the grove with the music of their melodious throats, and welcomed his approach in notes of swelling harmony ; here might be heard the rich tones of the thrush, there the clear notes of the blackbird, while the nightingale caused the air to vibrate with her varied warblings. On hedge and tree the dew drops, white with the frost of the previous night, hung glittering in the solar ray, and reflected a thousand everchanging colours to the charmed and pleased eye. The cold clear air, as it was inhaled by the early rustic, invigorated his frame and caused the ruddy glow of health to animate his cheek, or carried the blue and curling smoke of his beloved cottage (in a deep and woody glen) far above the trees, and marked the spot where resided all that he held most dear on earth. The woodman's stroke now sounded in the woods as his vigorous hand now plied the axe. The milkmaid's song now floated over the lea, while the lowing kine, rising from their grassy couch, prepared to meet her ; here and there the bark of the shepherd's dog, as he collected the straggling flock, came to the ear in sharp and tuneful notes, while the sound of a distant horn, and the rattle of a wheel caused the sight to be directed towards the early travellers.

As the sun gained power, his genial ray caused the morning dews to dissolve in thin and shadowy vapours, which by degrees became a thick and more substantial mist, and hanging o'er the vale and mountain side, appeared to the spectator on its summit like a white and foaming sea, and the dark tree tops peeping above its surface, like numerous solitary islands. All nature smiled, and dressed in her gayest garb of green, responded by its verdant beauties to its Creator's praise, in accents of silent joy, which manifested themselves from a thousand different sources. Here was food for contemplation, and as the delighted eye of some early riser wandered o'er the scene, his heart would beat in unison with the glories spread around, and this joyful soul was lost in rapture and admiration.

Alas ! How little, really in unison with Charles Leslie's feelings were all these varied charms of nature. He dashed a tear from his eye as he exclaimed :—

"Oh, how beautiful a world has God given us, if we knew but how to enjoy it !"

Then increasing his speed, he rapidly approached London.

CHAPTER CII.

"We'll sit beneath the overhanging limes,
And wonder how the world can be unhappy,
While Heaven has left us youth and love."
                                        BULWER.

ADELINE'S REQUEST.—THE BALMY AIR.—A MOTHER'S GRAVE.—THE VILLAGE
LOVERS.—HOME AGAIN.

THE day after Charles Leslie's departure from the Parsonage was unusually genial and calm. A bright glowing sunshine lent a Heavenly beauty to the meanest objects, and there was not a wild flower or a blade of grass that was not by the delicious flood of golden light that strewed from the Heavens changed into—

"Something rich and rare."

The air was loaded with delicious perfumes, the birds sung upon every branch—

"In very wantonness of joy."

and it seemed one of those precious days upon which nature was determined to hold a jubilee, and give her teeming subjects a taste of that delicious existence, which we may suppose to have mantled over every flower and shrub, when yet the world was young, and the lamb walked in fellowship with the lordly lion.

Mrs. Plumpjoy opened the window of Adeline's chamber, and expatiated loudly upon the extreme beauty and serenity of the day, and the sick girl herself, as if by some influence given her by the bounty of Providence, on that day sat up in her bed and looked out upon the blue sky and the green fields, and listened to the song of the lark as it mounted high into the balmy air to pay its tribute of musical prayer to Heaven.

"We shall not have many days like this, I am sure," said Mrs. Plumpjoy, with a prophetic shake of the head. "The poor dear major, who was a remarkably clever man in his way, always used to say when he saw a day like this,—'Martha, my dear, you may depend upon it, when this fine dry weather goes, we shall have some rain, and it's very strange, but I always, do you know, my dear Adeline, found that sooner or later, such was the case, which was very remarkable, and shewed what a judgment the major had."

"Mrs. Plumpjoy," said Adeline, suddenly.

The good lady gave a great jump, for Adeline's voice was so unusually strong and clear.

"Lor! you quite frightened me, I declare," she cried.

"Will you assist me to dress?" said Adeline.

"Dress!" cried Mrs. Plumpjoy. "Why, you don't mean surely to—to—to—"

No. 45

"To get up," said Adeline. "Yes, dear Mrs. Plumpjoy, I feel better to-day, and I think if I could get out into this balmy air—"

"Out?" screamed Mrs. Plumpjoy.

"What is the matter?" said the curate, who was passing the door and heard the exclamation of his sister.

"Dear Mr. Endsleigh," said Adeline, "I think it would do me good if I could get out a little."

"My dear Adeline," replied the curate, "is your strength equal to such an effort?"

"I—I think it is."

"It would rejoice me to see you once more abroad," said the curate, with much feeling, "and if you feel equal to getting up, I will borrow the little chaise from the post-house, and you can have the enjoyment of the fresh air without fatigue."

"Oh, yes—yes," said Adeline, eagerly. "You are very good to me, Mr. Endsleigh."

The curate left the room and hurried to the village, where he first called on the medical man, and asked him his opinion of the propriety of granting Adeline's request.

"There is little danger in her going out," was the reply, "but a great deal in thwarting her strangely-expressed wish to do so."

"Then she shall go," said the curate.

"If you please," added the medical man ; "I will go with you."

"There cannot be any occasion," answered Mr. Endsleigh, "although, believe me, I appreciate your kind offer. We will go no distance."

He then quickly procured the low easy chaise of the post-house, and in a short time was ready to give Adeline an airing.

"What do you think?" exclaimed Mrs. Plumpjoy, as the curate tapped at the door of Adeline's chamber. "There's that flaunting Anna Riley just gone past the door, and I know she is going to meet that beau of hers, that she boasts comes so far to see her."

"Well, sister, it's no business of ours," said the curate.

"Well, brother, who said it was?" cried Mrs. Plumpjoy, with a triumphant look as much as to say "ah, I had him there."

"Well, well, I cannot contend with you," remarked the curate. "It is now nearly two o'clock, and you know the sun sets before five now, so we have no time to lose, besides I have doubts of the weather, for the extreme mildness of the day is scarcely natural at this season."

Presently, with the assistance of both the curate and his sister, Adeline, with difficulty, got down the stairs, and she rested for a few moments on a chair in the garden. Then she was carefully seated in the little pony-chaise, the curate looked anxiously in her face, as he said,—

"Where shall we go, Adeline?"

"*To my mother's grave !*"

Mr. Endsleigh looked puzzled, for he was quite taken by surprise. He, however, adopted the very best course he could pursue.

"Certainly," he replied, as he stepped into the chaise. "We will drive to the wicket-gate, and see if you are strong enough to get out there."

Adeline looked a world of thanks, for she had expected opposition, and they started at a slow pace towards the churchyard.

"The idea," said Adeline, "of visiting once more my mother's grave before I died, has haunted me day and night. Oh, sir, I was so afraid you would not let me."

"Controul your feelings, Adeline," said the curate, mildly and calmly, although his heart was wrung by her words, "I think your wish exceedingly natural."

They soon reached the wicket-gate, and the curate stepping out of the chaise, said to Adeline,

"Do you think yourself equal now to walk?"

"Oh, yes—yes," she replied. "I—I am sure I can."

He gently assisted her to alight, and leaning heavily on his arm, they together entered the rural and picturesque churchyard.

Short as had been the distance from the Parsonage to the churchyard, still, when the curate looked to the sky, he saw that the sun was rapidly taking his western course, and he was most anxious that Adeline should return before it had sunk to rest, and the usual cool evening air began to blow.

They proceeded for some time in silence. Then, when Adeline came in view of her mother's grave, she suddenly quitted the curate's arm, and with a preternatural strength rushed forward and sunk upon her knees upon the green mound, beneath which lay the mortal remains of her mother.

"Mother! dear mother!" she cried frantically, "it is your child calls you. Your own Adeline."

The curate was alarmed at this sudden outbreak of feeling, and he advanced and gently tried to raise her from the grave.

"No—no!" said Adeline, faintly, "not yet—not yet." She then covered her face with her hands and wept bitterly, ever and anon calling upon her mother in such tones of frantic grief, that the curate was alarmed and afflicted beyond measure. In vain he urged her to return. More than two hours elapsed, and she would not move from the grave.

"Adeline—Adeline!" he said, at length, "this is unkindness. Let me implore you to return."

"Hush!" she said, suddenly. "Hush! I hear a step. See! see! 'Tis the young maiden coming to meet her lover; but, you know, Mr. Endsleigh, she will be deceived and left to die of a broken heart."

As she spoke the curate looked in the direction she pointed, and he saw the young girl his sister had mentioned, Anna Riley, walking towards a distant part of the churchyard.

Adeline slowly rose, and taking the curate's arm, led him after the girl, saying,—

"We will warn her. It is our duty."

The curate was bewildered, and allowed himself to be led by Adeline close to where Anna was waiting; then placing her hand upon her lips, she said,—"Listen! listen."

For some time Anna sat in a deep and contemplative reverie, gazing on the scene before her. The sun had just sunk behind the western hills, whose cloud-capt summits seemed to pierce the sky, which reflected the rich and gorgeous colours of his departing rays; the air was calm and mild, and, as it fanned her cheek, it wafted to her senses the fragrance of ten thousand flowers which variegated the parterre below.

Every sound was hushed, except the discordant bark of some shepherd's dog, as a distant flock were driven to the fold, or the busy hum of insects that now, "thwarted and convolved," revelled their short span of life in the dusky twilight hour. All nature breathed of love, and Anna felt its force as she leaned her broad and placid brow, pale with high thought and sentiment, upon a hand and arm that defied the power of art to imitate; while the moon's broad disk now peered above the distant wave and cast her long line of dancing light to the beholder's eye from the water's surface.

As the moon rose higher in the blue vault of Heaven, the evening star came following in her train, with its mild and silvery light, eclipsing the myriads of lesser spheres that spangled the azure firmament and seemed to keep a respectful distance, abashed by the presence of their queen.

The nightingale now, from the neighbouring bush, sent forth her plaintive notes; the glow-worm had lit his lamp, and, as a sigh of pensive melancholy escaped from the rose-bud lips of Anna, it was responded to by the chime of the distant spire, which now waked the echoes of the gentle night.

"Ha!" sighed the beauteous maiden, as the last echo of the bell tolled faintly on the balmy air, "he ought to have been here;" and she had scarcely finished before the sweet and silvery notes of her lover's lute fell harmoniously upon her practised ear. "He comes!" she continued; "how long the dreary day appears, and how ardently I sigh for the silent evening hour, that tranquillizes and soothes the heart to love."

She had no sooner finished this soliloquy than, throwing her mantle around her slender form, she rose to meet him. A slight rustling of the leaves was heard, and in another moment she was locked in the arms of her enraptured lover.

"Beauteous Anna," he exclaimed, as he embraced the sylph-like form within his arms, "what happiness can exceed mine, to possess a being whose very presence lends a double charm to the enchanting scene around?"

"Mine!" replied the playful girl, whose heart now palpitated with wild delight, as she yielded to his fond embrace; "my happiness must be greater than yours, for if I am what you would wish me to believe, I am not only that, but possess the love of the most generous of men."

"Could I persuade myself that I was worthy of so much loveliness, my happiness would know no bounds. Yes, dear Anna, I only sigh that the world is not at my disposal, that I might lay its treasures at your feet."

"Then cease to be unkind even to yourself," replied the smiling girl, "I sigh not for wealth or riches, and were I to possess what you would grant, I should not be happier than now. Two hearts that beat in unison need not any foreign acquisition to make them happy; and beneath the most humble roof, cheered with your generous love, I'd scorn the pomp and pageantry of a prince."

"Angel of light!" breathed her fervent lover, as he pressed her to his heart; "without your enchanting presence to cheer my days, the universe would be a dreary void. That moon which now sheds her limpid light o'er vale and stream, is not more pure than your spotless soul;—nor are the abodes of those blest spirits which have left this world of sorrow, more sacred than the spot your presence hallows."

"You think too highly of my worthless charms," replied the gentle female; "if they afford you pleasure I am happy; but when the cankerworm of care shall have stolen the damask hue from my cheek, and age and disease shall have dimmed my eye, what claim shall I have upon your affection?"

"Cruel fair!" exclaimed the youth, "shall we not then both be old?—shall I see you altered? Will not long attachment bind me to you?—and may my soul never see its Heavenly state, if I ever cease to love you!"

"Hush! hush!—to-morrow night!" exclaimed the timid girl; "here's some one coming."

A gentle kiss was exchanged, and the youth disappeared among the trees, and soon after his song was borne to her far upon the evening air, as he carolled gaily along the meadows.

This scene had passed very rapidly, and Adeline had cast upon the curate such looks of intense interest, that he had not spoken, nor made any movement to interrupt the lovers.

Now suddenly she sprang forward, and with a wild cry, she said :—

"Beware!—Beware! A broken heart!—Another broken heart!—God help her!"

She fell insensible upon the curate's arm, who was just in time to save her from falling on the cold and damp earth of the grave-yard.

CHAPTER CIII.

"The roses on her cheek were gone,
How beautiful they bloomed;
Her voice had wasted to a sigh,—
The gentle girl was doomed."

BYRON.

THE CURATE'S DESPAIR.—LONDON PHYSICIANS.—THE OPINION.

WHO could paint the grief and alarm of the curate at this sudden and unexpected termination to the little excursion, which he had fondly hoped would have been of some benefit to the health of the invalid. He raised Adeline from the ground, and calling upon the young girl to whom she had addressed such incoherent words, he claimed her assistance to carry his beautiful and insensible burthen back to the little chaise, which was waiting at the wicket-gate for them.

The distance was fortunately but short, and Adeline was soon placed in as easy a position as circumstances would admit of, and the curate urged the patient animal who drew the chaise homewards.

Mrs. Plumpjoy was standing at the door, anxiously looking out for the return of the curate and his charge, when they came within sight of the Parsonage. The chaise was stopped at the door, and when the curate's sister saw the pale face of the gentle girl reposing against a cushion, motionless, and without expression, she thought her dead, and clasping her hands she looked at her brother in too great dismay and consternation to speak.

The curate guessed her mistake, and said :—

"It is not as you suppose, Martha ; the pulse still tells of life,—she has fainted."

Hastily then dismounting, he, with the additional assistance he now had, quickly conveyed Adeline to her own chamber, where he left her to the care of Mrs. Plumpjoy, while he retired to his own study in an agony of painful thoughts.

"What can be done for her ?" he said. "Oh, Heaven! is there no hope ?"

For a time, then, the old man gave himself up to despair, then suddenly lifting up his head from his hands, he said :—

"Surely I am bound to use all human means for her recovery. There are, I have heard, in London men of rare skill in healing disorders and restoring the wasted energies of life. I—I will go to them ;—yes, I will go. They shall come and see my Adeline. How I thank God for these—these I so little valued."

As he spoke he opened a small drawer in which was some gold, old guineas were mixed with the more modern coinage. It was the curate's little store of wealth, from which, when occasion required, he relieved the distresses of all around him. He took out some of the gold pieces, and with a trembling hand he put them in his pocket. He had then taken two steps towards the door when it opened, and Mrs. Plumpjoy appeared.

"How is Adeline ?" said the curate eagerly.

"She has recovered, and is now sleeping, poor dear thing," replied the compassionate woman.

"Did she speak, Martha ?"

"Yes ; and I think she ain't just right in her mind. She wanders a little."

"Martha," said Mr. Endsleigh, in a tone of emotion, "I am going to London again."

"To London, brother?"

"Yes, for Adeline. There are physicians in that great city, who, if they can do nothing for Adeline, will kindly say so, and we shall have the melancholy satisfaction of knowing, Martha, that all that human means could do, he did for the dying girl who was so dear to us."

"Yes," sobbed Mrs. Martha Plumpjoy. "Go, brother, go."

"I knew you would say so," replied the curate. "The coach passes so early that I will trust to you to call me in time, Martha."

"I will. Indeed I will," sobbed his sister.

The curate then sought some repose before he again undertook the journey, which, although nothing to a young man, was to him, at his time of life, a serious undertaking.

Mrs. Plumpjoy was true to her word; and after hearing that Adeline still slept, the old curate left his once happy home on his melancholy errand.

The coach duly arrived, and Mr. Endsleigh, with all his troubles and fears, was whirled along at a rapid pace towards the mighty leviathan of cities—London.

It was at an inn yard in the city that the coach stopped, and after the curate had taken some slight necessary refreshment, he started on his errand of finding out the residences of some of those distinguished medical men, who he knew only by common reputation.

His task, however, was by no means difficult, for he took the best course he could, which was to ask at the first chemist's shop he came to, where he was very politely furnished with the names and addresses of the persons he was seeking.

The only mistake the old man committed was in his first call, which was in Old Broad-street, upon a medical man, whose name he had frequently heard, but who he did not know, and who was more distinguished for his vanity in being thought a scientific and moral philosopher than anything else.

The curate was admitted to this gentleman, and on his first entrance treated with all the silly courtesy for which he was so celebrated. Now poor Mr. Endsleigh unfortunately began his statement at the wrong place, and the first words he uttered were,—

"Sir, pardon my intrusion, but I am in great *distress*."

Now the moment the word distress caught the ear of the great philanthropist, Doctor B., the oily manner departed, and he said, quickly,—

"Aye—aye—I—never assist anybody; and I don't like to hear people's distresses. Good morning."

The curate looked for a moment in his face, then shaking his head, he left the room and the house without another word.

This was a practical lesson to Mr. Endsleigh, which, had he been a younger man, might have been valuable through life, viz., never to trust to the kind sympaties of an universal philanthropist, for his goodness is so very universal that it would puzzle any one to find a particular instance of it.

The next call which the curate made, was upon Mr. ——, a man as deservedly esteemed in his profession as he was in private life, and here the good curate's difficulties ended, for Sir —— not only entered kindly into the case and sympathised with the curate's feelings, but told him to go home again at once, and he, Sir ——, would bring with him another medical gentleman, whose advice, from practice in such cases, might be valuable; at the same time he positively refused all offers of remuneration.

It is needless to say how grateful Mr. Endsleigh felt for the kindness, contrasting so strangely too, as it did, with the universal philanthropist he had just left. He thanked Sir —— with tears in his eyes, and leaving the address with him, he departed, bearing Sir ——'s promise, to repair to Bracefield as early as his previous engagements would possibly permit him.

It was late in the afternoon before the curate again stood by his own door at Bracefield, and his first inquiry was for Adeline.

"She has been very restless and uneasy all day," replied Mrs. Plumpjoy "Are the doctors coming, brother?"

"Yes," he replied; "before night I am promised a kind visit from the most eminent man in his profession."

"Oh, brother, I am very glad," said Mrs. Plumpjoy. "Then, as you say, we shall know that we have done all we could for poor Adeline."

"We shall, Martha; and a dear consolation that will be when she is—in— Heaven."

"I will ask," said Mrs. Plumpjoy, "if she will see you now, for she has often asked for you."

The curate waited till his sister returned to say, Adeline was expecting him, and he at once repaired to her chamber.

She was sitting up in bed supported by pillows, and it was with a bitter pang at his heart, that Mr. Endsleigh saw she was much paler and more sickly-looking than when he had last seen her. Her voice, too, was strange and low, although still retaining its musical sweetness. She stretched out her thin wasted hand, and said faintly,—

"Mr. Endsleigh, you have not been to see me for so long."

"I have been from home, Adeline," he replied. "I hope you do not feel worse for, what I fear I must call, our imprudent excursion yesterday?"

"Excursion?" said Adeline, looking anxiously in his face. "What do you mean, my dear sir?"

He glanced in her countenance as he replied—

"Did we not go out yesterday in the little chaise?"

Adeline shook her head as she said,—

"No—no."

"She does not recollect anything about it," whispered Mrs. Plumpjoy. "I have asked her and she always says no."

With a deep sigh the curate dropped into a chair by the bed-side, and almost at the moment the rattle of carriage wheels struck upon his ear.

He rose and walked to the window just in time to see Sir —— alighting from his chariot in company with another gentleman. Then turning to Adeline, he said,—

"My dear, will you see two medical gentlemen that I have asked to visit you?"

Adeline turned her mild blue eyes full upon the curate's face, as she replied,—

"Yes—oh, yes. Your wishes are commands, for who have I to be kind to me but you? I will see them, but—but——".

"But what, Adeline?"

"'Tis all in vain."

"Nay, say not so. There is always hope."

"No—no; not always. Look at yon sunset. See the sun's disk is just disappearing in the western sky. To-morrow it will rise again and I shall see it. At the close of day it will again assume its present position and I shall see it—but *I shall* not see it rise a second time."

"Oh, Adeline—Adeline; do not indulge in such gloomy prophecies," said the curate. "Life and death are not in our hands."

"True," said Adeline; "but there is a something comes over the mind when it hovers on the confines of eternity, which cannot be described unless it be a communion with creatures of another world."

A low tap now sounded on the door; it was old Andrew, to announce the physicians.

"Bid them walk up, Andrew," said the curate, and in a few minutes Sir —— and his friend Mr. ——, were in the room of the sufferer.

The curate made way, and Sir —— sat himself down in the chair by the bed-side of Adeline, and taking her small delicate hand in his, he began to converse with her on indifferent topics.

After about ten minutes of such conversation, he rose and said,—

"Well, I will now bid you good day," and beckoning to the curate to follow him, he and his friend, with Mr. Endsleigh left the room.

When they reached the little parlour of the Parsonage, the curate could not speak, but he looked anxiously in the face of Sir —— with an expression which he well understood.

"My dear sir," said the humane physician, "this is a case which admits of no doubt — needs no kind of consultation. Your young friend, I grieve to say it, will not be long with you."

The curate sighed deeply.

"Make up your mind to the worst," continued Sir ——. "It would be cruelty to flatter you with false hopes even for one moment."

"It would!—it would!" gasped Mr. Endsleigh.

"I was greatly in hopes that we might do something, but here we are foiled."

"And can nothing be done?"

"Nothing."

"When, sir, when do you think the pure spirit that inhabits the earthly frame of her who is so dear to me—when will it take its flight?"

"That is difficult to say," replied the physician; "but I should not count upon her existence above twenty-four hours."

At this moment the last gleam of the setting sun suddenly vanished. The curate started.

"She said to-morrow," he sobbed.

"She herself said to-morrow?" cried the physician.

"Yes—yes, at sunset to-morrow."

"Then the probability is that she is right. I have seen many remarkable instances of such a prophetic feeling before death."

"Alas! alas!" said the curate; "and I must part with thee, Adeline,—the light of my old age,—the joy of my heart."

He wept bitterly, and Sir —— seemed much affected.

"Let it be a consolation to you now, sir," he said, "to hear me say that from my medical experience I can prophecy that her end will be peaceful and calm,—that she will resign her being into the hands of her Maker without a struggle. Sleep will precede death, and the two will be so blended, that the probability is you will scarcely be able to say where the one ends and the other begins."

"I thank you, sir," said the curate,—"from my heart and soul I thank you. You shall have an old man's prayers."

The physician then, after shaking hands with the curate, left Bracefield.

Then Mr. Endsleigh sought relief in prayer, and strove to reason himself into calmness and resignation—but oh, how difficult it is to give up hope! Unknown almost to himself, he had cherished a lingering supposition that something might yet be done to snatch Adeline from the grave. Now, even that last ray of hope was dragged from his heart, and he saw nothing in its place but blank despair. Long and fervently the old man prayed for strength of heart to bear his grievous trial, and he rose from

his attitude of fervent devotion calm and placid, if not resigned to the privations which his heart was to undergo.

"If," he murmured, while the tears coursed each other down his furrowed cheeks—"if it be the will of Heaven that I become a mourner, I need not question the decree, which, although it creates suffering for me, releases my darling adopted child from a world of care and suffering, to place her where there are no tears, and woe can never come."

CHAPTER CIV.

"Who knocks at this dread hour,
When all should be at rest?—
In faith and holiness I'll hold my lonely watch,
Perchance 'twill come again. I will not fear it."

AN ALARM.—A MYSTERY.—THE CURATE'S DETERMINATION.—A MIDNIGHT
VIGIL.—THE OLD CHURCH.

THE hour at which Mr. Endsleigh usually retired to rest was past, and still he remained absorbed in grief in his own little room. A thousand anxieties were gnawing at the old man's heart, and he felt that to retire to his chamber with the hope of tasting the sweet balm of sleep, would be an useless mockery.

Early in life, when the spring of his youthful spirits was still in its prime, he had suffered affliction—the heart-rending affliction of having torn from him, by the remorseless grasp of death, the being with whom he had hoped to pass the weary pilgrimage of life—she in whom had been centred all his

No. 46

fondest hopes—she who he had hidden in his heart of hearts as a pure and holy thing to be loved and worshipped next after Heaven and his God.

Death had then stepped in and claimed its victim, and the curate's heart had nearly sunk beneath the blow; but fifty years had winged their weary flight since then, and the remembrance of that young grief had faded away to a quiet regret and a cheerful hope, that the time was dawning each day nearer when he should meet the loved one of his youth in that better world where death is unknown, and the songs of joy from immortal lips fill the sunny air.

And many a time since then had the curate successfully battled against earthly affections. He had not shut up his heart against mortal affections, but with an enduring constancy he had resisted, trusting much of his happiness upon the frail tenure of a human life, and he had, therefore, passed calmly through existence after time had mellowed his first great grief.

Vain, however, had been all his resolves, and his most fixed determinations had melted into thin air. The gentle Adeline imperceptibly crept into the old man's heart, and filled a void there which it had been the incessant study of his life to keep vacant. Had she been some dear child of his own, he could not have loved her more than he did. Her innocence and her truthful tenderness won their way into his affections far more than earthly beauty. In her he had found all of virtue that he had ever hoped to find in so frail a structure as humanity, and now—now that she was about to go from him, he felt how truly dear she had become to him, and that unconsciously he had allowed his earthly happiness, even for the short sojourn he had to make in this world, to be wrought up with another.

All these thoughts passed through the mind of the aged man of God, and twice, thrice even he started and looked around him to assure himself he was not weeping for the darling of his young heart, and that the last fifty years of life had not been

"But the troubled fancy of a dream."

"Alas!" he cried, "it is too true. Here are my well remembered books. I hear the sighing of the wind among the trees. 'Tis too—too true, and Adeline—the beautiful and good—the second of God's creatures that have filled my heart with the joy of pure and exhaustless affection, is dying."

Solemnly now upon the night air came the boom of the church clock as it sounded the midnight hour.

The curate started. "So late?" he cried. "What a solemn stillness reigns around. It is the appointed time for rest—but I cannot sleep for my deep affliction."

As he spoke, and ere the murmured sound of his last word had ceased to stir the silent air, a heavy knock came upon the outer door of the Parsonage. Mr. Endsleigh cast an alarmed look around him, but before he could think even, the knock came again, and awoke the echoes of the silent house. A strange feeling came over the old man, and for one brief moment a superstition that he blushed to own to himself, crossed his mind, and he whispered—

"Is it death come for its victim?"

A summons for admittance at that hour of the night was certainly a most unusual thing at the Parsonage. The habits of the villagers took them to rest at least three hours before the clock tolled forth the hour of midnight, and the curate felt certain that something very unusual must have occurred to induce any one to disturb him at such an hour, the more especially as it was well known that sickness was in his house.

Before the knock could be again repeated, he heard the door opened by some one, and in a few moments afterwards the handle of his door was gently turned, and Mrs. Plumpjoy protruded her head into the room, saying, softly—

"Brother, are you here?"

"Yes, Martha," replied the curate.

"Bless you and save us, I thought you were in bed long ago," exclaimed Mrs. Plumpjoy; "and it gave me quite a turn when I went into your room and found it empty."

"How is Adeline?" said the curate, anxiously.

"She still sleeps," replied his sister. "But here's some one from the village, as says he must see you, your ownself."

"Indeed?"

"Yes. He seems quite in a fright. It's one o' the young Meadows's, but I don't know which, for as poor dear Major——"

"Hush—hush, sister," said the curate. "My heart is too ill at ease to listen to you. Forgive me if I appear unkind. I—I do not mean it."

Mrs. Plumpjoy looked in her brother's face for a moment, and her own eyes filled with tears as she said—

"Brother—you—you—I——"

"I know all you would say, my dear Martha," said the curate, kindly taking her hand. "Now go again to—to—her—who—who will not long be with us."

So saying, the curate walked softly down the staircase, and by a little lamp which burnt on a slab in the passage, he saw one of his young parishioners waiting for him.

"What has happened," said Mr. Endsleigh, "that you come to me at this hour, John Meadows?"

"Please ye, Muster Endsleigh," said the young man, "father and Simon would have me come, sir, to tell you all about it."

"About what, John?"

"Two nights now, Muster Endsleigh."

"What do you mean?" said the curate, mildly. "You have not told me anything yet, John."

"Well, father and Simon do always say I be the very worst to tell a story as never was."

The curate knew by experience that it would be quite useless to hurry John Meadows, so he merely remarked, quietly—

"Take your time, John; only recollect that it is very late."

"Please you, sir," said the young farmer, "for two nights, as brother Simon and myself have gone out late to lay eel-lines in the mill stream, we have seen a light in the church."

"What?" cried the curate, starting.

"A light in the church, Muster Endsleigh; as plain as I can see you now, sir."

"John, you must be mistaken."

"So I thought, you see, sir; and when I first saw it I says to Simon—'Simon,' says I; 'Well, John?' says he. 'Look at the church, Simon,' says I. Then he looks, sir, and says I to Simon—'Simon,' says I; 'don't you see nothing?' says I; then says he—'John,' says he—'there's a light in the church,' says he."

"'Tis very strange," remarked the curate.

"So we thought, sir."

"When did you first see this light?"

"Last night, Muster Endsleigh."

"Why did you not tell me of it earlier, John?"

"Why, father, he says, when we told him, says he, 'Oh, it's nonsense, boys; don't trouble Mr. Endsleigh unless you see it again. Then,' says he, 'go to him at once, mind, without any delay,' says he."

"That was very proper advice," said the curate; "and have you seen it again?"

"Yes, sir; not half an hour ago."

"To-night?"

"Yes, Muster Endsleigh. We all saw it; father and I and Simon, and they sent me off to tell you."

"It is exceedingly strange, John; for I have the keys of the church in the house at this moment."

"If you wouldn't mind coming out a little way, sir," said John Meadows, "you'd perhaps see it yourself, sir. It shines through the east window."

"Certainly I will come," said Mr. Endsleigh. "It is my duty to see to it."

He took his hat from the accustomed peg in the passage, and leaving the door upon the latch, he walked out into the cool night air with his young companion.

Walking in the direction of the church for some three or four hundred yards, they came to a spot which the curate knew commanded a view of the church.

"Here, John," he said, "if it were daylight we should see the east window plainly."

"Yes, sir," replied the young man; "it was but down in the hollow there, by the mill-stream, that I was, sir, when I saw it."

"All is darkness now," remarked Mr. Endsleigh, as he strained his eyes in the direction of the church.

"Yes," said John Meadows, in a tone of disappointment; "it has gone, sir."

"I will wait a few minutes," said the curate, "although I cannot help thinking you have all been deceived by the reflection of some distant light upon the church window."

John Meadows shook his head doubtingly, as he said—

"No, Muster Endsleigh; it moved about, and we all three felt so very sure."

Mr. Endsleigh was silent, and kept his eyes fixed on the church. All was still and black. There was no air stirring, and the sky was very dark, so that the circumstances were sufficiently favourable for such a phenomenon to have shown itself very distinctly.

"If you were not deceived by something which you mistook for a light," said the curate, after five minutes patient watching, "it will not appear to me, you see, John Meadows."

"Sir, I could take an oath I saw it," cried the young farmer.

"I believe you," said Mr. Endsleigh, suddenly clutching the arm of his companion. "There it is!"

A stream of light issued from the window of the church and fell clearly and distinctly upon the tombs in the old grave yard.

CHAPTER CV.

"Is it a portent of good or evil?"—SHAKSPERE.

THE MYSTERIOUS LIGHT AND THE CURATE'S DETERMINATION.

FOR a few moments only the mysterious light shone brightly and clearly through the latticed window of the ancient church, and then suddenly it disappeared, leaving the darkness ten times more palpable and black than before.

"What do you think of it, sir ?" said the young man.

"I know not what to think," replied Mr. Endsleigh; "but I am convinced, with you, that the light was within the church."

For a few moments the curate stood in an attitude of deep musing, then he said—

"It is possible that some of the simple ornaments of our little sacred edifice may have tempted a sacrilegious robber. John Meadows, will you go with me to the church; I am an old man now, and scarcely fit to go alone ?"

"Certainly, Mr. Endsleigh," replied the young man.

"Then I will wait here while you go to the Parsonage, and ask any one you see for the church keys and the lantern."

The villager departed with a quick step on his errand, while Mr. Endsleigh remained lost in anxious and apprehensive speculation.

"It is my duty," he said, sadly, "to see to this affair, although, Heaven knows, my heart is full to overflowing already with griefs. Adeline, God alone knows if I shall find you in life even when I return."

John Meadows soon rejoined the curate, bearing with him a dark lantern and the church keys.

"There is a small door," said the curate, "that will admit us through the chancel. Shroud your light, John, and should there be any unholy robber in the church, he will not be so likely to escape us."

They then, being so perfectly acquainted with the road, proceeded quickly towards the church.

Mr. Endsleigh scarcely took his eyes from off the window through which had streamed the mysterious light, but all remained perfectly dark, and they arrived at the chancel door without having again been able to detect the least glimmer from the interior of the sacred pile.

With a trembling hand the old curate unlocked a low arched door-way which led into the chancel, and thence through another small door into the body of the church.

"We cannot conceal our presence now," remarked Mr. Endsleigh, "so give what light you can, John, to our search from your lantern."

John did as he was desired, and holding up the light as high as he could, shed a dim ring of light around their two figures, as they stood in the centre of the building.

For a few anxious moments neither spoke or scarcely breathed; then, as no sound whatever reached their ears indicative of the presence of any living thing save themselves, the curate spoke.

"John," he said, "the church is not large, but it is old and has many curious nooks and corners about it. I hear nothing and see nothing suspicious, but before we go I would fain strengthen the belief which is creeping over me, that the light was a mere spectacle illusion by ascertaining that the doors are safe, and that no one is concealed in the church."

There was a slight tremor in the young farmer's manner as he replied—

"I be quite willing, Muster Endsleigh; I don't see why I should be afeard."

"Certainly not," replied the curate. "Come—to the door first, my friend."

They crossed the aisle, and carefully examined the large door, all seemed perfectly secure and safe, and then slowly traversing the whole of the building, the curate felt satisfied in his own mind that no one could be there.

This search occupied nearly half an hour, and when it was over, the curate's thoughts returned painfully to Adeline, and he longed again to be under the same roof with the dying girl.

"We must suppose, John," he said, "that we were both wrong, for you must be quite convinced that no one is here."

"That I could take my oath on, Muster Endsleigh," replied John.

"Let us go then, and to-morrow night——"

The curate paused, for a pang shot through his heart, as he thought that to-morrow night the pure spirit of Adeline would probably have flown to meet its God.

"To-morrow night, sir?" said John.

"No—no matter," sighed Mr. Endsleigh. "It is no matter. Come—come."

He locked the little chancel door, and buried in the agony of his own thoughts, he slowly followed the young villager, who held the lantern low to the ground to guide the steps of the aged pastor.

"Now go you home," said the curate, when they reached the spot from whence he had seen the mysterious light. "Give me the lantern and seek your rest."

The young man bade Mr. Endsleigh an affectionate and respectful good night, and trudged quickly to tell his story to his father and brother, while the curate stood for a moment in a state of silent abstraction on the spot where he had been left.

"Home—home," he said; "home to thee, Adeline."

He turned sharply, and even at the moment the same stream of bright light he had before seen, came from the eastern window of the church, and again fell in a long yellow streak across the head-stones and humble green mounds of the church-yard.

Mr. Endsleigh stood regarding it for several minutes in speechless amazement, then he said to himself in a low voice,—

"Shall I be superstitious and believe that this is some omen concerning my Adeline? or are my old eyes, at this most inauspicious time, marked by some optical delusion abroad, when I would fain be tending at home the sick couch of her who is going from me, and taking with her my heart's best hopes? Yet, it cannot be a delusion—'Tis too apparent—how very strange! I—I must go again to the church, and this time I will go alone; but first—first—Adeline, I will see thee.

The old man then hastily walked to the Parsonage, and opening the door, which he had left upon the latch, he noiselessly entered his own cheerless—but once happy and contented home.

It was now between one and two in the morning, and the curate felt sensibly the want of his usual repose. He ascended slowly the staircase leading to Adeline's chamber, and when he reached the door of the room in which lay the young being who he loved so dearly, he paused to wipe the unbidden tear from his eyes, as many melancholy thoughts came crowding over his mind. Then he tapped gently—so gently that it could scarcely reach the ear of an attentive watcher, and could not possibly disturb any one who slept.

In a moment Mrs. Plumpjoy opened the door, and the dim light from a shaded bed-room lamp fell upon the bent form of the old curate.

"She still sleeps, brother," whispered Mrs. Plumpjoy.

The curate spoke not, but glided tremblingly into the room, and with clasped hands stood by the bed-side of the slumbering girl.

The rest of Adeline, if rest it was, seemed profound and happy. Her long hair had escaped from beneath the cap which had confined it, and was streaming in graceful beauty upon the pillows which supported her head. One arm was thrown carelessly upon the pillow, and upon the delicate face there was a radiant flush of colour, such as a painter would have loved to place upon the fair cheek of some dying saint.

Her breathing was deep but regular, and there was little in the aspect of that young and beautiful girl, as she there lay, to indicate that she was so fast approaching the portals of the grave.

Mr. Endsleigh continued to gaze at her in silence until he could see her no longer for the tears that filled his aged eyes, then he murmured a blessing upon her, and coupled it with the name of God to hallow the blessed aspiration.

It might be that the very air that was loaded with so heartfelt and pure a wish had brought from Heaven some vision of beauty and dear happiness to the gentle slumbering girl, for she murmured something softly in her sleep, in a smile of such Heavenly loveliness, that the old man turned suddenly from the couch, whispering to himself,—

"I will go, now, while that smile is still playing on my heart like a sunbeam from the gate of Heaven itself. Bless thee, Adeline!—Bless thee!"

He then as carefully as he had ascended descended the narrow staircase, and just as the church clock gave out the hour of two, he again left his house to explore by himself the precincts of the sacred edifice, and discover, if possible, whose unhallowed presence had produced the alarm, which he knew would spread itself all over the village, in consequence of the mysterious light from the eastern window.

Shrouding as before the light which he carried, he took the same path towards the church, and soon arriving at the little door in the chancel, he, without fear, opened it, and entered alone the sacred building. The place was so familiar to the old curate, that at any hour of night or day he could have securely walked to any particular spot, or placed his hand upon any indicated part of the structure; but he held his light in as convenient a position as possible, to shed as much of its rays over the building as it would, and commenced a regular and systematic examination of every part of the basement of the structure.

He went into every pew, and closed the door of each behind him so firmly that it could not be opened noiselessly, except by some one exceedingly well acquainted with the place. Then he ascended to the pulpit, from whence for so many years he had preached the pure and exalted doctrines of faith and mercy, but all was empty—no indications of any disturber having been in the place could he find. Everything was in its accustomed situation. Then the old man leant against the railing of the little winding step that led to the pulpit, and strove to reason himself into a belief that imagination must have misled him into a conviction that the light was in the church, when in reality it was not. The only difficulty he had in bringing himself to this state of belief, was the fact that the extremely unimaginative John Meadows and his brother and father had seen the phenomenon; and when he considered that they were very unlikely to be effected fancifully in the same way as himself, he was thrown back upon the slender hope that the appearance might have arisen from some optical delusion altogether; and as minute after minute passed without anything occurring to confirm an idea of the presence of any one in the church, he became more and more confirmed in that supposition.

"And yet," he thought, "if any one should be concealed here, or in the churchyard, they are not likely to show themselves while I am here with a light. The watcher may be the watched in this case, and while I am waiting to see any one who may appear as the cause of the singular light, that one may be waiting for my departure to consummate some unholy purpose."

The curate continued in thought some few minutes after this idea had taken possession of his mind, and then suddenly taking up his light from a seat on which he had placed it, he walked with as noisy a step as he could towards the chancel door, and, opening it, he placed his lantern on the outside, then closing the little entrance with a slam, he remained in darkness in the church. His object, by this scheme, was to induce a belief in the mind of any one who might be listening to his movements, that he had left the church in despair of making any discovery concerning the light.

He did not move hand nor foot as he stood now by the little door which he had just closed, and he even suppressed his breathing as much as possible in that lonely place.

Full ten minutes passed away, and Mr. Endsleigh began to breathe a little more freely, from the conviction that no one could possibly be there. He was even upon the point of moving, when a low rumbling noise met his ear, and he stood as silent and as still as a statue, in mute wonderment as to what it could possibly mean.

There was another long pause, and then the same noise faintly echoed through the empty church. The kind of noise was different from that which Mr. Endsleigh had ever, to his recollection, heard before, and he was quite at a loss to form a conjecture as to its origin, or the particular part of the building from whence it proceeded.

He resolved to make no movement—to utter no sound, until by some means the mystery was solved, or the noise brought to his ears in some more distinct manner.

He had scarcely formed this determination, when his eyes were attracted to the roof of the church, nearly in the centre of which there appeared, suddenly, a small circle of light. It played and danced upon the time-blackened rafters of the old building, and the curate continued to gaze at it in intense surprise, until it began slowly to move along in a direction towards the eastern window. Mr. Endsleigh cast his eyes anxiously round the church, but he could see nothing, save that spectral-looking circle of light slowly taking its route along the roof.

For a moment the curate stood quite irresolute, and the feelings of superstition which the best and wisest of men are never able thoroughly to eradicate from their minds, came strangely across the old man's brain.

Mr. Endsleigh was, however, a man of too much good sense and real religion, to be long the victim of idle or superstitious fancies, and he quickly got rid of the first imaginative impression which the mysterious light made upon him.

"That reflection upon the ceiling," he thought, "must have a source, be it remote or close at hand;" and on the instant he made a movement forward into the body of the church.

The moment his foot sounded on the flooring, the light became stationary.

"Speak!" cried Mr. Endsleigh. "Whoever you are, speak! and say what is your purpose here!"

There was a deathlike silence for a moment, and then a shriek rang through the building with such awful and startling effect, that the curate clasped his hands, exclaiming,—

"God of Heaven, what is this?"

When the echoes of that fearful cry died away, the light was likewise gone, and darkness and silence again reigned within the church.

"Daylight must unravel this mystery, if possible," said the curate. "I will return here to-morrow, with younger and stronger arms than mine, and we will with Heaven's help, do our best to free the temple of God from desecration."

Taking his lantern, then, in his trembling hand, he left the building, and repaired homewards, deeply ruminating upon the singular occurrences of that night of alarm, sadness, and terror.

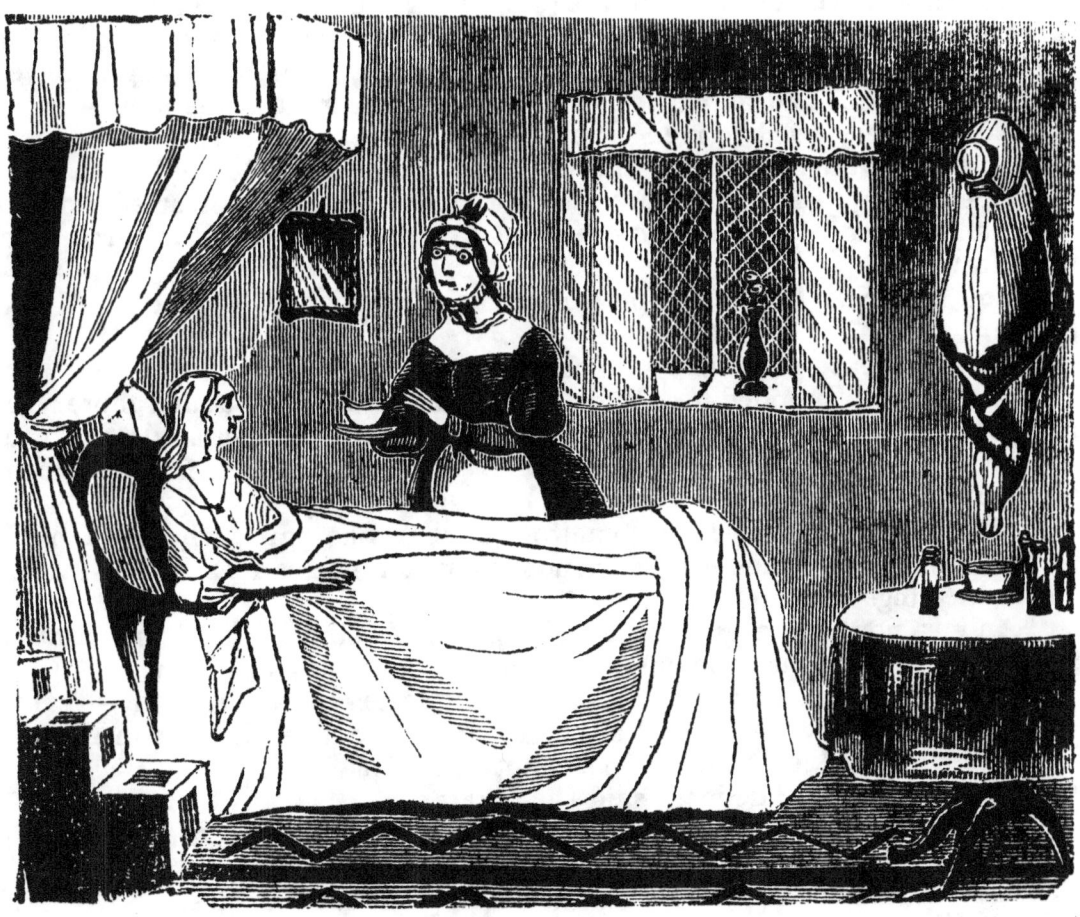

CHAPTER CVI.

"It is believed by many that the spirits of another world crowd the chamber of the dying, and sometimes whisper consolation to the departing soul.—And who shall deny it?"—Dr. JOHNSON.

CHARLES LESLIE SENT FOR.——THE RALLYING BEFORE DEATH.——THE WILD MUSIC.

THE curate determined to say nothing to any one concerning the awful cry that had smote his ears in the church, but to wait till the morning brought with it coolness and reflection to decide upon what would be the best and most proper course to pursue.

After receiving notice from Mrs. Plumpjoy that Adeline still slept, the old man lay down himself to endeavour to seek the repose which was necessary to enable him to go through what might be the distressing day which was now faintly dawning in the east.

Exhausted nature exerted her supremacy, and the curate fell into a deep and dreamless slumber, from which he did not awaken till the morning sun fell upon his aged face, and roused him to a consciousness of daylight by its glittering warmth.

Hastily rising, and consulting his watch, he found that the day was still but young. Feeling, however, greatly refreshed by his few hours sleep, he hastily rose, and dressing himself, descended to the parlour.

He was told by old Andrew that Mrs. Plumpjoy had gone to bed after procuring a kind dame from the village to take her place by the bed-side of Adeline.

No. 47

With this information the curate stole gently up the staircase, to ascertain the state of his dear young friend. As he neared the door, a gush of feeling came across his heart at hearing that voice, which he might never have heard again, and he paused to listen, as he heard Adeline say,—

"You are very good to me. Pray go to rest."

The words were simple, but they went to the heart of the old man.

He gently tapped at the door, and the homely but kind-hearted woman who had relieved Mrs. Plumpjoy, opened it, and dropped a low curtsey to the curate.

"You have been kindly sitting up with my dear young friend?" said the curate.

"Yes, an please you, sir," said the woman. "Bless her!"

"I thank you," replied Mr. Endsleigh. He would have added more, but Adeline turned her eyes upon him, and with a faint smile—a smile that was the twin brother of that which he had seen beam upon her face in sleep, said gently,—

"Mr. Endsleigh, you have come to see your poor girl, who is so much trouble to all her friends—dear friends, to whom she can make no return but in blessings and thanks."

"And is not that a great and rich return, Adeline?" said the curate, taking her hand in his, and looking at her with earnest affection.

She pressed his hand to her eyes filled with tears, as she replied,—

"I am going to where we shall meet again, to live in the sunshine of such blessings and joy as here we can but pray for."

"You are better, Adeline," said the curate.

"Were it not," she said, sadly, "that I know my hours are numbered, I should proclaim myself well."

"Alas!" said the curate. "Do not indulge in such fancies. Why will you, Adeline, prophecy so gloomily?"

"The gloom has passed away," she replied. "All is now hope."

"Hope?" said Mr. Endsleigh. "The hope of renewed health—the hope of life and strength to be long with us."

Adeline shook her head, and pointed upwards.

"No," she said, "my hope is now with God!"

Even as she spoke, the curate saw a remarkable change take place in her countenance. The colour which so doubtfully mantled on her cheeks, suddenly left them, and she became as pale and as beautiful as monumental marble.

She slowly sunk upon the pillow, and there ensued a few moments of silence, for the curate's heart was too full for speech, and it might be that Adeline could not make the effort to address him.

"Adeline," he said, after recovering himself a little;—"Adeline, how are you now?"

"Hark! there again!—Ah, 'tis beautiful. I never hear it but when my heart seems nearly to pause in its small pulsations;—then they sing it to me!"

"What is it that you hear, Adeline?" asked the curate, much affected by the solemn earnestness of her manner.

"Do you remember," she said faintly, "a long time since giving me a copy of that hymn of Bishop Hebers, that is so full both of poetry and true religion?"

"I do," said the curate.

"It is very strange," continued Adeline, "but they are singing that hymn to me now."

"Who are singing it, Adeline?"

"There are many sweet voices. Sometimes the sounds seem far off, as if they had but faintly penetrated through some small crevice in the blue vault of Heaven ; then they will seem even in the chamber, and hovering close—so close to me. The music is strange and unearthly, and yet so very sweet."

" And do you hear the words, Adeline?" whispered the curate.

" Hark ! hark !" she cried. " You hear them too !"

The curate shook his head.

" 'Tis very strange you do not hear them, Mr. Endsleigh. I am awake. Now they commence again !—The same low Heavenly strain !—I can repeat it with them !—Oh, what a faint murmur it is now !—Hark ! hark !"

She held up her finger in an attitude of listening, and then slowly repeated the tones to which she alluded, commencing with,—

> " Thou art gone to the grave, but we will not deplore thee,
> Though darkness and silence encompass the tomb,
> For the Saviour hath passed through its portals before thee,
> And the light of his love will illumine the gloom."

" How beautiful !—How beautiful !" she repeated.

The curate sat by her side awe-stricken, and he asked his own heart if he was justified in doubting that the pure beings of another and better world were hovering around the couch of the dying girl, who in her purity and goodness assimilated so closely to themselves, and smoothing her passage from a life of care and anxiety to a world without end and joy everlasting.

" Adeline," he said, " if you are to go from us that love you, it is we that will have to mourn, and that only because we are selfish."

" But the blessing of God," she said, solemnly, " will fall brightly upon those who sheltered the orphan, and were kind to the fatherless."

" Adeline," said the curate ; " you are the teacher now. I listen to you, and am instructed. If it be the will of Him who made the heavens and the earth, that you should be taken from me, I will repeat to myself those lines of pure faith and hope, and when my human heart is disposed to lament and murmer, I will fancy I hear your sweet voice, as even now I hear it saying,—

> " Thou art gone to the grave, but we will not deplore thee !"

Adeline looked up in the old man's face with sweet tenderness, and after the pause of a moment, she said,—

" Is Charles here ?"

" He has gone to London," reluctantly replied the curate.

Adeline sighed.

" I wished," she said—" I had hoped to see him again."

" He will be back in about two days, I think," said the curate.

" Too late—too late !" sighed Adeline.

" He would come if you send for him."

" I would fain—fain see him before——"

" Before when, Adeline ?"

" Before sunset."

Mr. Endsleigh was in hopes she had forgotten her prophecy of the previous day, and it inflicted a pang upon his heart to find that she still bore it in mind, and was by her manner still impressed with a belief in its accuracy.

" I will send for Charles, Adeline," he said.

" Will you be so kind ?" she said, quickly.

" Instantly. He begged me to do so at your slightest wish, that way tending."

" I—I want to see him,—I must see him," she murmured. " Yes—yes, I must see Charles."

The curate rose, saying,—

" Andrew shall saddle a horse and go at once to the address which he left me, and you will see him, I am quite sure, as quickly as it is possible he can reach here."

"Yes—yes, I must see Charles," she repeated, and her eyes gently closed in slumber again.

The curate waited till he was quite sure she slept, and then he gently left the apartment, and sought out old Andrew, his faithful servant.

"Andrew," he said, " I wish you to go to London."

The old man shook his head.

"No, master, no, I cannot go near him. I tell 'e I can't abide him. No—no—no."

"Why, Andrew," said the curate, " what do you mean ?"

"Besides, I be got a rheumatiz," continued Andrew, "and the horse be not very well, and ——"

"There are many objections, Andrew, to doing my bidding," said Mr. Endsleigh.

"Leave him alone, sir," cried the old servant. "Ah, sir, he be not worth looking to."

"Who do you mean ?" said the curate.

"Why—that—that—Master Mandeville, to be sure."

"And did you think I was going to send you to him ?"

"Y—e—s," said Andrew, looking rather sheepish.

"No, Andrew. It was at Adeline's request to Charles Leslie, that I wished you to go."

"To—to—Charles Leslie ?"

"Certainly. Adeline wishes to see him as quickly as he can come here."

" I be off," cried old Andrew. " Never fear me, master, he shall be here soon."

"Make what haste you can then, Andrew," remarked Mr. Endsleigh, "for the young thing, who we all love so much, will not be long among us now."

" You—you don't think, master, that Miss Adeline is really so very bad ?" faultered the old servant.

" There is no hope, I am told," replied the curate.

The old domestic said no more, but hurrying to the stable, saddled the horse, and with tears in his eyes, took the address of Charles Leslie from his master's hands, and waving his hand, he galloped from the Parsonage.

"This day will be a weary one," remaked the curate. "It will be one of deep anxiety and many griefs. Oh, Adeline, if it *should* please Heaven to spare thee yet to live, for the old man who loves thee so tenderly, until he has run his allotted span ; and—and yet why should I wish it ? 'Tis human selfishness that speaks !"

The church clock striking nine, put him in mind of his singular adventure of the preceding evening, and he paused in deep musing till the last recording stroke of the bell had died away, then he pursued his way slowly back into the house.

"Now that all is light," he thought, "and the sun is penetrating clearly into every spot, I cannot bring myself to believe in the events of the night. Could I possibly have imagined the awful sound which seemed to pierce my very brain, or was it the time—the place, and the deep silence that contrasted with it, that dressed it in such terrors. After all it may have been but the cry of some wild bird, which echoing through the old church at such an hour, and when my mind too was in expectation of something wonderful, that produced all the effect. And yet the light. There could be no imagination there. I cannot, however, think of ought to-day, but of Adeline. I cannot now leave home. If it be my duty to set to work to unravel this mystery connected with the sacred edifice committed to my care, it is a duty which must give way to the all-absorbing one of tending thee, my Adeline. No, I cannot leave thee now."

CHAPTER CVII.

"Oh, what an invocation is the name we love!"

SHAKSPERE.

THE DAY IS WEARING ON.—CHARLES LESLIE'S ARRIVAL.—THE INTERVIEW.

THAT day at Bracefield, was indeed one of unremitting anxiety and wretchedness. Mrs. Plumpjoy took her place again by the bed-side of Adeline. Mr. Arundel, the humane medical man of the village, called upon Mr. Endsleigh during the morning, and strove, with tender sympathy, to comfort the old man, although he gave him no hope.

"It would be as vain as wicked for me to say that human aid could aught avail this dying girl," said Mr. Arundel. "You must be prepared for the worst, Mr. Endsleigh, and seek consolation in that same source from whence you have so frequently brought dear hope and consolation to others."

The curate thanked him humbly and kindly, and then strove to talk of other matters, although Adeline alone possessed his thoughts.

The day seemed very long to all in that house of mourning. To the curate it was the most unhappy day he had ever passed. He was, as the reader is well aware, not one of those divines who surround the bed of sickness with horror and gloom. He felt it a necessary duty to assume as much cheerfulness as his heart would let him whenever he entered the chamber of Adeline, and in his heart he believed that young, pure, soilless spirit of the dying girl, would be acceptable to its God.

Mrs. Plumpjoy had lost all her redundant spirits, for she had by degrees really came to love Adeline very much, notwithstanding her first prepossessions against her. In fact poor Mrs. Plumpjoy was something in the same situation as her brother, with regard to the orphan girl, that is she never suspected how much she admired and loved her, till now, when in all probability she was about to leave them. So poor Mrs. Plumpjoy would sit by Adeline's bed-side, talking to her kindly and gently, and occasionally she would leave the room, to have, as she said, "a good cry," after which she would return again, with as serene a countenance as she could assume, to what she considered her dutiful watch by the bed-side.

Thus the day slowly crept. Adeline sometimes slept, and sometimes conversed wildly and sweetly to those about her. After the hour of mid-day, however, a perceptible restlessness began to be exhibitted in all her movements. She incessantly asked for Charles Leslie, and sometimes she would weep bitterly when told he had not come.

It was nearly three o'clock, when the curate, who was standing at the back of his house, casting a watchful and anxious eye to the London road, saw two horsemen in the distance approaching at a swift pace.

"He comes at last!" sighed the old man. "Poor Charles, this day will be a bitter one to thee as well as to me. It is a sore trial. We must endeavour to speak words of comfort to each other."

The sound of the horses' feet now plainly reached his ears, and he could see beyond a doubt that they were Leslie and Andrew who were approaching.

After a moment's thought he determined to apprise Adeline that Charles had come, as she had for the last hour expressed such earnest anxiety for his arrival.

Mr. Endsleigh accordingly entered the house, and ascending to the chamber of sickness, he knocked gently.

It was the voice of Adeline that said,—

" Come in."

The curate entered ; Adeline was in a sitting posture in bed, propped up by pillows, and as the old man came to the side of her couch of pain, she said hurriedly, but in a firmer voice than she had used for many days past,—

" Has he come ? Has he come ?"

" Charles is close at hand," replied the curate.

Adeline's eyes brightened for a moment, and she pressed her hands upon her breast, as if to suppress some powerful feeling that agitated her.

" You may hear his horse's feet," remarked the curate.

" Yes, yes, yes," repeated Adeline. " He is coming ! I knew he would come !"

" Do not agitate yourself, Adeline," said Mr. Endsleigh. " Whenever you wish to see Charles, he shall come to you."

" Now, now," she cried. " Oh, Mr. Endsleigh—my dear friend, there is but little time. Let him come now ! Let him come now !"

There was a wild anxiety about her manner which alarmed and afflicted the curate, and he replied gently,—

" My dear Adeline, calm yourself. Charles is here, and will come to you directly. I will fetch him."

Adeline watched him as he passed from the room, and continued to keep her eyes rivetted upon the door-way, in anxious expectation of his re-appearance with Charles Leslie.

When the curate reached the ground-floor of his house, the first person he saw was Leslie, pale, agitated, and unhappy. He grasped Mr. Endsleigh's hand, as he said in a voice husky from emotion,—

" Is—is it really true ? Can it be possible that she so very soon must—leave us ?"

" My dear Charles," replied the curate, " we must arm ourselves with patience and resignation."

" There is no hope, then ?"

The curate shook his head, and a deep sob burst from the breast of Charles Leslie.

" Hush, hush," cried the curate. " Oh, give not way thus, Charles."

" 'Tis the last ! 'Tis the last !" said Leslie. " My good friend, you shall see that I will take my sorrows gently. I will controul my grief."

" Charles, Adeline is momentarily expecting you. She seems most anxious for your presence."

" I—I will go," said Charles.

" Follow me then, quietly," whispered the curate. " Do not, for Heaven's sake, show agitation, Charles."

" I will not. Trust me, I will not. I am calmer now. Lead on, sir. You shall see I can be calm, even—while my heart is breaking."

The curate said no more, but very slowly, in order to give Charles time to conquer his feelings, preceded him up the staircase.

The door of Adeline's chamber was not closely shut, and Mr. Endsleigh pushing it gently open, said,—

" Adeline, Charles is here."

Adeline's eyes were fixed upon the door-way, and her hands were pressed upon her heart in the same manner that she had pressed them very frequently within the last two hours. It was indeed that she was deeply affected at the sight of Leslie, for her lips moved several times before she could speak, and when she did utter an audible sound, it was merely his name, and that pronounced in a tone of such exquisite anguish, that the curate was fain to turn to the window to hide his tears.

Charles Leslie walked to the bed-side, and in a much firmer voice than any one could have thought him capable of commanding at such a moment, he said,—

"Adeline, you see I have come to you again."

She stretched out her hand to him, and he took it, and bent his head over it as if to kiss it.

"Charles," cried Adeline, "you are weeping for me."

She withdrew her hand, which was bedewed with Leslie's tears.

He immediately lifted his head, and looked in her face, saying,—

"I am weaker, Adeline, than I ought to be."

"Do not weep for me, Charles," she said. "I have not used you well."

"Oh, Adeline, do not wring my heart by saying that," replied Charles. "You do yourself injustice."

"What's the time?" suddenly she cried.

"Nearly four," said the curate.

"Nearly four, nearly four," she repeated slowly; then turning her eyes upon Charles Leslie's face, she added, "I have something to say to you, Charles—alone."

"Come, Martha," said the curate, "let us leave our dear Adeline with Charles."

The curate and his sister left the room.

"Charles," said Adeline; "go—go to the window and tell me where you see the sun."

"The sun is high in the Heavens yet, Adeline," he replied.

"High in the Heavens yet," she said, solemnly, and slowly.

"Why do you ask, dear Adeline?"

"Because—because, Charles, I shall never see it rise again."

"Adeline, why will you give me so much ——"

"Nay, Charles, do not be grieved, but listen to my dying words. I have treasured them up for your ear alone, Charles."

He seated himself by her bed-side, and taking one of her hands in his, he gazed earnestly in her face, as she continued in her old, low, musical voice, broken occasionally by nervous catchings of the breath, to speak to him.

"When I was a young and thoughtless thing, Charles, with nothing but gaiety at my heart, and romance turning in my brain, you loved me; that love of yours was deep and sincere, you have proved, Charles. It is proved now, or you would not be now by the bed-side of—of—the dying girl, who had not sense to distinguish between deep and holy affection such as yours, dear Charles, and the gaudy glitter of a passion, alas! so different!"

"Adeline," said Charles; "I did love you, dearly, and fondly love you. You *were* indeed the dream of my heart. Such love as mine, dearest Adeline, is patient and enduring. The same to me you were ever as when I took you to my heart, and told myself that for ever it would be yours. Adeline, I love you now! Time has made no change! You—you are still—still my Adeline! My beautiful and good! my own fair, bright-eyed girl!"

He dropped his head upon the coverlid, and wept so bitterly, that his grief was an awful and solemn thing, and the chamber echoed to his heartrending sobs.

"Charles, Charles," whispered Adeline, bending her face close down to his. "Charles! I—I love you now!"

"Oh, forgive me!" he cried. "I thought to have avoided this. Say on, dear Adeline, and heed not my tears."

"I must say on, Charles, for the time is very short. Yes, I scorned your love, pure, holy, and ennobling as it was, because I was enchanted by the me-retricious glitter of attractions, which were new to me, and like the gaudy moth that flutters round the flame which it mistakes for a new sun, shining for it alone, I have fallen a victim to my grievous error. This, Charles, is my only atonement. Do not, oh, do not despise me when I am gone. Speak of me as weak—as vain—but still think that the poor and dependant Adeline, might with more discretion, and less feeling, have been happier, and made more happiness around her."

"You will be ever thought of," said Charles, "as a being too pure and beautiful for earth. You live in the hearts of all, as the one richly valued! dearly-loved being, without a reproach—without a stain."

"'Tis strange," sighed Adeline. "All, all have loved me so well, but him—him who I loved! Charles, my heart is broken!"

"Oh, say not so, Adeline," cried Charles. "Still live to be the wife of him who really loves you."

"The wife! The wife! Your wife, Charles?"

"Mine, dear—dear Adeline. My cherished wife!"

"Oh, God!" cried Adeline, clasping her hands; "now death has indeed a pang!"

She slowly sunk back on the pillows, and Charles Leslie, with a pang of consternation, saw that she had fainted.

CHAPTER CVIII.

"Weep—weep—for she we loved is dead!"
POPE.

THE HOUR IS COMING.—THE LAST WISHES.—A SUN SET.

CHARLES LESLIE hastened from the room, and summoned the curate and Mrs. Plumpjoy, who were both greatly distressed to find Adeline in a state of insensibility.

"She is gone! She is gone!" cried the old man, wringing his hands.

"No, no," said Charles; "she still lives! Oh, Mr. Endsleigh, if you grieve thus passionately, what can I do who am young and unused to sorrow?"

The curate said nothing, but sitting down on a chair near the bed, he with clasped hands regarded the various means which were taken to restore Adeline to sensibility. All, however, failed, and finally Charles Leslie hurriedly walked to the village for Mr. Arundel, who promptly attended.

By his skill Adeline was once more restored to consciousness, and Leslie followed him to the door, wishing to ask him what he thought now of the state of his patient, yet shrinking from putting the question, in dread of what the answer might be.

At length as Mr. Arundel was upon the point of walking from the door, he said,—

"I—I suppose—there is—no change?"

The medical man turned, and said in a low sympathetic tone,—

"Mr. Leslie, I am sorry to say there is a change."

"For—for—the worse?"

"Yes; your young friend cannot live long."

"I—I—thank you, sir," said Charles, as he staggered, rather than walked, into the house again.

He paused for a few moments at the foot of the staircase to endeavour thoroughly to master his feelings, then he slowly ascended, whispering to himself.

"Yes, I must be with her now till the last."

A striking change had indeed taken place in Adeline within the last half hour. Her eyes were bright, but it was a strange and unearthly radiance that shot from them, a hectic tint of colour was upon her cheeks, and the gentle and affectionate Adeline Mourdant, never, in the height of her health and joy, looked so delicately beautiful as she did now that she was upon the couch of death.

The old curate still sat upon the chair near the bed, and seemed petrified with grief. His hands were clasped before him, and his aged eyes were bent upon the face of Adeline, as if he were striving to catch some ray of hope from the varying expressions it pourtrayed.

Mrs. Plumpjoy was weeping by the window, and striving to stifle her sobs so that Adeline should not hear them.

When Charles entered the room, he walked quietly to the seat he had before occupied close to the head of the bed, and sitting down, he took Adeline's hand in his without saying a word.

There was deep silence for several minutes, which was broken by Adeline, saying faintly—

"Is the sun still sinking, Charles?"

"No," replied Leslie, as firmly as he could. "It is not yet fully in the west, dear Adeline."

"I—I would fain see it," she said, after a pause of a moment.

Charles Leslie silently rose and disposed the curtains of the bed and the window, so that, as Adeline lay half recumbent, she could command an extensive view of the open country. The sun was slowly sinking, but yet it wanted a large space of the horizon, and the sombre tints of evening had not yet began to appear.

"Thank—you—Charles," she said, in so low a tone that it sounded more like the lisping whisper of a child than anything else.

No. 48

Charles Leslie resumed his seat by the bed-side again, and took the small attenuated hand in his.

Adeline looked in his face with all the fond affection of a child, as she said—

" Dear Charles, can you tell me where Herbert Mandeville is now ?

" I—I hear," said Charles, " that he has left England."

" Left England ?" replied Adeline ; " and without a word of regret—or—or—farewell."

She seemed much affected by this intelligence, and the tears filled her eyes as she kept repeating the words—

" Left England."

" Dear Adeline," said Mr. Endsleigh, breaking the silence he had maintained so long. " Do not grieve for that. See around you those who really love you with all their hearts."

" Yes—yes," she said ; " but—I cannot help it. I forgive him all—may he be happy—far happier than the poor devoted Adeline could have made him with nothing to offer but a loving heart."

" Could there be a richer—dearer gift ?" said Charles.

" Will you, Charles, do me a last favour," suddenly said Adeline, turning her face to him.

" Can you ask," he replied. " Adeline, as I hope to meet you again in Heaven, I will perform your slightest wish."

" Will you then seek—Herbert, and—tell him—tell him that I forgive him all, and bid him not grieve for me."

" I will seek him," said Charles.

" I would not have him accuse himself with bitterness of grief concerning me," she continued. " Tell him, Charles, all was forgiven, and that I blamed myself far more than him."

" It shall be done, Adeline," replied Charles ; " I will seek him, and find him, if he be on the face of the earth."

Adeline thanked him with her eyes, and then pointing to the window, said, faintly,—

" The sun is setting."

Even as she spoke, a sweet crimson light slowly crept over the western sky, and long streaks of yellow radiance shed a golden light upon all things animate and inanimate.

" The sun is setting," she repeated.

Charles looked in her face, and oh, how more than earthly beautiful she seemed. The mixed light of gold and crimson from the clouds surrounding the retiring luminary imparted to her face a healthful glow, such as one might suppose to rest eternally upon the countenances of those blessed spirits who sit around the throne of God, and her attitude, as she pointed to the distant horizon, was such as might well beseemed the inhabitants of a world of love, joy, and beauty, lying among those bright clouds that tinged, by their reflected light, her cheeks with such a Heavenly lustre.

The old curate rose from his chair and tottered to the bed-side.

" Heed not the sunset, my child," he said ; " heed it not."

" And you too, my dear kind friend," cried Adeline. " Let me hope that you will not weep for me. Forgive me if I have been wayward and wilful, as I know I have been."

" God bless you," said the old man, fervently.

" Mrs. Plumpjoy, where is she ?" said Adeline.

" Here, my dear," replied the weeping woman.

" You have been kind and good to me as well as others," said Adeline. " Bless you all—dear—dear friends. See, the sun is setting."

The sun's disk had just touched the line of the horizon, and the fiery hue of the sky was at its height.

Charles would now have closed the curtains of the window, but Adeline shook her head, saying,—

"No, Charles—no. Leave them. Let me look still upon that sunset—it is the last."

Now the glowing tints in the sky began to fade, and the glorious and beautiful orb of day was rapidly dipping from mortal sight.

For some minutes there was a death-like stillness in the chamber—it was broken by Mrs. Plumpjoy's sobs.

"Do not—oh, do not weep," said Adeline. "Hark, Charles! oh, listen all—listen!"

She held up her finger in an attitude of deep attention.

"What is it you hear, Adeline?" whispered Charles.

"The hymn again—the hymn again!" replied Adeline. "Hark to that beauteous swell of harmony. Now I hear the words. How clear and musical,—

"*Thou art gone to the tomb, but we will not deplore thee.*"

Is it possible you do not hear it?"

"To you alone, dear Adeline, are such sounds given; they are not for us," said Charles.

"Charles—Mr. Endsleigh—God bless you both. If affection for me should prompt you to raise a record of my last resting place above the verdant soil that covers me, write on it 'The Grave of the Forsaken.' Charles, the sun has set!"

She stretched out her arms to Leslie, and pillowed her head upon his breast.

"God support me," sobbed Leslie, "in this hour of trial. Adeline, my Adeline!"

The old curate walked close to him with a trembling step, and in choking accents, said,—

"Charles—my dear boy—our—our darling is—is——"

"Sleeping," said Charles; "she is sleeping on the heart that loves her."

"*She is dead!*" said the curate.

Slowly Charles Leslie lifted from his breast the head of Adeline. With affectionate care he parted the long hair from the face—*it was the face of the dead.*

A sudden gloom came over the chamber, and the night wind moaned past the window. He laid his insensible burden upon the pillows, and then turning to the curate, seemed struggling to speak, but the effort was too much. Nature was overwrought, and with one deep convulsive sob, Charles Leslie, for the first time in his life, fainted, and fell at the feet of the aged man of God.

CHAPTER CIX.

"He lay beside her weeping,
And they watched him as he wept,'
Till they thought that he was sleeping
On the pillow where she slept.'
BAYLEY.

THE HOUSE OF DEATH.—THE CURATE'S DESPAIR.—SYMPATHY FROM HE POOR AND LOWLY.

HAD we the power, it were too painful to paint the grief which reigned in the Parsonage on that sad night which followed the death of Adeline.

The old curate's feelings seemed stunned by the shock, and he wandered about the house for some hours, wringing his aged hands, and exclaiming:—

"My poor Adeline! My gentle, beautiful child!" nor would he be persuaded until nearly the dawning of morning to retire to rest.

Charles Leslie had been recovered from his insensibility and had retired to his chamber, where, for many hours, he gave himself up to his mighty and overwhelming grief, a grief which he felt it was in vain to struggle with, and to combat which it would have required more than mortal philosophy.

The closed shutters of the Parsonage in the morning, announced to the villagers that death had snatched from their venerated pastor the adopted child of his old age, and the grief of all was clamorous and loud, for Adeline was universally beloved.

As the morning advanced, some of the youngest of the village girls brought wild flowers, and being admitted to the chamber where lay the mortal remains of the beautiful girl, they strewed the corpse with their simple offerings, and shed many a tear for the fate of one so young and so much beloved.

And how calm and beautiful she seemed in death. The despoiler had come but had left no harsh traces of his presence. Her last sigh had been at the moment that she laid her head upon Leslie's breast, and so calmly had her pure spirit

"**Winged its ærial flight,**"

that it had left a smile upon the cold lips of its earthly dwelling place.

One by one the weeping village maidens laid their simple offerings upon the orphan's bier, and all went home again to weep, for there was something in the scene more awfully impressive on account of the entire absence of anything that rudely spoke of death, than on any similar occasion had affected their young minds.

It was nearly mid-day before Charles Leslie and Mr. Endsleigh met in the Parsonage, and then their only salutation was a silent pressure of the hand, which, however, said more to the heart of each than could the most laboured set of words.

They tried then to converse upon indifferent topics, but the effort was in vain. There was that in the aspect of each of them, that plainly told the other how pre-occupied with the one great subject of distress and sorrow their minds were, and at length, after a painful pause, the curate said in a trembling voice,—

"Charles, we ought not to be afraid to speak of our Adeline, although she has—gone—from us."

"I am glad to hear you say so, my dear friend," replied Leslie; "for if we proscribe that subject between us, we shall but nurse a hidden sorrow which we may beguile by conversing with each other."

"Our dear Adeline," added the curate, "is now in Heaven."

"If ever," said Leslie, "a pure spirit flew straight to the presence of its Maker, that spirit was Adeline. I must grieve, Mr. Endsleigh, for when was deep grief for the loss of a loved one, amenable to sober reason?"

"When, indeed, Charles," said the old curate, shaking his head mournfully. "I am very old now, and I did not think I could have survived a grief like this. The time, however, must come, according to the common lot of humanity, when I shall hope to join my dear Adeline, never again to part."

"In that hope, my dear friend, seek for consolation," replied Charles.

"You," continued Mr. Endsleigh—"you must mix with the world, chastened but not weighed down by sorrow, Charles. What good you can do for God's creatures I know you will do, and always look forward with a cheerful, not a saddening hope, to that happy time of meeting when we shall know no more tears—dread no more partings."

"I will," said Leslie, "life may be to me a weary pilgrimage, but I will not make it worse by useless repining. My heart is sorely stricken, Mr. Endsleigh, but I shall endeavour to bring myself such consolation as I can extract from Adeline's own words to us who loved her, when she knew that she was passing from us."

"The blessing of that pure young heart, Charles," said the curate, " will hover ever around you, be assured."

" I will think so, sir," replied Leslie.

" Now then, my dear Charles, we must free ourselves from all afflicting sensations upon this subject. Let us never, hereafter, hesitate to talk of her and her acts."

" You are right," said Charles.

" Then, in the first place," said the curate ; " you will stay till—till——"
Suddenly the old man paused and burst into tears.

Charles Leslie knew what he was going to say, and he did not attempt to stem the current of affection.

When Mr. Endsleigh had recovered himself sufficiently to speak, he said—

" Charles, in me you see an instance of the vanity of human nature. I was preaching philosophy and firmness to you, when—my own heart was nearly breaking, and here you see a foolish word has brought these tears into my aged eyes."

Charles only sighed deeply.

" You know what I meant to say," continued the old man ; " I can say it better now. It was our—darling's funeral, I—I meant."

" I will remain here," said Charles, " until all that can be done for the memory of her who is gone is done, then I have a duty to perform."

" To seek *him* ?"

" Yes—I will go to Herbert Mandeville and carry to him the forgiveness of his victim.

" Charles," said Mr. Endsleigh, after a pause, " do not quarrel with this young man when you do see him, for your own sake, and for my sake, and for the sake of the gentle being who we loved so well, be content to deliver the message you have promised and no more."

" My dear friend," replied Leslie ; " your caution, believe me, is needless. My spirit is now bruised and nearly broken ; circumstances which some time since would have stirred my blood with indignation, will now pass me unheeded. The world and all its hopes, fears, joys, and sorrows is now much sunk in my consideration, and I fix my eyes upon an eternity which is to come, rather than upon the quarrels and jealousies of this existence."

" You are right, Charles," said the curate. " Be indifferent to the world, but not too much so, for we are all sent here to perform our allotted parts in the great drama of existence, and we must not slur over, or neglect that which it is the will of Heaven we should do."

" I will not neglect it, sir," said Charles, sadly ; " and you need not fear that I should add an angry word to the message of peace. I have promised to take to that man I had thought never again to see. If his heart is unmoved by the few simple words which Adeline desired should be taken to him—no laboured reproaches of mine or any earthly being could inflict a pang upon its flinty stubbornness."

" You are right, Charles—you are right. He will feel, for he is human ; and now, Charles, will you walk with me upon a melancholy errand ?"

" Alas, sir !" said Leslie ; " all our errands must now be melancholy."

" True—true. But this is one which I wish you to share with me, Charles. Come."

Leslie rose, and the old curate placing his arm within that of his younger companion, slowly walked from the Parsonage.

He led the way towards the narrow lane which terminated at the little wicket-gate opening into the churchyard, and Charles, with a sigh, guessed the old man's purpose. It was to select a spot in which the mortal remains of Adeline should be laid."

As they slowly walked onwards in silence and in sorrow, they were met by several of the simple and kind-hearted villagers, who, with instinctive delicacy, said nothing, but stood on one side to allow their aged pastor to pass on with his deep affliction unquestioned, contenting themselves with such humble and kindly recognition as they thought would be welcome but unobtrusive.

Mr. Endsleigh returned each salutation in his old kind way, but he did not smile as was his wont when he by chance encountered any of his humble friends. The old man tried to shape his face to a look of cheerfulness, but he could not, and although he kept the tears that glistened in his aged eyes, from falling down his furrowed cheek, and gave no words to his grief—yet all saw the deep affliction of the heart in the expression of the face, which no efforts could subdue.

Slowly as foot could fall, they passed up the green lane, and Charles Leslie opening the wicket-gate, preceded the curate into the churchyard.

Then there was a pause of many minutes before either could speak. It was broken by the old clergyman, saying—

"This spot, Charles, will be hallowed to us for ever."

"It will," replied Charles. "If I live I will often visit this humble depository of the dead, and with a chastened holy sorrow, gather philosophy and consolation from these tombs."

"Yes, Charles, yes. If the world use you roughly, and you feel resentment growing at your heart, come here and look upon these humble tombs, and while you do so, tell yourself that the oppressed and the oppressor, the rich and the poor, the strong and the weak, must alike sleep the long sleep which knows no waking, and that a few feet of earth will suffice to cover the proudest heart that ever beat in human breast."

"Yes," said Charles; "and at such moments I will learn to rejoice rather than lament that she, who I loved best of all, is free from earthly cares and earthly strifes, and that the fair casket which contained her spotless soul, is sleeping gently here, while the pure spirit itself is listening to its God."

The curate pressed the hand of his young companion, and the two stood side by side for many minutes in silent thought.

The sun was shining brightly upon the waving grass that grew in luxuriance over the dead, and the trees with which the old grave yard was sprinkled, rustled their leaves gently in obedience to the mild air that just sufficed to give them motion.

Both the curate and Leslie seemed sensibly to feel the charm of that silent and picturesque spot, and the old man said, softly—

"Charles, this is a fit resting place for our dear friend who is gone. Look at yon verdant spot, so sweetly speckled with light and shade by the sun as it glances through the foliage of the trees. Charles—we—we—will lay her there."

Leslie did not speak, but he bowed his head, and taking the curate's arm, he slowly walked to the spot indicated by him. It was a slightly elevated part of the churchyard, and commanded an extensive and varied view for many miles of the surrounding country. Charles gazed long and anxiously around him. There was the old church with the ivy crawling in graceful festoons far up its ancient porch, and mingling fantastically with the once rich carvings which had adorned the entrance. Some distance further stood the blackened and dismal-looking ruins of Rose Villa, just as the fire had left them, and still further in the landscape, was dimly perceptible the remains of the ancient mansion at which the soldiers had halted in their pursuit of George Mourdant.

How familiar were all these places to Charles, and yet with what different feelings he now regarded them, to what he used to do when death had not robbed him of the one charm of life which gave light, colour, and animation to all beside.

With a deep sigh he turned to the curate, saying—

"Yes, let her lie here, my friend. Let this spot be her quiet grave. Here we will raise the simple tablet to her memory which shall say more to our hearts, than the most laboured laudatory epitaph, or the most costly sculptured monument."

"Her own words shall alone find a place upon her grave," said Mr. Endsleigh.

"The Grave of the Forsaken," replied Charles.

"It shall be done," added the curate. "This day week, my dear young friend, we will consign to the quiet repose of the grave, the fairest and the best of earthly creatures."

"This day week," repeated Charles. "Be it so—and let us each day come to this spot, and with mild sorrow, speak of her we loved so well. So we shall accustom our minds to talk of her freely as one gone from us in sadness and sorrow, but still as one whose memory is a chosen and a beautiful remembrance."

"We will, Charles, we will. You will stay with us till then?"

"Yes," replied Leslie. "When she is laid here I go to perform my promise, and then again I shall return, for this spot will be to me a sacred and a holy one."

The curate again took the arm of Leslie, and having performed his purpose of choosing a resting place for his dear Adeline, he slowly returned to his now melancholy and desolate home.

CHAPTER CX.

"Ere yet decay's offensive fingers
Have marred the lines where beauty lingers."
BYRON.

MOONLIGHT.—THE LONELY HEART.—CHARLES LESLIE'S DEVOTION.

THE silver moon rose early upon the village of Bracefield, and being at the full, there was not a humble roof, or blade of grass, that did not borrow a strange and heavenly beauty from the pure flood of white glittering radiance which streamed from the orb of night. It lit up the old church, and it slept in more than earthly loveliness upon the silent graves. As far as the eye could reach, the meadows looked like sheets of molten silver, and the glistening leaves upon the trees seemed like those which the adventurous Aladdin found in the cavern of wonders, each one of which was a gem of price.

Upon the Parsonage house too, it streamed in a full flood of glory, and into one room it seemed to penetrate with a refulgence and intensity that banished every shadow, and filled it with a mild, white radiance, such as might become well the dreamy air in the abodes of blessed spirits above the blue ether, and out of the sphere of earthly influences.

That chamber into which the moonbeams came with so much beauty, was the chamber of death. On an open bier in the centre of the room, lay the gentle, the young, the confiding, the beautiful, and the forsaken Adeline Mourdant. There was no concealment of the mild quiet, features so still and beautiful in death. The angelic smile with which she had resigned her spirit into the hands of Him who gave it its earthly dwelling place, still lingered on the parted lips, and through the fringing lashes of her eyelids might still be caught a glimpse of those blue orbs which once had rivalled the clear arch of Heaven in brightness and lustre.

Death had not yet robbed Adeline of a charm, and as the moonbeams fell clear and cold upon the face of the sleeper, she might well have been taken for some recumbent statue, carved from the purest marble, of a saint, or it might be something more holy, still worked wondrously, to show the world a presentment of the beauty that once had been.

The wild flowers still reposed upon her breast, but the moon's ray robbed them of their colours and all were pale—pale as the small face of the young thing who lay there in her girlish beauty and innocence so awfully still, so lifelike, yet so lifeless.

The church clock solemnly sounded the hour of midnight, and the last echoes of the ancient bell had scarcely died away in the stilly air, when the door of the chamber of death was gently opened, and a tall figure entered with a quiet holy tread as if it feared to awaken the still form that could hear no sound now, till the voice of the Omnipotent should breathe to it the command to rise again.

Slowly the visiter of the dead approached the bier, and then he stood with clasped hands gazing earnestly upon the lifeless face, while occasionally a deep sigh from the bottom of his heart would attest the agonising state of the feelings that lay there hidden from every eye.

The mourner was Charles Leslie. He had risen from a restless couch to look in the silence of the night upon the face of her he had loved so fondly.

For a time he stood in silence, then suddenly he spoke in tones of heart-piercing anguish.

"My Adeline! My Adeline!" he cried. "Oh, why have you passed from me? Why was I permitted to see you, but that you should leave my eyes ever regretting that such a dear vision could never again bless them? Why was I endowed with a preception of your rare virtues but to admire—to love, and then to mourn you? My Adeline! My Adeline!"

He stooped and kissed the cold lips, then rising, with a burst of anguish he covered his face with his hands, and wept long and bitterly. Occasionally he would murmur the words,—"My Adeline! My Adeline! My beautiful! my good!"

Then as his frantic grief wore silently away in tears, he again bent his gaze earnestly upon the calm face, that with its marble beauty, seemed to mock his agony.

"Still beautiful!" he cried. "Still more than lovely as thou wert ever! Oh, Adeline, if I could have won thee when thou wert happy. If then I could have laid bare to you the heart in which your gentle image lived alone, how happy we might have been. If I could have shewn thee the difference between such love as mine, calm and deep as it was like a fathomless depth of the ocean, and that sparkling brawling passion which deceived thee, my Adeline, by its froth and glitter, what sunny days might we not have passed together. Oh, Adeline! Adeline! my loved—lost, mourned Adeline! If all that has passed were but the fitful fancies of a dream, how happy we still might be. Alas! no. 'Tis sad—too sad reality. Thou art there in death, my gentle, blue-eyed girl, while I—I—live a man of sorrow, a walking image of despair!"

Again the storm of wild grief swept across his soul, and he groaned and wept in the bitter agony of his spirits, and again too it passed away like the tempest's wrath, leaving an unnatural stillness and repose behind it.

"This is madness!" he said, suddenly. "My brain already reels, and reason totters on her throne. I—I must leave thee, Adeline. Cold and wan as thou art. Even I who love thee so dearly, so—so fondly, even I must leave thee!"

He stooped over the still face again, and again he kissed the lifeless lips. Then suddenly starting, he exclaimed, as he pointed to the corpse,—

"No, no, thou art not my Adeline. She was kind and gentle, and her heart beat ever responsive to another's woe. Thou art cold and still! N my Adeline! Not so! Oh, no!"

The door opened at this moment, and the curate in a night dress stood the threshold.

"Charles! Charles!" he cried. "For the love of Heaven leave this I heard your voice."

"Yes, yes," said Leslie. "I—I was talking with the dead! Look, Mr Endsleigh. This was once my Adeline. These pale lips once bloomed with the hues of health. These cheeks that now mock the moon beams, once bore the tints of vigour. These eyes which now lack fire and lustre, were once twin stars, that shone in beauty when the sun was high, to show the world two opposition lights, more lovely, because more intelligent. Look, sir; look, my old friend, upon the marble brow where noble virtue still sits, as it were enthroned!"

"Charles! Charles!" cried the curate.

"This hand, too," continued Leslie; "the taper fingers of which seem made to mould and fashion human hearts to do its owner's bidding. Now, sir, look on it! It is cold!"

"For God's sake, Charles!"

"Hush, sir! Hush! All you see here was once instinct! This is the casket in which God commanded the purest spirit that waited round His Heavenly throne to dwell in for a space."

The curate wrung his hands in despair.

"This was once the girl you loved. The being I adored," continued Charles. "'Twas sinful, very sinful, for now, when none but Heaven itself and the pale moon are looking on us, I will confess I—I—loved her, next, if not dearer than Heaven itself!"

No. 49

"God help him!" said the curate.

"And so—so—you see she was taken from me. My Adeline! My Adeline!"

His overwrought feelings would sustain him now no longer, and after several gasping efforts to speak, the heart-stricken Charles Leslie fell in a state of insensibility at the foot of the bed on which reposed the remains of his first, last, and only love!

The curate was inexpressibly shocked at the scene. He did not wish, if possible, that any one but himself should be witness to it, and kneeling by Leslie's side, he raised his head from the floor, saying,—

"Charles, Charles, for the love of Heaven and all you hold dear, rouse yourself from this fearful state of nervous excitement. Speak to me, Charles, oh, speak!"

Slowly Leslie opened his eyes, and fixed them on the tearful face of the old man.

"Mr. Endsleigh?" he said.

"Yes, Charles; 'tis I. Command yourself, let me entreat."

"Where am I?" asked Leslie.

"Here in Adeline's chamber."

"The—the chamber of the dead?"

"Yes, Charles. I found you here. But, come, rise and leave here with me. Lean on me, my dear Charles; I am old, but still can render you some assistance."

Charles rose, and leaning heavily upon the arm of the curate, he seemed lost for a few minutes in deep thought.

"What—what did I come here for?" he said. "I—I had some specific object."

"Specific object, Charles? You come to weep by Adeline."

"Now I recollect," cried Leslie. "I—I wished to have some relic of love—one of those ringlets which in graceful freedom shrouded her fair brow."

"My sister will procure you a lock of Adeline's hair," said the curate. "It would renew your grief and illness for you to take it now, Charles."

"No, no; I must now—now, Mr. Endsleigh."

"Nay, Charles, be persuaded."

Leslie shook his head, saying,—

"Let me have that remembrance of her to place next my heart, and I will go in peace."

"Then I will sever it," said the curate.

Charles leaned heavily against the wall, while by the pale moonlight Mr. Endsleigh took from a work-box that was in the room, a minute pair of scissors, that had belonged to Adeline, and severed two tresses of her hair. The one he thrust with a deep sigh into his own breast, and the other he presented to Leslie, saying,—

"Now, Charles, make me a promise that you will pay no more visits to this apartment.

"I—I will obey you," said Leslie, as he clutched the long waving lock of hair in his hand.

"Go now to rest, then, Charles." And with many more gentle words, the old curate got him from the room, and closed the door upon the cold and lifeless form, that was such an agony to him who was so wrapt up in her virtues and her beauty.

CHAPTER CXI.

" They laid her in her narrow home,
    And prayed to God to bless her sleep ;
They knew that angels guard her rest,
    And yet they cannot choose but weep."

MONTGOMERY.

THE FUNERAL,—THE CHURCHYARD.—OLD AND YOUNG.—THE GRAVE OF THE FORSAKEN.

We will not follow the curate and Charles Leslie from day to day in their deep grief: the task would be too—far too painful ; for time did not seem to alleviate the pangs of their hearts, and by the dawning of the morning on which Adeline was to be consigned to her last home, even Mrs. Plumpjoy wept bitterly to see the great alteration which grief had made in Charles Leslie. He was the shadow of his former self, and his once manly voice was weak and tremulous.

The morning had arrived, and it was known throughout the village that Adeline was about to be committed to the earth. Old and young forsook their various employments, and there was an universal feeling to show respect to their good pastor's adopted child, for such they considered Adeline.

Any stranger passing through Bracefield would have been surprised at the universal appearance of mourning that pervaded the place. All the little shops were closed, and every sound of ordinary labour was at rest, while the villagers themselves were gathered in small companies at their respective doors, conversing solemnly and sadly of the affectionate and kind being who in the flower and beauty of her youth was thus snatched from life and love.

In the meantime how sad and dismal were the awful preparations taking place within the parsonage.

The official persons who were conducting the last ceremonies were as kind and considerate as possible, but still there would every moment occur something to wound the feelings of the mourners.

The little party consisting of Charles Leslie, Mr. Endsleigh, Mrs. Plumpjoy, and Mr. Arundel, the humane surgeon, were assembled in the parlour of the parsonage. Several attempts at conversation had been made, but quickly abandoned. The one engrossing subject engaged every one's mind, and upon that one subject no one was inclined to speak, so that after a short time, not a word was exchanged, but the occupants of that parlour sat almost as still and motionless as the poor form that was above stairs, who they had met to mourn.

Then the door opened, and the undertaker entered, and whispered something to Mr. Endsleigh, who immediately rose and walked to the door.

" Whence—whence," said Charles, "are you going ?"

The curate hesitated a moment, then turning to the man, he signified by his hand that he should tell what he meant.

" Please, sir, we are going to screw down the lid," said the undertaker.

" Ye—yes," gasped Leslie ; " of—course ; and—and you thought we should like to take one last look !"

" Exactly, sir," said the man.

" I—I will—I will—yes—yes," repeated Charles, in a low hollow voice as he passed immediately from the room, followed closely by the curate and Mr. Arundel.

They ascended the staircase solemnly to the chamber of the dead, and when they reached the room, the curate drew Charles's arm within his own, and whispered.—

"For my sake, Charles, at this trying moment endeavour to controul your feelings. I would fain you had been spared this sight; but oh, be calm, and resist your feelings."

"I will—I will," said Charles Leslie. "You shall see that I will."

He approached the spot, where supported upon trussles, was the last narrow home of Adeline. There was the same placid calm face as before. It seemed as if corrupting time had shrunk from exercising its blighting power upon that fair form.

One long look Charles cast upon the face of the dead, and then for the last time he murmured,—

"Farewell, farewell, my Adeline!" and turned from the room.

The curate was scarcely less affected than Leslie, and it was perhaps happy for him that in that period of deep affliction he felt strongly the necessity of supporting his young companion, and preventing him from sinking beneath the pressure of his grief, which, however, could only be attempted by an external show of composure in himself.

They now again sought the little parlour, and before ten minutes more had elapsed, they were told that the mournful procession was ready. Then the curate and Charles rose, and in silence proceeded to the door, and joined the sad cavalcade, and as they moved towards the church, the inhabitants of the village fell silently and sadly into the rear of the procession, swelling its length considerably, and imparting to the solemn scene an imposing grandeur from the numbers that came to mourn.

The distance was but trifling between the church and the Parsonage, and now as they neared the sacred edifice, the first stroke of the tolling bell fell upon their ears, and sunk deeply to every heart.

The curate and Charles walked together as first mourners for the loved one who was dead, but when the bearers halted at the church-door, the venerable clergyman, with a tottering step, walked forwards, for he intended to receive the remains of his Adeline within the holy pile.

Arrayed then in the simple and dignified vestments of a minister of God, the old man stood waiting for the approach of the dead. A solemn and silent throng filled the church, and the coffin, covered by its pall, was placed before the rails of the communion-table. All were hushed! The sad and solemn bell ceased tolling, and the voice of the curate rose to Heaven in prayer— fervent and holy prayer for her who was with her God! It was a prayer full of divine hope and simple heart-felt religion. All who heard it were deeply affected, and when he had finished, there was a pause of many minutes, for a holy spell seemed cast over the multitude; then again the deep-toned bell smote upon their ears, and echoed through the church. The coffin was raised, and in solemn order the procession once more was in motion.

Mr. Endsleigh followed in his clergyman's habit, and soon all halted by the grave. The service of the dead was pronounced; the old man stretched his hands over the deep pit, which was to contain the mortal remains of his beloved Adeline. The coffin descended with a hollow sound, and the first handful of earth rattled on the tenement of the dead. Then, and not till then, the old man's heart failed him, and several of the by-standers had just time to catch him in their arms, or he would have fell into the grave of his loved and lost one.

And Charles Leslie, who shall describe what he felt on that awful occasion? What pen shall depict the bursting agony of his heart? With hands clasped motionless and mute, he stood by the brink of the grave till all was over. What thoughts were then crowding through his brain, none can tell.

Mr. Arundel marked his condition, and coming to his side, he said,—

"Mr. Leslie, take my arm."

Charles did so mechanically, and the kind-hearted surgeon led him from the spot.

There was an unnatural calmness upon Leslie's face—no sigh escaped him—sensation seemed to be dead within his breast. It was some hours afterwards in the solitude of his own chamber, that an agony of grief came over him too dreadful for description, and imprinted furrows on his cheek which twenty years of calm existence would have failed to produce.

The last sad office was performed, and the grave had closed over the heart of the Forsaken.

CHAPTER CXII.

" No more for her the moon shall come,
In gathering light and beauty."
COLERIDGE.
" 'Tis night eternal with that weary sleeper."
BYRON.

THE MORNING.—THE EARLY TRAVELLER.—THE HEAD STONE.—FAREWELL.—A NOBLE HEART.

THERE was a hushed and beautiful repose about Bracefield as the first streak of light indicative of the coming morn, irradiated the east. At first but a dim halo spread along the extreme verge of the horizon, then gradually it deepened into streaks of grey light. After a time these gave place to a sickly yellow tinge, which each fleeting moment was increasing in intensity. The birds lifted their heads from beneath their wings, and with many a chirrup and sweet strain of clear melody, welcomed the coming day. The drooping wild flowers slowly unfolded their closed cups, and shaking the sparkling dew from their radiant and many tinted leaves, awakened to greet the sun. The God of life and light, and warmth and beauty, was coming, and all nature, animate and inanimate, with one accord, seemed to rejoice at its advent.

And now from the rapidly lightening east there shot long streaks of upward light, gilding to thin fleecy clouds that floated in the azure sky, and soon the golden edge of the bright sun itself peered above the line of yellow light that heralded its coming, and a long flashing ray of glorious sunlight stretched far and wide through the realms of endless space, tinting with its Heaven-born beauty all things both high and low, and banishing before its refulgence the misty vapours of night, which had hung upon the world during its period of gloom and darkness.

The morning had come—a morning of life and beauty, full of sweet charms, like unto early youth ; full of hope like the young heart when first it looks abroad upon the face of nature, and dreams not that it cannot be immortal.

But what was all this life and beauty to the inhabitants of the Parsonage ? She who they loved was gone. No more for her would the bright morning sun gild the little casement of the chamber in which she slept the calm sleep of innocence and purity. No more for her would the distant sounds of awakening nature gather into sweet confusion, to tell her that the day was come. No more would she lie entranced to listen to the sweet strains of the wild birds,

" Singing in wantonness of joy."

Alas! she was gone! she who lent to every sight and sound of beauty, the last touch of delight which made them still more beautiful to those who loved her. She was gone, and with her had gone many of the charms of nature, for our appreciation of what is beautiful, depends more upon the feelings with which we view it, than upon the object itself. Now, therefore, as Charl

Leslie rose from a sleepless couch, and looked out upon the bright and glowing morning, it was with a sigh instead of a smile, for his heart was not allured to admiration, and his feelings were not in unison with what he saw.

It was still very early, but Leslie had determined to leave Bracefield, if possible, before any one was stirring. This resolve he had communicated the previous evening to the curate, and had taken leave of him, so that there was no obstacle to his leaving the Parsonage, wrapt in the gloom of his own painful feelings.

Hastily, therefore, preparing himself for departure, Charles Leslie crept with a noiseless step from his bed-room, and being familiar with the premises, he quickly saddled his horse, as he had done on former occasions, and leading the animal out into the lane at the back of the Parsonage, he mounted, and with one long lingering look at the old house, he, with a deep sigh, urged his steed forward, nor once more turned his head to the building, which had now for him so many melancholy associations connected with it.

He rode on for some minutes in silence, then as if by some sudden impulse, he reined in his steed, and remained for a few moments in anxious thought. Then, as a deep sigh burst from his heart, he suddenly exclaimed—

"I cannot—no—I cannot leave Bracefield without once again looking on the spot that hides from me my beautiful and true, my Adeline."

He turned the horse's head, and putting the animal to a canter, he soon reached a small bridle path which led into the village from whence he intended to proceed up the green lane to the churchyard.

No one impeded his progress; scarcely a soul in the village had risen, for the day was still very young, and it was a relief to the wounded spirits of Charles to meet no one with whom he would have been, by common courtesy, constrained to interchange the civilities of the morning. Making direct for the green lane, he soon reached its entrance, and allowing the horse to walk gently along the narrow pathway, he dismounted when he had reached the wicket. Charles then tied the bridle of his steed to the gate-post, and himself entered the churchyard.

His heart beat with emotion as he waned his way among the mounds of earth, each marking the repose of some one that had been loved and mourned, until he neared the spot on which his Adeline reposed.

As he came within sight of the little rising ground, on the summit of which the grave of Adeline had been dug, he caught the sound of a slow and measured footstep, and the next moment he saw some one approaching him through the grave-stones.

Leslie paused, and the intruder came close to him before he spoke. It was an old man who Charles knew as the mason of the village.

The old man paused, and leaning on a stick he carried, shook his head mournfully, as he replied—

"God bless you, Master Leslie, I am an old man now, and have put up many a head-stone in this ancient grave-yard."

"Many a head-stone?" said Leslie.

"Yes," continued the old mason; "that is a part of my trade of a mason, Master Leslie; a gloomy part though, but I never heeded it till now."

"And wherefore does it now affect you?" said Leslie. "There are tears in your eyes, old man. Have you lost one who loved you and who you loved?"

The old man again shook his head mournfully, as he replied to Charles' interrogatory.

"Young and old, the poor and the rich; even the vain, the proud, and the foolish—all—all loved Adeline Mourdant."

Charles clasped his hands as he said—

"Old man, you speak truth. She was a being formed to be loved—but oh, had those loved her who knew all her worth—who saw deeper into the pure depths of her innocent heart than——. But—but this is madness. I wish you a good morning, friend, and thank you kindly for what you have said of her who sleeps here the sleep of death."

"Mr. Endsleigh," said the old man; "Mr. Endsleigh ordered me, by daybreak, if possible, to place the head-stone by her grave, bless her."

"And—and," gasped Charles—"you have done it?"

"I have, Master Leslie"

Charles walked slowly onwards, and the old mason, after looking after him for a few moments, with slow steps quitted the churchyard, murmuring—

"It will be my turn soon—very soon—very soon."

A few seconds brought Charles Leslie to Adeline's grave. At its head was the stone which Mr. Endsleigh ordered to be placed there; on it was the simple and affecting inscription.

A. M.
AGED 19,
"THE GRAVE OF THE FORSAKEN."

Fresh green turf had been carefully laid upon the grave, and some one from the village had thrown upon it a few wild flowers. Charles was sensibly touched at this mute demonstration of affection for Adeline, and lifted one of the flowers from the grave and placed it in his breast.

"And this is all that is left to tell of thee, Adeline," he said mournfully, as through his gathering tears he gazed earnestly at the simple inscription. "The Grave of the Forsaken. Alas! alas! Those were thy own words, my Adeline, but thou wert not forsaken, for thou wert loved and cherished by many hearts—aye, by all but the one that had sworn to do so in presence of its God. Herbert Mandeville, wherever thou art, may Heaven forgive thee for the broken heart that lies beneath this verdant sod. If thou can'st stand as I now stand, gazing on that simple stone, and not feel a pang worse than the tortures of the damned, thou art as one in the great family of mankind—one destitute of feeling here or hope hereafter. I will seek thee, Herbert Mandeville, and deliver my message of forgiveness. If thou art in life I will find thee, to tell thee that an angel has broken her heart for thee, and yet prays that thou mayest be happy. Farewell, my Adeline, a long farewell to thee; for I may have many, many miles to traverse ere yet again I stand beside thy humble grave. This spot, while yet life is mine, shall ever fill me with holy thoughts. My Adeline, I will visit thy grave and rest my spirits from the turmoils of the world in sweet, yet melancholy remembrance of thy virtues. Farewell—farewell, I go to do thy bidding, gentle spirit, and I will live but in the dear hope of some day sleeping here by thy side, and they may place another head-stone by me, on which they may say, that here in peace eternal sleeps one who loved thee, Adeline; and whose only consolation when thou wert gone, was that he might await by thy side the summons of the Almighty to judgment! My Adeline, farewell."

He turned and left the spot, but many times ere he reached the wicket-gate, he strove to catch another, and yet another, parting glance at the Grave of the Forsaken."

At length it was hidden from his view, and with a deep sigh he mounted his horse; then waving his hand, he again cried—"my Adeline, farewell," and galloped from the spot.

CHAPTER CXIII.

" It gleamed forth at the midnight hour,
　　When all around was still,
Save the sweet sighing of the wind
　　As it swept down the hill.''

THE CURATE'S ILLNESS.—MORE ALARM.—THE MYSTERIOUS LIGHT AGAIN.

To the grief and consternation of Mrs. Plumpjoy and the whole village, it was found in the morning after Adeline's funeral, that Mr. Endsleigh had far overtaxed his strength, and that he was too weak and unwell to leave his bed.

Mr. Arundel was immediately summoned, and he sat for a long time by the bed-side of the aged man, for he saw that grief had made a terrible inroad upon his health, and he feared, that unless he could raise him from the state of deep dejection into which he had fallen, that he would never again rise from that bed a living man.

The old curate did not complain. He uttered no sounds of grief, neither did he weep, but there was a settled gloom upon his once calm and serene face, which was distressing to witness, and he spoke with a tone of such deep and melancholy pathos of his bereavement, that although his words were those of resignation and almost cheerful hope, the dreadful struggle that was taking place in the old man's mind, between his deep personal grief and his religious condition, was manifest by the tones of his voice, which, however, he might endeavour to modify then, would, in despite of all his efforts, follow the dictates of his heart.

The old man was unused to act a part ; for so many years the genuine feelings of his heart had always been fully and freely expressed, and all unskilled was the aged man of God in the expression of feelings that he did *not* feel, and in the varied expression of countenance which could hide a bleeding if not a broken heart.

Mr. Arundel gently nursed his grief until it was partially destroyed by its own intensity, and then prayer—prayer such as the bruised heart may justly offer at the throne of the Almighty, began slowly but surely to exert its benign influence upon his soul, and day after day the old curate spoke with a more cheerful tone. It was not that he lamented his darling less.' It was not that she occupied a smaller space in his heart now that she was gone ! but it was because the judgment began to assert its proper and constitutional supremacy over the feelings, as it seem to do in a mind so highly cultivated and well-regulated as Mr. Endsleigh's. His grief now was quite as great—aye, possibly it had sunk deeper than ever into his heart, but it was a totally different kind of grief that he now felt. At first, despite all his corrector and more religious feelings, there lurked in his mind a feeling that he ought not to have been deprived of his darling—the prop of his old age—the one dear joy that still made the world beautiful in the old man's eyes.

Now, however, his mind obeyed softer and better impulses. He told himself it was Heaven's will that she should be taken f om him, and with a truly Christian spirit, he brought himself to believe in the more perfect happiness of his dear Adeline in Heaven, than he, and all who loved her on earth, could have bestowed upon her.

The old man's first visit to the grave of Adeline was in company of Mrs. Plumpjoy and Mr. Arundel. It was early on the first Sunday morning that he felt well enough to enable him again to resume his spiritual functions. On that day he had determined to go through his accustomed duties, and to preach

the words of truth to his humble congregation for the first time since death had been in his once happy dwelling.

Mr. Arundel was apprehensive of some burst of feeling from the old curate, which would be most prejudicial to his precarious health, and even Mrs. Plumpjoy was nervous with apprehension as she felt his arm tremble within hers upon first obtaining sight of the little stone tablet erected to the memory of Adeline. Their fears, however, were groundless: it is true the old man's step tottered as he walked onwards, and his voice betrayed emotion, as he said,—

"Yes, yes, this is the grave of my darling child, Adeline. I shall come often here."

"Do so, sir," said Mr. Arundel, who was rejoiced to see the spirit in which the curate now took his bereavement. "If we make a proper use of such sorrows as these, they lose one half of their melancholy."

"You are quite right," said Mr. Endsleigh, "and—and now—I had better stay here no longer, just at present—or—or, perchance, my heart might yet betray me, and I might weep, not wishing, or scarcely knowing that I did so."

The curate then turned slowly from the spot, and entered the porch of the ancient church.

From that time forth he frequently visited the grave of Adeline, and each time he lingered for a longer space by the verdant spot, beneath which slept the beautiful and good. He ceased to weep for her, but with a mild and patient melancholy he would lean on his stick by the grave-side, and picture to himself over and over again all that she had at various times said to him, and find in every sweet remembrance food for contemplation, more than grief. Although this was not the way to forget his deep sorrow, yet it was the way to temper it with a chastened and holy resignation.

It happened, too, that shortly afterwards there was great sickness in the
No. 50

village of Bracefield, and Mr. Endsleigh stood by the bed-sides of many of the young, the hopeful, and the beautiful. He saw many dear and clinging ties of affection severed by the same stern decree that had torn from him his Adeline; and when his voice was in prayer to comfort the bereaved, and when he told them that their separation from the loved one was but for a season, for that he or she had but

" Gone on before "

to those mansions of eternal rest and joy, whence they would again meet to part never more; and, as his voice trembled, and his heart looked upwards with holy confidence, he borrowed consolation for his own sorrows from his own words. Thus is it often, that out of evil springeth good, and half a-year passed away over the head of the venerable man of God in greater serenity, if not greater happiness, than it seemed possible it should, considering the great shock his feelings and affections had sustained.

There was another subject, too, which, while it filled his mind with disagreeable sensations, still tended in some manner to withdraw him from dwelling too much upon individual sorrows, and that was that the mysterious light had been again seen issuing from the window of the old church at an hour when it was well known no living soul was within its walls.

The villagers were inexpressibly alarmed at the curious phenomena, and nothing would convince them of the extreme improbability that any supernatural visitation was the cause of the appearance. Indeed the curate himself was agitated and annoyed upon the occasion, and still more was he vexed when he was told that the light had been seen oftener than he had been informed of it, and that respect for his private sorrows had induced the kindhearted villagers to say nothing of it until his mind had in some measure recovered from the shock it had undergone by his domestic calamity, for all knew how much he had loved, and how deeply he mourned the beautiful young girl that, in the winter of his life, he had taken to his heart.

Sometimes the light had been seen at one window of the old church, and sometimes at another, and, upon making close inquiry, Mr. Endsleigh had learned that two of the more intrepid of the villagers, who had gone to the churchyard, in order to have a nearer view of the strange phenomenon, had been much startled by a spectral appearance in the churchyard—a form that had glided past them noiselessly—clad in the vestments of the grave, and curdling their very blood with terror.

All this Mr. Endsleigh felt it to be his duty, his imperative duty, to set right, or at least endeavour to clear up.

He was much attached to his ancient church, and he did not forget that beneath the shadow of its walls lay Adeline.

Things were in this state at Bracefield when Mr. Endsleigh received the following letter from Charles Leslie, dated Paris, and which will give the reader a better insight into the proceedings of that noble-minded young man, than we could possibly do by a mere narration of his progress in his search for Mandeville, who had unaccountably disappeared, no one knew whither; or, at least, those that knew, did not choose to tell, and were, doubtless, well paid for their silence.

"June, 1827.

" MY DEAR FRIEND,—My letters hitherto have consisted but of one statement, or, rather, one of its invariable accompaniments, namely, I am searching for Herbert Mandeville, and cannot find him.

" Now, however, I, for the first time, have a serious and well-grounded hope that I shall find him, and relieve my mind of the burthen of the sacred promise which you know I made to our dear Adeline, that if he were on this earth I would carry to him, in kind words, her forgiveness.

" I made that promise, my dear Mr. Endsleigh, as you know, in no light or idle mood, and, as you likewise know, I have travelled over most parts of Europe now for nearly ten months without being able, by the slightest clue, to fix upon the whereabouts of this unfortunate, and, I fear, in many respects, guilty young man.

"I always had a fancy that if I met him anywhere, it would be at Paris, and here, as you will see by the date of this, I am for the fourth time in that capital of frivolity, impiety, and vice.

"My prognostications as to meeting Herbert Mandeville here have not been verified ; but it is here, at length, that I have met with a clue to his retreat, and strangely enough I have met with it.

"The other day I met accidentally at a party at our ambassador's, a very agreeable, and most intelligent French gentleman, who entertained me very much by an exceedingly graphic account of a stupendous storm, which quite devastated the coast of France some time, and in which an English gentleman was exposed to some danger. He likewise added that the English gentleman had been exposed to a great deal of inconvenience, owing to being without a passport.

"All this, my dear friend, I listened to with some interest, in consequence of the amusing manner in which it was told ; but when he concluded, by saying that the Englishman's name was Mandeville, you may guess how much more interested I became.

"I pressed my informant with questions, and learned that since then he had met this Mr. Mandeville at Rome under an assumed name, which, to the best of his recollection, he believed was Armstrong.

"This is all the information I can collect ; but upon it, slender as it is, I shall start for Rome to-morrow ; and, should I be fortunate enough to find him I seek, and deliver my errand, you shall see me once again at Bracefield, my dear old friend, as quickly as may be, for I long again to visit the spot where lie the remains of her I loved so well.

"Believe me, my dear friend, yours ever,
"CHARLES LESLIE."

"To the Rev. R. Endsleigh."

The old curate was always pleased to hear from Charles Leslie ; but he was doubly pleased with this last letter, because it indicated a hope of Charles's speedy return, and he was now the only one to whom the old man most especially warmed.

Mr. Endsleigh loved mankind, aye, he loved even the meanest thing that God had made, but Charles Leslie he knew well, and all the affection which his heart had garnered up for his dear child—who was in Heaven—as he always called Adeline, he now longed to lavish upon Leslie.

The letter was therefore a comfort to the old man, and he felt himself better able to attend to the affairs of the next object of his affection, namely, his ancient church.

Summoning old Andrew to his study, he said, kindly—

"Andrew, I have received a letter from Mr. Leslie, in which he talks of coming to us soon."

"Does he, sir?" exclaimed the old man, evidently much pleased. "I am sure we shall be all now glad to see Master Leslie."

"We shall—we shall, Andrew," replied the curate ; "he gains all hearts."

"Ah, sir," remarked the old and licensed domestic with a deep sigh. "If so be——"

"If so be what, Andrew?"

"If so be, sir, as poor dear Miss Adeline, bless her, had but a tooked to Master Charles how happy we might all a been."

The curate was silent for a moment, and a tear stole down his check as he said—

"Man proposes, Andrew ; but God alone disposes. We are in His hands."

"So we is," said Andrew ; " only——"

"Hush—hush," said the curate ; " enough of that, Andrew."

"Very well, sir, only——"

"No more ; you—you will vex me, Andrew."

"Then I'd rather lose my tongue than say another word," responded the old servant.

"I sent for you, Andrew," continued Mr. Endsleigh, "about something else, only I knew it would please you to hear that Mr. Leslie might soon come to us, so I told you that first."

"That's just like you, sir," replied Andrew.

"Well, then—you have heard, of course, quite as much as I have about these lights in the church, Andrew ?"

"I believe you, sir," said Andrew ; " and a good deal more, I'll be bound."

"Very like—very like."

"Ah, sir, Bill Mathews he solemnly thinks as the ghostesses isen't more nor less than the evil spirit of his wife, and he says —"

"Well—well, never mind him," interrupted Mr. Endsleigh. "I wish you to watch with me in the church, I have myself passed one night in it, and not been able to clear up the mystery, but I think that two of us may have a better chance."

Andrew looked rather nonplussed at this sudden and most unexpected proposal, and stammered out—

"D—d—don't ye think, sir, as a dozen or so would stand a better chance ?"

"No, I do not," said the curate.

"Well—then—I—sup—pose as I must go."

"Not at all, unless you go with your own free will.   It is a duty which I have no right to command you to."

"You—you mean to go, sir, yourself ?"

"Certainly I do."

"Quite—quite surely ?"

"Quite !"

"Then—I must, so there's an end to it."

"Very well, Andrew, you shall."

"I will, sir.   When is it to be ?"

"Not till the light has been seen once more."

"Very well, Mr. Endsleigh. I—I only hopes as it won't be seen no more."

CHAPTER CXIV.

" 'Tis dangerous for woman to dissemble,
The passion she but feigns she yet may feel."
                                        POPE.

CHARLES LESLIE'S PROGRESS TO ROME.—A STRANGE ADVENTURE AND STILL STRANGER PROPOSAL.—THE FUGITIVES.

WE confess ourselves attached to Bracefield, and we would fain linger with the old curate by the grave of Adeline, but rougher scenes call us away, and it is our duty now, as faithful historians, to follow for a brief space the fortunes of Charles Leslie in his search for Herbert Mandeville.

Before the letter, which we have presented to the reader, reached its destination at Bracefield, Charles had made every preparation for quitting France and travelling to the Imperial City of Rome, among whose same solemn and gigantic ruins he now hoped to find the object of his search, to whom he so longed to deliver his errand of mercy and forgiveness from the pure heart of her he had injured.

The seasons' changes are frequently more bitterly felt in France than in England, and at that time, although the season was scarcely on the wane in our own country, an unusual wet season had set in in France, and heavy rains fell upon the coast, extending inland, even as far as Paris.

The air was comfortless and chill when Leslie left his hotel in Paris, to start by a crazy vehicle his first stage southward.

The rain was descending in torrents, but Leslie paid little heed to it, for the errand upon which he was bound had conjured up a fit of deep dejection and depression of spirits to which, despite his struggles of mind, he had been occasionally subject since the death of Adeline, and the consequent extinction of his purest, brightest dream of happiness, for it was really not until she was dead, that the last hope, lingering in his breast unknown even to himself, that she might one day be his, was totally extinguished, and he awakened to that feeling of despair in which there is no hope.

With his hand thrust deep in his breast, as was his custom when under such temporary feelings of despairing sorrow, Charles Leslie hurried onwards towards the place where the carriage, if such it could be called, was to start. That hand that was thus hidden in his breast, clutched his only momento of Adeline—the lock of hair he had severed from her pale brow as she lay before him in death. He heeded not the frowning aspect of the elements, for his own heart was at that moment far more gloomy than they. The rain fell upon him without his being conscious of its influence.

Now he reached the dilligence, and hastily threw himself into the seat which had been reserved for him.

"Why should I give way," he thought, "to this gloom of the heart? I will struggle again and again against it. The night is chill and cold—but, but my Adeline is where cold reaches her not ; she—is—gone."

One tear, and but one—for he made a powerful effort to suppress the tide of feeling from bursting forth and overpowering his reason—rolled down his cheek, and then he became calm and strove to think of other themes.

As he there sat waiting for the departure of the vehicle which was to carry him at least some short distance on his route, his ear caught the voice of some one singing with so melancholy and exquisitely saddened an intonation, that he felt in a moment it could not, by even the most consummate actress of woe, be assumed merely for the occasion.

The voice was a female one, and possessed considerable power and sweetness. What it had once been might have been fairly judged by what it was at present, at least by a lover of music and a person of imagination. The careless crowd that swept onwards and elbowed the unfortunate singer, stopped not to reflect upon what that voice might have been under more favourable circumstances ; they reflected not upon the different intonation which a happier destiny might have given to the notes of the singer, but Charles was not one of those who judge hastily or heedlessly of anything or anybody, and there was something in the deep pathos of the singer's voice that touched a sympathetic chord of woe in his own breast.

The unfortunate singer was evidently approaching to where the carriage was waiting, and a degree of curiosity to hear her closer, and even, if possible, to see and speak to her, took possession of Charles Leslie's breast.

It is true that

"There is a charm in melancholy,"

which none but those who have known much sorrow can at all appreciate, and the tones of this poor wandering street-singer sounded each to Leslie's ears, like the last sad despairing notes from a broken heart.

"Poor creature," thought Charles, "I can relieve her temporary poverty —for this night at least or a few nights to come, and can raise her above the painful necessity of singing thus, with the sad yet beautiful tones, in the public streets."

He waited for the slow approach of the singer who was but crawling, as it were, along the street, and as she neared, Charles Leslie, to his great surprise, heard that the words she uttered, although low and indistinct, were English.

"Here then, at least," he thought, "putting all false sentiment and feeling on one side—here is a proper object for my bounty. She is either a country-woman of my own, or long residence, possibly, in some English family, has made her very familiar with the language."

As yet he could not catch the words she uttered, in anything like sufficient connection, to tell what was the subject of her melancholy ditty, but as she was evidently approaching, although slowly, he would not leave the carriage, but contented himself by waiting till he should catch the first glimpse of her, when he intended to call her.

In a few moments more he saw a miserably-looking, ragged object close to the carriage, and now he heard the words of her song distinctly, they spoke of high wrought feeling, and he would not interrupt the melancholy strains.

It was this:

"Oh! could my sighs my wish impart,
    And whisper to his ear my love ;
Oh! could he feel the throbbing heart,
    Its tenderness and truth to prove.

"Oh! could he view my soul sincere,
    Though hopeless love disturbs its rest,
He'd find his image pictur'd there,
    For ever loved and still dearest.

"At morning dawn, or close of day,
    I'd prize with him the lowest cot ;
With him would join the rural lay,
    All else but love and him forgot.

"And when the term of life drew nigh,
    I'd wish my pillow were his breast ;
There breathe the last expiring sigh,
    And sink within his arms to rest."

The singer ceased, and in a low voice, broken by sobs, she begged for charity—charity to save her from starving in a foreign land.

Charles Leslie leaned anxiously forward, to speak to the poor woman, but he was interrupted by a coarse man, who sat on the opposite seat to him, who cried imperiously,

"So, English, are you, eh? *Sacre*, we want no English here. Sing a more sprightly ditty, or by the genius of France, the first and most glorious nation in the world, I'll give you to the guard. Ah! *sacre!*"

Charles Leslie felt his indignation rising, but by a great effort he restrained himself, and he saw the poor creature, with a shudder, and an expression of suffering, gaze earnestly and imploringly in the face of the man who had spoken to her so roughly before she commenced, in obedience to him, a gayer strain.

"Young Cupid lies enchanting
    In a face of dimpling smiles;
And with sunny laughter,
    The saddest heart beguiles.

"Young love and happy faces,
    Were ever near allied,
And Cupid lies in sunshine
    In wantonness and pride.

> " A tear will banish loving,
>   A smile will win a heart;
> Then who would live in sadness
>   With love and joy to part?
>
> " The sunshine of the bosom
>   Will dance in sparkling eyes,
> And all is joy and gladness
>   Beneath the smiling skies.
>
> " Then sigh not, lest young Cupid
>   Should gently fly away,
> That banish tears and sadness,
>   And welcome Love's fair day."

" Now, sir," said Leslie, calmly and firmly, when the song had ceased, " you are satisfied, I hope ?"

" Ah, *sacre !* satisfied—bah !"

" If you require anything more of that poor woman," said Leslie, " you had better ask it of me. I shall be able better to answer you."

There was something in Charles's manner that the arrogant Frenchman evidently feared, and he shrunk back in his own corner, without another word.

Charles turned to the poor singer. She was clinging to the carriage and weeping bitterly.

" You are an Englishwoman ?" said Charles.

" I—I am," she gasped.

" How is it, that you are here so badly off ?"

" I—I am wretched," said the woman.

" Your condition must, indeed, be bad. Have you no friends in Paris?"

" None—none. I have no friends anywhere."

" What has reduced you to this state of extreme destitution and misery ? Believe me, I do not ask from idle curiosity. I wish, if possible, to do something for you. You are a countrywoman of my own, and in a foreign land. I, therefore, consider it a duty to assist you, independent of my sympathy with your forlorn condition."

The poor creature wept bitterly, for some few minutes, before she replied, then taking from her breast a folded paper, she handed it to Leslie, saying,

" Read that, sir, some other time. It will tell you who and what I am. It will likewise inform you of the object of my weary and melancholy pilgrimage from my native land, and should you meet him, who is therein mentioned, give it to him, and—and—"

" And what ?" said Leslie.

" Will you then send a note, saying so much, addressed to me at the *Paste Restaute,* at Calais ? Farewell, sir ; farewell."

" Stay," cried Leslie. He placed as much money as he could spare in her hands, and the next minute, with a deep sob, she darted from the side of the vehicle, and was lost in the obscurity that reigned around.

CHAPTER CXV.

AN OLD ACQUAINTANCE.—CRIME AND ITS CONSEQUENCES.—ROME.

CHARLES LESLIE was very much struck by the singular manner of the unfortunate street singer. Her language evidently proclaimed her as belonging to a class of society, far—very far above her present condition in life, and he readily imagined that nothing but vice of some kind could have reduced her from her proper sphere of life, to the one she now moved in.

And yet, he thought, after all, she may be more of a victim than a victimiser, more of a sufferer than an inflictor. There was not light enough for him to read the paper she had handed to him, and which, in bulk, was not greater then a letter; he, therefore, waited with some eagerness for the completion of the next stage of his journey, in order that he might peruse the document, which he doubted not contained some interesting particulars concerning the unfortunate person who had given it to him.

The public carriages of France might be all truly denominated "infernal machines," for, out of all question, they are the heaviest, the slowest, and the most inconvenient that it is possible to conceive. The French character, in fact, abounds so much with national vanity, that improvement is very slow in its progress as concerns them, or any of their public conveniences.

At length, however, the distance was performed, after a fashion; the harness of ropes having broken at least once in every mile, and Charles Leslie, hastily leaving the crazy vehicle, entered nearly as crazy a hotel, and having ordered some refreshment, proceeded to read the paper, which interested his curiosity so much. It was as follows:

"I have written this paper, and several copies of it, for the purpose of placing in the hands of any of my kind countrymen I may meet, who may feel disposed to aid me in the accomplishment of the only object for which I drag on a weary and miserable existence.

"My name is Flora Waldon, but I have been better known in London, as Mrs. Delancey."

"Delancey!" cried Leslie, when he came thus far, "surely that was the name of the unhappy woman with whom it has been currently reported, Herbert Mandeville eloped? How strangely do things occur. Can it be possible that this unfortunate and destitute singer in the streets of Paris, is the woman who I have heard described as beautiful in the extreme, and possessed of the rarest accomplishments? Oh, guilt—guilt—into what depths of misery wilt thou not plunge thy votaries."

He resumed the manuscript.

"A conspiracy was hatched to entrap a young heedless man, of the name of Mandeville, to elope with me, supposing me the wife of Delancey. The sole object of that conspiracy was to extort money from him by the threat of an action, which money was to be divided between the person calling herself Clara Seagrave, the man Delancey, and one Dufours. The plot succeeded, and it was not until it had done so, that my woman's heart confessed that I loved Herbert Mandeville.

"I refused to allow the threatened action to be proceeded with, and was turned with blows and reproaches, into the streets, a houseless and destitute wanderer. Such were the fitting wages of my share in the guilty transaction. Mr. Mandeville, I found, had fled none knew whither, and now for many weary months I have wandered in search of him, to place in his hands this confession, and restore him to his home.

"I have subsisted upon charity. The streets have been my home;—a stone step my pillow.

"Sir,—If you, in your travels, should meet this Herbert Mandeville, I pray you to give him this paper, and accept the heartfelt thanks of the unhappy
"FLORA WALDON, known as MRS. DELANCEY."

"Unhappy woman," sighed Leslie; "I will do thy bidding. Alas! alas!

Herbert Mandeville, ruin and destruction seem to have followed ever in thy footsteps. It will be your duty, if your heart be not quite destitute of feeling, to restore this poor repentant woman to the comforts of a home."

Charles Leslie carefully placed the document in his pocket-book, and with a deep sigh, he reflected upon the strange combination of circumstances which had made him, of all men, the bearer of forgiveness, peace, and good news, to the very man who had blasted his happiness for life, and broken the heart of the being who was almost as dear to him as his hopes of Heaven.

Still Charles Leslie's noble spirit did not shrink from its self-imposed duty. It was Adeline's wish that he should carry her last words to Mandeville, and that wish became in his mind a sacred obligation. Over and over again he had constructed in his mind the very words in which he would address Mandeville when they should meet, and now he hailed with some degree of pleasure the prospect of speedily accomplishing the chivalrous and generous object that kept him from his native land, and that one spot of earth near which it was his earnest wish to pass the remainder of his days,—namely, Adeline's grave.

His progress through France was slow and wearisome, but the longest journey must have an end, and with a feeling of satisfaction, Charles Leslie found himself once again treading the classic regions of Italy.

The season of summer in the north of Europe was rapidly breaking, but still the fertile vales and smiling vineyards of Italy were glorious in their beauty. It was a beauty, however, which spake but sadly to the heart of Charles Leslie, for as often as he glanced from some vine-covered height upon the magnificent landscapes of

" The land of music and romance,"

his sense of the beautiful and the sublime was destroyed by the bitter obtrud-

No. 51

ing thought that she whose bosom would have throbbed with delight at such scenes—she whose eyes would have rivalled in their sparkling lustre, even the blue—the deep, impassioned blue of an Italian sky, was silent in the grave. Adeline was not there, and Charles Leslie would turn from all the gorgeous beauty with a sigh of regret, a sigh deeper and more mournful as the scene that called it forth was more lovely and replete with Heavenly charms.

Thus, with a patient and uncomplaining melancholy, Charles Leslie passed through that land which has been called

" The garden of the world,"

each murmuring rivulet, each rock, each time-worn tree and mouldering ruin of which is replete with associations of beauty and dear romance.

As he neared Rome, his anxiety to meet Herbert Mandeville there increased in intensity, and a nervous apprehension of missing him again, kept Charles Leslie in a constant perturbation of spirits.

A letter, which he sent to the curate by an English traveller, who promised to post it on his arrival in England, too well pourtrays the anxiety of his heart for us to omit transcribing it here.

"My Dear Friend,—Before you receive this I shall be at Rome, from whence I will write to you again. If I do not find him I seek there, I know not what to do. Oh, Mr. Endsleigh, I shall never know peace until I have fulfilled the requests—commands I should call them, of her who now I please myself with thinking looks down from Heaven upon those who loved her here, where she sojourned so brief a space.

"I have prayed to find Mandeville at Rome, and now that I am within a few miles of that city, my agitation is extreme. Forgive the incoherence of this letter. I could not resist the opportunity of writing to you.

"Believe me, my dear friend,

"Yours, ever truly,

"To the Rev. R. Endsleigh.   "Charles Leslie."

CHAPTER CXVI.

ROME.—THE INQUIRY.—DISAPPOINTMENT.—FOUND AT LAST.—THE AGONIZING MEETING.

It was early in the morning when Charles Leslie with a beating heart, entered the ancient city of Rome, in search of Herbert Mandeville. He looked not at the gigantic monuments of former magnificence and glory that other travellers came so many weary miles to gaze at. Alike at that time to him was the strange heterogeneous villa of the modern Italian grandee, and the purely beautiful remains of the classical temples of the race that had faded away many, many years ago, leaving behind but the record of their arts, their wealth, their civilization in grey ruins of their palaces and their temples.

He proceeded directly to a house of entertainment kept by an English family, of whom he knew something, and after the first salutations were over, Charles said :—

"Do you know of any one of the name of Mandeville staying at Rome ?"

"No," was the reply ; "unless a very recent arrival ; indeed, I am certain there is no such person at present in the city."

"I—I beg your pardon," said Charles, suddenly recollecting the assumed name which he had been told Herbert went by ; "I do not mean Mandeville. That is a mistake of mine. The name is Armstrong."

"Armstrong! Armstrong!" repeated the person. "Now I recollect there is a gentleman of that name staying on a visit with the Marquis de Lara."

"Indeed?"

"Yes, I am sure Armstrong is the name."

"On a visit with an Italian nobleman, you say?"

"Yes; the marquis's palace is close at hand. There, I make no doubt you will find the gentleman you seek."

"You are sure of the name?" said Leslie.

"Oh, quite. We have heard it often."

"Have you seen the gentleman?"

"Once, for a moment, merely."

"Was he a young man?"

"I should judge so. He was on horseback when I saw him."

"It must be he," thought Leslie. "I thank you for your information, my friend. I will go to the marquis's at once, if you can spare me any of your household to point out to me his residence."

"Certainly," was the reply; and in a few minutes, Charles Leslie, guided by a boy, was at length, he believed, fairly within a few minutes time of meeting Herbert Mandeville.

The boy pointed to a stately building that had evidently been repaired at the expense of many of the beautiful views in the vicinity, and exclaimed,—

"That is the marquis's palace."

"Thank you," said Charles, handing him at the same time a liberal reward.

With a slow step, and a composed mien, he ascended the steps of the spacious abode. His heart was full of Adeline, and his strong sense of what he had to do and say, overcome his nervousness, and he felt far more firm and collected than he had been when a hundred weary miles lay between him and Rome. There was an undefinable something about the manner and appearance of Charles Leslie, which bespoke the gentleman, and he was received by several servants in the hall with deferential respect.

"Is this the Marquis de Lara's?" asked Leslie.

"It is, signor," replied a servant, respectfully.

"Has he a gentleman visiting him at present from England?"

"He has, signor."

"What is his name?"

"Armstrong."

"'Tis he then I wish to see. Is he now within?"

"He is, signor. He and my Lord Marquis are breakfasting."

"Take this card to him," said Leslie, "and tell him the bearer will wait his leisure."

The servant bowed, and took Charles's card, after motioning him into an elegant reception apartment, adorned with choice paintings, and a beautiful vaulted ceiling.

In a few moments the domestic returned with Charles's card in his hand.

"Well?" said Leslie.

"Signor Armstrong says there must be some mistake, for he has not the honor of knowing your name."

"Indeed?"

The servant gave an expressive shrug.

"Wait one moment," said Charles, and taking the card, he wrote on it in pencil,—

"HERBERT MANDEVILLE,—I have travelled many miles to see you, for your own peace and happiness."

He then gave the card again to the servant, saying,—

" Take that back to him, and say I still wait."

" Certainly, signor," was the reply ; and the domestic bowed himself out of the room.

" So, he would avoid seeing me," thought Charles ; " but I must see him. He expects some reproaches, and an angry meeting. I must see him, however. I will perform my errand, if it cost me my life. Were he behind treple bars of adament, I would face him ! I have sworn it !"

The door now opened, and the servant again appeared with the card.

" Well, what says he now ?"

" Signor, pardon me," said the servant.

" Nay, never mind. You are not answerable for an unmanly message."

" Will signor have his exact words ?"

" Aye, to the letter."

" Then, Signor Armstrong says you must be some madman !"

" Indeed ?"

" Even so, signor. Those were his words."

" Was that all ?"

" No. He desires, as well as the marquis, that I see you off the premises."

Charles Leslie faced the servant so suddenly, that he gave a great jump, and looked very much alarmed.

" Where is Mr. Armstrong ?"

" In—in—the—the breakfast saloon."

" But where is that ?"

" T—the first door up the marble steps."

" Thank you," said Charles ; and he strode up the steps with an air that did not at all induce the gaping domestics to offer him any opposition.

At the top of the flight of steps was a handsomely-painted door, which Charles Leslie opened without ceremony. It conducted him into an apartment of great magnificence, in which were two gentlemen at their morning repast. They both rose, and Charles Leslie looked from one to the other in bewilderment ; neither bore the resemblance to Herbert Mandeville.

" To what circumstance," said the elder of the two gentlemen, " are we indebted for the honor of this familiar visit ?"

" I—I expected a Mr. Armstrong," stammered Leslie, fairly vanquished by the cold dignity with which he was addressed.

" And now that you have found him, sir," said the younger gentleman, " what is your business with him ?"

" Are you Mr. Armstrong ?"

" I am, sir."

" And—and—that is your name ?"

" I believe it is," said the young man, sarcastically.

" Gentlemen," said Charles Leslie, " I come from England to convey a dying message to one who I was told had assumed the name of Armstrong at Rome. I am the victim of some mistaken information, and I can only make to you both my earnest apologies for this most unwarrantable intrusion."

The gentlemen both bowed, and the elder said,—

" Sir, it is we who ought to apologise, for not seeing you at once when you would have found out your error."

" That's true," said the younger, " It was all the fault of my confounded hasty disposition ; I, therefore, apologise to you, sir, for my rudeness to a countryman and a gentleman."

" You are very kind, gentlemen," said Charles, " and I thank you both from my heart, for your great courtesy. I must renew my search elsewhere, and God send it may prove successful."

" I was myself told of another person of my name being at Rome," said Mr.

Armstrong; "and I can give you my informant's name, if you think it will aid you."

"I shall be most grateful to you, sir," said Charles, eagerly.

Mr. Armstrong wrote on one of Leslie's cards the name of Signor Peliani, and directed him to a house near the outskirts of the city, after which they separated with mutual expressions of civility.

"Once more foiled," said Charles, when he was again in the open air. "Alas! I meet with nothing but disappointment. This is my last chance, I fear."

A little inquiry, and a half an hour's walking brought him to the house he had been directed to, and the door, as is usual in Italian houses, being open, Charles entered without ceremony, and tapped at an inner door.

There was no reply, and Charles turned the handle, and entered the room. Seated at a table reading, was Herbert Mandeville.

CHAPTER CXVII.

"And could he once again have seen,
The well remembered form
'Twould ease the anguish of his heart,
Rob passion of its storm."

MORTON.

THE INTERVIEW.—THE MESSAGE.—REPENTENCE.—THE JOURNEY HOME.—
HOPELESS TEARS.

FOR one moment, and only for a moment, Herbert did not look up; but when he did so, and encountered the calm earnest gaze of Charles Leslie, he started to his feet with a cry of surprise and alarm, and gazed at him as if he had been some apparition from the dead.

"Herbert Mandeville," said Charles, solemnly.

"Do—do—I dream?" said Herbert; "or are you really Charles Leslie?"

"I *am* Charles Leslie. I am glad you know me! You do not dream, Herbert Mandeville! Would to Heaven it was all a fearful dream! What joy would there then be in the waking!"

"All—all—what?"

"Can you ask?"

Herbert was silent for a moment, then as his first emotions of surprise wore off, he assumed a cold and imperious manner, as he said,—

"Sir, I don't know by what train of reasoning you consider yourself justified in forcing your company upon me. It ought to be—nay, it is, and shall be sufficient, that I will hold no communication with you. This is my apartment, and there's the door, sir."

"I expected this," said Leslie. "But I have come too far to speak to you to be easily put off."

"But you shall be put off. Do you imagine you can force yourself upon me whenever you please with your canting hypocrisy?"

"Herbert Mandeville," said Leslie, "I have sworn not to quarrel with you——"

"Indeed!" sneered Herbert.

"Yes, and I will keep my oath."

"Oh, doubtless; discretion is the better part of valour."

"I have likewise," continued Leslie, taking no notice whatever of the taunt —"I have likewise sworn to deliver to you a message."

" A message ?"

" Yes, Herbert Mandeville, and I will keep that oath !"

" You are full of vows," sneered Herbert.

" For nearly twelve months I have now been seeking you, and I thank Heaven that at last I stand face to face with you to discharge my solemn trust."

" Your trust !"

" Aye, sir, my trust."

" Then do I not thank Heaven," said Herbert, " for a more hateful face to me there is not in the wide world than yours. Charles Leslie, I loathe—detest your very sight."

" Still I must do my duty," said Charles.

" Say your say, then, sir, at once, and let me be rid of you—you whom I hate."

" I bring you peace."

" Pshaw !"

" I bring you forgiveness."

" Forgiveness ? Go and preach to old women, Master Leslie, you have grown to dotage."

" It may be so," said Charles ; " but still you must hear me. I bring you the forgiveness of her you have injured."

" Indeed ; and so you have travelled to Rome on this fool's errand. Do you expect me to believe you ?"

" Your belief or not I little heed," replied Charles Leslie. " I promised Adeline Mourdant that I would search the world until I found you and breathed to you her words. When I have done so I have relieved my heart of a solemn vow—hear me."

" I suppose you expect to be burthened with some message back," sneered Herbert.

" No—no," said Leslie ; " the message would now be sent in vain."

" You—you do not mean to say that—that——"

" That what ?"

" That Adeline is your wife ?" cried Mandeville, all the jealousy in his disposition roused by the supposition.

" My wife ! No."

" Then—then why in vain should I send a message ? Surely it were but courtesy to answer a lady's message, whatever we may think of the messenger."

" And yet your message cannot be taken."

" And wherefore ?"

" Can you not guess ?"

" Guess. Is—is she wedded ?"

" She is."

" To whom—who dared—to whom, sir ?"

" *To the grave.*"

Herbert Mandeville turned ghastly pale, and he staggered close to Leslie as he gasped,—

" You—you mock me !"

" I do not."

" You do not mean that—she is—dead ?"

" She is."

" No, Leslie—no, Charles Leslie. Say you have done this to vex me —say it was out of revenge you told me this, and that it is not true—has no shadow of foundation."

" It is true !"

"No, it is not. I—I will forgive you all—I will bless you ; but—but do not tell me Adeline is dead."

"Adeline is dead!" echoed Charles Leslie.

With a deep groan Mandeville sunk into a seat, and covered his face with his hands, while bitter, scalding tears trickled through his fingers.

"Yes, Herbert Mandeville," continued Charles Leslie, in a voice of deep emotion, "the fond, the faithful, the beautiful, the good Adeline is no more. On this breast she breathed her last sigh ; these arms received her lifeless form—these eyes saw her laid in her last cold resting place."

"Spare—spare me!" gasped Herbert.

"Alas!" continued Leslie, "I wish to inflict no wound. Adeline is dead!"

Mandeville groaned.

"In those last hours," resumed Leslie, "when the soul is hovering on the confines of another and a better world, she spoke of you."

"Of—of me ?"

"Yes ; she charged me as I loved her, and that was, indeed, a mighty invocation. She charged me to seek you out, and carry to you her forgiveness."

"Forgiveness for me ?"

"Yes, and her blessing. I have promised, and I have done my duty."

Charles moved toward the door, but Herbert sprung after him, and seized his arm.

"Leslie ! Leslie !" he cried, "do not for the love of Heaven—do not leave me thus."

"I have fulfilled my vow," said Charles Leslie solemnly, disengaging himself from the grasp of Mandeville.

"No, no—she said more. Oh, tell me all, her every look—her lightest word."

Charles shook his head.

"No, Herbert Mandeville, you are forgiven, be content. Yet stay ; here is another matter I had well nigh forgotten. Read that paper when you think fit."

He laid upon the table poor Mrs. Delancey's confession.

"Oh, stay—stay," implored Herbert.

Charles waved his hand.

"I have injured you too," cried Herbert.

"And I forgive you with all my heart," said Charles, still moving towards the door.

"One moment, oh, but one moment. Tell me where—where——"

"What ?" said Charles, pausing.

"Where—is she—now ?"

Her earthly remains are in the humble graveyard of Bracefield ; her pure spirit is with its God."

"And—and I killed her ! I killed her ! You all think I killed her," screamed, rather than said, Herbert.

"Let Heaven judge us all," replied Leslie. "On the humble stone that covers her remains——"

"Yes—yes, on that stone ?" gasped Mandeville.

"On that stone, at her request, are placed these words——"

"The—the words, tell me."

"*The Grave of the Forsaken.*"

"She—she knew I killed her," gasped Herbert.

"I have fulfilled my vow," said Leslie.

He walked from the house, nor did he once turn to cast even a glance at the dwelling he had left.

"Home—home!" he cried, when he had placed some distance between him and the house inhabited by Mandeville. "Now, Adeline, I will pass the remainder of my days near to thee. Each well-remembered tree and flower shall speak to me of thee. To Bracefield—to Bracefield!"

CHAPTER CXVIII.

" He lay beside her weeping,
    And they watched him as he wept,
Till they thought that he was sleeping
    On the pillow where she slept.
But when they went to wake him
    From his chill and lonely rest,
His dream would not forsake him,
    For his sun was in its west."—BAYLY.

BRACEFIELD AGAIN. —A RETROSPECTION. — "THE GRAVE OF THE FORSAKEN."

Now again will we conduct the reader, who has so kindly gone with us in our chequered narrative, back to the humble graveyard of Bracefield on that eventful evening when the frantic horseman and his panting steed dashed into the village, and drew up at the curate's door.

Who that impetuous horseman was, and under what circumstances he thus came with a hurried and broken heart to Bracefield, our readers are aware.

The unfortunate, and in many respects guilty, Herbert Mandeville remained for a few brief moments after Charles Leslie left him at Rome, paralysed by the wild regret that now filled his mind upon hearing that the beautiful and gifted Adeline was no more.

Then suddenly rushing forth, he ordered a horse, and before another hour, had turned his back upon the imperial city, bending all his energies to the one object of reaching England as quickly as it was possible so to do.

It was Herbert, then, that, exhausted both in mind and body, dashed so recklessly through the village of Bracefield. It was he, with bitter self-accusations, begged, implored the good old curate to conduct him to the Grave of the Forsaken.

That there upon that grave he breathed his last sigh, and his spirit took its flight, we already know, and let us hope that his heart, freed from earthly passion and earthly vanities, found favour in the sight of Heaven!

The awful and mysterious disappearance of the body of Herbert Mandeville during the short space of time that the old curate had left it to itself, and the deep emotion of the man of God, we have recorded. Our duty now is to be near him in his lonely watch by the grave of Adeline after he had requested Andrew to leave him for an hour alone among the dead.

When the last echo of the old servant's footsteps had died away, Mr. Endsleigh knelt down upon the grave of Adeline, and lifted up his voice in humble supplication to Heaven to unravel the fearful occurrences of the night, and to make clear that which was dark, awful, and mysterious. Then he rose calmer in his heart, and more composed in spirit, and sitting down by the grave, he determined, with a holy hope that his prayer would not be in vain, to keep i ssolitary watch in that lonely spot till even morning should chase away the vapours of the night, and suggest other resolves.

The time passed heavily to the aged man, until casting his eyes accidentally towards the church, he again saw the mysterious light streaming from one of the windows.

Mr. Endsleigh immediately rose, and walked towards the little door in the chancel, of which he generally had the key about him. He opened it, and with a slow, but firm step, entered the sacred edifice.

The light streamed apparently from the floor of the church, and for one brief moment a feeling of terror crept over the heart of the ancient minister. It was but for a moment, however, and summoning resolution to his aid, he stepped calmly and noiselessly forward.

He had not emerged from the shadow which the pulpit cast along the sombre pews, when his steps were arrested by the sound of a human voice, exclaiming in smothered accents,—

"I tell you it is he."

"Then it's the oddest thing ever I heard of," replied another voice.

"Where is the cart?" said the first speaker.

"Oh, at the old place," was the reply.

"Then just carry the body between you, and throw it in. The clothes are worth something."

The curate felt paralysed and bewildered by what he saw and heard, for before he could resolve upon any course of action, the light glared more fully through the ancient edifice, and two men passed him so closely, as almost to brush his garments.

Between them they bore an inanimate form, and one glance shewed the curate that it was the missing body of Herbert Mandeville.

Then in one moment the whole truth seemed like a gush of light to flash upon his mind. These men were robbers of the dead, and had got possession by some means of one of the long since shut up and unused vaults beneath the church.

The confusion of the curate was but momentary, and then with a firm step

No. 52

and a voice which might have been that of a younger man, by at least thirty years, he rushed forward and exclaimed—

"Hold, ruffians! Would you thus profane the Temple of God with your unholy trafficking? Hold! I say, hold!"

The men stopped with every symptom of terror and consternation. They immediately dropped the body of Mandeville and stood glaring at the curate, who was now in the full gleam of the light they carried in bewildered amazement.

"Are you men?" cried Mr. Endsleigh. "Have you human hearts that you thus ruthlessly tread in God's holy sanctuary?"

"Damnation! who are you?" cried one of the men, fiercely.

"Are you alone?" said the other.

"No; I am not alone," replied Mr. Endsleigh, solemnly. "God is with me, and looks down upon the events of this night."

The men glanced at each other, and one of them drew from his bosom a horseman's pistol, as he muttered—

"Dead men tell no tales."

"No—no," cried the other. "D— it, let the old man go."

"Go!" shrieked the more ruffianly of the two. "Go indeed, and raise a hue and cry all over the country after me."

He made a movement forward, but the other struggled with him, and his hat falling off, disclosed upon his forehead, in fearful distinctness, the letter R.

The curate, with great presence of mind, ran to one of the aisles, and seizing the bell-rope, which for convenience had for many years been hung so low, he awakened all the echoes of the ancient building by the deep tones of the bell.

"Curses," cried Dufours, for it was he. "Curses, he will alarm the whole place; let me go I say."

Scarcely had the bell fully with its reverberating sound filled the night air, when the door of the church was flung open, and Andrew, accompanied by ten or a dozen young men from the village, appeared with lights and such rude weapons as they could in their haste lay hands on.

"Mr. Endsleigh! My dear master!" cried Andrew.

"Safe, quite safe," answered the curate.

For a moment Dufours glared around him like a wild animal at bay; the blue letter on his forehead gave him a singular and unearthly appearance, and more than one of the assembled villagers shrunk back in trembling alarm from his gaze.

"Seize him!" cried Mr. Endsleigh, pointing to Dufours.

"Not yet!" roared the ruffian, drawing another pistol from his breast, and presenting both at the throng that impeded the entrance to the church. "Not yet, I say. What'll stop me? As for you," addressing his companion; "curses on you. We might have been off but for you!"

"That man saved my life!" cried the curate; "injure him not, my friends. He will live to be a good man yet."

"Will he?" cried Dufours. "I'll prove you a liar!"

He discharged one of his pistols full in the face of his more timid and more compassionate companion, and before the confusion occasioned by the murderous act had ceased, he darted through the horrified throng of peasants, and made good his escape from the church. Several darted off in pursuit of Dufours, but the greater number grouped round the dying man. They raised him from the ground, and while the film of death was gathering on his eyes, he spoke faintly :—

"I—I am not so bad as—as Dufours," he gasped; "I—I never took a life."

"Happier, oh, far happier is the murdered than his murderer," said the curate.

"Ye—yes," said the man. "There is a—a gang of us. We have robbed the churchyard these two—two years."

"Where did you conceal yourselves?" said the curate.

"In—in the vaults. There is one that—that communicates with an old tomb in the churchyard. We scared the peasants by representing ghosts."

"There is one grave," said the curate, in an agonized tone; "the Grave of the Forsaken! Oh, tell me, you have spared that?"

"It—it is——"

He seemed struggling for utterance.

"One word! but a word!" said the curate.

"Un—un—touched!" gasped the man, and he fell dead in the arms of those who held him.

"God's will be done!" said the curate. "Remove the bodies both to my house, my friends. Adeline—my Adeline, you still sleep in peace, thank Heaven!"

Our tale is over. The old curate lingered still a few years in life. His only delight was to wander by the grave of Adeline, and when he died, which he did calmly, and like an infant passing into slumber, his last words were,— "Lay me along with my dear child."

His request was complied with, and the Grave of the Forsaken holds two faithful hearts that in life loved each other, and in death were **not** divided.

Herbert Mandeville was buried near to Adeline, and a simple monument marks the spot, on which are inscribed the words,—

"The repentant are welcomed in Heaven."

Justice overtook Dufours, who expiated his last crime on the scaffold.

Of the other personages of our story we can say but little. George Mourdant was never again heard of; he was believed to have perished in want and destitution in a foreign land. Mrs. Plumpjoy refused an offer of matrimony in 1829, and said she wondered what would happen next, unless a horse came to be shaved.

Charles Leslie never married. He is now a bright ornament of our senate.

No one could for a moment suppose, to gaze now upon the face of Charles Leslie, that he had suffered so much of that deep anguish of the heart that knew no parallel. He had not, however, forgotten Adeline—he had not forgotten the agony of that moment of unutterable woe when he held in his arms the lifeless form of the fair being in whom was concentrated all that he loved—all that would have gilded his existence, and lent to life the charm of constant and enduring affection; but his was a nature that hid its deepest feelings. His face was no speaking index of those griefs and treasured memories of the past that many allow every idle eye to scan. He resembled a deep and fathomless pool, the surface calm, unruffled, and placid; but below, who shall say what storms may lash to fury the contending waves of passion?

Moreover, Charles Leslie was one who had a strong sense of duty. He felt that he could be useful, and calming gently his own absorbing griefs, he plunged into the arena of public life and became one of the brightest ornaments of the House of Commons, and one of the most unblemished of patriots.

Still there were times when from the busy turmoil of the great world he would steal away to the green spot which marked the resting-place of Adeline—his Adeline, as he now permitted his heart to call her; and there, perchance, in the dreary solitude of a summer's eve, the stern legislator, the eloquent statesman, the patriotic Leslie, might have been seen weeping over the verdant sod which covered the loved, worshipped, and never forgotten form of the gentle girl who had but lived, loved, and died!

He would liken her in his mind to one of those pure soilless beings described by Byron :—

> "Earth's mists with their pure pinions disagree,
> And they regain their native stare,
> Unlaurelled upon earth."

These visits were frequent, and Charles ever believed that he returned a wiser, although perchance, a sadder man, from his lonely vigils by THE GRAVE OF THE FORSAKEN.